Vendetta: Lucky's Revenge
&
Dangerous Kiss

Jackie Collins brings the wild and sexy world of super-stardom alive. Her phenomenally successful novels have made her as famous as the movers and shakers, power-brokers and superstars she writes about with an insider's knowledge. With 200 million copies of her books sold in more than forty countries, Jackie Collins is one of the world's top-selling writers. In a series of sensational best-sellers, she has blown the lid off Hollywood life and loves. 'It's all true,' she says. 'I write about real people in disguise. If anything, my characters are toned down – the real thing is much more bizarre.'

There have been many imitators, but only Jackie Collins can tell you what *really* goes on in the fastest lane of all. From Beverly Hills bedrooms to a raunchy prowl along the streets of Hollywood. From glittering rock parties and con-certs to stretch limos and the mansions of the power-brokers – Jackie Collins chronicles the *real* truth.

Books by Jackie Collins

Jackie Collins

Vendetta: Lucky's Revenge & Dangerous Kiss

PAN BOOKS

Vendetta: Lucky's Revenge first published 1996 by Macmillan.
First published in paperback by Pan Books 1997.
Dangerous Kiss first published 1999 by Macmillan.
First published in paperback by Pan Books 2000.

This omnibus first published 2005 by Pan Books
an imprint of Pan Macmillan Ltd
Pan Macmillan, 20 New Wharf Road, London N1 9RR
Basingstoke and Oxford
Associated companies throughout the world
www.panmacmillan.com

ISBN 0 330 44366 6

1 3 5 7 9 8 6 4 2

A CIP catalogue record for this book is available from
the British Library.

Printed and bound in Great Britain by
Mackays of Chatham plc, Chatham, Kent

Vendetta:
Lucky's Revenge

For my Italian hero,
Ti amo,
Jake

Los Angeles

1987

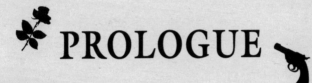

PROLOGUE

DONNA LANDSMAN'S icy slate eyes darted around the expensive mahogany conference table, fixing on her three high-powered lawyers and her mild-mannered husband, George. 'How much more time before we acquire enough shares to take control of Panther Studios?' she demanded impatiently. 'It's taking too long.'

One of her lawyers spoke up, a florid-faced man with close-together bushy eyebrows and a bulbous nose. 'Donna, it's true, it is taking longer than we anticipated. However, as you know, I've never been in favor of this—'

'Do you hear me, Finley?' she interrupted, and crushed him with a contemptuous glare. 'Because if you don't, get out of my sight. Negativity fails to interest me. If I want something, *nobody* tells me no. And ... I ... want ... Panther.'

Finley nodded, sorry he'd spoken. Donna Landsman never listened to anybody's advice. She was queen of the hostile takeover, every company she went for made her another fortune. This was one of the reasons Finley couldn't understand why she was so anxious to wrest control of Panther. It was a studio in trouble with massive debts and a rocky cashflow – hardly a money-making proposition.

'Yes, Donna,' he said. 'We all know what you want and, believe me, we're working on it.'

'I should hope so,' Donna said, making a mental note to tell George that, soon, it might be time to replace at least two of their lawyers. Finley would be the first to go.

She stood up, indicating that the meeting was over. No point in wasting more time.

George stood up, too. He was an undistinguished-looking man in his fifties with plain features, heavy spectacles, and flat brown hair cut too short. Everyone knew he was the financial brains behind Donna's empire. She was the flash and he was the cash. They were a formidable combination.

'I'll see you later,' Donna said to her husband, dismissing him with a wave of her hand.

'Yes, dear,' he replied, unfazed by her abruptness.

Donna strode from the conference room to her offices – a palatial suite of interconnecting rooms with a breathtaking view of Century City. For a moment she paused in the doorway, taking it all in.

Lawyers! What did they know? Exactly nothing. The only thing they were truly competent at was sending enormous bills. Fortunately she had someone in place who was able to do exactly what she required. Her team of lawyers had no idea how smartly she'd worked this one – even George had no clue.

Donna smiled to herself.

Everyone has a weakness.

Seek and ye shall find.

She'd found.

She entered her private bathroom, pausing before the ornate antique mirror above the sink and peering intently at her reflection.

She saw a woman of forty-three with streaked blond hair pulled back into an elegant chignon. A woman with sculpted features – the pride of her plastic surgeon. A slim woman who wore her Chanel suit and Winston diamonds with flair.

She was attractive in a hard, manufactured, *I-am-very-rich* way. She was attractive because she'd forced herself to become so.

Donna Landsman.

Donatella Bonnatti.

Ah, yes ... She'd come a long way from her humble beginnings in a dusty little village nestled on the south-eastern corner of Sicily. A long, long way ...

And when she brought Lucky Santangelo to her knees, she'd make sure the bitch knew exactly who she was dealing with.

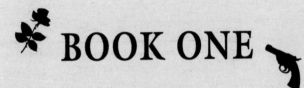

BOOK ONE

Chapter One

LUCKY SANTANGELO Golden steered her red Ferrari through the ornate metal gates of Panther Studios, waved a friendly greeting to the guard, then drove across the lot to her personal parking space located directly outside her well-appointed suite of offices. Lucky was a wildly beautiful woman in her late thirties with a mass of tangled jet curls, deep olive skin, a full, sensual mouth, black opal eyes and a slender well-toned body.

She'd bought Panther in 1985, and since then she'd been running the studio. After two action-packed years it was still exciting, for there was nothing she enjoyed more than a challenge, and running a Hollywood studio was the biggest challenge of all. It was more absorbing than building a casino/hotel in Vegas, something she'd done twice, or managing her late second husband's shipping empire, a task she'd now relinquished, having handed everything over to a board of trustees.

Lucky *loved* making movies – reaching out to America, putting images on the screen that would eventually influence people all over the world in a thousand different ways.

It wasn't easy. The opposition to a woman taking control of a major studio had been formidable. *Especially* a woman who looked like Lucky. *Especially* a woman who seemed to have it all together, including three children and a movie-star husband. Everyone knew that Hollywood was just one big boys' club, female members not exactly welcome.

The legendary movie mogul, Abe Panther, had sold her the studio only after she'd proved she was capable of taking over. He had challenged her to go in under cover as a secretary and work for Mickey Stolli, his devious grandson-in-law who had been running Panther at the time. Abe's deal was that if she could find out everything Mickey was into, he'd sell her Panther.

She'd found out more than enough to close the deal: Mickey had been skimming big bucks every way he could; his head of production was snorting coke and supplying two-thousand-dollar-a-night call-girls to movie stars and VIPs; the head of distribution was smuggling porno flicks overseas along with Panther's legitimate productions, scoring an under-the-counter bundle; the movies Panther was making were soft-core exploitation crap, full of sleazy sex and outrageous violence; producers were getting massive kickbacks; and women around the lot were treated as second-class citizens – it didn't matter whether they were star actresses or mere secretaries, chauvinism ran rampant.

Lucky offered Abe a lot of money and salvation for a studio whose reputation was being slowly ruined.

Abe Panther liked her style.

He sold.

Lucky took over in a big way.

Abe had warned her that bringing Panther back to its glory days was going to be a struggle.

How right he had been.

First of all, she'd refused to continue making the kind of cheapo garbage Panther had been churning out. Then she'd fired most of Mickey's key executives, putting a new, first-rate team in place. After that it had been a question of developing new projects – a slow process that took time and patience.

The studio had been running at a loss for years, with astronomical bank loans. Lucky and her business adviser, Morton Sharkey, had been forced to arrange another massive loan just to keep the studio operating. Then, after the first year's disappointing net loss of nearly seventy million dollars, Lucky had taken stock and decided it was time to recoup some of her initial investment and diversify. Morton had suggested selling blocks of shares to several corporations and a few private investors. It had seemed like an excellent idea.

Morton had taken care of everything: finding the right investors who would leave her alone to run the studio; setting up a board of directors who wouldn't interfere; and making sure she still owned forty percent of the stock.

The good news was that, currently, Panther had two big movies on release, both performing well: *Finder*, a showy vehicle for the controversial superstar Venus Maria, who also happened to be one of Lucky's best friends; and *River Storm*, a sharp-edged detective thriller starring Charlie Dollar, the middle-aged hero of stoned America. Lucky was especially delighted as both movies had been put together under her regime. She hoped that this was the start of the turn-around she'd been working toward. *Give them good, interesting movies and they will come* – that was her motto.

She hurried into her office, where Kyoko, her loyal Japanese assistant, greeted her with a lengthy typed phone list and a morose shake of his head. He was a slight man in his thirties dressed in a Joseph Aboud jacket and sharply creased grey pants. He had glossy black hair pulled back in a neat ponytail, and an inscrutable expression. Kyoko knew every aspect of the movie business, having worked as personal assistant to several top executives since graduating college.

'What's the matter, Ky?' Lucky asked, throwing off her Armani jacket and settling in a comfortable leather chair behind her oversized art-deco desk.

Kyoko recited the day's business. 'You have fifteen phone calls to return, a ten-thirty with the Japanese bankers followed by a production meeting regarding *Gangsters*. Then a noon appointment with Alex Woods and Freddie Leon, lunch with Venus Maria, another production meeting at three, your interview with a reporter from *Newstime*, a six o'clock with Morton Sharkey and—'

'Dinner at home, I hope,' she interrupted, wishing there were more hours in the day.

Kyoko shook his head. 'Your plane departs for Europe at eight p.m. Your limo will pick you up at your house no later than seven.'

She smiled wryly. 'Hmm . . . a twenty-minute dinner break! You're slipping.'

'Your schedule would kill a lesser person,' Kyoko remarked.

Lucky shrugged, 'We're a long time dead, Ky. I don't believe in wasting time.'

Kyoko was not surprised by her answer. He'd worked as Lucky's personal assistant since she'd taken over the studio. She was a dedicated workaholic who never ran out of energy. She was also the smartest woman he'd ever met. Smart and beautiful – a devastating combination. Kyoko loved working for her as opposed to his last boss, an edgy man with a relentless coke problem and a small dick.

'See if you can get Lennie on his portable,' Lucky said. 'He tried reaching me in the car this morning but the connection was deadly – couldn't make out a word.'

Lennie Golden, the love of her life. They'd been married four years and every day it seemed to get better.

Lennie was her third husband. Right now he was on

location in Corsica, shooting an action-adventure film. Three weeks apart was a killer and she couldn't wait to join him for a long weekend of lounging around doing nothing except making slow leisurely love.

Kyoko connected with the production office in Corsica. 'Lennie's out on a beach location,' he informed her, covering the mouthpiece. 'Shall I leave a message?'

'Yes. Tell them to have him call his wife pronto. Mrs Golden can be interrupted wherever she is.' She grinned when she said Mrs Golden – being Lennie's wife was the most fun of all.

Regrettably Lennie's movie was not a Panther production. Early on they'd both decided it wasn't a wise move for him to be seen to be working for his wife. He was a big enough star in his own right, and making a movie for Panther would only induce false rumors of nepotism.

'Get me Abe Panther,' she instructed Kyoko.

Occasionally she called Abe for advice. At ninety he was a true Hollywood legend. The old man had seen it all, done most of it, and was still as canny and quick-witted as a man half his age. Whenever she spoke to him he was always full of encouragement and wisdom, and since the banks were coming down on her big time, she needed his assurance that with two blockbuster movies their attitude would soon change.

Once in a while she drove up to Abe's grand old mansion overlooking the city. They would sit out on the terrace watching the sunset, while Abe regaled her with outrageous stories about Hollywood in the far-off golden days. Abe had known everyone, from Chaplin to Monroe, and he wasn't shy about telling fascinating tales.

She felt like visiting him today, but there simply wasn't time. As it was she was hardly going to see her children – two-year-old Maria and baby Gino, who was six months.

Bobby, her nine-year-old son from her marriage to deceased shipping billionaire Dimitri Stanislopolous, was spending the summer with relatives in Greece.

'Mr Panther is unavailable,' Kyoko said.

'Okay, we'll try him later.'

She glanced at her children's photographs proudly displayed in silver frames on her desk. Bobby, so cute and handsome; baby Gino, named for his grandfather; and Maria, with her huge green eyes and the most adorable smile in the world. She'd named Maria after her mother.

For a moment she let her mind wander, thinking about her beautiful mother. Could she ever forget the day she'd found her floating in the family swimming pool, murdered by her father's life-long enemy, Enzio Bonnatti? She'd been five years old, and it had seemed like her world was ending.

Twenty years later she'd taken revenge – killing the slime who'd ordered her mother's murder, getting retribution for the Santangelo family, for it had been Bonnatti who'd also masterminded a hit on her brother, Dario, and the first great love of her life, Marco.

She'd shot Enzio Bonnatti with his own gun, claiming selfdefense. 'He was trying to rape me,' she'd told the police, stony-faced. And she was believed because her father was Gino Santangelo and he had money and pull in all the right places. The case never even came to court.

Yes, she'd taken revenge for all of them and never regretted it.

'Shall we start with the phone calls?' Kyoko asked, interrupting her reverie.

She glanced at her watch. It was already past ten, the morning had flown by, even though she'd been up since six. She picked up her phone list. Kyoko had arranged the names in order of their importance – an order with which she didn't agree. 'You know I'd sooner talk to an actor than an agent,' she chided. 'Get me Charlie Dollar.'

'He wants a meeting.'

'About what?'

'He doesn't like the poster art for *River Storm* in Europe.'

'Why?'

'Says they've made him look overweight.'

Lucky sighed. Actors and their egos. It was never-ending. 'Is it too late to change it?'

'I spoke to the art department. It can be done. It'll be costly.'

'Worth keeping a superstar happy?' she asked, sounding only mildly sarcastic.

'If you say so.'

'You know my philosophy, Ky. Keep 'em smiling and they'll work all the harder to promote the movie.'

Kyoko nodded. He knew better than to argue with Lucky.

☆   ☆   ☆

Lennie Golden hated bullshit, and the worst thing about being a movie star was that half the time he was knee deep. People's reaction to fame was so weird: they either fell all over him, or insulted the hell out of him. Women were the worst. Getting laid was on their minds the moment they met him. And it didn't have to be him – any movie star would do, Costner, Redford, Willis, women had no preference as long as the man was a celebrity.

Lennie had learned to ignore the come-ons – he didn't need the ego boost of constantly scoring. He had Lucky, and she was the most special woman in the world.

At thirty-nine Lennie was a charismatically attractive man with an edgy style all his own. Tall, tanned and fit, he was not conventionally handsome. He had longish dirty-blond hair and direct ocean-green eyes, plus he worked out every day, keeping his body in excellent shape.

He'd been a movie star for several years – which surprised him more than anyone. Six years ago he'd been just another comedian looking to score a gig, a few bucks, anything going. Now he had everything he'd ever dreamed of.

Lennie Golden. Son of crusty old Jack Golden, a stand-up Vegas hack, and the unstoppable Alice. Or 'Alice the Swizzle', as his mother had been known in her heyday when she was a now-you-see-'em-now-you-don't Vegas stripper.

When he was seventeen he'd split for New York and made it all the way without any help from his folks. His father was long dead, but Alice still caused trouble wherever she went. Sixty-seven years old and frisky as an overbleached starlet, she'd never come to terms with getting older, and the only reason she acknowledged Lennie as her son was because of his fame. 'I was a child bride,' she'd simper to anyone who'd listen, batting her fake lashes and curling her overpainted lips in a lascivious leer. 'I gave birth to Lennie when I was twelve!'

He'd bought her a small house in Sherman Oaks, where she ruled the neighborhood – having decided that since she was never going to be a star, she would become a psychic. A wise move, for now – much to Lennie's embarrassment – she appeared regularly on cable TV and sounded off about anything and everything. Quietly he'd christened her 'My-mother-the-mouth'.

Sometimes it all seemed like a fantasy, his marriage to Lucky, his successful career, everything.

Leaning back in his director's chair he narrowed his eyes and surveyed the beach location. A blond in a bikini was busy strutting her considerable assets. She'd paraded in front of him several times with a definite yen to get noticed.

He'd noticed all right. He was married not dead, and

spectacular blonds with bodies to die for had once been his weakness. Earlier in the day she'd asked to have her picture taken with him. He'd politely declined: photos with fans, especially attractive ones, had a nasty habit of ending up in the tabloids.

She'd gotten the message and returned a few minutes later with a strapping bodybuilder type who spoke no English. 'My fiancé,' she'd explained with a dazzling smile. '*Please!*'

He'd obliged and had a photo taken with the two of them.

Now the blond did another turn. Long legs. Rounded butt in an almost non-existent thong. Firm tits with erect nipples straining the flimsy material.

Looking was okay.

Taking it any further was not.

Marriage was a commitment that worked both ways. If Lucky was ever unfaithful to him he'd never forgive her. He was confident she felt the same way.

The blond finally zoomed in for landing. 'Mr Golden,' she purred, in a Marilyn rip-off voice with a slight French accent. 'I *loove* your movies. It is such an honor to be appearing in this one with you.' Deep breath. Nipples threatening to break through.

'Thanks,' he mumbled, wondering where the fiancé was now.

Adoring giggle. '*I* should be the one thanking *you*.' Small pink tongue darting out to lick pouty pink lips. Invitation to fuck shining in her over-eager eyes.

Rescue swooped over: Jennifer, the pretty American second assistant. She wore shorts, a tight T-shirt and Lakers baseball cap. Temptation was everywhere.

'Mac's ready to rehearse, Lennie,' she said, ever protective.

He shifted his lanky frame out of the director's chair and stretched.

Jennifer raked the blond in the bikini with a condescending look. 'Try and stay with the other extras, dear,' she said crisply. 'You never know when you'll be needed.'

The blond backed off, not happy.

'Talk about Silicone City!' Jennifer muttered.

'How do you know?' Lennie asked, wondering why women were so much more knowledgeable at spotting fake tits than men.

'It's obvious,' Jennifer replied disdainfully. 'You men fall for anything.'

'Who's falling?' he said, amused.

'Not you,' Jennifer said, flashing him a friendly smile. 'It's a pleasure to work with a star who doesn't expect a blow-job along with his morning coffee.'

Jennifer, Lennie decided, was Lucky's kind of woman.

He couldn't help smiling when he thought of his wife. Tough exterior. Soft interior. Drop-dead gorgeous. Strong, stubborn, sensual, street smart, vulnerable and crazy. The package that was Lucky was really something.

Lennie had been married once before. A quickie marriage in Las Vegas to Olympia Stanislopolous, the willful daughter of Dimitri Stanislopolous, who – at the same time – had been married to Lucky.

Olympia had died tragically, overdosing in a hotel room with Flash, a drugged-out rock star.

Dimitri had suffered a fatal stroke.

Soon Lucky and Lennie were together, where they belonged.

Olympia left behind a daughter, Brigette, now nineteen and one of the richest girls in the world. Lennie was fond of her, although he didn't get to see her as often as he would have liked.

'I want you to meet Lucky when she's here,' he said to Jennifer. 'You'll like her, she'll like you. It's a done deal.'

'She won't be interested in meeting *me*,' Jennifer said. 'She runs a studio, Lennie. I'm just a second assistant.'

'Lucky doesn't care. She likes people for who they are, not what they do.'

'If you say so.'

'And hey,' he said, boosting her confidence, 'there's nothing wrong with being a second assistant – you're working your way up. One day you'll be directing. Is that the plan?'

Jennifer nodded. 'I've arranged a car to meet your wife at Poretta airport tomorrow,' she said, all business.

'I'll be in it,' Lennie said.

'You might be shooting.'

'Have them shoot around me.'

'You're in every shot.'

'Fake it.'

'I *never* fake it.'

Yes. Lucky would definitely like this one.

Chapter Two

ALEX WOODS had a smile like a crocodile – wide, captivating and ultimately deadly. It stood him in good stead with the movie executives he was forced to deal with daily. It caught them off-guard, unbalancing the delicate power structure between writer/producer/director and studio honcho who could usually make or break any film-maker – however famous and talented. Alex was a powerful presence, capable of making a lot of people nervous.

Alex Woods and his lethal smile had written, directed and produced six big-budget major movies over a ten-year period. Six controversial, sex- and violence-drenched masterpieces. Alex called them masterpieces, but not everyone agreed – each of his movies *had* been nominated for an Academy Award but he had never won. It pissed him off. Alex liked recognition – a lousy nomination didn't do it for him. He wanted the fucking gold statue on his Richard-Meir-designed beach-house mantelpiece, so he could fucking shove it up everyone's ass – metaphorically speaking, of course.

Alex was not married, even though he was forty-seven years old, tall and good-looking in a darkly dangerous way with compelling eyes, heavy eyebrows and a strong jawline. No woman had ever managed to nail him. He didn't go for American women; he preferred his female companions to be

Oriental and preferably subservient, so that when he made love to them he felt like the big conquering hero.

The truth was that Alex had a submerged fear of women whom he might in any way consider his equal. This fear originated from his mother, Dominique, a fierce Frenchwoman who'd dispatched his father, Gordon Woods, a moderately successful film actor who had specialized in playing best-friend roles, to an early grave when Alex was only eleven years old. They'd said it was a heart attack, but Alex knew – because he'd been a silent witness to many of their violent fights – that she'd tongue-lashed the poor man to death. His mother was a vicious calculating woman, who'd driven her husband to find solace in a bottle of booze whenever he could. Death was his cunning escape.

Shortly after his father's funeral, Madame Woods had sent her only child off to a strict military academy. 'You're stupid, exactly like your father,' she'd said, her tone allowing no argument. 'Maybe it'll make you smart.'

The military academy had been a living nightmare. He'd hated every minute of the rigid discipline and unfair rules. It didn't matter, because whenever he'd complained to Dominique about the beatings and solitary confinements she'd told him to stop whining and be a man. He'd been forced to stay there for five years, spending vacation time with his grandparents in Pacific Palisades, while his mother dated a variety of unsuitable men, virtually ignoring his existence. Once, he'd caught her in bed with a man she'd made him call Uncle Willy. Uncle Willy had been lying back with a giant hard-on, while Mommy was on her knees next to the bed, completely naked. It was a scenario that stayed with him forever.

By the time he left the academy and tasted freedom his anger was insurmountable. While his contemporaries had rocked and rolled their way through high school, screwing cheerleaders, getting drunk and high, he'd been shut in a windowless room on detention for some petty misdemeanor, or getting paddled on his bare ass because they didn't like his attitude. Sometimes detention lasted ten hours with nothing to do except sit on a hard wooden bench staring blankly into space. Torture for rich kids whose parents didn't want them around.

Alex often thought about the lost years of his youth and it filled him with rage. He hadn't even gotten laid until college and that had been no memorable experience – a fat greasy whore in Tijuana who'd smelt of stale tacos and worse. In fact, he'd hated it so much he hadn't tried sex again for a year.

The second time had been better: he was a film student at USC, and a serious blond who'd admired his budding talent had given him head twice daily for six months. Very nice, but not enough to keep him satisfied. Eventually, he'd gotten restless and enlisted in the Army. They'd sent him to Vietnam where he'd spent a shattering two years experiencing things that would haunt him forever. When he'd returned to LA he was a different man, unsettled and edgy, ready to explode. He'd left town after two weeks – leaving a short note for his mother that he'd be in touch and hitching his way to New York.

Ah . . . revenge . . . He didn't call her for five years, and as far as he knew she'd never sent anyone looking for him. When he finally called, she acted as if she'd spoken to him the week before. No sentimental bullshit for Madame Woods.

'I hope you're working,' she'd said, her voice as cold as cracked ice. 'Because you'll get no hand-outs from me.'

Big surprise.

Yeah, Mom, I've been working. Hustled my ass for a couple of months so I could eat. Kept door at a low-class strip joint. Ran interference for a busy hooker. Cut up carcasses in a meat factory. Drove a cab. Chauffeured a car for a degenerate theater director. Bodyguarded a criminal. Lived with a rich older woman who reminded me of you. Procured drugs for her friends. Managed an after-hours gambling club. Worked as an assistant editor on a series of cheapo slash/horror stories. And finally the big break – wrote and directed a porno movie for a lecherous old Mafia Capo. Tight pussies. Big cocks. Erotic porno. The kind that really turns people on. And a story. Next thing Hollywood beckons. They know good pornography when they see it.

'I'm on my way to the coast,' he'd said. 'Universal have signed me to write and direct a movie for them.'

She was unimpressed. Naturally. A long pause. 'Call me when you're here.' And that was it.

Some broad, his mother. No wonder he didn't trust women.

That had been eighteen years ago. Things were different now. Madame Woods was older and wiser. So was he. They maintained a love/hate relationship. He loved her because she was his mother. Hated her because she was still a mean bitch. Occasionally he dined with her. Severe punishment.

In those eighteen years his career had soared. From one low-budget no-brainer he'd risen to the top, gradually gaining a reputation as an innovative, risk-taking, original movie-maker. It hadn't been easy, but he'd done it, and he was proud of his success.

It would be nice if his mother was, too. She never praised him, although criticism still fell easily from her thin scarlet lips. Alex knew that, if he had lived, his father would have been happy and supportive of everything he'd achieved.

Now he had a meeting with Lucky Santangelo, the current head of Panther Studios, and it did not please him that he had to go to a female to try to keep his latest project – a movie called *Gangsters* – in a go position. He was Alex Woods for Chrissake – he didn't have to kiss anyone's ass, especially some broad who had a reputation for doing things her way.

Nobody did things their way on an Alex Woods movie.

All he needed was for her studio to put up the money because Paramount had dropped out at the final hour. Their excuse was that *Gangsters* was too graphically violent. But he was making a movie about Vegas in the fifties. Hoodlums, hookers and gambling. Violence had been a way of life back then.

The trouble with the studios was that they were running scared because of criticism from all those do-good politicians who were busy screwing whores on the side while their wives stood beside them with a fixed smile and a dry pussy. Some freaking double standard!

Alex hated hypocrisy. Tell the real truth and nothing but was his motto, and that's exactly what he did in each of his movies. He was a controversial film-maker, garnering either bitter criticism or brilliant reviews. His movies made people think and sometimes that could be dangerous.

When Paramount folded, his agent, Freddie Leon, had suggested taking *Gangsters* to Panther. 'Lucky Santangelo will do it,' Freddie had assured him. 'I know Lucky, it's her kind of story. Plus she needs a hit.'

He hoped Freddie was right, because if there was one thing Alex hated it was the waiting game. He was only happy when he was immersed in making one of his movies. Fulfillment was being in action.

Freddie had suggested they get together before their meeting with Lucky, and he'd asked Alex to meet him for a late breakfast at the Four Seasons.

Alex dressed all in black, from his sneakers to his T-shirt, and drove to the hotel in his black Porsche Carrera. When he arrived Freddie was already at the table skimming a copy of the *Wall Street Journal*, looking more like a banker than an agent.

Freddie Leon was a poker-faced man in his early forties with a quick bland smile and cordial features. He was not just another agent, he was *the* agent. Mr Super Power. He made careers and he could break them just as easily. He'd worked hard for the privilege. His nickname around town was The Snake – on account of the fact he could slither in and out of any deal. Nobody dared call him The Snake to his face.

Alex slid into the booth. A waitress appeared and poured him a cup of strong black coffee. He took a quick gulp, burning his tongue. 'Shit!' he exclaimed.

'Morning,' Freddie said, lowering his newspaper.

'What makes you think Panther will do *Gangsters*?' Alex asked impatiently.

'I told you, Panther needs hit movies,' Freddie replied evenly. 'And it's Lucky's kind of script.'

'How come?'

''Cause of her background,' Freddie explained, pausing for a moment to take a sip of herbal tea. 'Her father built a hotel in Vegas back in the early days. Gino Santangelo – apparently he was quite a character.'

Alex leaned forward in surprise. 'Her father's Gino Santangelo?'

'Right. One of the boys. Made himself a fortune and moved on. Lucky built her own hotels in Vegas – the Magiriano and the Santangelo. She'll understand your script.'

Alex had heard of Gino Santangelo: he was not as notorious as Bugsy Siegal or any of the other high-profile gangsters, but in his day he'd certainly made his mark.

'The story is that Gino named his daughter after Lucky Luciano,' Freddie added. 'From all accounts she's had quite a life.'

In spite of himself Alex couldn't help being intrigued. So

Lucky Santangelo was not just some ballsy broad out of nowhere. She had a history – she was a Santangelo. Why hadn't he put it together before?

He downed the strong black coffee in three big gulps and decided that this deal could turn out to be more interesting than he'd thought.

☆ ☆ ☆

Three Japanese bankers, very correct, very conventional. The meeting went well, although Lucky sensed they were not thrilled to be dealing with a woman.

Ah . . . the story of her life. When would men learn to relax and realize it wasn't all one big pissing contest?

She needed the Japanese bankers to put up the money for a chain of Panther stores around the world. Merchandising was hot, and Lucky knew the smart move was to get in at the beginning.

The bankers deferred to her head of marketing – a man – and seemed to be on the verge of saying yes when they left, promising a decision within a few days. As soon as they departed she called her father at his Palm Springs estate. Gino sounded fine, and so he should: at eighty-one, he – like Abe Panther – was married to a woman a little over half his age, Paige Wheeler, a sexy red-headed interior designer who took excellent care of him. Not that Gino needed looking after, he was as active as a much younger man, full of drive and vigor, channeling his considerable energy into playing options on the stock market, a hobby that got him up at six in the morning and kept him alert.

Lucky concluded her conversation with a promise to visit soon.

'Make sure you do,' Gino said gruffly. 'An' bring the bambinos – I gotta start teachin' 'em things.'

'Like what?' she asked curiously.

'Like never you mind.'

Lucky smiled. Her father was something else. Through the bad times, when they weren't even talking, she'd hated him with a burning passion. Now she loved him with an equal passion. They'd survived so much together. Fortunately, it had made them both stronger.

She remembered the time he'd exiled her to strict boarding school in Switzerland when she was sixteen, then punished her after she ran away from it by forcing her into an arranged marriage with Craven Richmond, Senator Peter Richmond's boring son. What a nightmare! But she'd had no intention of staying trapped. When Gino fled America to avoid jail for tax evasion, she'd seized her opportunity and moved in to run the family business. Gino had expected her brother, Dario, to take over. But Dario was no businessman, so Lucky had completed the building of Gino's new hotel in Vegas, proving herself capable in every way.

When Gino finally returned, there'd been a major battle for control. Neither won. Eventually they'd reached a truce.

That was all in the past. They were too alike to be enemies.

Lucky hurried into the boardroom for a brief production meeting before seeing Freddie Leon and Alex Woods. She'd already made up her mind to greenlight *Gangsters*. She'd read the script and considered it brilliant. Alex Woods was a fine writer.

After speaking to her team individually, she was pleased that they'd each agreed with her decision to go ahead. She needed assurance they were all in sync that the movie could make a lot of money for the studio. Alex Woods was a controversial and dangerous film-maker, but when he delivered, everyone knew he was worth the trouble.

The heads of production, domestic distribution, foreign and marketing were duly assembled. They were a top-rate group of people, and after a short meeting Lucky felt assured of success.

She returned to her office, and was just about to call her half-brother, Steven, in England, where he and his family had recently moved, when Kyoko put his head around the door. 'Alex Woods and Freddie Leon are here,' he announced. 'Should I keep them waiting?'

She glanced at the Cartier clock on her desk – a present from Lennie. It was exactly twelve noon. She replaced the receiver, reminding herself to call Steven later. 'Show them in,' she said, well aware that the most important and secure people never kept anyone waiting.

Freddie led the way with his bland smile and expressionless grey eyes.

Lucky rose to greet him. The thing she liked about Freddie was his business-like attitude. No phoney deal with him: he had a purpose and he got right to it.

Alex Woods followed Freddie into her office. She'd never met him, but had read many interview pieces about him, and had often seen his photograph in newspapers and magazines.

The photos did not prepare her for the man's actual presence. He was tall and well-built with powerful good looks and a killer smile – which he immediately flashed in her direction.

For a moment she was taken aback. It was a rare occurrence for Lucky to feel vulnerable – almost girlish – it was like she was seventeen checking out a hot number and in her single days she'd had enough hot numbers to last several lifetimes.

Freddie introduced them. She shook Alex's hand. His grasp was firm and strong – a secure man.

She withdrew her hand and started speaking a shade too quickly, pushing back her long dark hair. 'Uh . . . Mr Woods, it's a pleasure to finally meet you. I'm a big admirer of your work.'

Hmm . . . Spoken like a true dumb fan. What was *wrong* with her? Why was she reacting like this?

Alex flashed that smile again, giving himself time to digest this woman's extraordinary beauty. She was dazzling in an offbeat way. Everything about her was incredibly sensual, from her tangle of jet curls to her watchful black eyes and full soft mouth. Her very fuckable mouth.

He found his eyes dropping to her rounded breasts concealed beneath a white silk shirt. She was not wearing a bra and he could make out the faint shadow of her nipples. He wondered if she was wearing any underwear at all.

Jesus! What was going on here? He was half-way to a hard-on. Why hadn't Freddie warned him?

Lucky was well aware of his scrutiny. 'Please sit down,' she said, willing herself to keep her mind on business.

Freddie was oblivious to the sexual tension heating up the room. He had an agenda and he stuck to it. Smooth agent talk slipped from his lips like nectar. 'Panther needs a film-maker like Alex Woods,' he said. 'I don't have to tell you how many times his movies have been nominated.'

'I'm well aware of Mr Woods' illustrious record,' Lucky said. 'And we'd love to be in business with him. However, I understand the projected budget on *Gangsters* is almost twenty-two million. That's an enormous commitment.'

Freddie was right there with an answer. 'Not for an Alex Woods film,' he said evenly. 'His movies always make money.'

'With the right casting,' Lucky pointed out.

'Alex's casting is impeccable. He doesn't need stars. The public comes for him.'

Alex leaned forward. 'Did you read the script?' he asked, watching her closely.

31

Her eyes met his with a level gaze. She knew he was waiting for compliments. She also knew it was better to keep him off balance – for now. 'Yes, I did,' she said, without blinking. 'It's violent, but truthful.' A pause. 'My father, Gino, was in Vegas at that time. He built the original Mirage Hotel. You might enjoy meeting him.'

His eyes remained fixed on hers. 'I'd like that very much.'

She refused to be the one to break the look. 'I'll arrange it,' she said coolly, pretending they weren't locked into some subliminal eye-contact power struggle. 'He lives in Palm Springs.'

'I can drive down there any time you say.'

'So,' Freddie said, sensing closure. 'Do we have a deal?'

'More or less,' Lucky replied, switching her attention to Freddie, and then getting mad at herself for being the first to look away from Alex.

Freddie ignored the ambiguity of her reply. 'This is a winning combination,' he predicted enthusiastically. 'Panther Studios presents Alex Woods' *Gangsters*. I can smell the Oscar now!'

'Just one small thing,' Lucky said, picking up her favorite silver pen – another present from Lennie – and tapping it impatiently on her desk. 'I'm aware that Paramount passed on this project because of the graphic violence, and I'm not asking you to tone it down. However . . . about the sex . . .'

'What about it?' Alex demanded, challenging her to object.

'The script makes it clear that several of the actresses are naked in certain scenes – yet it seems our hero and his friends remain modestly covered.'

'What's the problem?' Alex asked, genuinely not getting it.

'Well . . .' Lucky said slowly. 'This is an equal opportunity studio. If the females get to take it off, so do the guys.'

'Huh?' Alex said blankly.

Suddenly Lucky was back in control. 'Let me put it this way, Mr Woods. If we get to see tits an' ass, we get to see dick too. And I'm *not* talking Dick Van Dyke.' A small smile as Freddie and Alex reeled at the thought. 'And if we can work that out, then, gentlemen, we've got a deal.'

Chapter Three

'HOW OLD ARE you, sweetie?' the fifty-five-year-old lech in the Brioni suit asked the exceptionally pretty fresh-faced honey blond sitting across his desk.

'Nineteen,' she replied truthfully, although she'd already lied about her name, substituting Brown as her surname instead of Stanislopolous. Brigette Stanislopolous was a mouthful, whereas Brigette Brown had a certain ring to it. Plus Brown was anonymous, and Brigette had no intention of anyone finding out who she was.

'Well.' Mr Fifty-five-year-old cleared his throat, wondering if anyone had nailed this delectable piece of female flesh. 'You've certainly got all the attributes to have a very successful career as a model.' His eyes lingered on her breasts. 'You're tall enough, pretty enough, and if you lost ten pounds you'd be thin enough.' A pause. 'Get rid of the baby fat and I'll arrange for you to have test shots taken.' Another pause. 'In the meantime, I'll take you to dinner tonight and we'll discuss your future.'

'Sorry,' Brigette said, rising to her feet. 'I'm busy tonight.' She paused at the door. 'But, uh, I, like, certainly appreciate your advice.'

Mr Lech jumped up. He was surprised she hadn't accepted his invitation – they usually did. Girls who wanted to be models were always hungry: usually they had no money and dinner with him was considered a coup.

34

'How about tomorrow night?' he suggested, with an encouraging leer.

Brigette smiled sweetly. She had a lovely smile, as innocent as spring flowers. 'Do you want to fuck me or get me started as a model?' she asked, shocking the socks off Mr Lech, who was not used to being spoken to in such a fashion by a junior piece of ass.

'You have a dirty mouth, little girl,' he said angrily.

'All the better to say goodbye with,' she said, slipping through the door, calling out a final, 'See you on the cover of *Glamour*!'

She hit the street, steaming at his condescending attitude. Men! What pigs! Lose ten pounds indeed! She was not fat – in fact, she was as thin as she'd ever been. And did he honestly think she would go to dinner with an ancient old cretin like him? *No way.* 'Read my lips, old man,' she said aloud, as she bounced along Madison Avenue. 'You are *not* a contender!'

Nobody took any notice. This was New York, and here you could get away with anything.

Brigette was five feet eight inches tall and weighed a hundred and ten pounds. She had sun-kissed honey-blond hair, which she wore shoulder length and straight. Her lips were full and pouting, her eyes blue and knowing, and her skin had a glistening luminous quality. She radiated health and energy. Most men found her fresh-faced sex-appeal irresistible.

Brigette loved the city. She was crazy about the hot dirty sidewalks and the way a person could get lost in the rushing crowds. In New York she was not Brigette Stanislopolous, one of the richest girls in the world. In New York she was just another pretty face, desperately trying to carve out a career.

Thank God Lucky and Lennie had understood when she'd informed them she wanted to skip college and take a shot at making it as a model in New York. They had not objected, in fact they'd convinced her maternal grandmother, Charlotte, she should go for it, but only on the condition that if it didn't work out in six months she'd go to college and continue her education.

No chance. Because it *was* going to work out. Brigette was a true believer; something good *had* to happen for her.

So far her luck had not been the best. Okay, so she was wealthy, but what did that mean? It wasn't like she'd earned the money herself. Her fortune was just sitting there – inherited from her billionaire grandfather, Dimitri, and her mother, Olympia. Both of them dead and buried. A lot of good the money had done them.

Her real father, Claudio Cadducci, was also dead, not such a sad thing for she'd never known him. Her mother had divorced him as soon as she'd given birth to Brigette because of his constant indiscretions. They'd been married when Olympia was nineteen and Claudio forty-five. According to all reports, Claudio had been a handsome Italian businessman with immense charm and an expensive wardrobe. Part of his divorce settlement had included two Ferraris and three million dollars. Unfortunately Claudio had never had time to enjoy the cars or the money because a few months later he'd stepped out of a limo in Paris and been accidentally blown to pieces by a terrorist bomb.

Olympia had married again immediately, this time to a Polish count who lasted exactly sixteen weeks. Brigette didn't remember the count at all. The only stepfather she'd known was Lennie, whom she adored.

Sometimes she missed her mother with a deep feeling of emptiness that nothing could fill. She'd been twelve when Olympia had died and there'd been nobody to take her place, except grandmother Charlotte, a New York socialite who led an extremely busy social life, and Lucky and Lennie, who were both so involved with their work and their kids that even though they made time whenever they could, it wasn't enough.

Brigette knew she had to find something to fill the void.

It certainly wasn't going to be a man. Men were not to be trusted. Men were only after one thing. Sex.

She'd had sex and she didn't want it again. Not until she was the most famous supermodel in the world.

Last year she'd gotten engaged for about ten minutes to the grandson of one of her grandfather's business rivals. They'd had a great time together, until she'd discovered he was a total coke freak. Brigette wasn't into drugs. She'd ended the engagement quickly and taken off for Greece, where she'd spent time with her grandfather's relatives.

Stopping off at Bloomingdale's, she perused the makeup counters, buying a pale bronze lipstick and some shiny lip-gloss. She loved makeup as long as it was natural looking. It was fun experimenting, trying new looks. When she was a star she planned on launching a personal makeup line. Oh, yes, she was going to amass her own fortune – it was merely a matter of time.

She'd been in New York for seven weeks and Mr Fifty-five-year-old lech was the third modeling agent she'd seen. It wasn't easy getting appointments, and since she had no intention of using her connections, she'd simply have to keep slogging away. An annoying thought, for Brigette was impatient, she expected it to happen yesterday.

She took a cab back to the apartment she shared with another girl in SoHo. Both Charlotte and Lucky had insisted she have a room-mate, although Brigette was sure she would've been perfectly fine on her own.

Lucky herself had found Anna, and Brigette suspected that she was a paid spy planted to keep an eye on her, but she wasn't bothered – after all, she had no secrets.

Anna was in her late twenties, a thin girl with long brown hair and dreamy eyes. She wrote poetry, stayed home most of the time, and was always available to do anything Brigette wanted.

She was cooking eggs when Brigette got in. 'How'd it go today?' she inquired, adding too much pepper.

'Okay,' Brigette said, thinking that it had not gone well at all. It never did. Oh, God! Maybe she was doomed to failure.

Anna brushed a lock of fine hair out of her eyes. 'Do they want you?'

'Ha!' Brigette replied, not pleased. 'They want me to lose ten pounds.'

'You're not fat.'

Brigette pulled a face. 'Don't I know it,' she said, smoothing down her extra short skirt. 'He said I had baby fat.'

'Baby fat!'

'Yes. What a retard!'

Anna continued to stir the eggs. 'So what next?'

Brigette shrugged. 'I'll keep trying.'

Later she ordered pizza and sat out on the fire-escape eating it because the apartment was so uncomfortably hot. She could have been living in luxury in an air-conditioned penthouse on Park Avenue, but that was not for her. She preferred the struggle.

Munching a slice of pizza, she thought about her life and the twisted turns it had taken.

Sometimes it was difficult to believe.

Sometimes she burst out crying for no reason.

Sometimes the memory of Tim Wealth came back to haunt her and she couldn't get him out of her mind.

Tim Wealth. Hot young movie star.

He'd taken her virginity at fifteen. And gotten himself murdered for his trouble.

How well she remembered him. How many nights she shuddered at the memories.

Poor Tim had gotten in the way of Santino Bonnatti – a lifelong enemy of the Santangelos – just when Santino was in the middle of a kidnapping attempt on Brigette and her younger uncle, Bobby.

Santino's men had brutally murdered Tim and left him dead in his apartment, while she and Bobby were forcibly taken to Santino's house and sexually abused. She could still recall in sickening detail cowering naked and terrified in the center of Santino's bed while the perverted freak, clad only in his underwear, stripped off her little brother's clothes and prepared to commit an obscene act.

It was then that she'd spotted the gun placed casually on a bedside table, and as Bobby's anguished screams filled the room, she'd known she had to do something.

Sobbing silently, she'd crawled across the bed and reached for the weapon.

Santino was too busy with Bobby to notice.

With shaking hands she'd picked up the gun, pointed it straight at the monster and squeezed the trigger.

Once.

Twice.

Three times.

Goodbye, Santino.

She shook her head vigorously, trying desperately not to remember.

Shut out the memories, Brigette.

Forget the past.

Concentrate on now . . .

☆ ☆ ☆

'She's a crazy bitch,' Alex said irritably.

'She's putting up the money for your movie,' Freddie replied mildly.

'What's her fucking problem?' Alex steamed.

'Didn't know she had one.'

'Christ! You heard her.'

Freddie sighed patiently. 'What?'

'She wants to see actors with their cocks hanging out. What kind of shit is that? Doesn't she realize there's a double standard?'

'Don't let it bother you.'

'It *does* fucking bother me,' Alex said angrily, as they reached their cars.

'Why?' Freddie asked, one hand on the door of his gleaming Bentley Continental. 'Whatever you shoot'll have to be cut. She can't afford an X rating, it'll kill the grosses, plus the theater chains won't book an X. She'll realize that.'

'She must be some sick broad,' Alex muttered.

Freddie laughed. 'Well, she sure got to you, I've never seen you like this.'

'Because she's stupid.'

'No,' Freddie said quickly. 'That's one thing Lucky's not. She took over Panther two years ago and she's doing an excellent job. She had no previous experience in the film industry, yet she's definitely turning things around.'

'Okay, okay, she's a fucking genius – but I'm not asking any of my actors to march around stark bollock naked.'

'Nicely put, Alex. I'll call you later.'

Freddie got into his Bentley and took off.

Alex stood beside his black Porsche, still fuming at Lucky's request. Didn't she realize women were not turned on by male nudity? It was a well-known fact.

He got in his car and drove to his production offices located on Pico. He'd called his production company Wood-

san Productions, because it sounded peaceful and still incorp-
orated his name. He owned the building – one of his better
business investments.

He had two assistants, Lili, a softly pretty Chinese woman
in her forties without whom he claimed he could not function, and France, an exquisite Vietnamese twenty-five-year-old,
who'd once been a bar girl in Saigon before he'd chivalrously
rescued her and brought her to America. He'd slept with
both of them, but that was in the past and now they were
nothing more than loyal assistants.

'How was your meeting?' Lili asked anxiously.

He slumped in a worn leather chair behind his enormous littered desk. 'Good,' he said. '*Gangsters* has a new
home.'

Lili clapped her hands together. 'I knew it!'

France brought him a mug of hot black tea, stood behind
him and began to massage his shoulders with relaxing kneading movements. 'Very tense,' she scolded. 'Not good.'

He could feel the pressure of her small firm breasts against
the back of his neck while her surprisingly strong hands dug
deep. It was comforting. Oriental women were the best.

'Let me ask you a question,' he said, still uptight about
Lucky's request.

'Yes?' both women chorused.

'Do you get off looking at naked guys?'

Lili's expression was impassive as she tried to figure out
the answer Alex wanted. France burst out giggling.

'Well?' Alex demanded, none too pleased by their
hesitation.

'*What* naked men?' Lili asked, stalling for time.

'On the screen,' Alex said shortly. 'Actors.'

'Mel Gibson? Johnny Romano?' France said hopefully.

'Jesus!' Alex exclaimed, fast losing patience. 'It doesn't
matter *who* they are.'

'Oh, yes, it does!' France retorted, abruptly stopping his massage. 'Anthony Hopkins – *no*! Richard Gere – *yes*!'

'Or Liam Neeson,' Lili added, a faraway look in her eyes.

'I'm not talking about just their upper torso,' Alex said ominously. 'I'm talking about everything – the whole caboodle.'

Lili figured out the answer he required, and even though she didn't mean it, she knew how to keep her boss happy. 'Oh, no,' she said quickly. 'We don't want to see that.'

'Exactly,' Alex exclaimed triumphantly. 'Women don't *want* to see it.'

'I do,' France murmured, low enough for him not to hear.

'Why are you asking?' Lili inquired.

''Cause Lucky Santangelo is a crazy bitch who's under the false impression women want to act like men.'

'Crazy bitch,' parroted France, thinking that Lucky Santangelo must be a really interesting woman whom she couldn't wait to meet.

'I don't get it,' Alex muttered, deciding that the next time he saw Lucky Santangelo he'd definitely set her straight. She had to learn a thing or two – and who better to teach her than the master himself?

Chapter Four

VENUS MARIA was in spectacular shape. She worked at it diligently, rising at six every morning to run up and down the Hollywood Hills with Sven, her personal trainer, before returning to her house for a punishing hour of aerobics and light weights.

Jesus! Staying in spectacular shape took some doing. Her routine was a major pain in the ass, but she never slacked off, because slacking off meant she would no longer have the best body in Hollywood. And fuck 'em, one thing they couldn't bitch about was her glorious bod.

Virginia Venus Maria Sierra had first come to Hollywood in her early twenties with her best friend, Ron Machio, a gay would-be choreographer. They'd hitchhiked their way from New York and survived in LA by taking any gig they could get. Venus had worked in a supermarket bagging groceries, as a nude model for an art class, a movie extra, and various one-nighters singing and dancing.

Ron had attempted waiting tables, running errands for a messenger service, and chauffeuring limousines. Together they'd managed to survive, until one night Venus was discovered by a small-time record producer who'd hung out at the same all-night clubs she and Ron frequented. With some heavy persuasion she'd gotten him to cut a record using her, then she and Ron had put together a sexy on the edge video to go with it. Venus had planned the look and the style, while Ron had come up with all the right moves.

Overnight they'd scored, for within six weeks their record was number one and Venus Maria was launched.

Now, five years later, at the age of twenty-seven, she was a major superstar with an enormous cult following. And Ron was a hot director with two hit movies behind him. It helped that Ron's current boyfriend was Harris Von Stepp, an extraordinarily rich show-business mogul who'd financed Ron's first film. As Venus often pointed out, if Ron hadn't possessed the talent, it would never have happened for him. She didn't like Harris, he was twenty-five years older than Ron and icily controlling.

As an actress the critics creamed Venus, even though every one of her movies did mega box-office. Her latest, *Finder*, had made over eight million its first weekend out. She was one of the few female stars able to open a movie.

It obviously pissed off the mostly male critics that a woman could be as daring and outspoken as Venus, and *still* manage to have a fantastic career. Journalists were always writing about her in derogatory terms – saying she was finished, tapped out, gone with the wind.

Finished! Ha! Her last greatest-hits CD had leaped into the charts at number one and stayed there for seven weeks.

Finished, indeed! Who were they kidding? She had legions of loyal fans, and if the critics didn't like her, too bad. She was around for the long haul and they'd better get used to it or bail out.

Two years ago she'd gotten married to Cooper Turner, a classically handsome movie star with a major stud reputation. Even though he was hitting forty-seven – twenty years older than she – she'd recently found out that her dear husband was unable to keep his dick in his pants. He adored women, and although she was sure he loved her, there was nothing she could do about his wandering cock. Cooper was a player who couldn't help it. Too bad, because they made a dynamite couple.

When they'd first met, she'd been involved in a liaison with one of his best friends, the New York property tycoon, Martin Swanson. At the time Martin was very hot for her and *very* married. Their affair had culminated in the suicide of Martin's wife in front of them. Cooper had been there for her all the way. Tragedy had brought them together and they'd fallen in love and gotten married.

At one time Cooper had mentioned wanting to start a family. She'd told him she wasn't ready, because she knew exactly what would happen: *she* would have the babies, while *he* cruised the club scene; *she* would lose her figure, while *he* stocked up on Armani suits; *she* would sit home with them, while *he* would be out showing off the famous Cooper cock.

No. Starting a family with Cooper was not for her.

Marriage, she realized, had probably been a mistake, and lately she'd been considering getting a fast divorce.

That would send the tabloids into a frenzy. She was their darling, their favorite. Ever since her dear brother, Emilio the slob, had sold them the story of her life, there'd been no getting rid of them. Every week they ran a sensational new story about her. According to the tabloids she'd slept with everyone from John Kennedy Jr to Madonna!

If they only knew the truth. She'd been the faithful wife, while Cooper put it about like a drunken hooker on a Friday night. Well, damn him, the time had come for a showdown.

After working out, Venus took a shower, then sauntered downstairs to greet her masseur, Rodriguez, a sizzling Latino of twenty-two with the experienced hands of a man twice his age. Rodriguez was all sinewy muscle, with dark wavy hair and smoldering eyes – just the way Venus liked 'em. She had a weakness for extremely handsome men – especially men with tight curved butts, and arms and legs to cream over.

Lately she'd been considering having an affair with him, but wouldn't that be baby snatching?

No way, she decided. Twenty-two was hardly a baby, and Rodriguez seemed *very* worldly. He was from Argentina, and delighted in regaling her with tales of his love trysts with older married women whose rich husbands failed to satisfy them.

That was one problem she *didn't* have. Cooper was an extraordinarily accomplished lover. He had a slow hand – the best kind. He truly loved women, and got off by making sure he gave them the ultimate pleasure trip.

Too bad the trip was soon coming to an end.

☆   ☆   ☆

Venus was late for lunch. This didn't bother Lucky, who'd taken advantage of the time by using her cellular to return a few calls.

When Venus entered the commissary all conversation stopped as the platinum blond casually sashayed across the crowded room to the private executive dining area in the back. There was something about Venus that screamed SEX! There were actresses in Hollywood taller, thinner, younger, more beautiful, but Venus had it over all of them: she managed to look vulnerable, smart and incredibly slutty all at the same time. It was an irresistible combination. Women admired her strength and men couldn't wait to fuck her.

Sliding into her seat she immediately ordered a white wine spritzer.

'Fifteen minutes, I'd like an excuse,' Lucky said, tapping her watch.

'I was considering screwing my masseur,' Venus murmured provocatively.

Lucky nodded. Nothing Venus said surprised her. 'Seems like a good excuse to me.'

'*I* thought so.'

'And what did you decide?'

Venus rolled her eyes and licked her lips. 'Mmmm . . . I'm sure he's *very* talented.'

'And you're *very* married.'

'So is Cooper,' Venus said sharply, her mood quickly changing. 'I don't see it stopping *him*.'

Lucky had been waiting for this moment. Everyone knew about Cooper and his out-of-control libido. Venus had never chosen to discuss it, and even though the two women were close Lucky hadn't wanted to rock the friendship. She'd simply assumed that Venus ignored her famous husband's indiscretions.

'I've about had it,' Venus said, with a defiant shake of her platinum curls. 'At first I thought flirting was his thing, which was okay with me, 'cause I'm not exactly a slouch in that department myself. Now I realize he's jumping everything that breathes.' She paused, shaking her head again. 'I don't get it,' she continued with a perverse twist of a smile. 'He's got *me* – every man's wet-dream fantasy. What more can he possibly want?'

'Have you confronted him?' Lucky asked, knowing that Venus was hardly the kind of woman to lie back.

'Fuck no!' Venus steamed. 'According to my hairdresser, who knows everything, my dear philandering husband is now in bed with Leslie Kane.' A defiant pause. 'As far as I'm concerned he can stay there. I'm not mad at him, I just want a divorce.'

'Well . . .' Lucky paused for a moment. 'If there's anything I can do . . .'

'Yeah,' Venus said fiercely. 'Don't believe a word you're gonna read, 'cause the rags'll come down on me big time.' She frowned, before adding indignantly, '*He*'s the one fucking his way through this town, and *I*'m the one who'll get the whore/slut headlines.'

Lucky agreed. It was a well-known fact that men were always the protected ones, while women got the blame for everything. If Meryl Streep starred in a movie that flopped she was instantly denigrated. If Jack Nicholson made three duds in a row they lined up to pay him millions of bucks for the next. Not at Panther. Lucky made sure women were treated equally in every way – including star salaries.

'Why couldn't I have gotten to Lennie before *you* picked him off?' Venus complained. 'Lennie's so great. You won't find *him* screwing his co-star.'

And if I did I'd probably kill him, Lucky thought calmly. She had a vengeful streak that was not to be messed with.

'Leslie Kane!' Venus snorted. 'Is Cooper the only guy in town who doesn't know she used to be one of Madam Loretta's hookers?'

'Have you told him it's over?'

'Leslie's having a dinner at her house tonight. I'm considering announcing it over dessert – that way everyone gets to share in the good news. May as well dump him with a bang.'

Lucky shook her head. 'You're really bad, you know that?'

Venus raised an eyebrow. '*I*'m bad? Try blaming the motherfucker who's screwing around on me.'

The rest of the lunch they discussed business, including the grosses on *Finder*, a couple of scripts Venus was interested in developing, and the future plans of her personal production company. Then Venus wanted advice on whether she should switch agents. Freddie Leon had been pursuing her and she felt like a change.

'Freddie's the best,' Lucky said, sipping Perrier. 'In fact, I had a meeting with him and Alex Woods this morning.' A casual pause. 'Do you know Alex?'

Venus didn't take a beat. 'Big talent. Big dick. Only fucks Orientals. Doesn't give head, but *loves* getting it.'

'How come you know everything?'

'Spent a stoned evening at a party with one of his exes – a spicy Chinese piece. She gave great detail.'

'We're doing his next project. A movie called *Gangsters*.'

Venus couldn't conceal her amazement. 'You're making an Alex Woods movie? *You*? Surely you know he's supposed to be a total chauvinist prick?'

'With a dynamite script.'

'Boy, lots of luck on this one.'

Lucky smiled. 'Thanks, but I don't think I'll need it.'

☆ ☆ ☆

The second production meeting of the day went smoothly; possible casting on *Gangsters* was discussed, and although some good names came up, Lucky knew Alex Woods would have his own ideas. She was aware that he didn't usually work with stars but Freddie had called her after lunch to tell her he was pushing Latino movie idol, Johnny Romano, for one of the leads. Lucky liked the idea: Johnny, with his huge following, could guarantee a big-bucks opening weekend.

'You've got *my* vote,' she said.

'Good. I'll tell Johnny.'

After the production meeting was over, the last thing she felt like doing was an interview for a magazine. However, she was well aware of the power of good PR, and bringing Panther Studios back to where it belonged was important. With *Finder* and *River Storm* doing so well, it was time to put out a positive PR spin, even though she was wary of the press and usually did everything possible to stay out of print.

Mickey Stolli, the former head of Panther – now running Orpheus – was constantly making negative statements to the press, saying Panther was finished, that none of its movies made money. Even though everything he said was a blatant lie, it wasn't good PR. The time had come to retaliate.

Lucky settled in with an earnest black man in his thirties and spoke eloquently about her plans for the future of the studio. 'Panther's making the type of movies *I* like to see,' she said firmly, pushing a hand through her unruly black curls. 'In my kind of movies women are smart. They are not relegated to the kitchen, bedroom or whore house. They're strong, well-rounded women with careers and lives of their own who do not live their life through a man. *That's* what intelligent women want to see. I'm putting into development and production the movies Hollywood *should* be making.'

Alex Woods called in the middle of the interview. 'Can I take you up on that visit to your father?' he asked, speaking in a low, fast voice. 'How about this weekend?'

'Uh, I don't know,' she said hesitantly. 'I'll have to arrange it with Gino.'

Alex sounded like a man on a mission. 'You'll come with me. It's important.'

She had not planned on accompanying him. 'I'm away this weekend,' she said, wondering why she felt the need to explain.

'Where?' he demanded, like he had a right to know.

None of your fucking business. 'Uh . . . I'm spending a couple of days with my husband.'

'Didn't know you were married.'

Oh, really? Where have you been? 'To Lennie Golden.'

'The actor?'

'Very good.'

He ignored her sarcasm. 'When *can* we go?' he asked impatiently.

'If you're that anxious I'll set it up for next week.'

Very insistent. 'And you *will* come?'

'If I can.'

Alex Woods was the kind of man she could have got into trouble with. Before Lennie . . . before her life had become so structured with kids and a studio to run and all the other things she was involved with.

She tried to return her attention to the interviewer, but two thoughts kept buzzing around in her head, vying for attention.

Alex Woods was a dangerous temptation.

Lucky refused to be tempted.

Chapter Five

DONNA LANDSMAN, formerly Donatella Bonnatti, resided in a fake Spanish castle perched atop a knoll above Benedict Canyon. She lived with her husband, George, who was her late husband Santino's former accountant, and her son, Santino Junior, a truculent, over-weight sixteen-year-old. Her other three children had all left home, willing to face anything rather than life with their domineering and controlling mother.

Santino Junior – or Santo as he was known – had elected to stay because he was the only one who could successfully manipulate her. Plus he was sharp enough to realize that *someone* had to inherit the family fortune, and that someone was going to be him.

Santo was Donna's youngest child and only son. She worshipped him. In her mind he could do no wrong.

For his sixteenth birthday, against George's advice, she'd bought him a green Corvette and a solid gold Rolex. Then, in case this was not enough, she'd handed him an American Express card with unlimited credit, five thousand dollars in cash, and thrown him an enormous party at the Beverly Hills Hotel.

She wanted her son to own the world.

Santo was in complete agreement.

George, however, was not. 'You're ruining him,' he'd warned Donna on many occasions. 'If you give him everything at such an early age, what does he have to look forward to?'

'Nonsense,' Donna replied. 'He lost his real father, he's entitled to whatever I can provide.'

George had given up arguing. It wasn't worth the battle. Donna was a difficult and complex woman. Sometimes he felt he didn't understand her at all.

☆　☆　☆

Donatella Cocolioni was born in a small village in Sicily to a poor, hard-working family. She'd spent the first sixteen years of her life taking care of her many younger brothers and sisters, until one day an older cousin, who lived in America, visited her village and picked her out as a bride for the important American businessman, Santino Bonnatti. Her father agreed it was an excellent match, and even though he'd never met Santino, he'd accepted a thousand dollars in cash, and sent her on her way to the United States without any thought for her feelings.

The truth was he'd sold her to a stranger in a far-away country, forcing her to leave the love of her life – Furio – a boy from her village. Donatella was heartbroken.

Arriving in America she was taken straight to Santino Bonnatti's house in Los Angeles. He'd looked her over with his beady eyes and given her cousin the nod. 'Okay, okay, she ain't no beauty, but she'll do. Buy her some clothes, have her taught English, an' make sure she knows who I am, 'cause I ain't puttin' up with no crap.'

Her cousin had taken her to his girlfriend's house – a parrot-faced blond imported from the Bronx. She'd stayed there several weeks while the blond attempted to teach her English. It was a disaster. The little English Donatella mastered came with a heavy Sicilian accent.

The second time she saw Santino was at their wedding. She wore a long white dress and a frightened expression. After the ceremony, Santino strutted around smoking a fat Cuban cigar, swapping dirty jokes with the boys while practically ignoring her.

Her cousin told her not to worry, everything would work out fine. Later she discovered Santino had paid him ten thousand dollars in cash for her delivery.

After the reception they'd gone back to Santino's house. Santino was not like the love she'd left behind in Sicily – he was older, short, in his late twenties, with thin lips, a rapidly receding hairline and an exceptionally hairy body. She found this out when he stripped his clothes off, dropping them on the floor with an impatient shrug. 'Get naked, honey,' he leered. 'Lemme get a load of t'goods.'

She ran to the bathroom, shivering in her satin wedding dress, tears staining her cheeks, until Santino marched in and, with no ceremony, unzipped her dress, ripped off her bra, pulled down her panties and bent her over the sink, entering her from behind, grunting like a hog.

The pain was so staggering that she screamed aloud. Santino didn't care – covering her mouth with a hairy hand he continued pumping away until he was satisfied. Then he walked out without a word, leaving her in the bathroom with blood dripping down between her legs.

That was the start of their marriage.

In quick succession she bore him two daughters, hoping this would make him happy. It didn't. His fury that she hadn't given birth to a son mounted daily – he desired an heir to carry on the great Bonnatti name.

When she didn't get pregnant again, he sent her to doctors, who poked and prodded and found nothing wrong. Santino belittled her, telling her she was a failure as a wife.

One day she suggested he have his semen tested. She'd been reading American magazines such as Cosmopolitan, *and it dawned on her that failure to conceive wasn't always the woman's fault.*

Santino was livid. He whacked her across the face so violently that she lost two teeth. It was the first time he had hit her. It certainly wasn't the last.

As time passed she discovered he kept many mistresses. She didn't care – the less he came near her the better.

She found solace in fixing big bowls of pasta which she consumed for breakfast, lunch and dinner. She baked soft doughy rolls and ate those too. In the supermarket she stocked up on cookies, chocolate and ice-cream. Soon she was huge.

Santino was disgusted. He spent more and more time with his svelte mistresses, although occasionally he fell on top of Donatella in the middle of the night, when he was drunk enough, forcing himself inside her.

He never gave her sexual pleasure, she was merely a receptacle for his maleness. All Santino required was a son.

She finally got pregnant again and he was ecstatic, but when their third child was another girl, he was so angry he moved out for six months.

Donatella considered those six months the happiest of her marriage.

When Santino came home, she hardened her heart against him. She was older and wiser and refused to take any more of his garbage.

Santino accepted her new attitude. From a stupid peasant girl she'd turned into a nagging balls-breaker. Finally he had a wife he could respect.

He made love to her once a month to keep her quiet until eventually she got pregnant again. This time she gave birth to a boy. They named him Santino Junior, and at last Santino was a happy man.

Donatella threw all the love she didn't get from her husband into her relationship with her son. Santino loved the boy, too. They vied with each other to see who could give little Santo the most attention. As soon as the child reached an age where he could understand, he played them against each other, although he always favored his father.

Donatella accepted that her life wasn't so bad. She lived in a three-million-dollar mansion in Bel Air, once the residence of a silent-screen star. She was the wife of an important business-man. She had four healthy children, and she was able to send money regularly to her relatives in Sicily.

Occasionally Santino suggested she learn proper English, claiming her strong accent embarrassed him. He also nagged her to lose weight.

She ignored both his requests, laughing in his face.

One day, in the summer of 1983, Steven Berkely, a black lawyer, turned up at her door and informed her that Santino was the lowest form of human life. Ha! As if she didn't know.

She invited him in, curious to find out what he had to say.

He threw a copy of a pornographic magazine on her coffee table and angrily told her the naked woman on the cover was his fiancée. 'Her face on somebody else's body,' he said harshly, thrusting the magazine at her. 'These are fake pictures.'

'I no look a' this dirt,' Donatella said, sorry she'd invited him in.

'My fiancée tried to kill herself because of these pictures,' Steven said roughly. 'All because your sick sadistic husband publishes this filth.'

She knew Santino owned a publishing company. He'd always told her they published technical books, not disgusting maga-zines. Now she had pornography in her own house, and an angry lawyer claiming Santino was responsible.

The phone rang. Glad of the diversion, she rushed to answer it. 'There's a house on Bluejay Way where your husband keeps his favorite mistress,' a husky female voice whispered. 'Come see for yourself. His car's outside.'

Donatella hustled the lawyer out. If she could catch Santino with one of his mistresses she'd make the lying swine pay. Muttering to herself, she hurried to her car, and set off to bust her cheating husband.

Donatella had no trouble finding Bluejay Way. She parked behind Santino's car and marched up the driveway of the house, ringing the doorbell.

Within moments the door opened an inch, and Zeko, one of her husband's bodyguards, peeked through the crack.

Donatella gave the door a hefty kick, hurting her foot in the process. 'Where you putta my husband?' she demanded.

'Mrs Bonnatti,' said a stunned Zeko, opening the door wider, failing to notice two men coming up the driveway behind her.

'FBI,' one of the men said, holding up identification.

Ignoring the two men, Donatella barged into the house, coming face to face with a willowy blond.

'Mrs Bonnatti,' the blond said, as if she was expecting her.

Donatella glared at her. 'You gotta my Santino?'

'He's here,' the blond replied calmly. 'Before you see him, you and I should talk.'

'He sleepa with you?' Donatella shouted.

The two FBI men shoved past Zeko and burst into the house waving guns. Zeko lumbered after them.

'Who's these people?' yelled Donatella.

'Get against the wall and shut up,' one of the men commanded.

Then an almighty crash came from the back of the house, followed by several gunshots.

Donatella crossed herself. Ignoring the FBI men, she rushed down the corridor toward the noise.

A man was hustling a child and a young teenage girl into the hallway. Donatella pushed past him and entered the room they'd come from.

Santino's body was sprawled on the floor next to the bed. He was covered in blood and very dead.

'My God! My God! My God!' shrieked Donatella.

A dark-haired woman was still in the room. Donatella recognized her as Lucky Santangelo, the Bonnatti family's long time enemy.

'Whore!' Donatella screamed hysterically. 'You shotta my husband. You killed him. I saw you!'

The rest was confusion. The police arrived and arrested Lucky Santangelo for Santino's murder. Months later, when the case came to court, it turned out that the real culprit had not been Lucky, but Brigette Stanislopolous, a teenage heiress whom Santino had held captive, and while he'd been molesting the girl's six-year-old uncle, Bobby, Lucky's son, she'd shot him. Everything had been captured on videotape, evidence that was produced in court.

Brigette walked and so did Lucky.

Donatella was left a widow with four children to raise. She was filled with an unforgiving rage. Santino might have been an unfaithful pig, but he was her unfaithful pig and the father of her children. Something had to be done to avenge his murder. After all, she was Sicilian, and in Sicily, if a family member is brutally murdered, their death has to be avenged. It was a matter of honor. It made no difference how long the vendetta took.

Carlos, Santino's older brother, came to see her, offering to take over all of Santino's businesses, cutting her in for a paltry five percent. Donatella told him she'd think about it, although she had no intention of doing so. Instead she met with Santino's accountant, George, and got herself an education. Santino's main business was import/export, which she soon discovered *brought in millions of dollars a year, most of it in cash. He also owned real estate, interests in two New Jersey casinos, and a very lucrative publishing company – which did, indeed, publish technology books, along with a selection of soft- and hard-core pornography.*

Donatella found out from George that she was Santino's legal partner. He'd often dumped documents in front of her, making her sign. She'd never dared question him. The pay-off was that everything was now hers.

George Landsman was an unassuming man who faded into the scenery with his mild manners and low voice. He'd been Santino's trusted lieutenant – there wasn't anything he didn't know about the various businesses. Quiet he might be, but George was a financial wizard. After watching him for a while, Donatella realized he was quite capable of keeping things running smoothly. With George's help and encouragement, she began to familiarize herself with everything, soon realizing that if she planned to take over, she'd have to rid herself of her cartoon accent, lose weight and get her long hair styled.

Once she started on her quest to improve herself she couldn't stop. First the accent went; then the weight; plastic surgery gave her a smaller nose, firmer chin and higher cheekbones; she had breast-reduction surgery, and got her hair cut and dyed; she purchased a closetful of designer clothes, and several pieces of important jewelry.

Somewhere along the road to improvement she married George, who, it turned out, had always lusted after her – even when she was fat and could barely speak English. The word 'orgasm' entered her vocabulary for the first time. She was considerably happier than she'd ever been before, especially when she discovered she possessed great skills as a capable businesswoman.

With George's tutoring she soaked up a lifetime of knowledge in a very short time. And when she finally felt she was ready, she began to make her own deals with George's sound advice to back her. First she sold the publishing firm, using the money she raised to take over an ailing cosmetics company. Months later she got rid of the cosmetics company and, with that profit, took over a chain of small hotels. Six months later she sold the hotel chain at more than double the price she'd paid.

From that moment on she was hooked. Takeovers became her game of choice.

Carlos, Santino's brother, was impressed. He came to see her again, this time suggesting a partnership. She turned him down, which didn't sit well with Carlos, who thought she should have kissed his ass.

'What're you doing about Lucky Santangelo?' she demanded of Carlos. 'We know the Santangelo family is responsible for Santino's murder, and you're letting them get away with it. If you *don't* do something, I will.'

Carlos glared at his dead brother's wife. This broad was something else. From a dumpy stupid hausfrau she'd turned herself into some kind of business dynamo, even learning to speak the language without that crazy accent. But did she really think she was capable of taking care of Lucky Santangelo?

No freaking way.

'Yeah. What'll you *do*?' Carlos asked, barely concealing a contemptuous sneer.

'Where I come from we honor our traditions,' Donatella replied ominously, thinking he was more of a deadbeat than his brother.

'Don't sweat it,' Carlos replied, angry that a woman would dare talk to him in such a way. What she needed was a proper man to slap the tongue right out of her plastic face. 'I got plans for that Santangelo cunt.'

Donatella arched her eyebrows. 'Really?' she said.

'Yeah, really,' he countered.

Carlos' plans did not pan out. In December 1985 he suffered an unfortunate fall from his Century City penthouse. Nobody knew how it happened.

Donatella knew.

Lucky Santangelo was responsible.

Donatella made the decision that it was up to her to ruin Lucky permanently. And with that end in mind she'd come up with a devastating plan to destroy her.

Every day at four o'clock, Santo arrived home from school. He made the most of the few hours of peace before his stupid mother descended and began fussing the crap out of him. Fortunately she and his wimpy stepfather were never home before seven, so that gave him plenty of time to do whatever he liked without either of them sticking their interfering noses in.

He hated his mother. Every day he thought about how much he hated her, and how unfair it was that she was still alive while his father was dead.

Why hadn't *she* been killed?

Why wasn't *her* dumb ass buried ten feet beneath the ground?

The only good thing about her was that she was easy. He could usually get anything he wanted – especially since all his siblings had taken off, leaving him in position *numero uno*.

As for George, he hated him, too. The man was an ineffectual wimp, whom Donna kicked around good. He was no stepfather. He was nothing.

Santo considered the hours between four and seven his special time. First he smoked a couple of joints; next he stuffed himself with ice-cream and candy; after that he flicked through his extensive pile of porno magazines hidden in a locked closet. If the girls turned him on, he jerked off – although mostly he saved that activity for HER.

SHE was the special one created for his pleasure.

SHE was everything a man could ever want.

Not that he was a man. He was sixteen, and being sixteen sucked.

Every morning when he got up and saw himself in the bathroom mirror, Santo wished he was older and thinner. If he was older he might have a better chance of scoring with HER. If he was thinner he might be able to make out with some of the more popular girls at school – the pretty ones with the Beverly Hills attitudes, nose-jobs, silky skin and long fair hair. These little tramps didn't care that he had plenty of money and a fancy car. They were too stupid to notice. Instead they ran after the dumb jerks who played football and worked out. Big sweaty assholes. He hated all of them. He didn't want them anyway. Not when he had HER.

SHE was a startlingly sexy blond with everything in the right place. And SHE didn't mind showing it. He'd seen her tits, her ass and her hairy pussy. He'd read her thoughts and knew what she wanted from a man.

Today he decided to concentrate on HER and forget about the other whores. After locking his bedroom door he went to his closet, reached in the back, and pulled out a suitcase filled with his collection, a collection that included early nude photos, where she sat around with her legs open exhibiting a big black bush of pubic hair, magazine lay-outs reflecting her rise to fame, CDs, posters, videos of her singles, taped TV appearances and interviews.

Reading her interviews was a major head trip. She was a maniac – talked about sex like she was one of the guys.

Santo devoured every word, memorizing her preferences. She liked men who went down on her – that was in *Playboy*;

she'd made love with a woman – *Vanity Fair*; she wanted sex constantly and fantasized about black men – *Rolling Stone*.

Yeah! She was some hot ticket. And he was rich enough to buy a ride straight up her wet pussy.

One day he knew he'd get the opportunity to do it with her.

One day Venus Maria would see him coming in more ways than one.

He leered at the thought. It made every day worth living.

Chapter Six

'I CAN'T BELIEVE I have an hour free before my next meeting,' Lucky said, collapsing into the leather chair behind her desk.

'Not exactly,' Kyoko said apologetically. 'Charlie Dollar's on the lot. I told him it was okay to stop by at five, and if you'd finished your interview you'd see him.'

'Oh, *great*,' she groaned. 'Why'd you do that?'

'He *is* one of Panther's biggest stars,' Kyoko reminded her. 'And I happen to know Mickey Stolli sent him a script he's interested in. So . . .'

'I know, I know . . . You're right, Ky. I should see him – keep him happy.'

'It would be prudent.'

She loved the way Kyoko spoke, he was always so proper.

'Okay, order two margaritas and a dish of guacamole from the Mexican place across the street. Then put on my Billie Holiday CD. I need a mind break and I suppose Charlie's the perfect person to have it with.'

Kyoko nodded, pleased she agreed with him.

The fiftyish Charlie strolled into her office five minutes later with a shit-eating grin and a bouquet of purple roses – her favorite.

Charlie, like most actors, could be a total pain in the ass. Lucky didn't care. She was fond of him because he didn't take himself too seriously, and he had a sardonic sense of humor, which made him stimulating company. In fact, if there hadn't been Lennie there might have been Charlie – he was certainly attractive enough in a Jack Nicholson off-center kind of way.

Charlie settled down on her couch and proceeded to light up a joint. 'Didja get my message?' he asked, dragging deeply.

'Couldn't miss it,' she replied, taking in his uncombed hair, scuffed Reeboks, rumpled T-shirt and ill-fitting pants. Somehow or other it all worked: the tramp look suited Charlie.

He patted his stomach. 'We're gonna dump the gut. Right?'

'Wouldn't want your fans to think you've lost it,' she said caustically.

'Smart lady.'

'You're so full of shit, Charlie,' she said, smiling affectionately.

He raised an indignant eyebrow. 'Why? 'Cause I wanna present the movie star image everyone knows an' loves?'

'Nope. You're just full of shit, period. Maybe *that*'s why I love you.'

Charlie took another deep drag before offering the joint to her. She declined. Maybe with Lennie, but not now, not with another meeting coming up.

Charlie mock-sighed. 'Lucky, Lucky, Lucky. What 'm I gonna do with you?'

She helped herself to some guacamole, savoring the tangy flavor. 'Certainly not the same as you do with every other woman,' she said tartly.

'Hey,' Charlie objected, extravagant eyebrows shooting up again. 'Can I help it if they all wanna jump my decrepit old bones? Lady, I do not encourage it. Truth is, I'm gettin' too old to choo-choo all night.'

'Oh, yeah, sure,' she said sarcastically.

He ignored her sarcasm. 'And I've *definitely* had it with baby chicks,' he continued. 'Went out the other night with one who'd never heard of Bruce Springsteen. Get *that* deal.'

Lucky shook her head. 'Life's tough, Charlie, when you won't date anyone over eighteen.'

They both laughed, enjoying their irreverent friendship.

'Word is you're off for a dirty weekend,' Charlie remarked, leaning back on the couch, examining his unmanicured nails.

She observed his comfortable gut, barely hidden beneath his baggy T-shirt, and wondered if he'd ever considered working out. 'Does it count as a dirty weekend if I'm spending it with my husband?' she asked.

'I sure hope so.'

She grinned, aching to see Lennie. 'I'll only be gone three days. Do me a big one, Charlie, try to save any other complaints until I get back.'

He nodded. 'Gonna do my best, Mafia Princess.'

'Don't call me that!' she protested.

He shook a knowing finger at her. 'C'mon, babe, y'know you love it.'

'I do not,' she said indignantly. 'My father was never into the whole mob scene. Gino was a very savvy businessman who just happened to have connected friends.'

'Sure, an' I drive a limo in my spare time.' A crooked grin. 'So, how's Gino doin'? The old guy's still got it goin' for him – I admire that in a senior citizen.'

'Balls of steel,' Lucky said drily. 'Runs in the family.'

Charlie blew a lazy smoke-ring. 'Never got a chance to see for myself,' he drawled.

'Is that a come-on?'

'Hey – balls of steel – my big turn-on.'

'Gee, I never knew you cared.'

'Sure I care.' A perfectly timed pause. 'Change my poster and I'll care even more.'

Actors! They always had an agenda. And, somehow or other, it always managed to put them in first position. 'Okay, Charlie,' she said with a small sigh, 'it's done. Now can we relax for five minutes?'

A big Charlie Dollar grin. 'Whatever you say, babe.'

☆ ☆ ☆

'Brigette?'

'Nona? Wow – Nona! How *are* you? When did you get back? And how did you *find* me?'

'Called your grandmother. After a brief interrogation she gave me your number. *Radical* security, babe. I could've been anyone.'

Nona Webster, ex-best friend whom she hadn't seen in two years because they'd drifted apart when Nona's rich Bohemian parents, Effie and Yul, had sent their only daughter off on a world tour. They'd attended boarding school together, and shared many an escapade.

'It's so great to hear from you!' Brigette exclaimed animatedly. 'Where are you staying?'

'Big downer. I'm stuck at home 'cause I haven't had a chance to scope out my own place. At least I've got a job – researcher at *Mondo*.'

Brigette was impressed. 'Wow! Cool magazine.'

'Yeah – Effie scored me the job. So . . . what are you doing in New York? Didn't you tell me LA was the only place?'

'It was, for a while. Then I, like, changed my mind.'

'I get it – you met someone.'

'I wish,' Brigette said wistfully.

'Listen, we've *gotta* get together. I've *sooo* much stuff to fill you in on.'

'How about lunch?' Brigette suggested, anxious to fill Nona in on a few things herself.

'Perfect,' Nona replied. 'Can't wait to see you!'

They met at Serendipity, devouring foot-long hot dogs while catching up on each other's news. Nona was more interesting looking than pretty. She had startling natural red hair, slanted eyes and a freckle-covered face. She dressed in a funky stylish way, and her personality was disarmingly direct. As soon as they sat down she confessed to three current boyfriends, each living in a different country.

'I can't decide which one's the best for me, so I made a daring escape,' she said, with a wicked grin. 'They all wanna do the marriage thing. I feel like such a slut!'

'You *are* a slut,' Brigette retorted crisply. 'What else is new?'

'Thanks!' Nona exclaimed.

'You always *were* the biggest flirt around,' Brigette pointed out. 'Made *me* look like an amateur.'

'That's true,' Nona agreed. 'But enough about me. What's going on with *you*?'

'Trying to be a model,' Brigette confessed.

'A model! Get outta here!'

'What's so funny about that?'

'I dunno . . . It's such a shitty profession. All looks no brains.'

'I can do it, Nona. All I need is a chance to get started.'

'Okay, so you're goin' for it, that's cool. I mean you *look* amazing – still got those fantastic tits and I must say you lost weight in all the right places.'

'So did you.'

'Ugh!' Nona said, pulling a face. 'The food in some of the countries I visited – pig's ears, snake bile, buffalo's balls. Who could eat!'

'Tell me about your three would-be husbands,' Brigette said, dying to hear every detail.

Nona rubbed her freckled nose. 'All *very* cute. One of 'em's black. My parents will freak – or maybe not, you know how liberal *they* are. Oh, by the way, they're throwing one of their parties tonight, you're invited.'

'How's Paul?' Brigette asked casually.

Paul Webster, Nona's handsome artist brother. Brigette had harbored a big crush on him – unreturned for a long time, until she'd gotten engaged. Only then had Paul stepped forward and declared his love for her. Too late. By that time she was over him.

'Married, with a *baby*!' Nona exclaimed. 'Amazing what happens to people.'

'Is he still painting?' Brigette asked, recalling Paul's ferocious talent.

'*Nooo*. He's a stockbroker on Wall Street. *Very* straight. Isn't that the funniest thing you ever heard?'

'I can't imagine Paul with a proper job and a family. He must've really changed.'

'Yeah – but I got a sneaky feeling he's still a bad boy underneath.'

'Do me a favor,' Brigette said earnestly. 'Impress upon your parents that I don't want *anyone* knowing who I am. Right now I'm Brigette Brown. After all the past scandal it's better this way.'

'Fine with me,' Nona said, looking at her watch and letting out a shriek. 'I gotta get back to work,' she said, grabbing the check. 'I'll see you tonight. Nine o'clock. Wear something outrageous!'

Brigette nodded. 'I'll be there.'

☆ ☆ ☆

Cooper Turner was a connoisseur of women, and Leslie Kane was irresistibly gorgeous. It was no surprise that in a short period of time America had fallen in love with this vision of clean-cut American beauty with her flowing red hair, full luscious lips and gorgeous body. She'd appeared in two movies and had become an instant star. Currently she was shooting a film with Cooper, and even though he was forty-seven and Leslie only twenty-three, they were an on-screen love match. Hollywood liked its leading ladies young and it didn't matter how old the guys were.

Leslie was in bed with Cooper on screen and off. He'd only had to look at her with his knowing ice-blue eyes and she'd turned to mush.

When she was fourteen she'd had his picture taped to the wall above her bed. Cooper Turner. Hunk. How she'd hated all the women she'd read about him dating in the fan magazines she'd so avidly collected. Didn't he *know* he was supposed to wait for her?

Whenever her stepfather had staggered into her bedroom late at night with beer on his breath and a swollen gut, she'd always clung to Cooper's image hovering above her rickety bed, watching over her, while her obese stepfather grunted and groaned on top of her. She'd yearned to kick him in his rancid balls and run. But she couldn't go, not while her mother lay sick in bed with a terrible cancer eating away at her.

The day her mother died she'd taken off with a thousand bucks in her pocket stolen from her stepfather and plenty of ambition to fuel her journey.

Goodbye, Florida.

Hello, LA.

She was eighteen and quite stunning, so it hadn't taken long for her to be discovered by Madam Loretta, a woman who recognized a money-maker when she saw one. For many years Madam Loretta had been supplying exquisite young girls to *tout* Hollywood. She required them fresh and unused, so as soon as she'd spotted Leslie, she'd lured her from the Rodeo Drive boutique where she was working, and set her up in a luxurious apartment.

Leslie was a natural. With her glowing looks, and small-time charm, she soon beguiled all her clients, who, much to Madam Loretta's delight, became instant regulars.

Leslie had harbored no intention of remaining a call-girl for ever. Servicing rich jaded men was not her life's ambition. She'd wanted more. She'd wanted true love, and one day – while waiting for her car at the Santa Palm car wash – she'd found it with Eddie Kane, a former child star who was then the head of distribution at Panther Studios.

Eddie Kane was a true Hollywood character and no slouch when it came to women. One look at Leslie and he'd mentally burned his fat black book. At first he'd had no idea she'd once been one of Madam Loretta's high earners, and although she'd gone to great lengths to make sure he never found out, eventually he'd discovered the truth, which caused an immediate split between them.

It was an unhappy time for Leslie, but she'd been determined not to return to her old life. Instead, she'd taken a job as a receptionist at a fashionable beauty salon, where several weeks later she'd been discovered by Mickey Stolli's wife, Abigaile. Abigaile had insisted Mickey screen test this incandescent beauty. In the meantime, a coked-out Eddie had smashed his precious Maserati into a concrete wall, leaving Leslie a very young widow.

The very young widow's screen test was a big success.

A year later she was a star.

Leslie often reflected that it was true, in Hollywood, if you wished hard enough anything could happen.

Now she was in bed with Cooper Turner and he was everything she'd ever imagined and more. He was her fantasy come to life.

She leaned over, softly trailing her manicured nails up and down his smooth bare back. It was lunch break and they were in a motel near the studio. Cooper's idea of lunch was eating her pussy for a solid half-hour. She'd come so many times she'd lost count. This man was an unbelievable lover.

Cooper lay beside her, asleep, a satisfied smile spread across his still boyishly handsome face.

The motel had been his idea. They'd sneaked off without telling anyone – highly unprofessional. Leslie knew that the hair and makeup people would kill her when she returned to the set because it would take at least an hour to put her back together before she could step in front of the camera, looking picture-perfect again.

'Sweetie-pie, wake up,' she purred, satisfaction coloring her breathy voice. 'C'mon, we have to get going.'

Cooper opened one eye, lazily reaching for her breasts. Gorgeous, like the rest of her. He pushed them together, gently caressing both nipples with his fingertips.

She sighed with pleasure, her nipples hardening to his touch.

He rolled over on his back, positioning her on top of him, her long legs spread wide across his thighs. Very slowly he inserted two fingers, savoring her anticipation. 'Lower yourself on me, baby,' he commanded, loving the fact that he could get her so hot and creamy. 'Do it slowly.'

'But, Cooper . . .' she protested, knowing it was useless to say no. She would do exactly as he asked and he knew it.

'C'*mon*, baby,' he urged. 'What're you waiting for?'

She caught her breath as she felt him slip inside her. Flexing her muscles tight, she held him a willing captive.

'That's it, baby, that's it,' he moaned, grasping her ass and squeezing. 'You're sensational!'

Chapter Seven

'WHAT'S YOUR mother like?' Tin Lee asked.

Insane, Alex wanted to reply. *Selfish. Mean. Self-obsessed. A tyrant. A nag. She drove my father to drink and an early death. And even now – with all my success and fame – she's constantly putting me down.*

'You'll like her,' Alex said shortly. 'She's a fine woman.'

'I'm sure,' Tin Lee said, with a gentle smile. 'After all, she raised you, Alex, and you are a wonderful man.'

Oh, Jesus. One good fuck and they think they know it all.

'I'm excited to meet her,' Tin Lee continued, clutching her tiny hands together. 'It is quite an honor that you wish me to accompany you and your mother on her birthday.'

Baby, baby, if you only knew. I can't be alone with dear old Mom. I can't stand her company. When we're alone together we rip the flesh from each other's throats. We're a fucking horror show.

They were standing in the front hall of Alex's Wilshire condo. He never took his girlfriends to his main residence, the modern house at the beach. That was private property not to be invaded by transient women.

In Alex Woods' life, Tin Lee was six weeks old. From Thailand, she was petite and pretty, an actress in her early twenties. She'd come in for an audition and he'd invited her out. He'd only made love to her once and had no real desire

73

to do so again. She didn't make him feel young, she made him feel old and decrepit. But tonight he desperately needed her as a buffer between him and his mother.

'I hope she likes me,' Tin Lee said, anxiously.

'She'll love you,' Alex assured her.

Right. And if you believe that you're dumber than I thought.

'Thank you,' Tin Lee said gratefully.

Oh, Jesus, Dominique would pick this poor girl to shreds. 'Another geek, dear?' she'd ask, when Tin Lee visited the ladies' room. 'Another Asian bar hooker? Why can't you settle down with a decent American girl? You're not getting any younger, Alex. You're forty-seven and look your age. Soon you'll be losing your hair, and then who'll have you?'

Sure, he knew exactly what his mother would say before the words left her brightly smeared crimson lips. She was going to be seventy-one years old and time had not mellowed her.

But what could he do? She was his mother and he was supposed to love her.

☆　☆　☆

Morton Sharkey was a tall, slim, hawk-nosed man in his late fifties. He was also a brilliant lawyer and well-respected business adviser. He was the man who'd helped Lucky to buy Panther, and even though he was a pessimist as opposed to an optimist, his instincts were usually impeccable.

They had their fights. Ever since she'd bought Panther, he'd been carrying on about it being a losing proposition.

'Don't sweat it, Morton,' she'd told him on numerous occasions. 'I've built hotels in Vegas, run Dimitri's shipping empire – I sure as hell know how to make a movie studio work.'

'The movie business is different,' Morton had warned, a stern note in his voice. 'It's the most creatively dishonest business there is.'

If he knew so much about the movie business, then surely he realized it took time to turn things around. Besides, when she'd sold off sixty percent at his insistence, she'd practically recouped her original investment. So what was he so worried about? Everything was under control.

Morton listened as she filled him in on her meeting with the Japanese bankers. 'If this merchandising deal goes through,' she said, 'it'll raise plenty. And that's exactly what we need to keep the banks happy. That, and our two hit movies.'

'Good,' Morton said.

'I thought you were going to be at the meeting,' Lucky added, noticing that Morton seemed somewhat preoccupied.

'I got held up.'

'Shouldn't wear a Rolex,' she joked.

He didn't get it.

'I'm visiting Lennie this weekend. When I'm back we'll discuss everything. If the Japanese deal is a go, and our two movies keep performing, I think we're finally in excellent shape, don't you?'

He cleared his throat. 'Yes, Lucky.'

There was something wrong with Morton today. She hoped he wasn't going through some bizarre mid-life crisis. He acted as if he couldn't wait to get out of her office.

'Are you all right?' she asked.

'Why wouldn't I be?' he countered defensively.

'I'm only asking.'

Morton jumped to his feet. 'Got a feeling I'm coming down with the flu.'

'Bed-rest and liquids,' Lucky said sympathetically. 'Oh, yeah, and *Nate 'n' Al's* chicken soup.'

'Have a nice weekend, Lucky.'
'I plan to!'

☆ ☆ ☆

Morton Sharkey left Panther in his pale beige Jaguar XJS convertible – his personal salute to middle-age. He drove two blocks before pulling over to the side of the street and speaking furtively into his car phone. 'Donna?' he questioned hoarsely when a woman answered.

'Yes.'

'We're nearly there. You'll have what you want shortly.'

'Make sure it happens as soon as possible.'

Click. She hung up without another word.

He'd met some ice queens in his time, but this one took the prize. She acted like she was ruler of the whole goddamn planet. He hated her attitude. Most of all he hated that she had something on him.

How could he have been so foolish?

How could he, Morton Sharkey, have gotten himself caught in the oldest trap of all?

Morton Sharkey, married with two grown children, a well-respected member of the business community, a family man with excellent values and a place on the board of several prestigious charity committees. All his life he'd worked hard and given back, helping others less fortunate than himself. His wife, Candice, was still an attractive woman. More than that, she was a caring faithful wife, and in twenty-six years of marriage he'd only strayed twice.

Until Sara.

Seventeen-year-old Sara with the long red hair and skinny white thighs and bitten nails and smart mouth and expressive lips and tiny breasts and tangerine pubic hair and . . .

Oh, God – he could go on and on about Sara. She was the

bittersweet dessert of his life, and even now, in spite of what had taken place, he still lusted for her.

Sara was younger than his daughter.

Sara was a free spirit.

Sara was a would-be actress.

Sara had accepted twelve thousand dollars to set him up.

And still he loved her.

Or obsessed over her.

It didn't matter which, because there was no way he was prepared to give her up.

What was that expression he'd heard so many times?

Ah, yes . . . *There's no fool like an old fool*.

How very true.

And yet . . . When he was with Sara, enveloped by her soft young flesh and wraparound legs, enjoying their fantasies together, nothing else mattered. Not even blackmail.

He hadn't wanted to betray Lucky. He'd been given no choice.

Donna Landsman had promised to destroy him if he didn't.

☆   ☆   ☆

Lucky's house in Malibu was set back from the ocean with a clear view of the coastline. It was a comfortable Mediterranean-style house, filled with simple rattan furniture and plenty of books, paintings, and objects she and Lennie had collected together. They'd both decided this was the perfect spot to raise children.

She arrived home just in time to catch little Maria toddling around the living room looking adorable in a cute orange jumpsuit. Sweeping her daughter up in her arms she swung her high in the air. Maria giggled uncontrollably – exactly like her mother, she craved action.

'She wouldn't go to bed until she saw you,' explained CeeCee, Maria's pretty black nanny.

'Wouldn't go to bed, huh?' Lucky teased, tickling her daughter until Maria screamed with even more excitement. When she quietened down Lucky kissed her forehead and said, 'Mommy's going away for a few days, so you be a very good girl and let CeeCee look after you nicely.'

'Mommy go,' Maria said, wriggling out of Lucky's arms and proceeding to race unsteadily around the room. 'Mommy, GO GO GO GO!'

'Mommy go, but I'll be back soon,' Lucky assured her.

'Good Mommy,' Maria crooned, running over and stroking Lucky's face with her soft baby hands. 'Nice Mommy. Mommy *good* girl.'

The joy of having such wonderful children was overpowering. After tucking Maria safely into bed, she crept in to check on baby Gino, asleep in his cot with his tiny thumb stuffed firmly in his mouth.

Watching her son sleep, she realized that moments like this made everything worthwhile.

She went into her bedroom, checked her weekend bag, then grabbed a quick snack in the kitchen before calling her father and telling him about Alex Woods. 'He's written a fantastic script,' she said enthusiastically. 'Very realistic. Can't wait for you to read it.'

'Yeah, yeah,' Gino said gruffly. 'I'll look at it, meet the guy, maybe give him an education, huh?'

'How about we come down to Palm Springs at the end of next week?' Lucky suggested, nibbling a chocolate cookie.

'You're comin' with him?'

'Well, yeah. I'm not leaving Alex alone with you – you'll frighten the crap out of him. Then he won't make his movie at my studio.'

Gino chuckled, 'Are you sayin' he's a chicken shit?'

'I don't know him that well.'

'Tell ya what, kid, I'll fill you in if he's got balls.'

'Gee, thanks!'

As soon as she put the phone down it rang again.

'Sweetheart!' said Lennie, calling long-distance.

Four years of marriage and her heart still jumped when she heard his voice. 'Lennie!' she said, smiling broadly. 'I've been trying to reach you all day.'

He chuckled. 'Here I am, babe. Bored and horny.'

She laughed softly. 'Don't try and sweet-talk me with your romantic come-ons.'

'Why not? You're so easy.'

'Yeah?'

'Yeah.'

'How's everything going?'

'Usual problems, nothing I can't deal with,' he paused, 'I need you, Lucky. Right here next to me.'

'I'm leaving for the airport any moment,' she assured him.

'I miss you so much, sweetheart. It's not the same when you aren't around.'

'I miss you too, Lennie,' she said softly. 'So do the kids. Maria runs back and forth all day chanting "Daddy! Daddy!" It's her new mantra.'

'How's her walking?'

'Impressive.'

'Takes after her mommy, huh?' He paused for a moment. 'Sweetheart, you're *sure* you want to do this? Fly all those hours just to spend two days with me?'

'Ha!' she exclaimed. 'Try stopping me.'

'No escape, huh?' he joked.

'My husband, the comedian.'

'Yeah, and don't you love it?'

'I love *you*,' she murmured.

'Love you, too. Kiss the kids, tell 'em Daddy's thinking about them.'

'How about *my* kiss?'

'You'll get yours in person.'

She gave a low laugh, anticipating their time together. 'Ohh . . . baby, baby, *that*'ll make the trip worthwhile.'

'I'll be at the airport to meet you. Fly safely.'

'If you say so I will.' She hung up with a big smile on her face.

Her limousine was on time, driven by Boogie, her long-time bodyguard, private investigator and driver. A Vietnam vet, Boogie was protective and smart. Lucky trusted him implicitly.

They rode in companionable silence to the airport. Boogie never spoke unless it was absolutely necessary.

The limo dropped her next to the Panther Lear jet. She didn't feel like talking, but the pilot insisted on giving her a full weather report. And the steward, a mop-top gay guy, regaled her with some outrageous gossip he'd recently heard about Leslie Kane and Cooper Turner. Like she hadn't had an earful at lunch with Venus. Why were people so fascinated with boring mindless gossip?

As the plane took off she leaned back, closing her eyes.

A weekend with Lennie . . . She couldn't wait.

Chapter Eight

'HI, GORGEOUS,' Cooper Turner said, entering Venus Maria's all-white luxurious bathroom.

She was sitting at the vanity, brushing her hair.

He sauntered up behind her, slid his hands onto her breasts, tweaked her nipples and kissed the back of her platinum-blond head.

She didn't move a muscle. This was her show and she'd run it her way. 'How'd work go today?' she asked casually.

'Pretty good,' Cooper replied, walking over and peering at himself in another mirror. 'Do I look tired?' he asked, turning back for her approval.

'Hmm . . . a little bit,' she replied, knowing this would drive him crazy. Cooper thrived on compliments.

'You really think so?' he said, frowning.

'It can't be helped, baby,' she said, falsely sympathetic. 'You're working hard. I mean, my *God* – you're at the studio morning, noon and night. I bet you hardly have time for lunch. What *did* you eat today?'

Pussy, he was tempted to reply. But he controlled himself. It wouldn't do for Venus to find out he was in bed with Leslie Kane. His wife had a fierce temper, and Leslie was merely a temporary distraction.

'Uh . . . just a salad,' he said vaguely. 'What about you?'

'Lunch with Lucky.'

'How's she doing?'

'Great. Panther's financing the next Alex Woods movie.'

'Jesus!' Cooper exclaimed. 'Alex answering to Lucky. They'll kill each other.'

Venus continued brushing her hair. 'Do you know him?'

'We've spent a few out-of-control nights together. Alex is a wild man.'

'Mmm . . .' Venus said, smiling slyly, going for the dig. 'With one of the biggest dicks in Hollywood.'

She had Cooper's attention. 'How do *you* know?' he asked quizzically.

''Cause *I* know everything.'

Cooper was fully confident of her answer. 'Bigger than mine?'

'You're so conceited.'

He grinned, 'No, just realistic, honey, just realistic.'

Yeah, Venus thought, let's see how realistic you'll feel after we have our little confrontation at Leslie's dinner tonight. Let's see how you'll handle that.

☆   ☆   ☆

Brigette strolled into the Websters' party as if she was already the most famous supermodel in the world. She'd watched the élite squad of girls strut the runways enough times to know the walk, to master the look. The look said, '*I own the world and you're all dogs.*' The walk confirmed it. Brigette had them both down.

She'd taken her time dressing for the party, discarding several outfits before settling on a drop-dead Hervé Leger black wrap dress and very high Manolo Blahnik pumps. She knew she looked hot with no bra and her honey blond hair casually caressing her shoulders.

It was her intention that tonight somebody was going to discover her, because she was determined that any moment would be the start of her modeling career.

Nona's parents greeted her at the door, startled at her transformation. They remembered Brigette as a cute, cuddly blond. Now this statuesque beauty marched into their party full of sass and attitude. She paused at the entrance to the living room.

'My dear, you look wonderful,' Nona's eccentric mother said admiringly.

'So do you, Effie,' Brigette replied, her bright blue eyes scanning the party, searching for the right people to impress.

'Nona tells me you're modeling now,' said Yul, a tall imposing man.

'Uh . . . yes.'

'That must be very exciting.'

'It is,' she lied.

'Well,' Yul said, leading her through the enormous room crammed with an eclectic group of guests, 'I'm sure you'll see dozens of people you know.'

'Thanks, I'm sure I will,' she said, looking around. The truth was she didn't know anyone. She couldn't even see Nona. *Great.* She'd made this fabulous entrance and now she was standing there like the town idiot.

For a moment she panicked, then she thought about how Lucky would handle a situation like this – Lucky, who was always in control. *Think Lucky! Think Lucky!* Head tilted high she headed for the bar.

'Brigette?'

The first person she bumped into *would* have to be Paul, Nona's brother and *her* ex-crush. She hadn't seen him for at least a couple of years. He looked different. Gone were the long hair, unshaven chin and single gold earring. Now he wore a respectable blue blazer, grey pants, white shirt and a conservative tie. As if this wasn't enough, his hair was cut short. He was a preppy nightmare!

'Paul!' she exclaimed.

'*You* look fantastic,' he said standing back with an appreciative smile.

'Hmmm . . . *You* look different,' she responded.

'Uh, this is my wife, Fenella,' he said, placing a proprietary arm around an anorexic brunette and pulling her into the conversation. 'Honey,' he said, 'meet Brigette Stanislopoulos. Remember I told you about her? Nona's best friend.'

'Nice to meet you,' Fenella said, in an uptight Bostonian accent. 'So you're Nona's friend?'

'Right,' Brigette replied, turning her attention back to Paul. 'By the way, it's Brigette Brown now. Please don't mention that other name.'

'Sorry.'

'That's okay.' An awkward silence. She broke it with, 'I hear you've got a baby.'

'A boy,' Paul said proudly.

Fenella clung to his arm possessively. 'Yes, little Military's the image of his daddy.'

Brigette stopped herself from laughing out loud. 'Military?' she said, shooting Paul a surely-you-can't-be-serious look.

'We wanted an unusual name,' Fenella said.

This is so weird, Brigette thought, once I would have done anything for this man. Now I'm standing here talking to a total stranger. A stranger who named his kid Military! What kind of a nerd has Paul turned into?

'Well, lovely seeing you,' she said, trying for a fast getaway. 'Guess we'll bump into each other later.'

She moved across the room, feeling Paul's eyes on her

back. Several men tried to start conversations. She ignored them and kept moving.

At last she spotted Nona, holding court by the window. She made her way over, still trying to maintain the walk and the look. From the attention she was getting it seemed to be working.

Nona leaped up and embraced her. 'I'm *so* glad you're here,' she said, smiling mysteriously. 'Big things have happened since lunch.'

'Like what?' Brigette asked curiously.

Nona pulled a handsome black man, dressed in a flowing African robe, to his feet. 'Meet my fiancé! Zandino,' she announced triumphantly.

Zandino bowed from the waist and beamed. His teeth were dazzling.

'Zandino,' Brigette repeated, slightly dazed.

'Yup. Zan flew in today and surprised me,' Nona said happily. 'We met when I was visiting Africa. Zan's father's a chieftain, but Zan went to college here, so it's not like he's a stranger to America.'

'Wow!' Brigette said, shaking her head. 'This is some surprise.'

'I know,' Nona said, grinning sheepishly.

Brigette turned to Zandino. 'Will you be living here?' she asked.

Zandino's wide toothy smile was irresistible. 'I shall be doing so,' he said, in very precise English. 'I hope to study law.'

Nona winked at her. 'Isn't he the *best*?' she whispered, leaning close to Brigette's ear. '*And* – he's got the biggest dick I've ever seen!'

'Nona! This is your future husband you're talking about!'

'It's true,' Nona said, laughing happily. 'Course, that's not the only reason I picked him. Zan is simply the kindest, sweetest guy I ever met.'

'That's great,' Brigette said gazing around the room. 'You know, Nona, I have to make connections tonight. Who do you think I should meet?'

'Well . . . I suppose I *could* introduce you to my boss from *Mondo*. And there's a couple of hot photographers here. And . . . let me see, hmm . . . Michel Guy – he's that aging French stud who runs the Starbright Modeling Agency.'

'I want to meet everyone,' Brigette said, a determined light shining in her eyes.

'Okay, okay, don't get anal about it. I'll take you on a tour, and we'll hit on anybody who can deliver.'

Brigette nodded. 'What are we waiting for?'

☆ ☆ ☆

Leslie Kane lived in a small but charming house on Stone Canyon Road in Bel Air. She'd bought the place as soon as she'd started making money, hired an interior designer, and was more than pleased with the results. For the first time in her life she had a home, a place that was truly hers. Now all she needed was a man to fill it, and Cooper Turner was the perfect candidate.

Minor detail: he was married.

Very minor detail: Leslie had supreme confidence when it came to men. After all, she'd been taught by the great Madam Loretta, and Madam Loretta had handled some of the most successful girls in the business – girls who had gone on to marry movie stars and major moguls.

Leslie knew she was on the right track with Cooper. He was certainly enthusiastic enough – every break they got he was hot to tango. Mr Permanent Hard-on. Quite impressive for a man of his age.

As she dressed for her dinner party, Leslie thought about Madam Loretta's three cardinal rules to keep a man happy.

Rule One: Find something about him that you consider the most wonderful thing in the world and praise him constantly.

Rule Two: Make sure you tell him he's the most exciting lover you've ever had.

Rule Three: Whatever he says, be amazed at his knowledge. Gaze adoringly at him and insist he says the most intelligent and clever things you've ever heard.

Leslie had put these three rules into practice and found it worked every time. Of course, now that she was a famous movie star she didn't need to impress anyone – men came running merely for the chance to say they'd stood next to her. Not that they got to do anything more than that because she was choosy. Sleeping around did not appeal to her.

What appealed to her was a settled relationship.

What appealed to her was a wedding ring.

What appealed to her was Cooper Turner.

She put on a clinging lace dress made especially for her by Nolan Miller. The neckline was demure, but the lace revealed her body down each side, clinging to her curves provocatively.

Admiring herself in the mirror, she wondered what Venus Maria would wear. Probably something trampy.

Leslie simply couldn't understand why Cooper had married Venus. The woman had no class, with her dyed blond hair and slutty looks. Leslie might have once been a whore, but she'd always managed to look like a lady.

Well . . . he wouldn't have to put up with Venus much longer, because when Leslie wanted something she usually got it. And she wanted Cooper.

Tonight she'd invited Jeff Stoner, a young good-looking actor who had a small part in the movie. In the past Cooper had often teased her about Jeff, saying he had a big crush on her, so she knew having Jeff at her house would irritate Cooper and hopefully make him jealous.

Good. She hoped he did.

Whenever Cooper had mentioned Jeff she'd laughed and dismissed him as just another boring actor. But tonight, when Cooper was sitting next to his trampy wife, and she was playing hand-on-the-thigh with Jeff, it would force Cooper into making some kind of decision about their future together. A serious commitment was exactly what she had in mind.

Satisfied with her appearance, she strolled into the living room ready to greet her guests.

Chapter Nine

'LET'S STOP FOR a drink,' Alex suggested, his nerves already on edge.

'Won't that make us late for your mother?' Tin Lee countered.

'She'll wait,' Alex said. His throat was so parched he had to have something. Before leaving his apartment he'd popped a Valium and smoked half a joint, not enough to get him through the evening.

Tin Lee nodded. 'Whatever you say.' She liked Alex and hoped he liked her. Meeting his mother was an encouraging sign.

Alex considered her to be most agreeable. They'd been out on several occasions and she'd never nagged him about anything. He liked that in a woman. A calm acceptance that the man is always right. None of that feminist shit.

In bed she'd ministered to him, unconcerned about her own fulfillment. There was nothing worse than a woman who expected equal everything, especially in the bedroom.

He gave his four-door Mercedes to a parking attendant at the Beverly Regent, and entered the bar, Tin Lee close behind him. He'd left the Porsche at home tonight so they could accommodate his mother.

They sat against the wall on the plush leather banquette seating. Tin Lee ordered cranberry juice, explaining she didn't care for alcohol. Alex ordered a double Scotch on the rocks and lit up a cigarette. He had all the vices and knew it. He smoked too much, drank too much, popped pills and smoked grass. The good news was he'd given up blow and crack. Even Alex knew the danger line. His shrink had explained that if he kept doing the hard stuff he couldn't expect to see fifty. Point taken.

Tin Lee coughed delicately. He continued smoking.

'Alex,' Tin Lee said, placing her hand on his thigh. 'Is something bothering you?'

Nothing that my mother dropping dead won't cure.

'Bothering me? What would be bothering me?' he asked, a feeling of irritation crawling over his skin.

'I don't know. That's why I ask.' A wistful pause. 'Is it something about me?'

Aw, shit, he was in no mood for a talk about 'their relationship', such as it was. And he knew it was coming. Women always took everything personally.

'Nothing's wrong with you,' he assured her, hoping he sounded sincere enough to stop her carrying on.

'Then why,' Tin Lee asked plaintively, not quite smart enough to leave a good thing alone, 'haven't we made love since the first time?'

No different from any of the others. Talk, talk, talk. Sex, sex, sex. Was that all women ever thought about?

'Don't I please you, Alex?' she asked, twirling a thin gold bracelet on her tiny left wrist.

He picked up his glass and gulped a couple of mouthfuls of Scotch as he contemplated his reply. Had to be careful, he needed her around this evening.

'No, honey, it's not you,' he said at last. 'It's me. I'm always tense when I'm preparing to shoot a new movie. I've a lot on my mind.'

'Sex is good for taking things off your mind,' Tin Lee said

boldly. 'Perhaps, later tonight, I can relax you with a massage. A very . . . personal massage.'

She wanted to be in his movie, that was for sure. And why not? Everybody wanted something.

A dark-haired woman entered the bar. He noticed her passing and for one unsure moment he thought it was Lucky Santangelo. Something about the way she moved across the room reminded him.

No. Lucky was much more beautiful – in a wild and intriguing way.

'One more drink and we're on our way,' Alex said, gesturing for the waiter.

☆ ☆ ☆

'What's *he* doing here?'

Cooper's furious whisper was enough to satisfy Leslie. 'Why *shouldn't* he be here?' she said guilelessly.

'You know he wants to fuck you,' Cooper fumed.

'So do a lot of men,' Leslie responded calmly, 'that doesn't mean I have any desire to return the compliment.'

He frowned. 'Are you sure?'

'Positive,' she said, waving a greeting at a well-known country singer and his plain wife as they entered her house. 'Excuse me, Cooper,' she said, secretly thrilled she'd gotten to him. 'I must go greet my guests.'

He watched her walk away in her tantalizing gown with half her body on show, and he couldn't help but feel a small frisson of jealousy – even though he knew she was doing it purposely, trying to piss him off because he was with his wife.

Meanwhile, Venus was settled at the bar downing shooters with charming Felix Zimmer, an aging producer known for his quirky habit of telling every woman he met that his specialty was eating pussy. Felix was oversized and no Mel

Gibson, but his conversational gambit sure helped him score with a lot of women – that and the fact that he was a very successful producer.

'Hey, babe,' she called, beckoning Cooper over. 'Do you know Felix?'

'Know him,' Cooper said with a thin smile. 'I taught him everything he boasts about!'

Venus laughed. Cooper thought she looked exceptionally pretty tonight in gold lounging pajamas with her hair arranged casually up. He decided he really should consider spending more time at home.

Leslie had put together an eclectic group: Felix and Muriel, his 'rumored-to-be-a-lesbian' wife; the country singer and *his* wife; Cooper and Venus; a hot director with his young model girlfriend; a sulky-faced woman who designed clothes for an Emmy-nominated TV show; and Jeff Stoner.

Cooper suspected Leslie had arranged the party solely for his benefit. For some perverse reason, she wanted Venus in her house.

For a moment he felt guilty. How would he feel if Venus did the same thing to him?

She wouldn't. Venus might appear sexually over the top and outrageous in her videos and movies, but in real life she was the perfect, faithful, supportive wife. He could trust her, and he did.

☆　☆　☆

'My son,' Dominique Woods announced, fluttering diamond-beringed fingers, 'used to be the most handsome man in the world – just like his father. Now look at him, he's dissipated, old. Time has not been kind to my Alex.'

'Excuse me?' Tin Lee said politely, shocked by the older woman's harsh words.

'It's true, dear,' Dominique continued matter-of-factly. 'He had enough talent to have been a famous actor like his father. The tragedy is that he threw it all away.'

'I never wanted to be an actor,' Alex said grimly. 'Always wanted to direct.'

'It's a damn shame,' Dominique said, her voice rising. 'As an actor you could have amounted to something – received *real* recognition.'

Jesus Christ. Six Oscar nominations were not enough for her. This woman wanted blood.

'Anyway, it's too late now,' Dominique continued, a cruel twist to her mouth. 'You lost your looks years ago. Soon you'll be losing your hair.'

Every time the same thing. What was her fucking problem? Anyone could see that his hair was thick, dark and wavy. No way was he anywhere near losing it.

His mother was insane – she seemed to take pleasure in putting him down. His shrink had advised him that fighting with her was pointless. All he could do was ignore her dumb comments.

'Alex has lovely hair,' Tin Lee said, rallying to his support.

'For now,' Dominique said ominously. 'However,' a meaningful pause, 'baldness runs in the family. His grandfather was bald as an ape's ass.'

'When he was eighty-five,' Alex muttered, ordering another drink.

'You can't avoid the march of time,' his mother said. '*I* fight it every day.' Now she turned coy. 'And I'm winning,' she added, focusing her attention on Tin Lee. 'Can't you see I'm winning, dear?'

Tin Lee nodded, too startled to say anything else. Alex took a long, cold, hard look at his mother. She was thin and very chic. Fashionably dressed, she wore a short-cropped black wig over thinning hair. Her problem was too much heavy makeup for a woman her age. Her skin was as white as alabaster. Her lips as red as blood. And her eyes were surrounded with charcoal black, which gave her an overly dramatic Norma Desmond look. From a distance she could pass for a woman in her late fifties, but close up the game was over. To his knowledge she'd had her face lifted at least twice. Even at seventy-one appearance meant everything to Dominique.

Alex had often tried to figure out what she was so bitter about and why she took it out on him. Was it because his father had died, leaving her with a child to raise by herself? Was it because she'd never married again? According to her, no man had been prepared to take on the responsibility of a woman with a son. Over the years she'd constantly reminded him. 'Who would have me when I had a boy your age to raise? It's *your* fault I'm alone now. Remember that, Alex.'

How could he ever forget?

Fortunately, she'd always had a certain amount of money. Not that she'd ever put any in his direction. Not that he'd ever wanted any.

Tin Lee rose to her feet. 'I'm going to the ladies' room,' she said.

His mother had the grace to wait until Tin Lee was out of earshot before she launched into her usual stream of criticism. 'Don't you know any American girls, Alex? Surely some of the actresses in your films would be suitable for you to take out? Why are you always with these Asian women? They arrive here searching for the good life, but I'm sure you're aware that in their own country most of them were no better than cheap street prostitutes.'

'You have no idea what you're talking about,' he said, trying not to get too pissed off at her stupidity.

'I certainly do,' Dominique replied, tapping a talon-like

94

finger on the table. 'I'm the disgrace of my ladies' bridge club because of you.'

'*Me?*'

'Yes, Alex, you. They read about you in those tabloid papers. They tell me appalling things.'

'What things?'

'Why can't you settle down with a decent American girl?'

How many times had they had this conversation?

How many times had he blown up and screamed at her?

He'd learned, after years of therapy, that it simply wasn't worth it anymore. What she said was completely meaningless, and he refused to take any notice of her cruel barbs.

By the end of dinner he was drunk. When they left the restaurant Tin Lee automatically slid behind the wheel of the Mercedes.

'I can drive,' he objected, teetering on the sidewalk.

'No you can't,' she said, firm but nice. 'Get in the back, Alex.'

'Smart little cookie this one,' his mother murmured, climbing into the front passenger seat.

Like *she* would know. Dominique knew nothing. *Nada.* Shit. She was a mean, bigoted, hateful woman. And yet she was his mother, so therefore he had to love her, didn't he?

He slumped across the back seat, moodily silent until they had dropped Dominique off at her condo on Doheny.

'It was such a pleasure meeting you, Mrs Woods,' Tin Lee said, still rallying. This girl had impeccable manners.

Dominique nodded imperiously, 'You, too, dear.' A pause. 'However, take a word of advice from an older and wiser woman. Alex is not for you. He's too old. Be a clever girl and find a boy your own age.'

Gee, thanks, Mom. Fuck you too.

Dominique swept into her building without looking back.

'She's uh . . . very nice,' Tin Lee said, groping for words.

Alex laughed uproariously. 'Very nice, my ass. She's a raving bitch, and you know it.'

'Alex, please don't talk about your mother like that. It's not good karma.'

'I don't give a shit about karma,' he said, drunkenly fondling her small breasts from behind. 'Drive me home, baby, I'm gonna show you how a bald, ugly has-been gets it on. I'm gonna light up your fuckin' world!'

☆　☆　☆

Jeff Stoner circled the room, summing up the action.

Cooper watched him, understanding every move. He'd been like that once – ambitious, hungry for the big time. Jeff had the look that Cooper knew so well, and he didn't like it, because he was well aware that if he didn't act to prevent it, tonight Jeff Stoner was definitely going to score with Leslie. She looked too delectable to be left alone after everyone had gone home.

Cooper knew exactly how Jeff would operate: he'd stay for a nightcap, bombard her with compliments, get her talking about herself and then POW – he'd zero in for his big chance. After all, apart from being gorgeous, Leslie was the star of the film, she had the director's ear, therefore – with a small amount of effort – she could convince the director to enlarge Jeff's minor role.

'Something wrong?' Venus interrupted his thought process with a hand on his arm. She'd finished talking to Felix, whose sexual boasting had finally bored her.

'Nothing,' Cooper replied vaguely.

Bastard, Venus thought. *Lousy, lying, cheating bastard.*

'Where's the john?' she asked.

Trick question. He knew enough not to fall into *that* trap.

'How would I know?' he said casually. 'I've never been here before.'

Big lie. He'd spent several steamy afternoons at Leslie's house when filming had quit early.

'Come find it with me,' she said, pulling him into the hall. Together they discovered a powder room near the front door. 'Come in with me, baby,' she said persuasively.

He followed her into the mirrored room.

She turned around, locking the door behind them.

Cooper peered in the mirror. Yes, he *did* look tired. When he finished the movie it was definitely health-spa time.

Venus didn't hesitate. Throwing her arms around his neck, she pressed his back up against the marble sink and began provocatively tonguing his lips.

He made a mild attempt to push her away.

'I'm *veree* horny,' she whispered, persevering. 'Humor me, baby. Got a little something I've been imagining doing to you all night.'

Instant reaction as her hand snaked down, unzipped his pants and rapidly began to free him from the confines of his Calvin Kleins.

'Nice . . .' she murmured with a throaty laugh, firmly caressing his positive response. '*Veree* nice.'

Venus could elicit a hard-on from a stone statue!

All of a sudden he forgot about Leslie and Jeff as she slid to her knees. His wife was a very accomplished woman. Very—

'God!' he groaned, arching his back as her tongue began flicking lightly back and forth across the tip of his penis.

'Shhh . . .' She silenced him by reaching up and placing a finger on his lips. 'We wouldn't want anyone to hear.'

Then, after a few moments of teasing, her full mouth enclosed his hardness and nothing else mattered as he gave himself up to the sensation of riding the wave as she sucked him dry of all desire, leaving him spent and extraordinarily satisfied.

The entire event took less than three minutes. Fast sex like fast food could sometimes do more than all the gourmet meals in the world.

'Jesus!' he exclaimed, totally content. 'That was really something!'

Venus rose from her knees, plucked a Kleenex from a box on the vanity and daintily dabbed her lips. 'Figured you seemed a touch tense, Coop. Thought I'd relax you.'

'You're unbelievable!' He laughed.

'I try to please,' she said, gazing at her reflection in the mirror.

'Well, you do,' he replied, stretching his arms high above his head.

'You'd miss me if we weren't married, wouldn't you, Coop?' she teased, staring at him through the glass.

He turned her around, cuddling her close. 'I miss you every minute we're not together,' he said seductively, the full Cooper Turner charm machine on alert.

Lying
cheating
sonofabitch.

Gently she pushed him away. 'We'd better get back. I'm sure Felix has plenty more to tell me about his talented tongue.'

'Talking of talented tongues,' Cooper said, 'when we get home tonight—'

'Yes?'

'You'll see,' he said confidently.

'I will?'

'Oh, yes, you will. I owe you one.' He zipped up, took one last glance in the mirror and unlocked the door. 'Let's leave early tonight, honey. I can't wait to be alone with you.'

'Whatever you like,' Venus replied, obliging to the end. 'Whatever turns you on.'

Chapter Ten

'HOW COME YOU haven't been in to see me?'

'Just your bad luck, I guess,' Brigette replied with exactly the right amount of sass.

Michel Guy's heavy-lidded eyes swept over her, lingering on her breasts, provocatively on show in her sexy Hervé Leger dress. 'Come to my office tomorrow,' he said. 'Bring your book.'

'I would,' Brigette replied agreeably. 'Only I'm kind of on an assignment.'

'Doing what?'

'A foreign catalog.'

'Which one?'

'Uh . . . it's a favor for a friend,' she said vaguely.

'Who's the photographer?'

'Uh . . . the photographer . . .'

Michel started to chuckle. 'You're a very pretty girl,' he said. '*Very* pretty. However, *ma chérie,* there are a lot of pretty girls in New York trying to be models. A word of advice – don't fake it, be truthful.'

'I'm always truthful,' she said, 'when it works.'

He scratched his chin. 'Have you done the rounds?'

'I've only been in New York a short time.'

'So you haven't seen any other agents?'

To hell with truthful. 'Not yet,' she lied.

'Here's my card,' he said. 'Be at my office ten a.m. tomorrow. There might be something you're right for.'

Brigette couldn't wait to find Nona and thank her for the introduction. 'This is like *soo* great,' she enthused, her eyes gleaming excitedly. 'I've been trying to get an appointment with Michel Guy for ages.'

'Michel's got a reputation as an ass-grabber,' Nona warned. 'He's living with that English model, Robertson – you know, the one who's so skinny you could slide her through a crack in a French window. Everyone knows he's taken. It doesn't stop him – he still hits on all the girls.'

Brigette was determined. 'If he's with Robertson, he's hardly likely to come on to me – she's incredible.'

'When has that stopped any man?' Nona said, tossing back her bright red hair. 'So, tell me . . . what do you think of Zandino?'

'Major cute. Only I thought you wanted somebody who was already, y'know, established.'

'Nobody *old*,' Nona said, wrinkling her nose. 'They have to be under thirty. I can't deal with anybody like, you know, older than that. Can you?'

Brigette hadn't really thought about it. So far all her relationships had been with younger men.

She took another look across the room at Michel Guy. He had crinkly greyish-blond hair, a weathered tan and faded blue eyes.

'How old do you think Michel is?' she asked.

'Forty-something. Pretty ancient.'

'Forty-something isn't ancient.'

'Keep it business,' Nona said sternly, wagging a warning finger.

'I'm not about to *sleep* with him,' Brigette laughed, 'although he *is* attractive.'

'There's my boss,' Nona said, on to the next subject. 'Charm her. Maybe she'll put you on the cover of *Mondo*.'

'You think?'

'Just kidding, but you may as well meet her.'

They headed across the room for another opportunity.

☆ ☆ ☆

'Get on top,' Alex demanded.

'It's enough, Alex, I've had enough,' Tin Lee cried, her compact, naked body slick with sweat.

Alex had been pumping away inside her for twenty minutes and, to her dismay, he remained ramrod hard. He'd popped two amyl-nitrate capsules and was still drunk.

Tin Lee was not enjoying herself. This man was big and rough and not a gentleman in bed. She wanted out.

Alex grabbed her around the waist, hauling her on top of him. She felt herself impaled, like a thing, an object. He wasn't treating her nicely. No foreplay. No touching. Nothing except a relentless pounding.

And yet . . . the truth was . . . she *did* want a role in his upcoming movie. And he *was* Alex Woods – a very important and famous director. And maybe . . . if he'd let her . . . she could teach him things in bed, like how to pleasure a woman because, right now, what she was going through was uncomfortable and humiliating. Wasn't he *ever* going to come?

Alex shut his eyes and attempted to concentrate. The problem was that when his eyes were closed the world took off leaving him dizzy and confused. God he hated drinking. Hated the effect. Hated getting up the next morning and suffering from his excesses.

His mother drove him to it every time. His fucking mother

101

and her fucking put-downs. Why couldn't she leave him alone?

Tin Lee moaned on top of him. Or was it more an anguished cry of exhaustion?

He didn't know. He didn't care. Dominique was right. Tin Lee should go out and find a nice boy her own age. What the fuck was she doing with *him*?

Abruptly he rolled away from her. Still hard, he finished himself off.

This did not make Tin Lee happy. She jumped off the bed and ran into the bathroom. When she emerged a few minutes later she was fully dressed.

'I'm going home, Alex,' she said, in a small, flat voice.

He nodded, too tired and disgusted to say anything.

She left his apartment and he heard silence – an eerie earth-shattering silence that was enough to drive a man crazy.

Burying his head under a pillow he fell into a troubled sleep.

☆　☆　☆

Leslie Kane was nervous. Something had happened and she didn't know what. Cooper had definitely cooled toward her and she couldn't figure out why. He sat on her right at the round dining table, Jeff was on her left. She'd imagined this would drive Cooper crazy with jealousy. It didn't. He seemed uninterested – almost cool as he chatted amiably to Felix's dyke wife. Leslie knew Muriel Zimmer was a dyke because in her past life, as a highly paid call-girl, she'd been summoned to the Zimmers' mansion one night with two other girls, and the three of them had been given diaphanous robes and elaborate Venetian masks and then they'd been led into an all-black bedroom with a huge circular waterbed where Mrs

Zimmer had awaited them wearing nothing but thigh-high rubber wading boots and a big toothy leer.

Leslie remembered the evening well. Mrs Zimmer obviously didn't. Thank God she was into masks!

Leslie could not stop herself from saying something to Cooper, although she knew it was hardly an appropriate time. 'Have I done anything to upset you?' she whispered, groping for his thigh under the cover of the long damask tablecloth.

'Huh?' He looked at her vaguely, like they were nothing more than casual acquaintances.

'Cooper,' she murmured, thinking of how he'd been earlier in the day, his head buried between her legs, his expert touch burning into her skin.

'Not now, Leslie,' he muttered, removing her hand as he turned once again to Muriel Zimmer.

Leslie felt a horrible lump in her throat. She . . . was . . . losing . . . him.

How had it happened so quickly? When he'd walked into her house two hours ago he'd been all over her.

Jeff Stoner leaned toward her, speaking in a low intimate voice. He resembled a young Harrison Ford. She didn't care – he didn't capture one iota of her interest.

'Leslie,' he said earnestly, 'inviting me here tonight was so damn sweet. In the Hollywood scheme of things I'm nothing, a nobody. Only you don't care, 'cause you see me as a guy you like, a friend. No bullshit. You're somethin' else.'

Oh, God, Jeff thought she was so sweet, yet all she'd been doing was using him. Now her clever scheme to make Cooper jealous was backfiring.

Venus Maria, who'd been holding court at the table with the country singer and the clothes designer, suddenly stood up, tapping the side of her champagne glass with a fork. 'Can I say something here?' she said, silencing the table. 'I think *somebody's* gotta say something 'cause this is such a special night.' She smiled at Leslie – a warm loving smile. 'Leslie, dear, you've put on such a *very* impressive show. Company interesting, food delicious – I mean, what more can any of us want? In fact, I feel so comfortable here tonight that I'm about to share a big secret with all of you.'

Cooper wondered what his unpredictable wife was going to share now.

'Everyone, raise your champagne glasses,' Venus continued. 'First, we're toasting our lovely hostess, Leslie Kane. Oh, and I know this might surprise some of you, or maybe not, but this toast is also for Cooper – my fantastic husband. You see, the truth is . . .' A long provocative pause. 'Leslie and Cooper are having an affair.'

Jaws dropped around the table, and a heavy silence descended.

'And although I'm a *very* understanding wife,' Venus continued brightly, 'and *extremely* open-minded, there comes a point in every relationship when one has to say enough is enough. So . . . dear Cooper,' she tilted her glass at him, 'I'm taking this opportunity to tell you and Leslie,' she lifted her glass toward Leslie, who sat in stunned silence, 'that you can continue your affair as long as you care to. Because, my dear Cooper, I'm divorcing you.'

Muriel Zimmer said, 'OhmiGod!'

The rest of them were silent.

Venus carried on. 'Even as we sit here, Coop, your clothes are being moved out of our house and into the Beverly Hills Hotel, where I'm sure you'll be very happy. That's, of course, if you don't move in with Leslie. I have no idea how accommodating she is. Maybe she's getting it on with young Jeff here – who knows? Anyway, Coop, I don't want you to be surprised when you try to get into our house and find your key doesn't work.'

Cooper stood up, his face flushed with anger. 'Is this some kind of joke?' he asked tightly.

'That's *exactly* what I thought in the beginning,' Venus said pleasantly, 'you screwing Leslie *had* to be a joke 'cause little Leslie here, *sweet* innocent Leslie, the darling of America, used to be a hooker.'

Leslie's stomach dropped.

Another 'OhmiGod!' from Muriel.

'Really, Coop,' Venus admonished. 'You must be the only guy in town who doesn't know Leslie was one of Madam Loretta's girls.'

A nerve twitched in Cooper's left cheek as he listened to his wife. No point in trying to stop her. She was on a roll.

Venus turned to Leslie again. 'Not that I hold it against you, dear, everybody has to do whatever they can to survive, *I* certainly did. But, you know what? You've also got to learn who you can fuck and who you can't. And if you jump into bed with *my* husband, you'd better be sure I approve, 'cause if I don't, I can be *very* mean, and you wouldn't want that, would you?'

Leslie sat absolutely still as her world crashed around her. She loathed Venus with a hatred she'd only felt for one other human being, and that was her stepfather – the man who'd molested her night after night with a sickening regularity.

'Anyway,' Venus continued cheerfully. 'Allow me to finish my toast. This evening was great, but right now I gotta go. I have a hot date waiting at my house, and I hate to keep 'em waiting when they're *really* hot. Oh, yes, and, Felix,' she added, winking boldly at the lecherous producer. 'Thought you'd like to know . . . Cooper gives great head.' She returned her attention to her errant husband. 'So . . . Coop, guess I'll see you around, babe.'

And with that she blew him a kiss and made a very effective exit. So effective that nobody noticed the tears in her eyes.

Chapter Eleven

 NONA'S BOSS, Aurora Mondo Carpenter, was a tiny brittle woman with watery eyes and cut-glass cheek-bones. She was of an indeterminate age, but Nona confided to Brigette that she had to be in her seventies.

Brigette was amazed. 'Wow!' she said. 'She doesn't look like any grandmother *I've* ever seen.'

Aurora's personal stamp was all over *Mondo*. She'd created the magazine and had been at the helm for over twenty-five years. She was married to one of New York's top architects, and often wrote coy little articles about him, claiming they had the best sex life in New York. Aurora was quite a character.

Nona was not in awe of her: she'd known her since she was a small child, Aurora was a close friend of her mother's, and she felt quite comfortable taking Brigette over to meet her.

'This is my friend,' she announced. 'Brigette's the hottest model in LA.'

'Really?' Aurora said, raising a thinly pencilled eyebrow. 'How many covers have you appeared on, dear?'

'Actually,' Brigette said, thinking fast, 'I recently returned from Europe.'

'How many *European* covers were you on?'

'Oh, God!' Nona said, quickly butting in. 'You can't even count them there were so many!'

'Why haven't you mentioned Brigette before?' Aurora inquired.

'She wasn't in the country. Thing is – Aurora, I had this brilliant idea that *Mondo* should be the first to use her. I mean, she's going to be *huge*. Michel Guy wants to sign her.'

Aurora nodded agreeably at Brigette. 'Come along to my office tomorrow, dear. We'll take tea together.'

'I'd love that,' Brigette said, bright blue eyes shining with enthusiasm.

'Bring your portfolio,' Aurora said, 'so I can peruse your covers. And don't forget your test sheets.'

'I'll be there,' Brigette assured her.

As soon as they were out of earshot Nona said, 'Have you *got* photographs?'

'I didn't think I'd need them until I landed a job.'

'You're impossible,' Nona said, shaking her head in disbelief. 'Surely you *knew* you had to be prepared? No wonder nothing's happened for you.'

'It's not as if I've been doing this all my life,' Brigette said huffily.

'Okay, okay, everything's under control, 'cause I've come up with a cool idea.'

'Like what?'

'Like *I'm* going to be your manager.'

'*You?*' Brigette exclaimed, choking back a derisive laugh. 'What do you know about being a manager?'

'Who got you an intro to Aurora Bora Alice?' Nona said. 'Who fixed you up with Michel Guy? Who's gonna get you test shots?'

'Well, since you put it like that . . .'

'Ten percent,' Nona said firmly. 'Which, right now, is ten percent of nothing. A deal?'

'I guess we could give it a try,' Brigette said hesitantly. After all, she had nothing to lose and everything to gain. The truth was there was nobody pushier than Nona.

Nona nodded, satisfied with her reply. 'There's Luke Kasway. I'll do the talking. The good news is he's gay. The bad news is he can be a bit testy. If he insults you, take no notice.'

'Why would he insult me?'

'It's his way. He calls it constructive criticism. Luke is such an awesome photographer that he gets away with it.'

Luke Kasway was short and compact with a spiky crew-cut. He wore a multicolored Versace shirt, baggy blue jeans, white sneakers and owl-like rimless glasses. Two gold earrings adorned one ear, while the other featured a small diamond stud.

Nona did her usual introduction, praising Brigette big time.

Luke didn't fall for it. 'Get real, Nona, your friend's never modeled in her life.'

'She's big in Europe and LA,' Nona insisted.

Luke laughed disbelievingly. 'I'm in LA all the time, I've never seen her.' He gave Brigette a penetrating stare. 'Be honest, have you done anything at all?'

Brigette brushed a nervous hand through her hair, wondering which way to play it. 'Actually,' she confessed, 'I haven't.'

'I like a girl who tells the truth,' Luke said, pushing up his glasses, which had a habit of slipping off his nose. 'When I've got time we'll take some test shots, 'cause I gotta admit you do have a certain quality.'

'Told you!' Nona said triumphantly.

'Whether that quality will shine through the lens is another thing,' Luke continued. 'Some girls can be insanely sexy in real life. Trouble is, if they can't make out with the camera, they're dead meat.'

'When can we do this?' Nona asked, grabbing the opportunity. 'She's got an interview with Michel Guy tomorrow, and Aurora's considering her for a cover.'

'I'm booked for the next three weeks,' Luke said. 'Then I'm off to the Caribbean, where I'm doing nothing but lying on the beach checking out hot young *cabana* boys.'

'Oh, *c'mon*, Luke,' Nona wheedled. 'You can do this favor for me.'

'Can't, sweetheart,' he replied, regretfully shaking his head. 'I'm booked solid.'

'What about now?' Nona pleaded. 'Let's go to your studio and take a few shots tonight. *Pleease*, Luke, it means so much to me.'

'You're pushy, exactly like your mother,' Luke said peevishly.

'Nobody's pushy like her,' Nona retorted.

He laughed. 'Okay, okay,' he said, turning to Brigette. 'Are you up for it?'

She nodded. *This* was the opportunity she'd been waiting for.

'Then let's go.'

'Can I bring my fiancé?' Nona asked.

'Didn't know you were engaged.'

'He's horny and major cute, you'll fall in love. Hands off!'

'Bring him, as long as he doesn't talk.'

Nona pouted. 'You're so mean, Luke.'

'Excuse me?'

'Nothing.'

☆ ☆ ☆

Luke Kasway's studio was in SoHo, near the TriBeCa area. Brigette, Nona and Zandino arrived by cab, following Luke who'd gone ahead in his own car. They piled out of the cab outside his building.

'This is so cool!' Nona said excitedly. 'Luke's the greatest!'

Zandino rang the bell downstairs. After a few moments Luke buzzed them in. The three climbed into an open freight elevator and rode to the top of the large industrial building.

'Welcome, kids,' Luke said, greeting them at the heavy stainless-steel door.

'We're here!' Nona exclaimed. 'Ready for action!'

'I can see that,' Luke said, ushering them into his enormous studio.

'Incredible space!' Brigette said, taking in the blow-up photographs of all the top models adorning the whitewashed walls.

'Who wants a drink?' Luke asked.

'I don't drink,' Brigette replied, still staring at the photographs, wondering if she'd ever be as famous as the girls in them.

'I'll have a bourbon and water,' Nona said.

'That's a very grown-up drink for a kid I've known since she was twelve,' Luke remarked, walking over to a functional all white and glass-block bar.

'I'm a *very* grown-up girl,' Nona retorted, following him.

'So I can see.'

'Oh, Luke, this is Zandino, my fiancé,' she said, beckoning Zandino over.

Luke did a double-take. 'Drink?'

Zandino beamed his toothy grin. 'Coca-Cola, please.'

Luke squinted at him. 'Nice robe,' he said.

'Traditional,' Zandino replied, still beaming.

Nona giggled. 'We thought we'd blow my parents' minds if he wore it to their party tonight.'

'Nothing would blow Effie and Yul's minds,' Luke said. 'They're the most liberal couple in New York, *and* the most interesting.' He handed them their drinks. Then he stepped back, taking a long critical look at Brigette. 'Okay,' he said. 'What are we doing here?'

'You're the photographer,' Nona pointed out.

Luke ignored her. 'Okay, babe,' he said to Brigette. 'Kick off your shoes and go stand in front of the camera over there.'

She stepped out of her Blahnik pumps placing herself in front of a plain blue backdrop.

Luke threw a switch on the stereo and Annie Lennox's throaty voice flooded the studio.

'Major point – relax,' he said, loading film into two cameras. 'I'll shoot a couple of rolls of black-and-white, some color, and we'll see what happens. No big deal. Don't get nervous on me.'

Now that she was finally in front of a camera Brigette felt her confidence level sink. She was suddenly awkward and unsure about what to do. She'd imagined herself on a Paris runway, strolling along snootily clad in a top designer's outfit, giving everybody that disgusted look like they should drop dead because she was so hot. But standing in front of an actual camera was intimidating.

'Imagine the camera's your lover,' Luke said, positioning himself behind it. 'You've had a lover, haven't you?'

'Of course,' she replied indignantly.

'Good. So make out with the camera, get those pretty eyes working. Let your hair fall over your face . . . that's it . . . now bring your head down, we're gonna see if we can create magic here.'

She began to pose, gradually getting into it as the music swept over her.

As soon as she did anything Luke considered obvious, he

111

started yelling. 'Be natural,' he shouted. 'Natural! Natural! Get it?'

He clicked off several rolls of film, then produced his Polaroid.

Nona and Zandino stood on the sidelines cheering her on.

After an hour of non-stop activity Luke was ready to quit. He yawned and stretched. 'I think we got it,' he said. 'Whatever *it* might be.'

'When can we see the photos?' Nona asked.

'Call my assistant in the morning.'

Brigette was on an adrenalin high. She began wandering around the studio again, still fascinated by all the photos on the walls. Among the models was a scattering of celebrities. Sylvester Stallone in a cowboy hat. Winona Ryder wearing a red bustier. Jon Bon Jovi bare-chested. 'Do you know all these people?' she asked Luke.

'Of course he does,' Nona replied, picking up a giant blow-up photograph of Robertson and Nature – another famous model, wearing nothing but skin-tight blue jeans and alluring smiles, their hands covering their breasts.

'*Some* picture,' Nona exclaimed.

'Yeah,' Luke agreed. 'That's the ad campaign I'm doing for Rock 'n' Roll Jeans – you heard of them?'

'Nope.'

'You will. They're gonna be bigger than Guess and Calvin Klein combined.'

'Really?' Nona said, her interest perking. 'The only thing is,' she added, studying the photo, 'there's nothing unusual about this ad. Two girls . . . every guy's fantasy, only it's been done a million times. Robertson and Nature have been on every cover from *Vogue* to *Allure*. It's not cutting edge, Luke. Using them for a hot new ad campaign is like, you know, kinda old news.' She paused, gazing at him innocently. 'You don't mind me saying that, do you?'

'Yeah, I mind,' Luke replied, not pleased with her criticism.

'I'm just being truthful.'

He pushed his glasses onto his nose. 'Do me a big one, Nona, go be truthful somewhere else.'

'Don't get uptight. I'm the girl who's going to buy the product.'

He looked at her, perplexed. 'Are you telling me you wouldn't buy these jeans simply because the models have appeared in ads for other things?'

She shrugged. 'It's nothing I haven't seen before.'

He snorted with aggravation. 'You're a pain in the ass, Nona – you always were.'

'I'm an *honest* pain in the ass,' she said, taking a long pause before adding, 'Now, if Brigette was wearing the jeans . . .'

'I suppose you want me to photograph her in them – is that your game?'

'What's to lose?' Nona said, wide-eyed.

Luke sighed. 'Okay, Brigette, go in the dressing room. You'll see a rack of jeans, pick out your size and put 'em on, then come back out here. No top.'

'I'm not doing nudity,' Brigette objected. Luke Kasway might be a top-rated photographer, but she wasn't taking off her clothes for anyone.

'Cover your boobs with your hands,' Luke said. 'Copy what those girls are doing in the photo.'

Nona nodded her approval. 'Go ahead.'

Oh, yeah, fine for Nona to say go ahead, it wasn't *her* stripping off.

She went into the dressing room, found jeans in her size and wriggled into them. She felt like an idiot covering her breasts with her hands, then she assured herself that, after all, models did a certain amount of nudity – it wasn't as if she was posing for *Playboy*.

She emerged, waiting for Luke's instructions.

'Okay, over there,' he said, gesturing to a different set-up – this time a brick-wall backdrop. 'Face the wall, legs apart, swing around when I tell you.'

She did as he asked.

Luke peered through his lens making grunting noises. 'Nice one, Brigette. Lower your head, bring your eyes up, lick your lips. That's it.'

Zandino, standing on the side-lines, said, 'It looks good.'

Luke glanced at him. 'You ever had any pictures taken?'

Zandino beamed. 'Snapshots when I graduated.'

'Another idea,' Luke said, snapping away. 'Does he have a body, Nona?'

She rolled her eyes. 'Does he have a body!'

Luke grinned. 'I should've known. We always shared the same taste, even when you were twelve!' He turned back to Zandino. 'Go in the dressing room, find jeans in your size.'

Nona saw the possibilities. 'Yes, Zan, do it,' she encouraged, giving him a little push. 'It's just for laughs.'

'Really?' Zandino asked, unsure.

'*Really*,' Nona assured him.

A few minutes later Zandino emerged. He *did* have a great body, toned, taut and a delicious deep chocolate hue. The jeans fit him as if they had been sprayed on.

'Wow!' Nona said, pointing gleefully at his crotch. 'Terrific view of your assets!'

Zandino frowned.

'Lighten up.' She giggled. 'At least they're major!'

'Okay, we're getting there,' Luke said, running his hands through his spiky hair. 'Over there with Brigette. Let's see how the two of you interact. Do stuff in front of the camera.'

'Like *what* stuff?' Brigette asked, nervous of Zandino invading her space.

'I dunno . . . Back to back, face to face. Zan, put your

114

hands over her boobs, whatever. We need to go for something different.'

'Wait a minute,' Nona objected. '*His* hands on *her* boobs? Forget it!'

'Listen, didn't you tell me you were her manager? This could fly.'

Nona nodded. 'I'm getting the idea,' she said. 'Black and white – Rock 'n' Roll Jeans.'

'Right!' Luke said enthusiastically. 'What's rock 'n' roll all about? *Black* music. *White* music. It's a fit!'

At first they were tentative, stiff.

'Get into it,' Luke screamed. 'Relax, for Chrissakes!'

Fine for him to say, Brigette thought. He wasn't standing there with some strange man holding his boobs.

Sting blasted from the speakers as gradually they started to relax and began to work together.

Luke moved fast, using several cameras as he shot roll after roll of film.

As soon as she relaxed Brigette found herself enjoying it. Posing was hard work, but exhilarating.

By the end of the session everyone was exhausted.

'Whew!' Brigette exclaimed, grabbing a towel. 'I'm dead, but what an experience. Awesome!'

'Don't go getting excited,' Luke warned. 'This could turn out to be a waste of everyone's time.'

'No,' Nona said, very secure. 'This'll be your new campaign. You'll see, Luke. I'm never wrong.'

Chapter Twelve

LUCKY SLEPT away most of the long flight to Europe, not even waking when they stopped to refuel. She'd planned on reading a couple of scripts, viewing the dailies on two of her movies currently in production, in fact, generally getting a lot done.

It was not to be. Instead she had a light meal, settled back with a glass of Cointreau, and fell into a deep sleep.

Before drifting off, her last thoughts were that she was going to forget about business this weekend and concentrate on having a wonderful time with Lennie. They both deserved it.

☆   ☆   ☆

After being out on the beach location all day Lennie wasn't tired so, instead of going straight to his room, he joined some of the cast and crew in the hotel bar and had a few beers.

He couldn't stop thinking about Lucky arriving. God, how he loved her. There was nobody else in the world for him, and this from a man who'd once been a major womanizer. Things had certainly changed. Now he was Mr Married and loving every minute.

'Gotta go,' he told Al, the first assistant director. 'Wanna get a good night's sleep.'

'Get an eyeful of *that* little beauty!' Al replied, nudging him as a blond with a body that didn't quit approached.

Lennie took a look. It was the same blond who'd been parading in front of him on the set earlier. Instead of a bikini she now wore a crotch-high skirt and midriff-baring tank top. Every guy in the bar was immediately transfixed.

She came right over to him. 'Hi, Lennie,' she murmured in her softly accented voice. 'Mind if I join you?'

What was with the 'Hi, Lennie' crap? He couldn't believe she was acting as if they were old friends.

'No, luv, he don't mind at all,' said the focus-puller, a randy Englishman with a Rod Stewart haircut and a lascivious leer. ''S matter of fact, y'can park it right here – next ter me.'

'Excuse me?' she said coolly, hardly glancing in his direction.

'I'm outta here,' Lennie said, quickly getting up. 'You guys can do what you like.'

'Thanks, *mate*,' Al said, with a ribald chuckle. 'Didn't know we needed your permission!'

Lennie made a swift exit before the blond had a chance to hit on him again. Instinct told him she was big trouble.

Up in his room he threw off his clothes, lay on his bed and began to study pages for the next day's shooting.

The phone rang. He grabbed it, hoping it was Lucky calling from the plane.

A provocative purr. 'Lennie? Are you lonely?'

'Who's this?' he said, although he was immediately aware it was the blond.

'How about buying me a drink?' A short pause, then – 'Say . . . in your room.'

'My mother told me never to drink with strangers,' he said, trying to make light of what could turn out to be an awkward situation.

'I wouldn't be a stranger for long,' she replied, her sexy voice full of promise.

'Hey, you know what?' he said shortly. 'Maybe tomorrow, when my wife's here, we'll *both* have a drink with you.'

The blond chuckled softly. 'Ooohh . . . you like three-somes. *Très* cozy!'

'Honey, go hit on somebody else,' he said, realizing this was not an easy one to get rid of. 'I'm not interested.'

'You would be if you saw what I had to offer.'

'I've seen it,' he said sharply. 'So has everyone else.'

She still wouldn't go away. 'So . . . you are Mister Straight and Faithful.'

'Get lost,' he said, slamming the phone down.

A few minutes later it rang again. He almost didn't answer it, thinking it was Miss Persistent. 'Yeah?' he snapped.

'Ha! *You* sound in a good mood.'

'Oh, Jennifer. What's going on?'

'I got your call changed. You're free to go to the airport tomorrow. I have a car picking you up at noon. Your new call's two p.m. Don't forget.'

'You're the best.'

'Thanks.'

'By the way, d'you remember the blond? The one who was trailing me on the set today?'

'What about her?'

'Can you believe she just called my room?'

'Yes, Lennie.' Jennifer sighed. 'I can believe anything about the army of silicone blonds who follow you day and night.'

'Let's not get carried away.'

'What did you tell her?'

'Let me see . . .' he said sarcastically. 'Oh, yeah, I told her to come up to my room with a bottle of vodka and a supply of condoms. What do you *think* I told her?'

Jennifer was unamused. 'Would you like me to accompany you to the airport?'

'No,' he said drily. 'I'm sure I can manage a reunion with my wife by myself.'

'Don't forget, Lennie, your new call is now two p.m.'

'Okay, okay.'

'I know what you're like. Write it down.'

'Got it.' He replaced the receiver, reached for his script and started to read.

A few minutes later there was a knock on the door. He knew it was Jennifer. She didn't trust him and was personally delivering his new call sheet to make sure he had it right.

He grinned, got off the bed and opened the door. Standing there was Miss Silicone City herself, wearing nothing but high heels, a loosely belted terrycloth robe and a seductive smile. .

'I'm sure you *are* lonely,' she purred. 'Big American movie star all by himself – it's not right.'

This woman never gave up. 'Listen,' he said patiently, 'I don't know how to tell you this, but I am perfectly happy, so go home, wherever that might be.'

'Are you sure, Lennie?' she said, staring directly into his eyes as she untied her robe and allowed it to fall open. Naturally she was wearing nothing beneath it.

'Oh, shit!' he muttered, taking in every inch of her incredible curves.

'Am I changing your mind, Lennie?' she said, sexy voice at full throttle.

'Listen,' he said sternly. 'Do everyone a favor and get out of here.'

She had no intention of going anywhere. 'You don't mean that,' she said confidently, a woman used to getting results.

'Yes, I mean it. I don't want to see it. I don't want to touch it. So make a fast exit, okay?'

She licked her index finger, bringing it down to caress an erect nipple. 'Don't you like what you see?'

'I'm calling hotel security if you don't leave right now.'

She shrugged off her robe. It fell in a heap at her feet leaving her totally naked. 'Go ahead, Lennie. I'll tell them you lured me to your room and attacked me.'

Now he was angry. 'Get the fuck away from me,' he said, attempting to slam the door on her.

Before he could do so, she flung her arms around his neck, clinging to him tightly.

From the end of the corridor a photographer appeared, camera flashing.

Lennie struggled to shove her away, realizing too late that this was a set-up.

Managing to disentangle himself from the naked blond, he made a run for the photographer.

The man with the camera immediately took off.

Lennie started to give chase before realizing that all he had on were his undershorts. What a picture *that* would make. Better to deal with the blond and find out what her game was.

He turned around, sprinting back to his room.

She was gone. They'd gotten their pictures and now they'd both vanished.

Grabbing the phone, he demanded security.

A few minutes later the manager of the hotel was at his door. 'Yes, Mr Golden?' the manager said, trying to appear formal, although it was obvious he'd been roused from a deep sleep.

What was he going to say? That there had been a naked woman in his room with a photographer? Somehow it didn't sound like anyone would believe him.

The smart move was to forget it and hope the photographs wouldn't surface, although he had a nasty feeling they would.

'Uh . . . thought I heard someone trying to break in,' he said lamely.

'I will take a look around personally, Mr Golden,' the manager said, with an almost imperceptible bow.

'You do that.'

Lesson to be learned. The *paparazzi* would stoop to any lengths to get the pictures they needed to sell to the tabloid rags back in America. Tomorrow he'd call his lawyers, tell them exactly what had taken place so they'd be prepared to stop publication if the pictures surfaced.

He picked up the phone and tried Jennifer's room.

'Yes, Lennie?' she said patiently.

'What was that blond's name?'

'Lennie!' Jennifer scolded. 'Your wife's coming in tomorrow. I thought you were one of the nice guys.'

'Get me her name and phone number.'

'Oh, yeah, right,' Jennifer said sarcastically. 'How about her measurements and diaphragm size?'

'It's not what you think.'

Jennifer gave an *all-men-are-pigs* long-suffering sigh. 'Whatever you say, Lennie. You're the star around here.'

He knew she didn't believe him, but Lucky would, and that's all that mattered.

In the morning, he was up long before it was time to leave for the airport.

This weekend he was going to make his wife a very happy woman indeed.

☆　☆　☆

Lucky was dreaming. She was lying on a raft in the sea while the water gently rocked the raft back and forth. Then Lennie was beside her, massaging her shoulders, telling her he loved her.

'Miz Santangelo . . . Miz Santangelo. We'll be landing in an hour. Thought you might want to freshen up.'

With a start she opened her eyes. Tommy, the plane's steward, was standing over her.

'Coffee and orange juice, Ms Santangelo?' Tommy inquired solicitously.

She yawned, still half asleep. 'Great, Tommy. I'll take a quick shower and be right out.'

The Panther jet was equipped like a luxurious hotel suite. In the bathroom she stood under a cold shower, jolting herself awake. When she emerged she felt refreshed and full of energy. She applied fresh makeup, fixed her hair, and dressed in a loose silk top and wide pants.

It was crazy, really. She and Lennie had been married four years yet she was as excited about seeing him as if they were going on their first date.

Whoever said passion didn't last?

'Is my car here?' Lennie asked the doorman.

The doorman snapped his fingers, and a chauffeur-driven old Mercedes pulled up. Different car, different driver.

'Where's Paulo today?' Lennie asked, getting in the backseat.

'Sick.'

'We're going to the airport.'

'I know,' the driver said, as the old Mercedes took off fast.

The Panther jet zoomed in for a smooth landing at Corsica's Poretta airport. Lucky couldn't wait to disembark, to feel Lennie's arms around her, see his face, just to hug him.

She hurried off the plane and was disappointed to discover he wasn't at the airport. An airport official asked if she'd like to wait in a private room. She agreed, although she was wild with impatience.

The first thing she did was call Lennie's hotel. They put her through to his room. A breathy female voice said, 'Hello.'

'Lennie?' Lucky questioned, frowning.

'Oh . . . Lennie . . . He left early this morning,' the voice said.

Lucky detected a faint French accent. Could it be the maid? 'Who's this?' she asked suspiciously.

'A friend of his. Who's *this*?'

'His wife.'

Whoever it was hurriedly hung up.

Lucky began to steam. Was it possible Lennie was screwing around?

No way. He wasn't the kind of man who would let her down. They had something special between them, they trusted each other. They had a special bond.

THEN WHO THE FUCK WAS IN HIS ROOM?

She marched from the little office and found the airport official. 'Get me a car and driver,' she said. 'I've decided not to wait.'

Chapter Thirteen

VENUS DIDN'T have a hot date waiting at her house – she'd made that up to infuriate Cooper. When she arrived home she wished that she *had* arranged for Rodriguez to be there. She needed a warm, sensual body. She needed to know somebody loved her.

Was it too late to call him?

Yes. It wouldn't do to look desperate.

God! Cooper's face. She'd certainly rattled his ego. All his life he'd screwed around on every woman he'd been with, never suffering the consequences. The day they'd gotten married he'd promised things would be different.

Well, guess what? He hadn't changed, and she wasn't waiting around for it to happen again.

So now she was alone in her mansion. Cooper's clothes and personal possessions packed up and gone, his presence removed as if he'd never lived there.

She kicked off her shoes and wandered around the house barefoot, staring at the numerous photos of them together.

It was too soon to remove his image from the silver frames, but she was sure she'd never take him back.

In the morning she was up at six to jog with Sven, her trainer. Jogging prepared her for the day, made her feel alert and focused.

They toiled up and down the Hollywood Hills puffing and

sweating. Back at the house they headed straight to the gym, where Sven put her through a vigorous workout that included an hour on the treadmill and three-quarters of an hour working her upper and lower body with free weights. Ha! And people thought it was easy getting this body.

At nine o'clock she asked him to put on the TV so she could watch Kathie Lee and Regis – their early-morning banter was always an entertaining exchange, especially when Kathie Lee was in one of her feisty moods.

The talk-show hosts were just getting into it when they were interrupted by a special news break.

Venus watched and listened to the newscaster's words in shock.

'Movie star, Lennie Golden, was reported killed early today in a fiery car wreck on the isle of Corsica, where he was currently on location shooting his latest movie. A spokesperson for Wolfe Productions issued a statement . . .'

Lennie Golden killed.

Lennie, Lucky's husband.

Lennie, her good friend.

'I've got to get to Lucky,' she mumbled, frantically running from the room.

☆ ☆ ☆

Cooper had not bothered going back to his house. If Venus said she'd moved his clothes and changed the locks, he sure as hell knew she'd done it.

After leaving Leslie's, he'd driven directly to the Beverly Hills Hotel where he'd found himself already checked into a bungalow. Venus had thought of everything.

Leslie had begged him to stay, something he'd had no intention of doing.

'How did Venus find out?' he'd asked. 'Who did you tell?'

'No one. People aren't stupid. They saw us together.'

He'd paced around the room trying to figure out how he'd gotten screwed. 'You *wanted* her to find out, didn't you?' he'd demanded.

'No,' she'd said stubbornly. 'It's the last thing I wanted.'

'Well, anyway, Leslie, it's not smart for me to stay.'

Her eyes had filled with tears. 'But, Cooper, I need you.'

'You should've thought about that before.'

He'd left her house, cursing himself for being so indiscreet. All he could think about was how he could make things right with Venus – because the truth was he truly loved her.

After sleeping fitfully, he woke late, immediately groping for the phone. He called room service requesting bacon, eggs, orange juice, muffins and coffee – the kind of breakfast Venus never allowed because she was always on a health kick.

When the waiter entered his bungalow, Cooper greeted him curtly. The man looked like a talker, and he wasn't in the mood.

'Terrible news about Lennie Golden,' the waiter remarked, as he removed the eggs and bacon from the hot-plate under the room service cart. 'He often used to lunch here. Everyone'll miss him.'

'What news?' Cooper asked, pulling up a chair.

'He was in a very bad car accident.'

'He's all right, isn't he?'

'His car went over a cliff.'

'IS HE ALL RIGHT?'

'No, Mr Turner. He's . . . he's . . . dead.'

Cooper shook his head in disbelief. Not Lennie. Not his friend Lennie. This couldn't be possible.

'Where did you hear this?' he asked.

'It's all over the news. I'm sorry, Mr Turner, I thought you knew.'

'No,' Cooper said blankly. 'No, I didn't know.'

☆ ☆ ☆

Alex rolled into his offices hung over and late. It was past noon and he was in a foul mood. All he could remember of the previous evening was his mother's insults. She did it to him every time, got him so crazy he couldn't think straight. Now she'd ruined his day because he'd blown an important meeting with his line producer and location manager and they were both pissed with him.

He felt like a drink. So far he'd resisted the temptation – last night was punishment enough.

'Good morning, Alex,' Lili, his assistant, greeted him with a faintly disapproving lilt to her voice. 'Or should I say "good afternoon"?'

'I know, I know, I shoulda been here at nine,' he grumbled. 'Something came up.'

'I called your house,' she said pointedly.

'Had the phone shut off.'

'Hmmm . . .'

France, his other assistant, brought him a mug of steaming hot black tea. 'Drink it,' she ordered sternly. 'Later you'll thank me.'

He held back an urge to throw up all over his desk. 'Send Tin Lee flowers,' he muttered.

'How much do you wish to spend?' France inquired.

'A lot,' he said ominously. God knew what he'd put Tin Lee through. She probably wasn't talking to him anymore.

'Alex,' Lili said. 'Have you heard the news about Lennie Golden, Lucky Santangelo's husband?'

'What news?'

'He was on location. There was a car wreck.'

'Where?'

'In Corsica. The car he was traveling in went over a mountain.'

'Jesus! When did this happen?'

'It was on the radio this morning.'

Alex remembered that Lucky had told him she was on her way to visit Lennie. 'Was Lucky with him?' he asked urgently.

'Don't know,' Lili replied, making a vague hand gesture. 'They didn't say.'

Alex jumped up. 'Get me Freddie.'

Lili hurried to the phone. 'Yes, Alex.'

☆　☆　☆

Brigette and Nona headed down Madison, laughing and talking non-stop about the previous night's party and the incredible photo session with Luke.

Brigette realized how much she'd missed her best friend, and how great it was going to be having Nona as her manager. Together they *could* make it happen – they'd always brought each other luck.

As they passed a newsstand on 65th Street, her eye caught the headline on the *New York Post.*

LENNIE GOLDEN KILLED
CAR CRASH IN CORSICA
MOVIE STAR MEETS FIERY DEATH

'OhmiGod!' she gasped, clinging onto Nona. 'OhmiGod! *No! No! NOOO!*'

☆　☆　☆

Donna Landsman was not surprised. She read the newspapers and smiled to herself. Everything was working out just fine.

Lucky Santangelo. How does it feel, bitch?

How does it feel to lose your husband, just as I lost mine?

How does it feel to be left alone with three young children to raise all by yourself?

Well, bitch, now you'll find out exactly how it feels.

And, I can assure you, this is just the beginning.

Chapter Fourteen

 LUCKY SAT VERY still, gazing straight ahead. She knew she should be crying, screaming, anything other than this icy calm that seemed to have crept over her, seeping into every pore deadening her feelings.

Lennie was dead.

Her Lennie was *gone*.

And yet . . . she remained lucid and in control as if her life moved around her in a kind of blurred slow motion.

She was numb with grief. Devastated. And yet . . . the tears didn't flow.

She sat on Lennie's bed in a hotel room in a foreign country and her husband was dead and she did not weep.

Little Lucky Santangelo. She was five years old when she'd discovered the mutilated body of her mother floating in the family swimming pool; twenty-five when they'd gunned down Marco; even younger when Dario was shot and thrown from a car.

Death was no stranger to the Santangelos. Lucky knew only too well what it meant.

And now Lennie was gone . . . her Lennie, the love of her life.

Or was he?

She considered the circumstances.

THE FUCKING CIRCUMSTANCES.

Riding from the airport to the hotel. Grabbing the key to his room from a surprised desk clerk. Noting a DO NOT DISTURB sign on his door.

She'd entered Lennie's world away from her and was disappointed to find that he wasn't there.

The bed was unmade, the room an untidy mess. Well . . . Lennie had never been known for his housekeeping skills.

Details . . . details . . . She'd absorbed them one by one. The overflowing ashtrays on both bedside tables. A nearly empty champagne bottle . . . two glasses, one rimmed with lipstick. A silk chemise crumpled on the floor, half hidden beneath the bed.

THIS MUST BE THE WRONG ROOM.

No. It wasn't. There was the picture of her with the children turned face down on a table. Lennie's clothes were everywhere, his script, phone book, his special silver pen – the one she'd bought him at Tiffany's, matching the one he'd bought her.

She'd called the production office trying to locate him. By that time news was trickling through of a horrible accident on the treacherous mountain roads.

They came and got her, the line producer and a production executive. They took her with them in a car up the twisting narrow road where they all stood in horror, watching as rescue teams went to work trying to recover the wrecked car hundreds of feet below where it had smashed onto rocks and burned before ending up in the angry sea swirling beneath them.

Lucky had known with an overwhelming feeling of dread that she would never see Lennie again.

Now she sat alone in his hotel room. Cleaned by maids, the champagne gone, the ashtrays washed and pristine, her picture with the children back in position.

FUCK YOU, LENNIE. HOW COULD YOU LEAVE US?

The phone kept on ringing. She ignored it, having no desire to speak to anyone. Her plane was on standby awaiting instructions. Right now, she was incapable of making a decision about anything.

They'd recovered the body of the driver, fished from the sea and identified through medical records. Lennie was still missing.

'They didn't have a chance,' one of the police detectives had explained through a sympathetic interpreter.

After a while Lucky got up and mechanically began to pack Lennie's things. His T-shirts, socks, sweaters. His workout clothes. A favorite jacket. His collection of denim workshirts that he liked to wear every day. She did it slowly, methodically, almost as if she were in a trance.

When she was finished with his clothes she gathered together his script, and several yellow legal pads – the first draft of a script he was writing.

Then she pulled open the drawer of the bedside table where she discovered several Polaroids of a naked blond. She stared at them for a long silent moment. The blond was exceptionally pretty, her legs spread wide, a seductive smile on her dumb-ass face.

FUCK YOU, LENNIE. FUCK YOU. YOU WERE SUPPOSED TO BE DIFFERENT.

No tears. Disappointment. Hurt. Anger. A tremendous feeling of let-down and betrayal.

She remembered when she'd walked in on her second husband, Dimitri, in bed with the opera singer Francesca Fern. She hadn't cried then. There was no reason for her to do so now.

Be strong, that was her motto. Over the years it was the only way she'd managed to survive.

There were more photos. Lennie standing with the blond,

her naked body wrapped intimately around him. Another shot of the two of them, apparently taken on the set. Lennie with his arm across her shoulders. Very cozy.

AND NOW YOU'RE DEAD, YOU SONOFABITCH. AND YOU CAN NEVER EXPLAIN.

Not that she wanted explanations.

Who cared?

Who gave a damn?

Lennie Golden was just another guy with a hard-on. Another horny actor on location.

WELL, FUCK YOU, LENNIE GOLDEN. FUCK YOU.

And the pain of loss was unbearable.

She finished packing his stuff into two suitcases and jammed them shut. The photographs she slipped into a zippered compartment in her purse.

After a while she picked up the phone and called her father in Palm Springs. They'd spoken earlier when she'd asked Gino to take the children. He had them safely with him.

'Come home,' Gino urged.

'I will,' she replied listlessly. 'I'm waiting for them to recover Lennie's body . . . I want to bring him back with me.'

'Uh . . . Lucky – it could take a while. You should be with your kids.'

'I'll give it another twenty-four hours.'

'There's nothin' you can do there. When they find him, the production office will make arrangements. You gotta come home now.'

'I . . . I need some time.'

'No!' Gino said harshly. 'You should be with your family.'

She didn't care to be lectured to. She didn't care about anything. 'I'll call you, Daddy,' she said, her voice quiet and low.

Before he could argue further, she replaced the receiver and began roaming aimlessly around the room. Lennie. So tall. So sexy. That great grin. Those penetrating green eyes. That lanky body.

Lennie. *Her* Lennie.

She couldn't put him out of her mind. She could feel his skin, smell his smell, and she wanted him more than she'd ever wanted anything in her life.

Lennie.

Cheat.

FUCK YOU, LENNIE.

YOU BETRAYED ME AND I CAN NEVER FORGIVE YOU FOR THAT.

BOOK TWO

Two Months Later

Chapter Fifteen

'HI,' LUCKY said. She was seated behind her massive desk twirling Lennie's silver pen as Alex Woods entered her office for their six o'clock meeting.

'Hello,' Alex responded, pausing at the door. He hadn't seen her since the tragedy, although it wasn't for want of trying. She'd been difficult to get hold of, elusive, always on the run. Even Freddie had been unable to arrange a meeting.

'People handle grief in different ways,' Freddie had explained. 'There's always problems at the studio. Lucky's thrown herself into work.'

'I'm work,' Alex had pointed out. 'And I've got to have a meeting.'

Actually there was no necessity for them to meet. Everything was being taken care of. Budget approval, casting, location choices – Lucky's head of production was on top of it, Alex had no complaints. If all continued to proceed at such a timely pace they'd be able to commence principal photography within weeks.

'Come in, sit down,' Lucky said.

He walked in, observing she looked tired; there were smudgy dark circles under her eyes and an edginess he hadn't noticed before.

She was still the most beautiful woman he'd ever seen.

'Look,' he said, 'before we get into anything, I want you to know how sorry I was to hear about Lennie—'

'Forget it,' she interrupted briskly. 'It's the past.' She knew she was probably coming across as hard and uncaring, but she couldn't worry about how Alex Woods perceived her. It didn't matter. Nothing really mattered.

She leaned back, automatically reaching for a cigarette. Her bad habits had come back to haunt her with a vengeance.

Earlier in the day she'd had a strangely disturbing meeting with Morton Sharkey. Her gut told her that Morton was up to something, only she couldn't figure out what. For once things were running smoothly at the studio, the banks were quiet, and the Japanese had said yes to the merchandising deal. The truth was that, business-wise, things couldn't be better.

After Morton left she'd downed a couple of Scotches, wondering what it was about him that was making her uneasy. Their meeting had gone well, except for one thing – Morton had been unable to look her in the eyes, and from past experience she knew this was a bad sign.

But she had other things to worry about. She was well aware that personally she was in big trouble. Something inside her was ready to explode. Something that had been deeply buried for the last two months.

Lennie was dead, and she was carrying on as if nothing had happened. Business as usual.

Well, fuck business. Fuck everything. She was tired and despondent and very, very angry.

Alex Woods was staring at her; she could feel the heat of his eyes. 'Everything going well?' she asked, returning to the present. 'Or are you here to complain?'

'As a matter of fact, I have no complaints,' he said, noting she was in a defensive mood.

'*That* makes a pleasant change,' she said coolly. 'Everyone else is driving me nuts.' She paused. He hadn't shaved, and the faint stubble on his chin added to his attractiveness. 'Congratulations on signing Johnny Romano,' she said. 'He's an excellent choice.'

'Glad you approve.'

'I wouldn't have okayed him if I didn't.' She picked up her list of phone messages, stared blankly at it for a moment, then put it down. 'How about a drink?' she suggested, anxious for another one herself.

Alex consulted his watch, it was past six, definitely martini time. 'You look like you've had a heavy day,' he said. 'How about we go to the bar at the Bel Air Hotel?'

'A fine idea,' she said, buzzing Kyoko. 'I'm outta here. Cancel my other appointments.'

'But Lucky—' Kyoko began.

'Don't give me a song an' dance, Ky,' she said sharply. 'I'll see you tomorrow.' She got up from behind her desk, grabbed her jacket and joined Alex at the door. 'Christ! If I can't do what I want occasionally, then what's it all about, huh?'

'You won't get a fight from me,' he agreed, smelling the faint aroma of Scotch on her breath.

She smiled, a dazzling smile. 'Good. Because I'm so bored playing the poor little widow.'

He was too surprised to say anything as they walked outside.

'My car or yours?' she said, standing still for a moment.

'Where's yours?' he asked, trying to keep his eyes off her long legs. After all, this was business.

'Parked over there, the red Ferrari.'

Naturally. 'I'm the black Porsche,' he said.

'Then, my dear Alex, the black Porsche it is – 'cause I've a feeling I will not be in a driving mood later.'

All he'd expected was a meeting, this was turning out to

be more than that. But he was into it, even though he had an eight o'clock date with Tin Lee, a date he knew it was highly unlikely he'd keep.

Lucky got in his car, leaned back and closed her eyes. Oh, how sweet it was making a daring escape. She'd had it with meetings and budgets and business decisions and SHIT SHIT SHIT. She'd had it with the goddamn studio. She'd had it with the responsibility of being a mother and a respectable pillar of society and the proper widow. It was too fucking much. She was going insane. She had no outlet for the fierce anger that was beginning to consume her.

Lennie had left. Checked out. Gone.

Lennie was an unfaithful sonofabitch and she couldn't forgive him for that.

They drove in silence for a few minutes.

'You're looking well,' Alex said.

She didn't bother with pleasantries. 'Do you have any family?' she asked.

'A mother,' he replied carefully, wondering what this was leading to.

'Are you close?'

'Like a snake and a rat.'

'Snakes eat rats.'

'You got it.'

Lucky laughed drily. It occurred to her she'd picked the perfect drinking companion, and that's exactly what she required tonight, someone who could keep up with her and not fall by the wayside.

'I need a joint,' she said, restlessly.

'No problem,' he said, reaching in his pocket and handing her a half-smoked roach that he just happened to have with him.

She pushed in the dashboard lighter, waited for the glow,

then lit up, taking a long satisfying pull. 'You're very obliging, Alex.'

'Not always.'

She gave him a quizzical look. 'Making an exception for me 'cause my studio's putting up the money for your movie?'

He went along with her mood. 'Yeah, sure, that's it.'

She gazed at him steadily. 'Or maybe you feel sorry for me 'cause I lost my husband?'

He kept his eyes on the road. 'You can take care of yourself.'

She sighed. 'That's what everybody thinks.'

He shot a quick glance at her. 'Are they right or wrong?'

'Hey,' she said. 'How about we drive to the Springs and visit Gino? You said you wanted to meet him. Catch me while I'm in the mood.'

'Sure.'

'Oh, boy, you're an agreeable one.'

If she only knew! Alex Woods had never been called agreeable. Difficult – yes. Sexist – yes. Moody, demanding, a perfectionist – all of those things. But agreeable? No way.

'You might be getting a false impression of me,' he said, speaking slowly. 'Y'know, nice guy helping out beautiful woman who seems to be troubled. I've got that chivalry thing buried somewhere inside me.'

'Glad to hear it,' she said, staring blankly out of the window. 'Let's get a drink before we hit the freeway.'

They stopped at a Mexican restaurant on Melrose. Lucky downed straight tequila, while Alex opted for a margarita. Then he ordered a pitcher to go, while Lucky visited the ladies' room, called home, told CeeCee she wouldn't be back tonight, and that she could be reached at Gino's house in Palm Springs.

Lucky was well aware she had nothing to complain about:

everyone around her had been incredibly supportive, from Gino to Brigette who'd flown in from New York and stayed at the house for several weeks. Even Steven and his wife had come in from London to attend Lennie's memorial service. The service had been special. She'd handled it with strength and grace. Little Maria had clung to her, while baby Gino stayed in CeeCee's loving arms. Later, she'd thrown a party at Morton's with all of Lennie's friends and colleagues, because that's what he would have wanted. His eccentric mother had insisted on making an embarrassing speech.

Dry-eyed, Lucky had gotten through it all.

Now, two months later, she was ready to crack.

Alex didn't bother calling Tin Lee. For a start he couldn't remember her number. And second, who cared? It didn't matter anyway, Miss Compliant was on a fast train out of his life.

'Hey – Alex.' Lucky touched his sleeve as they left the restaurant. 'Whatever I say tonight, promise not to hold it against me. I'm in a weird place.'

He looked at her somewhat intrigued. 'What might you say, Lucky?'

'Anything I feel like,' she answered boldly.

Alex had a strong suspicion this was going to be an interesting journey.

Chapter Sixteen

VENUS HAD A lot on her mind. Since she'd thrown Cooper out it had been almost like starting over. She'd given Rodriguez a chance to show his stuff but, to her disappointment, sexually he wasn't in Cooper's class. Too young and sure of himself. Every move planned to give pleasure, but with no real feeling behind it. Unfortunately, Rodriguez simply didn't do it for her.

The truth was she missed Cooper – not enough to take him back, even though he'd made several attempts. They'd seen each other at Lennie's memorial service where he'd cornered her and told her what a mistake she was making.

'It's *you* who made the mistake,' she'd said, trying not to get upset. 'You took me for granted, Coop, not a good move.'

'But, honey,' he'd said, attempting to embrace her, 'I love you, and only you.'

'You should've thought about that before,' she'd replied, and quickly escaped.

After that he'd sent her flowers every day, and phoned continually. She'd changed her private number and had had the flowers forwarded to a children's hospital. Eventually he'd stopped.

She'd wanted to talk to Lucky about it. Impossible, because since returning from Corsica, Lucky had gone back to work as if nothing had happened.

It puzzled Venus. She considered herself one of Lucky's best friends, but even *she* couldn't get her to talk about her loss. There was no getting close to her at all.

The good news was that she'd signed with Freddie Leon. He was the kind of agent she'd always dreamed of – a man with ideas bigger than hers. Recently he'd been trying to talk her into considering a pivotal cameo role in Alex Woods' *Gangsters*. 'It's not the lead,' he'd warned her. 'However, it's an Oscar nomination role, and you should do it.'

She'd read the script and was excited. Set in the fifties, *Gangsters* was a steamy, brutally honest film about Las Vegas and two powerful men. One, a sadistic mobster. The other, a famous Latin singer owned by the mob. Johnny Romano was playing the singer. They had yet to cast the mobster. The role Freddie had in mind for her was Lola, the original good-time girl who becomes involved with both men. It was not a huge role, but very showy.

'Alex has agreed to meet you,' Freddie said.

'How very generous of him,' Venus drawled sarcastically, wondering if Freddie really understood who she was and what she'd achieved.

Freddie chose to ignore her sarcasm. 'You'll read for him.'

Venus gave a brittle laugh. 'Not me, Freddie, I don't read. I'm *way* beyond that.'

'Listen,' Freddie said, his bland features unperturbed. 'Marlon Brando read for *The Godfather* and look what it did for *his* career. Frank Sinatra auditioned for *From Here to Eternity*. When big actors realize a role is special, they'll do anything to get the part. If you want to play Lola, you'll have to convince Alex. It's the only way.'

The meeting was set up for noon the next day at Alex's office.

Just as she'd expected, the tabloids had gone headline crazy with the news of her separation from Cooper. The two of them were spread all over the front pages of the super-market press. So was Leslie Kane, who somehow or other had managed to get herself portrayed as the sweet innocent girl next door, while Venus was painted as the sexually voracious superstar who'd driven her husband into another woman's arms.

God! These papers were so full of crap. If they only knew the truth about Leslie it would blow their minds.

The other bad news was that she'd heard her bum brother, Emilio, had returned from Europe where he'd been hanging out with an aging Eurotrash *contessa*. Emilio made a living out of being her brother, he was even now probably trying to sell more stories of her early days to the tabloids.

One of her spies told her Cooper had left the Beverly Hills Hotel and returned to his former high-rise penthouse on Wilshire. It made her sad to think of him going back to his old ways but, then, she wasn't responsible for him. If he chose to be an almost fifty-year-old playboy screwing a different woman every night, that was *his* problem.

More news flashes from the set informed her he'd broken up with Leslie. It wasn't important, their real problem had never been Leslie.

Rodriguez was on his way over again. She'd decided to give him another chance to exhibit his sexual skills.

The truth was, she was not fond of being alone in the house. At least Rodriguez was company.

Ah . . . the life of a superstar. Not as glamorous as everybody seemed to think.

☆ ☆ ☆

Leslie Kane had taken up with Jeff Stoner, the small-time actor from her current movie. Not because she'd wanted to – he meant nothing to her – but because she'd had to do *something*. Cooper's behavior was too humiliating toward her. After Venus' cruel and nasty speech at her dinner party, she'd hoped that Cooper would finally be hers.

No. It was not to be. He'd turned against her as if she had some unspeakable sexual disease, the bastard was barely polite to her. And what made it worse was the way he treated her on the set. When they were shooting their love scenes he was fine, then as soon as the director yelled, 'Cut!', he was cold and unapproachable.

What had she done to merit this kind of treatment?

Nothing. Except make love to him whenever he was in the mood. And before her dinner party he'd been in the mood all the time.

Was it because he'd found out she was once one of Madam Loretta's highly paid call-girls?

Probably.

Men were so two-faced.

Jeff, on the other hand, didn't seem to mind at all. Well, he was much younger than Cooper – by about twenty years. And younger men, she'd discovered, were far less judgmental.

Jeff *loved* being her boyfriend. He blossomed in the limelight. She was his career booster, giving him the high profile he'd always yearned for.

Cooper hadn't liked it when she'd spoken to their director and gotten him to enlarge Jeff's part. It wasn't much – an extra scene at the end of the movie and a few closeups – but it sure pissed Cooper off. And he couldn't do a thing about it, because *she* was the real star of the movie. Her career was sizzling hot, while Cooper's flame was turned kind of low and steady.

Sexually Jeff came nowhere near Cooper's stellar performances. He was a beginner – all stamina with no finesse. The trouble with a lot of men was that they had no idea how to make love, all they knew how to do was fuck. Jeff was no exception.

She missed Cooper's slow sensuality, the way he knew exactly where and when to touch her, his long kisses, his probing tongue and sensitive hands. Oh, yes, there was no substitute for real experience. Cooper's moves were still the best.

Jeff came bounding out of the bathroom, all hyped up because they'd been at a party where she'd introduced him to his hero, Harrison Ford.

'What a guy!' Jeff enthused. 'So *nice*. Kinda like you, Les.'

'I'm not so nice,' she said, casually brushing her long hair.

'Yes, you are,' Jeff said. 'Even if you won't admit it.' He took the hairbrush out of her hands, put his arms around her, and kissed her on the mouth.

His kisses were too hard, she could barely breathe. And he had this thing he did that she hated. He rolled his tongue and shoved it in her mouth. Not a winner.

If only he knew how to kiss . . .

Two minutes of kissing and his hands were on her breasts. One minute of fingering her nipples, a quick suck on each one, and he was inside her, pumping away, probably under the false impression that he was the world's greatest lover.

She wasn't in the mood to teach him otherwise.

Later, while Jeff snored beside her, she lay in bed thinking about Cooper and how to win him back. There had to be a way.

If there was, she'd find it.

☆　☆　☆

Back in New York Brigette was more determined than ever to make things happen. She'd truly loved Lennie, and now he was gone. His death had brought her up with a resounding jolt, forcing her to realize how fast a life could be snuffed out.

In LA she'd spent as much time as possible with his kids. Lucky was always at the studio, and seemed so completely swamped with work that Brigette hardly got to see her, even though she was staying at the house.

A few weeks after the memorial service for Lennie she'd told Lucky she was returning to New York. Lucky hadn't seemed to mind, she'd wished her luck and assured her good things were about to happen for her.

Now she was back, and there'd be no more sitting around. She was going to be somebody. And she was going to be somebody *soon*.

Anna was pleased to see her. 'Nona called three times today,' she said, as Brigette dumped her suitcases. 'She said for you to call her immediately.'

She'd only spoken to Nona a few times while she was in LA. Nona had promised she'd still get her in to see Aurora Mondo Carpenter and Michel Guy, and that Luke would have photos ready when she returned. At least she had *something* to look forward to.

She went in the kitchen, opened a Seven-Up, sifted through her accumulated mail, then called Nona.

'About time!' Nona exclaimed. 'Where *were* you?'

'On a plane. It was late leaving LA. I only just walked in.'

'Well, get ready to walk out again. Luke Kasway wants to see us at his studio. And he wants to see us now!'

☆ ☆ ☆

Rodriguez arrived on time, his smoldering eyes gazing eagerly into Venus'. 'My beautiful one!' he exclaimed, lifting her hand to his lips.

Venus, clad only in a short Japanese kimono, smiled. There was something delightfully decadent about the fact that she was paying Rodriguez. She got off on it, and even though he was not the lover she'd expected – who was?

'I'm tired,' she complained, in a little-girl voice. 'My bones are weary.'

'Ahhh!' he said soothingly. 'Rodriguez will make your bones sing, your muscles come alive. Your whole body will tingle from my special touch.'

He'd certainly mastered the art of corny English. They went to her massage room in her classic modern all-white house. She clicked on the CD player and k.d. lang proceeded to serenade them.

Rodriguez removed his jacket. He wore a sleeveless black T-shirt and thigh-hugging black jeans. The muscles in his arms rippled invitingly. He had a deep tan and minty breath. All in all he was some studly package.

He smiled at her, his dark eyes full of sexual promise. 'On the table, my beautiful one,' he commanded.

She slipped off her kimono, revealing a black lace thong and nothing else.

Rodriguez's eyes swept over her appreciatively, fixing on her full breasts. 'Perfect!' he exclaimed. 'You are perfection, my Venus.'

I am not your Venus, she wanted to say. *I'm your client. You're giving me a massage and we're both getting our rocks off, but that doesn't mean I belong to you.*

Without a word she climbed onto the table and lay face down, her arms stretched out above her head.

Rodriguez produced a bottle of exotic perfumed oil,

poured a small amount in the palms of his hands, and began lovingly to massage her shoulders and back.

Slowly, surely she felt the tension leaving her body. Oh, God, he did have extremely talented fingers.

'How long have you been in LA?' she questioned, her skin tingling.

'Since I was sixteen,' Rodriguez replied. 'I came here with a married woman running from her husband. She promised to buy me my own beauty salon.'

'What happened?'

'Her husband arrived to claim her. The man was a billionaire.' Rodriguez shrugged. 'She loved me, but she was forced to go with him. I was too young to fight it.'

'What did you do then?'

'Another woman. They have always been my weakness.'

'No, Rodriguez,' Venus corrected. 'You've been *their* weakness.'

His hands moved down to the small of her back, very slowly peeling off her lace thong. Tossing it aside, he began kneading her bare buttocks with his masterful hands.

'Wow . . .' she sighed luxuriously, feeling the heat. 'That's *sooo* damn good.'

'I learn from the best,' Rodriguez boasted. 'My father – he was the most famous masseur in Argentina. The women of Buenos Aires would do anything for my father.'

'I was thinking,' Venus Maria murmured, as his fingers hit the crack. 'How would you like to be in my new video?'

'Doing what?'

'Playing yourself. It's for the song I've written called "Sin". I see the video as being very surreal and sensual.'

'I would be honored.'

'My casting agent will call you.'

His hands were inside her thighs now, spreading her legs, delving down, exploring her most private places.

She did nothing to stop him, she needed the release.

So what if she had to pay him? That was part of the perverse thrill.

And best of all, she was in total control.

☆   ☆   ☆

Brigette took a cab over to Luke Kasway's studio. Nona had sounded excited on the phone, although she hadn't revealed anything other than *Get your ass over here fast*.

She knew she wasn't looking her best in baggy jeans and a shapeless plaid shirt, her honey blond hair braided down her back. Fortunately, she'd just purchased a pair of cool Porsche shades, so she covered her eyes with those even though it was dark out. She didn't want Luke to be disappointed when he saw her. After all, the last time they'd met she'd been all dressed up.

Nona was pacing the sidewalk waiting for her.

'What's going on?' Brigette asked, paying off the cab.

'Dunno. Luke was totally psyched when he called. Insisted on seeing us immediately.'

'Do you think he's got a modeling job for me?'

'I bloody well hope so,' Nona said. 'And even if he hasn't, we'll get to see the pictures. Tomorrow we'll take 'em up to show Aurora. Now you're back, I'll call Michel, we'll go see him, too.'

'Sounds good to me.'

'Don't worry, girl,' Nona said encouragingly. 'We'll get it going.'

Luke was in the middle of a session when they entered the studio. His assistant, a skinny girl in khaki overalls and scuffed combat boots, led them over to the bar and told them to wait.

Luke was busy shooting Cybil Wilde, the gorgeous blond model. Cybil wore lingerie of the seeing-through kind and a toothpaste-ad smile. It didn't seem to faze her at all that the studio was packed with people.

'Who *are* all these bodies?' Brigette whispered.

'Ad executives, hair, makeup, stylists,' Nona replied. 'When they shot my mom for *Vanity Fair* there were more people than this.'

Loud rock music blasted from several speakers. A side table was set up with a full salad bar and plenty of snacks. The atmosphere was tense, even though Cybil seemed to laugh a lot.

Every time Luke took a break, people sprang at Cybil, fussing with her hair, touching up her makeup, adjusting the tiny red lace bra and bikini panties that barely covered her luscious curves.

Brigette tried to imagine herself in Cybil's place. Would it be fun? Would she like it?

When Cybil finally went off to change, Luke came over to the bar. 'Hello, ladies,' he said, running a hand through his spiky hair.

'What's the panic?' Nona asked. 'You told me to get Brigette up here immediately.'

'Let me finish this gig,' Luke said. 'Then I'll take you two girls out for dinner.'

'I'm supposed to be seeing Zan later,' Nona objected. 'And Brigette's exhausted. She only just got off a plane.'

'Have Zan meet us. In fact, I want him there too.'

'Can we at least go home and change?' Nona grumbled.

'Yeah, yeah, whatever. I didn't realize this session was going to run over. Tell you what – let's meet at Mario's, eight o'clock. We'll get into everything then.'

Nona frowned. 'Exactly *what* are we getting into?'

'Oh, didn't I tell you?' Luke replied ingenuously, like it was no big thing. 'Rock 'n' Roll Jeans want Brigette and Zandino to carry the ad. You were right, Nona, they're gonna be superstars!'

Chapter Seventeen

LUCKY FINISHED off most of the pitcher of margaritas before falling asleep. When she awoke she experienced a fleeting moment of confusion – where the hell was she?

Then she remembered. She was in a car with Alex Woods and they were on their way to visit Gino in Palm Springs.

She glanced over at Alex. He had the demeanor of a man who'd always gotten his own way, strong profile, rugged jawline, probably a selfish sonofabitch with women.

She couldn't help wondering if he was a good lover.

Naw . . . too into himself.

'Hey,' she said, stretching languidly. 'Where are we?'

'On the road. You drank everything in sight and fell asleep.'

She laughed softly. 'It's a habit I have.'

'That's okay.'

'Gee . . . thanks,' she murmured, reaching for the pitcher of margaritas wedged precariously against the back of her seat. She took a couple of healthy swigs. 'Guess I should call Gino, warn him we're heading in his direction.'

'You didn't call him from the restaurant?'

'Don't sweat it, he'll be thrilled to see us.'

'He's *your* father.'

'Yeah, and he's the greatest, although . . . I have to admit . . . we didn't always get along.'

He had a feeling she wanted to talk. 'How come?' he asked, making it easy for her.

'Gino wanted a boy. Got me instead. I turned out to be more than he could handle.' She grinned at the memories. 'I was a wild child. Uncontrollable.'

'And now?'

'A mere shadow of my former self.'

'What was so wild about you, Lucky?' he asked, genuinely interested.

'Oh, the usual,' she said casually. 'Ran away from school, fucked a lot of guys, tried to take over my father's business, threatened to cut off one of his investors' dick if he didn't put up the money he owed.'

'A nice simple girl,' Alex said sarcastically.

'Trust me, it worked. When you mess with a guy's dick, it *always* works.'

'And now you're running a studio. Perfect.'

'Y'know,' she said thoughtfully, 'Gino always warned me to check on everyone around me – and to double-check everyone around *them*. In other words' – she put on a tough-guy voice – 'don't trust no one. *Capisci?*'

'He sounds like a smart guy.'

'Yeah,' she said ruefully. 'He sure is.'

'Want to tell me about it?'

'There's nothing to tell. I've simply got this gut feeling that something bad is about to happen. Don't ask me why.'

They drove in silence for a few minutes, then Alex said, 'I didn't think nice Italian girls fucked around.'

She laughed good-naturedly, 'Oh, baby, baby . . . what a sheltered life *you've* led.'

'*Me?*' he said incredulously. Hadn't she read his press clippings?

She paused and lit a cigarette. 'How come out of everything I said the only thing you commented on was that nice

154

Italian girls aren't supposed to screw around? Hmmm . . . Could it be that the bad boy of movies, Mr Sexually Anything Goes, is deep down – dare I say it? – a prude?'

'Are you out of your fucking mind?'

She smiled slyly. 'Girls do talk, y'know. Wanna hear what the word is on you?'

He couldn't resist falling into the trap. 'What?'

Dragging on her cigarette, she blew a steady stream of smoke into his face. 'Big boy on campus. Doesn't give head.'

'*Jesus!*'

'Oh, sorry,' she said innocently. 'Am I shocking you?'

He was completely perplexed. Lucky Santangelo was certifiably crazy.

'You say things to get a reaction, don't you?' he asked.

'Isn't that the whole point?'

He drove on in silence, trying to figure her out.

'Why'n't we pull off at the next exit?' she suggested. 'We're all out of margaritas.'

Alex had to admit he was intrigued. He hadn't expected Lucky to be so unpredictable. She had an aura of strength about her, as if she could handle any situation and come out on top. It was unnerving. He was not used to women who projected such confidence.

So far she hadn't mentioned Lennie, and it didn't seem appropriate for him to bring it up. If she wanted to talk about it she'd no doubt do so.

He changed lanes and pulled off the freeway. The territory was desolate, not much going on except a gas station, a hamburger joint and a seedy roadhouse with a neon sign flashing LIVE NAKED GIRLS.

Alex slowed the car. 'We're in the wastelands,' he said. 'This appears to be it.'

'Define *live* naked girls,' Lucky said, frowning. 'Is that as opposed to *dead* naked girls?'

'Not your kind of place, huh?'

'Seems our choice is limited.'

He shrugged. 'Don't blame me.'

'Alex, when you know me better you'll realize I *always* accept responsibility.'

'Former wild child straightens out. I like it.'

'Fuck you,' she said casually.

He looked her straight in the eye. 'Is that a threat or a promise?'

'You'd better leave me alone tonight, Alex. I wouldn't want to see you get hurt.'

And as she said it, it came to her. That's *exactly* what she needed to do. Hurt someone the way Lennie had hurt her. It was bad enough that he'd gotten himself killed, but when he'd gone he'd left enough evidence of infidelity to make her hate him for ever. There was only one way to even the score.

They parked the car and entered the crowded bar. Big surprise – it was filled with men, most of them swigging bottled beer.

A harassed under-age waitress in boots, a cowboy hat and micro-skirt darted about carrying a tray. She was topless with small droopy breasts and a lackluster smile. At one end of the bar was a circular platform where a large blond stripper undulated her out-of-shape body up and down a shiny pole wearing only a frayed pink G-string and fake silver cuff bracelets. Dolly Parton blared from the jukebox. Every time the stripper squatted down, rolls of excess flesh doubled over her stomach and hips.

'Lovely,' Lucky muttered, taking a seat at the bar while every guy in the place checked her out.

Alex slid on the stool beside her. He carried an unlicensed gun in his car: after taking a look around he was sorry he hadn't brought it in with him.

'Tequila,' Lucky said to the bartender, a gnarled old man

with sunken cheeks and a permanent scowl. He ignored her, waiting for Alex to give him the order.

'Tequila for the lady,' Alex said, getting the picture. 'And I'll have a bourbon and water.'

'Make mine a double,' Lucky said, impatiently tapping her fingernails on the bar. The bartender shuffled off.

The big blond stripper reached the end of her act, snatched off her G-string, turned her back to the crowd, bent over and shook her huge blob of an ass at the paying customers. There was a scattering of groans and catcalls.

'What a bunch of pathetic losers,' Lucky said, checking out the place. 'I mean take a look at these jerks. Why aren't they at home with their wives?'

'I didn't promise you the Ritz in Paris,' Alex said. 'And keep your voice down.'

'You didn't promise me shit,' Lucky replied, the booze finally getting to her. 'But, hey, we're here, let's make the most of it.'

The bartender returned with their drinks. Lucky downed her tequila in one shot. A John Travolta clone, perched on a stool the other side of her, let loose an admiring whistle.

'Another one,' Lucky said.

'Are we ever gonna make it to your father's?' Alex sighed, signaling the bartender.

'Tell me the truth,' Lucky said, swaying slightly on the rickety bar stool. 'Is that the only reason you're with me tonight? To meet Gino?'

'What do *you* think?'

'I think we're together 'cause we both have a need for something different.' She fixed him with a long knowing look. 'Am I right?'

'Perceptive.'

'Oh, yeah, that I am. So fucking perceptive that I truly believed Lennie was faithful.'

'And he wasn't?'

'Don't wanna get into it,' she snapped, sorry she'd mentioned something so private.

A short man clad in a too-tight leisure suit jumped up on stage. 'Okay, folks,' he bellowed, his cheeks red from the effort, 'here's the moment we've all been waiting for – the star of our show! Give her a great big hand – and we all know where!' Snicker, snicker. 'Here she is – our special queen of the night – Driving Miss Daisy!'

An ugly black woman with an incredible body hit the stage with a burst of unbridled energy. She was clad in a white fringed bra, bikini panties and a peaked chauffeur's cap. The Rolling Stones were on the jukebox and Driving Miss Daisy immediately began taking it off to the strains of 'Honky Tonk Woman'. The audience went wild.

Alex considered her almost naked ebony flesh. 'I should find a walk-on for her in *Gangsters*,' he mused. 'She's got quite a look.'

'Why not?' Lucky replied coolly. 'What would your movie be without the obligatory strip scene?'

She had a smart answer for everything. 'Hey, it's what's happening, Lucky,' he said, knowing she'd give him an argument.

'Maybe it is, but how come you movie makers are so predictable? It's always two actors sitting in a strip joint while the camera spends the entire scene zooming in for closeups of the stripper's tits and ass. When are you guys gonna realize those scenes have been done to death?'

'What *is* it with you? The first time we met all you could talk about was actors taking it off.'

'Did that offend you?'

'Women don't want to see that. It's a man's world.'

'You'd *like* it to be a man's world,' she said forcefully. 'You'd like it to *stay* a man's world. But women do what they want today, and women don't mind taking a peek at naked guys. Why do you think Richard Gere is a star today? 'Cause he flashed his nuts in *Looking For Mr Goodbar*, and women loved him for being so honest.'

Driving Miss Daisy did something obscene with the pole, causing quite a commotion among her audience. Several guys threw dollar bills on stage.

'A friend of mine was in hospital and I took her *Playgirl* to read,' Lucky continued, getting into it. 'Now, you'd think the nurses would've seen *plenty* of male equipment. But, let me tell you, they went ape-shit when they got a load of the guys in this magazine. They grabbed it, showed it to every nurse on the floor. They were *thrilled*.'

He shook his head. 'You don't get it.'

She smiled, unperturbed. 'No, Alex, *you* don't get it.'

Driving Miss Daisy was divesting herself of her clothes at a rapid pace. Flinging her bra into the audience, she twirled the two fringed pasties barely covering each erect nipple. Her bikini bottom was long gone, replaced by a hardly there G-string. Coated with a fine film of sweat, she moved like a sinewy gazelle.

'I wonder how she got here,' Lucky mused. 'This seedy two-bit bar in the middle of nowhere.'

'That's my deal,' Alex said. 'Finding out people's stories.'

'Then writing about them and turning them into a movie.'

'Beats packing meat.'

Driving Miss Daisy squatted down, cleverly picking up dollar bills between her thighs. The John Travolta clone on Lucky's left yelled his appreciation.

'Asshole,' Lucky muttered.

'From what I hear, yours is a pretty interesting story,' Alex ventured, curious to hear what she had to say.

'I told you, I was a wild child,' she said lightly. 'I didn't tell you about the guy I shot. Self-defense, of course.'

Jesus! She *was* a wild one. 'No, you didn't tell me that,' he said quietly.

'Enzio Bonnatti, he was the man responsible for killing my mother and brother, and, uh ... there were a few other minor incidents along the way that made me who I am today.'

She was actually sitting there calmly telling him that she'd killed somebody. Perhaps they had more in common than he'd thought. He'd killed in Vietnam, only he'd had an excuse: it was called war.

He wondered if she suffered from the same nightmares that often crept up on him without warning. Middle of the night panic attacks.

'You're a very unusual woman, Lucky,' he said, clearing his throat.

She watched him carefully for a moment. He didn't know the half of it. Maybe she was talking too much, it might be prudent to change the subject before he got too intrigued. 'And you, Alex? Ever been married?'

'No,' he said guardedly.

'Never?' she shook her head disbelievingly. 'How old are you?'

'Forty-seven.'

'Hmm ... that means you're either very smart, or you have a fatal flaw.'

He picked up his drink. 'What are you – a shrink?'

'Guys who aren't married by your age usually suffer from major hang-ups. Otherwise some woman would've picked you off long ago.'

'There's a simple answer. I've never met anybody I'd be prepared to spend the rest of my life with.'

'I've done it three times,' she said lightly. 'It's not so nerve-racking after the first time.'

'And the first time was ... ?'

'Craven Richmond. Senator Peter Richmond's little boy. God, was he a moron! And I was stuck with him.' She laughed at the memory. 'Gino married me off because he could. Peter owed him a favor.'

'Must've been some favor.'

'It was.'

'Do I get to hear about it?'

'Not until I know you better.'

'And after Craven?'

'Dimitri Stanislopoulos, a man old enough to be my father.' She paused for a moment. 'Actually, he *was* the father of my best friend, Olympia.' She giggled – recalling her juvenile delinquent past. 'We were two little bad girls who ran away from school together.'

'You must've really been something.'

'Oh, yeah! I gave jail-bait a whole new meaning.'

'I bet you did.'

'Anyway, while I was married to Dimitri, I caught him in bed with Francesca Fern – the opera singer. She was a rival of Maria Callas', and very demanding. He didn't want to leave me, but, boy, he sure wanted to fuck the life out of her.'

'The man was obviously insane.'

'After Dimitri, there was Lennie.' She stopped speaking, her eyes clouding over. There was a long silence. 'Lennie was my soulmate,' she said at last. 'We were everything to each other. I loved him so much.' She gazed deeply into Alex's eyes. 'Have you ever felt that kind of connection with another person?'

'No,' he said, wishing he had.

'It's the greatest feeling,' she said wistfully. 'There's this incredible chemistry . . .'

'It must have been hard for you, Lucky,' he interrupted. 'The accident . . . losing Lennie . . .'

'Some things are meant to be,' she said, abruptly reaching for her drink. 'I haven't told anyone this, Alex, but I found out Lennie was screwing around. There were photos in his hotel room with a blond draped all over him. Nude pictures of her stashed in the bedside drawer. He was obviously with her the night before I arrived. I don't know why he didn't cover his tracks – he must've thought the maid would clear everything up while he was at the airport.' She took a long deep breath. 'Anyway, it's been hard, because, uh ... I believe in fidelity. You know, screw around all you want when you're single, but when you marry somebody – well, for me that's the ultimate commitment.'

'Ah . . .' Alex sighed. 'She has old-fashioned values.'

'What's wrong with that?' she responded vehemently, sorry she'd revealed so much of herself. 'I find it crazy that we live in a country where everybody says it's okay if a guy goes out and gets laid because he's a guy. It's *not* okay with me. I loved Lennie and he let me down. That's not playing fair.' She stopped talking and lit another cigarette, angry with herself for becoming so emotional. 'I'm getting maudlin,' she said, making a rapid recovery. 'Let's have one more drink.'

'You're almost blasted, Lucky.'

She looked at him coolly. 'Sometimes you just gotta blow it out, Alex.' She clicked her fingers, summoning the bartender. The old man shuffled over. She waved a twenty-dollar bill under his nose. 'Give this to Driving Miss Daisy. Tell her we'd like her to join us, and bring me another double.'

'What are you *doing*?' Alex said, creasing his forehead.

'I'm curious to know how this ugly woman with this amazing body ended up here, stripping for a living. Aren't you?'

'I'm more interested in meeting Gino.'

'We'll get there. Don't worry.'

The John Travolta clone leaned into their conversation.

He wore a yellow shirt and mud brown pants. His hair was long and greasy. 'You all from LA?' he asked, rubbing the tip of his nose with a dirty fingernail.

'Now what makes you think that?' Lucky said, tilting her head.

He placed his bottle of beer on the bar, suggestively fingering the wet rim. ''Cause you sure don't look like you're from these parts.'

'Aw, shucks,' Lucky drawled, almost flirting. 'And I was hoping I'd fit right in.'

The young guy guffawed. 'Name's Jed. This here's the hottest place around,' he boasted. 'You picked good.'

'Really?' Lucky said, her dark eyes drawing him in.

Jed leaned closer, leering at her. 'You one of them Hollywood actresses?'

Alex could smell the dumb jerk's hard-on. 'She's with me,' he interrupted. 'And we're not looking to have a third party join us.' *So keep it in your pants, shithead, and get the fuck away.*

'No offense,' Jed said, backing off. 'Just bein' friendly.'

'Lucky,' Alex said in a low voice. 'I'm not interested in getting into a fight, so do me a favor and stop encouraging the local talent.'

She regarded him mockingly. 'Thought you might get off taking a walk on the wild side, Alex. Isn't the wild side your territory?'

'In case you haven't noticed, I'm considerably outnumbered.'

'Oh . . . *sooo* sorry.' She held her empty glass toward the bartender. 'Set me up again.'

'Jesus Christ!' Alex muttered. 'Whaddya have – a hollow leg?'

'Something like that.'

'I'm going to the john,' he said curtly. 'Try to stay out of trouble. When I get back we're taking off.'

She mock-saluted. 'Yes, *sir*!'

The moment Alex was out of sight the local stud returned to the business of picking her up.

'Didn't mean no offense,' he said, sliding nearer.

'None taken,' Lucky responded, noticing he had no side teeth. It did not add to his sex appeal.

'Would that be your husband?' Jed said, gesturing to Alex's seat.

'No. That would *not* be my husband,' she said, amused.

'Then mebbe I kin buy you a beer.'

'I'm drinking tequila.'

'I kin go for that.' He signalled the bartender. 'Put the lady's drink on my tab.'

The bartender was a man who sensed trouble long before it happened. 'Not a good idea, Jed,' he said warningly.

'The guy she's with ain't her husband,' Jed explained, as if that took care of everything.

'Still not a good idea.'

Jed stood up, red in the face. 'I'm fuckin' buyin' her a drink,' he said, angrily slamming the bar with his fist.

'Christ!' grunted the bartender, disgusted.

'Let's not make this a major incident,' Lucky said, staring at the crusty old man.

'You people should stay where you belong,' the bartender growled, glaring at her. 'Comin' in here as if y'own t'place. Drinkin' tequila like you're some kinda man.'

'Screw you,' Lucky said, starting to loose her temper.

Jed grabbed her arm. 'Better not insult t'old bastard. C'mon, I'll take you somewhere else.'

She shook her arm loose. The booze was clouding her judgment. Alex was right: encouraging the local talent was not a good idea.

Jed went for her arm again. She slapped his bony hand away.

'What's your freakin' problem, lady?' Jed exploded.

'Don't touch me, asshole,' she warned fiercely, her black eyes suddenly deadly.

His face reddened even more. 'Whaddaya call me, *bitch*?'

Alex chose that exact moment to return from the men's room.

Chapter Eighteen

 'YOUR FANS, THEY must drive you crazy,' Rodriguez remarked, lazily stroking Venus' platinum hair as they sat, naked, in her outside jacuzzi, the city lights spread out beneath them like a shimmering blanket of rare jewels.

'Sometimes,' she said thoughtfully. 'When I'm out in public, and they try to touch me. You never know if they've got a knife or a gun. You can never tell if they're the maniac who's going to get you.'

'Is that why you have a guard at your house?'

'Protection is necessary. Think about it, everything we do today needs some kind of protection.'

'Like sex.'

'Exactly. You told me you hate wearing a condom. Well, *I* hate having to live my life with guards. Sadly these are things we're forced to do.'

'Rodriguez does not have any disease.'

'I'm sure you don't.'

'Then we throw away the condoms?'

'No. We do not.'

'Why, my beauty?'

'Get an AIDS test and we'll see.'

He touched her breasts with his fingertips, rubbing insistently.

She shivered as her nipples became erect. Tonight he'd been better than the two previous times. Tonight he'd made her moan with pleasure. As a reward she was allowing him to stay a while.

He reached for the bottle of champagne perched on the side of the jacuzzi and held it to her lips. She allowed the golden liquid to trickle down her throat.

'Aren't you having any?' she asked, slowly licking her lips.

'I'll show you how Rodriguez drinks champagne,' he said, boldly picking her up and placing her on the edge of the jacuzzi.

'What are you *doing*?' she objected, but not too strenuously.

'Silence, my lovely,' he murmured, spreading her legs and caressing the soft inner part of her thighs. Then he took the champagne bottle and tipped the bubbly liquid over her pubic area. '*This* is how Rodriguez drinks champagne,' he said, lapping the liquid from between her legs, continuing to work his smooth Latin tongue, until once more she sighed with pleasure and decided that maybe Rodriguez was a keeper after all.

☆ ☆ ☆

Mario's was a noisy and colorful Italian restaurant packed with models, agents, art dealers and writers. 'It's *the* happening place,' Nona informed Brigette as they pushed their way past the jammed bar to Luke's booth, Zandino trailing behind them.

They'd both rushed home and changed. Nona wore a bright green satin Dolce and Gabbana shirt and tight black pants, while Brigette had settled on a skimpy white Calvin Klein shift dress and strappy sandals.

Luke was not alone. Cybil Wilde and her hair stylist were sitting in his booth. Cybil had a Christie Brinkley glow about her that automatically made her the center of attention. She was so glossily pretty that Brigette was immediately intimidated, even though they were about the same age.

'Squeeze in, everyone,' Luke said, greeting them warmly. 'I'm sure you all know Cybil, and this is the great Harvey, who makes even *my* hair look half-way passable.'

Harvey reached up and touched a lock of Brigette's honey blond hair. 'Nice, luv,' he said in a heavy cockney accent. 'No coloring, none of them stupid streaks all the girls are into. Keep it this way.'

'Thanks,' Brigette said, sliding in next to him.

'And as for *you*, madam,' Harvey added, checking out Nona's blazing red hair. 'Veree *au courant*. An' natural too, I bet.'

Brigette took a moment to study Harvey. A man of about thirty, he had a white blond buzz cut with a side streak of green, black leather wrist cinchers, and a small diamond embedded in the side of his nose.

'What would you do to my hair?' she asked, curious to get his opinion.

'Nuffin',' he said. 'You're a little darlin' just the way you are.'

Talk about an ego booster! Brigette was pleased.

Nona was more interested in getting down to business. 'Can we talk here?' she asked Luke.

'Absolutely,' he replied, waving at several friends.

'Well?' Nona demanded impatiently. '*What?*'

Luke grinned, behaving like an asshole.

'What?' she repeated, pulling on his arm.

'I showed the ad agency the pictures of Brigette and Zan. They took 'em to the client, and wham bam – we got ourselves a gig!'

'OhmiGod!' Nona exclaimed, nudging Brigette. 'Did you hear that?'

'Great.'

'Great,' Nona shrieked. 'GREAT. It's absolutely AMAZING!'

'I got *my* start modeling for a May Company catalog,' Cybil interjected, smiling prettily. 'I was sixteen.' Her smile widened, causing dimples in her cheeks. 'A very well-developed sixteen!'

'When will the photos appear?' Brigette asked Luke. 'And where?'

'We haven't taken 'em yet,' Luke said, laughing at her naïveté. 'First you get your agent to make a deal. Then we shoot a proper session. After that, my sweet girl, you'll be in every magazine from here to the moon! Rock 'n' Roll Jeans spend *money*.'

'How come *I* wasn't up for this job?' Cybil asked, pouting.

''Cause you're – as Nona so tastefully puts it – like dog shit. Oh, don't worry,' Luke added quickly. 'You're in excellent company – Robertson, Nature – they all got Nona's seal of disapproval.'

'Guess we need an agent,' Nona said thoughtfully. 'Like yesterday.'

Brigette thought of all the agencies who'd refused to see her. The only one who'd shown any interest was Michel Guy.

'Elite,' Cybil said, trying to be helpful. 'They're the best.'

'No. The Ford Agency,' Luke argued. 'They'll protect her. She's a virgin in this biz. She'll need armored guards to keep the aging playboys from jumping her innocent little bones.'

'Those men are so gross,' Cybil squealed, turning up her snub nose. 'Total *perverts*! Prince this and Count that, and all they want to do is snort coke, get head, and show you off to their equally disgusting decrepit old friends.'

'Tell us how you *really* feel, dear,' said Harvey, sipping a margarita through a straw.

'Be warned!' Cybil said to Brigette. 'I'll give you a list of the worst offenders.'

'Thanks,' Brigette responded. Cybil was so open and friendly it was impossible not to warm to her.

'What's your take on rock stars?' Luke asked Cybil with a sly smile.

Cybil giggled, she'd just started dating English rock star, Kris Phoenix. 'I'm in love!' she cooed. 'Kris is *sensational!*'

Brigette remembered another English rock star, the infamous Flash. Her mother had overdosed and died while in his company, both of them drugged out of their minds in a cheap hotel room in Times Square.

Oh, God! Nobody must find out her real identity. It was imperative she protect her anonymity. Maybe she should change her first name just to be sure.

'I can get you in to see any agent in town,' Luke boasted. 'Tell me who.'

'Michel Guy,' Brigette said quietly, hardly believing that this was finally happening.

'No problem,' Luke said. 'He's sitting two tables away with Robertson – only when she finds out she's not doing the Rock 'n' Roll Jeans campaign, you may not be a welcome addition to Michel's family.'

'We'll see,' Brigette said with a small, confident smile.

☆ ☆ ☆

After Rodriguez left, Venus found she could not sleep, so instead she did her usual night-time prowl around the house. It was not late enough for her to settle down. Rodriguez had satisfied her sexually, but mentally he was a blank. She must be getting old, because now she needed more than just a great body and a horny disposition. She craved a companion, someone she could talk to when the sex was over. Cooper excelled at both.

She tried to decide whom she could wake up at this time of night. Maybe Lucky, who never wanted to talk anymore unless it concerned business. Well, too bad, this might be the perfect time to reach her.

'Miss Santangelo is in Palm Springs visiting her father,' CeeCee informed her over the phone.

'How's she doing?' Venus asked.

'She works too hard,' CeeCee replied, sounding concerned.

'Tell me about it! I never see her anymore, she's always too busy.'

After putting the phone down, she attempted to read a magazine and found she couldn't concentrate. She was so restless it was crazy.

Hmm . . . she thought, who else would be up?

Ron, of course. Her best friend, Ron, who, since he'd been with Harris Von Stepp, was also on the missing list. She'd nicknamed Harris Major Mogul to get back at Ron, who'd called Martin Swanson the same thing when she and Martin had been an item.

Ron had not been amused. 'Don't *ever* let him hear you call him that,' he'd warned. 'Harris has no sense of humor, he'll throw a complete fit.'

'Harris is too tight-assed,' she'd replied. 'Couldn't you have latched on to a fun faggot?'

'Control your language, girl,' Ron had scolded. 'Faggot is *not* a politically correct word.'

She missed Ron. Not seeing him as much as she used to was like breaking off with a favorite lover.

The hell with it, she decided to call him.

'You'll never guess who this is,' she announced, when he answered the phone.

'Oh, like *quelle surprise*!' Ron said, totally unsurprised. 'Are we experiencing a crisis?'

'As a matter of fact, we are. I was kind of wondering if you could come over, sit around and talk, y'know . . . get cozy like we used to . . .'

'Certainly, popsicle,' he said crisply. 'That will go down *very* well with Harris. I'm sure he's simply *dying* for me to run into the bedroom and say, "Just shooting out to visit Venus." The man is a jealous wreck as it is. *Especially* of you.'

'Why *me*? I'm a girl.'

'*Ohh* . . . you've just answered your own question. Clever little minx!'

'When can I see you?'

'Seriously, poppet, if it's urgent I'll risk Harris' wrath and come over now.'

'No, no, it can wait, but I *do* miss you.'

'Miss you, too. How about lunch tomorrow?'

'Excellent.'

'I'm in the editing room all morning. Let's see, we could meet, say, one-thirty?'

'I can tell you all about Rodriguez.'

'Ahh . . . you finally did it with your masseur.'

'But of course!'

'Then I'll surely be there. Details are my life!'

When she hung up she had this insane desire to call Cooper. *Come back, all is forgiven*, she'd say. No, she'd learned at an early age that it was suicidal to repeat past mistakes.

Cooper would never change. And unless she was prepared to accept his infidelities she was better off without him.

Chapter Nineteen

 'AW, JESUS!' Alex groaned, as he approached the bar and caught the action.

'It's okay, I promise you, it's okay,' Lucky said quickly, jumping to her feet.

Jed was flexing his power. 'What's *with* you, bitch?' he demanded belligerently, facing her right on. 'Too freakin' good for us?'

'Back off,' Alex said, with a granite-like expression as he stared Jed down.

Jed swayed on his feet. 'Don't freakin' tell *me* what to do, Grandpa!'

'Fuck!' Alex muttered, wondering how he'd ever got caught up in this scene. And what was with the grandpa shit? He should knock this snot-nosed pisshead out of the ring.

Instead, he reached into his pocket, produced a wad of bills, threw them at the barman, and grabbed Lucky's arm. 'We're outta here,' he said, pulling her to the door without looking back. It was a trick he'd learned in Vietnam. If you want to fight, stay eyeball to eyeball with the enemy. If you don't, get the hell out. And do it fast.

'Hey,' Lucky objected as they reached the door. 'What about the twenty bucks I gave the bartender?'

Alex tightened his grip. 'What about getting in the car and shutting the fuck up?'

'You're a lot of laughs,' she complained.

'If it's laughs you want, you picked the wrong guy,' he said tersely.

'Let me jog your memory, Alex, you're the one who came running into my office asking me out for a drink.'

'I came for a business meeting,' he reminded her. 'Did I know you were going to be sitting there half ripped?'

'Half ripped?' she said, outraged. 'I'm perfectly sober.' Although, even as she said it, she knew she was teetering on the edge.

'Yeah, yeah,' he muttered, hustling her over to the Porsche. Out of the corner of his eye he observed Jed emerging from the bar with a couple of his rowdy friends. He shoved Lucky in the passenger seat, bent down and reached for his gun in the glove compartment.

'What are you *doing*?' Lucky said.

'Protecting us. Do you mind?'

'Are you *crazy*? You can't shoot the jerk just 'cause he came on to me.'

'I'm not planning on shooting anybody. I'm buying us time to split.'

'Gino taught me never to pull a gun unless you're prepared to use it.'

'He taught you well, 'cause if those punks come at me, I'm shooting 'em straight in their scrawny balls.'

'I can see the headline now,' Lucky said, not taking him seriously, even though his gun appeared to be the real thing. 'Studio head an' bad boy film-maker. Busted!' She broke up at her own humor.

Jed and his friends hesitated at the entrance. Maybe they'd seen the glint of the metal, or maybe they'd changed their minds. Whatever, to Alex's great relief they didn't venture further. Which was fortunate, because he'd meant what he'd said.

Lucky doesn't know me, he thought grimly. She has no idea that in Vietnam I was forced to kill people more than once.

It wasn't something he cared to remember, only in his nightmares.

He got behind the wheel of his Porsche, revved the engine and took off at high speed.

'Shame.' Lucky sighed, snuggling down in her seat feeling no pain. 'I was *sooo* interested in talking to Driving Miss Daisy.'

This woman is crazy, Alex thought as he got back on the freeway. What am I doing with her? She's crazier than me.

They'd been driving for five minutes when Lucky realized she'd left her purse at the bar. She sat up abruptly to announce the fact.

'We are *not* going back,' Alex said tersely. 'No fucking way.'

'Oh, yes, we *are*,' Lucky retorted. 'My credit cards are in it, my Filofax, driver's license – everything. We *have* to go back.'

'You're a difficult woman,' he said sourly.

'So I've been told.'

He couldn't believe he was doing it as he took the next exit off the freeway, making a sharp turn. 'Listen to me,' he said sternly, his eyes fixed on the road ahead. 'You stay in the car with the engine running while I go in and collect your purse. Understand?'

'You're not taking your gun in.'

'Don't tell me what to do.'

'No, don't tell *me* what to do.'

'Oh, I can see we're going to have a fascinating time making this movie.'

'You'd better believe it.'

Did she *always* have to have the last word?

☆　☆　☆

He pulled his Porsche up outside the roadhouse and got out. In spite of Lucky's warning he shoved his gun down his belt at the back of his pants. Better prepared than not, small-town hotheads were the worst kind.

When he walked in, another stripper was busily working the stage, grabbing everyone's attention. Chinese this time. They certainly went in for variety.

Alex hurried over to the bar. 'My companion left her purse,' he said.

The grizzled old barman fished under the bar, silently handing over Lucky's purse. 'We don't want no trouble in these parts,' the man said sourly. 'You LA people with your money and flashy cars. Stay away.'

'Listen, buddy, it's a free country,' Alex pointed out, putting Lucky's purse under his arm and walking out.

His Porsche was exactly where he'd left it. There was only one problem.

Lucky was not in it.

He stood by his car totally pissed off. He'd *told* her to stay in the goddamn car – was that so difficult? Too independent. That was the problem with Lucky Santangelo.

One thing was sure. He'd never met a woman like her. He considered teaching her a lesson, driving away and leaving her stranded. Then he decided he couldn't do that: nobody deserved to be left in this pisshole and, besides, her studio was financing his movie.

He went back inside looking for her.

The bartender was busy shifting heavy crates of beer, he shook his finger when he saw Alex, as if to say, *Not you again*.

'Did you see the lady I was with?' Alex asked.

'I told you,' the bartender repeated. 'Your kind ain't welcome here.'

Alex was fast running out of patience. 'Where's the ladies' room?' he asked.

'Out in the parking lot,' the bartender said. 'An' don't come back.'

Like he would ever want to.

☆ ☆ ☆

The outdoor ladies' room doubled as a dressing room for the strippers. They scurried in with their plastic makeup cases and see-through carry-alls, changing clothes in the cramped space. When Lucky entered, the black stripper known as Driving Miss Daisy had just finished getting dressed in an alarmingly tight scarlet catsuit.

'Hi,' Lucky said, 'my friend and I wanted to buy you a drink, only it didn't seem like we were welcome here.'

The stripper peered at her reflection in the cracked mirror over the once white basin. 'Girl, this place is two-tone shit,' she remarked, busily rubbing lipstick off her teeth. 'Why're you here?'

'I'm with Alex Woods, the film director,' Lucky explained. 'And we're both kind of curious to know why you're wasting the best body we've ever seen in this dump?'

Driving Miss Daisy adjusted what appeared to be a long red wig. 'Listen, girl, there's times a person don't have no choice. I work plenny a places – private parties, ole boys' reunions, crap clubs an' dives like this. Thing is, girl, *that's* what pays the rent.'

'We'd pay you—'

'Oh, *no, no, no,*' Driving Miss Daisy said, shaking a bony finger at Lucky. 'I ain't into any of them *kinky* scenes, so don' go gettin' no fancy ideas jest 'cause I take my clothes off.'

'Absolutely no kinky scenes,' Lucky assured her. 'All we want is to hear your story. Alex is interested in putting you in his new movie.'

'His movie, huh?'

'Would a hundred bucks give us twenty minutes of your time?'

'This is too weird,' the stripper said, shaking her long red wig.

'What's weird about it? It's an opportunity. Seize it.'

The woman pursed her lips. 'Never *had* no *opportunities*,' she said thoughtfully.

'So take it,' Lucky urged.

'I got another gig t'go to.'

'We'll come with you.'

'I dunno . . .'

'Where is it?'

'A pool hall . . . 'bout twenny minutes from here.'

'A deal,' Lucky said quickly, before the stripper changed her mind.

They walked outside, running straight into an irate Alex.

'I told you to stay in the car,' he said, glaring.

'I don't take instructions well.'

'That's obvious.'

'Alex, this is Driving Miss Daisy . . . or, uh . . .' She turned to the stripper. 'I guess you've got a name, right?'

'Why y' wanna know my name?' the woman asked suspiciously.

''Cause I feel a little foolish when I have to keep saying Driving Miss Daisy. It's not like I'm turning you in to Social Security or anything.'

The stripper narrowed her eyes. 'Jest 'cause I'm black, y' think I'm on welfare? That's *shit*!'

'Did I say that?'

'Lucky,' Alex interrupted impatiently, 'can we go?'

'We're going to see . . . what's your real name?'

'Daisy,' the woman muttered.

'Fine. We'll catch, uh, Daisy dancing at another place, and then she'll have a drink with us.'

'I'm *not* stopping at another one of these shitholes,' Alex said, still glaring.

'I promise,' Lucky said sweetly, 'no more trouble.'

Alex didn't believe a word. 'Yeah, like *you* can control it,' he said.

'I can,' she assured him.

He shook his head. 'You're something else, Lucky.'

'So are you, Alex,' she said. 'But we'll get into that another time.' She turned to the stripper. 'Daisy, we'll follow you, where's your car?'

'Y'all are *real* strange,' Daisy said, rolling her eyes.

'You can say that again,' Alex muttered.

'I'm the yellow Chevrolet over there,' Daisy said, pointing to a wreck of a car.

'We'll be right behind you,' Lucky said.

'Are you insane?' Alex asked, when they were settled in his Porsche. 'Why are we doing this?'

'If you're not into it, drop me at the next bar and I'll call a limo,' she said, fed up with Alex's nagging.

'I can't leave you here,' he said flatly, adding a surly, 'Much as I'd like to.'

She desperately wanted another drink, it seemed that every drop of alcohol she'd consumed had no effect. 'C'mon, lighten up,' she said, turning on the charm. 'It'll be a blast. Another tequila. A game of pool. What's so bad?' She nudged him, trying to lure him into the spirit of things. 'Twenty bucks says I can beat you.'

He studied her for a moment. 'You think you can beat me at anything, don't you?'

'Maybe I can,' she said, thinking that maybe she could.

'Your ego has a life of its own.'

'I suppose yours is just a shadowy little thing?' she countered, groping for a cigarette.

He couldn't help laughing. 'I bet you're always used to getting your own way.'

'Like you're not?' she said, wondering why she felt this continuing urge to needle him.

He regarded her steadily. 'I worked my ass into the ground to be able to get my own way.'

'What do you think *I* did?' she replied, meeting his gaze.

'Then I guess we're more alike than we realize.'

The yellow Chevrolet exited the parking lot.

'Let's go,' Lucky said. 'We're following an adventure about to happen!'

Chapter Twenty

MORTON SHARKEY met with Donna Landsman in the privacy of her fake Spanish castle. As he drove up the long winding driveway, he tried not to think about how he was betraying Lucky. He knew that what he was doing was wrong, but the downward spiral he was caught up in was too strong to stop. Besides, he was being blackmailed, so he was also a victim.

And yet . . . in spite of everything, he was still obsessed with Sara. When he was with her, nothing else mattered.

An Oriental butler opened the front door and led him through a baronial hallway into a grand, high-ceilinged living room. Morton noticed a lot of portraits of other people's ancestors hanging on the walls.

Donna stood in the middle of the room dressed in Escada, her face impeccably made-up, a martini glass in her hand. 'Morton,' she said, formal and cold, not offering him a drink.

'Donna,' he responded.

She did not ask him to sit down. 'I understand you have good news for me,' she said.

'It's the news you've been waiting for,' he replied evenly. 'All the investors are in place. As of tomorrow you will be in control of Panther Studios.'

She smiled a thin, almost evil smile. 'I'm delighted you decided to cooperate with me.'

As if he'd had a choice. He tried not to stare at her, a nerve began twitching under his left eye. 'When do I get the tapes, Donna?'

'The moment I'm sitting behind the desk in Lucky Santangelo's office.'

'Exactly what day are you taking over?'

'Tomorrow,' Donna said, her face an unemotional mask. 'I hope you'll be there to congratulate me.'

'I wasn't planning on it.'

'That's not very friendly of you, Morton,' she chided. 'Surely you wish to witness my moment of triumph?'

'Not really.'

'Too bad.' Her voice hardened. 'Because you *will* be there. I'm sure at this late stage you would not want the videotape of you and that *inventive* young lady becoming public property.'

Witch! Scheming witch! Why was she doing this? What made Panther Studios so important to her? That was something he hadn't figured out.

'Very well, Donna, I'll be there.'

Another evil smile. 'Good.'

She waited until Morton had left, then she went to the bar and fixed herself a second congratulatory martini.

She sipped it slowly, relishing the thought of what joy tomorrow would bring.

Revenge was sweet. So very very sweet.

☆ ☆ ☆

As soon as he was out of there, Morton drove directly to Sara's apartment, an apartment he paid for. When he'd met her, she'd lived in a place too dreadful to contemplate – he'd always imagined getting mugged on his way in. Now he'd installed her in a respectable high-rise, and he felt secure traveling up in the elevator from the private underground garage.

He let himself in with his key. At first she'd objected to him having one but, as he'd pointed out, if he was paying the rent, why shouldn't he?

Sara was not alone, which infuriated him. He'd told her repeatedly that when he visited he did not want her friends around.

Even though he'd informed her he was on his way over, her friend Ruby was there, a sulky looking girl with stringy black hair and a bad attitude. The two of them were sitting on the living room floor surrounded by trashy magazines, candies and an army of colored nail polishes. Both of them were barefoot, giggling as they painted each other's toenails.

'We're experimenting,' Sara said, waving.

'Hiya, *Morton*,' Ruby said, mocking his name.

He nodded, standing awkwardly over the two girls, expecting them to get up. Neither did.

'Sara,' he said at last. 'I'd like to speak with you.'

'Go ahead,' she said, busily painting black polish onto Ruby's big toe.

'Privately,' he said, annoyed that she didn't treat him with more respect.

She pulled a face. 'Say what you want – Ruby don't care.'

He wondered how much Ruby knew. Was she aware that Sara had put him in the most compromising position of his life? Did she know that Sara had banked twelve thousand dollars to do so? And she wasn't even embarrassed or sorry when he'd found out. 'It's a lotta money, Morty,' she'd said, completely without guilt. 'Couldn't turn it down.' Then she'd made love to him in a way that he'd never been made love to before. And he'd continued seeing her.

He was sick. He knew that.

Lovesick. Only now he made sure there were no hidden cameras concealed in the apartment.

Ruby took the hint. She stood up and yawned. 'I'm goin' by Tower Records,' she said. 'Want anything?'

'Wouldn't mind comin' with you,' Sara said, wistfully entertaining the idea until she noticed Morton's furious expression. She grimaced. 'Guess not.'

Ruby slipped on a pair of ugly sandals and left.

'I can't imagine why you're friendly with her,' Morton said, standing stiffly in place.

'That's 'cause you got no imagination,' Sara said, popping a Gummi-bear in her mouth. She jumped up, throwing her arms around his waist. 'That's okay, Daddy, 'cause I got 'nuff for us both, don't I, honey-buns?'

'Yes, Sara, you do,' he said, feeling an overpowering rush of excitement, the kind of sexual anticipation he hadn't experienced in twenty-five years.

Sara pulled her skimpy tank top over her head and dropped her shorts. She wore no underwear. She was skinny as a ten-year-old boy, but her lack of curves only heightened Morton's ferocious excitement. His eyes fastened on her almost pubescent nakedness, drifting down to her thick tangle of tangerine pubic hair.

'What's it gonna be?' Sara asked with a sly smile. 'Waitress? Lawyer? Schoolgirl? Or maybe you're in the mood for the little *boy* thing . . .' She smiled knowingly, twisting her pubic hair. 'C'mon, bunny rabbit, it's your call.'

'Little boy,' he said, his voice constricted.

'Ohhh . . . you *are* naughty today. If I was playing Nanny I'd be forced to spank a bad boy like you.'

And so the games began.

And Morton Sharkey gave no more thought to his betrayal of Lucky Santangelo.

☆ ☆ ☆

Santo had noticed that his mother was in an extremely good mood. This meant he could ask her for anything he wanted and more than likely get it.

He wandered into the kitchen where she was busily preparing pasta sauce.

'Hi, Mom,' he said, slouching over to stand beside her.

Donna beamed. 'Santo. Come. Taste,' she said, shoving a spoonful of steaming rich meat sauce into his mouth.

It burnt his tongue. *Dumb cunt!* he wanted to yell. Instead he said, ''S good,' hating the garlicky flavor almost as much as he hated her.

Donna knew that when she cooked, which wasn't often, she was the best. 'Only good?' she questioned, confident of his answer.

'Awesome!' Santo responded. He knew what was expected of him.

'I'm freezing a batch of it,' Donna said. 'You can invite friends over and enjoy it together.'

She was so stupid she didn't even know he had no friends. The kids at school shouted names at him like Rich Jerk and Fat Greasy Wop. They hated him, and he hated them back.

He didn't care. One day he'd burn the whole friggin' school down with everyone in it, then she could meet his so-called friends all laid out in the morgue – burnt to a crisp.

'I was thinkin', Mom,' he said, perching his considerable bulk on a stool. 'Wouldn't it be bitchin' if I got a new car?'

'What are you *talking* about?' Donna exclaimed, expertly chopping zucchini. 'I bought you a Corvette for your birthday.'

'Since I had that dumb accident it's not the same,' he complained, hunching his shoulders.

'We had it repaired.'

'I know – but, Mom . . .' He waited until he had her full attention. 'I *really* want a Ferrari.'

'A *Ferrari*?' she said, shocked.

'Why not?' he whined. 'Mohammed's dad bought him one, and Mohammed's the geek of the decade.'

'It's not a practical car for school,' Donna said sternly, adding the chopped zucchini to her pasta sauce.

'I'd drive it weekends, and take the Corvette to school,' he explained, making it sound like a sensible idea.

'Well . . .' She hesitated. It was so damn difficult saying no to her son.

'C'mon, Mom,' he said persuasively. 'It's not like I do drugs, or go out an' get wasted like most of the kids in my school. I could, like, *really* do things that'd bum you out.'

Donna shook her head. Was this a veiled threat? No, not from her sweet boy. Santo was too good. 'Two cars,' she mused, thinking it over. 'George will never agree . . .'

'Who cares what George says?' Santo said bitterly, his puffy features hardening. 'He's not my father. My father was killed, and you can't replace him with George, so don't try.'

'I would never do that,' Donna objected.

Santo went for a new angle. 'Putting George's feelings first sucks,' he said, scowling.

'I put *you* first, Santo,' Donna replied, crushed that he would think otherwise.

He glared at her accusingly, as if he didn't believe her.

'When I was your age we had nothing,' Donna said, shaking her head at the memories. 'We were so poor—'

''S not the same,' Santo interrupted. 'You lived in some little village.'

'A village I shall take you to one of these days,' Donna

promised, remembering her humble roots with a certain amount of nostalgia. 'My relatives will be so proud of you. I'm so proud of you.'

'If my dad was alive, *he'd* buy me a Ferrari,' Santo said, going for the full guilt trip. If this didn't get her, nothing would.

Donna stared at her son, finally capitulating because it was too difficult to say no. 'If it's what you really want.' She sighed.

He beamed. She was so damned easy.

'Go to the showroom, pick out the model you like.'

He jumped up and hugged her. 'You're the best mom in LA.'

The title alone was worth the expenditure. 'George is staying in Chicago overnight,' she said. 'If you like, we can catch a movie, then have dinner at Spago.'

Much as he wouldn't mind pigging out on the delicious pizza at Spago he couldn't face an evening alone with his mother. 'No, Ma, I can't,' he mumbled. 'Too much homework.'

'Oh,' she said, her face sagging with disappointment. 'Can't it wait?'

'You'd be bummed if I fell behind on my grades, wouldn'tja, Ma?'

'I suppose so.' She paused. The two martinis she'd had earlier were giving her a nice steady buzz. 'It's just that this afternoon I concluded a very exciting deal. I thought we could celebrate.'

Like her closing some big deal was anything new. 'What deal?' he said, not interested, but smart enough to know that since she'd agreed to the Ferrari he should jolly her along.

'I'm taking control of a Hollywood studio,' she announced proudly. 'Panther Studios.'

This was more like it. Thoughts of stardom raced through his head. 'Can I be an actor?' he asked, imagining the possibilities.

Donna's thin mouth curved into an indulgent smile. 'You can be anything you want.'

Shit! This was good news. A Hollywood studio. Venus Maria was an actress, and all actresses were prepared to do anything to get into movies, everyone knew that. If his mother owned a studio the power would reflect on him. In fact, he'd be able to make sure Venus Maria starred in every film the studio made.

This was a sign. First the Ferrari, now a big movie studio. The time had come to contact Venus.

Of course, he wouldn't reveal his identity yet, instead he'd write her an anonymous letter informing her he was on her side, and that soon, when the time was right, they'd be married, joined together in every way.

'Gotta go, Mom,' he said, sliding toward the kitchen door. 'See ya later.'

Once up in his room he hunched over his computer and began composing his first letter to HER.

Recently he'd purchased a stars map and looked up Venus' address. Then he'd taken an investigative drive up to her house in the Hollywood Hills, got out of his car and peered through the large wrought-iron gates. A guard had emerged and waved him away.

Freaking moron. Didn't he know that one day he, Santo, would live there with Venus? It was only a matter of time. He'd thought about telling the asshole that's what was going to happen. The jerk probably wouldn't believe him.

No. He could wait. One day everyone would know.

He did his best to concentrate on the letter, but somehow or other it was impossible to stop his mind from wandering.

He imagined Venus without her clothes, naked and

available, licking her jammy lips, prancing around the stage just for him . . .

And when she saw what he had to offer . . . Oh boy! Venus Maria would be some happy babe.

Jeez! He was getting the biggest boner just writing to her. Why hadn't he done it before?

He unzipped his pants, fumbled for his dick, and thought about her some more. She was some horny piece of ass, and one day she would be all his.

He decided he had more exciting things to do with his hands than play with a computer. Her letter would have to wait.

Chapter Twenty-one

IT WAS PAST ten when Lucky and Alex drove up to Armando's Strip Palace and Pool Bar – a gaudy, sprawling place that once again appeared to be in the middle of nowhere.

'Another classy joint,' Lucky remarked, taking in the signs, which proclaimed the usual LIVE NUDE GIRLS, and the unusual NAKED WICKED WILD WILD WIMMIN!

'Sure you wanna go in?' Alex asked, pulling into the jammed parking lot right behind Daisy's yellow Chevrolet.

'Yes,' Lucky said, feeling light-headed and ready for anything. 'This looks like a happenin' place.'

Alex realized there was no way she was backing out. Not Lucky Santangelo. Not this woman. 'Okay, let's go,' he said, resignedly parking his Porsche.

Daisy met them as they got out of the car. 'I gotta go in the back way,' she mumbled. 'Armando's shitty rules. Where's my hundred bucks?'

'Don't you trust me?' Lucky asked, thinking this woman was the least likely candidate to have a name like Daisy.

'I ain't in this business t'trust no one,' Daisy retorted, hands on hips.

Lucky fumbled in her purse, pulled a hundred-dollar bill from her wallet and handed it over.

'Tell the guy at the door you're friends a' mine,' Daisy

cackled. 'That'll get you a bad seat.' She teetered off on stiletto heels, still laughing.

'Lucky,' Alex said, with a deep sigh of resignation, 'what the *fuck* are we doing here?'

'Getting a drink,' she said, pushing back her long dark hair.

'How about food?' he said, adding a *sotto voce*, 'to put in your hollow leg.'

'Ha ha!'

They entered Armando's. It was four times as big as the last place and just as overcrowded. Three pool tables lined up on one side of the room. A live band blasted their version of a well-known Loretta Lynn song, and a long curved bar on which a red-haired stripper cavorted was jammed with beer-swigging cowboys and a scattering of women all dressed up in their cowgirl best.

'Hmm . . .' said Lucky, surveying the room with a jaundiced eye. 'It seems to be one of those country-and-western deals with a twist. Wanna do a little quick-stepping, pardner?'

'There's something seriously wrong with you,' Alex said sternly.

'Why?' she replied, feeling pretty good.

'You're not normal.'

'What's normal?' she asked flippantly, deciding that in spite of himself Alex was quite a sport.

'Well . . .' he thought for a moment, 'you're not exactly quiet.'

She burst out laughing. 'Oh, I see. You're into quiet, subservient women, is that it?'

'You know what I mean,' he said, aggravated.

No. She didn't know what he meant, and quite frankly she didn't care. He was here for a purpose, and that purpose was to entertain her.

God! Her world was starting to spin. Better get a grip. Better get it together.

There were no free tables, so once again they found two seats at the bar, crowding in between a couple of surly cowboys. Alex slipped the hostess a twenty, informing her he expected the next available table.

'Jesus!' he muttered, as they sat down. 'If I don't get into a fight tonight, I'm the luckiest guy around.'

Once again Lucky brushed back her long hair and laughed. She knew she was drunk, but it didn't matter. Tonight she wasn't Lucky Santangelo, businesswoman, head of a movie studio, mother. Tonight she was single and free, and she could do whatever she felt like. And right now she felt like having another drink. Only problem, Alex wasn't keeping up with her.

'One tequila,' she said, concealing a hiccup. 'We'll watch Daisy do her thing, play a game of pool, then we're on our way. That's a Santangelo promise.'

'You and your promises,' he said grimly, glad that he'd stayed comparatively sober. Somebody had to know what they were doing.

'No, really,' Lucky insisted. 'You *will* meet Gino later. You're gonna love his stories.'

Alex knew there was no way he was getting anywhere near Gino tonight. 'Yeah, yeah,' he said.

'Y'know, Alex,' Lucky said, placing an understanding hand on his shoulder. 'I've been doing all the talking. Isn't it about time we got into you?'

'Why?' he said, stone-faced.

'I still can't get over the fact you never married.'

'Hey, listen, just because *you* were married three times . . .'

'My take is you must have an overpowering mother whom you secretly hate.'

'That's not funny,' he said, frowning.

'Did I hit it right on?'

He didn't reply.

The waitress came over and told them she had a ringside table ready for them. They moved over just as Daisy bounced onto the stage like a dynamo.

Instead of a pole, Armando's had a fake silver palm tree stuck in the middle portion of the long bar. Daisy worked the palm tree like it was her most intimate lover, doing things to it most people only dreamed about.

The audience began throwing money, stamping and whistling their approval. Daisy got off on the applause. She squatted down, thighs spread, and began collecting dollar bills.

'Amazing muscle control,' Lucky murmured. 'I hope they bring a guy on next.'

'Are you *crazy*?'

'C'mon, Alex, surely you're into equality among the sexes?'

'Bullshit.'

'Scratch a movie director and find a chauvinist,' she taunted.

'What is it with you?' he asked, exasperated.

'Nothing you'd understand.'

By the time Daisy had taken it all off, the audience was out of control. Daisy sure knew how to play a crowd. When she was finished she joined them at their table, out of breath and triumphant, her jet skin glistening with perspiration.

'What you wanna know?' she asked, flopping into a chair.

'Alex, *you* do the talking,' Lucky said.

He shot her a look. *She* was the one who'd dragged him to this joint, and now she expected *him* to ask the questions. Surely she knew he couldn't give a damn about this black stripper, even if the woman did have an unbelievable body.

Still . . . visually . . . in his movie, Daisy would definitely score. Especially the picking up the money with her thighs bit.

'What's your story, Daisy?' he asked, with a bitter twist. 'Fucked by your father? Beaten by your stepfather? Raped by an uncle? Then you ran away from home. Am I getting there?'

Daisy twirled her fingers through her long red wig and ordered a beer. 'My ole man was a Baptist minister,' she said primly. 'Wouldn't allow no sex talk in our house. My daddy was one strict motherfucker. Me? I'm a workin' girl with two kids an' a lover. I make enough t' see my kids are done right by.'

'Not exactly the story you were expecting, huh, Alex?' Lucky said, needling him again.

'Where's your lover tonight?' Alex asked, ignoring Lucky and concentrating on Daisy.

'Babysitting. She's into stayin' home.'

'She?' Alex questioned.

Daisy winked at Lucky. 'Honey, *y*'know what I mean. Once you all had pussy, y' don' wanna bother with some big dirty ole *man*. Cock ain't all it's cracked up to be – right, baby?'

'Thanks for sharing that,' said Alex, not fond of the direction this conversation was taking.

'So,' Lucky said, amused at Alex's discomfort. 'Where can we reach you?'

Daisy swigged beer from the bottle. 'Why you wanna reach me?'

'In case Alex puts you in his movie.'

Daisy held out both her hands, admiring her long curved nails painted a deep sparkly purple. 'I ain't no actress,' she said modestly.

'No acting involved,' Alex said.

'Absolutely not,' Lucky added. 'You'll be in the strip scene. Y'know, that's the one where two guys are talking—'

Daisy got it. 'Yeah, *that* ole scene,' she said. 'Two guys

with some babe behind them shovin' her big titties in their faces.'

'Right!' Lucky said. Daisy was smarter than she'd thought.

They both laughed.

'Write down a phone number where my casting people can reach you,' Alex said, handing her a packet of book matches and a pen.

Daisy scrawled her name and number.

Alex wanted out. 'Can we go now?' he said to Lucky.

'One game of pool. You promised.'

He looked over at the pool tables and was relieved to see they were all occupied. 'No free table,' he said, trying not to sound too pleased.

'I'll get us one,' Lucky said, jumping up.

'No,' he said forcefully. 'We're outta here while we're still walking.'

Her eyes were dark and challenging, she liked a man who fought back. 'Don't wanna get beat, huh?'

He was too sober and she was too drunk. It wasn't worth an argument.

They said good night to Daisy and headed for the parking lot.

The cold night air hit Lucky like a block of cement. She stumbled, almost falling.

Alex caught her in his arms. 'Whatever happened to your hollow leg?' he asked, breathing in her sensual musky scent.

'Don't feel so good,' she mumbled, leaning heavily against him.

He couldn't help enjoying her sudden vulnerability. This was a new dependent Lucky. This is how women were meant to be.

Without thinking, he brought his lips down on hers, kissing her roughly, passionately.

It was an electric kiss, surprising both of them.

Lucky knew she was drunk, knew she shouldn't be doing this, knew it was a big mistake. But all she could see were the pictures of Lennie with the naked blond flashing before her eyes. And all she could feel was hurt and disappointment that he'd let her down.

Lennie had deserted her so cruelly. There was only one way to get even.

And Alex was it.

☆   ☆   ☆

Two lovers in a cheap motel. Thrashing around on the bed, their clothes leaving an untidy trail across the threadbare carpet. They both felt the urgency of instant sex. No foreplay required. He was harder than he'd ever been and she was ready.

He touched her breasts, so very beautiful . . .

She touched his cock, thrilling to the urgent throbbing of his desire . . .

She moaned when he entered her. An anguished moan of passion and carnal abandon.

They were both into the ride. It was pure lustful pleasure tempered by no inhibitions – nothing more than a great uncomplicated fuck.

It was exactly what Lucky needed. And when she came, it released the pent-up anger and hurt and pain and all the other frustrations she'd been holding onto.

Alex shuddered to a climax simultaneously. 'Jesus *Christ*!' he exclaimed.

She didn't respond. She rolled away from him, curling into a tight ball, hugging her knees to her chest.

He didn't pursue her.

Within minutes they were both asleep.

BOOK THREE

Chapter Twenty-two

LYING NEAR THE south-eastern corner of Sicily, high above the dusty road from Noto to Ragusa, was the tiny village that was Donna's birthplace. She had been born in a small house still occupied by her eighty-seven-year-old father, two of her younger sisters and their husbands, her brother Bruno and his wife, and various nieces and nephews. Donna supported everyone, sending them regular food packages, clothes and luxuries unheard of in such a primitive place.

Since her father had sold her off as a young girl she'd only visited once. However, she was a legend in the small village and spoken of in revered terms.

Donna's village was mostly on rugged terrain, but a forty-five-minute walk down through the steep hills led to a cliff, below which was the seashore and a catacomb of mysterious caves. Folklore said they were haunted and very few people ever went near them.

As children, Donna, Bruno, and her young love, Furio, had spent much of their spare time exploring the caves. They were not frightened of ancient rumors, although the village elders spoke of ghosts and even worse. Legend had it that after the disastrous earthquake of 1668 had destroyed many towns, the caves became a place where thieves and murderers made their home. When one of them raped and killed a local girl, the village men, filled with wrath, raided the caves and butchered them all, burying them in a mass grave.

Donna, Furio and Bruno did not believe the stories, the caves were their playground and nothing could spoil it.

When Donna was taken off to America to become a bride, Bruno and Furio stopped going there.

It wasn't until Donna sent for Bruno and told him of her plan that he even thought of going back. When she explained what had to be done to avenge the murder of her husband, Bruno was in complete agreement that the caves presented the perfect solution. Located at the bottom of the cliff – dank, deserted, difficult to get in or out of – they were a natural prison.

Lennie Golden knew this to be true. For Lennie had been held captive for eight long weeks, his left ankle shackled to an unmovable rock, allowing him only to hobble around the musty cave.

Every morning he awoke to the same demoralizing sight: a shaft of light filtering in from somewhere high above; the walls of his cave mossy and damp; and he could hear and smell the sea somewhere close.

How close? The damp made him think that it was dangerously close. What if there was a storm? Would his cave be flooded? Would he die a grim and watery death because there was no way he could escape?

His home.

His cell.

His place of incarceration.

And the worst thing of all was that he had no idea why he was there. He could only assume he'd been kidnapped for ransom. But if that was the case, why hadn't Lucky or the studio paid the money?

He'd been imprisoned for eight interminable weeks of

misery. He knew exactly how long it was because he'd been gouging marks in the walls of the cave as each day passed. During that time, the only people he'd seen were the two men who brought him his daily meal of bread and cheese. Once a week they replaced the cheese with a hunk of indigestible meat, and twice they'd given him fruit. Right now he was so hungry he would have eaten anything.

Neither of his captors – both surly-looking men in their late thirties – spoke English. They avoided having anything to do with him, shunning eye contact and all conversation.

One or other of them appeared every day at the same time, placed the food on an upturned crate and left immediately. Every few days they emptied the bucket that was his makeshift toilet, at the same time replacing another bucket, filled with murky water, that was his only washing facility.

There was no mirror or anything to groom himself with. He suspected he resembled a wild man with long, matted hair and an eight-week growth of beard. His clothes were filthy. Once he'd tried to wash them, but discovered it wasn't worth freezing to death while waiting for them to dry.

He could accept the food and toilet situation. He could even accept the bone-chilling cold and damp, and the rats that scurried around the cave all night long, sometimes running over his legs as he lay on the stiff wooden planks that did duty as his bed.

What he could not accept was the hopeless despair and never-ending boredom of having nothing to occupy his mind. Day after day, sitting there, unable to read or write, listen to music or watch TV.

Nothing.

HE . . . WAS . . . SLOWLY . . . GOING . . . CRAZY.

Lately he'd begun talking aloud. Listening to himself was a small comfort, for at least it was the sound of a human voice. He'd started going over old routines from his stand-up comedy days, and scenes from his movies. Sometimes he spoke to Lucky as if she was there with him.

In his mind he often retraced the events of that fateful morning. He remembered being so happy because Lucky was flying in. He'd created a vivid mind picture of her running off the plane into his arms. They fit so well together, they always had.

He recalled leaving the hotel, the doorman pointing to his car. A new driver, not his regular one. Shortly after they'd set off for the airport the driver had offered him coffee. He'd accepted, gulping down the hot liquid, enjoying the strong almost bitter flavor.

After that – nothing – no more memories until he'd woken on the floor of the cave chained like a rabid dog, with nobody there to explain what was happening.

When the first of the men had appeared he'd thought he was saved. But no, it was merely the beginning of his nightmare.

Now there was nothing he could do except wait, desperately trying to keep himself sane. And to hope that Lucky was searching for him.

Sometimes he wondered . . .

Was he dead?

Was this hell?

HE DIDN'T KNOW.

Chapter Twenty-three

 IT WAS FIVE-THIRTY in the morning when Lucky awoke. Her mouth felt like a rat had died in it. Her head was pounding relentlessly. She was aching all over and craved a cigarette.

She turned her head and sneaked a look at Alex. Naked and snoring, he was sprawled across the rumpled bed, completely relaxed.

Oh, God! What had she done?

Moving quietly, she got off the bed and set about stealthily gathering her clothes from the floor. Then she crept into the cramped bathroom and hurriedly dressed, not bothering to shower because she had only one thought in mind – a fast silent exit.

Outside the motel room in the middle of Nowheresville, it was murky and still dark. Bypassing Alex's Porsche, she walked briskly to the deserted renting office where she punched a bell on the desk, waiting impatiently for someone to respond. A mangy dog sniffed her ankles and wandered off. She shivered, pulling up the collar of her jacket.

Finally a tousle-haired teenager appeared, tucking a grubby *Star Trek* T-shirt into his pants. 'Kinda early, ma'am,' he said, with sleep in his eyes. 'What kin I do for you?'

'I need a limo,' Lucky said, drumming her fingers on the

counter, fervently hoping she could be on her way before Alex discovered she was missing.

'A what?' the teenager asked blankly.

'Limousine. Hired car. Anything to get me out of here.'

'I dunno . . .' the boy said vaguely. 'The gas station won't open till six, an' I don't reckon they got no limousines. My grandad'll know. Only thing is he's sleepin', an' it ain't worth my butt t'wake him.'

'Do *you* have a car?'

He rubbed his chin. 'Me?'

'Yes. You.'

'I got me a 'sixty-eight Mustang,' he said proudly. 'Souped it up good.'

'Will it get me from here to LA?'

'Lady—'

'*Will* it?'

Wrinkling his brow he mumbled, ''Scuse me, ma'am, but ain't you in that foreign car parked outside cabin four?'

She sighed impatiently. 'Let's make this a short story. I have to get out of here now. How much will it cost me to borrow your Mustang?'

Five hundred dollars later she was on her way, putting as much distance as possible between herself and Alex. She didn't regret what had happened. She'd wanted it – in fact, she'd been moving toward it ever since Alex had stepped into her office.

In retrospect, though, maybe she would have been better off sleeping with the Travolta clone from the bar. Less complicated.

Oh, God! She hoped Alex wasn't going to turn out to be a problem.

No way. He used women, she was sure of that. It shouldn't bother him that the situation had been reversed.

Alex Woods.

In future she'd make sure it was all business.

The teenager in the *Star Trek* T-shirt had told the truth: his old Mustang sped along the freeway like a revved-up sports car. She tuned the radio to a soul station, listening to Otis Redding sing the classic 'Dock of the Bay' as she cruised along.

Instead of heading for LA, she drove toward Palm Springs. She'd promised Alex he would meet Gino, but it was not to be: she wanted to be alone with her father. If Alex insisted on meeting him he could do so on his own time.

When she arrived at Gino's estate she found him up and dressed, busily screaming at his stockbroker on the phone, red in the face and happy as a teenager who'd just gotten laid.

'Kiddo!' he exclaimed, covering the mouthpiece. 'What in hell *you* doin' here? Doncha know it's earlier than shit?'

Dear old Daddy. He certainly had a way with words.

She hugged him, marveling that he never seemed to age. Gino was eighty-one years old and looked about sixty-five, with his thick, slightly graying hair and youthful grin. He was fit and feisty with all his own teeth and, from the smile on Paige's face, an active sex life. In his Brooklyn youth he'd been nicknamed Gino the Ram. Oh, yes, her father certainly had a colorful past, and he'd traveled a long way from his humble beginnings.

He finished with his stockbroker and banged the phone down. 'The guy's a putz,' he complained. 'Always tellin' me the wrong thing t'do. Dunno why I listen to him, the dumb bastard costs me money every goddamn day.'

'Why *do* you listen?' Lucky asked, collapsing into a chair, rummaging in her purse for a cigarette.

Gino peered at her. 'What's up, kiddo? I got a strong suspicion it ain't a social call at this time of mornin'.'

'I got blasted,' she said ruefully. 'Thought I'd share my hangover with you.'

'Still livin' your life like a guy, huh?' Gino said, shaking his head disapprovingly. 'Doncha know ladies don' get shit-faced?'

She found a cigarette and lit up. 'I told you once, Gino, a long time ago,' she assumed a tough-guy voice, 'I ain't no lady, I'm a Santangelo, just like you.'

He grinned. 'Yeah, yeah, could I ever forget it? You were some problem kid.'

She fixed him with a winning smile. 'The problem kid turned out good, huh?'

'I got no complaints.' He paused a moment. 'How're you *really* doin'?'

She shrugged, edgy, tired and confused. 'I'm getting there,' she said, not sure *how* she was feeling.

He looked at her knowingly. 'It takes time, kid.'

'Yes, Gino.' She nodded, wishing for a split second that she was a little girl again and could run into the protective custody of his arms. 'I know that.'

'We've been through a lot together, kiddo,' he said, studying her with the black eyes that matched hers.

'I know that too,' she said quietly.

'Okay, so you're a Santangelo, don't ever forget it.'

She smiled softly. 'As if I could.'

He stood up – even at his age, always on the move. 'You want some tea? Coffee?'

'Nothing, thanks,' she said, stifling a yawn. 'Is it okay if I take a shower?'

'Use the guest room. I'll tell Paige you're here.'

'Don't wake her.'

'Ha! The friggin' Russian army wouldn't wake *my* wife if she wasn't ready!'

The guest room was decorated in English country pastels. It wasn't Lucky's taste, although she had to admit Paige had done a good job.

She wandered over to the large picture window and gazed

out over a manicured green lawn, a profusion of lush, purple bougainvillaea bushes and an azure kidney-shaped pool. Swimming pools gave her a bad feeling – ever since that fateful day she'd discovered her mother's body . . .

No! She was not taking that soul-destroying trip down Memory Lane. Not today.

Throwing off her clothes, she entered the bathroom, pausing for a moment in front of the full-length mirror, studying her reflection. Youthfulness ran in the family: her body, even after three children, was lithe and slender, olive-skinned, with firm breasts and long legs.

Alex Woods hadn't seen it. After that one passionate kiss in the parking lot, things had moved at a rapid pace. A roadside motel. No conversation. Such was their lust they'd fallen on top of each other with none of the sexual niceties. Dark, fast fucking. The driven kind.

It reminded her of her wild years when she'd bedded as many men as she'd felt like with absolutely no guilt. *Don't call me I'll call you* – that had been her motto.

God! It seemed like a million years ago. Long before AIDS.

And then she'd met Lennie. Her true love. Her soulmate. And for the first time her life was complete.

Thinking of Lennie, the tears finally came. She slumped down on the bathroom floor, silently sobbing out her anger and hurt and frustration until she was totally spent.

It was a cleansing, a renewal: she'd exorcized Lennie's unfaithfulness. Now, finally, she could mourn him properly.

She jumped up off the floor, took an icy-cold shower and dressed quickly. She had a sudden great yearning to see her children, hold them close and love them more than anything in the world. Gino would understand if she left immediately, so she decided to drive straight back to LA and spend some time with them before going to the studio.

Family first.

Business second.

And she'd still make Panther the biggest success story in town.

Lennie would want her to go on.

Lennie would want her to achieve nothing but the best.

☆ ☆ ☆

Alex surfaced slowly. Light was creeping into the room, playing tag on his eyelids. He tried throwing his arm across his face to block the rays of early-morning sun. It didn't work.

He stretched and groaned, slowly opening his eyes. It was definitely time to get up.

For a moment he lay there, completely disoriented, until gradually it all started to come back.

Lucky Santangelo. The girl with the hollow leg.

Lucky Santangelo. A beautiful, exciting woman.

They'd made love in this godawful motel room, urgent, passionate love. Now it was morning and . . . where was she?

He got off the bed, tripping over his shoes on the way to the bathroom.

She wasn't in there.

He went to the window, pulled back the shade and peered outside. His Porsche was parked where he'd left it last night. Good sign, it meant she couldn't have ventured far.

He hoped she'd gone to get them coffee. Boy, he could sure use a cup of strong black coffee.

Picking his clothes off the floor he returned to the bathroom. The shower was broken, spewing a thin stream of rust-colored water. Forget that.

Glancing at his watch he was shocked to see it was almost nine. He was always up by six-thirty. Must have really needed the sleep.

Jesus, he felt good – didn't even have a hangover. *She* was the one with the hangover.

Lucky Santangelo. Thinking of her brought a smile to his face. In a strange way she was a mirror image of him, a rebel, completely unpredictable. And so wildly beautiful . . .

The smart move would be to take a shower back in LA. He threw on his clothes and left the small, depressing motel room, walking the few yards to the renting office where he encountered a weather-beaten old man, sitting outside shelling peanuts while chewing tobacco.

'Morning,' Alex said cordially.

'Morning to you, too,' the old man replied, barely raising his head as he continued to shell his peanuts.

'Where's the nearest place for coffee around here?'

'There's a café across the street, kitty-kat to the gas station,' the old man said. 'Try some a Mabel's blackberry pie, 's damn good.'

'Thanks,' Alex said. 'I'll remember that.' He began to walk away, stopped and came back. 'Did you see the lady from cabin four go across there?' he asked.

'That woman took off over three hours ago,' the old man said, his lined and weathered face impassive. 'Borrowed me grandson's car. Gave him five hundred bucks.' The old man chuckled. 'He reckoned you people was drug dealers with that kinda money t' throw around.'

'She gave your grandson five hundred bucks to borrow his car and then *left?*' Alex said incredulously.

The old man spat a wad of tobacco onto the ground. 'That's what I said.'

'I can't believe she did that.'

'Wimmin,' the old man said, wearily shaking his head. 'Once they got you, it's damn trouble all the way. Tol' my grandson that. He don't take no heed a me – the boy's out chasin' skirt like a trackin' dawg after a bitch in heat.'

'How's he getting his car back?'

'Said she's sending a driver with it. Gave him her fancy card an' everything. When he read she was with a big Hollywood studio, he said okay. If he don't get his car back, it's his own sorry fault.'

Alex was in shock. How could she take off and leave him? Something about Lucky should have warned him she was not to be trusted.

On the other hand, maybe she'd observed how soundly he was sleeping and hadn't wanted to disturb him.

Whatever. The least she could have done was left a note.

Coffee would have to wait. He had to get back to LA immediately.

Chapter Twenty-four

 MORNINGS WERE always a busy time at Venus' house. Anthony, her handsome blond assistant, arrived early, Sven was there to take her jogging and work her out, several maids cleaned the house, and the phone never stopped ringing.

As soon as she awoke she began studying the *Gangsters* script. Lola was such a complex character – ballsy, sexy, sad – and Venus was sure she could get inside her, really capture the despair and heartbreak of the woman.

She couldn't decide what to wear for her meeting with Alex Woods. Should she dress as herself? Or should she take a chance and go as Lola?

In a quandary, she called Freddie. 'What do *you* think?' she asked. 'I could be me, provocative, sensual, all of that.' She paused. 'Although he's probably seen *that* me in my videos. I mean, he *does* know who I am, doesn't he?'

'Why do you think I had such a hard time getting you in?' Freddie said, making a point.

Sometimes Freddie pissed her off. 'Oh, that's nice. You sure know how to make a person feel secure.'

'It wasn't easy, Venus. I had to break the image barrier, shatter his preformed opinion of you.'

'Keep going, Freddie, you're really pumping my ego!'

'Go as Lola. If I know Alex, it'll impress him.'

Next decision. *What* was she going to wear?

She scoured her wardrobe, rejecting everything in sight, mad at herself for not thinking of it yesterday. She should have gone to one of those vintage shops on Melrose and gotten something really sensational.

What would a good-time girl in the fifties wear? Hmm . . . think Marilyn, or even Jayne Mansfield.

Digging deep in her closet she finally found the perfect dress, a silk number, cut on the bias, ending just above her knees. It revealed plenty of cleavage and was form-fitting, with cute little cap sleeves that hugged the top of her perfectly shaped arms. With it she wore very high heels, gold hoop earrings, and arranged her hair on top of her head in a kind of bird's nest.

As soon as she was dressed she ran around her house eliciting opinions. 'You like this look?' she asked Sven, who was still in the gym arranging for new torture equipment to be delivered.

'Very nice,' he replied, hardly noticing.

She showed her English assistant, twirling in front of him. 'What do *you* think, Anthony?'

Anthony had shoulder-length white-blond hair, a muscled body and a beauteous smile. 'Divine!' he exclaimed.

Why were all the best-looking men gay? It was such a waste. Mental note – introduce him to Ron. Perhaps Anthony with his precise English accent and extra long eyelashes could lure Ron away from Major Mogul and they could all live happily ever after.

'This was on the doorstep this morning,' Anthony said, handing her an envelope marked personal.

She tore open the letter, it was short and to the point.

Hi Venus,
    You're hot stuff, sexy and horny. I know everything

about you. Your big tits and your hairy pussy turn me on. Don't worry – I'll never let anyone harm you because you're mine. I'll always love you, even after we're married. You'd better wait for me – it won't be long.

X X X
An Admirer

P.S. I jerk off thinking of you every day – I don't have sex with anyone except you. I hope you feel the same way.

'Oh, Jesus!' she said, throwing the letter down in disgust. 'Another obsessed sex maniac. How do these morons get my home address?'

Anthony shrugged. 'It was here when I arrived this morning.'

'What did he do? Climb over the gates? Where was my guard?'

Anthony shrugged again. 'I have no idea.'

'I hate this!' she said, feeling vulnerable. 'It makes me nervous. The last time this happened some freak got into my *bedroom*. Fortunately I was in New York at the time.'

'What did he *do*?' Anthony asked, eyes bugging.

'I dunno, 'cause I didn't press charges. Couldn't face going to court.'

'Maybe it's *him*,' Anthony said dramatically. 'Is he dangerous?'

'Quit making a big deal out of this,' she said sternly, not liking his tone. 'Call my security people and have them check the letter out. And always be careful who you let in.'

'Yes, Venus,' he said obediently.

Just as she was leaving for her meeting Rodriguez appeared at the door. He carried a bunch of white roses and had dressed for the occasion in a dark brown silk shirt, impeccably cut beige pants, a thin alligator belt that showed off his slender waistline, and snappy two-tone leather shoes.

'My princess!' he exclaimed.

Enough of the flowery shit, she wasn't pleased that he felt free to show up unannounced.

'What do you want?' she asked, none too politely.

He handed her the roses. 'I am here because my heart would not stop beating, and as each beat took place I thought of you.'

'Rodriguez, you really have to get some new dialog,' she said, frowning.

'What do you mean, my sweet?'

She tossed the roses at Anthony. 'I don't appreciate you turning up here without calling first. I'm on my way to an important meeting.'

'I thought we could have lunch.'

'Not today. I'm very busy.'

'Did you call your casting person? I so look forward to being in your video.'

So that was the reason for his enthusiasm. Everybody wanted to be a star.

'I'll have Anthony do it,' she said abruptly. 'Go home and wait for the phone call.'

His face drooped with disappointment.

Too bad. If he thought he was going to move in on her, he could think again.

☆　☆　☆

Brigette was alive with energy. It was so great waking up in the morning with something to look forward to. She couldn't wait to phone Lucky in LA, although right now it was too early. Instead she raced into the kitchen where Anna was sitting at the table, writing.

'Guess what?' she said excitedly.

'What?' Anna asked, putting down her pen.

'Everything's starting to happen for me. I told you it would! I'm *so* buzzed!'

'I gather last night was a success.'

'Brilliant! Michel Guy asked me to come to his office today, and the photo-session with Luke is set for next week. Isn't that *fantastic*!'

'You deserve it,' Anna said.

'I do, don't I?' Brigette replied, laughing because she couldn't quite believe it.

Later she met with Nona, who'd devised a plan of action. First they were going to see Michel Guy, then visit Aurora to tell her about Rock 'n' Roll Jeans, and ask her if she wanted to be the first to put Brigette on *Mondo*'s cover.

'Sounds good to me,' Brigette said.

'Listen,' Nona said. 'Zan and I are going to move in together. His father has a shitload of money so rent's no problem, and I can't wait to get out of my parents' house. We wondered if you'd be interested in sharing an apartment with us?'

Brigette giggled. 'That'll be a laugh riot,' she said. 'Zan, you and then *me* tagging along. I don't think so.'

'It's a terrific idea,' Nona said persuasively. 'After all, we'll be working together, and what better than to be living in the same place?'

'Well . . .' It was kind of an interesting thought. 'Maybe I'll mention it to Charlotte.'

'You're nineteen, Brigette, you don't need anybody's permission.'

'Okay, so I'll *tell* Charlotte.'

'Good. 'Cause I see wild times ahead!'

'I'm all for that,' Brigette said, thinking that it was about time she started enjoying herself again. 'When am I moving?'

☆ ☆ ☆

Alex drove back to town in a state of confusion. He couldn't believe Lucky had walked out on him. Women never left him, it was always the reverse. How many times had he instructed his answering service to call at a certain hour to inform him of an emergency. 'Sorry, gotta go,' he'd say regretfully. And his female companion would obediently get up and drive herself home. Damn! This just didn't happen to him. There had to be an excuse, a good excuse.

He tried calling the studio from his car. Kyoko informed him that Ms Santangelo was not in yet. He felt like a fool because he didn't have her home phone number, and he wasn't about to ask her assistant. Of course, he could probably get it from Freddie. *Oh, hey, Freddie, it's me, Alex. I fucked Lucky Santangelo last night, only I never got her private number, and now she's walked out on me. Can you give it to me?*

No way.

He got through to his office.

'Where are you, Alex?' asked Lili, with her usual disapproving sniff. 'Everyone is worried. Your mother called three times.'

'My mother's worried about *me*?' he asked, not believing it for a moment.

'Apparently Tin Lee panicked when you didn't show up for your date last night. She waited at your apartment three hours, then called Dominique. Now they've bonded. They imagined you'd been kidnapped, murdered – something like that.'

'I got sidetracked.'

'By a bottle of Scotch?'

'Not your business, Lili.'

There was a twist of venom in her voice. 'Well, Alex, if you expect me to run your production company *and* make excuses for you, I'd appreciate it if you'd let me in on your secrets.'

He hated it when Lili got pissy. 'I had to go to Palm Springs to see Gino Santangelo about the script,' he explained.

'You could have told me.'

'You're beginning to sound like a wife, Lili, and I don't even get to fuck you!'

She was unamused. 'May I remind you, Alex, that you've missed two meetings this morning. And Venus Maria will be here at noon. Also, you're due to go on a location scout to Vegas this afternoon. Your plane leaves at three.'

'What's Venus coming in for?'

'She's reading for Lola. You promised Freddie you'd see her.'

'Does she have to?' He groaned, not looking forward to it.

'You made an appointment. It's unprofessional to cancel at this late hour.'

'Fine, Lili, stop worrying, I'll be there.'

'What shall I tell your mother?'

'Exactly nothing.'

Chapter Twenty-five

Lucky did a lot of thinking on the drive back from Palm Springs. In a way she felt as if she was emerging from a dense fog – Lennie was gone and, hard as it was, she had to learn to accept it.

She drove directly to her house, where she spent time with her children. She picked up baby Gino, holding him close, allowing herself to be enveloped by his soothing warmth and helplessness. The realization swept over her that her children needed her. One thing she knew for sure – she would always be there for them.

Maria was racing around the house as usual. She had more energy than her mother – which was really saying something. She jumped up and down with delight when Lucky told her they'd spend the morning together. 'Mommy, Mommy, me story . . . I wanna story . . . *Pleeease!*' she begged.

'Okay,' Lucky said, and sat down and read to Maria from a colorful book about Larry the Lamb and Petey the Petunia.

Maria collapsed with mirth as she listened to her mother assume the various voices. 'Now we go swimming, Mommy. Now! Now!' she shrieked, when Lucky finished reading.

Instead of swimming, Lucky took her daughter for a long walk along the beach, then promised that over the weekend they'd go out and choose her a puppy. Maria was ecstatic.

CeeCee informed her that Venus had called. Lucky was

well aware she'd been neglecting her friends and resolved to do something about it.

Arriving at Panther after twelve, she drove across the lot, parking in her usual spot.

Kyoko was at his desk in the outer office.

'I'm sorry about yesterday, Ky,' she said, on her way into her private domain. 'I had to get out of here or go totally insane. Did you reschedule the appointments I missed?'

'Everything's taken care of,' he replied, following her in. 'I thought you might be late, so I canceled all your morning meetings, too.'

'Why?' she said wryly. 'Was I that out of control yesterday?'

'It seemed like you were about to be.'

'Very astute, Ky. I had an interesting trip, and now I'm back.'

'You probably needed the break,' Kyoko said sympathetically.

'I did. Only today I'm being punished big time. I have a *major* hangover. Any aspirin around here?'

He fetched her some, with a mug of strong black coffee and a large glass of fresh orange juice. Then he placed her phone list in front of her.

She scanned the names, noting that Alex Woods had called twice. She had no intention of calling him. It was probably better to give him time to cool off, then, when they met again, it would be merely business.

For a moment she allowed her mind to wander, remembering Alex in bed . . . hot, fast sex . . .

No! Alex was a one-night revenge fuck. It would *never* happen again.

'Uh, Ky . . .' she said, trying to sound as casual as possible. 'If Alex Woods phones back, find out what it's in reference to. I don't want to speak to him unless it has something to do with *Gangsters*. Take care of it, okay?'

'Yes, Lucky,' Kyoko said. It was not for him to ask questions that were obviously none of his business.

'And get Venus for me,' Lucky added, gulping down two aspirin with the orange juice.

Kyoko connected with Venus' house and spoke to Anthony. 'She's not home,' he said. 'Shall I try her on her car phone?'

'Please.'

A few seconds later Venus was on the line sounding delighted. 'This is like telepathy,' she said. 'Did CeeCee tell you I tried to reach you at home last night?'

'I'd *really* like to see you,' Lucky said. 'It's been too long since we got together. You don't happen to be free for lunch?'

'Unfortunately, no,' Venus said, sounding disappointed. 'How about dinner tonight?'

'Works for me. I'll have Kyoko make a reservation at Morton's.'

'Great! We can trash every guy in town, I love doing that!' Venus paused for a moment before continuing. 'Uh ... I wasn't going to mention this, 'cause I know it's your movie, but I'm on my way to see Alex Woods. I'm reading for Lola in *Gangsters*.'

'Lola?' Lucky said, surprised that Venus would consider such a small part. 'That's not a starring role.'

'I know, but your friend and my agent, Freddie, assures me I should do it 'cause it'll showcase me in a different light.'

'Trust Freddie to come up with a good idea.'

'I've been studying the script, which I *love*. Now I know why you wanted to make this movie.'

'Are you seeing Alex today?'

'In about ten minutes. So ... if he should ask you about me ...'

'Alex has the final say on who he casts. If it was my decision, you'd be Lola – although you'd bust the budget. Last week Alex signed Johnny Romano.'

'According to Freddie, he had to fight to get me in to see the great Mr Woods, which, as you can imagine, does not thrill me.'

'I'm sure it doesn't.'

'You've been working with him, what's he like?'

Lucky reached for a cigarette, her addiction worsening every day. 'I thought *you* were the one who knew all about him,' she said, in a noncommittal tone.

'Only the stuff one of his ex-girlfriends couldn't wait to tell me.'

'What was it she said again?'

'Hmm . . . Let me see . . . oh, yeah – only screws Orientals and doesn't give head.'

'Sounds like a great guy,' Lucky said drily.

'You should know.'

'What do you mean by *that*?'

'C'mon, Lucky,' Venus pleaded. 'Give me the goods. Is he the pain in the ass everyone says he is?'

'Alex seems to be an okay guy,' Lucky said, choosing her words carefully. 'He's gotten a bad rap in the press. I'm sure you'll get along with him.'

'If you happen to speak to him later, find out what he thought of me.'

'Sure,' Lucky said casually. 'Maybe I will.'

And then again, maybe I won't.

☆ ☆ ☆

By the time Venus had finished talking to Lucky she was pulling up to Alex's production offices.

A guard waved her into the parking lot with a welcoming beam and an enthusiastic, 'Can I have your autograph for my sister? She's your biggest fan.'

How many times had she heard *that* line?

She got out of her car, smoothing down the skirt of her clinging silk dress. The guard's eyes were all over her, inspecting every available inch as she scrawled her signature on the grubby slip of paper he thrust her way. Her security advisers had warned her never to drive around LA by herself. Too bad – she enjoyed being alone in her car, listening to the latest CDs, thinking about things, generally relaxing. If she used a driver it was a whole different trip – although since she and Cooper had broken up, she never went anywhere unaccompanied at night.

Marriage to Cooper had been fun while it lasted, she'd been comfortable being faithful to one man.

A pity he hadn't felt the same way.

An exquisite Oriental girl met her at the entrance to Alex's building. 'Hi, I'm France,' the girl said, extending a small, well-manicured hand. 'Welcome to Woodsan Productions. We are honored to have you here. Please follow me.'

Nice greeting. Perhaps Alex Woods was anxious to see her, after all.

France led her into a large reception area with framed posters of all of Alex's movies on the walls. An impressive collection.

'Alex is running a few minutes late,' France said apologetically. 'May I get you something? Tea? Coffee? Spring water?'

Venus settled for an Evian and the latest issue of *Rolling Stone*. This was a new experience – she hadn't been kept waiting in years. Was he testing her? Seeing if she was a prima donna?

After a twenty-minute wait, by which time she was getting more than a little impatient, another Oriental woman appeared. This one was older and strikingly attractive.

'I'm Lili, Alex Woods' executive assistant,' the woman said, introducing herself with a warm smile. 'Alex had to go out of town unexpectedly last night. He extends his heartfelt apologies for being late, and should be here momentarily.'

'How momentarily?' Venus asked. She was not inclined to wait much longer, it wasn't good for her image.

'Very soon,' Lili assured her, adding a convincing, 'He's so looking forward to meeting you.'

I bet, Venus thought, her confidence level sinking fast. Freddie forced me on him. He's never heard of me, and if he has, he hates everything about me.

Why was she putting herself in this vulnerable position when she didn't have to? She was a star, for Chrissakes, she didn't have to wait around for anyone – especially Alex Woods with his chauvinist reputation.

'Another Evian?' Lili inquired.

Venus stood up. 'You know what?' she said pleasantly. 'I can't wait any longer. Please tell *Mr* Woods, it was, uh . . . a pleasure *almost* meeting him.'

What she really wanted to say was, *I'm pissed off, I'm out of here, and tell your rude fucking boss to shove it.*

Lili looked visibly distressed as she tried to think of a way to stop Venus from leaving. 'He'll be right here,' she said soothingly. 'I spoke to him on his car phone minutes ago and he was almost downstairs.'

'That's all right,' Venus said graciously. 'We'll reschedule.'

Freddie Leon's image flashed before her eyes. 'No Oscar,' he said sternly. 'Forget about your pride and stay.'

Sorry, Freddie, not even for you.

She was at the door, with Lili trailing her, when Alex made

his entrance. Unshaven and harassed, he brushed past Venus, not even noticing her. 'Shit!' he said to Lili. 'The goddamn traffic. Don't blame me.'

'Alex,' Lili said evenly, but with an underlying edge of steel, 'this is Venus Maria. She was just about to leave. However, I am sure *you* can persuade her to stay.'

He took a look at the platinum-blond superstar. Not bad. She'd dressed as her interpretation of Lola and it almost worked.

'Sorry, honey,' he said, flashing the little-boy killer smile that had gotten him out of a million predicaments, 'why'n't you come back in, an' we'll talk.'

The honey didn't please her. Too patronizing.

The smile was cute. Calculated, though. He probably used it on women purely to get his own way.

He was not perfectly handsome like Cooper. He was bigger, rougher, more masculine. In fact, he was quite attractive in an overpowering macho way.

Bet you love getting blow-jobs, she thought. Wonder why you don't return the compliment.

'Five minutes,' she said boldly. 'I'm sure that's long enough to convince you I'm your Lola.'

Chapter Twenty-six

 A CHANEL SUIT seemed appropriate. Navy blue with a white braid trim and neat gold buttons. Daytime diamonds. Her hair styled to reflect the life of an extremely successful businesswoman.

Donna Landsman, formerly known as Donatella Bonnatti, stood back from the full-length mirror admiring her reflection. Yes, she looked the part – no vestige of Donatella visible. There was no way Lucky Santangelo would ever know. And Donna was not about to tell her. Not yet.

Donna often wondered what her late husband's reaction would be if he could see her now. So cool and sophisticated. So worldly. In her new role, she wouldn't look twice at an uncouth lout like Santino, with his disgusting bathroom habits and foul mouth. In spite of his faults she'd willed herself never to forget that, in spite of everything, Santino had been her children's father, and as such he deserved the respect of having his death properly avenged.

So far she was doing an excellent job. First Lennie Golden, and today Lucky's precious Panther Studios. She'd even discovered where Brigette Stanislopoulos was, and she had a plan in mind to deal with her too.

Yesterday she'd spoken to her brother, Bruno, in Sicily. He'd assured her that everything was under control. Lennie was their prisoner and nobody except he and Furio knew.

Just as she'd thought, the caves were the perfect hiding place.

It gave her a great sense of exhilaration to know that she had Lucky Santangelo's husband captive in a place where nobody could find him. In fact, even better, everyone thought he was dead. What a masterful piece of planning *that* had been.

Of course, eventually, Lucky would find out – Donna would make sure of that. But not until Lucky was involved with another man – maybe even planning marriage. *That* was the time Donna would arrange to have Lennie set free and returned to his wife. *That* would be Lucky's real punishment.

In the meantime, after taking over Panther, she would give the order to deal with Lucky's father, the infamous Gino. He was an old man now, he'd be easy to take care of.

It made her proud that she was going to be responsible for the downfall of the Santangelo family. Bad blood had existed for so many years and the Santangelos had always come out on top.

Well, she, Donna Landsman, was finally changing all that.

With that thought foremost in her mind, she set off for Panther Studios and retribution.

☆　☆　☆

'See if Charlie Dollar's on the lot, and ask him if he'd like to lunch with me,' Lucky said, thinking that she wouldn't mind a dose of Charlie's light relief.

Kyoko did as she asked, and informed her that Charlie was on the lot and would be delighted to see her.

They met in the private dining area in the commissary, Charlie as dapper and mismatched as ever in baggy corduroy pants, a flapping Hawaiian shirt and blacker-than-black shades. Lucky cool in a white Armani suit.

Charlie grinned his maniacal grin. 'Hiya, gorgeous,' he said. 'It's about time you came up for food an' conversation.'

'It's great to see you, Charlie. How was Europe?'

He gestured expansively. 'The old movie star slayed 'em. My film's doin' boffo biz – a direct quote from *Variety*.'

Lucky nodded, 'I know, I'm excited with the figures.'

Charlie pressed his stubby, nicotine-stained fingers together. 'I'll tell you what it is. Give the great unwashed something they wanna see, and they'll fight their way into the theater.'

'You underestimate yourself, Charlie. It's you and your special magic that pulls them in.'

'No, babe,' he quipped. 'It's that scene in the shower where they get an eyeful of my bare butt. *Nobody*'s seen an ass like that in years!'

'Same old Charlie,' she said, reaching over and squeezing his hand affectionately.

''S' good t'see you, too, Lady Boss.'

'Hey,' she objected, 'how come you've always got some crazy title for me?'

He raised his extravagant eyebrows. 'Maybe you prefer Mafia Princess?'

'Let's not start with that again,' she said sternly.

He threw up his hands in mock dismay. 'Okay, okay, don't shoot!'

'Very amusing.'

'I always like t'go for the laugh.'

'Don't you just?'

He raised his black shades, peering over them.

'So what's happenin'?'

'I saw Gino this morning.'

'Is the big man in town?'

'No, I drove down to Palm Springs last night.'

'How come you didn't call? I'm the best on a car ride.

I sing, give directions, eat crackers, make twenty-five pit stops—'

'You're always good company, Charlie.'

He chuckled. 'That's what my proctologist says!'

She smiled. 'Was the European trip fun? Did you finally meet *the* girl?'

'My love life sucks,' he drawled. 'They only wanna fuck me 'cause I'm a movie star. An' they wanna do it *fast*, so they can run off an' boast about it to their friends. That's their whole deal.'

'I'm sure there's a nice girl out there for you somewhere.'

He laughed sardonically. 'A nice girl? In Hollywood? Baby, what planet are *you* from? They're all hookers or actresses. Take your pick – there ain't much difference.'

'Mr Cynicism.'

'Hey,' he said, waving at a couple of producers, 'here's your task. Find me a nice girl, and you can be best man at my wedding.'

'How about Venus?'

'How about checking your sanity?'

'She and Cooper are split.'

'Big freakin' surprise.'

They were in the middle of lunch when Kyoko rushed over to their table in an agitated state. 'Lucky, you'd better come to your office right away,' he said.

'Is it the children? Has something happened?' she asked, imagining the worst.

'No, no, they're fine. It's business,' Kyoko said. 'Please, Lucky, come with me right now.'

'Anything you need my help with?' Charlie offered. ''Cause you know I'm your resident movie icon in shining armor.'

Lucky stood up. 'Stay here. I'll be right back.' She

followed Kyoko from the restaurant, waiting until they were outside before she turned on him. 'What the *hell* is going on?'

'There's a woman in your office. She refuses to go.'

'*What* woman?'

'I don't know. Morton Sharkey's with her. They walked right past me into your private office. They wouldn't stop.'

Lucky felt a shiver of apprehension. She'd suspected Morton was up to something – she'd sensed it the other day. But what?

They walked across the lot without speaking. She entered Kyoko's office and strode through it into hers. Sitting behind her desk was a woman in a Chanel suit. Hovering nearby was an uncomfortable-looking Morton Sharkey.

'You'd better have a good explanation for this,' Lucky said, her voice full of steel. 'A *very* good explanation.'

Donna swung around in Lucky's chair locking eyes with the enemy. 'I'm Donna Landsman, the new owner of Panther Studios,' she said, her voice even colder than Lucky's. 'And you, my dear, are fired.'

'What?' Lucky gasped.

'I'm taking over as of now,' Donna said, satisfied to note that not a flicker of recognition had crossed Lucky's face. 'You have thirty minutes to clear out your personal possessions and get off the lot.'

'What the *fuck* is going on?' Lucky said, angrily turning to Morton.

He cleared his throat. 'It's true, Lucky,' he said, in a strained voice. 'Mrs Landsman has gained control of fifty-five percent of Panther stock. This gives her a controlling interest.'

'It's not possible,' Lucky said, in shock.

'Oh, yes,' Donna gloated, savoring the moment. 'It's *very* possible. And, I can assure you, it's done.'

An icy calm came over Lucky. She was under attack, had to get a grip, find out exactly how this had happened. 'Did you know about this, Morton?' she asked, her voice a tight coil of anger about to erupt.

He couldn't look at her. 'I . . . heard something was going on.'

Lucky's black eyes were suddenly deadly. 'Don't give me that bullshit, Morton. You knew. You *had* to know. There's no way this could have happened without you.'

'Lucky, I—'

Her heart was beating so fast she thought it might explode. 'I bet you even helped her. Didn't you? *Didn't you, Morton?*'

He shrugged helplessly. 'Lucky . . . I had no choice.'

'No choice? *No fucking choice!*' She was well aware she was screaming, but it was impossible to stop herself. 'How can you stand here and say that to me? Have you no shame, you double-dealing hypocrite?'

'This is no time for name-calling,' Morton muttered, truly ashamed, but caught in a trap from which there was no escape.

'Oh, isn't it?' she said furiously. 'Whatever happened here, Morton, you're responsible. *You* were the one who put together the stock deal for me. *You* brought in all the investors and told me I never had to worry. Now this woman marches in and informs me she has control of my studio.' She turned on Donna. 'Who the fuck are you, anyway?'

'Unbecoming language for a supposedly smart business-woman,' Donna said cuttingly, relishing every second of her triumph.

Lucky was enraged. 'I need to see proof of this.'

'I have all the papers here,' Morton replied, handing them to her. She flicked through the papers. 'You still own forty percent—'

'You set me up,' she interrupted violently. 'Nobody could have done it except you.'

'The Board called an emergency meeting and made a decision that your services as head of the studio are no longer required,' Morton stated. 'You will, of course, be paid off on your contract.'

'Paid off?' she said, incredulously. 'They're paying *me* off? Don't any of you get it? This is *my* studio. Everything that's going on here now is because *I* turned it around.'

'You shouldn't worry about the studio, dear,' Donna said patronizingly. 'I'm bringing Mickey Stolli back to run it.'

'You've *got* to be kidding!' Lucky exploded. 'Mickey Stolli ran this studio into the ground.'

'He's thrilled to be returning,' Donna said, still savoring Lucky's fury.

'Why are you doing this?' Lucky demanded, shaking with anger. '*Why?*'

Donna consulted her watch, 'Ten minutes have passed. That leaves you exactly twenty more to collect your personal belongings and vacate this office. I wouldn't want to have you thrown off the lot.'

'Fuck you,' Lucky said, her black eyes filled with rage. 'Whoever you are. *Fuck you.* Because I'm going to get this studio back. Don't you doubt it for one minute. In fact, you can bet on it!'

Chapter Twenty-seven

 'YOU'RE LATE,' Michel Guy said sternly. 'By about eight weeks.'

'Excuse me?' Brigette replied. This was not the greeting she'd expected.

'You were supposed to be here two months ago, remember? When I met you at Effie's party, I told you to come and see me the next day.' He leaned back in his chair, regarding her quizzically. 'Y'know, an invitation from me is considered a big deal in this town.'

'The reason I didn't take you up on your offer,' Brigette said, 'was that my stepfather died. I went to LA for the funeral.'

'I'm sorry,' Michel said. 'I didn't know.'

'Anyway, I'm back now.'

'Yes,' Nona said, joining in. 'She's back, and I'm her manager.'

'You?' Michel said, barely concealing his surprise.

'Yes, me,' Nona answered defiantly. 'We could have gone to any of the top agencies, but Brigette wants you to represent her. I guess she gets off on your accent.'

Michel Guy's faded blue eyes crinkled with amusement. 'This is a new way of persuading an agent to sign you,' he said. 'I thought Brigette was the one looking for representa-

232

tion, and I was the one supposed to be doing her the big favor.'

'Things have changed,' Nona said. 'Brigette has a fantastic deal pending.'

'And what might that be?'

'Will you represent me?' Brigette asked, fixing him with her blue eyes.

'I was considering it,' Michel replied slowly. 'Although first, I must see how you are in front of the camera. And, Brigette,' he added, 'models don't need managers, not until they're superstars.'

'I plan on being much more than just a model,' she replied confidently.

'It takes time to build a name for yourself,' Michel pointed out.

'We know that,' Nona rushed in. 'The thing is, we're coming to you with a fantastic shot at an immediate score.' She paused for dramatic effect. 'Rock 'n' Roll Jeans want Brigette to be their new spokesmodel.'

Michel nodded, thinking fast. So that's why Rock 'n' Roll Jeans hadn't signed the deal with Robertson and Nature – both girls his clients.

'When did this happen?' he asked, doodling on a yellow desk pad.

'Luke Kasway photographed her before she went to LA. The ad agency saw the photos and they're crazy for her.'

Michel knew Robertson would be furious if he signed Brigette to the agency. So what? With Michel, money always came first. He addressed his next words to Brigette. 'If this is true, I will make you the best deal in the business.'

'That's what I want,' Brigette said determinedly.

'We're on our way to see Aurora at *Mondo*,' Nona offered. 'I figured if we told her about the Jeans thing she may want to put Brigette on the cover.'

'No, no, no!' Michel said, almost shouting. '*You* don't do that. *I* do that. And this is *how* I do it. I throw a dinner party at my apartment. We invite Aurora, her husband and several other interesting guests. During the course of the evening, I let it drop to Aurora that both *Allure* and *Glamour* are vying with each other to get Brigette on their cover because of the new deal that will make her bigger than any of the Guess girls. I can assure you, the next day Aurora will come to us *begging* for Brigette to appear on her cover first.'

'Sounds good to me,' Brigette said, smiling broadly.

'Ah!' Michel tapped his head. 'The brain must always be working.' His crinkly blue eyes met hers. 'Am I not right, *ma chérie*?'

'Oh, yes,' she said enthusiastically, quite impressed with him. 'Absolutely.'

☆　☆　☆

'What's your background?' Alex asked. 'Where are you from?'

Venus realized that Alex Woods obviously didn't know too much about her. What the hell – she'd go along with the game, humor the big film-maker. 'I'm originally a Brooklyn girl,' she said amiably. 'Gotta hunch half of Hollywood started off there.'

'Not me,' Alex replied. 'I'm a local boy.'

'Oh, c'mon,' Venus said, flirting ever so slightly. 'You can't possibly be from Los Angeles. *Nobody*'s a native.'

'I am.'

'I'm surprised,' she said. 'Your work has such a New York edge.'

'I spent a lot of time in New York,' he said. 'But let's not get off track here. *I'm* supposed to be interviewing *you*.'

'It's not exactly an *interview*, Alex. I came in to see you

234

because you've written a sensational script, and I want to play Lola. I know I can do an incredible job.'

'You're pretty sure of yourself.'

'Why wouldn't I be? I've accomplished a lot,' she threw in some flattery to soften him up. 'Kind of like you.'

He looked amused. 'You don't have to sell yourself. I know who you are.'

'*That*'s a relief!' she said mockingly, convinced he had no idea who she was.

He stood up. 'Well, now we've got that straight, will you excuse me for a moment? I gotta use the john.'

Oh, God, she thought. He's a coke snorter. Can't even hold out for five minutes.

'Sure,' she said, off-handedly. 'Why should I mind? I've already spent the last hour hanging out here.'

'Be understanding,' he said, flashing the grin. 'Nature's screaming.' He went in the bathroom, closed the door and immediately buzzed France.

'Yes, Alex?' she said.

'Flowers,' he said. 'Lucky Santangelo. Make certain the florist puts together something very special. Roses, in fact, lots of them.'

'How much do you want to spend?'

'Be sure it's a big deal. In fact, make it six dozen red roses. Have them delivered this afternoon so they're waiting for her when she gets home.'

'What should the note say?' asked France. 'The usual?'

'No, not the usual, France,' he said, irritated. 'I'll write my own card.'

'How about Tin Lee?'

'What?'

'Flowers because you stood her up?'

'I suppose so.'

He returned to his office where Venus was lolling on the couch in a typical Lola pose. 'Hiya, baby,' she said, winking suggestively. 'Wanna slide in beside me?'

It was a line from the script and she delivered it with relish.

'We can't afford you,' Alex said.

'I know. You overshot your wad on Johnny Romano.'

'I don't usually work with stars.'

'I don't usually work with star directors who've hardly heard of me.'

'Not true.'

Venus sat up straight. 'Admit it, Alex, you don't know anything about me.'

'I'm not into gossip. I'm too busy working.'

'Oh,' she said crossly. 'Is that what you think I'm about?'

'No. I didn't say that. C'mon, Venus, tell me more about yourself. You're from Brooklyn. What kind of family?'

'What is this? My biography?'

'Why're you getting so uptight?'

'I'm not.'

'Then go ahead, tell me.'

She plunged into a shortened version of her life story. 'Hmm . . . let me see,' she said. 'Well, my father was a charming Italian chauvinist. My mom died when I was quite young. I had four older brothers, so I became their caretaker – y'know, washing, cleaning, cooking them pasta, all that housewife crap. Boy, did they get a shock when I took off with my best friend, Ron Machio. We were out for adventure, a couple of desperadoes, so we hitched our way to LA where I did everything from performing in underground clubs to nude modeling for an art class. Then I met a record producer who decided to record me. Ron put together my video. It was so outrageous that I was, like, y'know, an instant hit.'

'It certainly got you where you wanted to be.'

'The top, Alex,' she said, very seriously. 'That's where I wanted to be. And that's exactly where I am now.'

'So why are you coming to see me about a cameo role?'

There was a determined thrust to her jaw. 'Because I want to prove that I *can* act. That I'm not some freako sex machine who can't cut it on the big screen. The critics hate me. I've made four movies and each time they've shredded my ass.'

Alex said, 'They do that to me all the time.'

'They don't pull you to pieces physically, calling you everything from a sex machine to a vulgar untalented whore!'

'I've been called a lot of names in my life,' Alex said, with a smile, 'but "vulgar untalented whore" ain't one of 'em.'

'You know what I mean.'

'Ignore the critics. I do.'

'It's not that easy – but I manage. I have this huge army of loyal fans, and in their eyes I'm always the best. They're my silent support group.'

'You want to read a scene for me?' Alex said. It was possible that she did, indeed, have potential, and he liked her.

'I'm kind of insulted you're forcing me to read,' she said, determined to let him know how she felt.

'I don't know your work, Venus,' he explained. 'I haven't seen any of your movies. And if what you're telling me about the reviews is true, I'd be insane if I didn't ask you to read.'

She nodded, stood up and wandered over to the window. 'I'll do it if *you* read with me,' she said, turning to face him.

'My casting people are waiting to join us. Lindy will read with you, she's good.'

'I'm sure she is, but she's not a man,' Venus said determinedly. 'I need interaction, sexual tension. I gotta get it going here, Alex.'

He studied her, drawn to the vulnerable streak he sensed beneath the high gloss. If he could only capture that quality

237

on film, she'd be a perfect Lola. 'What scene do you want to read?' he asked.

'I'll take a shot at the one where Lola has the breakdown, where she's really in trouble and doesn't know who's gonna help her out.'

Alex picked up the script off his desk. 'Good choice,' he said. 'Okay, Venus, go ahead and convince me.'

Chapter Twenty-eight

 SURFACING FROM yet another nightmare, Lennie imagined he heard a noise that was different from every other sound he knew so well. He thought he heard a woman laughing.

He sat up straight, straining desperately to hear.

Nothing – except the relentless pounding of the sea.

He had no idea of time. From the light filtering down into the cave he assumed it was early morning.

He stood up, stretching his aching bones. Recently he'd started working out, which wasn't easy with his ankle chained. The challenge was not to lose any more of his physical strength.

He'd also realized it was important to give himself a reason for living, so he now followed a stringent routine to which he forced himself to adhere.

With order there was hope.

Without, there was nothing.

Today was one of those days he simply couldn't get it together. Instead he sat down again on the makeshift wooden bed and began thinking about the time he and Lucky first met in Vegas. He'd been performing at her hotel as a stand-up. She'd come along, fired him, then tried to lure him into bed. He smiled at the memories.

A year later they'd bumped into each other when he was

married to Olympia and she was married to Dimitri. One look and they'd both known that this time they were never going to be parted.

His wonderful, stubborn, beautiful Lucky.

What he wouldn't give to be with her now.

He wondered what she was doing. Had his kidnappers contacted her? Was the ransom demand so big that she wasn't able to pay it?

Not possible. He knew his Lucky. She'd find a way to pay it even if it was a billion dollars.

He heard the noise again – a woman's soft laugh. This time he was certain he wasn't imagining it.

'Is anybody there?' he yelled out. 'Anybody around?' The echo of his voice came back at him. Apart from that there was the usual silence.

Was his mind playing cruel tricks on him? Perhaps he was truly going crazy.

If only he could get this goddamn shackle off his foot. His ankle was raw from trying.

He fell back on the so-called bed, throwing his arms across his face, covering his eyes. Despair enveloped him like a heavy cloak of unremitting gloom.

Lucky, Lucky, Lucky. Ah . . . my sweetheart . . . Why aren't you saving me?

He drifted back into a light sleep, imagining he was driving a speedboat on the sea, a fast boat carving its way through the heavy waves, heading for freedom.

A girlish shriek jolted him awake. He sat up abruptly. Hovering in the entrance to the cave stood a young woman in her early twenties, with clouds of curly brown hair and a Madonna-like face.

Surely he was dreaming. She must be a vision.

The woman's hand flew to her mouth as she gasped something in Italian, a language he didn't speak.

My God, she's real, he thought. *She's flesh and blood*. SHE'S MY SAVIOR.

'Thank God you're here,' he shouted. 'Thank God!'

She stared at him, her eyes registering fright and surprise. Then she turned and ran, vanishing from sight.

'Come back!' he screamed after her. 'Come back, whoever you are. I'm not going to hurt you. Goddamn it – COME BACK!'

She was gone.

He hoped and prayed she was going for help, because without her, he was lost.

Chapter Twenty-nine

THE ONLY THINGS Lucky bothered taking were the silver picture frames on her desk containing photos of her children and Lennie. She snatched them up, and without another word marched from her office.

Kyoko ran alongside her as she headed for her car. 'What happened?' he asked, almost as distressed as she was.

'That deceitful lying sonofabitch sold me out!' Lucky seethed. 'I'm going to bury him. Do you hear me, Kyoko? I'm going to *bury* that man.'

'Can I help?' Kyoko asked.

'Yes. Arrange to have all my things removed from my office immediately. I want my desk out of there, my leather chair, I want every piece of furniture that belongs to me. And if that woman gives you any trouble, call my lawyer.'

'It doesn't seem possible that this could happen,' Kyoko fretted.

'It's very simple,' Lucky said resolutely. 'I was set up by my confidant and business adviser, Mr Morton Sharkey. But don't worry, Kyoko, I'll find out why – and I'll shred his sorry ass.'

'Should I inform Charlie Dollar you've left?'

'Yes, please do that,' she said, trying to control her anger and think straight. 'I don't want this going around the studio. Tell Charlie I had an emergency to deal with.'

'Certainly, Lucky.'

'You'll work for me at home, Ky, until we get this straightened out. Is that okay with you?'

'It will be an honor.'

She got into her car and sat behind the wheel, placing the pile of silver frames on the passenger seat. Lennie's image gazed up at her. Impulsively she picked up his photo, kissing his face through the glass. 'I miss you, my darling sweetheart,' she murmured softly. 'I miss you so very, very much.'

Oh, God, what was happening to her life? First Lennie, now this. Everything was falling to pieces . . . everything.

She fought off tears, and drove off the lot with nowhere to go except home. Recovering her composure, she called her personal lawyer, Bruce Grey, informing him of the situation.

Bruce was as shocked as she was. 'How could Morton allow this to happen?' he said.

'*Allow* it?' she steamed. 'Somehow or other he engineered it.'

'Why?' Bruce asked, puzzled.

'Beats me,' she said bitterly. 'However, I intend to find out. In the meantime, I'll messenger all the relevant papers over to you. Get me a complete rundown on everybody who owned the stock. Let's see if they sold, or if they merely voted in this woman's favor.'

'That should be easy.'

'Her name's Donna Landsman. Sound familiar?'

'Never heard of her.'

'Prepare a full profile on her. Oh, yes, and, Bruce, get me this information before the end of the day.'

The children were out when she arrived home, everything peaceful and quiet. She walked over to the window and stared out at the spectacular ocean view.

On impulse she ran upstairs, changed into shorts and a T-shirt and made her way down to the beach. She loved the sea – walking along the edge of the surf was the perfect place to get her head together and think this through.

Why was this happening to her?

What had she done to deserve it?

Wasn't it enough that she'd lost Lennie?

It seemed that things were stacking up against her, but hadn't it been that way all her life?

Yes.

And hadn't she always been able to overcome?

Yes.

Okay, so this time she'd fight back and win. No question.

By the time she returned to the house she felt better. She could deal with it. She *would* deal with it. There had to be a way.

She wished that Boogie was here. Right now he was on vacation, fortunately due back tomorrow. At a time like this she needed the support of familiar faces around her – and there was nobody more loyal than Boogie.

The kids and CeeCee were still out. Settling in the den, she phoned Abe Panther. 'I hope you're sitting down,' she said, wondering if he'd already heard.

'What's your problem, girlie?' he cackled hoarsely.

Automatic response, 'How many times have I told you not to call me that.' A beat. 'Panther's been taken over. And – this is the shocker – your favorite grandson-in-law, Mickey Stolli, has been rehired to run it.'

Abe began to choke on the other end of the line.

'I know it's difficult to comprehend,' Lucky said. 'Thought I'd drive over and see you, get your advice.'

'Sounds like you need it.'

'The bottom line is I was double-crossed. I'll tell you about it when I get there.'

She went upstairs and dressed hurriedly.

As she was leaving the house, a flower-delivery van pulled up to the door. The driver got out and handed her a small arrangement of mixed flowers.

She tore open the card, quickly reading the scrawled message.

> Sorry about last night.
> Call you soon.
> Alex

What was *that* all about? Ten out of ten for not being the romantic type.

Not that she wanted him to be.

Not that she needed him at all.

Throwing the card on the hall table she left the house.

☆   ☆   ☆

Alex got the news on the plane to Vegas. Lili informed him, via phone, that there was a rumor going around that somebody had taken over Panther Studios and dismissed Lucky Santangelo.

'No way,' he said. 'Who'd do that?'

'Reports are it's a businesswoman. Nobody seems to know who.'

'How could this happen so suddenly?'

'Apparently she ordered Lucky off the lot this afternoon.'

Alex frowned. 'She did *what*?'

'Everybody's talking about it.'

'See what else you can find out, Lili, and call me at the hotel.'

'Tin Lee phoned.'

'What did she want?'

'She said she'd be delighted to see you later, and to thank you for the fantastic roses *and* the invitation.'

'*What* invitation?'

'I don't know, Alex. I can't keep up with your love life *and* run your production company.'

Alex hung up, puzzled. The invitation had gone to Lucky. *Can I see you tonight? Call me.* So had the roses.

Fuck! It was obvious there'd been a mistake. Tin Lee had gotten Lucky's flowers and note, while Lucky must have received Tin Lee's.

He grabbed the phone and tried reaching Lili again, but the line was out due to turbulence.

Russell, his location manager, a cheerful man, moved over from the seat across the aisle, and strapped himself in next to Alex.

'How did the Venus Maria reading go today?' Russell asked.

'Pretty damn good,' Alex replied, not really in the mood for conversation.

'Are we hiring her?'

'I'm not sure.'

'You should grab her,' Russell said. 'My kids buy every one of her CDs. They're first in line for her concerts. She's got a lock on the young audience.'

Russell had worked on his last three movies and Alex valued his opinion. 'How do you think she'll come across with Johnny Romano?' he asked.

'They'll generate plenty of heat,' Russell said.

'You could be right,' Alex replied, thinking about it. 'I'll call Freddie when we get to Vegas – suggest we run a test.'

'Will she test?'

'She came in and read, didn't she?'

Ron Machio, Venus' best friend, arrived at Orso's, a busy Italian restaurant on Third Street, a few minutes late. He was tall and lanky with straight brown hair worn back in a ponytail, and a long bony face. 'Well, madam,' he said, scrutinizing Venus, who was already sitting out on the patio sipping white wine. '*Very* fifties.'

She grinned, delighted he'd known immediately what period she was going for. 'Sit down,' she said. 'I ordered for you. Wine and pasta. It's my check.'

'Have we reinvented ourselves yet again?' he asked, flopping into a chair, stretching out his long legs.

'No, Ron,' she said. '*This* is the me that went up for a role in Alex Woods' new movie. *This* is the me who's going to win an Oscar.'

Ron's thin eyebrows shot up. '*Really?*'

'Yes, really. I believe if you want something badly enough, you can get it. Look at us – we're the perfect example. We came out to LA with zilch, and now I'm, like, Miss Superstar Big Deal and you're this hugely successful director. It's pretty amazing when you consider that neither of us graduated college.'

'Very successful people never graduate college,' Ron said knowingly. 'They're all former drop-outs. All these poor schmucks who sweated their youth away in college ended up slaving in the mail room.'

'Very philosophical, Ron. Major Mogul's influence?'

'I wish you wouldn't call him that,' Ron said irritably. 'If you got to know him, you'd find he's quite nice.'

'I'm sure Harris Von Stepp has been called a lot of things in his time, but never nice.'

'Well, he is. He's just . . .'

'Uptight,' she offered. 'Is that the word you're searching for?'

'Venus,' Ron scolded, shaking a finger at her. 'You can be a *very* mean little girl.'

The waiter delivered two plates of linguini with clam sauce.

'Anyway,' Venus said, 'I read for Alex, and he seemed to like me. He's calling Freddie.'

'Freddie?' Ron questioned, picking up his fork.

'Didn't I mention it? Freddie Leon represents me now.'

'My, my, we *are* in the big league.'

'It was about time I changed agents,' she said, taking a mouthful of pasta.

'And, naturally, you had to have the best.'

'But of course!'

'Minx!'

'Did I tell you about my new assistant, Anthony?'

'Noo . . .'

'He's a gorgeous blond,' she teased. 'Isn't that your passion, Ron – gorgeous blonds?'

'Trying to tempt me?'

'Would I do that?' she asked, all innocence.

'Yes,' Ron said, curling pasta around his fork. 'That's *exactly* what you'd do.'

'How *old* is Major Mogul?' Venus asked, as if she didn't know.

'What has age got to do with anything?'

''Cause you shouldn't get into that older man, younger man routine. It's so *passé*. And you don't need it.'

'You're a fine one to lecture,' Ron responded crisply. 'Does Madam recall Mr Martin Swanson, the big New York tycoon who was at least twenty years her senior?'

'Yeah, and look where it got me,' she said ruefully.

'And talking of relationships,' Ron continued, 'what's happening with your masseur?'

'Ah . . . Rodriguez.' Venus sighed, twirling the several thin silver bracelets that enclosed her wrist.

'Is he what you expected?'

'Nobody's ever what you really expect.' She smiled wistfully. 'I guess he's okay.'

'Just okay?'

'The thing is, Ron, after Cooper—'

'Oh, you mean Cooper's reputation was actually true?'

She laughed softly. 'Cooper was the best lover I ever had. I'll have to go a long way to find another as good as him.'

'Ah . . .' Ron said. 'If only he'd kept it in his pants.'

'Yeah,' Venus agreed, going for the joke. 'Every time he unzipped 'em his brains fell out!'

They broke up laughing.

'About this Anthony . . .' Ron ventured.

Venus grinned. 'You're such a slut!'

'Takes one to know one.'

'I think it's coffee at *my* house, right?'

'Well, if you insist.'

Chapter Thirty

ABE PANTHER HAD not left his crumbling old mansion for over ten years, ever since a major stroke had forced him out of the day-to-day machinations of the film business. When he'd sold his studio to Lucky, he'd been convinced it would be hers until his death, and long after that. The news of somebody else taking over Panther had infuriated him, especially if it was true that his thieving grandson-in-law, Mickey Stolli, was being reinstated as studio head.

Before Lucky arrived, he'd called up his granddaughter, Abigaile, to find out what was going on. Abigaile was a true Hollywood princess: pushy and grasping, she lived for entertaining and huge parties.

After Abe had sold his studio to Lucky, a bitter Abigaile hadn't spoken to him for a while. It was only when Mickey was appointed the head of Orpheus that Abigaile had finally made peace with her grandfather.

Now he was on the phone, attempting to elicit information.

Abigaile was uncooperative. 'There'll be an announcement in the trades,' she said crisply, unwilling to reveal more.

'I'm sure there will,' Abe replied sternly. 'However, I wish to know now what's taking place.'

'It's confidential information,' Abigaile said, still miffed with her grandfather for marrying his long-time companion, the obscure Swedish actress, Inga Irving. 'Mickey will kill me if I tell anybody.'

'I'm not anybody,' Abe reminded her gruffly. 'I'm your grandfather.'

'I'll speak to Mickey and call you later.'

Abe was sitting out on his terrace puffing on a large Havana cigar when Lucky arrived. She kissed him on both cheeks, marveling at the old man's tenacity.

'Sit down, girlie,' he said and repeated his conversation with Abigaile.

'Typical,' Lucky said, lighting a cigarette.

'Who betrayed you?' Abe asked, leaning toward her, his less than white dentures clenched tightly together.

'Morton Sharkey,' she said, expelling a thin stream of smoke. 'I intend to find out why.'

'It seems inconceivable that this could have happened without you knowing,' Abe said, unclenching his teeth to puff on his cigar. Their smoke intermingled mid-air.

'Not really,' Lucky said. 'It was all done secretly. They called a Board meeting, and failed to notify me.'

'Nobody alerted you?'

'They wanted me out, Abe,' she said forcefully. 'The last thing they'd do is warn me.'

'Right, right,' he muttered.

'Why did I allow Morton to talk me into selling off so much of my stock?' she fretted. 'What's *wrong* with me? I should have kept fifty-one percent to protect myself.'

'Why didn't you?' Abe asked, squinting at her.

'Because I needed the cash flow, and I trusted Morton.'

'Never trust a lawyer.'

'Don't make it worse,' she snapped. 'I'm burning up.'

'Do you have a plan, girlie?'

She got up and paced around the flower-bordered terrace.

'I'm getting Panther back, Abe. You'll see. I'm doing it for both of us.'

Abe cackled. 'That's the spirit,' he said, puffing on his large Havana. 'If anyone can get 'em, my buck's on you!'

Inga Irving emerged from the house, greeting Lucky curtly. Inga – once a great beauty – was a big-boned woman in her late fifties, with a broad face of discontent. Long ago, when Abe was *the* Hollywood tycoon to beat all Hollywood tycoons, he'd brought her to Hollywood from her native Sweden in the hope of making her a movie star. It hadn't happened. Inga remained forever sour about her lack of success. Two years ago Abe had finally married her. It had not put a smile on her face.

'Lucky,' Inga said, nodding in her usual haughty manner.

'Inga,' Lucky responded, used to the Swedish woman's moody demeanor.

'Time for your nap, Abe,' Inga announced, in a no-nonsense voice.

'Can't you see I'm visiting with Lucky?' Abe said crossly, stabbing his cigar in her direction.

'She'll have to come back another time,' Inga said, with a stern expression.

Abe continued to object, but Inga was having none of it. His ninety-year-old balls were firmly in her pocket and that's exactly where they were staying.

'It's okay, Abe,' Lucky said, kissing him on the cheek. 'I've got to go anyway.'

A flicker of triumph crossed Inga's face. She'd finally found a role she could excel at. Keeper of the once great Abe Panther.

Lucky got in her car and drove home. She had work to do.

☆　☆　☆

'How stupid can you get!' Alex yelled over the phone.

'I'm sorry,' France said, apologizing for the third time.

'*Sorry*? How could the wrong fucking note and the wrong fucking flowers go to the wrong person?' he screamed. 'I went to the trouble of writing that note myself, France. What are you – a moron?'

'I'm sorry, Alex,' she repeated yet again, holding the phone away from her ear.

He wondered if she'd done it purposely. Even though their romance was long past, Alex knew that both she and Lili were still very possessive of him. They'd obviously assumed he'd spent the night with Lucky, and now they'd plotted to make sure she received the wrong message. Loyalty and jealousy did not mix.

'What can I do?' France wailed.

'Nothing,' Alex said sourly. 'Cancel Tin Lee. Tell her I had to stay in Vegas overnight. I'll call Lucky myself. Get me her home number.'

Lili picked up the extension line a few seconds later. 'We don't have it on file, Alex.'

He was sure they were making it difficult on purpose. 'Call Freddie's secretary,' he snapped.

'Certainly, Alex. Will you be reachable on your mobile?'

'Yeah, we're leaving the hotel now.'

'I'll get right back to you.'

'Wait a minute,' he said, totally irritated by both his assistants. 'I haven't finished.'

'What is it, Alex?' said Lili, ever patient.

'Have Freddie call me.'

'Is there any message if we can't reach him?'

'Yes. Set it up for Venus Maria to test with Johnny Romano tomorrow afternoon.'

'It's done, Alex.'

He banged down the phone and walked through the hotel

to meet Russell and the rest of his crew out front. As he strode purposefully through the crowded lobby, the lure of the tables was powerful. Once he'd been a degenerate gambler. Reluctantly, with the help of his therapist, he'd given it up after he'd dropped a million dollars over a year. Right now his only addiction was work.

His team was gathered outside the hotel watching huge water fountains erupt with fire. On the location scout were his cinematographer, line producer, first AD, set designer and a couple of assistants.

Russell introduced him to the area location man, Clyde Lomas, a florid-faced Las Vegas native, with a small snub nose that seemed out of place in his long, mournful face.

They shook hands. Clyde had sweaty palms, which put Alex in a bad mood because all he could think about was getting to a bathroom to wash the man's sweat off his hands.

'We got some fancy places for you to look at,' Clyde announced, in a loud booming voice. 'Set 'em up myself. Five houses and three hotels.'

Alex glanced at his watch. 'Are we going to have time to cover all this?' he said, turning to Russell.

'I hope so,' was the reply. 'We're booked on an eight o'clock plane back to LA. If you feel like staying the night I can arrange that, too.'

'I wasn't planning on it,' Alex said, thinking that if he could reach her, he wanted to spend the evening with Lucky.

'Let me know if you change your mind,' Russell replied. 'I can go either way.'

They climbed into a large air-conditioned van and set off.

☆ ☆ ☆

Lucky thought about canceling dinner with Venus at Morton's, then she reconsidered. Why should she? That's exactly what everybody would expect her to do – crawl off somewhere and vanish.

Hollywood. A town with no conscience. Just one big happy boys' club. And wouldn't they be thrilled to hear that Lucky Santangelo had been ousted.

She refused to give them that pleasure. She'd be out there, head held high for all to see. This was merely a temporary setback.

CeeCee and the kids were home when she got back. She played with Maria a while, then fed baby Gino his bottle. After that she handed them over to the ever cheerful CeeCee to put to bed.

Shortly after six, a messenger delivered a large manila envelope from her lawyer. She took it into the den, ripped it open and began to study the contents.

Donna Landsman. Businesswoman. Queen of the hostile takeovers. A corporate raider with a thirst for buying small companies, stripping the assets and then reselling them at a profit.

Lucky couldn't figure it out. If Donna Landsman was such a high-powered business tycoon, what did she want with Panther? The studio had massive debts, it would be a long while before it was profit-making. There were no assets to strip unless, of course, she abandoned the whole studio deal and sold off the valuable land.

Yes! That's what she planned to do. That had to be it.

As far as the other investors were concerned, on paper it showed they'd been paid twice the amount they had paid for their original shares. She assumed that since Morton had brought them in, it was on his advice they'd gotten out.

Take the money and run. Why not? It was good business.

It seemed that Donna Landsman had acquired thirty-nine percent of the stock. The remaining shareholders were Conquest Investments, a company based in the Bahamas, who'd retained ten percent. And Mrs I. Smorg, whose address was care of a lawyer in Pasadena – she owned six percent. Then there was Morton Sharkey with his five percent. It was a sure thing he'd pushed the remaining shareholders to vote in Donna Landsman's favor.

Screw Morton Sharkey, because that's what he was doing to her.

She sat back, her mind racing.

There had to be a reason he was doing this to her. There was always a reason.

Tomorrow, when Boogie returned from his vacation, she'd put him on Morton's case. Boogie had worked as her security for years, and if there was anything to find out, he'd discover it. No problem.

Until then all she could do was wait.

Chapter Thirty-one

 ROBERTSON HAD malevolent violet cat's eyes. They followed Brigette wherever she went at Michel Guy's dinner. They radiated, *Get out of my face and don't come back.*

'She hates me,' Brigette whispered to Nona.

'Of course she hates you,' Nona agreed. 'Why wouldn't she? You're going to be the star now.'

'Oh, c'mon,' Brigette said. 'She's, like, *sooo* famous, why would she care?'

'Modeling careers are short,' Nona said wisely. 'She's aware of that. You're the one on the rise.'

'Really?'

'Don't play coy with me. You know it. *Everyone* knows it.'

They'd had an interesting few days. True to his word, Michel Guy had pulled off a lucrative deal with Rock 'n' Roll Jeans. As soon as the company signed her to an exclusive big-bucks contract, she was rushed into the studio for a major photo-shoot with Luke Kasway. The ad agency had wanted her with Zandino, but Nona had vetoed his appearance because she didn't like the idea of her future husband modeling – in some ways Nona was a bit of a snob. Instead they used Isaac, a young black model with ratted hair and a rap attitude. Brigette thought he was cool. They'd exchanged phone numbers, but so far he hadn't called. She was contemplating phoning him.

It had taken all day to shoot the photographs: the ad agency had everyone on an accelerated schedule and the pace was frantic.

When she'd seen the finished results, Brigette was in shock. Luke Kasway was a genius who'd made her look utterly amazing.

Nona had said, 'Don't get carried away, it's all lighting. Let's not forget how you look in the mornings!'

But both of them had known – along with Michel and Luke – that she was a star about to happen.

Nona had lucked into a spacious duplex apartment overlooking Central Park. It belonged to a friend of her mother's, who'd taken off to live in Europe for a year. The three of them moved in immediately.

In a way Brigette was sorry to say goodbye to Anna – she'd gotten used to the security of always having somebody around. However, she realized the time had come to be out on her own and to stop brooding about the past.

Brigette Stanislopoulos was dead.

Brigette Brown was into a whole new deal.

She'd phoned Lucky to tell her of the move.

'As long as you're not living by yourself,' Lucky had said. 'And watch it! It's easier to get into trouble than out of it.'

'Enjoying yourself?' Michel asked, sneaking up behind her.

'Oh, yes,' she said, flattered that he was taking so much notice of her. 'It's an awesome party.'

'You're an awesome young lady,' he murmured, '*formidable*.'

'Really, Michel?' she said, gazing up at him with crush written all over her glowingly pretty face.

He leaned down and whispered in her ear, his breath heavy with garlic. 'Aurora has said yes to your cover. She wants it immediately. You're to go see Antonio – the photographer – tomorrow, and he'll shoot the next day. I'll give Nona the details.'

'You're so clever!' she exclaimed.

A smile played across his face. 'No need to flatter me, *ma chérie.*'

She loved it when he spoke his native language, it was so sexy. 'Do you and Robertson really live together?' she asked boldly.

His faded blue eyes studied her carefully. 'Why do you ask?'

She hoped he didn't think she was being too inquisitive. 'I just . . . wondered,' she said vaguely.

'Sometimes we do, sometimes we don't,' he replied ambiguously. 'We have an . . . understanding.'

She caught Robertson still watching her. Maybe *her* idea of an understanding and Michel's differed.

'So, my dear girl, are you happy with the way things are going?' he asked, touching her arm.

'Very happy.'

'Are you glad I came into your life when I did?'

'Impeccable timing,' she said, smiling.

'You know, Brigette,' he said, reflectively, 'you're not like one of these pretty little American girls from the Midwest. You seem almost European.'

'I *am* European. My mother was Greek – she died several years ago. My father was Italian.'

'Ah, an interesting combination! That explains why you're so sensual for one so young.'

'Do you think I'm sensual, Michel?' she asked eagerly.

'Yes, *ma petite.* America will fall in love with you.'

It had been a long time since she'd allowed herself to flirt with anybody, it was quite a heady feeling. That Michel was older attracted her. Maybe a mature man was what she needed, she certainly hadn't had any luck with the young ones.

Michel took her hand, squeezing it gently. 'Stay after the

guests have left,' he said persuasively. 'We have much to discuss.'

'What about Robertson?'

'She has her own apartment. Tonight she will go home.'

Brigette couldn't wait to find Nona. 'I'm staying after the party,' she announced. 'Michel wants to talk to me.'

'Oh, *I* get it,' Nona said, not impressed. 'He's finally coming on to you, right?'

'No way,' she said indignantly. 'It's just business.'

'I'm telling you,' Nona warned. 'He's a womanizer with a fancy accent. You're just fresh meat, that's all.'

'Thanks a lot.'

'And what about Robertson? Is she going to sit back and watch while you two discuss business?'

'They have an arrangement.'

'Ha! You're falling for the oldest line since "Let me just put it there." The next thing he'll say is, "Sorry, it was fantastic, but now I gotta go back to my girlfriend 'cause she's pissed off."'

'You don't give me much credit, do you?' Brigette said crossly.

'I *care* about you,' Nona said. 'Your experience with men is limited. Tim Wealth – Mr Rat-Pack Movie Star. My brother – the hippie maniac. And that rich coke freak you were engaged to. That's about it, or am I missing someone?'

'I haven't led a normal life,' Brigette admitted. 'That doesn't mean I can't in the future.'

'Michel Guy is *not* normal,' Nona said, frowning. 'Jump into bed with him and you're on a fast track to nowhere.'

Brigette had no intention of being lectured to by Nona. 'I'll see you later,' she said, cutting her off. 'Don't wait up.'

☆ ☆ ☆

'Freddie Leon called,' Anthony said, surreptitiously eyeing Ron and liking what he saw.

'What did he want?' Venus asked.

'To set up a test tomorrow afternoon with you and Johnny Romano.'

'A *test*,' Venus said, pulling a face. 'I don't test.'

'You don't read either,' Ron said, crisply. 'But for Alex Woods you did.'

'Why doesn't he just run film on me?'

'I presume you've read what the critics had to say about your previous performances?' Ron inquired tartly. 'You're fortunate he wants to test you.'

Venus glared at him. 'Don't forget that one of those movies was yours.'

'Mr Machio,' Anthony interrupted, trying to stave off a fight, 'I'm such a fan. Your choreography and direction in *Summer Startime* were quite wonderful.'

'Why, thank you,' Ron said, noticing Anthony for the first time.

'I'm sorry, Ron,' Venus said, enjoying the moment, 'I haven't introduced you to my very proper English assistant – Anthony Redigio.'

'Isn't Redigio an Italian name?' Ron asked, with a neat little smile.

'My father's Italian,' Anthony replied.

'Mine, too,' Ron said. 'Our Venus likes Italians.'

'So do I,' Anthony said boldly.

Their eyes met. Venus hid a triumphant smile. Was this a Venus match made in heaven or what?

'Did you check out that letter, Anthony?' she asked.

'I sent it over to Security,' he replied, busily stacking papers on the desk.

'Good. Get me Freddie on the phone, and after that fix Ron coffee. I'll be in the other room.'

Ron shook his head and half smiled. 'You're such an obvious little brat,' he whispered.

'Takes one to know one,' she replied gleefully.

Freddie was his usual bland self. 'Definitely test,' he said.

'What if it gets out?' she fretted. 'Doesn't that make me look desperate?'

'Not at all. Personally, I think you'll get the part. Alex liked you.'

'He did?' she said, perking up. 'What did he say?'

'He thought he could bring things out in you that nobody's seen before.'

'Did he think I was unbelievably sexy?' she asked, jokingly.

'What difference does it make whether he thought you were sexy or not? You're not going to fuck him, you're going to work for him.'

'Oh, Freddie!' she gasped, mock-shocked. 'You used the F-word! I've never heard you swear before.'

'It's your bad influence, Venus.'

She couldn't believe Freddie actually sounded human – he was usually such a cool proposition. 'Okay, I'll do it,' she decided. 'Only because you say so.'

In the office Ron and Anthony were getting along fine. 'I love *all* your work,' Anthony was saying, with the proper amount of deference. 'I've seen everything you've done.'

Ron was busy soaking up every word of praise. 'Where are you from, Anthony?' he asked, sipping his coffee from a mug emblazoned with Venus' picture.

'Born in Naples,' Anthony said. 'My parents moved to London when I was two. I came to LA a year ago. Venus is my second job.' He glanced over at her. 'She's divine to work for.'

'You *would* say that, wouldn't you?' she said, grinning.

'Of course! I'm no fool,' Anthony replied archly, a touch of camp surfacing.

'Where do you live?' Ron asked.

Venus imagined what Ron was thinking. *Where do you live, Anthony, so I can come up one afternoon and crawl all over your fine muscular body?* He was such a randy sod.

'West Hollywood,' Anthony said. 'In an apartment.' He paused for a moment. 'Actually, I shared with a friend for a while, but he . . . got sick and went home.'

'Sorry to hear that,' Ron said, immediately sympathetic. 'Are you—'

'Oh, I'm fine,' Anthony interrupted quickly. 'I get myself tested twice a year.'

Ron nodded. 'It's not like it used to be.' He sighed nostalgically. 'Ah, the wild times.'

'Ron was *king* of the wild times, weren't you, cutie?' Venus said.

'Yes, my sweets. If my memory serves me correctly, *I* was the king and *you* were the queen.'

'We shared an apartment at one time,' Venus said, grinning at the memories. 'It was so funny. The desk clerk would take one look at any handsome stud who walked in and automatically say, "Venus or Ron?"'

'I'm sorry to admit I was too young to experience the wild times,' Anthony said, with a wistful sigh.

'How old are you?' Ron asked.

'Twenty-one.'

'A mere puppy.'

'An experienced puppy.'

'Glad to hear it,' Ron said, perching on the edge of Anthony's desk. 'And is the puppy currently involved?'

'No,' Anthony said, batting his eyelashes in a slightly girlish way. 'Are you?'

'I am,' Ron admitted, a tad reluctantly.

Anthony threw him a bold look. 'Shame.'

'Let's go, Ron,' Venus said, deciding they'd had enough

of each other for now. Best to let the sexual tension build. 'I'm taking you to see my gym. It's *so* incredible, you'll crap!'

'Such a lady!' Ron sighed.

'Isn't that why we became friends in the first place?' she said, grabbing his hand and dragging him off.

☆　☆　☆

Clyde Lomas was driving Alex slowly crazy. The man and his loud voice were an irritating pain in the ass. Every time they entered a house, Clyde went into some kind of insane realtor riff.

'This here's the wet bar. Over there's the entertaining area. I can assure you, this house has a wonderful flow for parties. Two barbecues, an outdoor *and* indoor jacuzzi, a black-bottomed pool and seven bedrooms with bathrooms *en suite*. The kitchen has four ovens and two dishwashers.'

'I'm not *buying* the fucking house,' Alex said, exasperated. 'All I want is to walk through and take a look.'

Clyde's long, mournful face became even more so. 'Sorry, Alex,' he said, crestfallen. 'I thought I was being helpful.'

'You're very helpful,' Russell said, trouble-shooting as usual. 'It's just that Alex has his own way of doing things.'

Alex strolled through the third house on their agenda, the close-knit members of his crew hovering behind him. As soon as he walked into a location he knew if it was right or not, he didn't need any instructions. He certainly didn't need Clyde Lomas.

The third house – a large mansion situated on the edge of a golf course – was perfect. He conferred with his cinematographer and set designer who both agreed with him.

He turned to Russell. 'Go ahead and cut a deal.'

'How many days?' Russell asked.

'What's on the schedule?'

'Four. I'll be safe, and book it for five.'

Alex walked outside to the pool area and called Lili on his mobile. 'You were supposed to get back to me with Lucky's home number,' he said, irritably.

'I can't find it,' Lili confessed.

'Excuse me?' Alex said, not used to being told no.

'Freddie's assistant has an embargo on her number. He's not allowed to give it out to anybody.'

'Fuck Freddie's assistant. Tell Freddie I want it.'

'Sorry, Alex, I tried. He said not without her permission.'

Alex knew he couldn't push it further without coming across like an over-anxious love-sick schmuck. 'What's the latest on Panther?' he asked, abruptly changing the subject.

'I found out a businesswoman bought Panther. The story is she went into Lucky's office and ordered her off the lot.'

'Does this affect *Gangsters*?'

'According to Freddie, everything will proceed as before.'

'Does he know this woman?'

'Apparently not.'

'Fuck!' Alex exclaimed angrily. 'I've really gotta speak to Lucky. What's that guy who works for her?'

'Kyoko?'

'Yeah, get her number from him.'

'I tried reaching him, he's no longer at the studio.'

'Use your smarts, Lili. Call him at home.'

'Yes, Alex. How's everything going there?'

'Fine. What's happening with the test?'

'All set for tomorrow afternoon. Makeup and hair are standing by. Venus will be in at one, Johnny at two. Both of them will be camera-ready by three. Does that suit you?'

'Organized as ever, Lili. Did France tell Tin Lee I'm not coming back?'

'I believe she did. And your mother's called twice.'

'What does *she* want?'

'Perhaps you should phone her yourself.'

'You do it, say I'm out of town.'

'Will you be flying back later?'

'Get me Lucky's number and I'll let you know.' He clicked off, stuffed his portable in his pocket and rejoined his crew.

'Ready for the next location?' Russell asked.

'Take me to it,' Alex said. 'I definitely want to get out of here tonight.'

Chapter Thirty-two

 MORTON'S WAS *the* industry hang-out. It was always packed with Hollywood movers and shakers, *the* place to be seen. When Lucky entered, every head turned to stare. Today she was big news and they all knew it.

She arrived before Venus and, rather than wait at the bar, she followed the maître d' to her table, navigating her way past tables full of people she knew. She kissed Arnold Kopelson, the producer, and his smart wife, Anne. She waved at the Marvin Davises, stopped to have a word with Joanna and Sidney Poitier, greeted Mel Gibson, blew a kiss at Charlie Dollar, and finally arrived at her destination.

As soon as she sat down, Charlie got up and ambled over. 'Hey,' he drawled, tucking his shirt in his pants, disheveled as usual. 'The phrase stood up is not in my vocabulary.'

She managed a wan grin. 'Sorry, Charlie. Unforeseen circumstances.'

'Yeah . . . I heard,' he said, pulling out a chair and sitting down.

She sighed. 'So did everyone else in this restaurant.'

'Hey, you should've come and got me. I'm the world's greatest expert at packing up.'

'It's only temporary, Charlie. I'll be back.'

He leaned across the table. 'Wanna give me the real scam? There has to be more to this.'

'I got screwed. Let's put it this way, it won't happen again.'

'Well, Lucky,' he said, looking sincere for once in his life. 'Don't forget, I'm always here for you.'

'Thanks, Charlie, I appreciate your concern.'

His stoned eyes restlessly scanned the room. 'Who're you having dinner with?'

'Venus.'

'Oh yeah, Venus. Didn't ya wanna fix me up with her?'

'You can join us for coffee if you like.'

'Maybe,' he said, getting up.

'Playing hard to get, Charlie?'

A crazy grin swept across his face. 'Baby, the only thing hard about *me* is my head. Ain't age a bitch!'

A few minutes later, Venus entered, pausing in the doorway just long enough for everybody to turn and stare. She looked just sexy enough in a white Thierry Mugler suit and funky lace-up boots.

The maître d' led her over to Lucky. She followed him without stopping, knowing that if she paused at one table, she'd have to stop at them all. Behaving like a star gave Venus a vicarious thrill, for she never forgot her humble beginnings. If people wished to greet her, they'd pay homage when she was settled.

Lucky stood up as she approached. They hugged and kissed.

'I'm *so* glad we're doing this,' Venus said. 'I've really missed you.'

'Missed you, too,' Lucky responded. 'Although I'd better tell you before somebody else does, this isn't the greatest night of my life.'

An attentive waiter appeared at their table. Lucky ordered Perrier while Venus opted for a margarita.

'What happened?' Venus asked, as soon as their waiter was out of earshot.

'Panther was taken over today,' Lucky said, drumming her fingers on the table. 'I was canned as head of the studio.'

'You've *got* to be joking!' Venus exclaimed.

'I wish I was. But hey, don't start sobbing in your milk and cookies, I'll get it back and then some.'

'I've no doubt you will. Who took over?'

'That's the weird thing. It's not one of the big conglomerates, it's a woman with a reputation as a corporate raider. She wanted Panther big time, and somehow or other she got it.'

'Will she run the studio?'

Lucky laughed humorlessly. 'You'll *really* get a kick out of this one. *Guess* who she's bringing in? *Your* favorite and *mine* – Mickey Stolli.'

'Get outta here!'

'It's true,' Lucky said. 'The woman is obviously deranged. Anybody with any sense would know Mickie's going to steal anything that's not nailed down. Hey,' she added with a brittle laugh, 'maybe that's what she deserves.'

'I'm confused,' Venus said. 'How did this happen?'

'That's what I have to find out.'

The waiter brought their drinks to the table. 'Compliments of Mr Dollar,' he said with an I'm-an-out-of-work-actor-hoping-to-get-discovered smile.

'Thank Mr Dollar, and tell him next time it'll be a bottle of Cristal or nothing,' Venus said, picking up her margarita. The waiter nodded and left. 'Y'know, Lucky, I've tried calling you so many times. How come you wouldn't let your friends in?'

'Lennie's death was such a horrible shock,' Lucky said, her eyes clouding over. 'I guess it was numbing . . .' She paused for a long moment before continuing, 'I opted for work – not friends. That way I didn't have to deal with my true feelings.'

'I can understand that,' Venus said quietly.

'You want to know the truth?' Lucky said softly. 'I miss Lennie every single moment of every single day.'

'I'm sure,' Venus murmured.

'Anyway,' Lucky said, making a supreme effort to change the subject, 'enough about that. Tell me how it went with Alex.'

'I'm testing tomorrow with Johnny Romano.'

'Alex is making you test?'

'Freddie says I should.'

'It's a control move. Mr Woods is showing you who's boss.'

'Oh, God!' Venus wailed, 'Now you're not running the studio, what'll happen with *Gangsters*?'

'I'm sure this woman isn't dumb enough to mess with the schedule.'

'Yeah, well, Mickey hates me,' Venus ruminated, sipping her drink. 'Remember that movie where he insisted I take off my clothes when all the male actors weren't asked to show shit? We had a battle royal over *that* one.'

Lucky remembered it well. 'You're a big star now,' she reminded her friend. 'Mickey won't give you any trouble.'

An agent came over to their table, an agent with a mission to get Venus to read a client's script. He greeted Lucky briefly – after all, what good was she anymore? – and zeroed in on his main prey.

Lucky allowed her mind to wander to Alex Woods. She'd had a good time with him, but that was all. He'd served his purpose. And the note he'd sent with the flowers proved she meant nothing to him. Fine with her. Over and out.

Jack Python, the talk-show host, stopped at their table. 'Lucky,' he said, penetrating green eyes probing hers, 'sorry to hear the deal.'

'What deal, Jack?' she said evenly.

'I understand you're not with Panther anymore.'

'Isn't it strange?' Lucky said. 'Good news travels real slow, but bad news gets around faster than a hooker chasing a client.'

'Hey, I didn't mean anything by it,' Jack said. 'Come on the show and we'll talk about it. I'll give you the full hour.'

'What would *I* have to talk about, Jack?'

'People are fascinated by the inner workings of Hollywood, and you're one of the few women – probably the only woman – who owned and ran her own studio. We could make it an interesting program.'

'How come you didn't ask me when I had the studio?'

''Cause your publicist wouldn't let me within twenty feet of you.'

She wasn't about to get mad at him. Jack Python was one of the good guys, his talk show was intelligent and fast-paced, far superior to the rest of the late-night mindless chat.

Jack drifted off and Venus got rid of the agent. They ordered steaks and a bottle of red wine. Venus started telling hilarious stories about Rodriguez, mimicking his accent and describing his lovemaking techniques.

Lucky found herself relaxing as she listened to her friend. Venus was a strong, outspoken woman. Unlike most female superstars she had an earthy humor and a kick-ass attitude. When it came to movie-making she also refused to put up with men's crap. Directors and producers were forever trying to coerce her into doing things on screen she deemed unacceptable. Venus always stood firm: she was never afraid of anything or anyone.

'He's really very sweet, problem is he tries so hard it's painful!' Venus said, finishing up her Rodriguez stories.

'How about Cooper?' Lucky asked. 'Do you miss him?'

'What's to miss?' Venus said dismissively, because she didn't want to get into the fact that, yes, she missed him a lot, and yet there was no going back.

Lucky scanned the room. Charlie was paying his check, which meant it wouldn't be long before he came over. 'What do you think of Charlie Dollar?' she asked casually.

'Old Charlie's the greatest,' Venus said, chewing a piece of steak. 'Trouble is, he's always so stoned.'

'Isn't that part of his charm?'

'Coke and charm do not mix,' Venus said firmly. 'Although I hear he's a pretty good lay.'

'Really?'

'Not that I'm planning to find out,' Venus added quickly.

'Would you go out with him?' Lucky asked.

Venus shook her head vigorously. 'Dangerous territory,' she said. 'There's no way Charlie would be capable of sustaining a decent relationship – he's been a movie star too long. Women are easy for him and he doesn't give a shit about any of them.'

Lucky agreed. 'Commitment is not exactly his bag,' she said. 'It's not mine anymore either. The only commitment I have is to my children and to getting my studio back.'

By the time Charlie ambled his way over to their table, Lucky had called for the check.

'Here comes your favorite movie star,' he said, with his usual maniacal grin. 'Ready to delight and entertain.'

'You don't have to bother,' Lucky said lightly. 'We entertained each other.'

He zoomed in on Venus. 'Wanna hit the clubs? Tango the night away with a decrepit old icon?'

'Gotta get an early night, Charlie,' she said apologetically. 'I'm shooting tomorrow. Besides,' she added with a wicked grin. 'What would you do with me? I'm over eighteen!'

He favored her with another maniacal grin. 'I could give you bags under your eyes you'd never forget,' he offered.

'Thanks, this time I'll pass.'

Much to Charlie's chagrin they departed shortly after, leaving him in the company of an aging movie star with a bad toupée, and a Lakers cheerleader with enormous silicone breasts. Charlie got along with everyone.

Outside the restaurant they waited for their cars.

'We gotta do this again *soon*,' Venus said. 'You're more fun than a date any day!'

'Gee, thanks,' Lucky said, laughing. '*And* you didn't even have to put out!'

'What a relief!'

'Call me after the test.'

'I'll do that,' Venus said, getting into her all-black limo, driven by an armed security guard.

The valet pulled up in Lucky's red Ferrari.

They waved their goodbyes and took off into the night.

☆ ☆ ☆

Lucky drove home fast, taking the San Vicente/Pacific Coast Highway route. It had been an exhausting twenty-four hours and she couldn't wait to collapse into bed and get a good night's sleep. Had to get her head straight so she could work out how she was going to deal with this latest setback.

As soon as she'd apprised Boogie of what needed to be done, she planned on taking the kids and staying at Gino's in Palm Springs for a long weekend.

She picked up the car phone to warn him.

'You again.' Gino sighed. 'You gotta be after somethin', kiddo. First an unexpected visit, now the late-night phone call.'

'I'm not waking you, am I?'

'No way. Paige an' I are sittin' here watchin' *The Godfather*. I take a look at it once a year. *Godfather One* and *Two* – forget *Three*.'

'Getting in touch with old friends, huh?' Lucky joked.

'One of these days I'll tell you my real life story, kiddo.' He chuckled. 'Gino, the early years. What a movie it'd make!'

'I don't doubt it. I heard stories about you from more people than you'd care to know about.'

'So what's up now?' he asked. 'Anythin' I can help with?'

She decided not to tell him the real truth. Why burden him with her problems? 'I was thinking of bringing the children down for a long weekend.'

'You mean I actually get to see my grandkids?'

'Oh, c'mon, Gino, you see them all the time.'

'I'm teasin' you, kiddo. I'll have Paige get everythin' ready.'

Gino sounded so content. He didn't seem to miss big-city life at all. It was obvious he loved living in Palm Springs in his big house with Paige to keep him company.

She wondered if that's what she should do – buy a house in Santa Barbara and forget about the film business, just veg out and be with her kids.

No way. She'd be bored within days. She needed action, and plenty of it.

She pressed in a tape and listened to Joe Cocker's raspy growl on 'You Are So Beautiful'. It was one of Lennie's favorites.

Recklessly she drove faster, breaking the speed limit on the Pacific Coast Highway, racing all the way home.

Zooming into her driveway, she jumped out of the car and entered her house. Everyone was asleep. First she peeked in at the children, then she went up to her bedroom on the second floor and walked out onto the small terrace, remembering the times she and Lennie had made love on the sand below with only the sound of the roaring surf to keep them company.

The phone rang. She picked up the portable.

'Do you know how difficult it's been reaching you?' said a pissed-off Alex Woods.

Somehow or other he'd gotten her home number, she wasn't pleased.

'I haven't exactly been available,' she said, not inclined to get into a fight with him.

'I called you at the studio this morning,' he said accusingly. 'Left several messages.'

'I'm sure you're aware of what went on today. I wasn't exactly in a returning-phone-calls mood.'

'Yeah, I heard.' A long pause. 'Are you okay?'

'I'm fine, thank you.'

'Uh . . . about the note that came with the flowers. You got 'em, didn't you?'

'You shouldn't have bothered.'

'Wrong flowers. Wrong note.'

'Really?'

'Although it beats me why I sent you anything at all after you walked out on me this morning.'

She took a deep breath, 'Listen, Alex, let's be truthful with each other. We were a one-night fling. I needed to be with somebody, and you happened to be there.'

'Oh, that's nice,' he said. 'How do you think that makes me feel?'

'It didn't mean anything to either of us. I did it to get back at Lennie. I'm sorry.'

There was a long silence.

'When I didn't hear from you, I stayed in Vegas,' he said at last.

'What are you doing there?'

'Location scouting. I'll be back tomorrow.' Another long silence. 'Can we get together tomorrow night?'

She sighed. 'Didn't you hear what I just said?'

'Lucky,' he said persuasively, 'you need me at a time like this.'

'What can you do, Alex?' she said wearily. 'Hold my hand while other people take control of my studio?'

'I didn't call you to argue.'

'What did you call for?'

'To say that last night was . . . special.'

'No, Alex,' she said flatly. 'Please hear what I'm saying. It was just another one-night stand on both our parts.'

'You're wrong, Lucky. I've had enough one-night stands to know when it's special.'

Why couldn't he just go away? She didn't need complications. 'I'm sorry if I gave you a false impression.'

He couldn't believe she was giving him the run-around. That he, Alex Woods, was actually getting shut out by a woman. 'I can tell you're not in the mood to talk,' he said abruptly. 'I'll call you tomorrow.'

'You're wasting your time.'

'That's my problem.'

She shut the phone. Alex Woods was not going to be put off easily.

☆　☆　☆

Venus' long black limousine glided through the gates of her estate. As it passed the guard-house, the man emerged, waving for the car to stop.

The driver lowered his window. 'Anything wrong?'

'No, no,' the guard answered. 'Please tell Miss Venus her brother's here.'

'My *what*?' Venus said, jumping to attention in the backseat.

'Your brother Emilio, miss,' the guard said, peering into the car.

'And you let him in my house!' she exploded, horrified.

'Well, er, yes. He had proof he was your brother,' the guard said, taking a step back.

'*What* proof?' she demanded.

'Pictures of you together, his passport. I know your real name is Sierra, so I thought it was all right to allow him in.'

'Well, it's *not*,' Venus said angrily. 'How many times have I got to tell you people that *nobody* enters my house unless I say so.'

The guard took umbrage at her tone. 'I was only doing my duty.' He sulked.

'Your duty is to keep *everybody* out unless I leave *specific* instructions.'

She was so furious she could scarcely breathe. Emilio Sierra. Slob brother number one. He'd sold her out to the tabloids so many times it was ridiculous. Then he'd gone off to live in Europe, and she'd hoped and prayed he'd never come back. Recently she'd heard he'd returned, and she'd known it was only a matter of time before he turned up again.

Goddamn it! Why did it have to be tonight?

She instructed her driver to wait while she picked up the car phone and summoned Rodriguez.

'My darling,' Rodriguez said, delighted to hear from her, 'I waited by the phone all day. Nobody called from Casting.'

Did he have to be so obvious? His eagerness to be in her video was a turn-off.

'What are you doing, Rodriguez?'

'Waiting for you, of course.'

'I feel like a long sensual massage,' she murmured seductively. 'Can you come over now?'

'Of course!'

'Let's go,' she instructed her driver.

The limo drove smoothly up to her house, pulling up in front. She got out and marched inside.

Sitting in her living room, feet up on her marble coffee table, guzzling a bottle of beer while watching a cable porno movie on her big-screen TV, was her dear brother.

Déjà vu. Hadn't this happened to her before?

'You're not welcome here, Emilio,' she said, trying to control her fury at his nerve. 'I can't believe you're back. Have you no idea what you've done to me?'

'What?' he asked, barely able to drag his eyes away from two blonds busily stroking each other's implants on the TV screen.

She grabbed the remote, switching the set off. 'You sold me out,' she said angrily, 'time after time after time.'

Emilio lumbered to his feet, placing his beer on the marble table without a coaster. Then he attempted to turn on the charm, of which he had none.

'I was in a bind, sis,' he said, in a whiny voice. 'Had debts to pay off. Now I'm clean. I bin in AA, drug rehab, the whole bit. You gotta give me another chance.'

'I don't have to give you anything,' she said, outraged he would dare to even ask.

'Look,' he said, gesturing around her sumptuous living room. 'You got everything. Me – I got zilch.'

'I worked hard for what I've got while you sat around on your fat ass doing nothing.'

Emilio's small eyes turned crafty. 'If our mom was alive, what d'you think *she'd* want you to do?'

'Shove it, Emilio. Don't start with that guilt-trip shit. It doesn't work anymore.'

'I'm your brother,' he whined, still trying. 'We're the same flesh and blood. I'm one of the few people who care about you.'

Now he was going too far. 'Get the fuck out of here!' she said contemptuously.

'No,' he mumbled sulkily. 'You want me out, call the cops.'

'You think I won't?' she threatened, glancing toward the door, hoping Rodriguez would put in an appearance soon. 'What happened to your big romance in Europe?'

Emilio pulled a face. 'She was too old,' he said. 'I wasn't sittin' around for twenty years waiting for the old bag to drop.'

'You really are a piece of work,' Venus said, shaking her head. 'What did she do – dump you when she discovered what a loser you really are?'

'I left on my own,' he said resentfully.

'And you couldn't *wait* to come mooching off me again.'

Fortunately, Rodriguez chose that moment to arrive. He swept in, stopping short when he spotted Emilio.

'Ah, Rodriguez,' Venus said, 'meet my brother, Emilio. He was just leaving.'

'No, I wasn't,' Emilio contradicted.

'Yes, you are,' Venus insisted.

They glared at each other.

Rodriguez glanced from one to the other and decided it wasn't prudent to get involved.

Venus was not allowing him that privilege. She turned to him, giving a short impassioned speech. 'I don't speak to my brother,' she said hotly. 'I don't even *like* my brother. Now he's here in my house. How do I get rid of him?'

Rodriguez shrugged.

'How about throwing him out for me?' Venus said hopefully. 'I'll have the guard help you.'

'Throw me out, little sis, and you'll regret it,' Emilio warned. 'If you think what I've done up until now is bad, just you wait. I'll give the tabloids somethin' that'll blow your cushy life to pieces.'

She could see she was getting nowhere. 'I'll tell you what, I'll give you fifty bucks, go get yourself a hotel room for the night. Then, tomorrow, find yourself a job.'

Emilio's expression turned cunning. 'Make it a thousand and I'm outta here.'

'This is *not* a negotiation,' she said coldly, close to losing it.

He scratched his chin. 'I don't get it. A thousand's nothin' to you – you buy shoes cost more than that.'

Rodriguez drew her to one side. 'Give him the money,' he suggested. 'Then maybe he'll go away.'

'Emilio will never go away,' she moaned.

'At least it'll get him out of your house.'

He was right. Getting rid of her brother was the important thing.

'You don't happen to have a thousand bucks on you, Rodriguez?' she asked.

He didn't even bother answering that one.

Leaving the two men downstairs, she hurried up to her bedroom safe, closing the door behind her, remembering the time when Emilio had gotten hold of her combination, stolen pictures of her and Martin Swanson together and blackmailed her.

She took out a thousand dollars in cash and returned downstairs.

Emilio practically had his hand out.

She gave him the neat stack of bills. 'Goodbye,' she said. 'Don't come back.'

He shoved the money in his pocket, shaking his head as if *she* was the bad one. 'Little sis,' he said sadly. 'You don't have a good memory, do you?'

'For what?'

'Our childhood. The good times.'

Who was he kidding? Four brothers and a father to look after. She'd been their unwilling slave, and they'd all treated her like shit.

'Goodbye,' she repeated, hustling him to the door.

She needed a good night's rest: tomorrow was her test with Johnny Romano, and she had to impress Alex Woods. But Rodriguez being there was okay – sex would give her that special glow, better than makeup any day.

When Emilio was gone, she took Rodriguez's hand and led him upstairs to her bedroom. 'Tomorrow I must look relaxed and beautiful,' she said. 'So . . . I'd like it if you made long, leisurely love to me and then went home. Can you oblige?'

'My princess,' he said, passionate Latin eyes boring into hers, 'you are asking the right man.'

Chapter Thirty-three

'MORE CHAMPAGNE?' Michel suggested.

'Thanks,' Brigette said, allowing him to refill her glass.

The two of them were alone in his apartment now. All the guests had departed, including an angry Robertson. Brigette had overheard them having a heated discussion at the front door.

'You make me sick,' Robertson had said, in a low, furious whisper. 'You remind me of a randy old dog.'

'Don't say foolish things you will regret,' Michel had replied, remaining calm.

'The only thing *I* regret is that I moved in with you in the first place,' Robertson had said. Then she'd left, slamming the door in his face.

Brigette knew she was intruding on another female's territory, but she couldn't help herself, she found Michel hypnotically attractive, even though he was old enough to be her father.

She sat on the couch in his living room, waiting to see what kind of moves an experienced, older man made.

A waiter removed several used glasses from the coffee table and left the room, discreetly shutting the door behind him.

'A toast to you, Brigette,' Michel said, raising his glass and clinking it with hers. 'We do it the French way,' he said. 'Twist your arm around mine – like so.'

She tried to do as he asked. His arm slipped, accidentally nudging her breasts. She giggled.

'Is something amusing you?' Michel asked.

'I don't know,' she said, feeling the effect of several glasses of wine and now the champagne. 'You, me, here. A few weeks ago I couldn't even get an interview with you. Now you're my agent and I'm sitting in your apartment.'

'I will tell you what I like about you, Brigette,' Michel said, lightly touching her cheek with his fingers. 'Your naïveté. It is so refreshing.'

She didn't tell him that her mother had been a famous heiress, and that her stepfather was Lennie Golden. She didn't tell him about growing up surrounded by luxury and riches, or that she was also an heiress, due to inherit millions of dollars when she reached twenty-one.

She certainly didn't tell him about Tim Wealth or Santino Bonnatti. These were *her* secrets, and she was not about to reveal them to anyone.

'I'm not naïve,' she objected. 'I've been around.'

'You haven't been anywhere, my darling girl. You know nothing of life. You have no idea what will happen when your name is famous and your face is everywhere.'

Bingo! He was the man of her dreams, sent to protect her.

'Are you a virgin, Brigette?' he asked in a fatherly concerned voice.

She sensed he required a yes. Not that it was any of his business.

'Sort of . . .' she lied. Tim Wealth had taken her virginity when she was fifteen. Maybe one day, when she knew Michel better, she'd tell him the story.

'How charming you are,' Michel said, moving closer.

'Charming and so very sweet. Untouched by the dark side of this business.'

'What's the dark side?' she asked curiously.

'A lot of the models do drugs. Uppers, downers, cocaine . . . even heroin.'

Big secret. She knew about drugs – her coke freak fiancé had taught her plenty. Not that she'd ever indulged, she was too smart. Drugs had killed her mother.

'Does Robertson? Is that why she's so thin?'

'Too thin,' Michel said, without responding to her question.

'I wouldn't mind being thinner.'

'No!' he said forcefully. 'You are a peach, ready to be split open so the right man can gently suck the virgin nectar.'

She shivered as his arm enclosed her shoulders, long, sensitive fingers gently stroking her skin.

He was moving very slowly, too slowly, for she felt a sudden rush of desire. It was eighteen months since she'd broken up with her fiancé. Eighteen long months since a man had been anywhere near her. She wanted him to touch her breasts without waiting another moment.

She leaned back against the couch feeling quite light-headed. Michel bent to kiss her neck.

'That's nice,' she murmured encouragingly, smelling his strong aftershave and the faint whiff of garlic on his breath.

He reached behind her, clicking off the light. Then, without any warning, he rolled on top of her and began pulling at her skirt, attempting to push it above her waist.

'No!' she said sharply, sitting up. He was French – weren't Frenchmen supposed to be incredible experienced lovers? Especially *old* Frenchmen. Michel was behaving no different from any other male. Five minutes of romance then bingo – he was on an unstoppable mission to score. She hadn't waited eighteen months for a fast roll on his couch.

'Something the matter?' he asked, his crinkly blue eyes not quite so kindly.

'I – I don't want you to do that,' she said, drawing away from him.

He stood up, placing himself directly in front of her. She could see his erection straining his dark grey pants. It was practically in her face.

'Am I going too fast for you?' he asked matter-of-factly, as if there was a certain procedure they had to follow.

'Yes,' she said, averting her eyes.

'Then I apologize,' he said, picking up the champagne bottle and refilling her glass.

She waited patiently. The neck kissing was very pleasant, more would be acceptable.

He rubbed his erection as he sat down beside her. 'Drink up,' he said.

'No more, thank you,' she said, thinking that maybe it was time to go home.

'I frighten you, don't I?' he said, his voice sounding strangely thick.

'No – why would you?'

'Sex . . . growing up . . . the unknown . . . it's always frightening. I can teach you many things . . .'

A warning voice sounded in her head. Michel was not the man she'd imagined. It was definitely time for a fast exit. 'I think I'll be going now,' she said, trying to sound casual.

She went to stand up. With one swift, unexpected move he grabbed both her wrists, pinning them together and raising them above her head. Then he lay half on top of her, crushing her body beneath his on the couch.

'What are you *doing*?' she yelled, trying to push him off.

Reaching down the side of the couch, he produced a long silk scarf with which he expertly bound her wrists together.

'Stop it!' she shrieked, truly alarmed.

'Initiation can be harsh,' he said, as if speaking to himself. 'Later, when you realize what gratification you'll get from the things I will teach you, you'll thank me.'

Oh, God! Just like Santino Bonnatti, he was some weirdo sex freak.

Stay calm.

Don't panic.

'Get . . . off . . . me . . .' she said, striving to shift his weight. 'If you release me now I won't tell anyone.'

'Brigette,' he said pleasantly, 'surely you must be eager to learn?'

'Stop it, Michel. I'm warning you—'

'Warning me of what, *ma chérie?*' With another swift move he pulled the top of her dress down, exposing her breasts. 'Ah . . .' He sighed. 'Just as beautiful as I imagined.'

Then he picked her up as if she weighed nothing, and carried her into the bedroom where he threw her down in the center of his oversize four-poster bed. Before she had a chance to move, his strong hands clawed at her panties, ripping them off.

She attempted to kick him, but he was too fast for her. With a firm grip on her left ankle, he tied it to the bedpost. Then he did the same with her right one.

She began to scream.

'This is the penthouse, *ma petite coquette*. The staff have left. There is no one to hear,' he said calmly.

Except for her dress bunched around her waist she was completely naked and exposed.

Oh, God! He was going to rape her, and she was totally helpless. Tears filled her eyes, rolling silently down her cheeks.

'Don't cry,' he said, his voice gentle. 'You have my solemn promise I will not touch you.'

'Why – are – you – doing – this?' she sobbed.

'It is better this way,' he said soothingly. 'You look so

sweet . . . your furry little pussy begging for attention, so pink and ready.'

'Let me go,' she begged. 'Please – it's not too late.'

He walked to the door and threw it open. Robertson entered the room wearing a short Roman toga and nothing else.

'Thank God!' Brigette gasped, thinking rescue was at hand.

'Now,' Michel said, settling into a chair angled so that he could comfortably view the bed. 'You will learn what real pleasure is all about.'

Chapter Thirty-four

 EARLY IN THE morning Boogie ambled into her house.

Lucky was waiting for him. 'We need to have a meeting,' she said. 'Immediately.'

Boogie followed her into the den without saying a word.

Maria ran out from the kitchen, falling into step behind them. 'Me come, too, Mommy! Me too!' she sing-songed.

'No, sweetheart,' Lucky said firmly. 'You stay with CeeCee. Mommy's got business to conduct.'

'Bus-a-nez,' Maria giggled uncontrollably. 'Me come, too.'

'CeeCee,' Lucky called out.

CeeCee appeared.

The little girl began kicking and yelling. 'Wanna be with Mommy. *Wanna be with my mommy.*'

'I promise we'll go see Grandpa later,' Lucky said, 'but only if you're a good girl and eat up all your breakfast.'

CeeCee scooped Maria up and carried her back to the kitchen.

'Maria's exactly like me,' Lucky said ruefully, running a hand through her curls. 'When she wants something, she wants it now.' Boogie nodded. 'Nice vacation, Boog?' He nodded again. 'Okay,' she said. 'Let's get down to it. Here's the big news. While you were away Panther was taken over.'

Boogie let out a long low whistle.

'Yeah, I know, it was a shock to me, too.' She lit up a cigarette, drew deeply and continued. 'What I need is a full report on the woman who did this – family, where she's from, information on any company she's involved with, who are her business partners, all of that. If you have to put other people on it that's okay, but keep it confidential. And I want everything as soon as possible.'

'Right,' Boogie said, his long, thin face alert.

'And put Morton Sharkey under surveillance. Something's wrong – I don't know what. Get me stuff on his wife and kids, too. Maybe his behavior has something to do with them.'

'No problem,' Boogie said.

'Then there's a Mrs Smorg, whose only address is care of a lawyer in Pasadena. Find out who she is, where she lives. And everything about Conquest Investments, a company based in the Bahamas.'

'You got it.'

She walked over to the drinks tray and contemplated pouring herself a Scotch.

Too early. Not the answer. Besides, she still had a lingering hangover. 'Okay, I guess that's it for now.'

Boogie followed her across the room. 'Are you all right?' he asked.

She shrugged. 'The truth is I feel totally helpless until I get a full picture.'

'I'll do my best. Some of the information might not be accessible until the beginning of the week.'

'I understand that. I'm taking the kids to Gino's for the weekend.' She handed him copies of all the relevant papers. 'The moment you have something, contact me there.'

As soon as Boogie left, she hurried into the kitchen. Maria was sitting happily at the table gobbling down Frosty Pops, her big eyes tracking a Bugs Bunny cartoon on television. She seemed perfectly happy. 'Hi, Mommy,' she said, with an angelic little smile.

Lucky frowned, 'Who *was* that girl?' she said sternly. 'The one doing all that screaming.'

'Don' know, Mommy,' Maria said, gazing innocently at her mother.

'Hmm . . .' Lucky said, still pretending to be cross. 'I *think* it was . . . *you!*' She pounced on her daughter, tickling her tummy.

'No, Mommy!' Maria screamed.

'*Yes!* I think it was a naughty little girl with big eyes and a big mouth,' Lucky teased.

'Wanna see Daddy,' Maria said, her lower lip suddenly quivering, not quite sure if Lucky was mad at her or not. 'Wanna see my daddy.'

'Daddy can't be here now, sweetheart,' Lucky said softly, thinking, How do you tell a two-year-old that her daddy is dead, and that she'll never see him again? 'He's away . . . making a movie.'

'Wanna see Daddy,' Maria repeated, her small face puckering, a single tear rolling down her cheek. 'Wanna see Daddy *now.*'

Lucky picked her up, holding her close. 'Tell you what, angel. Later we'll go visit Grandpa in Palm Springs.'

'Okay, Mommy,' Maria said, the tears stopping as she stroked her mother's face. 'Love you, Mommy.'

Lucky hugged her even tighter. 'And I love you too, baby. I love you the whole wide world.'

☆ ☆ ☆

On the plane back to LA Alex slumped in his seat suffering from a monster-sized hangover. He hadn't meant to but he'd laid one on the night before with a reluctant Russell, who had been more interested in getting back to his hotel room and phoning his wife than accompanying Alex on a tour of the strip clubs.

They'd covered them all, and at each place Alex had gotten more and more despondent. These girls, these lap dancers, would throw their tits in anybody's face, wriggle their ass all over your lap, come on to you like you're the most attractive man in the world. And all they really wanted was the big buck. There was something completely soulless about sex when it was presented in such a purely commercial way. Although once they recognized it was him, Alex Woods, the famous film director, they were all over him like a pack of vultures picking away at fresh meat.

Everybody was a star-fuck.

He was pissed off at Lucky's response to his phone call: she was not reacting as planned. Too bad for her, there were plenty of women who'd cream at the chance to spend ten minutes in his company. Tin Lee would do anything he asked and so would a lot of other females he could think of.

He had that I-just-wanna-lie-down-and-die hungover feeling. And now he had to arrive back in LA ready to deal with the vast egos of Johnny Romano and Venus, because he knew it wasn't going to be Disneyland once those two got together.

When he arrived at his office he found a stack of messages to be dealt with. In his absence Lili could only do so much, many things needed his personal attention.

'Johnny Romano requires a script conference,' Lili informed him. 'He's also insisting Armani design his clothes, and as Wardrobe have quite rightly pointed out, Armani was not around during that time period.'

He'd known when Freddie had talked him into using Johnny Romano that the superstar actor was going to be trouble. He'd hired him anyway, because Johnny was exactly right for the part. Thank God he'd gone with an unknown actor for the other lead role.

'I'll deal with it,' he said shortly. 'He's coming in to test with Venus today, right?'

'He said to be sure to tell you he's only doing it as a personal favor for you.'

Alex laughed drily. 'Some thrill, huh? Dealing with stars.'

'You'll handle him,' Lili responded in her usual unruffled fashion. 'You always do.'

'You coming to the set with me today, Lili?' he asked, feeling like some sympathetic female company.

'If you want me to,' she said. She liked it when Alex was in one of his needy moods.

'What would I do without you, Lili?' He sighed, flashing a wan version of his killer smile, well aware that whatever he did she would always be his faithful fan.

'You'd manage,' she said crisply, knowing full well he wouldn't. He'd fall to pieces without her smooth organizational skills keeping everything together. Alex was not easy to work for but she'd mastered the art of keeping him happy. She met his every need – except sexually. Lili was glad that part of their relationship was over: he'd been a selfish lover, but that was okay, she'd understood he was damaged. Alex didn't know how to give because he'd never had to. His domineering mother had ruined him in that area.

'Okay, let's go,' Alex said, always on the move. 'And bring the aspirin – I'm half dead.'

☆ ☆ ☆

Every day Leslie Kane read the trades from cover to cover. She felt it was important to know exactly what was happening in town – it gave her an edge.

Today she noted that Lucky Santangelo was out at Panther

Studios. Interesting. Then she went on to read that Mickey Stolli was being reinstated as studio head. Very interesting, because it had been Mickey's wife, Abigaile, who'd discovered her and made Mickey give her her first big break.

Next she read about Venus testing for the part of Lola in Alex Woods' hot new movie *Gangsters*. She immediately grabbed the phone and called her agent.

'Why aren't I up for this role?' she demanded.

'Because it's only a cameo,' her agent replied.

'I don't care. It's a cameo in an Alex Woods film. Get me a script.'

'I'll talk to Alex today.'

'You do that. Oh, and, Quinne, in future, kindly apprise me of everything. Let *me* make the decisions.'

Who did he think he was dealing with? The same naïve girl who'd been discovered in a beauty parlor? No, she was Leslie Kane, the current darling of the American screen and, as such, she should be treated with the right amount of respect.

She decided to play it out without using her connections, as far as Mickey and Abigaile were concerned. They were her insurance: Leslie knew if she put on the pressure the part was hers.

Sometimes Leslie wondered what Abigaile would say if she knew about her sordid past. Mickey didn't remember her – even though he'd once attended a bachelor party for a big producer in her call-girl days. He and his friends had behaved appallingly: all they had been interested in was humiliating and degrading the women and getting their dicks sucked. A bunch of out-of-control pigs.

Thank God she'd had the strength to get out of that particular business after meeting Eddie. At least he'd done *something* for her.

Jeff Stoner entered the bedroom, a towel tied casually

around his waist. He had wet hair and a big grin. He looked happy, and so he should – he was living with one of the most successful young actresses in Hollywood.

'Can we go see the new Mercedes today?' he asked.

She'd told him she wanted to buy another car, and she knew Jeff was thinking that if he helped pick it out, he'd more than likely be the one to drive it.

'Maybe,' she said, keeping him hanging.

Jeff was a nice guy, but nobody could live up to Cooper.

For over two months now she'd been plotting and planning how to get Cooper back. He was ensconced in his former apartment and refused to take her calls.

What had she done? Nothing, except love him. The fact that he'd gotten caught wasn't her fault. He was blaming her and she didn't like it.

She'd loved him, now she was beginning to hate him.

But what could she do?

☆　☆　☆

Johnny Romano had the look of a true movie star, with his thick, sensual lips, sly smile, and deep-set, sexually inviting brown eyes. He was Hispanic, six feet tall and of slender build, although he'd developed his upper body enough to boast a powerful set of muscles.

Women couldn't get enough of Johnny Romano.

Johnny Romano couldn't get enough of women.

They were his addiction. Conquering them was everything. Johnny had an insatiable sexual appetite – it was not unusual for him to bed one or two women a day. Ever aware of the peril of AIDS, he protected himself with two condoms and a cavalier attitude, although he'd assured himself AIDS could never happen to *him*. He was a megastar, for God's sake, and what's more, he was a *straight* megastar. The condoms were merely a gesture in the right direction, a nod to the good Lord, because Johnny was also a devout Catholic boy.

Eighteen months previously he'd been stood up at the altar by Warner Franklin, a black lady cop. The ungrateful witch had run off with a six-foot-ten American basketball player just before they had been due to wed in Europe. Johnny had never forgiven her. As far as he was concerned, Warner had given all women a bad name.

He was pleased to be testing with Venus Maria – he'd always had a thing for her, even though in the past when he'd invited her out she'd turned him down. Now that she wanted to be in *Gangsters* it could be his chance to score.

He strode onto the set, his entourage hovering protectively around him, ready to zip into action in case any uninvited mortal approached their star without express permission.

Alex moved over to greet him. 'Johnny,' he said, as they exchanged a firm macho handshake. 'I appreciate you doing this, so does Venus.'

'That's okay, man,' Johnny said magnanimously. 'Anything for you.'

Yeah, sure. When it suits you.

'So . . .' Alex said. 'What's all this crap I hear about you wanting Armani to design your clothes? We all know Armani wasn't around then. Whoever came up with that idea is just plain dumb.'

Even the slightest hint of being thought of as dumb sent Johnny into a spin. 'Sure, Alex,' he agreed. 'Armani – ha! Who the fuck thought of *that*?'

Alex said, 'I knew it wasn't you.'

Johnny said, 'No way, man.'

'Wardrobe are designing special outfits for the character. You'll love 'em. This part is made for you, Johnny, you'll be great in it.'

'I know,' Johnny said immodestly. 'And, Alex, we gotta sit down for a script conference. There's a few things I wanna change.'

'Of course,' Alex said pleasantly, while thinking, *Fuck you, asshole. I'm not changing one word of my script.*

'Where's the lady?' Johnny asked, strolling behind the camera.

'On her way.'

'Haven't seen Venus in a while,' Johnny said casually. 'Tough broad . . . stupid, too – she made the mistake of marrying Cooper Turner when she could've had me.'

Oh, Christ! Alex thought. She never fucked him, and he's pissed.

'Good morning, Johnny,' Lili said, with a welcoming handshake.

Johnny favored her with a sleepy smile. 'Hiya, gorgeous. How come the man let you out of the office?'

'To see you, of course,' Lili replied, right on cue.

Alex smiled to himself. Lili always knew the right thing to say to keep a superstar happy.

A few minutes later Venus walked onto the set, dressed in a low-cut, clinging scarlet dress, her hair blonder than ever. She looked spectacular. Accompanying her was a smaller entourage than Johnny's: three people, hair, makeup and Anthony, whom she'd allowed to come along as a special treat.

'*Wheeew!*' Johnny whistled admiringly as he watched her approach. 'Lookin' good, girl. Lookin' creamy *hot*!'

'Hi, Johnny,' she said casually, knowing full well he wanted to get her into bed.

'You know what, baby?' he said, enveloping her in a crushing hug. 'I gotta notion it's finally gonna be *you* an' *me*. It's time, girl.'

'Let's rehearse,' Alex said, anxious to get started before they got on each other's case.

'I'm ready,' Venus said, moving out from Johnny's crushing hug.

She wasn't in the best of moods on account of Emilio: he'd called this morning saying he wanted more money. And on her way out of the house, the same stupid guard who'd let Emilio in had handed her a letter that had been left in the guard-house when the jerk was away from his post taking a leak – and it had turned out to be another porno love outpouring from her number one fan. What a weirdo! The letters made her very uneasy.

On the good side, the previous evening Rodriguez had made love to her with a great deal of finesse. She had to admit he improved every time they did it. She decided she'd definitely put him in her video, give him a thrill. He was young and eager – he deserved a reward.

Alex was a dynamo on the set. Moving fast, like a prowling black panther, he knew everything that was going on, and was into everybody's business. Nobody lagged behind on an Alex Woods set – they didn't dare.

The test went smoothly. Johnny was on his best behavior, and Venus was really into it.

When they were finished, Alex said, 'You both did a fine job, thanks.' He was impressed with Venus's performance. If it translated onto the screen, the role was hers.

'Yeah,' Johnny agreed. 'My Venus here is one hot little *tamale*, ain't'cha, baby?' He patted her intimately on the ass.

She patted him right back, pinching his butt so he felt it. 'Don't call me names, Johnny,' she said pleasantly. ''Cause I got a few I can call you. Okay?'

Johnny roared with laughter. 'She's something!'

It occurred to Venus that working with him would be a

nightmare: his ego was probably as big as the Empire State Building.

Johnny turned to Alex, his expression turning serious. 'Hey, man,' he said, 'when we gonna meet on the script? I need my changes.'

'Tell you what, Johnny, have your notes typed up and I'll take a look. Right now I'm in the middle of pre-production – no time.'

Venus knew Alex was giving Johnny the run-around. She wasn't surprised, Johnny was too stupid to get it. He was so busy being Mr Big Movie Star he didn't get anything except himself. It was a shame he wasn't more self-deprecating like Charlie Dollar. He took the whole star trip far too seriously.

She walked away from them both, proud of her performance, sure she'd done well.

Anthony was glowing with the excitement of being on a film set in such close proximity to Johnny Romano.

'You were *wonderful!*' he assured Venus on the way out. 'I'm *completely* impressed.'

She decided Anthony would also get a reward. She'd lure Ron over again, all they needed was a touch of encouragement.

Smiling, she headed for her limousine. As far as she was concerned, she'd snagged the part.

Chapter Thirty-five

BRIGETTE AWOKE in her own bed in the apartment she shared with Nona and Zandino. She lay very still for a moment, gazing blankly at the ceiling. Her tears were long gone. Everything about last night was a hazy blur. She remembered Michel bundling her into a cab with the words, 'Whatever you do, Brigette, this is *our* secret. It will only harm you if you tell stories. I know you wouldn't want our very private photo-shoot becoming public property, would you now?'

For several endless hours Michel and Robertson had made her their plaything. True to his word Michel hadn't touched her, but he'd watched *everything*. And Robertson had done everything, in spite of Brigette's protests.

She still felt vulnerable and exposed, even though her ordeal was over.

Why hadn't she listened to Nona? Although Nona had no idea Michel was such a pervert. She'd thought he was nothing more than just another sleazy playboy.

The sad truth was that Michel got off on watching women together, especially when one of them was an unwilling victim, bound and helpless.

When Santino Bonnatti had abused her, there'd been a weapon at hand and she'd used it, never experiencing a moment of remorse.

There'd been nothing to fight Michel with. She'd had no choice but to lie there and take it.

When she'd gotten home, Zan and Nona were asleep. She'd crept into the bathroom and stood under a long cleansing shower before crawling miserably into bed – where she'd lain awake for hours before falling into a troubled sleep.

Now it was morning and she could hear Nona and Zan in the kitchen. She realized she'd better get up. Be cool, she warned herself. Don't tell them what happened. It could spoil everything.

She climbed out of bed and reached for her robe, noticing purple bruises on her wrists. Looking down, she was dismayed to discover more bruises on her ankles and the insides of her thighs. She wrapped the robe around herself, pulling it tight.

'Hmm . . .' Nona said, glancing up when Brigette entered the kitchen. 'What happened to you last night?'

Did Nona suspect? No. It was just her way of eliciting information.

'Nothing much,' she said vaguely, opening the fridge and taking out a carton of milk.

Nona was determined to find out everything. 'Don't give me that nothing much bit. Did he jump you? Did the great lover get it on?'

'No,' Brigette said evasively. 'He was a gentleman.'

'Michel, a *gentleman*?' Nona snorted, not believing a word. '*Now* I've heard everything.'

Brigette poured herself a cup of coffee. Although she appeared outwardly calm, inside she was shaking.

She sat down at the table and picked up a newspaper. Zan beamed at her. Nothing ever bothered him.

'Okay, so you don't want to talk,' Nona said, a little bit put out. 'C'mon, Zan, we've got to go over to my parents' this morning.' She turned to Brigette. 'Don't forget to drop by Antonio's studio today to meet the stylist, makeup and hair people. It's all been arranged.'

Brigette nodded. 'Okay.'

'Here's the address,' Nona said, handing her a slip of paper. 'Shall I meet you there?'

'I can handle it.'

'We're catching the new Al Pacino movie tonight. Wanna come?'

'I – I don't think so.'

'Seeing Michel again?' Nona said disapprovingly.

'No, thought I'd get an early night, y'know, what with the shoot tomorrow . . .' She trailed off, wishing Nona would leave.

'Good thinking,' Nona said briskly, grabbing Zan's hand. 'By the way, my parents are planning another one of their little bashes next Friday. Keep it free.'

As soon as Nona and Zan left the apartment she picked up the phone and called Isaac, the model from the Rock 'n' Roll Jeans shoot.

He sounded as if he was asleep. Too bad. 'Remember me?' she said brightly. 'Brigette Brown, your partner in jeans.'

'Hey – baby,' he said, rousing himself. 'Gotta say I had a blast that day.'

'I need a favor,' she said, getting right to it.

'Like what?'

'Like I can't discuss it over the phone. Can we meet for lunch?'

'Sure,' Isaac said, and suggested a small Italian restaurant on Second Avenue.

Brigette arrived first and waited outside, impatiently pacing up and down the sidewalk.

Isaac pulled up five minutes later on a second-hand Harley. He parked it on the street and gave her a big embrace as if they'd been friends for years. He looked like a rap star, with his ratted hair and baggy clothes. 'I was gonna call you,' he said. 'You got there first, girl.'

'I'm good at that,' she said, summoning up a small smile.

A pretty young black woman greeted Isaac at the entrance with a familiar, 'How's it goin', man?'

'Everything's cool, Sadie,' he replied.

Ignoring Brigette, Sadie led them to a window table and handed Isaac menus.

'She's got a thing for me,' Isaac confided, as Sadie walked away. 'It's kinda dumb shit, her bein' married to the owner an' all. No use dissin' him – this bein' the best pasta in the city. I get off on their spaghetti an' clam sauce. Wanna try some?'

The thought of food made her stomach turn. She studied the menu anyway. 'Maybe I'll just have a salad.'

He settled back. 'Did ya see the pictures?'

'I did. You look good.'

'Only good?' he said ruefully. 'How 'bout *fine*, baby? Real fly an' *fine*.'

She smiled again. Had to keep smiling, otherwise she'd break down and cry. 'Okay – fine.'

'Hey,' he said, 'I heard they're takin' the big billboard in Times Square.'

'Yes, I heard that, too.'

Sadie returned, pencil poised. 'The usual, Isaac?'

He winked at her. 'Ya got it, babe. An' my friend'll have a Caesar.' As soon as she walked away he said, 'So what's the favor?'

Brigette leaned toward him, big blue eyes wide and appealing. 'Can you get me a gun?'

'Hey, *whoa*!' he said, throwing his hands up in a defensive gesture. 'What gave *you* the idea *I* can get you a gun?'

'You told me the other day if I needed anything in the city *you* were the person to ask.'

'*Sheeit!* An' I thought you were into me for my *baaad* personality.'

'*Can* you get one?' she repeated.

He pulled at his ratted hair, glancing around to make sure they weren't being overheard. 'What're you gonna do with a gun?' he asked, lowering his voice.

'It's for protection.'

'You carry a piece, baby, you gotta know how to use it.'

'Maybe you'll teach me.'

His eyes darted to a nearby table where a man and a woman sat. Satisfied they weren't listening, he mumbled, 'Lemme see what I can deliver.'

Sadie returned with their order, slamming Brigette's salad in front of her with a surly glare.

Isaac shoved a forkful of pasta into his mouth. ''S good,' he said. 'How's your salad?'

She forced herself to choke down a lettuce leaf. 'Fine.'

'No, baby,' he joked, '*I'm* fine,' adding a cavalier, 'So . . . you wanna go dancin' tonight? Hit the bars? Chow down on some soul food?'

'Sorry, I'm booked,' she said, hoping her refusal to go out with him wouldn't come between her and a gun. 'Another time would be great.'

After lunch she took a cab over to Antonio's studio, the famous Italian photographer.

A business-like young man ushered her into a side dressing room and, in reverent tones, said, 'Shh, we mustn't disturb Antonio, he's shooting. I'll let everyone know you're here.'

She sat down in front of a large makeup mirror studded with tiny theatrical lights, and stared at her reflection. She didn't look any different. She certainly didn't look as degraded and debauched as she felt. In fact, she looked exactly the same.

Only she *wasn't* the same. She was used goods. Debased by that French pig and his vile girlfriend.

After a few minutes Antonio's favorite makeup artist, Raoul, came in to check her out. Raoul was Puerto Rican with a thick greased pompadour and arched eyebrows. 'Antonio likes the idea of a retro look,' Raoul said, studying her reflection in the mirror. 'I'm into thin eyebrows. We will pluck yours out and pencil them in high and sharp. Then I shall give you beautiful cheekbones and full ruby lips.'

Sami, the hairdresser, entered next. He was tall, with a pale complexion and long fair hair worn in a braid down his back. 'Maybe we cut your hair and dye it black,' he said, standing next to Raoul, both of them inspecting her thoroughly in the mirror.

She felt like an object. 'Maybe not,' she said quickly.

'Excuse me?' Sami said, hands on hips, not used to an unknown girl answering back.

'I refuse to cut my hair,' she said stubbornly.

'And may I ask why?' Sami asked in a who-do-you-think-you-are voice.

'I have a contract with Rock 'n' Roll Jeans. They don't want me to.'

'Oh,' he said huffily. 'In that case, sweetie, I'll have to put you in a black wig.'

'This is my first cover and it's important I present my own image, not your idea of how I should look,' Brigette said, surprising herself.

Both men glared at her. How dare she have an opinion? She was a model. Models were supposed to look good, shut up and listen to the experts.

'Does Michel know you have this feeling?' Raoul said, with a bitchy edge.

'Michel's my agent, not my keeper,' she snapped.

Raoul and Sami exchanged raised-eyebrow looks and stalked from the room – obviously to report to the great Antonio that she was a difficult little bitch.

Parker, the stylist, came in next. She was a tall woman with close-cropped grey hair and a bored smile. 'I hear you're giving Tic and Tac a hard time,' she said, in a gravelly voice.

'I'm speaking my mind,' Brigette said wearily, deciding she'd had about all she could take.

'Ignore them,' Parker said breezily. 'The important thing is what you're going to wear.' She narrowed her eyes and stood back. 'I see a very contemporary look. How about this?' She plucked a short white Ungaro dress off a rail packed with clothes. 'And with it these *faux* tigerskin shoes,' she added, sweeping down and choosing them from a box full of footwear. '*Very* now. No jewelry. Pure and simple.'

'I like it,' Brigette said.

'Good. I thought you'd throw me out, too.'

'I'm not trying to be awkward,' Brigette explained. 'I simply feel I must have some say in the image I present.'

'You're absolutely right,' Parker replied briskly. 'Although, I should warn you, Antonio has *very* strong ideas, so don't be nervous tomorrow when he starts telling you *exactly* how *he* sees you. He's shooting Robertson now – do you want to take a peek?'

Brigette felt a shudder of revulsion. She never wanted to set eyes on Robertson again. 'No, thank you,' she said quickly. 'I have another appointment.'

'I'll tell Antonio. As soon as he takes a break he'll be in to see you.'

'Do I have to wait?'

'If you want Antonio to shoot your cover tomorrow. He's *very* temperamental.'

'So am I,' Brigette muttered.

'What?' said Parker, not quite sure she'd heard correctly.

'Nothing.'

Antonio entered five minutes later, Raoul and Sami hovering behind him. He was a short, flamboyant Italian, whose big specialty was photographing superstars. Brigette remembered coming to his studio when she was ten with her mother. He'd photographed them both for a mother/daughter photo spread in *Harper's Bazaar*. He'd fawned all over Olympia and ignored her. She was not about to remind him.

'You have the problem?' he asked, glaring at her with small beady eyes.

She glared right back. 'Only if you think it's a problem that I want to look like myself on my first cover.'

Antonio shrugged. What did he care? It wasn't worth a fight for one measly cover. And this girl was naturally pretty, she'd do.

'Is okay,' he said, sending Raoul and Sami into a major snit. 'Ten tomorrow. You don't be late.'

'He liked you,' Parker said, when he'd left.

'I couldn't care less,' Brigette replied. And it was true: one night and all her dreams were smashed, broken into a thousand pieces. She was tired of being the helpless victim. From now on, she realized, she had to force herself to be as hard and unfeeling as everyone around her. No more Miss Sweetness. She was on the road to recovering her self-esteem – and if she had to be tough to do it, then so be it.

Chapter Thirty-six

PALM SPRINGS was a pleasant haven. Gino was crazy about his grandkids and spent every moment with them while his wife, Paige, sat back with an indulgent smile. Paige, who was in her fifties, was still an attractive and very sexy woman.

On Sunday she and Lucky sat out by the pool watching Gino splash with little Maria in the shallow end while baby Gino kicked on a blanket under a striped beach umbrella.

'You should bring them here more often, Lucky,' Paige said, sipping a piña colada through a straw. 'Gino loves spending time with them.'

Lucky gazed out at the world through black Porsche shades. 'You're right, I will.'

'It'll make him so happy.'

Lucky picked up a Diet Coke. 'Y'know, Paige,' she said, reflectively, 'seeing you and Gino together makes me feel good. You're really great for him. You keep him in line, and that ain't easy!'

Paige smiled softly. 'Gino's the love of my life,' she said simply. 'I can't imagine why it took me so long to make a decision.'

'Well, you did have a husband in the way,' Lucky pointed out.

'Yes, that was a touch difficult. However, your father is a *very* persistent man.'

'*Nooo?*' Lucky joked.

'I wish I'd known him when he was young,' Paige continued. 'Or maybe not. I'd probably never have lived to tell the tale.'

Lucky agreed. 'He told me the other day I should make a movie of his life. I said there wasn't a rating would cover it.'

They both laughed.

Gino walked over holding Maria's hand. 'The kid an' me, we're goin' shoppin',' he announced.

'Shopping? It's ninety-two degrees,' Paige said, her copper-colored hair hidden beneath a large straw hat. 'Why not wait until later?'

Gino patted her on the thigh – a move not lost on Lucky.

Ah . . . Gino the Ram – he'd probably still be at it when he was ninety! What a guy!

'The kid an' I are gonna buy a puppy,' Gino said, fixing Lucky with an accusing look. 'It seems you promised.'

'I forgot,' Lucky said, with a sudden flash of guilt.

'Gonna get a doggie, Mommy,' Maria sing-songed proudly.

'Shall I come, too?' Lucky asked.

'No, kid, stay here with Paige – discuss girl things. Maria an' I, we got a lot to talk about.'

Maria giggled uncontrollably.

'Okay, honey, let CeeCee put you in your shorts and top, then you can go with Grandpa.'

'Doggie!' Maria screamed excitedly, jumping up and down. 'We go get doggie!'

Lucky watched Maria run off to change. She was trying hard to relax and clear her mind. It was difficult to let go, but she was determined to have these few days of peace before battle. And there *would* be a battle for she had no intention of allowing her studio to be taken over without a fight.

Before leaving LA she'd tried calling Morton Sharkey at home and his office. He'd changed his home number, and an embarrassed secretary in his office informed her Mr Sharkey was unavailable.

Yeah. Sure.

Morton Sharkey was behaving like a very naughty boy. And naughty boys got punished. Big time.

When Maria was dressed, Lucky walked out to the car with her and Gino. 'Don't choose a large dog,' she warned Gino, as he lifted Maria into his blue station wagon, securing her in her own special car seat. 'I can't deal with some giant monster roaming around my house.'

Gino cocked his head on one side. 'What's the matter, kid? You don't trust me?'

She laughed and hugged him. 'Of course I do,' she said, feeling sentimental.

'Then leave it to us, we got good sense.'

When she returned to the pool Paige asked if she wanted to go to the golf club for lunch. She declined. Much as she liked Paige and found her amusing company, sitting around at a golf club eating lunch with the ladies was not exactly her idea of a good time.

Besides, she had too much on her mind.

Nobody was getting away with taking Panther from her. Nobody.

☆　☆　☆

Venus was rehearsing. Clad in a white leotard, her hair piled on top of her head and no makeup, she sweated along with her talented troupe of dancers. She loved shooting her videos, discovering the right moves, creating a mini scenario. She regarded her videos as three-minute movies. It was always a challenge coming up with something new, raw and exciting.

This time she was using Dorian Loui, a young Chinese choreographer recommended by Ron. Dorian had created a smoky mysterious bar setting, in which Venus would slink up and down the line from man to man, seducing them one by one, dropping an item of clothing at each stop. Exactly the kind of deal she was into. Sinful sex, glossily packaged. The secret of her brilliant career.

True to her word, she'd included Rodriguez in the video. He was man number eight – the last in the line. He'd arrived at rehearsal dressed as if he was going to lunch at the Bistro Gardens. She'd taken one look and sent him out to get rehearsal clothes. Now, clad in a tank top and shorts, he was really into it. And Dorian was really into him.

'Forget it,' she whispered in Dorian's ear during a break. 'This one is definitely straight.'

'Damn!' exclaimed Dorian. 'And such manly thighs!'

She hadn't heard about her test yet. Freddie said he hoped to know by Monday. 'It's a done deal, Freddie,' she'd wanted to tell him. But she'd held back. Wouldn't do to look too cocky.

Since she'd thrown Cooper out, career-wise things seemed to be moving in a better direction. She was delighted with the video of *Sin*: it should be another controversial sensation – exactly what the public expected from her. And if she landed the role in *Gangsters*, it would give a new dimension to her career. Working with Alex Woods was a definite coup: it sent out a message that if she was good enough for Alex Woods, she was good enough for anybody.

She'd invited Ron for lunch. He arrived on the set five minutes after Anthony, who'd appeared with her mail and phone messages.

'I believe you two know each other,' she said, throwing a towel around her neck, as she strode from the set.

Ron caught up with her on the way out. 'You're a naughty little girl,' he scolded. 'What *are* you trying to do?'

'You know *exactly*, Ron. Harris Von Stepp is old, boring and controlling. You're too young to hang out with the over-the-hill gang.'

'He's an extremely powerful man,' Ron said.

She stopped walking and stared at him challengingly. 'You've got a great career going. Why do you feel you need a powerful man behind you?'

'Hmm . . .' Ron said, unable to come up with a suitable reply.

'Listen, Ron,' she continued, 'I learned a lesson when I dumped Cooper. I could have stayed and accepted his infidelities. Instead I decided to be true to myself. It works.'

'And you don't miss Cooper?'

'No,' she lied. 'Anthony's joining us for lunch. Ask him out for a drink later. What've you got to lose?'

There was a pizza restaurant in the shopping complex beneath the studio. Everyone convened there to eat.

Venus commandeered a corner table with Ron, Anthony and Dorian. 'Three fags and a superstar,' she joked. 'Who's the odd one out?'

'It's always you,' Ron remarked sagely.

'Talking of odd ones out,' she said, 'guess who turned up at my house last night?'

'Let me see,' Ron said, waspishly. 'Pacino? Stallone? De Niro? Stop me when I'm getting warm.'

'Try Emilio.'

'He's back?'

'Unfortunately. I had to give him a thousand bucks to get rid of him.'

'Mistake.'

'He wouldn't have left otherwise. I told him I was calling the police, and he said, "Go ahead." I didn't know what to do.'

Ron nodded. 'The truth is you're screwed. If you let him back in, he sells everything about you to the tabloids, and if you shut him out he's still got a story.'

'Maybe my lawyer can get him to sign a release saying he can't sell anything to the press if I pay him a couple of thousand bucks a month. What do you think?' she asked hopefully.

'I think Emilio is about as trustworthy as a rabid dog.'

Rodriguez appeared at the door of the restaurant, pausing for effect.

'Take a look at *that*,' Ron said, staring admiringly.

'*That*, my dear,' Venus said, with a possessive smile, 'is Rodriguez. *My* Rodriguez.'

☆ ☆ ☆

Lucky awoke with a start. She'd fallen asleep by the pool. Gino was still out with Maria, CeeCee had taken baby Gino inside for his nap, and Paige had gone off to the golf club for lunch.

God! Falling asleep in the middle of the day. What was happening to her?

The sun was impossibly hot. She stood up, feeling slightly dizzy, and dove into the pool, swimming several lengths.

This was insane. Her life was falling to pieces and she was sitting around a pool in Palm Springs getting a tan. When Gino arrived home she'd tell him she'd been summoned to an urgent meeting in LA and had to leave immediately. The children could stay, there was no need for them to rush back.

Boogie hadn't called. It was unlike him to lag behind on

an assignment. He'd better have plenty to tell her tomorrow, because she was getting extremely restless.

She got out of the pool and went over to the bar where she fixed herself a Scotch on the rocks.

Great! Now she was drinking in the middle of the day. Could things get any worse?

Picking up her purse, she extracted a cigarette and, without really thinking about it, opened the zippered compartment where she kept the photographs of Lennie she'd found in his hotel room.

She took them out and stared at them.

Why torture yourself? a little voice screamed in her head. *Why not tear them up and throw them away?*

No. There was something about the pictures. Something not quite right . . .

She kept on staring at them. What was it that bothered her? Was it the blond? The way Lennie was standing? He seemed almost startled as the blond wrapped her naked body around him.

It was time to find out exactly what Lennie had done on the day before the accident. She had a feeling it was important to know.

☆　☆　☆

Alex sat at an outdoor patio table at the Four Seasons with Dominique and Tin Lee. He didn't know how he'd gotten there. Somehow it all seemed to have been arranged without him. 'You're taking your mother for lunch on Sunday,' Lili had informed him. 'With Tin Lee.'

If he was forced to see Dominique, he may as well have Tin Lee along, so he'd agreed.

When he'd arrived both women were already sitting at a

table chatting away. His mother appeared quite cheerful for a change.

Tin Lee was positively glowing. 'Alex,' she said, jumping up and kissing him on the cheek.

'You look tired,' Dominique said, her critical eye sweeping over him.

Ah, yes, that was his mother – quick with the compliments as usual.

'I'm in pre-production,' he pointed out. 'There's always too much to do. I need another ten hours a day.'

'I've left several messages over the last few days,' Dominique said, concerned only with herself.

Didn't she listen to him? 'Been busy,' he explained again, signaling the waiter and ordering a vodka martini.

'It's lunch time,' Dominique pointed out, crimson lips pressed together in silent disapproval.

'Hey, guess what?' he said drily. 'I'm over twenty-one.'

'And you look it,' she responded.

Tin Lee placed her hand on his arm. 'Alex, it is so good to be here with you,' she said. 'I've missed you.'

'You see,' said Dominique, as if she was personally responsible for Tin Lee's feelings. 'The poor girl has missed you.'

'Thank you for the beautiful roses,' Tin Lee said. 'And your nice note. I'm sorry you had to stay in Las Vegas. If you had asked me, Alex, I would have flown up there to keep you company.'

He wasn't impressed that his mother and transient girlfriend were obviously bonding.

'Tin Lee and I have been talking,' Dominique said. 'Did you know, Alex, that she comes from a very good family in Saigon? Her father was a surgeon.'

'Before the troubles,' Tin Lee said quickly. 'I was a baby when the troubles began.'

'That's irrelevant, dear,' Dominique said, quietening her with a look. 'The point is, you are well bred.'

Tin Lee nodded. The waiter came over with menus. Alex ordered eggs, potato pancakes and smoked salmon.

'Fattening,' Dominique said disapprovingly. 'You're putting on weight, Alex. You should be on a diet, you're of an age where you could get heart disease.'

Jesus Christ! Why did he have to put up with this shit?

Somehow or other he managed to get through lunch.

When the waiter served coffee, Tin Lee stood up and said, 'I'm going to the little girls' room.'

As soon as she left the table his mother started. He had been expecting the usual complaints. Instead, she said, 'Alex, you've finally made an excellent choice.'

'Excuse me?' he said, by this time on his third martini.

She patted her lips with a napkin, leaving a deep crimson stain. 'Tin Lee is a smart girl from a good family.'

Was he hearing right? 'Huh?'

'It's time you were married. This is the girl for you.'

Was she fucking *crazy*?

'I've no intention of getting married,' he said, almost choking on his martini.

'You're forty-seven,' Dominique admonished him. 'People are starting to talk.'

'Yeah? What're they talking about?' he asked belligerently.

'A woman at my bridge club asked me the other day if you were gay.'

'Gay!' he exclaimed. 'Are you fucking out of your mind?'

'Kindly do not use foul language in front of me,' she said haughtily. 'I do not appreciate it.'

'Listen,' he said, endeavoring to remain calm. 'I am *not* getting married, so banish that thought. Besides, what happened to "all Asian women are hookers"?'

'Tin Lee is a *very* nice girl,' Dominique repeated. 'You could do a lot worse.'

'I've met an American woman I like,' he muttered.

Now why had he told her that? She didn't deserve any information about his life.

'Who is she?' Dominique asked, quick to pounce.

'Nobody you know,' he responded vaguely.

'I'm fond of Tin Lee. She's young and pretty. She'll make a good mother for your children. I'm ready for grandchildren, Alex. You're depriving me.'

It was always about her. 'Hey, Ma,' he said roughly. 'I got news for you. Tin Lee ain't in the running.'

Dominique gave him a crushing look. 'It's time you grew up, Alex.'

'No!' he exploded. 'It's time you minded your own fucking business and left me alone.'

And with that he got up and walked out.

☆　☆　☆

Lucky was on her way inside from the pool when Inca, the housekeeper, ran from the house flapping her hands in the air.

'Miss Lucky! Miss Lucky!' she yelled hysterically. 'Important telephone!'

'Calm down, Inca. What is it?'

'Miss Lucky – come quick! Come quick! The man on the phone – he say Mr Gino – he's been shot.'

Chapter Thirty-seven

 EVER SINCE THE night at Michel's apartment, Brigette had managed to avoid seeing him or Robertson. It hadn't been easy, but somehow or other she'd done it.

The photo session for the cover of *Mondo* had gone well. Antonio had behaved himself – in fact, he was quite charming in a gay-Italian-star-photographer way. Score one for Brigette.

Parker had been most impressed. 'He sees stardom in your future,' she'd informed her. 'Otherwise he'd shred you with his Cuisinart tongue – adorable little queen that he is.'

After the Antonio session she'd spent several days doing a series of promotional photos for the Rock 'n' Roll Jeans campaign with Luke. He was a delight to work with: the more she got to know him, the more comfortable she felt in his presence.

Nona kept on mentioning that Michel wanted to get together. She'd nodded and said, 'Yeah, sure, we'll do it.' But she never allowed Nona to pin her down to a date.

She refused to attend Nona's parents' party. Instead, she went and stayed with her grandmother, Charlotte, for a few days in her Park Avenue apartment.

It was not an enjoyable experience. Charlotte was a social shark: all she did was attend numerous parties and luncheons, and spent the rest of her time shopping for an even more extensive wardrobe. It wasn't Brigette's scene.

Without telling anyone she found a realtor and rented her own apartment. 'I'm moving out,' she informed Nona over breakfast the next day.

Nona put down the *New York Times*. 'You're doing *what*?'

'It doesn't work – you, me and Zan living together.'

'Why not?'

'I need to be by myself.'

'If that's what you want . . .' Nona said unsurely, thinking that since Brigette had signed the big jeans contract, she'd changed.

Brigette was disappointed Isaac hadn't come through with a gun. She called him. 'Well?' she demanded aggressively. 'What's happening?'

'Hey, girl, cool it. I'm tryin' . . .'

'Either you can get it or you can't,' she said flatly.

'I might have somethin' by tonight. Wanna meet?'

'Okay,' she agreed, surprising herself.

There was no reason for her to sit alone in her apartment when she could go out and have a good time.

She was ruined goods anyway. Whatever she did – it didn't matter anymore.

☆　　☆　　☆

School made Santo physically sick. He hated everything about it – the students, the teachers, the work, as far as he was concerned everybody was shit. Whenever possible he cut class and roamed around Westwood, visiting the movie theaters, catching all the latest films. What did grades matter anyway? He had plenty of money. One of these days when his mother dropped he'd inherit everything.

Sometimes he fantasized about what life would be like after Donna was gone. He'd have the big house, the cars, the money. He'd be able to do whatever he liked.

Of course, if George was still around, he'd be a problem. The ideal situation would be for the two of them to go together. In fact, he wouldn't mind blowing them away himself – taking a shotgun and zooming the two of them into oblivion.

He had a gun, a Luger pistol he'd bought from a boy at school who was desperate for money. He kept it hidden under his mattress along with a box of bullets. Anything was available at school: at lunch break the schoolyard was a virtual bazaar of drugs, weapons, porno magazines and videos.

Mohammed, the nephew of an Arab potentate, was a one-man pharmacy. He could supply anything – Quaaludes, Valium, Librium, Halcion, coke, speedballs, grass. Another boy, son of an action-movie star, was into weapons: Uzis, pistols, semi-automatics. He was capable of filling any order.

'I wanna buy a shotgun,' Santo told him.

'You got it,' the boy said. 'Gimme a coupla days.'

A shotgun would be useful to have. Then, maybe one night when George came home late from one of his business trips, he'd go downstairs and blow the miserable old bastard away.

Jeez, Ma, sorry. Mistook him for an intruder.

That would settle George – get him out the way permanently.

Mohammed was busy doling out drugs in a corner of the yard. Santo sidled over, scoring his weekly supply of grass. 'Gimme some coke, too,' he requested.

'Didn't know you were into coke,' Mohammed said, his Middle Eastern face impassive. He didn't do drugs himself, only sold them.

'Figured I'd try something stronger.'

'Something stronger?' Mohammed said, stroking his chin. 'Smoke heroin, s'better than crack.'

'Never tried either.'

'Then it's time. Girls get off on it.'

'I'm buying a Ferrari,' Santo boasted, hoping to impress.

Mohammed nodded. 'Nice wheels. Got one myself.'

Santo said, 'Yeah. Beats the shit outta my Corvette.'

Mohammed said, 'We gotta go drag racing one day.'

'Yeah,' Santo agreed.

His first friend. It felt good.

☆ ☆ ☆

Once a week at a prearranged time Donna's brother Bruno phoned to assure her everything was all right. This week he hadn't called, and Donna was nervous.

The thought of Lennie escaping always lurked at the back of her mind even though she knew it was unlikely, because the caves were like a maze – impossible to get out of if you didn't know the way. And even if he *did* escape, he was too far from anywhere to summon help.

Still . . . Bruno not calling was worrisome.

Just as she was beginning to panic, Furio phoned to inform her that Bruno had gotten in a car accident, but she was not to worry, that he, Furio, was taking care of everything while Bruno was in the hospital with a broken arm and leg.

Talking to her lost love was strange. She remembered him so vividly, and yet he had no connection to the woman she was today.

She had an empire. Furio had nothing. The love they'd once shared no longer existed.

She was still flush from her triumph with Lucky Sant-angelo. Sitting in Lucky's office and firing her had been one of the best moments she'd ever experienced.

Lucky, who considered herself such a winner, was a winner no more. Donna had reduced her to a loser in every way.

She'd taken her husband.

She'd taken her studio.

And today she was taking her father.

Yes. Revenge – Sicilian style – was extremely sweet.

Chapter Thirty-eight

IT WAS UNBELIEVABLE. Gino had been shot.

As soon as Lucky established what had happened, and found out that Maria was unhurt and safely in police custody, she raced to the hospital, desperately trying to contact Paige on the car phone, reaching her at last and telling her to get to the hospital as fast as possible.

When she arrived, Gino was being wheeled into surgery. 'OhmiGod!' she whispered, leaning over the trolley taking him into the emergency operating room. 'Daddy ... Daddy ...'

Gino had the strength of a horse, he was still alive and talking. 'The bastards – finally – got – me,' he gasped in a strange gurgly voice.

She clutched his hand, running alongside the trolley. '*Who* finally got you?' she asked urgently. 'Tell me who.'

'Dunno,' he mumbled. 'I'm an old man. Thought the wars were long over ...' He trailed off, unable to continue. Blood bubbled from a corner of his mouth and trickled down his chin.

She tried to remain calm. 'Where was he hit?' she asked the doctor.

'Missed his heart by a fraction of an inch,' the doctor replied. 'The other bullet's in his thigh.'

Her throat was dry with the fear of losing him, but she said it anyway. 'Will he make it?'

'We'll do our best.'

What if their best wasn't good enough?

What if her father died?

It was unthinkable.

She left the hospital and broke all records driving to the police station to fetch Maria. Her little daughter was sitting forlornly in the corner of the precinct room, thumb stuck firmly in her mouth, eyes wide with fright, clutching the lead of a frisky Labrador puppy. 'Mommy, Mommy!' she cried, jumping up when she spotted Lucky. 'Bad man shot Grandpa! Baaad!'

'I know, sweetie, I know,' she said, picking Maria up and hugging her tight. 'How did it happen?' she said, turning to the policeman on duty.

'Our report says Mr Santangelo was walking to his car in the open parking lot of the shopping mall. According to eye witnesses a man came out of nowhere and fired two shots at him. Then the perpetrator took off in an unmarked car and a shopkeeper called the police.'

'Was it a robbery?'

'This kind of random crime happens all the time.'

'Was it a robbery?' she repeated, her voice rising slightly.

'Doesn't look like it.'

She turned to leave.

'Uh, ma'am,' the cop called after her, 'Detective Rollins would like to speak to you.'

'Not now,' she said. 'I'm on my way back to the hospital. Have him contact me tomorrow.'

Her mind was considering all possibilities. First Lennie's death, then the loss of her studio, now Gino getting shot. This was starting to look like more than just a run of bad luck.

She drove Maria back to the house, made sure she was all right, then left her and the new puppy with CeeCee, and immediately rushed back to the hospital where Gino was still in surgery.

Paige was huddled on a seat in the corridor, her face streaked with tears. She stood up as soon as she saw Lucky and clung to her. 'Why would anyone shoot my Gino?' she sobbed.

'Nobody seems to know, Paige.' She hesitated before continuing. 'Uh . . . was he involved in any new business dealings?'

Paige shook her head.

'Do you know if he has any enemies?'

'The police were here asking the same thing.'

'What did you tell them?'

'That he's an old man who loves his garden.'

'Right,' Lucky said thoughtfully. She knew what Gino would say if he was around. *You heard of criminal justice, kiddo? You know what that means? Justice for the freakin' criminals. You gotta keep the cops out of it. We'll deal with it ourselves.*

Ah, yes, he'd taught her well. The police would never catch the man who'd shot him. Therefore, it was up to her to track him down.

If he lived she'd have the strength.

If he didn't . . .

After what seemed like an eternity the doctor emerged from surgery. He had grey hair and hang-dog bushy eyebrows. At least he looked capable, not like some slick-haired TV actor.

Lucky tried to read his face as he approached. Was it good news? Bad? She couldn't tell. Taking a deep breath she composed herself and stood up to greet him, for Paige was immobile.

'We were able to remove both bullets,' the doctor said, in a deep sonorous voice. 'However, there was considerable loss of blood, and due to your father's age . . .'

Her stomach dropped. She was icy cold with the fear of losing him.

Gino . . . Daddy . . . I love you so much . . .

Paige suddenly sprang into action. 'Is he alive?' she cried, jumping to her feet.

'Yes,' the doctor said. 'Depending on his constitution there's a possibility he'll pull through. I advise you not to get your hopes up. We'll do our best.'

Their best might not be good enough. Then what? Lucky knew Gino couldn't live forever, but she'd never imagined the end would come with an assassin's bullet.

'He'll make it,' she said, a determined thrust to her jaw. 'Gino's strong.'

'I hope so,' the doctor said, his eyes revealing that he didn't think so.

'When can we see him?' Lucky asked.

'He's in recovery now. We'll keep him there for a few hours. If all goes well we'll transfer him to intensive care later. You can visit him then.'

Lucky took her stepmother's arm. 'C'mon,' she said, noticing how pale Paige looked. 'I'm taking you home for an hour.'

Paige shook her head. 'I'm not leaving,' she said stubbornly. 'I have to stay close to Gino in case he needs me.'

Lucky understood. 'Okay. I'll be back soon. Is there anything I can get you?'

'No, nothing.'

Lucky hurried from the hospital, her mind in overdrive. As soon as she got in her car she picked up the phone and called CeeCee. 'I'm on my way home,' she said. 'Try to reach

Boogie on his pager. When he calls back, keep him on hold until I get there.'

Gino's words repeated in her head. *Thought the wars were long over* . . .

What did he mean? *What* wars? He'd made a few enemies over the years, but that was long ago. Gino had been a legitimate businessman for at least thirty years. They'd had a life-long battle with the Bonnatti family, but when Carlos Bonnatti had fallen from the nineteenth floor of his Century City penthouse, the battle had been finally over, for Carlos was the last of the Bonnattis.

She couldn't get a handle on it. Who would want to shoot an old man? Maybe the police were right and it *was* a random crime, a robbery gone wrong.

Only what were they robbing Gino of? He was an old man driving a station wagon, accompanied by a child and a puppy. He was hardly a potential victim dressed the way he was – in casual shorts and a shirt. He wasn't even wearing a watch.

As she drove toward the house it occurred to her that Gino might not be safe in the hospital. Should she put a guard on him? If it hadn't been a random crime, and somebody *had* been out to get him, they'd be monitoring his progress. Yes it would be prudent to have somebody at the hospital and another armed guard at the house, especially as her children were alone with only CeeCee and Inca to protect them.

She shuddered when she thought of what could have happened. If Maria had gotten in the line of fire . . . If the bullet had smashed into her little girl . . .

It didn't bear thinking about.

CeeCee greeted her at the door. 'I gave Maria a mild sedative and put her to bed.'

'How's she been?' Lucky asked anxiously.

'The puppy kept her distracted.'

Lucky sighed. 'I guess she's too young to understand what really happened.' CeeCee agreed. 'Did Boogie call back yet?'

'He's waiting on the line.'

Lucky hurried into the library, sat behind Gino's desk and picked up the phone.

'I had to be sure of my facts before I contacted you,' Boogie said.

'Forget it, Boog. Gino's been shot.'

'*What?*'

'He's in intensive care. They removed two bullets. I want guards at the hospital and at the house. Arrange it immediately.'

'It's done, Lucky. I'm on my way there. I have a lot to tell you.'

'Everything else can wait,' she said. What did her studio matter when her father was lying in hospital battling for his life?

She put down the phone and began opening the drawers of Gino's desk, searching methodically for a clue, some indication that he was involved in any kind of business venture.

There was nothing to be found except a pile of betting sheets. She picked one up and studied it. Gino enjoyed betting basketball, two hundred here, three hundred there, he'd never been a big gambler – after all, he'd owned hotels in Vegas and seen how recklessly people could lose their money.

So it wasn't like they were after him for an unpaid gambling debt. This was minor stuff.

Inca knocked on the door. 'Miss Lucky,' she said hesitantly, 'there's a Detective Rollins here.'

'Show him in.'

Detective Rollins was a balding middle-aged man with an unfortunate smirk. He spoke in a gruff voice. 'Sorry about your father,' he said, not sounding sorry at all. 'You *are* Lucky Santangelo?'

'That's right,' she replied, wondering how he knew her name.

'I've been looking up the family history,' he said, with a smug little sneer. 'Thought there might be something you wanna share with me.'

'Like what?' she said blankly, drumming her fingers on the desk.

Detective Rollins shrugged. 'You know . . .'

'*What?*' she repeated, fast losing patience with this jerk.

He managed to wipe the smirk off his face long enough to say, 'If this is a mob hit we don't appreciate it around here. This is a quiet community.'

'What the hell are you talking about?' she said sharply, black eyes flashing.

He moved closer, leaning across the desk, his big fat fingers splayed across the dark wood.

'I'm talking about your family's reputation. I got a file on the Santangelos from the FBI.'

She was outraged. 'My father's lying in the hospital, and all you can do is get files from the FBI. Why aren't you out finding the man who shot him?'

The sneer was back. 'I was hoping you'd be able to tell me who that might be.'

She jumped up. 'I don't believe this!' she exclaimed angrily. 'My father isn't connected in any way, if that's what you're implying.'

'C'mon, Lucky,' he said, like she was the biggest liar he'd ever come across.

'Miz Santangelo to you,' she said icily.

The detective shifted his weight and glared at her. 'Okay, *Miz* Santangelo, your father has a rap sheet. He fled the country on tax avoidance. He's done jail time for murder. You wanna tell me this wasn't mob-related?'

She hated this man, he was a moron. 'If you were doing your job, you'd be telling *me* what happened. Not making dumb assumptions.'

He backed off. 'Okay, okay, I know you people went legit years ago, but that doesn't mean you don't have enemies.'

Yeah, right – like she'd tell *him*. 'Detective Rollins, if that's all you have to say I suggest you leave.'

He walked to the door and stopped. 'If Gino comes out of this, we'll be watching him,' he said, wagging a warning finger at her.

'Fuck you,' she said.

'Yeah, you're a Santangelo all right,' he sneered.

She slammed the door behind him. She didn't need some moronic detective poking his long nose into their affairs. Everything was legitimate and had been for years. It wasn't fair that Gino got shot and the cops regarded *him* as the criminal. *We'll be watching him.* What kind of shit was *that*?

'I'm going back to the hospital,' she informed CeeCee. 'When Boogie gets here, send him over.'

She stopped in Gino and Paige's bedroom and grabbed a sweater for Paige. On the way out she went by the bar and took a swig of Scotch from the bottle. She needed something to keep her going.

At the hospital there was no change in Gino's condition. 'He's fighting,' Paige said, her eyes puffy and red-ringed.

'He'll win,' Lucky assured her, putting a comforting arm around her stepmother's shoulders. 'Here, I brought you a sweater. Put it on, you're shivering.'

'Will he be all right?' Paige asked hopefully. 'Will he, Lucky?'

'Of course,' she said, more confident than she felt. 'You know Gino, he's not going out this way. Gino will go in his own bed, most likely making love to you.'

'That's a cheerful thought,' Paige said, summoning a weak smile.

'And he'll probably be around ninety-eight at the time,' Lucky added. 'Yeah, ninety-eight and feisty as hell.'

She used her influence and commandeered a small office with a phone. Then she sent out for food and forced Paige to eat. Around seven o'clock Boogie arrived, accompanied by two men both in their early thirties.

'This is Dean and Enrico,' Boogie said. 'Dean will stay here, Enrico's gonna cover the house. They're both aware of the situation.'

Lucky nodded her approval.

'We must talk,' Boogie said.

'Drive Enrico over to the house,' Lucky instructed. 'When you get back we'll sit down.'

'Who were those men with Boogie?' Paige asked, as soon as they'd left.

'I'm putting a little protection in our lives,' Lucky explained, trying not to alarm her. 'Y'know, Paige, we're both aware of my father's, uh . . . colorful past. This is called taking precautions.'

Paige plucked a Kleenex from her purse and blew her nose. 'I don't understand any of this.'

'I'm being extra careful,' Lucky continued. 'Gino would do the same if it was me lying in that bed.'

When Boogie returned, he and Lucky took the elevator down to the hospital cafeteria. Lucky sat at a Formica-topped table, while Boogie went up to the counter and got two cups of coffee. He came back and handed one to her.

She sipped the hot liquid. 'I'm anxious to know about Donna Landsman,' she said. 'Only I'm not sure if this is the time for you to fill me in. It's more important that you find out who shot Gino, and why.'

'They could be connected,' Boogie said.

She frowned. 'Connected? How?'

'When you hear what I have to say, you'll understand.'

She felt a shudder of apprehension. 'Go ahead.'

'I found out about Donna Landsman – the companies she's involved with, the takeovers she attempted and didn't succeed. The ones she won. I also have information about her personal life.'

'Yes?'

'She's married to George Landsman.'

Lucky took another gulp of hot black coffee. 'Is he an active business partner?'

'Very active. He manages the money. He's also a former accountant with a surprising history.'

She leaned across the table. 'Like what?'

'Like he was Santino Bonnatti's accountant.' A long, silent pause. 'Lucky, Donna Landsman is Santino Bonnatti's widow, Donatella.'

A chill pervaded her body. 'Oh my God!' she exclaimed.

And suddenly everything became startlingly clear.

Chapter Thirty-nine

AFTER WALKING OUT on his mother, Alex drove directly to his beach-house, his private domain – pristine and modern. He never allowed anybody to visit. Women, he took to his apartment; business meetings were office affairs; and since he never entertained, the house was his – no intruders.

He'd made the mistake of bringing his mother there once. That was enough. 'It's cold,' she'd said, inspecting everything with a critical eye. 'You need a woman's touch.'

What did she know? She lived in an apartment that was so over-decorated it was ridiculous. The minimalist style he'd settled on suited him. He liked clean-cut lines and flowing rooms.

He employed a Japanese couple who lived on the property. They never disturbed him unless he requested their presence.

The house stood on a high bluff overlooking the ocean. It was spacious with a huge terrace that swept around in a half-circle incorporating two waterfalls, lush greenery and a pond with exotic fish. When he had time to meditate – which wasn't often – this was where he came.

Alex considered his house to be the most peaceful place on earth. It was his private retreat where he could not be touched by the outside world.

Although he'd had several martinis at lunch, he'd promised

himself to never drink at the beach-house. Today he made an exception, pouring himself a large vodka. Then he picked up a copy of his script, and strolled out to the terrace.

He hadn't realized it before he got her private number, but Lucky also lived at the beach. This did not exactly make them neighbors, as he'd found out her house was in Malibu. His was further along the coastline at Point Dume. Still . . . it was nice to know that she probably enjoyed the ocean as much as he did.

He'd left several messages on her answering machine. So far she'd failed to call back.

He pulled out a lounger, took off his shirt, and began going through his *Gangsters* script with a red pencil. He drove his production people crazy. Every day he made changes, and he'd continue to do so throughout the movie.

At around five o'clock the doorbell rang. He let it ring three times before he got up, put on his shirt, and went to the door.

Standing there was Tin Lee.

'What the *hell* are you doing here?' he asked, frowning ferociously.

'Alex,' she said, standing her ground. 'Your mother was worried about you. She insisted I came.'

'What *is* this shit?' he roared, furious at her intrusion. 'That woman doesn't run my life. She has no right to tell you where I live. *Fuck!*'

Tin Lee stood up for herself. 'What do you mean, Alex, no right? We have been lovers. How can you be so cold toward me?'

Goddamn it! This was just what he didn't need.

'Sorry,' he muttered, realizing it wasn't her fault. 'My mother drives me insane – you know that. You've seen what she's like when she's in action.'

Tin Lee stretched out her hand. 'Alex, this is a tense time

for you. Your movie is starting, everything is happening. Please . . . may I come in for a moment?'

He did not want his house invaded. Yet how could he send her away? She'd driven for over an hour to get here. 'Sure, come in,' he said reluctantly.

She stepped into the front hall, pretty and petite in her white sundress and strappy sandals. 'This is wonderful!' she exclaimed, looking around. 'Why do you not live here all the time?'

'It's my weekend retreat,' he said. 'I come here to think, to work.'

'I'm sorry if I'm intruding.'

'Hey, listen, it's not you. I'm fucked up because Dominique drives me so goddamn crazy.'

Tin Lee was sympathetic. 'Why do you let her drive you crazy, Alex?'

'Because she's my mother. Don't you understand? It's like a conundrum. There's no rhyme or reason for it.'

He walked out onto the terrace. Tin Lee followed him.

'Do you want a drink?' he asked, thinking about another vodka for himself.

'No, Alex,' she said boldly. 'I would like you to make love to me.'

It was the last thing he felt like doing.

Before he could stop her she unzipped the back of her white sundress. It fell in a heap at her feet.

'No!' he said.

'Yes, Alex,' she said persuasively. 'Why shut me out, when you *know* you want me?'

She moved toward him – a perfectly formed, exquisite creature in white bikini panties and nothing else, her small breasts bouncing only slightly, the dark brown nipples startlingly erect.

He shouldn't have drunk so much. He felt himself becoming aroused.

Her hand reached for the zipper on his pants, quickly pulling it down.

What was that famous expression? Ah, yes . . . *A standing prick has no conscience.*

Hey, he was free, white and over twenty-one, he could do what he liked. He didn't have anyone to be faithful to.

Tin Lee sank to her knees, grappled with his belt and pulled his trousers and underwear down around his ankles.

He placed his hands on the back of her glossy black hair, driving himself hard into her petite mouth.

She almost gagged, managed not to, pulled back and said, 'Please, Alex, can we go in the bedroom?'

'No,' he said, hard as the proverbial rock. 'I like it out here.'

She'd come to him, he hadn't invited her. Now she could take the consequences.

☆ ☆ ☆

The music was loud, throbbing and sensual, the set smoky and dark, with moody lighting creating just the right decadent atmosphere.

Venus was high on the adrenalin of performing, she loved what she did. The only problem was that this was their eighth take, and Rodriguez was blowing it every time. He simply wasn't a professional.

It was her fault. She had only herself to blame for including him.

'Honey,' she said, drawing him to one side, thinking she only had herself to blame for including him. 'You've *got* to relax. All you have to do is stand at the bar while I slither down your body, rip off your shirt and kiss you. Now, we've done that enough times in real life, so what's the big deal?'

He was embarrassed. Rodriguez liked to excel at everything he did, and this was not turning out well. 'I'm sorry,' he said, eyes downcast, long lashes casting a faint shadow.

'Think of me, baby,' she purred seductively. 'Forget about the camera and concentrate on *me*.'

'I will,' he assured her.

'Oh, and, Rodriguez, whatever you do, *don't* stare into the camera lens. Okay?'

'Yes, my darling,' he said. 'Next time will be perfection.'

'It better be 'cause you're wearing me out,' she muttered under her breath as she went over to confer with Dorian.

'We can't replace him now,' Dorian said. 'We have to finish shooting this set-up today.'

'I know.'

'When *are* you girls going to learn?' Dorian sighed, pursing his lips. 'There's only one place for a hard cock and that's at home.'

Venus couldn't help giggling. 'Maybe I should take him to my trailer and fuck him,' she mused. 'That'll relax him!'

Dorian raised a startled brow. 'Ooh, you've got a mouth on you, girl!'

'And I suppose *you* don't,' she retorted sharply.

Finally, after another two hours, Rodriguez got it. Everyone sighed with relief.

As soon as they were finished Venus rushed to the phone and spoke to Freddie. 'I was supposed to hear from you today,' she said accusingly.

'I'm waiting to get a call from Alex,' he said. 'With the changes at Panther, everything's chaos.'

'I know, Freddie, but *Gangsters* starts shooting any minute. I have a schedule to work out.'

'As soon as I reach Alex I'll contact you.'

She wasn't satisfied with his reply. 'Is it Mickey Stolli?' she demanded. 'Is *he* against using me?'

'I haven't discussed it with Mickey.'

She wasn't sure she believed him. 'Okay, okay, call me when you hear.'

One of the background dancers passed by. 'Just wanna say it was a pleasure working with you, Venus,' the guy said, with exactly the right amount of reverence in his voice.

'Thanks,' she replied, checking him out. He was almost as good-looking as Rodriguez.

What was this thing she had about handsome men? *All package and no calories*, that's what Ron said.

She stifled a giggle, observed Rodriguez chatting up the makeup girl, and beat a hasty retreat.

Her car and driver were waiting outside the studio. 'Home!' she exclaimed, collapsing on the backseat. She wasn't in the mood for sex or conversation. Every muscle in her body ached. All she wanted to do was soak in a hot tub.

As they entered her driveway, the same guard who'd stopped them before waved the limo to a halt.

Venus wound down her window. 'What now?' she asked impatiently.

'Your husband, Cooper Turner, is here.'

'Where?'

'I thought it was all right, since he's your husband, to let him in the house.'

Her green eyes narrowed with fury. Was this guy the moron of the century or what? 'You're fired,' she said.

☆ ☆ ☆

'You havin' a good time?' Isaac asked.

'I'm having a *great* time.' Brigette giggled.

And, yes, she was having a good time. Sitting in a crowded

restaurant with Isaac, eating soul food, surrounded by his friends. She'd downed a couple of vodkas and shared a joint with one of the girls in the ladies' room.

She'd started off the evening uptight, but the drinks had relaxed her, and the joint had made her feel a lot more at ease with this new group of friends.

'Hey, you gotta get down,' Isaac said. 'You got this uptight thing goin'.'

'That's 'cause I usually mix with uptight people.'

'Yeah, well, now you gotta hang loose, y'know what I'm sayin'?' He handed her a spare-rib. 'Chew down on it, girl, get your hands good an' greasy. Y'know how to do that, doncha?'

'I know how to do that,' she replied, taking the rib and suggestively sucking off the meat.

'That's more like it,' Isaac said, laughing.

An hour later they piled out of the restaurant and made their way to a private club. Brigette had been to several of the more upscale Manhattan discotheques, but the one Isaac took her to was down in the Village, dark, smoky and very funky.

He had not gotten her a gun. 'I'm workin' on it,' he'd assured her.

By this time she didn't care.

The group they were with consisted of Isaac, two anorexic black models, one spaced-out white guy, one over-excited Puerto Rican, and a gay Chinese dancer in drag. Nona wouldn't approve. Nona liked to run with the more successful crowd. This group was on the edge – exactly where Brigette had decided she belonged.

They stayed at the first discotheque until three in the morning, then they moved on to another place in Manhattan, which didn't start until dawn. On the way they stopped at a coffee shop devouring pastrami sandwiches and cheesecake all round. 'We need our strength,' Isaac joked. 'You're gonna be dancin' all night, girl – an' then some!'

He was very cute and friendly. When he kissed her on the dance floor it seemed totally natural. She responded with plenty of heat.

'Wanna come back to my place?' he whispered in her ear.

She didn't know what time it was. She didn't care. 'Yes,' she said.

They took a cab back to his one room in the Village. As soon as he closed the door, he began to kiss her, starting with her mouth, quickly moving down to her neck. His hands were all over her, and she could feel his urgent desire.

She responded eagerly.

She wanted to be with a man.

She wanted to be with Isaac.

It was the only way to block out all memories of Michel and the humiliating things he'd forced her to do.

Isaac peeled her dress off. She didn't mind at all. In fact, she was into it.

They fell on the bed, and he was on top of her, his hands on her breasts, luring her to the point of no return.

Just as he was about to enter her she had a hazy thought. 'Do you have . . . protection?' she gasped.

'Sure, baby,' he responded, not stopping what he was doing for one moment. 'Around here there's a dude with a gun on every street corner.'

He laughed. She giggled.

Who cared anyway?

She gave herself up to the night.

Chapter Forty

GINO WAS RELEASED from hospital a week after being shot. His doctor remarked that he had the constitution of an ox. Yeah, Lucky thought, he should only know. It would take a lot more than a couple of lousy bullets to finish Gino Santangelo.

Lucky hadn't wanted to tell Gino what was going on while he was in the hospital, but as soon as they got him home and settled in his own bed, she laid out the facts.

'Santino Bonnatti left a widow,' she said, restlessly pacing up and down next to his bed. 'Donatella.'

'So?' Gino said.

'So,' Lucky continued, 'Donatella resurrected herself. After Santino died, she married his accountant, got herself an education and a make-over, and today she's a successful businesswoman going by the name of Donna Landsman.'

'What're you tellin' me?' Gino said, struggling to sit up.

'It's Donna who's carrying on the vendetta against the Santangelo family.'

'A goddamn *woman*?' he bellowed, his face grim.

'Yes, Gino, a woman.'

'Are you sayin' the bitch put a hit on me?' he said heatedly.

'I'm certain she did,' Lucky replied. 'It was her who plotted to take over my studio. And somehow she arranged

340

to have Lennie killed.' A beat. 'That car crash was no accident.'

'What're we gonna do about it?' Gino said furiously. 'What the fuck we gonna do?'

Lucky's eyes were black and deadly. 'There's no we, Gino. You're eighty-one years old. You've just been through a very traumatic experience. You can't be involved.'

Gino clenched his jaw. 'Says who?' he demanded.

'Says me, Gino.'

Their eyes locked. Once he would've tried to control his willful daughter. Now he had no chance.

'I've sent Maria, the baby and CeeCee to stay with Bobby and his relatives in Greece,' Lucky continued, matter-of-factly. 'This time I'm dealing with things *my* way.'

'What's your way?' he asked warily, knowing full well what a wild one his daughter was.

She laughed mirthlessly. 'Remember the family motto? "Don't fuck with a Santangelo".'

He shook his head. 'Whaddya think you're gonna do, Lucky? Blow this fuckin' bitch away?'

'No . . . not yet, anyway. Right now I'm working on regaining control of enough shares so I can throw her out the same way she did me.'

'Listen t' me, Lucky,' he said warningly. 'Things are not like they used to be. This ain't the old days when violence ruled.'

'I know,' she said, thinking that he was finally growing old.

'Paige tells me there's some detective poking his dick into our business, tryin' to find out things. In your position you gotta be careful.'

'Detective Rollins,' she said dismissively. 'Don't worry about him, he's an asshole. He's under the impression this was a mob hit.'

'In a way it was, huh?' Gino shook his head disbelievingly. 'How *about* that?'

'The main thing is that you're protected. I've arranged for round-the-clock guards. Now that you're safely home I'm leaving for LA this afternoon. You still have your gun, don't you?'

'Does the Pope keep a Bible?'

She smiled in spite of everything. 'You take it easy, Gino. Remember, you're not as young as you used to be, even though you *think* you are.'

He laughed ruefully. 'In my mind I kinda stopped at thirty-five. Hey, kid, I was pretty hot at thirty-five.'

'You're pretty hot now,' she said, going over to the bed and kissing him.

'Listen,' he said, his tone suddenly serious. 'One phone call an' this bitch is taken care of. Not one fuckin' problem.'

'No, Gino. That's not the way I want to handle it.'

'It's the clean way.'

'It's not my way.'

'Okay, okay.'

She stood back from the bed and repeated a phrase from her childhood. 'So I'll see ya, Gino.'

He grinned, remembering. Then his black eyes met her black eyes, a match in every way, and he said, 'So I'll see ya, kid. Don't do nothin' *I* wouldn't do.'

She grinned back at him. 'That's what I like – plenty of leeway.'

Boogie was waiting downstairs. He already had her luggage loaded in the trunk of the car and was ready to go. Lucky slid into the passenger seat. 'You drive,' she said, impatient to get back to LA.

Boogie had put together an excellent team of security. Two armed men were on alternate duty at the Palm Springs estate; Enrico had accompanied the children and CeeCee to Greece; and Dean was staking out her beach-house.

On the ride back she tried to sleep – a useless exercise, for too many thoughts were buzzing around in her head.

Donna Landsman – Donatella Bonnatti. The woman had waited four years to exact revenge for her low-life, child-molesting husband's death, and she'd done it in a clever and devious fashion. As far as Lucky was concerned, Donna was a far more dangerous adversary than the male Bonnattis had ever been.

However, clever as she was, she had no idea how swift and deadly Santangelo justice could be.

☆ ☆ ☆

Lucky relived the scene in her office. She should have known, she should have seen it in Donna's eyes. Why hadn't she noticed the hate there? Why hadn't she realized before?

She killed Lennie. My Lennie. My love.

Donna Landsman doesn't deserve to live.

Lucky knew she was going to have to take care of her personally. Whatever Gino said, there was no other way.

First she'd get her studio back. *Then* she'd exact the appropriate revenge for the shooting of Gino and Lennie's death.

Boogie drove fast, respecting her silence. She reflected that in times of trouble Boogie always came through – he'd proven himself so many times in the past. He was also the best investigator in the business: within forty-eight hours he'd discovered everything there was to know about Donna Landsman. He'd accessed her tax returns, bank statements, credit lines. He knew who her doctors were, her dress size, where she lived, what cars she drove. He even came up with a full record of all the plastic surgery she'd undergone. 'You know me,' he'd said, with a modest shrug. 'Once I start digging, it's all over.'

He'd also found out that Morton Sharkey kept a very young girlfriend. Her name was Sara Durbon and she lived in an apartment Morton paid for.

The lawyer in Pasadena who looked after Mrs Smorg's shares had refused to give up the address of his client. 'Don't sweat it,' Boogie assured Lucky. 'I've got someone on it. We'll be into his files any moment.'

As far as Conquest Investments were concerned, Boogie's contacts were still digging through reams of red tape, trying to find out exactly who controlled the company.

They arrived at the Malibu house just past noon. Boogie followed Lucky into the front hallway. 'What's our first move?'

'When I have all the information in front of me, that's when I'll strike,' Lucky said. 'Today I have to take care of some personal business. Tomorrow I'll visit Sara Durbon – see what she has to tell us about her very married boyfriend.' She paused for a moment, reaching for a cigarette. 'Y'know, Boog, Morton Sharkey is the key to my getting back the studio.'

'There's somebody I'd like you to see later,' Boogie said. 'I can have him here at six.'

'Who?' she asked curiously.

'A person you'll be interested in talking to.'

She'd learned never to question Boogie.

It was a relief to be home, even though her mailbox was full and the answering machine jammed with messages, including several from Alex Woods.

She summoned Kyoko, who hurried over, anxious to return to work. Although he'd quit Panther with Lucky he knew everything that was going on there, because a close friend of his still worked at the studio: according to all reports, Mickey Stolli was running riot like a crazed despot, firing people and replacing them with his own team.

'Is he changing the schedule?' she asked.

'Not on anything in actual production,' Kyoko replied.

'How about *Gangsters*?'

'It's still a go.'

'And the Landsman woman, is she around?'

'Lunches every day in the commissary at your table.'

Lucky burned with fury, imagining Donna sitting there, gloating, thinking she'd won, thinking she'd outsmarted Lucky Santangelo.

Not for long . . .

Oh, no, not for long . . .

And retribution will bring with it a taste of hell.

Never fuck with a Santangelo.

Chapter Forty-one

WHEN WAS THIS torture going to end? Lennie didn't know how much more he could take.

The last time one of his captors had come to the cave with food, he'd kicked it back in his face.

The man had yelled a stream of foreign curses and fled.

Lennie hadn't cared. 'FUCK YOU – I DON'T GIVE A SHIT ANYMORE,' he'd screamed after him. 'DO YOU HEAR ME, ASSHOLE? I DON'T CARE IF I EAT, I DON'T CARE IF I SLEEP. I'D SOONER BE DEAD THAN TRAPPED IN THIS HELL-HOLE.'

He knew he must look like a crazy man with his long straggly beard, matted hair and filthy torn clothes – but what did it matter? There was no one to see him.

A week ago he'd discovered a jagged piece of rock embedded in the walls of the cave. It had taken him a while but eventually he'd managed to pry it free. Ever since, he'd been concentrating on grinding the chain around his ankle. For several hours a day he worked on the rusty chain praying for results.

Yeah. Who was he kidding? Maybe in another six months.

For the last few days only one of the men had appeared with his food. Nobody had told him why. Nobody spoke to him and it was driving him *fucking crazy*!

What would happen if they both dropped dead? Would he be left to starve to death? Did anyone else know he was there?

Over the weeks, months, he'd tried to communicate with them. They refused to listen. They were robots, fucking robots.

Today he was putting into operation a plan he'd been thinking about for a while. When the man came in with his food, he was going to grab him and hold the jagged piece of rock to his throat. Then he'd threaten to slit the bastard's jugular unless they released him.

Desperate people did desperate things.

'HEY, LUCKY,' he yelled, 'HOW YA DOIN' TODAY, KIDDO?'

No, mustn't call her kiddo – that's what Gino calls her. Mustn't get between her and Daddy.

She had a strong bond with her father. Lennie wasn't jealous, he knew how much they'd gone through together.

'You love me even more, don't you, babe?' he muttered feverishly. 'You an' me – we're soulmates.' Then he began yelling again. 'WHERE ARE YOU, LUCKY? WHAT ARE YOU DOING? WHY AREN'T YOU GETTING ME THE FUCK OUT OF HERE?'

Sometime in the late afternoon he heard someone approaching. Whenever his captors came, he could make out the echo of their footsteps long before they appeared. He braced himself – ready for anything. This was it. This was the day he was either going to die or escape.

Fuck! He could feel his heart pounding in his chest as he waited, bouncing around like a ping-pong ball.

He hovered in the shadows, listening as the footsteps drew closer. Tensing up, he prepared for action. All the working out he'd done had paid off – in spite of his meager diet he was stronger than he'd been at the beginning. Stronger and determined to survive.

When the man entered, he jumped him, taking the bastard by surprise, grabbing him around the neck with a blood-curdling scream.

Only it wasn't the man, it was a girl, and she began screaming too. '*Aiuto! Aiuto!*' The plate of food she was carrying smashed to the ground. '*Aiuto!*' she shrieked again.

She was speaking Italian, of which he knew little – although he understood enough to know she meant 'Help'. He had a firm lock around her neck. 'Who are you?' he demanded savagely. '*Who the fuck are you?*'

She struggled, trying to kick back and throw him off balance. She succeeded. They fell to the ground, knocking over the bucket of water that was his washing facility.

Now they were rolling in the mud, struggling for position. She was like a frightened deer, whimpering with fear.

He managed to get on top of her, pinning her arms above her head.

When he had her in position, he stared into her face, soon realizing it was the same girl he'd seen before.

She cried out in Italian. It sounded as if she was praying. '*Mi lasci in pace!*'

'Speak English,' he said harshly. '*Parli inglese.*'

'Who – who are you?' she whispered, her pretty face a mask of sheer panic.

'Who are *you*?' he responded.

'Furio a-a-away,' she stammered. 'He say I bring food.'

'You bring me fucking food, huh? Who is Furio anyway?'

Tears welled up in her eyes.

'Who is Furio?' he repeated.

'My poppa,' she whispered.

'Are you alone?' he asked.

She nodded, petrified.

'I'm a prisoner here – did you know that? *Prigione.*'

She tried to wriggle out from under him. The softness of her body, the smell of her, was like ripe nectar, luring him with all the comforts he'd missed.

'Do you have a key to get this off my ankle?' he demanded.

She shook her head blankly.

What was he going to do? Right now he had her in his power. But how long before he had to let go?

'You have to help me,' he said, very slowly to make sure she understood. 'I'm desperate.'

'My poppa . . . he say you bad man,' she said, in broken English. '*Uomo cattivo.*'

'No. Not me. Your father's the bad man. He kidnapped me. *Kidnapped. Capisce?*'

She nodded silently.

'I can't let you go,' he said, 'not until you figure a way to get me out of here. Can you do that?'

She gazed up at him.

'Can you?' he demanded. '*Può?*'

'I try . . .' she said at last.

There was no way he could trust her.

Unfortunately he had no choice.

Chapter Forty-two

THE FACT THAT Mickey Stolli was a major prick was not lost on Alex. There were dozens of men like Mickey running around Hollywood. Short, unattractive guys with a shitload of power. Guys who never got laid in high school. Guys with no fucking talent who leeched onto the true film-makers and took credit for all the successful movies that got made.

Alex called them the Hollywood executives who didn't know their ass from a hole in the ground. Mickey Stolli was one of them.

What happened when these guys acquired power was they made up for all their shortcomings. The movies they greenlighted were always about hookers, strippers and beautiful girls searching for the right man to come along and save them.

Fantasy time in Hollywood. Put all your hang-ups on the screen for every poor jerk to identify with.

Some of the guys used their power to sleep with as many famous women as possible. There was one particular producer who made a lot of big-budget movies. His casting sessions were legendary – and they always took place in his home. He interviewed many important actresses. When they came to his house he had a hidden video camera running, and if they *really* wanted the part in his latest epic, he ended up screwing them on film.

Saturday afternoons he entertained his male friends with his library of videos. Their wives thought they were over at his house watching football.

Other guys got power by marrying it. Mickey Stolli had married Abigaile, the granddaughter of the once big Hollywood mogul Abe Panther. From his relationship with Abigaile, Mickey had been able to parlay himself into a studio head. Not bad going.

Alex knew that to survive as a film-maker in Hollywood he had to keep cordial relationships with these guys, otherwise he was screwed. So when Mickey Stolli came to him and announced how pleased he was that Panther was making *Gangsters*, Alex was sure there would be a price.

'You got an estimated budget of twenty-two million dollars,' Mickey pointed out. 'That's major, Alex.'

Alex said, 'You'll see every dime on the screen.'

'Yeah, yeah, I understand that. You're a great film-maker, Alex. Not good, *great*. I'm proud t' be associated with you.'

What the fuck does the little prick want?

'Thanks, Mickey.'

'Uh, I gotta favor t' ask.'

Here it comes. 'Yes?'

'The role of Lola. Put Leslie Kane in it.'

'Leslie *who*?' Alex said.

'She's starred in a couple of hit movies. America loves her. Leslie's the girl every guy wants to take home to meet dad.'

'I was planning on casting Venus Maria.'

'Venus?' Mickey snorted. 'She's movie poison. Believe me. I should know – I've had her in a couple of flops.'

'She tested with Johnny, she was dynamite. This could be her breakthrough movie.'

Mickey ran a chubby hand over his bald head. 'Breakthrough,

schmake-do – who cares? Do me this favor with Leslie and there'll be no grief with your budget. Are we reading each other?'

Alex didn't say yes immediately, he told Mickey he'd think about it.

Lili got on to his case big time. 'Mickey Stolli will cause us nothing but problems,' she said. 'You'd better use Leslie Kane, it's not a big role.'

'Have you ever seen her act?' Alex asked.

'She'll be fine. It's too late to go to another studio with *Gangsters*, we're almost at our start date. You have to do this.'

Finally, he'd said yes. Now all he had to do was meet Leslie Kane and see what a big mistake he'd made.

☆   ☆   ☆

'*What?*' Venus yelled. 'Alex Woods cannot do this to me. The sonofabitch simply can't do it.'

She sat in Freddie's office, cheeks flushed with fury. Freddie had just informed her that Leslie Kane would be playing the role of Lola in *Gangsters*.

'I'm sorry,' Freddie said, his bland features perfectly composed. 'Alex wanted you, but the studio insisted on Leslie. There's nothing he can do.'

'Nothing he can do!' she shouted, filled with frustration. 'It's *his* movie, Freddie. *He* calls the shots. Leslie is completely wrong for the part. She's the boring girl next door, for Chrissakes!'

Freddie shrugged. 'I have three other scripts for you to read. You'll find something you like better.'

'Oh, yeah? *What?*' she said sarcastically. 'A Scorsese film? Something with Oliver Stone? I'm sure they can't *wait* to hire me. I wanted *this* role.'

She left his office in a state, muttering to herself. Leslie

Kane, indeed. First she went after Cooper, now she had *her* role in *Gangsters*. It wasn't fair. Mickey Stolli had screwed her again.

It hadn't been a good week: Emilio driving her crazy with his insane demands, phoning several times a day; then Cooper turning up at her house, begging her forgiveness. Fortunately, just when she'd begun to weaken, Rodriguez had arrived and she'd bid Cooper a fast goodbye. Cooper was not used to competition – especially younger, equally good-looking competition. He'd been furious.

She slumped in the back of her limo and made an impulsive decision. 'Take me to Panther Studios,' she instructed her driver.

Mickey Stolli was on the phone in his office when she burst in. 'Remember me?' she said, standing in front of his desk, hands on hips, glaring at him.

He glanced up, covering the mouthpiece of the phone. 'Hey, Venus, baby, what're *you* doing here?'

A flustered secretary followed her in. 'I'm sorry, Mr Stolli,' the secretary said. 'I couldn't stop her.'

'That's all right, Marguerite, we're old friends,' Mickey said, gracious for once in his life.

Mickey was fifty years old, short, bald, with a permanent suntan, all his own teeth and a hard body, thanks to daily tennis, his passion. He had a rough-edged voice, tinged with memories of the Bronx only when he was angry. Recently he'd been running Orpheus Studios, but he hadn't gotten along with the Japanese who owned it, so when Donna Landsman had approached him about returning to Panther, he'd quit immediately. Panther was his prize. His studio. Coming back was like coming home.

'I'll call you later, Charlie,' he said into the receiver. Slamming down the phone, he gave Venus his full attention. 'What can I do for you, sweetie?'

'Alex Woods *wants* me in *Gangsters*,' she said agitatedly. 'I want to be in *Gangsters*. I did a great test, and now you're casting that wimpy little Leslie Kane. What's *wrong* with you, Mickey?'

'Leslie Kane brings 'em into the theaters. There are times Alex Woods keeps 'em out.'

'Don't talk crap,' she snapped. 'Alex is a brilliant film-maker, and you know it.'

Mickey shrugged. 'He wants Leslie. What can I tell you?'

'You're lying, Mickey. Just because we've had our outs—'

'Does Freddie know you're here?' Mickey interrupted.

'No,' Venus replied. 'I figured since we had such a convoluted past together, I should come see you myself.' She leaned across his desk. His eyes feasted hungrily on her cleavage. 'This role means a lot to me, Mickey. How about reconsidering?'

'What's in it for me?' he asked, sweat beading his bald head as he watched the platinum-haired superstar show off her big tits.

She licked her full pink lips. 'What do you *want* to be in it for you?'

'A blow-job.'

She laughed mockingly. 'A blow-job, Mickey? Is that all?'

He could feel the hard-on springing to life in his pants. 'Do I hear a yes?' he said hopefully.

'Show me a signed contract and we'll see.'

Mickey watched her sashay her delectable ass out the door. She was something, Venus Maria. He'd always had a hot nut for her – even when he'd been banging Warner Franklin, the black cop, and she was no slouch in the getting-it-up department.

Mickey fantasized about Venus on her knees in front of him, his legs spread while her blond head dipped between them, licking and sucking – doing all the things he knew she'd excel at. He got off on the picture.

He wouldn't get shit out of Leslie. She was Abigaile's friend, and even though he'd heard the rumors that she used to be a hooker, he wasn't sure he believed it. Leslie was too straight.

Venus was right. Leslie *was* completely wrong for Alex's film. He'd had to put the screws on Alex to get him to use her, now he could reverse them.

Hey, as the new head of Panther he had complete autonomy. If he wanted to hire Venus Maria, he could do so.

And if she wanted to give him a blow-job, well . . . she just might get lucky.

☆ ☆ ☆

Abigaile Stolli and Leslie lunched at the Ivy. Leslie was her usual fresh-faced self, long red hair swept back into a girlish ponytail, a simple paisley granny dress covering her killer body. The look suited her: in spite of past indiscretions she was still only twenty-three and had kept her innocently sexy demeanor.

Abigaile Stolli was in her early forties, a short woman with shoulder-length auburn hair and snubbed features. She was not a beauty, but Abigaile had no need to be: she was a powerful Hollywood wife with a pure bloodline. Abigaile was true Hollywood royalty.

Everyone fussed around Leslie, calling her Miss Kane this and Miss Kane that. She enjoyed every moment, and why shouldn't she? She'd had to struggle to get where she was today.

'Thanks for your help, Abbey,' she said, raising her glass of freshly squeezed orange juice toward Abigaile, toasting her friend.

'Here's to *Gangsters*,' Abigaile responded. 'You'll be wonderful in it, dear.'

'I hope I'll get along with Alex Woods,' Leslie worried. 'He has quite a reputation.'

'Any problems, go right to Mickey,' Abigaile said expansively, enjoying herself because she liked to be seen lunching with a star. 'He'll take care of Mr Woods. Mickey runs the studio with an iron hand.'

'I'm glad to hear that,' Leslie said. 'I'm sure I'll enjoy working for him again.'

'Above all, Mickey's a professional,' Abigaile said.

A professional what? That was Leslie's question. When she'd been married to Eddie he'd had plenty to say about Mickey Stolli, who, at the time, was his boss at Panther. 'The guy's a thievin', no-good, two-timin' rat bastard,' Eddie had often fumed. 'And he's getting me in big trouble.'

Leslie had never found out exactly what the big trouble was: all she knew was that it had something to do with skimming money and drugs.

'By the way, dear,' Abigaile said, 'we're giving a small dinner for Donna and George Landsman, tomorrow night. Just a few people. Alex Woods, Cooper Turner, Johnny Romano. We'd love you to come. And bring . . .' She trailed off, unable to remember the name of Leslie's live-in, although she'd met him on several occasions.

'Jeff,' Leslie filled in.

'Ah, yes, Jeff, of course. Can you make it?'

As if there was any way she'd miss it. 'We'd be delighted,' she said.

Jeff picked her up from the restaurant in her new bronze Mercedes, happy in his role as resident stud and glorified chauffeur. It was better than going on endless auditions for pilots that never got made. Leslie didn't feel sorry for him – if he ever became a star Abigaile would remember his name.

'We're going to dinner at Mickey Stolli's tomorrow,' she informed him.

'Okay with me, hon,' he said, maneuvering the Mercedes into the flow of traffic.

I'm sure, she thought. And began planning what she'd wear to win Cooper back.

☆   ☆   ☆

Mickey called Alex late on Monday night. 'I changed my mind. If you wanna use Venus, y'can.'

'What happened?'

'It's kind of involved – it's gotta do with my wife and her friendship with Leslie. Listen, don't mention to Venus or Freddie she's got the part until I tell you. Let it hang for a few days. I'm givin' Leslie a script she'll like better. That way we'll ease her out of *Gangsters* – no sweat.'

Alex couldn't believe he was putting up with this shit. 'I'm not used to working like this, Mickey,' he said tightly.

'Aw, c'mon, Alex,' Mickey cajoled. 'Bend a little. You're gettin' what you want.'

'Sure, Mickey,' he said, hating himself for kissing up – it wasn't his style.

'Good. Oh, an' Abigaile told me to remind you – you're having dinner at our house tomorrow night. Leslie will be there. Act as if she's doing *Gangsters*, okay?'

Alex complained to Lili, who shook her head wisely. 'You have taught me much about Hollywood, Alex,' she said. 'One of the things you impressed upon me was never to ask a question when you already know the answer.'

'Okay, Lili, okay.' He went into his office and shut the door. Every day he interviewed dozens of actors for minor roles. His casting people made recommendations, then they'd bring five or six actors in to try out for each role. Alex saw them all personally. It was time-consuming, but he refused to work any other way.

He had a few minutes before the casting calls started so he picked up the phone and tried Lucky again. He'd been calling her constantly, getting nothing but her answering machine. He'd heard about Gino being shot, and he was anxious to find out more. He also wanted to make sure she was all right, and to let her know that he was there for her. Even if she didn't want a relationship, he could still be her friend.

This time an actual human being answered the phone.

'Alex Woods calling for Lucky Santangelo,' he said.

'I'm sorry, Mr Woods, she's stepped out.'

'Who's this?'

'Kyoko, her assistant.'

He cleared his throat, feeling foolish. 'Hey, Kyoko, I've been trying to reach her for a week now. Have her call me back.'

'Yes, Mr Woods.'

'She can find me at my office or my house.' He put the phone down. What was it about Lucky that he found so attractive?

Her spirit. She was a wild one, just like him.

And he yearned to get to know her better.

☆　☆　☆

They were in Brigette's apartment, arguing. Nona had turned up unexpectedly, and Brigette wasn't pleased.

'What?' she said irritably.

'I'd like to know what your problem is?' Nona repeated. 'You've become a total pain in the ass.'

'Why am I a pain in the ass?' Brigette said. 'Just because I don't do everything you want me to?'

'You don't do a *thing* I suggest. I'm supposed to be your

manager, Michel's your agent, and you refuse to have anything to do with either of us.'

'I have my reasons,' Brigette said mysteriously, not wanting to get into it on account of a lousy hangover.

'*What* reasons?' Nona demanded. 'Isaac – whom you can't seem to live without anymore? You're out every morning till four or five, then you sleep all day. Your career is just getting started, Brigette. Now's the time to work it.'

'I can do whatever I want,' Brigette replied truculently. 'Nobody owns me.'

'What does *that* mean?'

'I don't need this modeling crap if I don't want to do it.'

Nona sighed her displeasure. 'Oh, that's nice, isn't it? Coming from the girl who was all starry-eyed and would do anything to get on the cover of *Mondo*. Now you're suddenly into "I don't need this modeling crap" bit. Hey, I can walk away from it, too, if that's what you'd like.'

'Okay, walk,' Brigette said. All she wanted to do was crash into bed and sleep for a week – maybe forever.

'I don't get it,' Nona said, shaking her head. 'Did something happen I don't know about?'

Brigette turned away from her and went into the kitchen.

'I'm right, aren't I?' Nona said, following her.

As each day passed Brigette was becoming increasingly unhappy. She couldn't keep it to herself any longer. 'Look,' she said, turning back to Nona, speaking furiously, 'nothing happened that you didn't warn me about.'

'So something *did* happen. I'm right. Is it Isaac?'

'Michel,' Brigette muttered, sitting down at the counter.

'What did he do?'

'I can't tell you,' Brigette said, laying her head on her arms.

Nona went over to her and put her arm around her shoulders. 'C'mon, Brig, it can't be *that* bad.'

'You warned me he was a sleaze.'

'So? He made a pass at you? Big deal. I'm sure you handled it.'

'It's worse than that,' Brigette said, her eyes downcast. 'He tied me up – spread-eagled like a chicken – and then brought Robertson in to do all these things to me while he watched and took photographs. It was the most degrading thing I've ever experienced. Why do you think I don't want anything to do with him?'

'Oh, God, Brigette. How come you didn't tell me about this before? We could've reported him to the police.'

'Oh, yeah – I can see the headlines now. "Heiress tied up and forced to experience lesbian sex." Don't you understand? It would ruin my life if this got out.'

'I'm so sorry . . . I had no clue . . .'

'I guess I'm just unlucky with men.'

'What a fucking *bastard*!'

'Nona,' Brigette said urgently, 'you've got to promise me you won't tell anybody, not even Zan.'

'You know I'm your friend, but we've got to do *something*. We can't let him get away with it.'

'What?' Brigette asked despairingly. 'He's got photos . . .'

'You know who we *should* tell?' Nona said.

'Who?'

'Lucky. You've always said she can deal with anything. She'll know what to do.'

'I can't tell Lucky.'

'Why?'

'Lucky's got her own problems right now – what with Gino getting shot, and losing the studio. I can't lay this on her.'

'Lennie would want you to. Listen, we could fly to LA immediately.'

'It's too humiliating.'

'Surely you feel better now you've told me?'

'Yes . . .'

'Well, think how you'll feel when you tell Lucky, and she does something about it.'

'Oh, God, Nona, why did he do it?'

'Because he's a sick pervert who deserves to get his. Now you've got to listen to me, my idea's the right one. We go to Lucky. I'll fly to LA with you.'

Brigette nodded. 'Maybe you're right.'

'I *know* I'm right. We're getting on a plane first thing tomorrow.'

Chapter Forty-three

 WHILE KYOKO was taking care of the mail, Lucky studied the call sheet from Lennie's movie, ticking off the people she wished to talk to. Dealing with Lennie's death was private business, something she had to look after on her own.

First she called Ross Vendors, the Australian director. He was at home in Bel Air, between jobs. Ross told her how sorry he was about Lennie, that he'd been so great in his movie and any time she wanted to view the half-finished assemblage of film it was fine with him.

'I was wondering,' she said tentatively, 'how did Lennie spend the day before the accident?'

'He was in great shape, Lucky,' Ross said, in his booming one-of-the-boys Australian twang. 'All he could talk about was you flying in the next day, he couldn't wait. In fact, he drove us all nutty – "Lucky will be here tomorrow . . . love her so much . . . never thought marriage would be like this . . ." I'm telling you, the man wouldn't shut up.'

She smiled softly. 'Really?'

'I would've told you this before, only I didn't like to disturb you in your time of grief.'

'That was thoughtful of you, Ross.' She paused for a moment before continuing. 'Uh . . . maybe you can tell me – who did Lennie hang out with on the set?'

'Lennie didn't really hang out. He dropped by the hotel bar a few times after work. Mostly he went to his room and studied his script. Jennifer was the only one who had a lot of contact with him.'

'Jennifer?' she asked, sounding casual, although her heart began pounding uncontrollably.

'Our second AD,' Ross said. 'Great kid. She fussed over Lennie. Made sure he got to the set on time, that his car was there whenever he needed it. In fact, on the day before you arrived, she got his call changed so he could go to the airport to meet you.'

'Oh, yes, Jennifer, I think I *do* know her.' Another pause. 'She's a pretty blond, right?'

'That's our Jennifer. Cute girl.'

Yeah. Especially naked in my husband's arms.

She scanned the crew list until she found the name Jennifer Barron. Then she called the number listed.

An answering machine picked up. 'Hi, this is Jennifer. If you need to reach me I'm working on *The Marriage* at Star Studios for the next six weeks. Leave a message and I'll get back to you.'

Lucky phoned Star Studios, got through to the production office of *The Marriage*, and spoke to an assistant.

'The whole crew's on location,' the assistant said. 'They're shooting down at Paradise Cove.'

Paradise Cove was ten minutes away from her house. She told Kyoko she had to run out, informed the guard she would not be needing him, jumped in her car and drove there.

The huge parking area above Paradise Cove beach was filled with enormous location trucks and luxurious trailers. She parked her Ferrari, got out and walked around. 'Where is everyone?' she asked a passing extra.

'They're on the beach shooting the wedding scene.'

She made her way toward the beach, going by the Kraft

service set-up and a gaggle of extras stuffing their faces with free snacks.

What if Jennifer was the blond from the photographs? What was she going to say to her? What was she going to do?

You bitch, you were fucking my husband!

No. All she wanted to ask was why – nothing more.

The crew were up ahead on the sand, everyone running around preparing for the next shot – everyone except the actors, who were sitting in a row in their personal director's chairs, makeup, hair and various assistants hovering in attendance.

'Excuse me,' she said, stopping a grip. 'Can you point me in the direction of Jennifer Barron – I think she's one of the ADs.'

He gestured to the line-up of actors. 'She's over there, talking to Sammy Albert.'

'Thanks.'

Thirteen years ago, Sammy Albert had been the hottest actor in town, now he was king of the second-rate features – a faded star with a bad hairpiece and bleached teeth. Lucky had never met him, although she certainly knew who he was.

More important to her was the blond standing next to his chair. The girl was in disguise. Baseball cap, dark shades, an LA hard body in brief shorts and a T-shirt. Lucky had no idea if it was the woman from the photographs or not.

She strode over and tapped the girl on the shoulder. 'Jennifer?'

'Yes.'

'I'm Lucky Santangelo. You were working on my husband's movie in Corsica. Lennie Golden.'

'That's right.'

'Can we go somewhere and talk?'

'Sure.'

They sat on the sand under a shady palm tree. 'Jennifer,'

Lucky said, choosing her words carefully, 'everyone's told me how . . . close you and Lennie were on the location. Well, what I need to know is – exactly *how* close?'

Jennifer was startled. 'You think there was something going on between me and Lennie?' she exclaimed. 'All he ever spoke about was you, Lucky.' She hesitated. 'Is it okay if I call you Lucky?'

'Go ahead.'

The girl was flustered. 'Where did you get the idea Lennie and I had something going?'

'I uh . . . saw the pictures,' Lucky said.

Jennifer looked puzzled. '*What* pictures?'

Reaching into her purse, Lucky undid the zippered compartment and produced the photo of Lennie with the blond on the set. 'This is you without the hat and glasses, right?' she said, handing it to Jennifer.

Jennifer studied the photo and burst out with relieved laughter. '*That* silicone babe – are you kidding me?'

'It's not you?' Lucky asked.

'No way,' Jennifer said vehemently. 'It's some dumb bimbo who kept trailing Lennie around the set.'

'Was she working on the movie?'

'She was an extra,' Jennifer said, adding a thoughtful, 'Y'know, a funny thing – Lennie called me to find out her name the night before he was killed.'

'Why?'

'Don't know. I was joking with him – I said something like, "Sure you don't want her measurements and diaphragm size, too?" Uh . . . just my sense of humor, Lucky. Lennie got it.'

'What did he say?'

'As far as I remember he said, "It's not what you think."' Jennifer took the picture and looked at it again. 'Where's her boyfriend? He was there when it was taken. Somebody's cut him out.' She shook her head. 'I'm telling you, Lucky, Lennie didn't even *know* her.'

'But he *did* ask you her name?'

'She was on his case,' Jennifer said. 'Earlier in the evening he said she'd called him in his room.'

'And?'

'And nothing. He told her to get lost.'

'Do you think he could've changed his mind later?'

'I doubt it. You know your husband – he wasn't into anyone except you. And if he *was* planning a one-night stand with this blond, he'd hardly ask *me* for her name and number. He must have had another reason for doing so.'

Lucky reached into her purse and took out the other photographs. 'These were in his room,' she said, handing them to Jennifer. 'When I arrived, it looked as if a woman had spent the night.'

Jennifer stared at the photos for a moment. 'I don't get it,' she said, puzzled. 'Why would he be with a naked woman in the doorway of his hotel room? It seems more like he's trying to push her away.'

'Do you think so?'

'Take another look.'

Jennifer was right. It did seem as if Lennie was uncomfortable. Why hadn't she noticed before?

Because you were too busy getting pissed off.

'How can I find out who she is?'

'My friend Ricco was responsible for hiring the extras. I heard he's working on a movie in Rome now, I'll call him – maybe he can help.' She paused before continuing. 'Y'know, Lucky, your husband was my favorite. I'm so used to movie stars hitting on me – it's always, "Come on, baby, how about a blow-job?" I used to joke with Lennie that he was the only one who never came on to me.'

'You've been a big help, Jennifer. Here's my home number. As soon as you find out anything, call me.'

'I will.' She glanced up. 'Oh, God! Watch out. Here comes Sammy Albert. When he heard your name, he was in heat.'

'Surely he knows I'm not the head of a studio anymore,' Lucky said drily.

'Guess not,' Jennifer said with a sly smile. 'And *I'm* not telling him!'

'Lucky Santangelo,' Sammy said, clapping his hand on her shoulder, 'you're some gutsy gal. I've always had a thing about meeting you.'

'Sammy Albert,' she said, copying his tone. 'I'm a big fan.'

'Of course you are,' he joked. 'To what do we owe the honor of you visiting our humble set?'

'I live nearby.'

'Does that mean lunch at your house?' he said, with a knowing wink.

Sometimes she *hated* actors! They honestly believed that all women were theirs for the taking. 'You'll have to excuse me, Sammy, I'm late for an appointment.'

'Shame.'

'It was a pleasure meeting you.'

'*My* pleasure, babe,' he said, with another knowing wink.

Back at the house she checked on Gino in Palm Springs. 'What are you doing?' she asked.

'Bettin' the ball games, what else?'

'Are you bored?'

'Naw . . . bored is for chicken-shits,' he said chuckling. 'What's happenin' there? Anythin' I should know about?'

'I'm waiting for Boogie to get me all the information.'

His tone became serious. 'Remember what I said, kiddo, ya gotta be careful.'

Boogie arrived promptly at six. 'Come out to the garage, Lucky,' he said.

'What's going on, Boog?'

'You'll see.'

She followed him through the house, through a side door to the garage.

Tied to a chair, his arms and legs bound, a gag in his mouth, was a small, weasel-faced man with a bad case of the out-of-control sweats. He wore a mud-brown suit, black shoes and a grubby yellow T-shirt. His hair, what there was of it, lingered around his shoulders in greasy ringlets.

'Meet Sami the Mutt,' Boogie said. 'He's the fuckhead responsible for pumping two bullets into Gino. Here,' Boogie reached into his belt and handed Lucky his gun, 'in case you feel like using it.'

Sami's eyes almost popped out of his head.

Lucky knew the game Boogie was playing. She weighed the gun in her hands, staring threateningly at Sami the Mutt. 'Maybe I should put one right between your shriveled-up balls,' she said, cool as ice. 'What do you think, Sami? Retribution for my father?'

Sami struggled in the chair, making panicked gurgling noises.

Boogie strolled over to him, slid a knife from his pocket and cut the gag from Sami's mouth.

'I was doin' a job, I was hired t' do a job,' Sami said, his words tumbling over each other in his haste to explain. 'If I'd known the mark was Gino Santangelo, I wouldn't have touched him.'

Lucky continued to stare at him, lacerating him with her deadly black eyes. 'Who hired you?' she said.

'I dunno . . . Some guy in a bar gave me cash. Di'n't know the hit was Gino Santangelo.'

'You're full of crap,' Lucky said. 'You knew who it was.

You went out and shot my father for money. What kind of a dumb shit are you?' She lifted the gun, pointing it directly at his crotch.

He peed in his pants.

'Not such a big man now, huh?' Lucky said. 'How much were you paid?'

'Four thou – cash,' Sami muttered, hanging his head.

'And who did you say hired you?' Lucky repeated, not lowering the gun.

'Some guy in a bar.'

'In LA?' Boogie said.

'Yeah, there's this strip joint near the airport. This guy, he comes in there sometimes.'

'What's his name?'

'Dunno.' He looked at Boogie pleadingly. 'Can you get her t' put the gun down?'

'I suggest you find out,' Lucky said, deliberately calm. 'Because if I don't have his name by tomorrow, I'm shooting your scrawny little balls all the way to Cuba. And, believe me, I've done it before.'

'You and I – we're leaving now,' Boogie said, going over and putting a blindfold on Sami. 'Miz Santangelo is giving you twenty-four hours to come up with a name. I'm driving you back to town and letting you loose. I'll bring you back here tomorrow – same time. And you *will* have a name for her.'

Lucky returned to the house. She felt nauseous. So many memories drifting back to haunt her. Memories of her childhood, men coming to the house, Gino in whispered conversations, the knowledge that she was different from other little girls because her daddy spent half his life on a plane back and forth to Las Vegas. And then her mother's brutal murder. Gino had been in Vegas when it happened. She was at home.

Was there anything she could have done to save her beautiful mother?

No.

At times the guilt was so overwhelming it almost suffocated her.

She'd gotten revenge years later.

Now she'd have to do it again.

It was a grim thought.

Chapter Forty-four

ABIGAILE SET a good table. She loved entertaining stars, it was her favorite pastime – a pastime at which she excelled. Giving a dinner party for Donna and George Landsman seemed appropriate, since Donna was technically Mickey's new boss. Not that Abigaile had ever heard of the Landsmans, but so what? In Hollywood, if you had money, you could rise to the top quickly.

Her guest list was stellar. It included Cooper Turner, who had not revealed whom he was bringing; Johnny Romano, who'd told her secretary he'd be accompanied by a date, but had not supplied her with a name.

What did these men do? Call a woman a half-hour before they left their house, and tell her to put on a dress? Whatever happened to social niceties?

Alex Woods was bringing someone by the name of Tin Lee; and Leslie Kane would be with her live-in boyfriend.

Donna Landsman's secretary had called yesterday to say that Donna would have her sixteen-year-old son with her. This absolutely infuriated Abigaile, she certainly didn't want some unknown teenager sitting at her table. Besides, it ruined her table placements.

Graciously she'd said it was okay, then told her own daughter, Tabitha, who was also sixteen, that she would have to attend the dinner with them.

Tabitha, home on vacation from her Swiss boarding school, pulled an uncooperative face. 'C'mon, Mom,' she complained. 'Have I really gotta sit down with a bunch of boring old farts?'

'I would hardly call Cooper Turner, Alex Woods and Johnny Romano boring old farts,' Abigaile said frostily, annoyed by her daughter's lack of respect.

'*I* would,' Tabitha groaned. 'Why can't you invite Sean Penn instead?'

Tabitha was a problem. At fourteen she'd run off with an eighteen-year-old Hispanic waiter; at fifteen she'd accidentally set the house on fire during a wild party while her parents were on vacation; and at sixteen she'd insisted on having her nose fixed, her hair streaked magenta, and several unspeakable body piercings. Quite frankly, Abigaile didn't know what to do with her.

It was only ten a.m., but Abigaile insisted her maids prepare everything early just to make sure there were no mistakes. She inspected her dining-room table: a perfect fantasy of crisp beige linens, expensive crystal and fine old Victorian silver. 'Very nice, Consuela,' she told her housekeeper.

Abigaile considered herself one of the great Hollywood hostesses. Her dinner parties were legendary, and a ticket to the Stollis was a much sought after invitation. She recalled, with a small triumphant smile the party she'd thrown a couple of years ago, when a certain black politician and an extremely famous feminist had gotten into a screaming match across the table.

'Cunt!' the black politician had screamed at the feminist.

'What did you call me, you black prick?' the feminist had screamed back at him.

And from there it had turned into a wild free-for-all. The two of them had run from the Stollis' house, yelling at each other all the way. According to the servants, they'd then proceeded to make out in the back of the politician's limo. That particular dinner party had been the talk of LA for months.

Yes . . . Abigaile certainly knew how to throw a party.

She continued smiling to herself at the memory and left the dining room. She had much to do before sitting down with her guests. Manicure, waxing, pedicure, facial, hairdresser, yoga, Pilates, a fitting at Nolan's . . . Abigaile didn't know how she managed to get it all in.

☆ ☆ ☆

'How about stepping out with me tonight?'

'Who is this?' Venus mumbled into the phone, barely awake. She'd kill Anthony for putting a call through to her this early.

'It's Johnny, baby.'

Her mind refused to function. 'Johnny?'

'Hel*lo* – Johnny Romano. What planet are you zoomin' on today?'

'Oh, Johnny, sorry, it's early. I was asleep.'

'It's past noon, baby.'

'Impossible!'

'Check it out.'

She groped for her bedside clock and was amazed to see that it was, indeed, twelve-fifteen. She must have needed the sleep – usually she was up at seven.

'Whaddya say, baby?' Johnny persisted. 'Dinner at Mickey Stolli's? There's no one I'd sooner take than you.'

'Who'll be there?' she said sleepily.

'It's a dinner for the broad who took over Panther,' Johnny said. 'Got no idea who's invited. Maybe Alex.'

It occurred to Venus that he hadn't heard she wasn't

playing Lola. She decided not to tell him, although it might be a good idea to elicit his support. She could always tell him later, if she agreed to go.

'I'm not sure if I can make it,' she said, giving herself time to think.

'Hey, c'mon, babycakes,' he urged. 'You an' me – we're an explosion waitin' to happen. Let's do it.'

'If I go with you, it's a strictly platonic deal – get that straight up front. I'm not one of your legion of open-legged starlets begging for action.'

'Hey, why d'you think I'm into you?' he said indignantly. 'You ain't easy. I go for that in a woman. It's an unusual thing.' He paused. 'Course, it beats me how you're able to resist me.'

'Y'know what, Johnny,' she said caustically. 'I'll try my hardest.'

'Is that a yes, baby?'

She yawned. 'It's a maybe. Call back in an hour.'

'Venus, Venus.' He sighed. 'You're a difficult one.'

Why was she even considering it?

Because she wanted to see Mickey again, and if Alex was there, that would be even better.

Anyway, why shouldn't she go? Get in their faces, force them to change their tiny minds.

She buzzed Anthony. 'How come nobody woke me?'

'You left a note last night,' Anthony said. 'Not to be disturbed before noon.'

'I did?'

'You certainly did. Rodriguez called three times. He wants to know when you'll be viewing your video, said he'd like to see it with you.'

'I bet,' she replied, deciding that Rodriguez was getting to be too much of a good thing. 'Do I have any appointments, Anthony?'

'Yes, you do.'

'Cancel everything. I'm taking today off. My plan is to sit by my pool, eat whatever I want, and do absolutely nothing. Wait a couple of hours, then call Johnny Romano and tell him I'll go to the Stollis' dinner tonight. Find out what the dress is, and what time he'll pick me up.'

Yes, she decided, it would be good to confront Alex Woods and Mickey Stolli in the flesh. Remind them that she *was* Lola, and that they were making a big mistake by casting anyone else.

Chapter Forty-five

'HI,' SAID LUCKY.

'Hi,' said the girl in the revealing bra top and ripped denim shorts, barely glancing at her.

They stood side by side at the makeup counter in the Dart drug store on La Cienega.

'You tried this color?' Lucky asked, holding up a bronze lipstick.

Sara gave it a perfunctory glance. 'No, but it looks kinda interestin'.'

'I think so, too,' Lucky said, putting down the lipstick. 'Hey,' she said, staring at her, 'aren't you Sara Durbon?'

This got Sara's attention. 'Well, yeah, I am,' she said, tugging at her shorts, which were caught in the curve of her butt. 'Do I know you?'

'Not really,' Lucky said, picking up another lipstick. 'We have a mutual friend.'

'Mutual friend?' Sara said, rubbing her chin with a skinny index finger. 'Like who?'

'Morton Sharkey.'

'Morton's a friend of yours?' Sara said, wrinkling her nose.

'That's right.'

'I've never met any of Morty's friends,' Sara giggled. 'How d'ya know me?'

'He talks about you a lot. I've seen your photo.'

'He talks about *me*?' Sara said in surprise. 'I thought I was his dirty little secret. Y'know, on account of the fact that he's married an' all.'

'He must really be fond of you.'

'I don't get it,' Sara said, her forehead creasing. 'I'm, like, *never* supposed to say nothin' to nobody.'

'What do you do, Sara?' Lucky asked. 'Are you an actress, a model – what?'

'Oh, I get it,' Sara said, nodding knowingly. 'His wife sent you, didn't she? The old bat found out 'bout me, an' now you're here to tell me to get lost, or pay me off or somethin'.'

'*Could* I pay you off?' Lucky asked, wondering what the hell Morton saw in this raggedy teenager.

'*Did* his hag wife send you?' Sara demanded belligerently.

'No, she didn't. However, I am interested in exchanging money for information. How do you feel about that?'

Sara narrowed her eyes. 'What's with this Morton Sharkey guy?' she said. 'First I get all that money—'

'What money?' Lucky asked quickly.

'It don't matter,' Sara said, censoring herself before she got into trouble.

'Sara, you and I should sit down and talk. I can be very useful to you.'

'Like how?' she asked suspiciously.

'Well, if you're an actress maybe I can get you a job. If you're a model, same thing.'

Mistrust filled Sara's eyes. 'Why'd ya do that for me? I'm nobody.'

'I have my reasons. How old are you?'

'Twenty-one,' she lied.

'The truth?'

Sara shrugged. 'Seventeen,' she admitted, with a giggle. 'Goin' on seventy!'

'What did you do? Run away from home?'

'How d'ya know?'

'I'll be truthful with you, Sara. I have a personal score to settle with Morton Sharkey, and I'm ready to pay anything to do so. Tell me what you want, and I promise you it's yours.'

'Anything?' Sara said, a touch of greed creeping into her voice as she considered the possibilities.

'Name it.'

'Lady, you got yourself one big deal.'

☆　☆　☆

'She never called me back, Kyoko.'

'I'm sorry, Mr Woods. I gave her your messages.'

'Yeah, yeah.' Alex was starting to feel like a fool. Lovesick movie director in hot pursuit of woman who didn't give a shit. 'Is she in town?'

'Yes, Mr Woods.'

'I'll call later.'

'She'll be home by four,' said Kyoko, feeling sorry for him.

Alex put the phone down. He was about to start a twenty-two-million-dollar movie, and all he could think about was Lucky Santangelo. Wasn't she at least interested in knowing what was going on at her former studio?

Lili buzzed him on the intercom. 'Alex.'

'What is it?'

'Everyone's waiting downstairs.'

'Tell 'em I'll be right there.'

'Don't forget you have a dinner at Mickey Stolli's. Tin Lee will be at your apartment at seven-thirty.'

'Christ! Why did I say yes?'

'I don't know, Alex, but you did.'

'Okay, okay.' He marched out of his office annoyed with himself; social dinners were not his thing.

Lili stopped him at the door. 'Johnny Romano called about the script changes again.'

'Stall him, Lili. You know how to do that better than anybody.'

Downstairs Russell greeted him. All their locations were in place except one, and today was their last opportunity to find it.

'You got some good things lined up?' he asked.

'You won't be disappointed,' Russell said.

They got into the van, where the other members of the crew waited, and set off.

Luck was on his side. The second location they visited was exactly what he was looking for. 'A done deal,' he told Russell. 'No need to see anything else.'

The van dropped him back at his car early. He glanced at his watch: it was around three-thirty. For a moment he considered going back up to his office, he had plenty to do. Instead, he got in his Porsche and drove directly to Lucky's house at the beach.

If Lucky Santangelo wouldn't speak to him on the phone, he'd be there to greet her when she got home.

Too bad if she didn't like it.

☆ ☆ ☆

Lucky sat with Sara at a corner table in the Hard Rock Café. Loud rock music blared out – instinctively, Lucky had known the noise would make Sara feel comfortable and, therefore, more talkative.

She'd already given her two thousand dollars in cash, now she was waiting for the pay-off.

'Okay, Sara,' Lucky said, watching the girl devour a double-size cheeseburger. 'Tell me everything, and after you've done that there's another two thousand in it for you.'

Sara, who liked money better than anything in the world, was quick to spill the goods as she gobbled down her cheeseburger. 'I met Morty when I was workin' in a massage parlor on Hollywood Boulevard,' she began. 'He came in one day – like he was all sneaky an' desperate to get it on. Only I was smart, told him I din't do that kind of thing.' A sly smile. 'Course, I did, but when you work in that business you kinda learn what the guy's trip is. You can tell if they're gonna give you money or trouble. I knew he was the money kind, so I played it all innocent. An' before I knew it, he'd slipped me five hundred bucks for a hand-job.' She rolled her eyes as if she couldn't believe anyone would be that stupid. 'Five hundred freakin' bucks for a sixty-second jerk-off! After that he kept on coming back.' She stopped to take another large bite of her cheeseburger. Tomato ketchup dribbled down her chin, a few red spots landing on her top. She didn't seem to notice. 'Okay, then he was after me t' see him outta business hours, so I had him over to my place. He took one look an' said he was gonna set me up in my own apartment. This dude is puttin' me on, I thought. But *nooo* – Morty was serious. Then I get, like, a visit from this woman.'

'What woman?' Lucky asked.

'She was, like, this fancy-dressed woman. She turned up at my door with some guy. They offered me a lot of money if I let them set up a hidden movie camera. Big freakin' deal. I said yes.'

'What was her name?'

'No idea.'

It had to be Donna. 'What happened then?'

'They put the camera up in my bedroom closet, an' told me how to angle myself so they could get some hot shots of Morty in action.' Sara giggled. 'Morty was *always* in action. Guess his wife never gave him any, 'cause he's the horniest old man *I've* ever been with.'

Lucky sighed. A horny old man with a hard-on. Guaranteed to betray you every time. 'Did he know there was a camera?'

'Course not,' Sara scoffed, taking another bite of her burger. 'So I get the videotape of him, give it to them, an' they paid me mucho bucks like they promised. Then Morty found out what I'd done.'

'How did he find out?'

'The woman started blackmailin' him. Boy, was he pissed! Beat the crap outta me – didn't think he was that tough.' She grabbed a handful of french fries, stuffing them in her already full mouth.

'He hit you?'

'I s'pose I deserved it. But like I told him, I *needed* that money. Where else was I gonna score like that?'

'What happened next?'

'Well,' she screwed up her face, 'after a few days he forgave me. Moved me out of my place 'cause he di'n't trust me no more. Now I'm like in this 'spensive apartment, an' he gives me an allowance. Truth is, if a better deal came along I'd grab it.'

'Am *I* a better deal?'

'Depends on what you're offering.'

Lucky sat back, laying out her rules. 'First, this meeting is confidential. That means you can't tell anyone. Second, I want a copy of the videotape.'

'Don't have it.'

'Quit with the lying.'

Sara giggled. Lying was a natural way of life to her. 'How d'ya know?'

'You had a copy made, didn't you?'

'It'll cost you big,' Sara said with another sly smile.

'How big?'

Sara sucked in her cheeks and blew out air. 'Ten thousand,'

she said, making up an amount on the spot. 'Yeah, ten thousand – cash. That'll do it.'

☆ ☆ ☆

As soon as he saw Lucky's red Ferrari driving down the private road, Alex jumped out of his car and stood in the middle of the road waving her to stop.

'What the hell are you *doing*?' she said, swerving to an abrupt halt. 'I could've killed you.'

'What does it look like I'm doing?' he said, strolling over to her window. 'Obviously, I had to take drastic measures to speak to you since you never return my calls.'

She ran a hand through her long dark hair. 'You're crazy,' she said, shaking her head.

'Yeah, yeah. Did you know we're almost neighbors? I live down the street.'

'Really?' she said, unimpressed.

'How about coming to my house for a drink?'

'Alex,' she said patiently, 'I thought I explained how I felt on the phone.'

'I know,' he said. 'You only slept with me to get back at Lennie. That made me feel really good about myself. But, okay, if that's the way you want it, I can live with that. Come see my house.'

'Why?' she said, still thinking about her meeting with Sara.

'Because I'd like you to,' he said persuasively, flashing the smile that always got him his own way.

She didn't want to encourage him, yet she couldn't help liking him. Hey, if Alex wanted to be friends, fine with her, as long as he realized there was no romance. 'I can only stay ten minutes,' she said firmly. 'I'll follow your car.'

'Drive with me. You know how much you like my driving.'

'I said I'll follow you, Alex. That's the only way I'm coming there.'

'Don't lose me.'

'Wouldn't think of it.'

He got in his Porsche and set off, checking his rear-view mirror. She was right behind him in her Ferrari.

Fifteen minutes later they arrived at his house.

'Down the street?' she questioned with an arched eyebrow.

'We share an ocean,' he said, grinning, ridiculously happy to see her.

She got out of her car, checking out his house from the outside. 'Hmm ... very nice,' she said, admiring the clean architectural lines.

'I built it,' he said.

'In your spare time?'

'Very funny.'

They walked toward the house. 'Aren't you about to begin shooting?' she asked.

'Next week.'

'And you're wandering around Malibu trying to kill your-self in front of my car.'

'Unfinished business plays on my mind.' He regarded her silently for a moment. 'I had to see you, Lucky.'

'So you're seeing me,' she said, trying to avoid direct eye-contact.

He opened the front door and led her inside.

She stood in the enormous soaring hallway with the huge skylights and let out a long, low whistle. 'Magnificent,' she said admiringly. 'And I thought all you could do was direct.'

'This house is very special to me,' he said, gesturing around the open space. 'Very private. I never bring anyone here.'

Lucky walked through the hallway, into the living room and out onto the terrace. 'Breathtaking,' she exclaimed. 'My house is a shack compared to this.' She turned to him with a smile. 'Wanna sell?'

He smiled back at her. 'Nope.'

'Don't blame you.'

'Can I get you a drink?'

'Water.'

'With Scotch?'

'Water,' she repeated, remembering their last encounter.

He went into the house and fixed himself a vodka and her a glass of ice-cold Perrier. When he returned outside she was sitting down. 'I'm pleased you came,' he said, handing her the drink.

'I guess you're right, Alex,' she said thoughtfully. 'We *are* unfinished business.'

'Glad you realize it.'

'Y'know,' she said reflectively, 'if we do continue to see each other as friends, you have to respect the way I feel.'

'I can do that.'

'It'll be a long time before I'm over Lennie.'

'That's understandable.'

'The truth is, I really regret what happened between us the other night.'

'Was it that bad?' he asked ruefully.

'You know what I mean, Alex. It was hot and exciting and we were both in the mood. But my reasons for doing it were wrong. I can't forget Lennie that quickly.'

'What you're saying is, if I play the good friend role and stay around long enough, things could change.'

'I have no idea what the future will bring, Alex.'

They held a long, intimate look. 'I was upset to hear about your father,' he said, breaking the silence. 'What happened?'

'I'm in the process of finding out,' she said. 'It's more complicated than I thought.'

'Is he doing okay?'

'Gino's strong. He'll recover.'

He felt totally at ease having her in his house. 'How about staying for dinner?' he suggested. 'My cook'll fix us anything you like. We can sit out here, watch the sunset . . .'

'Sounds tempting, only I'm busy tonight,' she said, standing up.

Hey, he wanted to say, *so am I, but I'm prepared to break my date.*

Then he started thinking – was she seeing someone else? Did he have competition?

'I have to get back,' she said.

He had a sudden insane desire to take her in his arms, hold her and kiss her. He'd never felt like this about any woman. Before Lucky, he'd considered they were only there to put a smile on his face. Now he had this juvenile crush.

She walked inside. 'By the way,' she said, over her shoulder, 'anything going on at my studio I should know about?'

He liked the way she still called it her studio. The woman had a no-defeat attitude he truly admired.

'I haven't met Donna Landsman yet,' he said, following her into the house. 'I have that pleasure in store tonight.'

She looked at him quizzically. 'Didn't you just invite me to dinner?'

'Hey, come with me.'

'Where?'

'Mickey Stolli's having a dinner for Donna at his house.'

'Jesus!' Lucky said. 'Trust Mickey to be right in there kissing ass.'

'So, like I said, come with me.'

Lucky considered the possibilities. Face to face with Donna Landsman in a social situation. Donna unaware that she knew her true identity. Mickey would shit himself if she turned up at his house. It was a tempting prospect. 'Who else is going?'

'I can have my secretary find out.' Now it was his turn to look at her quizzically. 'I thought you had other plans.'

'I can always change my mind.'

So can I, he thought. Once more, Tin Lee would be left at the altar. 'So,' he said. 'Dinner here, watching the sunset, wasn't good enough. But you'll consider coming to Mickey's?'

She laughed. 'The only reason I *might* consider it is because I wouldn't mind sitting across the table from Donna Landsman, seeing what she has to say. And as for Mickey – well, he and I are deadly enemies. Just to see his face when I walk in . . . the kicker being he can't do a damn thing about it because I'll be with you.'

'You know, Lucky, you have a way of making a guy feel really good about himself. First of all you sleep with me, then tell me it doesn't mean anything. Now you'll go to a dinner party with me only to get back at the people who're there. Thanks, babe, my ego's in overdrive.'

'You want me to come or not?'

His eyes met hers. There was electricity in the air. 'Yeah, I want you to come.'

'Then call me in half an hour.' She laughed softly. 'I promise I'll take the call.'

He walked her out to her car. She got in her red Ferrari and drove home.

Things were shaping up.

Chapter Forty-six

BEING THE majority shareholder of a big Hollywood studio was far more rewarding than Donna Landsman had imagined. The day her takeover of Panther Studios was announced in the trades, she'd received flowers from dozens of people she didn't know, including several movie stars and many important executives in the film industry.

Donna had never met anyone famous in her life, so when Abigaile Stolli called, informing her she'd like to throw a dinner party in her honor, Donna had been delighted – especially when Abigaile revealed the stellar guest list. It was an impressive line-up.

Donna had her secretary call to get Santo invited. When she told him, he immediately sulked. 'Don't *wanna* go,' he complained.

'Of course you do,' she replied, in her *I'm-taking-no-shit-from-you* voice. 'You'll meet all those famous people. They might do you some good in the future, connections are everything.'

On reflection he'd decided it wouldn't be such a bad idea. At least he'd get a decent meal, for a change. He hated his mother's cooking, and the cook she employed was even worse. The old bag made nothing but dried-up pasta and unappetizing tomato sauce with dull salads. Hint, hint, his mother wanted him to lose weight. Well, screw her – before all that dieting and plastic surgery she'd been no beauty. He remembered when she was his father's wife – the old Donatella. It was like that woman had died and this over-madeup cow had come to take her place.

'Is George going?' he asked.

'Of course he is,' Donna replied. 'I wish you'd try to get along with George. You make no attempt.'

'Maybe if he stopped pretending like he's my father,' Santo said with a surly glare. 'The way he acts sucks.'

'George has *never* tried to take the place of your father,' Donna admonished him.

'Yes, he has,' Santo mumbled. 'He's always on my case.'

He knew George had disapproved when his mother had informed him about the Ferrari – he'd heard them screaming from his room. Well, Donna was screaming, George never raised his voice. Donna, of course, had won.

Santo considered George an ineffectual worm. Donna kicked him around good. Santo couldn't understand why she kept him when it was quite obvious she'd be better off divorcing the spineless creep. Maybe, if she was going to meet movie stars, she'd find somebody she liked better. Arnold Schwarzenegger or Sylvester Stallone. Yeah! That was the ticket! A stepfather he could respect.

'You have to wear a suit and a tie,' Donna informed him.

'Why? Are we going to church?' Santo replied, with a rude smirk.

'It's only proper,' Donna said, concerned about her own outfit. She was not used to mixing with movie stars – it made her feel insecure.

Santo was aware he could get away with almost anything, but tonight he knew she'd force him to put on a dumb suit. He went to his room and sulked. Didn't she realize he looked even fatter in the one suit he possessed?

Locking his bedroom door, he crossed the room and opened his closet. Hidden in the back was the shotgun he'd recently purchased from the movie star's son at school. Yeah! He'd gotten himself a shotgun and two boxes of bullets. Shit! Talk about a power trip! Any time he wanted he could blow them both away.

Donna first.

George second.

POW! Just like that.

The fact that he owned the gun made him so psyched that he decided to write another letter to Venus. In his mind they were getting closer every day, bonding, exactly like people in love should.

He imagined her reading his letters, wondering who he was, wishing and hoping they'd meet soon and be together forever.

He'd started delivering his letters personally, choosing the early hours of the morning to do so. He'd creep down the hillside above her estate and force his way through the brush with not much effort. Then he'd scale the wall and deliver his latest offering. The stupid guard was always asleep. Her security sucked big time.

He had a favorite routine. Write Venus a letter. Jerk off.

Write another one. Jerk off again.

Life wasn't so bad after all.

☆   ☆   ☆

Venus had the best day doing nothing. In the afternoon Ron came over and sat by the pool with her. She'd noticed that, lately, he'd been spending more and more time at her house.

'Have you and Anthony closed the deal yet?' she inquired with a mischievous smile.

'Don't ask things like that,' Ron replied testily. 'You're just a nasty, curious little girl.'

'Why? 'Cause I want you to move out of that mausoleum you're living in?'

'No, because it's none of your business.'

'I tell *you* all about Rodriguez,' she said, sipping a Diet Coke through a straw.

'Where is he today?'

'Driving me crazy. I mean, he's under the false impression that he and I are a couple. He thinks that after a few great lays, we're Mr and Mrs America. Poor Anthony's running interference on the phone.'

'I notice you've hired a new guard.'

'Yeah, that other one was a moron. Every time I came home there was somebody else waiting in my house. This one seems more together. I'm hoping he can catch the crazy who keeps on hand-delivering letters to my house.'

'What letters?'

'Didn't I tell you? I've been receiving porno crap from some nutcase who thinks we're gonna be married and run off into the sunset. I mean this guy is *really* out there.'

'I presume you've handed them over to the authorities?'

She removed her sunglasses and threw her head back, catching rays. 'I will when I get around to it. Anthony's keeping a file.'

'It only takes one deranged fan to shoot a bullet into you.'

'Thanks, Ron. That's very encouraging. You've made me feel much safer!'

Late in the afternoon, after Ron had left, Anthony buzzed to inform her that Rodriguez was at the front door practically in tears.

'Okay,' she relented. 'Send him over to the house.'

Rodriguez burst through the front door, carrying flowers.

'Have I offended you, my princess?' he asked, liquid eyes full of love.

'No, Rodriguez,' she said firmly. 'Only you must realize we're not *living* together. We're not even girlfriend/boyfriend. I need my space.'

'What are we, then?' he asked, looking hurt.

'You're my masseur,' she said, deciding to go the honest route. 'And I pay you for your services.'

He was crestfallen. 'Is that all I am?' he asked mournfully.

She figured it was better to let him down sooner than later. 'Yes, Rodriguez, that's all you are.'

She knew she probably sounded cold and unfeeling, but surely it was best to end it this way before he got too caught up in the whole scene.

'I'm sorry if I disturbed you,' he said tightly.

'That's okay,' she said, glancing at her watch. It was around five. 'Do you have time to give me a massage now?' she asked, attempting to soften the blow.

'Of course,' he said stiffly.

'I'll meet you in there.'

She went upstairs, took a shower, wrapped a towel around herself toga-style, and strolled into the massage room.

Rodriguez had changed into white cotton chinos and a short-sleeved T-shirt – his working clothes.

She observed, as she always did, that he was incredibly good-looking. Maybe someone would discover him and make him into a star.

She got onto the table, lying on her stomach. Rodriguez whisked the towel from under her. She didn't have any false modesty – he'd seen it all, and then some.

'Use the lemon oil today,' she suggested. 'I love the smell.'

'Certainly,' Rodriguez replied obligingly, pouring a small puddle of oil in the center of her back and rubbing it in with his firm fingers. He began humming a Latin song under his breath. A good sign – at least she hadn't broken his heart.

She closed her eyes and let go, thinking about Cooper. The other night he'd been so convincing in his quest to win her back. 'I've changed,' he'd told her. 'We can get back together any time you say. I'll never stray again, it's not worth it.'

Sure, Coop, she'd thought. *You've been doing it for thirty years. Why would you change for me?*

Fortunately, she was not naïve.

Rodriguez's hands were on her ass, kneading, moving in circles, creeping closer and closer to the crack.

'Rodriguez,' she murmured sleepily. 'Remember this is a business arrangement. I can't be your girlfriend.'

'I understand,' he said, hands still working it, spreading the cheeks of her ass.

'No, don't do that,' she said, not too convincingly.

'In Argentina,' he said, 'when a woman says no . . . sometimes it is safe to assume she means yes.'

She felt the tip of his insistent tongue.

Oh, God! One more time. After that she would never encourage him again.

Chapter Forty-seven

 'HE'S HERE,' Boogie said.

'How did you get him to come back?' Lucky said.

'He tried to skip town. I persuaded him not to.'

'Does he have an answer for us?'

'Listen for yourself.'

She followed Boogie to the garage. Same scenario. There was Sami the Mutt trapped in a chair, red-rimmed eyes darting furtively around the closed space like a trapped animal searching for a way out.

This time she carried her own gun – a small silver automatic she'd owned for several years. She had no intention of using it on this pathetic excuse for a man. However, there was nothing wrong with scaring the crap out of him. He'd shot her father, narrowly missing little Maria by inches. His intention had been to kill Gino for money. If it had happened she'd have blown him away without another thought – this worthless piece of human excrement.

She stood in front of him, casually holding her gun down in front of her so he couldn't miss seeing it. 'Do you have a name for me, Sami?' she asked, her voice echoing around the empty garage. 'I hope you do, because today I'm not in the mood to fuck around.'

Sami glanced first at the gun, then over at Boogie, who'd

propped himself against the wall. 'Go ahead,' Boogie said easily. 'Tell her.'

'John Fardo, he hired me,' Sami mumbled, sweat bubbling on his forehead.

'Tell her who that is,' Boogie encouraged him.

'John's a limo driver. One of his clients had him set up the job.'

'What client?' Lucky asked, her black eyes deadly and watchful.

'Dunno,' Sami said in a strained voice. 'John works at Galaxy Star Limo – it's on Sepulveda.' Sweat dripped down his rat-like face as he squirmed in the chair. 'You gonna let me go now?'

'Get this piece of shit out of here, Boogie,' she said, walking to the door. 'And make sure he takes the money he was paid and gives it all to charity. Every cent.'

She returned to the house, thinking that they didn't make hit men like they used to. Fortunately for Gino, Sami the Mutt was a blundering amateur with no balls.

She sat in the den, dialed information and got the number of the limo company. Then she called them. 'You have a John Fardo working there,' she said, very businesslike. 'He usually drives Mrs Landsman, Mrs Donna Landsman ... Is that correct?'

The receptionist asked her to hold on a moment, came back and said, 'That's right, ma'am.'

'Fine. I need to contact Mrs Landsman later. Will John be driving her tonight?'

'Yes, ma'am. He drives her every night.'

Big surprise.

☆　☆　☆

Alex was delighted when Lucky called and said she could make it. He told her he'd pick her up at seven, then immediately tried reaching Tin Lee to cancel. She wasn't home.

This made him very nervous as Tin Lee knew the dinner was at Mickey Stolli's. He phoned Lili at home.

'How did the location scout go?' Lili asked.

He could hear her TV playing in the background and wondered if she was alone. 'Fine,' he said. 'Uh, listen, I've had a change of plans. I can't take Tin Lee to the Stollis'.'

'Did you call her?'

'I tried, she's not home. What can I do?'

Lili turned her TV down. 'You'll have to meet her at your apartment and tell her the bad news.'

'I was planning on staying at the beach.'

'Shall I call the Stollis to cancel?'

'No, don't do that,' he said quickly. 'I'm still going.'

'*You're* still going,' Lili repeated patiently, 'only you're not taking Tin Lee.'

'You got it.'

'Do you have another date?'

'As a matter of fact I do.'

'Then I suggest you reach Tin Lee as fast as possible.'

'That's smart of you, Lili, but I thought I just told you, I can't fucking reach her.'

'I'm sorry, Alex,' she said, unfazed by his growing anger, 'there's nothing *I* can do.'

He had a sneaking suspicion that Lili quite enjoyed his romantic screw-ups. 'Okay, okay,' he said, pissed off that she wouldn't help. '*Don't* come up with a solution.'

He called the hall porter at his apartment building on Wilshire. 'I'm expecting a guest at seven. When she arrives, tell her I've been held up on business and can't make dinner tonight. She's to go home and wait for me to call her. Have you got that?'

'Yes, Mr Woods,' said the desk porter.

'You're *sure*?'

'Absolutely, Mr Woods.'

Alex didn't know what else he could do. If he drove back into town to take care of it himself, he'd be late picking Lucky up. The smart thing was to stay at the beach.

He went into his bathroom and tried to decide what to wear. Black, of course, because he never wore anything else. A black silk shirt, black Armani jacket, black pants. It was a look.

Christ! He was as nervous as a teenager going on a first date. This was a joke.

After dressing, he went to his bar, stared at a bottle of vodka and decided against it. Half a joint would take the edge off. Had to be alert.

He consulted his watch, nearly seven.

One joint, and he'd be ready for anything.

☆　　☆　　☆

Mickey got in his car and left the studio. He hadn't heard from Venus since her surprise visit. He didn't know if this was good or bad. What the hell? She'd come around. Now he was head of Panther again, anything could happen. And he wanted it to happen desperately, because Venus was one hot babe, and it was time for him to get a piece of that juicy action.

Being back at Panther was a relief. Running Orpheus Studios had never been his kind of deal – answering to the Japanese, keeping everything above board and respectable. Mickey was used to doing things his way, he did not enjoy kow-towing to anyone.

He called Abigaile from the car to check on their party. She immediately started bitching because she didn't know the name of Cooper Turner's or Johnny Romano's date.

'Who gives a shit?' Mickey said, eyeing a blond in a black Mercedes who'd pulled up alongside.

'What am I to write on their place cards?' Abigaile wailed.

'Write it when they arrive,' he said impatiently. The blond zoomed past. He didn't give chase.

'Calligraphy is not one of my talents,' Abigaile snapped. 'I have a person who writes my cards.'

His wife could be a real pain in the ass, although he had to admit that since they'd reconciled, things were better than they'd been before the split. Two years ago she'd thrown him out after she'd caught him with Warner. Being out on his own was no fun. Hotel life was a drag, he'd yearned for the comforts of home. In fact, to his amazement, he'd even missed Abigaile.

Yes, Abigaile who gave great party *and* organized his social life was a definite asset.

But that didn't mean he couldn't screw around when the feeling hit him.

☆   ☆   ☆

Abigaile hung up on Mickey, annoyed because he didn't understand. 'Consuela,' she called, summoning her housekeeper. 'We do not have the names for these two place cards.'

Consuela shook her head. Like it mattered – these American woman worried about the craziest things.

Abigaile held up the card with Mickey's name on. 'Can you copy this calligraphy?'

Consuela stared at her blankly.

'The *writing*,' Abigaile said, raising her voice. 'Can you *copy* it?'

'Sure, Mrs,' Consuela said, with a *what-do-you-think-I-am –an-idiot?* shrug.

'Tell the butler to give you the names of the ladies with Mr Turner and Mr Romano, then write them on the blank cards.'

'Yes, Mrs.'

'Make sure you do it properly.'

That problem solved, she now had to decide what to wear. She had two outfits on stand-by: a Nolan Miller beaded two-piece evening suit, or a blue Valentino dress. They were both hanging in her vast closet, awaiting Mickey's approval.

She went upstairs and peered in her makeup mirror. A professional makeup artist had come by earlier in the day to do her face. Abigaile was very fussy about her skin and insisted on certain products. For cleansing and skin-care she used Peter Thomas Roth – his line was fragrance-free and helped reduce the appearance of fine lines and wrinkles. Anything to get rid of wrinkles. She'd discovered these products on a vacation in Aspen, and refused to use anything else. Over Peter Thomas Roth went Estée Lauder, with a touch of Revlon around the eyes.

Satisfied with her face, she began worrying about her daughter. What bizarre creation was Tabitha going to spring on them tonight? Last week they'd taken her to Trader Vic's for a family dinner. She'd worn a torn satin slip, fake tattoos all over her arms, and clumpy Doc Marten boots. Not a pretty sight. Mickey had sworn he'd never be seen with her in public again.

Abigaile decided she'd better check, so she hurried up to her daughter's room.

Tabitha was lying on her bed clad in a T-shirt and striped man's underpants, watching Axl Rose on MTV. Bon Jovi blasted from the CD player. The combination of noise was deafening.

'Aren't you getting ready?' Abigaile screamed over the din.

''S okay,' Tabitha replied, waving vaguely in her mother's direction.

'I hope you're wearing that dress I bought you at Neiman's,' Abigaile said, still shouting.

'Yeah, yeah,' Tabitha replied, casually twirling the gold ring she'd recently had stapled to her navel.

Abigaile shuddered and backed out of the indescribably messy room.

She wouldn't admit it to anybody, but she couldn't wait for Tabitha to move out.

☆   ☆   ☆

Venus decided on red – a drop-dead Alaïa dress with practically no back and plenty of daring cleavage. She hoped it would drive Mickey insane with lust. Even Alex might be impressed – he had to have *some* feelings.

Anthony was working late. She had him come up to her bedroom and check her out.

'Divine!' he exclaimed, with just the right amount of genuine adoration.

'Divine enough for them to cast me as Lola?'

Anthony nodded respectfully. 'There *is* no other actress for the role.'

He certainly knew the correct things to say.

Johnny's limo arrived shortly after. It was a double stretch – bigger than any she'd ever seen.

She wondered if his dick was as big as his limo. Ha, ha! She was *not* about to find out.

Johnny whistled at her dress. She complimented him on his grey shark-skin suit and black gangster-type shirt. He helped her into the car, copping a surreptitious feel. She pretended she didn't notice.

Johnny's limo driver was a beautiful black woman. Two female bodyguards sat ramrod straight up front.

'Do you really need all this?' Venus asked, settling in the back seat.

'Sure, babe, an' you should have the same,' he said with a sly smile. 'It's tax deductible.'

My – what big teeth you have, she thought, as he reached for a bottle of Cristal and poured her a glass. Rap music on low volume serenaded them.

She accepted the glass of champagne and thought about the letters she'd been receiving. 'Who deals with your fan mail?' she asked.

'Never read it – don't wanna see it,' he replied, gulping the champagne as if it was water. 'I get a lotta crazy letters.'

'Me, too. Lately I've had obscene letters arriving at my house. The envelopes turn up on my doorstep.'

He refilled his glass. 'How does your guard let this happen?'

She shrugged. 'It's a mystery.'

'You gotta deal with it. Beef up security, put a couple more guards on your property.'

'You're right.'

'I'll recommend some people to you,' Johnny said, his hand falling casually onto her thigh. 'When we're working together, we both gotta be surrounded at all times.'

'I've been meaning to talk to you about that,' she said, casually removing his hand. 'Alex has decided to go with Leslie Kane. I'm out of the movie.'

'No way!' Johnny exclaimed, frowning.

''Fraid so.'

'Impossible. Who told you this?'

'Freddie Leon.'

'You want I should do something about it?'

'If you like,' Venus said. 'Only don't expect any favors in return.'

'Don't worry, babe,' Johnny said, swigging more champagne. 'When Johnny says he'll do somethin', consider it done.'

'Thank you,' Venus answered demurely.

☆   ☆   ☆

'It's late,' Leslie said, as Jeff ran into the house. 'Where were you?'

'Jeez! I got held up at the gym, didn't realize the time,' he said, totally out of breath.

'I'm dressed and ready to go,' Leslie pointed out. 'We have to leave at seven-fifteen.'

'Sorry,' he said. 'I'll throw myself in the shower and be out in a minute.' He raced into the bathroom.

What did he think she was? A moron? He'd been with another woman, she could smell it all over him. And even if she couldn't, his wife had phoned to gloat. Yes, Jeff was married. Somehow he seemed to have developed a mild case of amnesia when it came to telling her. 'I'm Amber,' the woman had said on the phone. 'Jeff's wife. If you don't believe me, look in the back of his photo book – our marriage license is concealed behind the last photo.'

'Why are you calling?' Leslie had asked blankly.

'Thought you should know.'

'Thanks. Now I know.'

That had been several days ago. She had no idea why the wife had called and, quite frankly, she didn't care, because Jeff wasn't around to stay. Jeff was merely a convenience until she got Cooper back.

She'd checked out his photo book. He *was* a married man. A *lying* married man.

How foolish of him to pick tonight to liaise with his wife. How foolish of him to pick any night when he was with her.

She followed him into the bathroom. He was already in the shower, scrubbing his body with a soapy washcloth.

'Who was at the gym?' she asked. 'Anybody I know?'

'No, it was kinda quiet,' he shouted, over the noise of the running water.

God, he was a bad actor, no wonder he hadn't gotten a break.

She picked up a bottle of scent from the counter top, spraying a generous amount behind her ears and between her cleavage. Cooper loved scent – smells turned him on.

She wondered who Cooper was bringing tonight. She'd read in the gossip columns he'd been seen out with several women. One, the divorced wife of a sports star; another, a TV talk-show hostess; and, the third, a German supermodel.

She hoped it was the first one – less competition.

Jeff emerged from the shower and began vigorously toweling his balls.

'Your hair's wet,' she said.

'It'll take me two minutes if I borrow your hair dryer.'

'You know where it is.'

She walked out of the bathroom. He was dumb. Plain dumb.

What was it with men?

Obviously brains and a hard-on did not mix.

☆　☆　☆

Cooper's date, Veronica, was a famous runway and catalog model, specializing in sexy but respectable lingerie. He'd met her on a plane, taken her out a few times, and found her to be attractive and quite intelligent for a model. She didn't cling. He liked that in a woman. The one thing he didn't like was her deep guttural voice – she sounded like a man.

'Hi, Cooper,' she said, when he buzzed her apartment. 'I'll be right down.'

Veronica traveled a lot, from New York to Paris to London – she was always on the move. She had apartments in LA and New York.

'Sure you don't want me to come up?' he asked through the speaker, automatically thinking that maybe a blow-job wouldn't be a bad idea. Up until now he'd been behaving like a gentleman. Tonight he planned on closing the deal.

'Okay,' she said, not exactly enthusiastic.

He took the elevator to the fourteenth floor.

'Come in,' she said, greeting him at the door, chic in a cream-colored sleeveless dress, her long arms faintly tanned and muscled. She was almost six feet tall, with shoulder-length streaked hair, cat eyes, an intriguing overbite and a slightly too long nose. It all worked.

Cooper walked into her apartment, hard-on firmly in place.

'Cooper,' she said, noticing immediately, 'you're incorrigible! I've never met anyone like you.'

'Can I help it if I'm pleased to see you?' he said, taking her hand and placing it on his erection.

'Save it,' she said, chuckling hoarsely. 'For later.'

If he'd done that with Venus Maria she would have whipped it out and given him what he wanted. Veronica was a little too cool for his liking. She was a star in her own field, maybe too much of a star. Although like every other success-ful model she harbored the dream of becoming a famous actress. That was her weakness.

He changed tactics, snaking his hand down her neckline,

taking her by surprise. She was not wearing a bra. 'Beautiful tits,' he said.

'I know,' she said, smiling confidently. 'Shall we go?'

☆　☆　☆

Tea with Dominique was an enlightening experience. Tin Lee sat stiffly on the heavy damask-covered couch perusing Dominique's photograph albums, observing Alex as a child. In the beginning of the book there were pictures of him with his dad, playing on the beach, riding horses, swimming. Then came the birthday photos in which Alex was surrounded by both parents – all three carefree and laughing. Morbidly, Dominique had devoted three pages to Alex's father's funeral. The photographs of Alex were heartbreaking – his little face a solemn mask of grief as he stood next to the casket. After that the smiling stopped, and Alex was serious in all the photos. There he was sitting with his grandparents, staring out of a window, standing awkwardly in the yard. At the back of the album there were several pictures of him in his military academy uniform, a forlorn figure in the austere grey, his face sad and lonely.

'Alex needed the discipline,' Dominique said, a touch defensively. '*I* couldn't look after him, I had my own life to lead. I was a young woman when my husband died. I had certain . . . needs. I'm sure nobody expected me to give up everything.'

'I understand,' Tin Lee said quietly, not understanding at all.

'Alex doesn't,' Dominique said bitterly. 'He blames me for everything.'

'What does he blame you for?' Tin Lee asked curiously.

'The death of his father,' Dominique said, her scarlet mouth turning down. 'Alex thinks I nagged Gordon to death.

He doesn't know the real story. Gordon was a hopeless drunk and a worthless womanizer. I had every reason to nag.'

'Have the two of you ever discussed it?' Tin Lee asked, sipping tea from a fragile china cup.

Dominique shook her head. 'No, Alex refuses to talk about anything personal. He only sees me because his guilt tells him it's his duty to do so.'

'If I may say something,' Tin Lee interjected, 'perhaps the two of you fail to get along as well as you should because you're always criticizing him.'

'I criticize him to get his attention,' Dominique said sharply. 'If *I* didn't criticize him, who would?'

'I think it makes Alex unhappy,' Tin Lee ventured tentatively, hoping she wasn't going too far.

'Don't become an expert on him, dear,' Dominique said, caustically. 'What takes place between me and my son is no business of yours.'

Duly chastised, Tin Lee stood up. 'I have to go,' she said. 'Alex hates being kept waiting.'

'Come with me before you leave,' Dominique commanded, leading her into her bedroom.

Tin Lee followed obediently. Dominique went over to her bureau and opened an old velvet jewel box that stood on top. She picked out an exquisite diamond cross hanging from a thin platinum chain. 'You see this?' she said. 'It belonged to Alex's grandmother. I want you to have it. Wear it tonight.'

'Oh, I can't accept it,' Tin Lee said, startled. 'It's too expensive.'

'No, dear, go ahead,' Dominique said, handing it to her. 'It's comforting to know Alex has someone who cares for him, a girl who's not after his money.'

Tin Lee stood in front of the mirror, placing the diamond cross around her delicate neck. 'Beautiful!' she gasped.

'Enjoy it,' Dominique said. 'And enjoy tonight. Alex taking you to an industry party is a good sign.'

'I hope we can all have dinner later this week,' Tin Lee said.

'Yes,' Dominique said. 'I'd like that. I don't have many friends. I get lonely by myself.'

'I'll make sure Alex arranges it.'

Tin Lee hurried downstairs and waited for the valet to bring her car.

Anxiously she glanced at her watch. She was running late. She hoped Alex wouldn't be too annoyed.

Chapter Forty-eight

ALEX PICKED a yellow rose from his garden and took it with him on his way to meet Lucky. When he emerged from his car outside her house, he held it gingerly by the prickly stem, not used to making romantic gestures.

Lucky answered the door herself, looking stunning in a black Yves Saint Laurent evening suit, plunging neckline white blouse, and diamond hoop earrings, her dark hair framing her beautiful face with wild jet curls. Alex noticed a security guard hovering in the background. Idly he wondered why she needed security.

'Come in,' she said. 'My place is a dump compared to yours.'

'No, it's not,' he said, looking around. 'It's very comfortable.'

'Yours is the *Architectural Digest* version of mine,' she said ruefully. 'But, then, I've got kids and you don't, because you never married, right?'

'You can remember what we discussed the other night?'

She nodded. 'Of course.'

'You were blasted, you know that.'

'Hey – I can hold my liquor. I might have been bombed, but I know exactly what happened.' She laughed softly.

407

'Remember . . . what was her name? Ah, yes, Driving Miss Daisy, that's it.'

'How could I ever forget?'

'Will you put her in *Gangsters*?'

'Maybe,' he said, handing her the yellow rose. 'By the way, you look beautiful tonight.'

'Thank you,' she said, placing the rose on a table. 'I didn't know you were a horticulturist.'

'Thank my gardener. I just go out and pick 'em.'

'Do we have time for a drink?'

'Only if you have one, too.'

'I don't plan on a repeat performance.'

'One drink, Lucky. We're both grown-ups.'

Their eyes met for an intimate moment. Lucky looked away first, a sign of weakness. 'What'll it be?' she said pleasantly, refusing to allow herself to be sucked in. Alex was an extremely charismatic man but, as she kept on telling herself, it was far too soon for her to consider a relationship.

'Vodka martini.'

The phone rang.

'You get your phone, I'll make the drinks,' he said, heading for the bar.

She reached for the phone. It was Jennifer.

'My friend Ricco, the guy I said was working in Rome, is in LA, staying at the Chateau Marmont,' Jennifer said, sounding out of breath. 'I think you should hear what he has to say. We can meet him in half an hour.'

'How about later?' Lucky suggested.

'No. He's on a midnight plane back to Italy and he has dinner plans, it's got to be now.'

Lucky glanced over at Alex busily mixing martinis. 'Okay, now,' she said, making a fast decision.

'Meet me in the hotel lobby as soon as possible.'

'I'll be there,' Lucky said, replacing the receiver.

Alex walked toward her carrying her drink. 'I'm good at this,' he said, uncharacteristically happy. 'Used to be a bartender.'

'How would you feel if I met you at the Stollis'?' she said. 'Something important just came up. I have to stop somewhere first.'

Lucky Santangelo was a difficult woman. 'You're kidding, right?' he said.

'Sorry, no.'

'Then I'll come with you.'

She was silent for a moment, trying to decide if she wanted him along. 'It'll make us late for the Stollis',' she said at last.

'Big deal,' he responded, filled with curiosity.

'Okay, let's split. I'll fill you in while we drive.'

He gulped his drink.

Why was it that every time he saw Lucky it turned out to be an adventure?

☆　☆　☆

The American Airline plane took off from Kennedy airport on time.

'Are you sure we're doing the right thing?' Brigette asked.

'Yes,' Nona said firmly. 'Neither of us is equipped to deal with Michel. He's a sick psycho. Lucky will know how to handle him.'

'I feel so bad about screwing up,' Brigette said. 'Every time I screw up Lucky has to come and rescue me.'

'What do you mean?'

'Well, last time with the kidnapping and everything . . .' She trailed off. 'Lucky took the blame when I shot Santino Bonnatti.'

'Yeah, but you stood up at her trial and told the truth. Shit happens, Brigette. You have to learn how to cope.'

'So why am I running to Lucky?'

''Cause you're strung-out. Every night it's you and Isaac out on the town getting stoned and drunk. Is that what you want your life to be?'

'Not really.'

'So it's time to stop running. Besides, I want you straight so you can help me plan my wedding.'

'I asked Isaac to get me a gun, y'know.'

'You *didn't*.'

'Oh, yes, I did.'

'And what were you planning on doing if he'd gotten you one?'

'I dunno. Blow Michel away.'

'I don't think so. You're in enough trouble as it is.'

'I suppose I am.'

'It's not too late to straighten things out,' Nona said comfortingly. 'When we're rid of Michel we'll find a reputable agent. Your career is only just beginning.'

'I know you're right – Lucky's my only chance.'

After dinner and a movie they both fell asleep until the steward announced it was time to prepare for landing.

'Great flight,' Nona said, buckling her seatbelt and nudging Brigette awake. 'I booked us into the Hilton. I didn't think it was wise for us to descend on Lucky unannounced.'

'I want you to be there when I tell her.' Bridgette said anxiously.

'Course I will be.'

Brigette put her hand over Nona's. 'Thanks for being such a good friend.'

'Hey,' Nona replied lightly. 'All I'm doing is protecting my ten percent!'

☆　☆　☆

Leslie and Jeff were the first to arrive at the Stollis', Jeff in his one and only suit – an Armani, purchased for him by Leslie – and Leslie in a white silk dress.

Abigaile greeted them at the door. The women exchanged air kisses and compliments. Jeff beamed happily. How did he get so lucky? Mixing in this company was a major plus. Thank God he had an understanding wife who was letting him do his thing for the benefit of their future.

'Mickey will be down in a minute,' Abigaile said, leading them through the spacious front hallway to the bar.

A handsome barman sprang to attention.

'White wine,' Leslie requested, nervously smoothing down the skirt of her dress.

'Tequila on the rocks,' Jeff said, feeling insecure.

She threw him a warning look, he did not hold his liquor well and they both knew it.

'Just one, cutie,' Jeff said, catching her look.

She hated it when he called her cutie.

Abigaile wished somebody else would arrive fast, or that Mickey would get his ass downstairs. She didn't relish being in sole charge of the guests. It was okay when there were lots of them and they could mingle. Now she had to entertain these two until somebody else arrived when all she really wanted to do was be free to supervise. Not to mention checking on Tabitha, who'd refused to come out of her room to show off what she was wearing. Little madam.

Abigaile heard the doorbell in the background. A few moments later Johnny Romano strolled in, accompanied by Venus Maria.

Abigaile frowned. How *dare* Johnny not announce who his guest was when she was as famous as Venus. The man had no manners – but then, what could you expect from an actor? Especially a Latin actor, who happened to have gotten rich in a string of disgustingly raunchy movies. Abigaile conveniently forgot that Mickey had been responsible for most of them.

'Abbey, baby,' Johnny purred, favoring her with the famous Latin-lover leer and a quick pinch on the butt. 'Who's my favorite Hollywood wife?' He bent to kiss her.

'Johnny, dear,' Abigaile responded, wrinkling her nose as she breathed in a strong whiff of his strangely exotic aftershave, 'you look *wonderful*. And, Venus, it's been ages! *So* good to see you again.'

'Thanks, Abbey,' Venus said calmly, although inside she was seething because she'd spotted Leslie, and Johnny hadn't mentioned *she* was going to be there.

Abigaile led them over to the bar. 'Do you know Leslie and . . .' She blanked on Jeff's name again.

Leslie, wide-eyed with shock, managed to stammer out, 'J-Jeff.' She had not seen Venus since the dreaded night at her house. This was a disaster. Now she'd have no chance with Cooper.

'Hi, Leslie,' Venus said coolly.

For a moment Leslie considered ignoring the tramp. Instead, she mumbled an uptight, 'Hello.'

Jeff seemed to have forgotten where his loyalty should lie. 'Venus!' he exclaimed, with a big I'm-your-greatest-fan grin. 'We met at Leslie's, remember? Some night *that* was!'

Both women shared the same thought. *What an asshole!*

Johnny, who as far as he knew hadn't encountered Leslie before, shook her hand, holding it a few seconds too long. 'Been readin' a lotta good things about you,' he said. 'Welcome to the stratosphere.'

Leslie managed a strained smile. 'Thank you.'

She guessed he didn't recall their one night of unadulterated lust in a bungalow at the Beverly Hills Hotel – her and two other girls. He'd paid ten thousand dollars for the three of them and behaved like a greedy pig.

'No, thank *you*,' Johnny replied, putting in some heavy duty eye-contact. If he didn't score with Venus, this red-headed lovely could be a definite contender.

At which point Mickey put in an appearance, showered and shaved, bald head glistening, Turnbull & Asser shirt, Doug Hayward English suit and red Brioni tie. 'Welcome, everyone,' he said, beaming at his guests, doing a classic double-take when he spotted Venus. 'Good evening, my dear,' he said, turning on as much suave charm as he could muster. 'We weren't expecting you.'

'I know how you like surprises, Mickey,' she said, automatically flirting. 'So here I am.'

'Yeah,' Johnny added. 'Me an' Venus, we're an item.'

'An item?' Abigaile chimed in, thinking Venus's dress was ridiculously low-cut.

Johnny squeezed Venus's arm. 'Hey, Mickey, we figured since we're makin' *Gangsters* together, we'd give you some extra PR. The tabloids're gonna cream over *this*.'

Mickey quickly glanced at Leslie. She was talking to Jeff and didn't seem to have heard. Thank God.

Abigaile, however, *had* heard. She took Mickey's arm and said, 'Excuse us a moment.' Whereupon she led him over to the other side of the room and said a sharp, 'What's Johnny talking about? Hasn't anybody *told* Venus she's out of *Gangsters*?'

Mickey nodded. 'Yeah, yeah, honey, it's all taken care of. Don't worry your little head about it.'

'My *little head*?' she said, haughtily. 'Who do you think you're talking to – one of your brain-dead starlets?'

'There's been a change of plan,' Mickey said, scowling. He couldn't stand it when Abigaile got uppity.

'What do you mean, a change of plan?' Abigaile snapped.

'I found a better movie for Leslie. Figured I'd send the script to her first, get her excited. She'll be starring with Gere.'

'Richard?'

'No, *Maxie*,' he said, raising his eyebrows. 'What do you think? Of course Richard.'

Big change of attitude from Abigaile, who imagined Richard Gere attending one of her future dinners. 'Oh, that's nice. She'll be thrilled.'

'I told ya, didn't I? Alex is too tough for Leslie. He'll give her nothin' but grief. I'm doin' the kid a favor. We won't announce it tonight.'

'Why not?'

''Cause I don't want Venus finding out. She's probably pissed at me. So is Alex. They're all pissed at me. I run a studio, nobody likes me.'

'That's ridiculous, Mickey, everybody loves you.'

He had *her* back on track. 'Thanks, honey. Now let's relax and have a nice evening. Keep your mouth closed, that way we won't get into trouble.'

'No, Mickey,' Abigaile said grandly. '*You* keep *your* mouth closed. *Yours* is the big one.'

She hurried back to their guests. Venus and Johnny had wandered outside by the pool. Leslie and Jeff were having a heated conversation at the bar. And Cooper Turner and his date were making an entrance.

'Abigaile, sweetheart,' Cooper said, kissing her on both cheeks. 'This is Veronica.'

'Hello, dear,' Abigaile said, craning her neck to greet the tall model.

Leslie, who had been haranguing Jeff for being so nice to Venus, glanced up and saw Cooper approaching. Her attitude immediately changed. 'Cooper,' she said, with a welcoming smile, 'how lovely to see you.'

'Hi, Leslie,' he said. 'Meet Veronica.'

Leslie nodded, continuing to smile while thinking, *Oh, God, he's with that trashy model who poses in those sexist lingerie catalogs that get dropped in your mailbox whether you want them or not. She's not so hot in real life. Too tall and horsy, with enormous teeth!*

'Veronica,' Cooper said easily, 'say hello to Leslie Kane and her boyfriend, Jeff.'

'Hiya, Cooper,' said Jeff, extending his hand, completely unconcerned that Leslie and Cooper had once been lovers.

Venus and Johnny strolled in from outside. Perfect timing, as the guests of honor – Donna and George Landsman – were entering the room, a sulking Santo trailing behind them.

Abigaile went into hostess overdrive. 'Donna,' she gushed, 'I'm *thrilled* to meet you. Mickey has told me *so* much about you. Welcome to Hollywood! We're *delighted* Mickey is back at Panther.'

An alert Mickey jumped into action. 'Donna,' he said, unwittingly ignoring George, 'welcome to my house.'

Donna had already spotted Cooper Turner, Johnny Romano and Venus Maria, and was completely intimidated. She could deal with anything business-wise, but mixing with these famous people was a new experience. She grabbed Santo, who was lurking behind her, and pushed him to the forefront. 'This is my son, Santo,' she said.

'Hello, Santo, dear,' Abigaile said, wondering why they'd allowed the boy to get so fat.

Santo spotted Venus across the room and his heart began to pound.

Venus. *His* Venus. In the flesh, only a few yards away from him. A dull red flush spread over his face.

'Gotta use the bathroom,' he mumbled.

'Now?' Donna hissed, not pleased.

'Yeah, now.'

Graciously Abigaile said, 'It's to the left of the hallway, dear.'

Santo rushed from the room. Had Venus noticed him? Oh, Jeez! He hadn't planned on them meeting like this.

He darted into the john, slamming the door behind him. Fortunately he'd brought a joint with him. Groping in his pocket, he lit up and inhaled deeply, frantically trying to compose himself.

On her way downstairs, Tabitha saw the fat boy enter the guest bathroom. She chuckled to herself. This was a good one, she'd burst in and embarrass him. Ha! Ha! That would teach her mother to force her to attend one of her moronic dinner parties.

She reached the door of the guest bathroom and flung it open. Santo, who'd forgotten to lock it, nearly jumped ten feet in the air. He was caught with a joint half an inch from his lips.

Tabitha took in the scene. Quick as a flash she closed the door. 'You must be that Donna person's son,' she said.

'Yeah,' he mumbled. 'Santo.'

'I'm Tabitha – the Stollis' daughter. I notice you've got a nice, fat roach. Give me a drag and I won't tell anybody.'

☆ ☆ ☆

Aaron Kolinsky, the desk porter on duty at Alex's apartment building, had a bad stomach-ache. Some of the tenants were enough to make any man ill with their stupid demands.

'Walk my dog.'

'Get my car waxed.'

'Run to the market for me.'

What did they think he was? A one-man service? The other guy working the shift was a young punk. He didn't know shit. Aaron found that he had to take care of everything.

At seven o'clock he quit for the night. He'd had enough. Seven o'clock in the morning until seven o'clock at night was enough for anybody to have to put up with these rich people and their constant demands.

He left long before Tin Lee put in an appearance. It didn't matter anyway. He'd completely forgotten Alex's instructions.

Tin Lee walked up to the desk, announced she was going to Alex's apartment, took the elevator upstairs and rang his bell.

No answer.

After five minutes she came downstairs again. She was running over half an hour late, Alex was probably furious and had gone on ahead.

'Did Mr Woods leave a message for me?' she asked.

'No, ma'am,' said the new desk clerk, more interested in reading his hidden copy of *Playboy*.

'Are you sure?'

'Nope. Nothing here.'

'Do you have a phone book?'

He handed over a big fat LA phone book. Fortunately Mickey Stolli was listed. She copied down the Beverly Hills address and collected her car from the valet, thinking she'd arrive at the dinner in time to be seated. Alex would be delighted that she was so resourceful.

Somehow she felt their relationship was about to step up to another level. And not a moment too soon. Tin Lee felt it was time she asserted herself.

Chapter Forty-nine

 SITTING IN ALEX'S Porsche on the way to the
Chateau Marmont, Lucky started talking and found
she couldn't stop. 'I don't know why I'm telling you
this,' she said. 'It's family history.'

'So what you're saying is that the Bonnattis always held a
grudge against the Santangelos, and Donna is carrying on the
tradition?' Alex said.

She nodded. 'It goes way back to Gino and Enzio Bonnatti
in the twenties. They were business partners in the beginning,
bootlegging, speakeasies – they made a lot of money. Then
Enzio got an urge to move into hookers and drugs, and Gino
wasn't into that, so they split their partnership. Gino went
to Vegas where he built hotels. Enzio took a different road.'
She paused for a moment, lighting a cigarette. 'Enzio was
my godfather. I was over at his house all the time. In a way I
was closer to Enzio than I was to Gino. Until one day I
discovered the truth. Enzio was responsible for my mother's
murder, Marco's death, *and* my brother's. It was a shattering
revelation.'

'Jesus!'

'I was devastated. But there was absolutely no doubt I had
to do something about it.'

'Why you?' Alex questioned, his eyes fixed firmly on the
road.

'Gino was in hospital, he'd had a heart-attack.' She pushed back her long dark hair, remembering the experience in vivid detail. 'I went to Enzio's house, lured him upstairs and . . . I shot him.' She took a long deep breath. 'Everybody thought it was self-defense. I told the cops he was trying to rape me.' Another beat. 'It wasn't self-defense, Alex. It was pure revenge.'

'And they never arrested you?'

'Nope. Gino had connections. Plus I really made it look like I was defending myself.'

Alex took his time before answering. 'That's some story,' he said at last.

'Y'know, Alex,' she said thoughtfully, 'if you wait for the law to take action you may as well forget it. If somebody close to you was murdered, would you sit in a court room watching them pussy-foot around for a year or two? Or would you deal with it yourself and get real justice?'

He stopped at a red light and turned to look at her. 'I don't know what I'd do, Lucky.'

'The Arabs have it right – an eye for an eye.'

'Maybe . . .' he said slowly.

'Hey – you want the murderer locked up in jail working on his appeal while *we* pay the bills?'

'Not me.'

'And how about hearing how he's found God, what a changed person he is – all that shit. Because we both know that's what happens. Believe me, Alex, if somebody does something to me or my family, they're going to get it back in spades.'

'I agree the death penalty *is* a deterrent, and they should put it into effect more often. But taking the law into your own hands . . .'

'Why not?' she demanded angrily. 'The law is so fucking clever? I don't think so.'

For a while they drove in silence until they reached the hotel. Lucky stubbed out her cigarette and got out of the car. The Chateau Marmont had a history of Hollywood scandals and was much beloved by actors and the artistic community. 'I'm crazy about this place,' she said, as they walked through the hotel entrance. 'I always expect to see Errol Flynn or Clark Gable in the lobby.'

'I didn't know you were an old-movie fan,' he said, surprised.

'I *love* old movies. That's all I ever watch on television. Old movies and soul music are my two passions.'

'You like soul music?'

'Crazy about it. Marvin Gaye, Smoky Robinson—'

'David Ruffin, Otis Redding . . .'

'Hey, you're into it, too,' she said, smiling.

'I have a large collection of original records.'

'Me, too!'

'So,' Alex said, 'what are we trying to find out tonight?'

'This guy, Ricco, was in charge of the extras. Jennifer said the blond in the photos was hanging around the set. She probably got herself hired purely to set Lennie up.'

'And you think Ricco can help you?'

'He did all the hiring. With unions and stuff it's not that easy to get into a movie.'

'Even in Corsica?'

'It was still an American production.'

'And if you find out Donna Landsman *was* responsible, what then?'

She gave him a long, mocking look. 'Now, c'mon, Alex, you wouldn't want to be an accessory, would you?'

He felt like he'd wandered into a scene from one of his own movies. Lucky's rules were different from everyone else's.

Jennifer was waiting in the lobby. 'Glad you could make it,' she said, hurrying toward them.

'Meet Alex Woods,' Lucky said.

'A pleasure,' Jennifer said, her pretty face flushed. 'Ricco wants us to go straight up to his room. I'll call and tell him you're here.' She went over to the desk and picked up the house phone.

'Pretty girl,' Alex remarked.

'Your type?' Lucky asked.

'No, Lucky, *you're* my type.'

'Hmm . . . not into California blonds, huh? That makes you unusual.'

Jennifer returned and the three of them got into the elevator.

In a way Lucky was glad that Alex was with her. It was hard discovering how Lennie had been set up, and gut instinct told her it *was* a set-up. Not only had they taken Lennie from her, but they'd wanted her to think he'd betrayed her too. Donna Landsman was a cold and devious bitch.

Ricco flung open the door. He was a short, dark Spanish man with an animated expression, a pencil-thin moustache and a way of speaking rapid English, repeating words, while waving his arms wildly in the air.

'Jennifer, my Jennifer,' he greeted, giving her a big hug. 'Is she not the most gorgeous girl you've ever seen?'

'Ricco,' Jennifer said, embarrassed by the compliment, 'this is Lucky Santangelo and Alex Woods.'

'I think perhaps I have died and gone to the heaven of the film-makers,' Ricco exclaimed, rolling his expressive eyes. 'Mr Woods, an honor to meet you. I have worshipped every one of your movies. One day, perhaps you let me work on them. And Miss Santangelo, you have made some fine films at Panther.'

'Thanks,' Lucky said. 'I guess Jennifer told you what this is about.'

'Exactly, exactly,' said Ricco. 'Jennifer has told me and I do recall . . . yes, I recall the blond very well indeed, very well indeed. A beauty. She come to me and say, "Ricco, put me in the movie." I tell her no lines. She says "Fine, fine." I cannot understand why a beautiful woman like this want to be an extra, but I obliged.'

'Where can I contact her?' Lucky asked.

'Yes, yes. My assistant has gone to my files, and we give you an address in Paris. I have it for you – here.' He handed her a slip of paper.

'I appreciate it,' Lucky said.

'For you, madame, anything.'

They left his room.

'I thought it was important you spoke to him yourself,' Jennifer said.

Lucky nodded. 'I'm glad I did.'

'It looks like somebody wanted you to think Lennie was playing around on you,' Jennifer said. 'Although they couldn't have known he was going to be in a terrible accident the next day.'

'Don't be so sure about that.'

'What do you mean?'

'I mean this was planned,' Lucky said slowly. 'I can assure you, Jennifer, Lennie's death was no accident.'

☆ ☆ ☆

Tin Lee drove directly to the Stollis' mansion. When she arrived, she gave her car to a parking valet and entered the front door. A butler looked her over. 'Can I help you, madam?'

'I'm Mr Woods' guest,' she said, giving the man her name.

He consulted his list. 'Ah, yes, please go in.'

She walked through the spacious front hall into the living room. Abigaile saw her coming. 'You must be with Alex, dear,' she said. 'I'm Abigaile Stolli.'

'Yes, Mrs Stolli,' Tin Lee said, feeling uncomfortable arriving on her own.

'Where's Alex?' Abigaile asked, peering behind her.

'Isn't he here?'

'Oh, I see . . . He told you to meet him. Don't worry, dear, I'm sure he'll arrive any moment. Go to the bar and have a drink.'

Tin Lee went to the bar, where she was immediately pounced upon by a slightly inebriated Jeff.

'Tin Lee,' he exclaimed with a sloppy grin. 'How ya doin'?'

She was relieved to see a familiar face. Jeff and she had attended the same acting class. 'I'm fine, Jeff. How are you? It's been almost a year.'

'You're pretty as ever,' he said, slurring his words as he pawed her arm.

'Who are you here with?' Tin Lee asked, backing away from his touch.

'I'm living with Leslie Kane,' he said proudly. 'She's my gal.'

'*The* Leslie Kane?'

'You bet your cute little Japanese ass.'

'I'm not Japanese, Jeff,' she said stiffly.

'Whatever,' he said vaguely, unaware that he was being offensive. 'Who're *you* with?'

'Alex Woods.'

'Holy shit!' He laughed too loudly. 'Didn't *we* do well?'

☆ ☆ ☆

Leslie had gone over to Cooper and was trying to engage him in conversation. Unfortunately, Veronica was sticking to his side like Super-glue, plus he had one eye on Venus, who was busy talking to Mickey.

'I've been asked to do a press junket for our movie,' Leslie said. 'They want me to fly to London and Paris. Will you be going?'

'Hadn't really thought about it,' Cooper said, still watching Venus.

'I'm sure it would help the movie.'

'You'll do a good job on your own.'

She was bitter about his attitude. When their affair was secret and he could bang her whenever he wanted, he'd been all over her. Now they'd been found out, he was treating her badly and she didn't appreciate it.

'Are we allowed to smoke in this house?' Veronica asked, looking bored.

'Smoking's bad for you,' Cooper admonished her.

'I do *everything* that's bad for me,' Veronica retorted, displaying horse teeth in a nasty smile.

Cooper laughed.

'I'll take a smoke by the pool,' Veronica said, perfectly secure that she could do whatever she liked.

'I'll come with you,' Cooper offered.

'No, wait a minute,' Leslie said, placing a restraining hand on his arm. 'I have to talk to you.'

'Don't worry, Cooper,' Veronica said, her deep voice jarring his nerves. 'I'll see you in a minute.' She strolled out to the terrace.

Cooper stared at Leslie as if they were no more than casual acquaintances. 'What?' he said, aggravated.

'I need to ask you a question,' she said.

'Go ahead.'

'What have I done to you to make you behave so coldly toward me?'

'Nothing,' Cooper said, feeling trapped.

'We used to make love every day until your wife found out. Now you act as if you hardly know me. It's not as though you're with her anymore.'

Cooper was silent for a moment. He knew he hadn't treated Leslie fairly, but that didn't mean she could hang on forever. After all, the girl was an ex-hooker – not exactly a sweet little virgin. 'Listen, honey,' he said, hoping to get rid of her permanently, 'consider it a movie fuck.'

Her eyes filled up. 'What?'

'It lasted while we were making the movie. This happens a lot in the business.'

'Are you telling me I didn't mean anything to you?'

'At the time, Leslie. Not now.'

She was filled with mixed emotions. She hated him. She loved him. There was a lump in her throat, and she wanted to scream.

'Don't make a big thing of this,' Cooper warned. 'You broke up my marriage, Leslie. That's why we can't be together again, because – and maybe I'm being unfair – I blame you.'

'You blame *me*?' she gasped.

'Yes,' he replied. 'So stay away from me, Leslie. It's better for everyone.'

☆   ☆   ☆

'I need a drink before we go to the Stollis',' Lucky said. 'Can we stop somewhere?'

'We're late anyway,' Alex replied. 'May as well.'

'One drink, that's all. I don't plan on doing what I did the other night.'

'Why not?' he said lightly. 'I enjoyed every minute of our adventure.'

They went into the bar at Le Dôme. He ordered a vodka and Lucky requested a Pernod and water.

'So now what you're telling me is that you think Donna Landsman was responsible for Lennie's death?' Alex said when their drinks came.

Lucky nodded, sure she was right. 'Exactly.'

'Even with no proof?'

'Oh, come on, Alex. Who needs proof? I know for sure she hired a hit-man to take care of Gino – her driver was the go-between.'

'*How* do you know?'

''Cause I had the man at my house earlier, tied to a chair in my garage. Fortunately the jerk was a total amateur. He confessed. She may have business smarts, but she certainly doesn't know what she's doing when it comes to hiring muscle.'

He was shocked. 'You had him at your house?'

'That's right.'

'Why didn't you hand him over to the police?'

'Get serious, Alex. What was I going to say? "Oh, hi, Mr Detective. Please arrest this hit-man. Oh, yes, and I think Donna Landsman is responsible for setting up an accident in which my husband was killed. And she also hired a guy to shoot my father – this guy, in fact. She's been a very bad girl and needs to be put in jail." I don't think so!'

'Guess you're right.'

'I *know* I am.'

'Jesus, you really say what's on your mind.'

'You do the same thing in your movies.'

He downed a shot of vodka, and clicked his fingers for another. 'Yeah, I put the feelings I'm unable to express in real life up there on the screen. A lot of my anger comes out in my movies. My theory is that's why I never won an Oscar. Sure, my films get nominated because I know how to make a hell of a powerful statement, but the anger in them turns some Academy members off. Result – they don't vote for me.'

'Is this a recent revelation or are you in therapy?'

'Had a shrink. The guy told me plenty. Listening to you is better. I *do* know I have to take control of my own life. That's the key to inner peace.'

'You've got that right. Look at me, I haven't had an exactly peaceful life but I've learned to go with it. You can bet I'll never have an ulcer.'

'You're a fortunate woman, Lucky. You were married to a man you loved, you've got three beautiful children.' He paused. 'You know, I've never been in love with anyone, never had a meaningful relationship or even wanted to. My only close relationship is with my mother, and that's about as fucked up as you can get.'

'Take control,' Lucky said. 'The power's within you. Use it.'

'Maybe you're right.'

He looked at her for a long moment. She suddenly felt very close to him. It took every ounce of willpower she possessed to finally break the look.

She realized Alex was right: they were unfinished business, but now was not the time.

Chapter Fifty

'I'M STONED,' Tabitha giggled. 'This is like real heavy shit, where'd you score?'

'School,' Santo replied, thinking she was really weird-looking in her orange Spandex micro-skirt, which barely covered her crotch, and the cut-off skimpy top that revealed most of her midriff. His eyes rested on the gold ring attached to her belly-button. He controlled an insane urge to rip it out. Would she scream? Would her ripped flesh bleed? He wouldn't mind giving it a try.

'Hey, what school you go to?' she said, running a hand through her spiked magenta hair.

'Why?' he asked suspiciously.

''S not polite to answer a question with a question.'

'Where do *you* go to school?' he asked, noticing that her fingernails were painted a creepy black – like she was out of some vampire movie.

'Boarding school,' she said. 'Switzerland. Here,' she snatched the joint from him again, jamming it between her lips, 'more for me. Otherwise, I'll tell 'em you were in here jerking off.'

'You wouldn't do that,' Santo said, still recovering from the shock of seeing Venus in the flesh, more gorgeous and sexy than her photos.

'I can do anything I want,' Tabitha boasted. 'I'm the daughter of the house.'

He'd seen girls who looked like her hanging around the strip on Saturday nights. Usually they were sitting on a curbside throwing up, or fighting with each other before crowding in to see some sleazy rock band. Rich punks. He'd never been into that scene. He preferred the gold Rolex, unlimited credit and a very expensive car.

'So,' Tabitha said, sucking on the joint, 'your mom's the one who kicked Lucky Santangelo out at Panther, right?'

'I guess so,' he mumbled.

'My dad hates Lucky Santangelo,' Tabitha said, matter-of-factly. 'She threw *him* out of Panther. I've never met her, but *I* think she sounds cool. And my great-granddad says she's the best.'

'You've got a great-granddad?'

'Yeah, doesn't everyone? Do you know who he is?'

'Who?'

'Abe Panther,' she boasted. 'He founded Panther Studios.'

'Yeah, well, *my* father was murdered,' Santo said, scoring points.

Tabitha ignored that pertinent piece of information. 'Why are you so fat?' she demanded.

'Why are *you* so rude?' he countered, hating her and her stupid outfit and her ugly hair. Who was she to call him fat? She was a total freak.

''S'pose we gotta join the party,' Tabitha grumbled. 'Okay, fat boy, let's go.'

'Don't call me that,' he said, hating her even more.

She giggled. 'Give me another joint and I won't.'

☆ ☆ ☆

Abigaile looked around. To her relief, everyone appeared to be having a good time. She glanced at the clock. It was eight-thirty. Where was Alex Woods? He was the only guest missing. She didn't think it was polite to summon everyone to the dining table until he was present.

'Tin Lee, dear,' she said, going over to the bar, 'did Alex give you any indication of what time he was arriving?'

'I thought he'd be here before me,' Tin Lee replied. 'He must have gotten held up. As you know, he's starting production on Monday. He's very busy.'

'He could've phoned if he was going to be late,' Abigaile said, hardly able to conceal her irritation.

'I'm sure he wouldn't mind if you went ahead without him.'

'Hmm . . .' Abigaile said, not pleased.

She was on her way to the kitchen when she spotted Tabitha, dragging Santo behind her. Oh, God, the out-fit! Mickey would have a heart-attack when he saw it. She swooped into her daughter's path, blocking her way. 'Tabitha,' she said, quietly seething. 'May I see you for a moment?'

'Mom,' Tabitha said, her orange Spandex micro-skirt riding up. 'Have you met Santo?'

'Yes, I've met Santo,' Abigaile said, through clenched teeth. 'Come, dear, I wish to speak with you.'

Tabitha, who was feeling the effects of the grass, giggled stupidly. 'What're we gonna talk about, Mom? Sex? Do you and Dad still do it?'

Abigaile gripped her daughter's arm and was on her way to maneuvering her out of the hall, when in walked Alex Woods accompanied by Lucky Santangelo.

Abigaile stopped short. Tabitha took the opportunity to wriggle from her grasp and escape.

'Sorry, Abbey,' Alex said, not sounding sorry at all. 'Got

held up in a meeting.' And before she could say a word, he and Lucky were on their way into the living room.

She hurried behind them, desperately trying to catch Mickey's eye. He was in such an intimate conversation with Venus that he didn't notice.

Tin Lee jumped down from her bar stool and ran to greet Alex. 'I was late getting to your apartment,' she started to explain, then she saw Lucky and stopped.

Alex's worst nightmare was coming true. 'What are *you* doing here?' he said, completely exasperated. 'Didn't you get my message?'

'What message?'

'You must be Alex's date,' Lucky said, getting the picture, and feeling sorry for the poor girl, who, pretty as she was, was way out of her depth. 'I'm sorry I kept him. Alex and I had a business meeting. He asked me to come here for a drink.'

'I'm sure it's okay if you stay for dinner,' Alex said quickly. 'I'll tell Abigaile.' He made his way over to Abigaile, who was still trying to get Mickey's attention. 'Abbey,' he said, 'Lucky's staying for dinner.'

'Lucky Santangelo is not Mickey's favorite person,' Abigaile responded tartly. 'They have a history.'

'She happens to be my date.'

'No, Alex,' Abigaile responded, 'your *date* is Tin Lee – who, I might add, has been here for half an hour without you.'

'My *date* is Lucky Santangelo,' he said, refusing to back down. 'Tin Lee is the one you're fitting in.'

'There's no room at the table, Alex.'

'Pull up another chair, Abigaile.'

They glared at each other.

'I'll see what I can do,' she said crossly.

☆　☆　☆

Lucky assessed the situation. She knew all the players, except George, Donna Landsman's husband. Without hesitating she walked right up to the woman and said, 'So, we meet again.'

Donna was shocked to see her. She tried to compose herself, aware that it would be unwise to make a scene. Mickey inviting Lucky was a big mistake, one he would pay for. 'How are you?' she said coldly.

'Pretty good, as a matter of fact,' Lucky replied, staring at Donna, trying to reconcile the new image with the old Donatella. There wasn't the slightest resemblance. 'Thing is, I've had time to reflect, get myself organized, consider the way things have been going.'

Cooper snuck up and grabbed her from behind. 'Hi, gorgeous! Great to see you.'

'Cooper! Have you met Donna Landsman?'

'Sure.'

'Isn't it nice to know we have such an *experienced* woman at Panther? You *are* experienced in the film industry, aren't you, Donna?'

George answered for her. 'Mickey Stolli will do an excellent job.'

Lucky raked George with a look, summing him up instantly. Worshipped his wife, probably never got laid before, a whiz with finances, had no idea what Donna was up to.

She turned back to Cooper. 'Are you making any deals with Panther?' she inquired.

'You'll have to ask my agent,' Cooper said, with a smooth smile.

'Oh, I'm sure Donna will pursue you. She probably has all the agents and managers crawling up her ass *begging* for deals. And, Donna, I must say, it certainly looks like it could accommodate them.'

Before Donna could respond, Lucky moved away, leaving

Donna fuming. She was not fat. How dare the skinny Santangelo bitch make a comment like that? And why was Lucky walking around so cool and collected? Wasn't it enough that she'd lost her husband, her studio and almost lost her father? What else would it take to bring her down?

'Did you hear that?' Donna said to George, her face red with anger. 'Did you?'

George tried to calm her. 'No scenes,' he said quietly. 'You mustn't let these people see she's upset you.'

'What's she doing here?' Donna muttered. 'I thought Mickey hated her.'

'I'll find out.'

'You'd better,' Donna snarled, her triumphant entry into Hollywood society ruined.

☆　☆　☆

Abigaile finally managed to prise Mickey away from Venus. 'Have you seen who's here?' she said, amazed that he hadn't noticed.

'Everything's going great, honey,' he said, a stupid smile spread across his face. 'What's your problem?'

'My *problem* is Lucky Santangelo.'

'What about her?'

'She's over there! Alex brought her. *And* he has a date here.' She glared at her husband as if it was his fault. 'What are you going to do about it?'

Mickey shrugged. 'There's nothing we *can* do. What did Alex say?'

'He told me to lay another place at the table.'

'Go ahead and do it.'

'I don't *want* that woman in my house. She *fired* you from Panther.'

'True, but in this town you gotta get along with everyone

– you never know when you'll need 'em. So, Abbey, go tell your maid to set another place. It's no big deal.'

'It *is* a big deal,' Abigaile fretted. 'It'll ruin my placement.'

'Honey,' Mickey said mildly, 'take your goddamn placement and shove it up your ass! Now do as I say.'

Still glaring, Abbey retreated.

Mickey headed straight for Lucky. 'I see Lucky Santangelo has decided to honor us with her presence.'

'Hi, Mickey,' she said coolly. 'How's everything?'

'Pretty damn good. I'm back at Panther where I belong. Now all I gotta do is dump that line-up of crappy movies on your schedule. The only good one is *Gangsters*.'

'I'm sure you'll turn things around, Mickey. Only *you* can put Panther back where it was before.' A meaningful beat. 'In the crapper.'

Johnny strolled over, joining in the conversation. 'Lucky, baby,' he said. 'No shit – you are my favorite.'

'*Everybody's* your favorite, Johnny,' she said. 'Do yourself a big one and get a new line.'

'Why?' he said, grinning. 'The old one's always worked for me.'

Jeff stumbled and almost fell off a bar stool on his way over to join the illustrious group. This was an opportunity too good to miss. 'I've always wanted to meet you,' he said to Lucky, his words slurring even more. 'You're beautiful, rich and powerful. There should be more of your kind of woman in Hollywood. I'm Jeff, I'm an actor.'

'Big surprise, Jeff.'

He grinned at her, swaying slightly. 'An' you're as beautiful as everybody said.'

Alex walked over and took Lucky's arm. 'Come here, Lucky. Talk to Venus for me.'

'What – now?'

'Here's the deal,' he said quietly. 'Mickey wanted Leslie

to play Lola, then changed his mind. Now he wants Venus, only she's under the impression she didn't get the part. You'll tell her she did, and not to mention anything tonight.'

'What am I? The mediator around here?'

'Do this for me, Lucky. Please.'

She sighed. 'Yeah, sure, like I have nothing else on my mind.'

☆ ☆ ☆

Tabitha sat Santo on a couch and proceeded to give him a brief rundown of the players.

'You see the woman with the long red hair? She's Leslie Kane, used to be a hooker. My father doesn't believe it, nor does my mother. I *know*.'

'How do you know?' Santo asked.

'My mom's manicurist told me – she's into everything. And the guy with her – he's some freeloader out-of-work actor who's living with her. That's Lucky Santangelo over there, the one with the black hair. The dude with her is Alex Woods. You know who he is?'

'Course I do,' Santo said, thinking that this girl wasn't treating him very nicely.

'Okay, so he's meant to only like slit-eyes. I guess that's his date – the one with the funny name.'

'How do you know all this?'

'I *observe*,' Tabitha said, twirling the gold ring in her navel. 'See Cooper Turner – he fucks anything that moves. And Venus Maria – so does she.'

'What did you say?' Santo said, his face reddening.

'You heard. Venus is a *major* slut. Fucks everyone.'

'Don't say that about Venus,' he said furiously.

'Why? Do you know her?'

'Yes. She's a wonderful person.'

'Ha! Shows how *much* you know. Right now, she's fucking her masseur 'cause she can't find anybody else since she booted Cooper Turner out. Tonight she's hitting on Johnny Romano. He screws all his girlfriends in the back of his limo. Bet he gets it on with her tonight.'

'You've got a dirty mouth,' Santo said.

'Yeah?' Tabitha jeered. 'And I bet you'd give anything to have it wrapped around your tiny little dick.'

☆　☆　☆

'What are we doing here?' Lucky said to Venus. 'And *what* are you doing with Johnny Romano?'

'Okay, okay, you caught me! This is pretty low,' Venus said, grinning sheepishly. 'I wanted to come tonight – if only to see Mickey's face when I walked in. He's under the impression I'll blow him if he gives me the role in *Gangsters*. I'm kind of stringing him along, then maybe I'll slap him with a sexual harassment suit.'

'Great idea,' Lucky said. 'You slapping Mickey Stolli with a sexual harassment suit is definitely a *Newsweek* cover.'

Venus laughed. 'Yeah, but nobody would believe it. They'd say *I* was the one harassing *him*.'

'I've got good news for you,' Lucky said. 'There's some complicated thing going on here involving Mickey. However, according to Alex, you *are* Lola, and Leslie's out, but you're not supposed to say anything tonight.'

'Are you *sure*?' Venus said.

'Alex told me himself.'

'Oh, God what a relief! Now I don't have to blow Mickey!'

'You weren't seriously considering it?'

Venus laughed. 'What do *you* think? And by the way, how come you're with Alex Woods?'

'He's . . . a friend.'

'Oh, c'mon, Lucky, it's *me* you're talking to. Alex is following you around with that look. You know the look I mean.'

'Let me ask you something.'

'What?'

'Am I an Alex Woods type?'

'Honey, you're so cool you'd be anybody's type.'

They both laughed.

Alex walked over.

'Done,' Lucky said.

He smiled at Venus. 'How are you?'

'Better since I heard the news.'

'Let's keep it to ourselves. We'll talk tomorrow.'

'I'll have to put a muzzle on Johnny – he's decided to defend my honor and get me the role.'

'Don't tell him why.'

'Of course not.'

'And talking of muzzles,' Lucky said. 'What do you plan on doing with him on the way home?'

'Not a damn thing,' Venus said, smiling. 'Exactly *nada*!'

☆ ☆ ☆

Abigaile did as Mickey asked, and had the maid set another place at the table. She hated it when things didn't go the way she wanted them to. Her daughter looked like a refugee from a bad Madonna video; the Landsmans' son was fat and unattractive; Lucky Santangelo was making everyone uncomfortable; and Mickey was behaving like a horny schoolboy, lusting after Venus as if he'd never seen a pair of tits before.

However, Abigaile refused to let anything ruin her perfect evening. Putting on a proper smile, she clapped her hands together. 'Dinner is served, everyone,' she trilled. 'Shall we make our way into the dining room?'

Chapter Fifty-one

 HER NAME WAS Claudia and, as far as Lennie was concerned, she was an angel. She'd given him back the will to live and that meant everything. It gave him hope that there *was* a future.

He'd found out he was in Sicily. How he'd gotten there or why was still a mystery. Claudia had told him everything she knew. She'd discovered that her father, Furio, and his friend, Bruno, were being paid to keep Lennie in the cave. Someone in America had hired them to do so – she suspected it was Bruno's sister.

'Who's she?' he'd asked.

Claudia said she was a very rich woman who lived in Los Angeles. As far as Claudia knew, nobody was aware of his existence except Bruno and Furio. Recently Bruno had been involved in a car accident and was in the hospital with a broken leg. Furio was away from the village on business, which is why she'd been entrusted to bring him food.

Claudia was twenty-one, and worked as a seamstress in a neighboring village. She'd learned English at school, and lived at home with her five brothers and sisters.

'My father . . . he trust me,' she said. 'He no trust others. Now I hear your story . . . I am not sure what I think.'

Several hours after capturing her that first day, Lennie had been forced to let her go – but only after they'd talked for a long while. He'd tried to explain to her who he was, that he'd been kidnapped, and exactly who she should contact in America. He'd even given her Lucky's number to call.

'Not possible,' she'd said.

'Why?' he'd demanded.

'Not possible,' she'd repeated.

Before she'd left the cave he'd made her promise to return, to help him. 'You *have* to find a way to get this chain off my ankle. You must, Claudia, otherwise they're going to let me die here.'

She'd returned the next day fetching him two cigarettes, an apple and a box of matches. Precious treasures.

Now she visited him every day, bringing whatever she could and talking to him. He learned about her life in the tiny village where there was not even a movie theater; her boyfriend, whom her father hated; and her abusive older brother whom, according to her, everybody hated.

'You've got to get to a phone,' he begged her. 'Get help—'

'No,' she said, shaking her head. 'My poppa would know it was me. I must help you my way.'

'When's that going to be?' he said roughly. 'I'm going insane trapped here.'

'Be patient, Lennie. I will help you. That is my promise.'

'When, Claudia, *when*?'

'One day I want to go to America,' she said, her eyes shining at the thought.

'Help me, and you will,' Lennie assured her.

The next day she brought him a crudely drawn map.

'When I get the key I bring it. You leave immediately. I replace key before Poppa finds it missing. You follow map.'

'Why can't you lead me out of here?'

'No.' She shook her head, her long hair swirling around her beautiful, innocent face. 'I go to my village. You travel other way. They come after you.'

'When can we do this?'

'On the weekend my poppa drinks beer . . . he sleeps. I try to get key.'

Only a few more days. He couldn't believe it.

Only a few more days and maybe he'd be free.

Chapter Fifty-two

 As THE GUESTS trooped into the Stollis' dining room, Mickey grabbed Abigaile. 'I've handled it,' he said, pleased with himself. 'Gave that Santo kid a hundred bucks and told him to take Tabitha out to a movie and a hamburger.'

Abigaile frowned. 'What will Donna say?'

'Who gives a shit? If you think my daughter's sitting at our dinner table dressed like that, think again.'

'Was Santo all right with this?'

'He took the money, didn't he?'

'If you say so,' Abigaile said, with a put-upon sigh. 'I'd better remove their places.'

'I've already had the maid do it.'

'Thank you, Mickey.'

He winked. 'I deliver in a squeeze.'

'Yes, you do,' Abigaile agreed, nodding. It was quite possible that Mickey was right: with Tabitha out the way she'd be more relaxed, although tonight's gathering was not her ideal group.

She considered her seating plan. She'd placed herself between Cooper and Johnny Romano – the best seat in the house; Mickey was flanked by Leslie and Donna Landsman; she'd squeezed Lucky in between Venus and Alex, placing Tin Lee on his other side – let's see how he'd deal with *that*;

George was next to Tin Lee; and on the other side of Leslie was Jeff, then Veronica.

All in all, she thought she'd done a masterful job. Seating was never easy, but Abigaile liked to think she excelled.

☆ ☆ ☆

Alex took Lucky's arm as they entered the dining room, Tin Lee trailing behind them.

'I don't want to be here,' Lucky whispered. 'Not one little bit.'

'You're here – accept it,' Alex said.

'Nobody forces me to do anything I don't want to.'

'This is a favor for me,' he said persuasively. 'After all, I came with you to see Ricco.'

'Nobody had a gun to your dick,' she said flippantly. 'You *wanted* to.'

He steered her in another direction. 'How are you planning on dealing with that situation?'

'Maybe I'll fly to Paris,' she said casually. 'And *no*, Alex, you can't come with me. This will be a solo trip.'

'You'd fly all that way on spec?'

'Not on spec. I've already called Boogie, he's put people on the case.'

'And Boogie is . . . ?'

'My private investigator. He's a pretty sharp guy – he can find out anything about anybody.'

'You employ your own private investigator?'

'I have to meet this woman face to face. We all know money can buy most things. I'm positive it can buy her.'

'Why not wait until your man has some credible information?'

'I have to do this now.'

'You're *very* impulsive.'

'Look at her,' Lucky said, nodding scornfully toward Donna as she entered the dining room. 'I remember when Santino had her shipped in from Sicily. She was a peasant who couldn't speak a word of English. Do you know that I went to their wedding?'

'Whatever else, you have to admire what she's achieved.'

'Fuck you, Alex!' Lucky said, turning on him. 'She's a murderer. I don't admire anything about her, and neither should you.'

'I didn't mean—'

'I don't care *what* you meant. Go look after your girlfriend, she's feeling neglected.'

☆ ☆ ☆

Mickey caught up with Lucky before she sat down at the dinner table. 'You got a lotta balls coming here,' he said, his voice low and rough-edged.

Lucky stared at him. 'Wasn't it Abigaile who used to go around wearing yours for earrings?'

'Once a cunt, always a cunt.'

'Hey, throw me out,' she challenged. 'It'll make for good dinner conversation.'

'I wish I could,' he said hoarsely.

Her black eyes narrowed. 'You think I *want* to be here? I promise you, Mickey, I'm only staying to piss you off.'

☆ ☆ ☆

Tabitha and Santo sat in Tabitha's BMW with the engine running outside the Stollis' mansion.

'I hate my freaking parents,' Tabitha said glumly.

'I hate mine, too,' Santo agreed.

She bit at a hang-nail. 'At least we've got something in common.'

'Your dad gave me a hundred bucks. Like I need *his* money – I got plenty of my own.'

'I have to drive this boring car 'cause *Mommy* thinks it's *safe*,' Tabitha sneered. 'What do you drive?'

'I'm getting a Ferrari,' he boasted.

'Not bad.'

'My mother buys me anything I want 'cause she feels guilty.'

'About what?'

'That she married this dweeb George after my father was murdered.'

Finally he had her attention. 'Really? Honestly? Murdered?' she said excitedly. 'Like *how*?'

'Shot,' he said, knowing he sounded real cool.

'Like *ambushed*?'

'No. The cops said he was molesting some kids. One of them put a bullet through him.'

'*That's* a weirdo story.'

'It's not true.'

'So, like, what *is* the truth?'

'It had something to do with my mother catching my dad with another woman.'

'Who shot him? Your mom?'

'I wouldn't be surprised. They were always screaming at each other. Yeah . . . I think the old cow could've done it.'

'Wow!' said Tabitha, completely impressed.

'Did you see what my mother looks like?'

'Like every other Hollywood old bag – a face full of plastic.'

'She used to be fat.'

'Like you?'

'Bag the insults.'

'You could work out. Look at me, I'm real skinny 'cause I throw up a lot. I'll teach you how t' do that if you like. It's pretty gross at first. After a while you get used to it.'

'As soon as she got rid of my dad, she made herself real thin and stuff. Then she married the geek. I hate 'em both.'

'Don't blame you,' Tabitha said, shifting restlessly.

'We could go to my house and pick up my Corvette,' Santo suggested, trying to hold her attention.

'You got more dope there?' she asked hopefully.

He nodded.

'What are we waiting for?'

'Weren't we supposed to go to a movie and get a hamburger?'

Tabitha threw him a scornful look. 'Get a life, Santo. We'll smoke a little weed, then come back later. They don't give a crap *what* we do.'

☆ ☆ ☆

'And so,' Veronica said, guttural voice too loud for the table, 'there I was on the runway in Paris wearing nothing but a bra and panties, and this Japanese dignitary is staring at my crotch when I tripped and fell right into his lap. I nearly crushed the poor little man.'

Jeff roared with laughter. Cooper smiled politely. Veronica's harsh voice was starting to drive him completely crazy.

He glanced across the table at Venus. She was busy talking to Lucky. He tried to attract her attention. She refused to acknowledge him. What a fool he'd been to cheat on someone as loyal as Venus. He missed her desperately and would do anything to win her back.

Leaning past George and ignoring Tin Lee, Donna said to Alex, 'I'm delighted we're making your movie at my studio.'

Alex gave her a stony look, wondering if everything Lucky suspected was true. 'Where are you from originally?' he asked.

'Italy,' Donna replied. 'Why?'

'I thought I detected a slight accent.'

'No,' she said fiercely. 'I have no accent.'

George interjected, 'Your *parents* are from Italy, Donna. *You* were born in America.'

'Yes, that's right, I was,' she lied.

'Really?' said Lucky, who had the uncanny ability of being able to tune into several conversations at once. 'What part of Italy were *they* from?'

'Milan,' Donna lied.

Lucky fixed her with a steely look. 'My grandparents came from Bari. The Santangelos.' A meaningful pause. 'Perhaps you've heard of them?'

'No,' Donna muttered, furious that she had to put up with this. She loathed being out of control, sitting with these Hollywood people who thought they were better than everyone else. She especially loathed having to deal with Lucky Santangelo face to face. This was *not* part of her plan.

It seemed Lucky Santangelo was indestructible. What else could she possibly do to bring the bitch to her knees?

Donna began to consider the possibilities.

Chapter Fifty-three

LUCKY LEFT the table on the pretext of visiting the ladies' room. Once she was out of the dining room she walked through the front door, gave the valet-parker twenty bucks to drop her at the nearby Beverly Hills Hotel, and from there took a cab back to her house.

She knew she should have told Alex she was leaving, she also knew he would have insisted she stay, and she was not in the mood. Sitting in the same room as Donna Landsman was sickening: breathing the same air as that woman was beginning to stifle her.

Donna Landsman had killed Lennie.

She didn't deserve to live.

Earlier, when she'd spoken to Boogie, he'd told her he had news on the shareholders. She'd arranged to meet him later at her house.

Driving down the highway she found herself thinking about Alex. He was interesting and talented and attractive and a challenge. The more time she spent with him, the more she felt herself being sucked in.

It was no good. She was not ready for an involvement.

She wondered what her children were doing. It broke her heart that they'd never see Lennie again. Even though she knew it was safer for them to be out of the country, she couldn't help missing them. Kids were so resilient: they got through every day, no matter what. They were probably having a wonderful time.

Back at the house the guard waved to her as she drew into the garage.

Boogie was already there, sitting in the kitchen watching CNN. He clicked off the TV and jumped up when she walked in.

'Let's go in the living room,' she said, impatient to hear what he had to say.

They sat on the couch and Boogie started talking. 'It's taken a while,' he said, 'but we finally discovered who Mrs Smorg is.'

'Yes?' Lucky said, tapping her fingers on the coffee table.

Boogie's long face was impassive. 'Inga Smorg – alias Inga Irving – is currently Mrs Abe Panther.'

Lucky was shocked. Inga. Abe's wife. This was a big surprise.

Abe would have a fit if he found out Inga had helped oust her. Inga must have bought the stock behind Abe's back as an insurance policy. The stoic Swede had always been jealous of Lucky's closeness with Abe, so when the opportunity arose to vote, Inga had elected not to support her.

'What about Conquest Investments?' she asked, reaching for a cigarette from a pack on the table, her addiction totally out of control.

'Another of Mrs Smorg's little secrets,' Boogie said. 'She and Morton Sharkey are in partnership. Conquest belongs to them – fifty-fifty.'

'Are you telling me they control an offshore company together? One that Abe doesn't know about?'

'That's right. She operates under the same name that was on her passport before she married Abe.'

'So,' Lucky said thoughtfully, 'if I can get Inga and

Morton to vote in my favor, I'll have enough stock to regain control?'

'That's the way it is.'

'This is easy, Boogie. All I have to do is tell Abe what's going on.'

'Be careful, Lucky. Abe's an old man – you don't want to get him excited.'

'I'll speak to Inga first. Maybe the *threat* of my telling Abe she owns stock in Panther will be enough to make her change her mind.' She stood up and walked over to the window. 'Okay, now fill me in on the blond in Paris.'

'Her name's Daniella Dion. She's a very expensive call-girl who works for an infamous French madam, Madame Pomeranz – a woman known for supplying beautiful girls to politicians and visiting VIPs.'

'That figures.'

'Daniella is a real pro. She's been doing this since she was fifteen – eight years. For a while she was the mistress of an octogenarian industrialist until he died. He left her money, the wife contested his will, Daniella ended up with nothing. She went back into the business two years ago.'

'When can I see her?'

'For twenty thousand dollars a day and all expenses, she'll fly to Los Angeles for an "appointment".'

'Arrange it.'

'I already have. She'll be here in two days. She's under the impression a friend is buying her time as a birthday present for Johnny Romano.'

'*Very* inventive, Boog.'

'I had to make sure she came.'

Lucky laughed drily. 'For twenty thou a day it's hardly likely she'd hang back. That's the most expensive fuck I've ever heard of.'

'There's women who go for higher,' Boogie said knowledgeably.

Lucky blew a stream of smoke toward the ceiling. 'Since when did you become an expert?'

☆　☆　☆

Nona and Brigette sat in their hotel room debating whether to hire a car and drive over to Lucky's to surprise her, or telephone first.

'I vote we phone,' Brigette said. 'It's too late to go running over there.'

The truth was, she was reluctant to tell Lucky her story. She felt embarrassed and foolish and, quite frankly, she didn't know how Lucky could deal with it.

Nona handed her the phone. 'Go ahead,' she urged. 'I bet she's up.'

Reluctantly, she dialed Lucky's number. 'Guess where I am?' she said brightly, when Lucky came to the phone.

'Here?'

'How did you know?'

'Because when somebody says, "Guess where I am", you can guarantee they're around the corner. What are you doing here?'

'Uh . . . I had to come out for a modeling assignment. I'm staying at the Hilton with Nona.'

'Why are you at a hotel when you could've stayed here?'

'We didn't want to bother you. Anyway, your house is full with the kids and everything.'

'The children are in Europe with Bobby.'

'I didn't know that.'

'Perhaps if you kept in touch you would.'

'Lucky, um . . . Nona and I were thinking – can we have lunch tomorrow?'

'This is not the greatest time for me. How about dinner at the house tomorrow night?'

'Sure.'

'And if you change your mind,' Lucky added, 'come stay. Spend the weekend.'

'We kind of, like, only came for a day.'

'I'll send a car. It'll be outside your hotel at five-thirty.'

'Don't use my real name. Brigette Brown's my name now.'

'I understand,' Lucky said, wondering why Brigette sounded so edgy. 'See you tomorrow, sweetheart.'

'She wanted us to stay with her,' Brigette said, hanging up the phone.

'Why didn't you say yes?' Nona said. 'We could have spent tomorrow at the beach.'

'I thought we'd go shopping, drop some money.'

'Oh, Brigette, Brigette, what am I gonna do with you?'

'Shopping is therapy, Nona.'

'Sure.'

'Should I phone Isaac?' Brigette asked, feeling better now she'd spoken to Lucky. 'He'll be wondering what's happened to me.'

'Why would you want to be with a guy who's only interested in getting high?'

'What's wrong with that?'

'You're at the start of a big career. Don't mess it up.'

'You sound like my mother.'

'Oh, great. Just 'cause I'm trying to be the sensible one around here.'

'No. You're right. My mother would never say anything like that. She'd be too busy out screwing rock stars.'

'We all know you didn't have a normal childhood,' Nona sighed. 'Neither did I.'

'I guess if we can survive our parents we're pretty fortunate, right?' Brigette said.

'Right,' Nona agreed. 'Let's go to bed.'

'Bed?' Brigette exclaimed. 'It's only eleven-fifteen.'

'Brigette—'

'Okay, okay.'

☆   ☆   ☆

Alex watched the door waiting for Lucky to reappear. After five minutes he knew she wasn't coming back. 'Excuse me,' he said, getting up from the table. He walked outside, found a waiter, and said, 'Where's Miz Santangelo?'

'Don't know, Mr Woods.'

He went to the front door and asked the valet-parker. 'Did Miz Santangelo leave? Did she take my car?'

'No, Mr Woods, she ordered a cab.'

He had half a mind to make a quick exit, but Abigaile and Mickey would never forgive him, not to mention Tin Lee, who was sitting beside him with a frozen smile on her face. God, how had he gotten himself into this position?

Lucky did what she wanted to do. He'd been like that once. Now he was a typical Hollywood player, toeing the line so he could get his fucking movie made, and Lucky had run out on him yet again.

He returned to the dining room. 'Abigaile,' he said, 'Lucky wasn't feeling well. She went home.'

Abigaile exchanged a look with Mickey.

Donna smiled, bitterly triumphant. She'd won. She'd driven the bitch away.

Now all she had to do was figure out how to get rid of her permanently.

Chapter Fifty-four

THE STOLLIS' dinner dragged on.

Jeff got drunker; Leslie got sulkier; Mickey got bolder; Abigaile got fussier; Alex got angrier; Tin Lee got tenser; Johnny got hornier; Venus got flirtier; George got quieter; Donna got gloomier; Veronica got louder; and Cooper got more detached.

As soon as coffee was served, Alex was on his feet. 'C'mon,' he said to Tin Lee, pulling her roughly to her feet. 'Say goodbye.'

They stood outside the house next to their respective cars.

'Would you like me to come home with you?' Tin Lee asked, tentatively placing her hand on his arm.

'Y'know, Tin Lee,' he said, realizing it was not fair to string her along any further, 'this isn't working out for either of us.'

'Excuse me, Alex?' she said, removing her hand.

'I can't make you happy.'

Oh, she thought miserably. The *I-can't-make-you-happy* speech, which, roughly translated, means *You-can't-make-me-happy*.

Her eyes filled with tears. Over the months she'd grown attached to Alex, and even though he was not the world's greatest lover, she had a need to be with him. Deep down she felt he needed her, too, because she was a calming influence on his otherwise turbulent life. Surely he realized it.

'Alex—' she began.

He cut her off. 'I don't want to talk now,' he said abruptly.

'If we don't talk now, when will we?'

'Look, I'm starting my movie, I'm very busy. I shouldn't even be out.'

'I visited your mother tonight,' she said quietly. 'We had an interesting talk. I saw your family photo albums. You were a sweet little boy, Alex.'

'Why did you do that?' he asked, mad at Dominique for allowing such intimacy.

'Your mother is lonely, Alex. She loves you very much.'

'I'm not interested in hearing what you think about me and my mother,' he said angrily. 'Dominique is *not* your friend, okay?'

Tin Lee sighed. 'What do you want from a woman, Alex?' she asked. 'What would make you happy?'

He didn't answer immediately. He considered her question. 'Peace,' he said at last. 'That's what I want. Peace.'

☆ ☆ ☆

Venus and Johnny Romano made their exit shortly after Alex. Lounging comfortably in the back of his limo, Johnny stretched out his long legs and poured Venus more champagne. 'Really boring, babe,' he announced. 'Those people got no clue how to get down.'

'Maybe that *is* their idea of getting down,' Venus remarked.

Johnny smoothed back his Latin-lover, heavily greased black hair. 'Well, they got one dull life.'

'Abigaile doesn't think so.'

He swigged from the champagne bottle. 'So how come you told me not to say anything about the movie?'

She gave a small triumphant smile. 'Because . . . I've got the role.'

He smiled broadly. 'Hey, baby, must've been something I said.'

'I'm sure it was, Johnny.'

'We gotta celebrate,' he said. 'Wanna stop by my place?'

'What kind of celebration is that?'

'Don't put it down till you've seen it.' He leered. '*Wanna* see it, babe?'

'See what?' she asked, as if she didn't get his double entendre.

He grinned lasciviously, patting his immediate erection, quite obvious in his tight-fitting black pants.

Venus averted her eyes, feigning a yawn. 'I'm more interested in getting a good night's sleep . . . by myself.'

'Hey – baby, Johnny Romano *never* forced himself on anyone. Never had to. But I'm telling you,' he added boastfully, 'you got no idea the goodies you're missing.'

'My – what a big ego you have,' she drawled.

'Yeah, all the better to eat you up with.'

She couldn't help laughing. Johnny's lines were outrageously corny.

'Hey,' he said, reaching for more champagne, 'did you catch the face on that fat kid when he saw you?'

'What fat kid?'

'The Landsmans' son. He took one look at you and nearly came in his pants!'

'Johnny!'

'Maybe he's your number-one fan, babycakes.'

'I didn't notice him.'

'You're so cool. He's gonna be talking about you for months, and *you* didn't notice the poor kid.'

'I saw the Stollis' daughter twirling her little navel ring in your direction.'

'Sixteen? Too young.'

'What?' she said, amused. 'By about three months?'

He laughed. 'You're funny. We're gonna have good times on this movie.'

'You bet we are, Johnny. First we'll work *very* hard, *then* we'll have good times.'

'I'm renting a house in Vegas. There's room for one more.'

'Thanks, Johnny, I'll get my own house. That's the nice thing about being a star – I can afford to do whatever I want. And what *I* want right now is to be left alone.'

☆ ☆ ☆

'I have an early photo shoot tomorrow,' Veronica said, glancing meaningfully at Cooper.

He took the hint and stood up.

'I enjoy those catalogs you appear in,' Mickey said, absently rubbing his bald head. 'Very sexy, Veronica. Very sexy indeed.'

'Thank you, Mickey,' Veronica replied, towering over him.

Mickey moved a little closer. He liked tall women – they gave a whole new meaning to going down. 'You ever thought about being in a movie?' he asked.

'As a matter of fact I have. Last week I signed with William Morris for film and commercial representation.'

'Good move.'

She favored him with a horsy smile. 'I'm glad you think so.'

He licked his fleshy lips. This one was a definite turn-on. He'd like to squeeze his cock between her big tits and come all over her. 'Give me a call at the studio sometime. Maybe I can help.'

'I'll do that, Mickey.'

Cooper kissed Abigaile on both cheeks. 'Nice dinner, Abbey, thanks,' he said, not meaning it.

'We must do this again,' Abigaile gushed, always delighted to have Cooper as a guest.

'Absolutely,' Cooper said, thinking, *No way!* He took Veronica's arm and led her out of the front door. 'Sorry about that,' he said, in a low voice, as they waited for his car.

'I'm sure you're planning on compensating me,' Veronica purred provocatively.

'Definitely,' he answered, on automatic pilot, although his mind was on Venus. Seeing her with Johnny Romano had really upset him.

He drove to Veronica's apartment, got out of the car and escorted her inside.

In the elevator she suddenly pounced, pinning his shoulders up against the wall, kissing him with the most inventive tongue he'd ever come across. God, she was strong!

This was a switch. *He* was the one usually calling the shots.

'Hey,' he objected, as her hands traveled intimately down his body, rubbing his penis. 'Let's not get carried away.'

'Don't be a tease, Cooper,' she said, exploring his left ear with her probing tongue. 'I've heard about your reputation. The girls are all dying to know.'

'What girls?'

A low, throaty laugh. 'We have a little supermodel club. Y'know, see who can fuck the most billionaires and movie stars.'

'That's really impressive,' he said sarcastically.

'No,' she said, her hand pressed firmly against his dick. '*This* is what *I* call impressive.'

And before he could say anything, she reached for the stop button and, as the elevator lurched to a halt, urgently began unbuckling his belt.

Cooper felt like a girl with a guy who was coming on too strong. Was this date rape? *Oh God, Venus, where are you when I need you?*

Before he knew it, Veronica had his pants down around his ankles and was busily working on removing his undershorts.

It occurred to him that, any moment, somebody could buzz for the elevator, the doors would open, and he'd be exposed for all to see.

'Let's go to your apartment,' he said.

'I want to do it here,' she countered, breathing heavily as she unzipped the back of her dress, allowing it to fall from her long, lean body.

The most famous underwear model in the world didn't wear any. She was tall and smooth-skinned with a shaved pussy and prominent nipples. She was also very, very naked. 'Kiss this,' she said, shoving one of her boobs toward his mouth. 'Kiss it, suck it – c'mon, lover boy, show me what you can do.'

'Am I about to make your list of billionaires and movie stars?' he groaned, chewing on a nipple.

'Maybe you'll be top of the list,' she promised, throwing a long leg around his waist, deftly trying to maneuver him inside her.

'Are you sure they don't have security cameras in these elevators?' he said, feeling his erection slipping away.

'Get with the program, baby,' Veronica encouraged in her guttural voice. 'Do it to me – do it to me good.'

A standing-up fuck. Just what he felt like.

He wondered what Venus was doing now. Was she in

Johnny's infamous limo? Was he plying her with champagne while telling her she was the sexiest woman in the world?

Johnny was too obvious. Venus wouldn't fall for his corny crap.

As he thought about Venus, so his erection completely deserted him and he slipped out of Veronica, who was not pleased. 'What's the matter?' she said sternly, sounding like a drill sergeant.

Oh, God, he didn't want her running back to the super-model squad reporting that he was a dud.

'Can't do it in an elevator – too public,' he explained. 'It's not my thing.'

'Public sex excites *me*,' Veronica said, flicking out her extra-long tongue and wriggling it at him, kind of a snake-like come-on. 'I once did it in a bathroom at the White House. Nobody knew.'

'Except the President,' he joked.

She didn't get it.

'Let me see if I can persuade you to overcome your fear of elevators,' she said, falling to her knees, and taking his penis into her mouth, ramming in his balls along with it.

This little move made him nervous, not horny. She had the biggest mouth he'd ever come across. He felt himself shrinking more as each moment passed.

'This isn't going to work,' he said, attempting to remove himself from her mouth before she crushed his precious balls to pieces.

'Don't I turn you on, Cooper?' she said, in her deep brown voice. 'Every man in America wants to fuck me. They leaf through my catalog, then look at their fat wives, and go, "Ah . . . Veronica . . . my fantasy woman. I want her tits in my mouth, my tongue in her pussy."'

'The problem is that I don't have a fat wife at home,'

Cooper said, groping for his pants on the elevator floor and hurriedly pulling them on. 'I need a drink,' he added tersely.

'Oh, you have to drink to get it up, is that it?' she said nastily.

He was beginning to dislike her more and more; in spite of her outward appearance, there was nothing feminine about her.

'I was married to Venus Maria,' he said. 'In fact, I still *am*. We're separated.'

'She's shorter than I expected.'

'She's a very special woman.'

'Then why are you separated?'

Good question.

Someone yelled down the elevator shaft. 'Are you stuck?'

Calmly Veronica stepped into her dress. 'Zip me up,' she commanded.

He did as she asked and flipped the on switch. The elevator rumbled into action.

Veronica smoothed down her dress. 'How old are you, Cooper?' she asked.

'It's public record,' he said, with an unperturbed smile, secretly livid that she would ask such an intimate question.

'Hmm . . .' she said knowledgeably. 'Perhaps you need a shot of testosterone.'

Bitch! 'Not when I'm with my wife I don't,' he said, wiping the smile off her horsy face.

☆　☆　☆

The only people left at the dinner party were Abigaile and Mickey, Donna and George, a drunken Jeff and an uptight Leslie. She'd been dying to go for the past half-hour, but it was impossible to get Jeff to move. He sprawled on a couch with a sloppy smile stuck on his face. 'Y'know, Mickey,' he said. 'One of these days I'd like to produce.'

You'd better learn to act first, Mickey thought sourly. There was nothing he hated more than the slew of good-looking guys who came to Hollywood figuring they could be actors, producers, directors. This Jeff guy was an out-and-out loser. Somebody had to talk some sense into Leslie.

'Where do you think the children are?' Donna said, her lips pressed into a thin, disapproving line.

'Dunno,' Mickey said, not too concerned. 'Maybe the movie ran longer than they expected.'

'I'm disappointed,' Donna said, ignoring George's warning look.

'How's that?' Mickey said.

'You invited Santo here for dinner, then sent him out to a movie. That's not very polite.'

'The kids didn't want to sit around with a bunch of old people like us,' Mickey said expansively. 'Tabitha will take care of your boy.'

'He doesn't need taking care of,' Donna said frostily. 'He also doesn't need to be led astray.'

'What do you mean by that?' Abigaile said, quickly joining in. Nobody was going to criticize *her* daughter.

'Santo is a good boy,' Donna said.

'Are you implying that Tabitha is a bad influence?' Abigaile said, bristling.

'Maybe I should call our house,' George suggested.

'Yes,' Donna said, trying to control her aggravation.

'Use the phone behind the bar,' Mickey offered.

Leslie got up to go to the guest bathroom.

'May I have a word with you, dear?' Mickey said, following her into the hall.

'Sure, Mickey,' Leslie said, listless since Cooper had left with the skinny six-foot model with the phony tits.

'You're looking tired,' he said.

'Do you think so?'

'Y'know, Leslie,' Mickey continued, putting his arm around her shoulders, 'leading ladies, they gotta be sparkling at all times. Who *is* this schmuck you're with?'

'You mean Jeff?'

'What are you doing with a loser like him? Is he a great fuck? 'Cause I can find you another guy who's better in bed *and* has brains to go with it.'

'I really don't appreciate you interfering in my personal life, Mickey,' she said, huffily. 'I might be doing a movie for you, but that doesn't give you the right to comment on who I see.'

'Honey,' he said patiently, 'I'm trying to teach you street smarts. *Never* live with an actor. They're ego-inflated pricks. Surely you've worked that out by now.'

'Look, I admit Jeff is a little, um . . . happy tonight, but that's only because he's glad to be here.'

'I bet he is,' Mickey snorted.

'Anyway, Mickey, don't worry, he's not around perman-ently. I'm using him, the way you guys use women.'

'I've never used a woman in my life,' Mickey said indignantly.

No, of course not, she thought. *How about that bachelor party where you had a girl spread-eagled on the buffet table while you ate the celebration cake out of her pussy for the boys' amusement?*

'Anyway, I'm taking him home now,' Leslie said. 'By the way, Mickey, I had an idea.'

'What?'

'Wouldn't Cooper be great in *Gangsters*?'

'The movie's cast, Leslie.'

'I know,' she said, her eyes gleaming. 'But can you

imagine? Cooper Turner in *Gangsters* with Johnny Romano and me – what a combination!'

'Didn't you just finish a movie with Cooper?'

'Yes, and it's going to be big. Why don't you find another script for us to do together? We have sensational screen chemistry.'

'Yeah,' he said, thinking that this was exactly the out he was looking for. 'That's not a bad idea. If I come up with something, would you sooner do that than *Gangsters*?'

'Yes,' she said. 'As long as it's with Cooper.'

'A nice romantic comedy – right?'

'Perfect.'

'I'll definitely get into it, baby. Come by the studio for lunch.'

'My pleasure, Mickey.'

'Meanwhile, take the loser home. I don't want him throwing up on my couch.'

☆　☆　☆

'I can hear a phone ringing,' Tabitha sing-songed, completely out of it. They were both lolling in the middle of Santo's bed in a drugged-out stupor.

When they'd gotten back to his house they'd shared another joint, then Tabitha started exploring his room, begging for something stronger.

He remembered the heroin Mohammed had sold him. 'Girls get off on it,' Mohammed had said. Tabitha was a girl. She had perky little tits almost exposed by her flimsy top. He wouldn't mind touching them – he'd never touched a real girl. So they smoked the heroin and ended up floating on a beautiful blue cloud above the world watching everyone.

Santo was overcome with a feeling of goodness. Everything

was so nice, and he was filled with joy. Wow! Tabitha felt the same way.

They were both so mellow and calm, that it seemed only natural they should take off their clothes and fling them at each other, screaming with laughter.

Santo kept thinking about Venus at the party, her blue eyes, blond hair and the way she looked in her daring red dress.

He got naked, glanced down and couldn't believe how hard he was. His cock resembled a rocket ready for take-off.

Before he knew it, Tabitha was sitting astride him and they were making out.

She moved fast, riding him like a show horse. All he could see were her perky little tits and her belly-button with the gold ring bouncing up and down. It was a mind-blowing experience.

When she fell off him they both started laughing uncontrollably and rolling around on the bed.

He wondered if he should show her his collection, maybe read her some of the letters he'd sent to Venus which he'd dutifully copied.

Something warned him she might be jealous. It wouldn't do to have her and Venus fighting over him.

'You're not bad, Santo,' Tabitha said grudgingly, stretching out her arms. 'We should do this again.'

'Any time you say.'

'I'm starving,' she said, jumping off the bed.

Naked, they ran downstairs and raided the fridge in the kitchen. Fortunately the servants had retired for the night, to their own separate quarters behind the pool house.

'Where's your *parents'* bedroom?'

He took her into Donna's room. She threw herself onto the middle of the huge old-fashioned four-poster bed, flinging the velvet embroidered cushions at Santo, screaming with high-pitched laughter.

'How we gonna clear this up?' he said, worried for only an instant. 'My mom'll know we were in her room.'

'Who cares?' Tabitha said. 'Come over here. Let's do it again on her bed.'

He hadn't taken much persuading.

Now they were back in *his* room and the phone was ringing.

'Ignore it,' he said, grabbing her pointy little tits.

'You sure?'

'Wanna show you something.'

'What?'

He got off the bed and went to his locked closet.

'*What?*' Tabitha repeated impatiently.

Unlocking the closet, he reached in the back, pulling out his new prized possession.

'Holy shit!' she exclaimed. 'That's a *big* gun.'

'All the better to kill them with,' Santo replied, laughing like a maniac.

'Huh?' Tabitha said, blinking rapidly.

'One of these days,' Santo boasted, 'I'm gonna blow their fucking heads off!'

Chapter Fifty-five

 JOHNNY ROMANO was not as pushy as Venus had thought. When she turned down his invitation to go back to his place, he accepted her refusal good-naturedly. His limo was now parked outside her house.

'Gotta say I'm buzzed you're doing the movie,' he said, flexing his long, surprisingly elegant fingers.

'So am I,' she said, noticing his huge diamond pinkie ring, and diamond-studded identity bracelet. He had to be wearing half a million bucks worth of diamonds at least. 'The script's brilliant, you'll be terrific.'

As big a star as he was, Johnny still enjoyed receiving praise. 'You think so?' he asked anxiously.

'Absolutely.'

'I got me this acting coach,' he said, his voice filled with boyish enthusiasm. 'Don't laugh – the guy comes to my house twice a week. He used to work with De Niro.'

'That's smart, Johnny. You can never know enough about your craft.'

'I got Lucky to thank for gettin' my career back on the straight.'

'How come?'

'Remember when she first took over Panther?'

'How could I ever forget? From undercover secretary to studio mogul in one quick move.'

'I was doin' a lot of shit movies then. Violence. Sex. She called 'em my motherfucka movies 'cause that's all I ever said! They made me a fortune – but Lucky pointed out I was never the hero. "Be a hero," she told me, "that's what the audience wanna see." An', goddamn it, she was right.'

'Good for you, Johnny. There's nothing like moving on.'

He edged across the seat, getting closer. 'Did you enjoy tonight, baby?'

'It was okay.'

'Didn't bother you seein' your old man with that luscious piece?'

'Cooper and I are history.'

'Shame for him.' His thigh was now pressed up against hers. 'Fortunate for me.'

'Don't bet on it, Johnny,' she said, moving away.

'I got somethin' funny to tell you.'

'What?'

'Veronica used to be a man.'

'Get *outta* here!'

'I met her in Sweden years ago when I was workin' as a waiter. She'd just had the operation.'

'Come *on*.'

He laughed. 'Cooper'll never know the difference.'

'You're bad, you know that. Why didn't you *tell* him?'

'And spoil a beautiful romance? No way.' He laughed again. 'So . . . I saw you bending Mickey's ear all night.'

'He's got a hot dick for me – what can I do?'

'Oh, baby, baby, you got a way of sayin' it the way it really is.'

'Secret of my success,' Venus said, with a confident smile. 'And now, Johnny, I'd appreciate it if you'd let me out of the car.'

He did as she asked and said goodnight without pushing it.

She was relieved, not being in the mood to fight off an overly amorous Latin movie star.

The first thing she did was play her answering machine. There was a plaintive message from Rodriguez begging to see her, and a happy one from Ron.

'Taking your advice, sweet thing,' Ron said. 'I'm moving out.'

He didn't say where he was moving otherwise she would have called him back.

She went into her all-white dressing room, stepping out of her red dress on the way.

The phone rang. Hoping it was Ron, she ran to pick it up in the bedroom.

'Hi, it's Cooper.'

'Oh . . . hi.'

'You looked *veree* sexy tonight.'

'What do you want, Coop?' she said, sitting on the edge of the bed, wondering if he'd discovered the truth about Veronica.

'Just wanted to say hello.'

'That's not very original.'

'I'm fresh out of lines.'

'You? *Never!*'

'I was thinking—' he said.

'What?'

'Oh, about what a great marriage we had.'

'How can you say that when your mission was to screw as many other women as possible?'

'I know,' he said, sounding repentant. 'All my life I did exactly what I wanted, and women came along for the ride. Then I met you, fell in love and got married. I didn't think I *had* to change. I was selfish and incredibly dumb. Now I realize I made a big mistake.'

'What happened? You strike out with the model? Didn't get any, huh?'

'I got plenty. Problem was I didn't want it.'

'Really,' she said, not about to ruin his evening with Johnny's story.

'How 'bout you? Was Romano all over you in the car? You know, he jokes about it to his pals – tells everybody that once he gets a girl in the back of his limo, a blow-job goes with the territory.'

'You should know me better than that.'

'Can I come over?'

'What for?'

'To talk . . . That's all, I promise.'

She knew she should say no, but she felt herself weakening.

He took advantage of her silence. 'Strange coincidence,' he said. 'Right now I happen to be on your block.'

'Okay,' she said, against her better judgment. 'Come on over.'

☆ ☆ ☆

Johnny Romano's limo cruised down Sunset. He sat back, chatting on the car phone to Leslie.

She cradled her portable while taking a good look at Jeff. He was sprawled in the middle of her bed, still in his clothes, snoring like a stuffed-up hog. Mr Romance strikes again.

'You gave me your number an' I'm usin' it,' Johnny said. 'An' this man is wonderin' what you are doin' right now.'

'Where's Venus?'

'Why would I be with Venus when I've got *your* number, baby?' he said, putting on the sexy, macho voice he used for imminent seduction. 'How 'bout havin' a drink with me?'

Jeff burped and rolled over on the bed, reeking of booze.

Leslie thought of Cooper. He was probably real cozy with

that big horse model and her big horse teeth. She felt sad: she'd loved Cooper all her life, and for a few magical weeks she'd had him to herself. Now he didn't want her anymore. It wasn't fair.

'I can pick you up in five minutes,' Johnny said. 'Just tell me where I gotta point my limo, an', baby – believe me – I'm there.'

☆　☆　☆

Alex drove directly to Lucky's house at the beach.

A security guard stopped him at the door. 'Good evening, Mr Woods,' the guard said politely. 'Ms Santangelo mentioned you might drop by.'

'She did? Good.'

'She also said she doesn't wish to be disturbed.'

'She left me that message?'

'Ms Santangelo said she'd talk to you tomorrow, Mr Woods, and to please not call her tonight.'

'Oh . . . fine . . . okay.'

Alex got back in his car, furious with Lucky for playing games. One moment she was confiding in him. The next she was treating him like a total stranger. He understood that she had problems, but why wouldn't she let him help her?

He drove home experiencing a feeling he'd never had before. Was this love? Because if it was, then love was a crock.

He decided he had to get himself together, forget about Lucky Santangelo and concentrate on what he did best. Making movies.

☆　☆　☆

The guard waited until Alex drove off, then buzzed Lucky. 'Mr Woods was here. I told him you'd speak to him tomorrow.'

'Thanks, Enrico,' she said.

You're doing the right thing, she told herself. *Mustn't encourage him. Alex is getting too close, and it's not what I want.*

She sat on her bed and reached for Lennie's photograph in a silver frame. She missed him so much. His smile, his company, his lovemaking, his conversation.

There could be no substitute.

Not yet, anyway.

☆ ☆ ☆

'There's no reply at our house,' George said, replacing the receiver. 'Perhaps we should wait for Santo at home.'

'I agree,' Donna replied, glaring at Mickey. 'I wish you'd consulted me before you sent my son off with your daughter.'

Mickey shrugged. 'Thought I was doing the kids a favor. How was I to know they wouldn't get back on time?'

'They'll be here soon,' Abigaile said. 'Tabitha's a very reliable girl.'

'Yes, from her appearance I would judge her to be *really* reliable,' Donna said sarcastically.

'Excuse me?' Abigaile said, not liking Donna's tone.

'Do you actually let your daughter walk around dressed like that?' Donna said.

'At least she's not bloated and overweight,' Abigaile responded, not caring if Mickey got mad.

Mickey moved in quickly, nudging his wife to shut up. 'I'm sure they'll be here any moment,' he said. 'As soon as they arrive, I'll personally drive Santo home. He'll be fine.'

Donna glared at him. How dare they send her son off just because they didn't want him sitting at their boring dinner table? She hated the Stollis. She had a good mind to fire

Mickey as soon as she found somebody else to take his place. In fact, the entire evening had been a disaster.

Their limousine was parked in the driveway. Donna marched over, waiting for her driver to spring out and open the door.

The man didn't move, he was slumped over the steering wheel obviously asleep. Donna tut-tutted her annoyance, while George tapped on the glass.

No response. George opened the door and the driver, John Fardo, fell out onto the concrete driveway.

'Oh, my God!' Donna shrieked.

George bent over the man, feeling for his pulse. 'Get help,' he said tersely.

Donna hurried back to the Stollis' front door and rang the bell. Mickey opened the door. 'Our driver's sick,' Donna said. 'Call the paramedics.'

Mickey walked outside. 'He looks drunk to me,' he said, staring at the man on the ground.

John Fardo groaned, gradually regaining consciousness.

'Are you all right, John?' Donna asked.

'Yeah, yeah, I'm fine . . . fine,' he muttered, embarrassed about the incident.

All he could remember was somebody dragging him out of the car, beating the shit out of him and shoving him back behind the wheel with the curt warning, 'Don't ever fuck with the Santangelos again.' After that he must have passed out.

Making a supreme effort he pulled himself together and staggered up off the ground. 'Sorry, Mrs Landsman, dunno what happened. I, uh, guess I musta fallen.'

'Fallen?' she said, imperiously.

He hoped they wouldn't notice his swollen face in the dim light. 'I'm okay now. Lemme drive you home.'

The Landsmans got in the car.

Mickey shrugged and went back in the house. 'Their driver was drunk,' he informed Abigaile, who was already on her way upstairs.

'What did you think of the party?' she asked, over her shoulder.

'Your usual success,' he said, following her up the stairs.

'How would *you* know?' she said tartly. 'You spent the entire evening drooling down Venus's neckline.'

'Honey, you can't possibly be jealous of me and Venus. She works for my studio.'

'You paid her too much attention, Mickey. It's disrespectful to me.'

'Gotta keep the actresses happy.'

'Ha!' Abigaile snorted, stopping for a moment.

Mickey grabbed her ass. 'Come here, hon,' he cajoled. 'You know you're the only one for me.'

☆   ☆   ☆

The first thing Donna noticed as they approached their house was Tabitha's BMW parked in the driveway. 'Thank God they're here,' she said to George. 'I was beginning to worry.'

'He's sixteen, Donna. You worry about him too much. Santo needs discipline, not coddling.'

'Why would he bring Tabitha here?' Donna mused. 'I know, it's probably because those stupid Stolli people made out he wasn't a welcome dinner guest. Santo was upset.'

That'll be the day, George thought. Donna had no idea what a spoiled monster she was raising.

They entered the house.

'Santo!' Donna called out in the dark hallway, reaching for the light switch.

'They must be up in his room,' George said.

'Why would he take her up there?' Donna said.

Why do you think? George thought, following his wife to their private elevator.

'I can't believe they invited Lucky Santangelo tonight,' Donna grumbled. 'A true lack of judgment on Mickey's part. I shall be watching him very closely from now on.'

'Yes, dear,' George said, standing next to her in the small but luxurious elevator.

The door to Santo's room was closed.

'Knock,' George said.

'Why should I?' Donna said, flinging open the door. 'This is my house.'

Santo was sprawled on his bed passed out. Lying across him was a half-naked Tabitha, also in a drugged stupor. Loud rap music blared from the CD player. On the bedside table was a half-eaten pizza, a spilled bowl of popcorn, half a joint and an empty bottle of Scotch precariously balanced on its side.

'Oh, my God!' Donna wailed. 'What has she done to my baby?'

Chapter Fifty-six

 LUCKY TOOK Boogie with her to meet Sara and deliver the money. They met at the Hard Rock, where Sara had seemed comfortable the last time. Sara ran in, sat down, and immediately ordered a double cheeseburger.

'Is this the only time you eat?' Lucky inquired.

'I got me a healthy appetite,' Sara replied, grabbing her burger as soon as it arrived, taking huge bites, stuffing her mouth until she couldn't jam anything else in. 'Okay, how we gonna do this?' she asked, as soon as she'd finished. 'I gotta get the money before I hand over the tape.'

'You'll come with me to my car where I have a VCR,' Lucky said. 'We'll play the tape, and if it contains what you say it does, you'll get your money. It's as easy as that.'

'Oh, yeah, like really easy,' Sara sneered, eyeing Lucky with deep suspicion. 'How'd I know you won't kidnap me? Sell me into white slavery, that kinda shit.'

'You have to trust me,' Lucky replied calmly, wondering if the girl was on drugs – she was certainly manic enough.

'Me, I don't trust no one,' Sara said, proud of her spiky attitude. 'Everyone's out for their own thing.'

'If you want your money, you'll *have* to,' Lucky said coolly.

'Who's he?' Sara said, gesturing rudely toward Boogie.

'My associate.'

Sara squinted her eyes. 'How do I know *he* ain't gonna do something to me?'

Lucky was starting to lose her patience. 'Either you want the money or you don't,' she said curtly.

'Okay, okay,' Sara answered quickly, not wanting to blow such a windfall. 'Where's your car?'

'Outside.'

'I may as well tell you,' Sara said, her expression turning crafty. 'My friend knows where I am, an' if I'm not home in an hour, she'll call the cops.'

'Very sensible,' Lucky said drily. 'I'm glad you've figured out how to protect yourself.'

They walked outside to the waiting limousine.

'Cool,' Sara said, liking the fact it was a limo. 'Y'know,' she continued chattily as she climbed in, 'I had this customer . . . uh, I mean, like, friend. He'd arrive at the massage parlor in his big freakin' limo, an' then he'd wanna get a very *personal* massage in the backseat, while his driver took us around town. This big old car had black windows so nobody could peek in. Sometimes he opened that glass thing so's his driver could get himself an eyeful. I di'n't go for that, but the old lech paid good.'

Why had Morton picked this sad little girl to get himself in trouble with? They were a total mismatch. 'Does Morton know you had all these adventures before you met him?'

Sara giggled hysterically. 'Morty thinks I was workin' the massage parlor thing like a *good* girl.'

Lucky leaned over and inserted the tape in the VCR. The picture scrambled for a moment before becoming clear.

She stared at the screen. There was Morton in Sara's bedroom sitting on the side of her bed fully dressed in a three-piece suit. Enter Sara in a schoolgirl outfit.

Sara: 'Hi, Daddykins.'

Morton: 'Were you a good girl at school today?'

Sara: '*Very* good, Daddy.'

Morton: 'Are you sure?'

Sara: 'Yes, Daddy.'

Morton: 'Come sit on my knee and tell me all about it.'

Sara: 'I did do *something* bad . . .'

Morton: 'Am I going to have to spank you?'

Sara: 'I don't know, Daddy. Were you a good boy at the office today?'

Morton: 'No, I did something bad, too.'

Sara: 'Then I think *I'll* spank *you*.'

And so it went on. Lucky watched in a trance-like state. She knew some people could only get off by indulging their fantasies, but as far as she was concerned it was kind of a sick obsession. What was wrong with normal sex? Who needed fantasies and props?

As soon as Morton began to divest his clothes, she clicked off the machine and said, 'Okay, I've seen enough.' Opening the window, she spoke to Boogie who waited outside. 'Give her the money and let's go.'

Sara climbed out of the car and stood awkwardly on the sidewalk. Boogie handed her a paper shopping bag. 'Here,' he said. 'You want to count it?'

Sara grabbed the bag and peered inside, barely concealing her excitement. 'Is this all I have t' do?'

'That's it,' Lucky said. 'Put the money in a safety deposit box and go home. Not a word to Morton.'

'Won't he find out?' Sara asked.

'Maybe,' Lucky said. 'It didn't bother you last time – nor him. He's still paying your rent.'

'I'm usin' the money to get outta town with my girlfriend,' Sara confided. 'I've had LA. You should've *seen* some of the weirdos who came into the massage parlor. Games, games, games – that's all they were into. An' most of 'em wished I was ten!'

'Spare me the details,' Lucky said.

'Well,' Sara said, clutching the shopping bag to her side, 'we're gonna try our luck in Vegas. Me and my friend. If there's anything else I can do . . . you got a phone?'

'Don't worry, Sara, if we need anything, *we'll* contact you.'

Boogie got into the car, and the limo sped off.

☆　☆　☆

Santo blamed George. His mother would never have punished him in such a vicious fashion if George hadn't encouraged her. He was sixteen, for Chrissakes. If he couldn't make out with a girl in his own room, what *could* he do?

George suggested a list of punishments and Donna agreed. Santo had never seen her so angry. Her face was white and pinched, she could barely look at him.

1. No Ferrari.

2. No allowance for six weeks.

3. No going out after school.

4. No credit cards.

Shit! He'd been caught having sex, not murdering the freaking President.

Donna didn't say a word while George confronted Santo with his punishments.

'C'mon, Mom,' he whined, turning to her. 'It wasn't so bad.'

'Drugs are very bad,' George said ominously, like it was a Federal offense – which, of course, it probably was. 'Your mother and I will not tolerate them in our house.'

'Her house,' Santo muttered sourly.

'No,' Donna said, appalled by her son's behavior. 'It's George's house, too. And he's taking care of this problem until you learn to behave.'

He couldn't believe that she was siding with George. It was unthinkable. What a freaking cow!

He wondered what kind of punishment Tabitha had gotten after her father had come to fetch her. 'I never want to see her with my son again,' he'd heard Donna say as Mickey whisked Tabitha off.

After George had finished yelling at him, and Donna refused to intervene, he went to his room and sat glumly in front of his computer staring blankly at the screen.

No Ferrari.

No allowance.

No privileges.

No TV.

What a sack of shit.

He was confused. He hadn't meant to do it with Tabitha, when all along he'd been saving himself for Venus. Now freaky Tabitha had gone and spoiled everything.

What if the things she'd said about Venus were true? That Venus was nothing but a slut and a whore.

It suddenly occurred to him that all this wasn't Tabitha's fault at all. *Venus* was to blame. If he hadn't seen her at the Stollis' party, and if Tabitha hadn't told him all those things about her, he wouldn't have gotten so stoned that he'd ended up not knowing what he was doing.

Yes. *Venus* was responsible for him not getting a Ferrari. It was *her* fault. She'd ruined his life, and he was going to make sure she paid for it.

☆ ☆ ☆

'This is for you,' Cooper said, standing over Venus.

She rolled over in bed, stretching lazily. 'What?' she mumbled, half asleep.

'Orange juice, raisin toast, coffee, the trades, and this . . .'

She struggled to sit up. Cooper held a silver tray with all of the things he'd mentioned on it. He was also stark naked, and carefully balanced on the edge of the tray was his erect penis.

She began to laugh hysterically. 'What are you *doing*?' she exclaimed, sitting up.

'Nothing,' he deadpanned.

'What am *I* doing?' she groaned, realizing she'd spent the night with the husband she was about to divorce.

'Falling in love with your husband again?' he suggested, charming her with his handsome smile.

'Oh, no . . . once was enough, thank you, Cooper. You're a lot of fun, but I've finally realized you are *not* husband material.'

'How many other guys make you breakfast?' he asked, plaintively. 'Where else can you get this kind of service?'

'Mmm . . .' she said, still smiling. 'Orange juice, raisin toast, coffee, a hard-on . . . Maybe I should reconsider.'

'Look, you,' he said, removing his dick from the tray and sitting on the side of the bed, 'I know what I did was unforgivable. If you'd done the same to me, I probably would've walked. Truth is, I learned my lesson and now I want us to get back together.'

'Hmm . . .' she murmured languorously.

'Last night I was with one of the most desired women in America. And you know what? I left her, and came running over to be with you.'

'Ha!' she exclaimed, sitting up further.

'What does "ha" mean?'

'According to Mr Romano – who knows about such things – Veronica is a sex change.'

'Jesus, Venus! That's ridiculous. And not true.'

She giggled. 'Guess you made the right decision, Coop.'

He frowned. Could that explain his lack of interest? His survival instinct must have kicked in, saving him from . . . what?

'We belong together, Venus,' he said persuasively, refusing to allow her to get him off-track. 'You know that.'

'Cooper,' she replied, her face serious, 'this new movie I'm about to start is very important to me, and—'

'Wasn't last night special?' he interrupted, fixing her with his ice-blue eyes. 'Wasn't it the greatest? We really are something together, everyone says so.'

She smiled at the memory of his incredible lovemaking. 'I must admit, Coop, you do have a technique like nobody else . . .'

'And let me assure you, from now on I'm saving it all for you.'

She wanted to believe him. However, this was Cooper Turner speaking – a man with a life-long reputation of screwing around. She'd taken a chance with him once. Was she foolish enough to do it again?

He was right in there with a fresh pitch. 'All I'm asking for is another shot. C'mon, honey, you *know* it's right.'

She felt herself weakening. 'Well . . . maybe we *could* see each other – kind of get reacquainted.'

'I thought we got reacquainted last night.'

She giggled again. 'Oh, yeah, and I'd like more of that tonight, tomorrow, and – if things work out – well, eventually we could talk about moving back in together.'

'Deal,' he said, smiling broadly.

'Now you'll have to excuse me,' she said, jumping out of bed. 'I must speak to my agent.'

'I love it when you get serious,' he said, grabbing her arm and pulling her back on the bed.

She smiled. What the hell? One more chance wouldn't kill her.

☆ ☆ ☆

Lucky stepped out from behind a marble pillar, accosting Morton Sharkey in the lobby of his Century City office building. 'Hi, Morton,' she said, removing her Porsche shades and fixing him with her black eyes.

He stepped back startled.

'Surprised to see me?'

'Uh . . . Lucky.' He was almost stammering. 'This, uh . . . *is* a surprise. What are you doing here?'

'I came to see you.'

'You did?' he said, agitated.

She moved closer. 'Ever since you pulled your little stunt at Panther, I haven't been able to reach you, even though I've left messages every day, told your secretary it's urgent, and repeatedly faxed you. Didn't your mother teach you it's very rude not to respond?'

'I'm sorry, Lucky, I've been extremely busy.'

'You sold me out, Morton,' she said flatly. 'And I don't like that.'

He adopted a defensive attitude. 'I did what was best.'

'For whom?' she said coldly. 'You were my business adviser. You helped me gain control of Panther, then you went behind my back and screwed me.' A pause. 'I don't get it, Morton. Unless, of course, somebody was *forcing* you to behave in such an unethical way.'

He began edging toward the elevator, trying to distance himself from her. 'Uh, Lucky, you still have forty percent of Panther. I'm sure with Mickey running it again it'll go into profit . . .'

She moved in front of him, blocking his way. 'Just like

before, huh? You, better than anyone, know he ran the studio into the ground.'

'These things happen,' he muttered, too ashamed to look at her. 'Business is business.'

'Mistake number one, Morton – you sided with Donna Landsman.'

'Mrs Landsman is a respected businesswoman.'

'No. For your information Mrs Landsman is the widow of Santino Bonnatti.'

Alarm spread across his face. 'What are you talking about?'

'Remember the Bonnattis? I'm sure I must have told you the story many times.'

He stared at her silently, thinking, so that's why Donna Landsman was so anxious to gain control of Panther.

'Fortunately for you I'm in a good mood,' Lucky continued pleasantly. 'Therefore, I'm giving you a chance to redeem yourself. My lawyer will immediately arrange for you to sell me your five percent of Panther, plus your half of the Panther shares you have in Conquest Investments. That'll give me back a controlling interest. Then I want you to set up the same scenario – just like you did for Donna. I'll be sitting in my office when you bring her in and *I* tell her *she's* out. Oh, yes, and make sure Mickey Stolli is with her. I want to personally fire his fat ass.'

Morton's voice faltered. 'I – I can't do that.'

'Oh, yes, Morton, you certainly can.' A long pause. 'By the way, how's your wife? And children?' Another long pause. 'I guess Donna hasn't shown them the tape yet.'

The color drained from his face. 'What tape?'

'Morton, you're a good businessman, but, you have to realize that when you're dealing with somebody like Donna – or, in fact, someone like me – you're out of your league. Not only does Donna still have your balls in a vise, but now I also have a copy of the tape.'

'Oh, God!' he groaned. 'Please don't do this to me.'

'Cooperate, Morton,' she said coolly. 'And I'll see every copy of the tape – including the original – is destroyed. And if you don't, well, I'll personally make sure your wife views it, because you've been a *very* bad boy and you deserve to be punished.'

His shoulders slumped and he looked ready to collapse. 'Jesus! What have I done?' he muttered.

Lucky sighed and shook her head. 'Don't you get it? Nice guys aren't supposed to screw around on their wives – especially with a teenage hooker. It's not proper. Marriage is a contract. And in my world a contract means something.'

She turned and walked away, leaving an ashen-faced Morton standing alone.

☆ ☆ ☆

Leslie spent the night with Johnny Romano, not bothering to return to her own house until early in the morning. She entered her bedroom and was annoyed to see that Jeff was exactly where she'd left him, fully clothed and snoring. The idiot wasn't even aware she'd been out all night.

She went into her bathroom, took a shower, dressed and applied fresh makeup. Then she hurried into Jeff's closet and packed all his clothes into a suitcase which she dragged to the front door.

That done, she sat down and wrote him a short note.

Dear Jeff:
    This isn't working for me. I will be out until three. When I get home I would like you to be gone. Please leave my keys on the kitchen table.
                       Leslie

She left the note on top of the suitcase and drove to the Four Seasons, where she checked in for the day.

If there was one thing Leslie hated, it was confrontations.

☆　☆　☆

Alex hit his office like a dynamo, energized and full of vigor. He'd woken up early and decided he'd better forget about Lucky for now and get back to concentrating on his movie. Once he'd made that decision he'd started feeling good.

'What's goin' on?' he asked, as he burst in, slapping France on the ass as he passed.

'Alex!' France said. It wasn't an objection, more another way of saying, *Thanks!*

Lili was delighted to see him in such good form. 'Do we have our old Alex back?' she asked, following him into his office.

'What do you mean?' he responded.

'You've hardly been yourself lately,' Lili said, crisply.

'Don't talk crap,' Alex said.

'I'm merely being truthful.'

'Okay,' he said briskly, moving on to more important things. 'This is the deal. Leslie's out. Venus is in. Talk to her agent, confirm with Mickey and arrange for her to come in at four. I want to check out Johnny's clothes today. Then put together a full readthrough with the entire cast on Thursday. Got it?'

'Yes,' Lili said, smiling happily. 'Are we sending flowers to anyone?'

'Absolutely not,' Alex said firmly. 'It's back to business, Lili. We're making a movie here. Let's get it together.'

☆　☆　☆

After seeing Morton, Lucky met with Inga. She'd called her early in the morning and suggested they should talk.

'What about?' Inga had asked suspiciously.

'Something I'm sure you don't want Abe to hear.'

That was enough to spur Inga into action. She'd agreed to meet Lucky for lunch in the dining room at the Beverly Wilshire Hotel.

When Lucky walked in, Inga was already sitting at a table. 'Hi,' Lucky said, settling into a chair, her back to the window so she could view the room.

Inga nodded, her broad, unlined Swedish face impassive as usual.

'I could have come to the house,' Lucky said. 'Only I didn't think you'd want Abe to hear our conversation.'

'Is it *about* Abe?' Inga asked, her strong jawline thrust forward.

'No,' Lucky replied, wondering if Inga would object to her smoking at the table. 'Well, I say no, but in a way it does have to do with him.'

'How?' Inga asked.

Yes. Inga would definitely be put out if she smoked. 'Shall we order?' she said, waving to the captain. He hurried over with menus.

'I usually don't eat lunch,' Inga said. 'Perhaps an apple and a piece of cheese.'

'How frugal of you,' said Lucky, consulting the menu and ordering a steak and french fries. 'I need my strength,' she said, with a small smile. 'So many people have been stabbing me in the back lately I'm positively weak. This afternoon I might lift weights – have you ever done that? It's great therapy.'

'No,' Inga said. 'For exercise I swim ten lengths in the pool every day.'

'*Very* good for you,' Lucky said, imagining Abe sitting pool-side, watching.

Inga ordered a salad, waiting impatiently to see what Lucky had to say.

'How well do you know Morton Sharkey?' Lucky asked at last, leaning her elbows on the table.

Inga shrugged. 'Not very well at all,' she said warily.

'Tell me how you met him. Through Abe?'

'Yes,' Inga said.

Lucky nodded. 'I remember when I was looking to buy Panther. Abe recommended Morton. He'd used him for a couple of deals and trusted him. I must say, I trusted him, too. Silly me. I even trusted him when he persuaded me to privately sell off a large block of shares. He suggested I diversify, sell sixty percent of Panther and use the money for other investments. I agreed. Of course, I should have kept fifty-one percent, but . . . I went with Morton's advice. He said he had investors in place who were controllable, nothing could ever go wrong . . .'

Inga was starting to look uncomfortable. 'What's your point?'

'You know what my point is, Inga,' Lucky said, her voice hardening. 'You're not a stupid woman. Or should I call you Mrs Smorg?'

'Abe is ninety,' Inga said brusquely, 'I've lived with him for the last thirty years. By obtaining a piece of Panther Studios, I protected my future.'

'Fine with me,' Lucky said calmly. 'But why did you side with Donna Landsman?'

'Morton advised me to do so.'

'Oh, you mean your *partner*, Morton Sharkey, the person you own Conquest Investments with?'

'Abe has never done anything for me,' Inga said, bitterly.

'I have no money, nothing in my name. I know when he dies his great-grandchildren inherit everything.'

'You're married to him, Inga,' Lucky said evenly. 'California law states you get half of his estate.'

Inga stared into space, reciting her reasons. 'Abe made several irrevocable trusts before we were married. I signed a pre-nuptial *and* a quit claim on his estate. In his will he has left me a hundred thousand dollars. That's it.' She gave a heavy sigh. 'I am not a young woman anymore. I have a certain lifestyle to maintain.'

'By protecting yourself you screwed me,' Lucky said tersely. 'By siding with Morton you gave me no chance.'

'I had to do what he said – he takes care of my investments.'

Lucky laid out her terms. 'This is the deal, Inga. If you don't want Abe to know about your outside activities, sell me your shares immediately. You hold six percent personally and half of Conquest is another five. That'll give me back eleven percent.' She paused for breath. 'My lawyer has drawn up the papers. You'll get top dollar. Be smart – buy yourself IBM with the money.'

Inga realized she had no choice. 'Very well,' she said stiffly. 'I will do as you say.'

☆　☆　☆

'I've a bitch of a headache,' Mickey grumbled.

'I'm sorry to hear that,' Leslie replied sympathetically.

They sat together in the commissary at Panther Studios.

'Not exactly a hangover,' Mickey said, hunching his shoulders. 'Although I *was* drinking.'

'Your party was very nice,' Leslie said, not meaning it, but, what the hell? May as well make Mickey feel good.

'It might have been nice for you,' he said vehemently.

'But *I* had a situation where my daughter ended up fucking that Santo kid in his house – and *I* had to go get her.'

'No!' Leslie said, suitably shocked.

'What is it with kids today, Leslie?' he asked mournfully. 'They treat sex and drugs like it's no big deal. When I was sixteen, buying *condoms* was a big deal.'

'I'm sorry to hear Tabitha's giving you trouble,' Leslie said. Obviously the kid took after her father.

He drank half a glass of Evian water. 'Trouble, schmubble . . . I suppose the kid's gotta do her own thing. She goes back to boarding school in a couple of weeks.'

Leslie picked at her salad. It was time to talk about *her*. 'Well, you'll be pleased to know I took your advice.'

'What advice, sweetie?'

'Jeff is history.'

Mickey nodded his approval. 'Smart move. A girl like you can have anybody you want.' He jabbed his finger at her. 'You gotta work the stardom thing, Leslie. Work it.'

'I'm sure you're right,' she murmured.

'An' talking of working it, have *I* found a script for you.'

'Really?'

'I've been thinkin' about your career. *Gangsters* is not right – you're too nice to pull off that kind of sleazy role.'

'What script, Mickey?' she asked eagerly.

'It's about a guy and a gal who meet in Paris, fall in love, fall out of love, then fall back in love. Hokey shit – the public'll eat it up.'

'It sounds wonderful. Are you sending it to Cooper?'

'Yeah, yeah, I'll send it to him. But, Leslie, you gotta realize, Cooper's like an old whore – give him the right amount of money and he'll stand on his head and recite the alphabet. He does it for the loot.'

'That's not a very nice thing to say,' Leslie said, springing to her former lover's defense.

'I keep on telling ya, ya gotta wise up to actors.'

'I'll read the script,' she said sweetly, ignoring his criticism. 'If I like it, I'll do it.'

'Honey,' he laughed rudely. '*I* like it, *you'll* do it. Have I ever given you bad advice?'

It wasn't worth arguing. Better he was on her side. 'No, Mickey, you and Abigaile have been very good to me.'

'Okay, sweetie – remember that,' he said, squinting across the table at her. 'You look better today, not so pinched. Throwing Jeff out agrees with you.'

'Thank you, Mickey,' she said demurely.

And she did not tell him about her night's adventure with Johnny Romano. It had been a one-off to get over her disappointment with Cooper. And not a very exciting one-off. Johnny Romano was still a greedy pig, only interested in his own satisfaction.

It would never happen again.

☆   ☆   ☆

'Outfit – sensational. Attitude – just right,' Alex said.

'Thanks.' Venus smiled. She was sitting in his office, enjoying their meeting. 'Coming from you that's a big compliment.'

'I spoke to Freddie.'

'So did I.'

'Everything's under control,' Alex said. 'Contracts are on their way.'

'You don't know how thrilled I am to be doing *Gangsters*,' Venus said. 'I guess I told you before – the critics hate me. This time I don't want them seeing Venus on the screen, I want to *be* Lola.' She looked at him intently. 'I *know* you can bring the performance out in me that I've never been able to give before.'

'If I can't get it out of you, nobody can,' Alex said, never modest about what he knew he could achieve. 'I'll personally work on the script with you. Today you'll do clothes, hair and makeup tests. Tomorrow there'll be a readthrough with the rest of the cast.'

'This is such a special day for me,' Venus said, brimming with enthusiasm. 'Not only have I gotten the part of my career, but I've decided to give my husband another chance.'

'Cooper?' Alex said, raising an eyebrow.

She laughed happily. 'He's the only husband I've got.'

'Taking him back, huh?'

'The truth is,' she grinned sheepishly, 'he's irresistible.'

'That's what *you're* gonna be in *Gangsters*,' Alex said, killer smile at full force. 'Irresistible.'

☆　☆　☆

On the drive back to her house Lucky had plenty of time to think. Finally it was all coming together.

She would get her studio back.

She would never get her husband back.

After she regained control of Panther, she knew she'd eventually have to deal with Donna Landsman. There was no way she could allow Donna to get away with murdering Lennie.

She'd been putting the thought to the back of her mind. Soon she'd have to face it.

She sighed – a deep sigh. When would the Bonnatti family learn?

Chapter Fifty-seven

 'MY POPPA is back,' Claudia said, clasping her hands nervously together. 'He say I no come here again.'

'Jesus, Claudia,' Lennie said, desperately trying to control his frustration. 'When are you getting the key?'

'This weekend . . . when my poppa sleeps.'

'Why can't you call the American Embassy? Get help. Get me *out* of this fucking place.'

Her pretty face was serene. 'Lennie,' she said seriously, 'my life is here – in my village. I help you escape, my poppa cannot know. No one can. We must do it my way.'

Sometimes he felt he was in the middle of an Italian movie acting out scenes. Beautiful peasant girl with incredible voluptuous breasts and sturdy thighs rescues handsome American stranger from a life in captivity. Shit! Universal would make it in a minute!

'Claudia,' he said, purposely speaking very slowly so as not to frighten her away. 'Isn't there a way to get me out of here today? What about your boyfriend? Can't he help?'

She turned on him with a ferocious, 'No!'

He'd upset her. Had to be careful. He sensed she was in two minds about betraying her father. Now he realized she hadn't even told her boyfriend.

'Okay, okay,' he said soothingly. 'You can't blame me for being impatient.'

'Where is the map I gave you?' she asked. 'If my poppa sees it . . .'

'Don't worry. I've hidden it.'

She was edgy today, full of fear. What if she changed her mind and left him here to rot?

No. She wouldn't do that. They'd forged a connection, a bond. She had a little crush on him, and he felt the same about her. Not that it lessened his love for Lucky. This was merely circumstances.

'Claudia,' he held out his arms, 'come here.'

Warily she walked toward him. Today she had on a dress like Sophia Loren had worn in the movie *Two Women*. A clingy cotton dress that buttoned all the way down the front, exposing her bare legs and lightly tanned skin. On her feet were simple sandals. She wore no makeup except a soft pink lipstick. Her long auburn hair fell to below her waist. He noticed she had a little scar on her left cheek, and her eyelashes were impossibly long.

She stood close to him. He could see she was near to tears. He breathed in her scent and asked her what was wrong.

Her lower lip began to tremble. 'I – I am confused . . .' she stammered.

'I know this is difficult for you,' he said, trying desperately to reassure her. 'You feel you're betraying your father, and yet you know that what he's doing is very wrong. Criminal, in fact.'

She nodded silently.

He reached out his hand, touching her arm. 'When I'm free, Claudia, I won't forget you. I want you to come visit me in America.'

'Not possible,' she said, shaking her head. 'No one can know I helped you.'

'Look,' he said. 'If you bring me a paper and pencil, I'll write down my address and phone number. Any time you want anything I'll be there for you, or I'll send you money. Whatever you want.'

'I know what Poppa has done is bad,' she said. 'This is why I help you.'

'Is that the only reason?'

'Lennie,' she said. 'I feel . . . close to you. So very close.'

He pulled her to him, kissing her passionately. She struggled, but only for a second. Then she gave herself up to his kiss, throwing back her head, her lips soft and giving and so very sweet.

Forgive me, Lucky, but I have to make sure she comes back, and this is the only way I know how.

Besides, the touch of another human being, the feel of her body, filled him with hope. There was a future. He wasn't dead yet.

She explored his face with her hands, stroking, caressing. 'My American prisoner,' she murmured lovingly. 'I will set you free. I will.'

Automatically he began to undo the buttons of her dress, exposing her full breasts.

She was truly one of the most luscious women he'd ever seen, her skin smooth, her nipples ripe and inviting as he bent to kiss them. She tasted so sweet he couldn't stop himself.

She lay down on the damp ground and threw her arms above her head in a gesture of pure abandonment. Her underarm hair was thick and somehow very sexy. He teased her nipples with his tongue.

'We shouldn't be doing this,' she said, breathing heavily. 'It is not right.'

He noticed she didn't move away.

'No one will ever know – this is between us,' he said,

quickly unbuttoning the rest of her dress, his fingers fumbling on the material.

She wore old-fashioned underpants that reached up to her waist. Recklessly he plunged his hand down them, feeling his way through a thick forest of pubic hair to reach the warm moistness of her desire.

She caught her breath, gasping with passion. She was his last chance of freedom.

'This weekend . . . you'll come back, you'll help me,' he said, plunging into her welcoming softness.

'Oh, yes, Lennie, oh, yes – you have my promise.'

Chapter Fifty-eight

 'So,' BRIGETTE said, nervously pulling at her hair. 'That's the story. I'm sorry, I don't know how I get caught up in these things...' She bit her lip, anxiously waiting for Lucky's reaction.

Lucky stood up from the outdoor table where they were finishing dinner. 'There's no need for you to apologize,' she said soothingly. 'You've been very unfortunate. Not all men are like Santino Bonnatti and Michel Guy. Although, you do seem to have a way of attracting the worst elements.'

'Michel seemed so nice,' Brigette said miserably. 'I mean I *trusted* him. He was older and gentle, and ... maybe I even encouraged him.'

'He took advantage of you, Brigette,' Lucky said vehemently. 'Any man who ties a woman up and forces her to have sex against her will with another woman – well, this is definitely a bad guy.'

'I tried to warn her,' Nona said, joining in. 'Although I had no idea he was such a sicko.'

'And Robertson, did she go along with it?' Lucky asked.

Brigette shrugged. 'He told her what to do and she did it. I guess she was stoned.'

'Yeah,' Nona agreed. 'A lot of those models think of nothing else except getting stoned and laid. It's all one big kick.'

'It might be a kick,' Lucky said curtly. 'But Michel Guy's not getting away with it, I can promise you that.'

'I told you,' Nona said, shooting Brigette a triumphant look.

'What'll you do?' Brigette asked.

'I'll make time to visit Mr Guy in New York.'

'He'll deny it,' Brigette said. 'He'll say I encouraged him – I know he will.'

'Who do *you* think I'll believe?' Lucky asked softly. 'You or him?'

'Me?' Brigette said in a small voice.

'Of course, you, sweetheart.'

Brigette jumped to her feet and hugged Lucky. 'Thank you,' she said. 'You're the best!'

'Y'know, if Lennie was alive he'd break this Michel prick's balls,' Lucky said.

'I miss Lennie so much,' Brigette murmured sadly. 'I miss him every day.'

Lucky nodded, her eyes misting over. 'So do I,' she said quietly. 'We all do.'

☆   ☆   ☆

Early the next morning Lucky chartered a plane and flew to New York.

She'd instructed Brigette and Nona to stay at her house in LA until she got back, which, if all went according to plan, would be later that same day. Daniella Dion was coming to town, and she was next on Lucky's list of people to deal with.

In the meantime, her personal lawyer was finalizing the details of getting her studio back.

Morton had called late last night, sounding panicked. 'What if Donna Landsman shows the tape to my wife?' he'd asked. 'How can I stop her?'

'That's something you'll have to work out with Donna,' she'd replied, not really concerned with his problems after what he'd done to her.

'Jesus, Lucky, if this gets out I'll be ruined.'

'You should have come to me in the first place,' she'd said, in a way feeling sorry for him. 'I could've taken care of it.'

'I made a mistake,' he'd said miserably.

Big mistake, Morton.

Today she felt invigorated, invincible. Sometimes the power within her was so strong she was convinced she could do anything.

The plane came in for a smooth landing. There was a car at the airport to meet her. The driver took the freeway to the city, riding the pot-holed streets to the center of Manhattan where Michel Guy's office was located. Lucky marched in without an appointment, bypassing two secretaries.

'You can't see Mr Guy without arranging it first,' one of the flustered secretaries said, dashing after her.

'Let me correct you,' Lucky said. 'I can do what the hell I like.'

Michel Guy was sitting in his office, legs propped on his desk, smoking a big fat Havana cigar.

Lucky took him completely by surprise. His legs came off the desk, the cigar came out of his mouth and he said, startled, '*Oui?* What can I do for you?'

'Do you know who I am?' Lucky said, staring him down.

He stared back at her. She certainly wasn't a model, but she was an extremely beautiful woman with a vaguely familiar face. 'No,' he said at last. 'Should I?'

'Maybe you'll recognize my name. Lucky Santangelo?'

Ah, now he knew exactly who she was, he'd recently read an interview with her in *Newstime*. 'You own a studio in Hollywood,' he said, wondering what the hell she was doing in his office. 'How can I help you?'

'I thought you might be interested to know the identity of my stepdaughter.'

'Your stepdaughter,' he said blankly.

The secretary stood by the door, glaring at Lucky.

'Okay, Monica, you can leave us,' Michel said, waving her away.

Lucky sat down uninvited and lit a cigarette. 'It seems she didn't tell you.'

'Who didn't tell me what?' Michel said, irritated and intrigued at the same time.

Lucky's voice was suddenly cold and hard as she stood up and leaned over his desk. 'You know something, Michel? You're a mean fuckhead with a small dick.'

'Excuse me,' he said, becoming alarmed at her behavior.

'*Schifoso*. You know what that means in English?'

'I'm French,' he said.

'Piece of filthy garbage,' she said, blowing smoke in his face. '*That's* what it means.'

'What do you want?' he said, deciding he'd better summon help.

'I want to tell you a little story,' Lucky said, sitting down again. 'Pay attention, Michel, it's short and simple.'

This intrusion had gone on long enough. 'I'm busy right now,' he said. 'I suggest you make an appointment and come back another time.'

'I built hotels in Vegas, two of them,' she said, ignoring his request. 'During construction, one of my investors balked at putting up the balance of the money he owed, even though we had a firm agreement. That night I broke into his apartment with a couple of friends to assist me in case he was foolish enough to get out of line. He awoke to find a nice sharp knife poised at the base of his penis.' A long, meaningful pause. 'Now . . . what do *you* think he did?'

'I don't know,' Michel said, thinking she was totally crazy.

'He put up the money – plus, of course, he kept his precious cock – and I kept my hotel.' A short silence. 'In the end, everyone was happy.'

He stood up, one eye on the door. 'What do you want from me?'

'My stepdaughter's name is Brigette Stanislopoulos. Perhaps you know her better as Brigette Brown.'

The color drained from his face. 'Oh,' he said blankly. 'I had no idea who she was.'

'I bet you didn't. I bet you thought she was some little girl you could fuck with. Blackmail, perhaps? Use as your toy?' Her voice cut into him like a knife. 'She's only nineteen, Michel. Aren't you ashamed of yourself?'

He'd read all about Lucky Santangelo. She was powerful. She had connections. He didn't want to find himself on a plane back to Paris with his balls in his mouth.

'I'm telling you,' he said, speaking fast, 'I had no idea. When that woman asked me to get the pictures—'

'*What* woman?' Lucky asked, knowing immediately who he meant.

'She paid me a fortune,' Michel said, his words tumbling over each other. 'If I'd known Brigette was related to you, I'd never have done it.'

'*What woman?*' Lucky repeated icily.

'Donna Landsman. She paid me to get compromising pictures of Brigette. I – I feel bad.'

'Really? Bad, huh?' Lucky said calmly, picking up an ivory-handled magnifying glass from his desk. 'You see this, you fucking pervert,' she said, her tone changing. 'I should shove this right up your French ass, because that's exactly what you deserve. But, instead, you and I are going to get the pictures.'

'I sent them to Mrs Landsman,' he said quickly.

'I'm sure you kept the negatives and a set for yourself.'

'No.'

She turned the magnifying glass in her hands, examining the sturdy ivory handle. 'Were you listening to the story I just told you? I can promise you, Michel, a knife at your cock is *nothing* compared to what I have planned for you if I don't get everything immediately. So let's go to your apartment, or wherever you have them. And let's not waste any more time. *Capisce?*'

The look in her deadly black eyes convinced him to do exactly as she said.

☆ ☆ ☆

Lucky didn't linger: she was on her way back to LA as soon as she'd obtained the photos *and* negatives from Michel Guy. She'd also made him sign a letter relinquishing all rights as Brigette's agent. 'Believe me, Michel,' Lucky had told him. 'You're getting off easy.'

He believed her. Fucking with Lucky would be a big mistake, and Michel was too smart to make that kind of mistake.

Boogie met her at LAX. They drove in silence to her house. Brigette was asleep when she got there. Lucky slipped the envelope containing the incriminating photos and negatives under her door, then she went to bed herself.

In the morning she awoke early and switched on the TV, watching while she dressed.

Morton Sharkey and Sara Durbon were on the morning news.

At eleven p.m., the previous evening, he'd blown both their brains out.

Chapter Fifty-nine

THE NEWS OF Morton Sharkey's demise was a big shock to Lucky: she hadn't realized he was in such an unbalanced state. According to the police report, Morton had walked in on Sara when she was preparing to split for Vegas. They'd had a big fight, overheard by the woman in the next apartment. It had culminated in two gunshots. The neighbor had called the police. Before they could get there, Sara's girlfriend had arrived to fetch her, and discovered the bodies. She'd run screaming from the building. Lucky felt sad, because whatever Morton had done, he didn't deserve to die. It was especially tragic that he'd taken Sara with him – poor little Sara, who'd only wanted to eat hamburgers and make money.

Lucky immediately tried to contact Morton's wife. Candice was too distraught to come to the phone. Instead Lucky spoke to his grown-up daughter, who accepted her condolences.

There was only one person to blame for his death. Donna Landsman. If she hadn't blackmailed Morton, he'd never have reached such a desperate state of mind.

Lucky knew she had to get hold of Donna's set of photographs of Brigette, and also the incriminating tape of Morton with Sara. At least let the man rest with dignity. He had the decency to transfer his shares back to her, and her lawyer assured her that everything would be cleared with Inga by the end of the day. Tomorrow Panther would be hers again.

Through Kyoko's studio connection she found out Mickey Stolli's movements for the next day. He was lunching with Freddie Leon at The Palm.

'As soon as he leaves the studio,' Lucky instructed Boogie, 'arrange to have his furniture cleared out, and mine put back in. When he returns from lunch, I'll be waiting to greet him. Make sure Donna Landsman is there, too.'

Boogie nodded. 'There shouldn't be a problem.'

Brigette was ecstatic when she'd found the photographs under her door. 'I promise I'll *never* do anything to make you ashamed of me again,' she said fervently. 'I'm going to do nothing but work, work, work, you'll be really proud of me.'

'It wasn't your fault,' Lucky said. 'Don't ever think it was.'

'Did you, uh, look at the photos?' Brigette asked, embarrassed.

'No,' Lucky lied. She'd had to check them out to make sure they were the right ones and didn't mention there was another set. Boogie was already arranging for a professional safe-cracker to stage a raid on Donna's house.

'What did Michel *say*?' Brigette asked.

'Forget about that low-life,' Lucky replied. 'The good news is, your contract with him is null and void, he collects no commissions on the Jeans deal, and I'm setting you up with another top agency.'

'Thanks, Lucky,' Brigette said, relieved and happy. 'Nobody could have done it but you.'

Later in the day Lucky called Johnny Romano. 'Have you got ten minutes if I drop by?'

'For you, baby, anything.'

She drove over to his house, a neo-classical mansion in Bel

Air with more marble than a mausoleum. A stunning black girl, dressed in a tight white suit and high stiletto heels, led her into the games room where Johnny was playing pool with a couple of go-fers. He greeted her with a hug and a kiss.

'I need a favor,' she said. 'It's kind of a weird one.'

'Nothing's too weird for me,' Johnny said, leading her over to a futuristic pin-ball machine.

'Well . . .' she said, watching Johnny play with his new toy. 'There's this very expensive French call-girl.'

'Tell me more,' he said, intrigued.

'She's flying to LA from Paris because she's under the impression she's been bought as a birthday gift for you.'

He laughed. 'For me?'

'That's right.'

'Baby – it ain't even my birthday!'

'I know that.'

His sleepy eyes lit up. 'Is this some kind of kinky sex thing you're into? 'Cause if it is, y'know I'm into it, too.'

'It's more complicated than that. It's to do with Lennie,' she said, proceeding to tell him of her suspicions. 'While you're with her, I'll be in the other room with a listening device.'

'Detective work,' he said, nodding to himself. 'I like it! When do we do this?'

'She's arriving tonight. I've booked her into a bungalow at the Beverly Hills Hotel. Boogie will pick her up at the airport and bring her straight there. Will you do it for me?'

'Baby, you can count on Johnny Romano – he's your man!'

☆　☆　☆

The immigration officer eyed the delectable blond in the Chanel suit, reeking of some incredible exotic scent, and decided she was worth his full attention.

'How long do you plan on staying in America?' he asked, eyes dropping to her rounded breasts with the prominent nipples straining the material of her blouse.

'Maybe a few days,' Daniella Dion said vaguely.

'Is your trip business or pleasure?' he inquired, craning over his desk to get a better look at her sensational legs, showcased in an exceptionally short skirt.

'A little bit of both.'

'And what business are you in?'

'Lingerie,' she said.

'Lingerie,' he repeated, his throat suddenly dry.

'That's right,' she said, with a small provocative smile.

He stamped her passport and reluctantly watched her step away from his desk. He couldn't wait to get home and throw a fuck into his overweight wife – this blond definitely had him revved.

Daniella sauntered through Customs and located the driver standing outside with her name printed on a large white card.

'Please follow me, Miss Dion,' Boogie said politely, taking her carry-on bag. 'Is this your only luggage?'

She nodded.

'Then we can go straight to the car,' he said, leading her down the escalator, through the doors to where the limousine was parked.

Holding open the back door he watched her slide onto the shiny leather seat. She was spectacular. Even Boogie was impressed.

He got behind the wheel of the limo and took off. 'We'll go straight to the Beverly Hills Hotel,' he said, keeping an eye on her in the rear-view mirror. 'Unless you wish to stop somewhere first?'

'No,' she said. 'You may take me to the hotel directly.'

'There's Evian, Scotch or vodka in the back. Please help yourself.'

'Nothing, thank you.'

'Your first trip to LA?' he asked conversationally.

'I'm tired,' she said, a touch petulantly. 'I don't wish to talk. Please close the partition.'

He shut the dark glass partition and called Lucky at the hotel. 'We're on our way,' he said.

☆　☆　☆

'Hey, baby, I want you to know I broke a date to accommodate you tonight,' Johnny said, prowling around the luxurious bungalow at the Beverly Hills Hotel.

'So, I owe you one,' Lucky said. 'After I get the studio back, you can come to me with any script you want to make and we're in business. That's a promise.'

'You don't owe me anythin', Lucky. You're the one who turned my career around.'

'You'd have worked it out eventually.'

'Yeah, but you *made* me change.'

'No. All I did was make you realize the smart way. Why do you think Clint Eastwood has lasted all these years? And Robert Redford. They won't play guys who beat up on women. They're the hero everybody loves. I knew you could be that guy, too. And now you are.'

'You bet your fine ass,' he said, grinning.

His sexism didn't bother her. She was used to Johnny – he reminded her of a boisterous puppy.

'Can we go over the questions again?' she asked.

'Go ahead, baby,' Johnny said.

'Okay. When you've got her in bed, you say, "I know about you and Lennie in Corsica." Then she'll probably say, "What are you talking about?" Then *you* say, "You were paid to set him up."'

'And after that?'

'Well, you'll have her naked in bed – vulnerable, in a strange country. I guess, depending on what she says, I'll come into the room and ask her myself.'

'Hey, Lucky,' he grinned slyly, 'you're payin' all this money, you want I should do the deed?'

'Whatever turns you on.'

He shook his head and laughed. 'I never paid for pussy – an', baby, I *ain't* startin' now.'

'Let me remind you, *I'm* paying, and she's *very* expensive. Maybe you *should* get our money's worth.'

'There's not a condom big enough for me to stick Romano, the magic eye, into a hooker.'

Romano – the magic eye! Was he kidding! 'Very delicately put,' she said, trying to keep from laughing.

'Just tellin' you the way it is.'

'Okay,' Lucky said, hoping Johnny could handle it. 'Just remember, she's your birthday present. When I've got my answers, you can do whatever you like.'

☆   ☆   ☆

Daniella sat in the back of the limo, gazing blankly out of the window. She wasn't fond of traveling and the plane journey had been long and tiring, although she should be used to long hours on a plane because her business often took her out of Paris. One of her regular clients was a Saudi prince, who paid an enormous amount of money for her to visit him at the palace in Saudi Arabia once a month; another was an Indian maharaja, who sent for her in Bombay several times a year; then there was the Australian media king who summoned her to Sydney twice a year to entertain him and his wife on their birthdays.

She'd made up her mind that the day her bank balance reached a certain level, she would quit altogether and vanish. She'd take her small daughter and buy a quaint old farmhouse in Tuscany where they could live in peace.

Daniella didn't care if she never saw another man again. They were animals, all of them. They paid for sex and then imagined they owned her. Stupid fools. They never owned her, they merely borrowed her body for the time it took.

She opened her purse, removed an elaborate solid gold compact – a gift from the prince – and inspected her face. *I am beautiful*, she thought, *but is that all they see?*

Yes, she told herself, *that's all they see.*

She took a Valium from her purse, and popped it in her mouth, washing it down with a bottle of Evian. Then she reached beneath her blouse, touching her breasts with the tips of her fingers, twisting her nipples until they began to harden.

As soon as she'd aroused herself, she reached under her skirt, parted her legs and methodically began rubbing her pussy.

She was so practiced in the art of self-gratification that it took only seconds before she reached a satisfying orgasm.

Gasping aloud, she fell back on the seat, closing her eyes, allowing the sweet sensation to wash over her.

Early on in her career she'd decided that no man would ever be allowed the privilege of making her come. She wanted the power over them, not the other way around. Since then she'd always taken care of herself before an appointment. That way she made sure that whatever they did to her, she was always in control of her feelings.

Adjusting her skirt, she sat up straight, preparing herself

for the evening ahead with Johnny Romano. He might be a movie star, but that was not an unusual client for Daniella. She'd had many other movie stars before him. She'd had kings and princes. She'd had politicians. She'd once had a president.

Tonight was going to be no different from any other night. Business as usual.

Chapter Sixty

DANIELLA DRANK Pernod and water.

Johnny drank Cristal champagne.

Daniella smoked a strong French cigarette.

Johnny smoked a joint.

And he stared at her . . . and couldn't stop staring, because she was the classiest blond he'd ever seen. Like a young Catherine Deneuve she sat opposite him, cool and collected, legs crossed, expression attentive, everything about her perfect.

They'd exchanged a few pleasantries – like, how was your trip, this is a lovely hotel. Now she waited patiently for him to make the first move. And even though he knew Lucky was prowling impatiently around in the second bedroom with a radio device picking up everything they said, he wasn't inclined to rush this little scene.

Daniella realized she'd better initiate the action. 'What do you like, Johnny?' she asked, in her low throaty voice. 'What *really* turns you on?'

I like the look of you, he wanted to say. *I like your accent . . . I like your smooth, creamy skin . . . your legs . . . your face . . . I like the whole classy package.*

He couldn't believe she was a hooker, there had to be some mistake. 'You seen any of my movies, baby?' he asked, snapping his fingers – a nervous habit he'd acquired after Warner dumped him. 'Am I big in Paris?'

'Oh, yes, Johnny,' she replied, not sure if he was or wasn't. 'Very big.'

The truth was she'd barely heard of him, and she'd certainly never seen any of his movies. Although she did remember a cover story in *Paris-Match*, where he was photographed at the Playboy mansion draped in blonds. Typical.

'I guess they dub me in French over there, huh?' he asked, desperately trying to impress.

'I'm sure,' she murmured.

'I hope they hire the right actor,' he said anxiously. 'What do *you* think of the voice they use?'

'Excellent,' she said, although she had no idea what he was talking about.

☆ ☆ ☆

Sitting in the other bedroom Lucky couldn't believe it. What was Johnny after – a review?

Maybe she should have met with Daniella by herself and asked the questions. Too late now.

While she was at the hotel, Boogie was organizing a raid on Donna's safe. He'd paid off one of the Landsmans' servants to get a map of her house and knew exactly where it was located. The Landsmans were out to dinner, and the man they'd hired to do the job was an expert who could get into the safe, remove the items Lucky wanted, close it, and Donna would never know anything was missing until she went looking.

Lucky took a deep breath. Tomorrow she'd get Panther back. She couldn't wait to see Donna's face. Mickey's, too. Those two deserved each other.

Johnny was still droning on about his movie career in

France. What was the matter with him? She'd picked Johnny because he was supposedly the stud of the century. Apparently he was a slow starter – either that, or this woman didn't turn him on.

☆ ☆ ☆

Daniella stood up, sensually slipping off the jacket of her pink Chanel suit. Underneath she wore a white sleeveless blouse. 'I'm hot,' she murmured, fanning herself with her hands.

'Yeah, it is hot in here,' Johnny agreed. 'Should I put on the air conditioning?'

American idiot, Daniella thought. He might be a movie star, but he was an idiot. Why didn't he make a move?

Ah, well . . . it was obvious the seduction was up to her. She hoped he wasn't going to be like her last American movie star . . . Lennie Golden. Lennie had been completely resistant to her charms.

Daniella had never had that happen to her before. At the time she'd been quite shocked, then impressed, because there was nothing more attractive than an incorruptible man.

She slowly unbuttoned her blouse, shrugging it off, revealing a white lace nippleless bra. Her breasts were enclosed, the nipples bursting free. Johnny gave a low groan of appreciation. Next, she unzipped her skirt and stepped out of it. Underneath she wore an old-fashioned white garterbelt, sheer stockings and a white lace thong.

She leisurely sashayed over to Johnny, standing in front of him, legs apart so that her crotch was eye level. 'Your move,' she purred provocatively.

He was immediately aroused. This woman was his all-time fantasy: a lady in the living room; a whore in the bedroom. He wondered if she cooked, too.

'Have you ever thought about being in movies?' he asked, squeezing the insides of her creamy thighs.

'No,' she replied, 'I never have.'

'You could be. You're gorgeous, baby.'

'Thank you,' she said, hitching his fingers into the edge of her thong, slowly helping him pull it down until her blond fluffy pubic hair was only inches from his face.

He stared at her bush, then gazed up at her nipples – so rosy and erect. Jesus! Enough was enough. He could only take so much. He stood up. 'Put your arms around my neck,' he commanded. She did as he asked. 'Now wrap your legs around my waist.'

She did that also.

He carried her into the bedroom, placing her on the edge of the bed.

She lay back, gazing up at him expectantly. He gripped her ankles, spreading her legs.

'Shall I undress you?' she asked, noting his bulging erection.

'Later,' he said. 'Right now I'm gonna eat your pussy.'

'No!' she said quickly, knowing it was foolish to object to anything a client required, but too tired to care.

Johnny was not to be put off. 'Baby, most women are *beggin'* for a little mouth action.'

'Why don't *I* eat *you*?' she suggested, attempting to sit up.

He pushed her back down. 'You're *my* present – *I* get to choose. So close your eyes an' have yourself a *good* time.'

Johnny had completely forgotten that Lucky was in the other room waiting. And even if he'd remembered, it wouldn't have mattered. This was something he had to do *now*!

☆ ☆ ☆

It occurred to Lucky she'd definitely picked the wrong guy. Was Johnny trying to turn her on? What was the matter with him?

Her cellphone rang. She grabbed it.

'Mission accomplished,' Boogie said.

'Both items?'

'Everything.'

'Lock them in your safe. I don't want them in my house. Once she finds out, she may retaliate. Oh, and Boog – job well done.'

She clicked off the phone and continued listening to the noises coming from the bedroom.

Groaning and sighing. Gasping and moaning. Somebody was having a good time on her dime.

Twenty minutes must have passed before the grunts and groans stopped and Johnny finally got down to business. 'Uh, Daniella,' she heard him say.

'Yes?'

'I know what happened between you and Lennie Golden.'

Lucky held her breath. *Here we go*, she thought, *this is where I find out the real truth.*

'Excuse me?'

'Lennie was my good friend,' Johnny said. 'He was in Corsica making a movie, you came on to him . . . set him up.'

A long pause. 'How do you know this?' Daniella said at last.

'I saw the photographs.'

Another long pause. 'I do what I'm paid to do. With Lennie I was paid to seduce him. It did not work out.'

'You mean you didn't fuck him?'

'No. He insisted on talking about his wife all night.'

'No shit?'

'He would have nothing to do with me.'

Lucky was listening intently. *Lennie . . . her Lennie . . .* Oh, how she'd misjudged him.

Johnny was into it now. The questions were coming fast and furious. 'Who paid you?' he asked.

'I can't reveal that.'

'Sure you can.'

Daniella went to get out of bed. Johnny grabbed her arm, keeping her there. 'I really like you,' he said.

'Rule one,' Daniella said. 'Never be nice to the whore who services you.'

'You're no whore. You're a beautiful woman who happens to charge for what most babes in this town give away for free. The way I see it, you got a moral edge. You also got the best set of tits I ever seen.'

'They're yours, Johnny – for the night. Tomorrow I return to Paris.'

'I could pay more for you to stay.'

'Why would you?'

''Cause I kinda like bein' with you. You could stay at my house for a week.'

'I'm sure you can afford me, but I'm not sure you'll have such a good time.'

'Why not?'

She shrugged.

'So . . . you don't wanna be in a movie, you're not gettin' off on my fame, which means you're not with me 'cause I'm Johnny Romano. You're here 'cause you got paid. That's okay. A nice clean business arrangement. You know what? You're the first broad I ever fucked for money – only it's not my money.'

'How interesting,' she said, concealing a bored yawn.

He jumped off the bed. 'You gotta meet a friend of mine.'

'I charge extra for *ménages à trois*.'

'No sex, baby, only conversation. Wait here.'

'Jesus!' Lucky said, when he entered the room. 'You took your time.'

'I thought you wanted me to get our money's worth.'

'You sure did that and then some. I'm not thrilled I had to listen.'

'You *should* be thrilled with what she said. You heard – Lennie didn't screw her.'

'Can you put something on other than your jockeys? I know you're well endowed, Johnny – you don't have to shove it in my face.'

'Daniella's really something,' he said dreamily. 'Wait till you see her. Lennie must have loved you a lot to have resisted *her*.'

'We loved each other, Johnny,' she said quietly.

'You got any idea what it's like on location? By the third week you'd fuck a sheep you're so bored.'

'How eloquent,' Lucky said, following him into the bedroom.

Daniella was sitting up in bed, a sheet covering her nudity.

'This is Lucky Santangelo,' Johnny said. 'Lennie Golden's wife. You might wanna repeat what you told me. I'll leave you two alone.' He left the room.

Lucky stared at the French call-girl. She was very lovely – much more so than in her pictures. 'Uh . . . I'm sure you know that after the night Lennie supposedly spent with you, he was in a car accident,' she said awkwardly.

'I am very sorry,' Daniella said, lowering her eyes. 'There are two things I should assure you of. One, he did not spend the night with me. And two, I had no idea they were planning to kill him.'

'So you're aware he was murdered?' Lucky said, her heart starting to beat erratically.

'I am not a fool,' Daniella said. 'I realized they were setting him up in some way. My job was to seduce him. The photographer was to capture us in bed. However, your husband had no desire to make love to me.' A short pause. 'I've never had a man turn me down if the situation was right, and the situation with your husband was exactly right.' Daniella let the sheet drop, revealing her perfect breasts. 'Look at me, Lucky. I am not modest, my beauty is all I have. I exist to service men.'

Lucky took a deep breath. 'Who hired you, Daniella?'

'My madam in Paris set it up. She was contacted by a woman in America. I was told to go to Corsica, see this man who could get me on the film, and seduce your husband.'

'What about the photos of you and Lennie together?'

'They removed my so-called boyfriend from the picture taken on the set. I was acting like a naïve fan, Lennie was extremely gracious.'

'And the other photo?'

'I went to his hotel room at night, stood at his door and dropped my robe, begging him to invite me in. The photographer caught us in the hallway.'

'Why are you being so honest with me?'

Daniella shrugged. 'I have no reason not to be. It cost you plenty to fly me here, so it must mean a lot to you. Your husband is dead. I'm sure it soothes you to know he was not unfaithful.'

'I appreciate your honesty.'

'Sometimes honesty is all we have.'

Lucky went back into the living room. Johnny was smoking a thin cigar and watching wrestling on TV.

'I'm leaving,' she said. 'Thanks, I owe you one.'

She got in her car and drove to her house.

Lennie, my darling Lennie, what did I do? I slept with Alex to get revenge. Now I realize I had nothing to get revenge for.

I betrayed you and I feel so bad, because I should have known you would never betray me.

Forgive me, sweetheart. I will always love you.

Chapter Sixty-one

 'I'M GETTING my studio back today,' Lucky announced.

'That's so cool,' Brigette exclaimed. 'How did you pull *that* off?'

'Don't you know?' Lucky said, with a self-deprecating grin. 'I can do anything.'

'I'm beginning to realize that.' Brigette giggled.

She and Nona stood in the front hallway, their suitcases packed.

'I wish you'd stay longer,' Lucky said.

'We would,' Nona replied. 'Only Brigette's billboard goes up any moment, and there's all kinds of press things planned. Plus we're meeting with the new agent you arranged.'

Lucky pulled Brigette to one side. 'What about that guy you were seeing?'

'Isaac's fun,' Brigette said. 'But now I understand he's not for me.'

'Don't go off men just because you've come across a few bad ones,' Lucky warned.

'I won't. I promise.'

'Lennie's watching over you – he'll make sure you find the right one.'

Brigette hugged her. 'Thanks, Lucky. I'm going to miss you *so* much.'

'You, too,' Lucky said, hugging her back. 'Plan on visiting again soon.'

She saw them into the limo, then returned to the house and checked in with Gino, who sounded like his old self. Nothing kept Gino down, he was a true survivor.

When was her life going to return to normal? Sadly she realized that, without Lennie, things could never be the same.

At one-thirty she was sitting behind her desk at Panther, with her own furniture and Kyoko stationed at his desk in the outer office just like old times.

'Donna Landsman will arrive at two-thirty,' Boogie said. 'She thinks she's attending a meeting with the heads of production.'

'Good,' Lucky said. 'That's exactly the way I want it.'

'Mickey has a two-thirty here with one of his overseas distributors. The timing should be right on.'

Boogie was correct. Mickey drove onto the lot exactly one minute behind Donna Landsman. They ran into each other as Donna was getting out of her limousine, entering the building together. It couldn't be more perfect.

Mickey saw Kyoko in the outer office and frowned. 'Where's Isabel?' he asked irritably.

'She'll be right back, Mr Stolli.'

Grumbling to himself about secretaries, Mickey led Donna Landsman into his office and stopped short.

Lucky swiveled around in her chair to greet them. 'Surprise!' she said. 'Isn't this just like old times?'

Mickey's jaw dropped.

Donna Landsman's face hardened.

'What *is* this?' Mickey shouted. 'What the hell is going on?'

'I'm back,' Lucky said calmly, enjoying their frustrated rage. 'Exactly like I said I'd be.'

'How is this possible?' Donna said, her pinched face white with anger.

'Simple,' Lucky replied easily. 'I acquired another sixteen percent of Panther shares and voted myself back in. And you know what, Donna? You'll *never* get control again, so you may as well start selling your shares back to me.' A short pause while Donna digested the news. 'Of course,' Lucky continued, 'you may have to take a substantial loss, but, hey, it's only money.'

'What the *fuck* . . .' Mickey fumed. 'I have a frigging contract.'

'Sue me,' Lucky said evenly. 'I'd love to meet you in court.'

'Where's my furniture? My files? My goddamn awards?' he yelled.

'I had everything delivered to your house, Mickey. I'm sure it's all sitting safely in your driveway. Abigaile will be *very* happy.'

'You won't get away with this,' Mickey fumed, blue veins bulging in his forehead.

'Hey – whoever wins, right? Sorry, Mickey, this time you backed a loser.'

Donna glared at Lucky, her arch enemy. 'You will live to regret this,' she said through clenched teeth. 'Nobody crosses me. Nobody.'

'Oh,' said Lucky, 'I'm shaking in my boots.'

Donna turned and swept out, Mickey close behind her.

'Kyoko,' Lucky called, feeling pretty high, 'bring in the champagne. We're celebrating.'

☆   ☆   ☆

'Who's that with Johnny?' Alex asked France, as Johnny Romano walked into the big banquet room where the readthrough was taking place.

'No idea,' France said. 'Maybe it's his girlfriend.'

'I didn't know he had one.'

'One a day according to Alex,' France said impishly.

A few moments later Venus ran in and sat down next to Johnny.

'Meet a very good friend of mine from Paris,' Johnny said. 'Daniella, this is Venus.'

'Hi, Daniella,' Venus said, smiling warmly.

Daniella nodded warily. Her job did not usually include attending the readthrough of a movie, but Johnny was paying so what did she care? She'd phoned Paris and told her babysitter she would not be back for a few days. Johnny had walked in while she was on the phone. 'Who you speaking to?' he'd asked.

'I'm telling my sitter I won't be back as promised.'

He'd looked surprised. 'You have a kid?'

'She will be fine. She's used to my being away.'

'How old is she?'

'Eight.'

'You must've been a baby when you had her.'

'Sixteen.'

'So I guess you were by yourself, had to support her. Is that why you started . . . uh . . . in the profession?'

'That is correct.'

Alex entered the room and settled at the head of the table, his first assistant on one side, line producer on the other. After a few minutes he stood up to address his actors. 'Now I don't expect anybody to give a brilliant performance today,' he said, looking along the table. 'Remember, this is just a readthrough to see how the lines run, what kind of interaction we get. In fact, it's a working experience you should all enjoy.' He pushed back a rogue lock of black hair and flashed the killer smile. 'If anyone has any objection to their dialog, make a note of it and come to me. I'm very open to other ideas. Okay, any questions? If not, let's get started, and let's have fun, because that's what movie-making *should* be.'

Venus nudged Johnny, her face glowing. 'This is the first time I've done this on a movie. They usually just throw you into Makeup and Hair and shove you in front of the camera.'

'Yeah,' Johnny said. 'It's cool.' He turned around and checked out Daniella, sitting behind him, then he turned back to Venus. 'You ever been into that kind of soulmate thing?' he asked. 'Like when you meet somebody, an' you know that's *it*, man, you're fuckin' *dead*.'

Venus smiled. 'Is she the one?'

'Could be,' Johnny said.

'Congratulations,' Venus said, squeezing his arm. 'Another stud laid to rest.'

'I've got one regret, though,' he said, grinning broadly.

'Tell me.'

'That you an' I never got it together.'

'Too late now.'

'Baby, it's *never* too late.'

☆   ☆   ☆

Donna sat in her limousine, stomach churning with fury. Lucky Santangelo had won again. This could not be happening. And Morton, the coward, had killed himself. If he was still around, Lucky could never have wrested control.

Why was it that everything she'd done to punish Lucky had failed?

Even the hit-man she'd hired had not managed to kill Gino, merely wounded him.

Her plan had been eventually to return Lennie to Lucky but in her mind she started writing a different scenario. Why *should* Lucky get him back? Why not kill him and deliver his fingers one by one to the bitch? That would wipe the smile off her face once and for all.

She wondered if either Bruno or Furio were man enough to do it. Or would they expect her to hire somebody?

She had to think about this, it could not be a casual decision.

And then it came to her. She'd do it herself. *She'd* go to the cave and shoot Lennie, then she'd photograph his dead body and send the photographs to Lucky.

Yes, she'd let the bitch know her husband had been alive all this time, and if she'd had any brains she might have figured it out and saved him instead of concentrating on getting her damn studio back.

Donna was pleased with her solution. She couldn't tell George: he knew nothing about Lennie. She'd say her father was sick and that she had to go to Sicily for a couple of days. Then she'd stay in a hotel, hire a car, drive to the caves and do the deed.

Lucky Santangelo thought she was so smart. She regained her studio, but she'd lost her husband forever.

It served her right.

☆　　☆　　☆

Congratulations started coming in immediately – news traveled fast in Hollywood.

Freddie was one of the first people to phone. 'I couldn't be more pleased,' he said. 'What happened?'

'An aberration,' Lucky said. 'A power play by a woman who didn't know anything about the movie business.'

'All I can say is I'm delighted you're back.'

'Thanks, Freddie.'

'Does Alex know?'

'I don't think so.'

'He's having a readthrough of the movie. Go tell him yourself.'

'Maybe I will,' she said thoughtfully.

☆   ☆   ☆

Alex was pleased with the way things were going. Sometimes readings could be a disaster – there'd been times he'd realized he'd cast the wrong people and changes had to be made before filming could start. This time everything clicked. Venus was quite wonderful as Lola, and Johnny was really into his role. The rest of the cast of mostly unknowns were excellent.

When they broke for lunch, Alex sat with Venus and Johnny – and his new girlfriend, Daniella, who seemed nice if quiet. She was certainly a beauty.

Alex had a nagging feeling he'd seen her somewhere before.

Everyone reconvened at two-thirty. Shortly after that, Lili whispered in his ear that she'd just heard Lucky Santangelo had regained power at Panther.

'You're kidding!' Alex said. 'Where did you hear this?'

'It came from a very reliable source,' Lili assured him.

'So,' he said, 'we're back in business with Miz Santangelo.'

He'd decided that since Lucky had made it clear she wanted space and time, he'd give it to her. Right now he had his movie to keep him busy, and making movies was the most demanding mistress of all.

At four-thirty they were finished. Johnny shot out of there with Daniella in tow.

Venus stood up and hugged Alex. 'This is the greatest week of my life,' she said happily. 'I know things'll work out with Cooper, and making *Gangsters* with you is the break-through I've always dreamed of.'

'You're a good actress,' Alex said. 'It's clear to me that nobody bothered to bring it out in you before.'

'Thanks,' she said, thrilled at such extravagant praise.

'Did you hear Lucky got the studio back,' he said.

'Fantastic!' Venus exclaimed. 'When?'

'Today. Lili heard about it before it happened!'

'Wow, that's so cool. And *guess* who's walking through the door?'

He turned to stare. It was Lucky herself.

'Hey—' Alex said, thinking how beautiful she was. 'We were just talking about you.'

Lucky smiled. 'All good or all bad?'

'Always good,' he said, returning her smile.

'Well, I figured as your new boss I should pay you a visit.'

'Hey you,' Venus said, with a big grin. 'You pull it off every time. Anybody else would, like, creep away. You just kind of got it together and turned it around. *How* did you do it?'

'I have my ways,' Lucky said mysteriously.

'Okay, I'm outta here,' Venus said. 'Got a husband waiting at home.'

Lucky raised an eyebrow. 'A husband?'

Venus continued to grin. 'It's second-chance time. See ya!' And she was gone.

Alex cleared his throat.

'Alex,' Lucky said, 'now I'm back *in* control, I think I should mention your projected budget is totally *out* of control. Can we talk?'

He laughed. 'There's nobody I'd sooner talk to than you. Only you're a little difficult to get a hold of.'

'Hmm . . . trust me, I'll be watching your budget big time. In fact you can bet on it.'

'I hope you'll visit the set sometimes, too.'

'I'm here today.'

'Maybe a weekend in Vegas?'

'Who knows? When do you leave?'

'Three days' shooting in Malibu, then Vegas the end of next week.'

'Don't be surprised if I turn up.'

'Lucky,' he said, giving her a long meaningful look, 'it would be the best surprise you could possibly give me.'

'Well,' she said, slightly flustered, 'this was a quick visit. I have to go.'

He took her arm and walked her to the door. 'You like my new attitude?'

'What attitude is that?' she asked.

He smiled, high because the reading had gone so well. 'I'm into my concentrated movie-making mode. That means I'll leave you alone for six months.'

'Is that a threat or a promise?'

'Take it any way you like.'

They smiled at each other and she got in her car and drove off, thinking about all the events of the past few weeks.

Donna Landsman.

No more delays.

It was time.

Chapter Sixty-two

'IT'S BEEN THREE days – I thought you'd deserted me,' Lennie said, so relieved to see Claudia he could barely stand it.

'I'm sorry, my poppa – he returned,' Claudia apologized.

'Yeah, I know,' he said bitterly. 'Mr Cheerful's back. He dumps food in here like he's feeding a dog. I gotta tell you I hate your father, Claudia. You should get away from him, he's full of bad karma.'

'What is . . . karma?'

'I hope you never have to find out.'

'Tonight my poppa will drink too much *vino*. When he sleeps, I steal the key and bring it to you. You have the map?'

He patted his pocket. 'It's safe.'

She handed him a small flashlight. 'Here – we will need this.'

'Thanks,' he said.

'If they discover you're gone, they will come after you,' she fretted. 'But they will not know until tomorrow, when Furio brings food.'

'How'll you get here late at night?'

'I shall be careful, too.'

'Shouldn't your boyfriend come with you?'

'No!' she said sharply. 'If he knew, he would not allow me

527

to help you.' She hesitated, obviously distressed. 'If he found out about us . . .'

'There's nothing to find out, Claudia,' he reassured her. 'You were here for me, that's all. I'll never tell anybody what happened between us.'

She nodded, satisfied that he would not betray her. 'As soon as I get the key I will be here. You must be ready to leave at once.'

He didn't know how he was going to get through the next few hours until she returned. Somehow he knew he'd find the strength.

Chapter Sixty-three

 Donna arrived home from the studio seething. She screamed at the maid, who promptly quit. She marched into the kitchen and screamed at the cook, who wanted to quit but needed the job.

George was still at the office. She phoned him and spewed venom. 'Do you realize our lawyers are incompetent fools?' she yelled. 'Somehow or other, Lucky Santangelo has gained back control of Panther. I want to know how this happened, George. I *demand* to know.'

'It was never a good business proposition,' George said, not sounding upset at all. 'And you have to admit, Donna, you know nothing about the film business. This could be a good thing.'

'Good!' she screamed, infuriated by his stupidity. 'Good! Whatta kinda moron are you? *Stupido!*'

'Excuse me?'

'Our lawyers are stupid,' she said, embarrassed, realizing she'd inadvertently slipped back into her former accent.

'I'll look into it,' George said.

'You do that.'

She suddenly thought about the pictures she had of Brigette Stanislopoulos – the true murderer of Santino. It had taken time and money to track her down but she'd done so, just after the girl had signed with a modeling agency. A small investigation of Michel Guy had revealed his predilections. A large sum of money had assured his cooperation.

What a stroke of genius! Now she had the pictures she'd sell them to every porno magazine in the world. How would Lucky Santangelo like *that*? Her stepdaughter exposed for all the world to ogle at.

A small cold smile. *You can't control everything, Lucky. You're not invincible.*

She was on the way to her safe to get the photographs when Santo arrived home from school.

'Why are you home early?' she demanded, catching him in the front hall.

'Why are *you*?' he retorted, seemingly unrepentant about the incident with Tabitha.

Lately they hadn't been speaking much. She yearned for her little boy back, the innocent boy she'd fussed over and raised. Now he was this big hulking lout with a smart mouth who did unspeakable things with dirty little girls. He'd betrayed her and she didn't like it one bit.

'Where are you going?' she said, as he tried to dodge past her.

'Upstairs,' he said sullenly. 'Locked up in my room.' He threw her a filthy look. 'That's what you want, isn't it?'

'It's your own fault, Santo,' she said, her voice rising. 'What you did was disgraceful.'

'No,' he said, scowling. 'What I did was normal.'

It infuriated Donna that he was still trying to justify his actions. 'If your father knew you'd turned into a sex-crazed drug addict, he'd kill you rather than have you as his son,' she said darkly.

'I'm no drug addict,' he sneered. 'Get with it, Mom. Everybody smokes pot.'

She had the last word. '*My* son doesn't. Not anymore.'

He ran up the stairs, slamming his way into his room, convinced his mother was the most hateful woman on earth.

Donna waited until he was gone, then she went into the library, closed the door and moved quickly to her private safe, concealed behind a tasteful Picasso. It contained important documents and a modest amount of jewelry – the good stuff was locked safely in the bank.

She entered the combination, and flung it open. She rummaged around, searching for the videotape of Morton Sharkey and the pictures of Brigette.

This was ridiculous – she'd put them there herself – now she couldn't find them. Surely she wasn't losing her mind?

Methodically she removed everything from the safe.

No tape. No pictures.

Was it possible that George had gotten hold of the combination?

No. George wouldn't dare invade her private safe.

She had to stay calm, and deal with this in a rational way. They were misplaced, and she *would* find them.

☆ ☆ ☆

Santo went straight to his computer. He'd gotten out of school early because there was no one to stop him. What did he care about math or history? He didn't need to know any of that shit because one of these days *he* was inheriting the Bonnatti fortune. His father had left him money in trust, and when Donna dropped he'd get her money too. So screw school. Right now he was more interested in settling the score with that tramp, Venus Maria.

He sat down at his computer and began to compose a new letter. A letter of hate.

She had it coming.

Chapter Sixty-four

LENNIE WAITED impatiently, the hours crawling by at an interminably slow pace.

He wondered if Claudia was ever coming back.

The thought of freedom was so intoxicating he could barely keep still, but he knew he had to reserve his strength for the escape – if it ever happened.

The man he now knew was Claudia's father arrived with his food, practically threw it at him and vanished.

He stuffed a chunk of bread in his pocket for the journey. Then he sat on the edge of his makeshift bed studying the crudely drawn map Claudia had given him. She'd promised she would lead him out of the maze of caves. After that he was on his own – they each had to go in different directions.

Freedom. What a beautiful word. He said it aloud a few times simply to reassure himself.

He thought about his children. If it was up to him he'd never leave them again. He'd take his movie career and shove it up the studio's ass, because from now on he was staying with his family. *Nothing* would separate him from Lucky.

After a long while he reached the conclusion that something must have gone wrong. Claudia wasn't coming back.

His head began to ache until he thought it would split

open. He lay down on his so-called bed, overwhelmed with disappointment.

Eventually he must have drifted off to sleep, because when Claudia finally arrived she had to shake him awake. 'Lennie,' she said tensely. 'Get up, hurry.'

He opened his eyes, dazed for a moment. Was this another dream? No, Claudia was actually standing over him.

'We must leave immediately,' she said, handing him the key. 'If my poppa wakes . . .'

She didn't have to say more. He sat up, and with fumbling hands inserted the key into the rusty lock enclosing his swollen ankle.

The lock was so stiff and corroded it refused to open. 'Jesus!' he said, panicked. 'This isn't the right key.'

'It is,' she insisted, bending down to help.

They both struggled with it, until somehow he managed to force the key in and wrench the lock apart.

At last he was free! He picked up the chain, and flung it violently across the cave.

Claudia slipped the key in her pocket. 'Come, we must go,' she said. 'It is already late.'

For a moment he was overcome with trepidation. He'd been a prisoner for so long he didn't know if he could handle freedom.

Claudia grabbed his hand. 'Follow me,' she said. 'When we leave the caves we must climb the side of the cliff.'

'What cliff?' he said, alarmed.

'It is not dangerous,' she assured him. 'I do it all the time in the light. Now it is dark, it might be more difficult.'

'Are you telling me that when we get out of here we've got to climb a cliff?'

'Yes, Lennie,' she said steadily. 'If I can do it, so can you. Come.' She took the flashlight from him and began moving swiftly through the pitch-black labyrinth.

He stuck close behind her, trying to ignore the slime and the scurrying rats as they made their way through with only the slim flashlight to guide them.

As they progressed, the sound of the sea started getting louder. Jesus! How close *was* the ocean?

'The tide is in,' Claudia said matter-of-factly. 'We have to walk through water – don't be nervous.'

As they emerged from the maze of caves, moonlight lit their way. The sea was lapping at the entrance and the night wind was howling.

Now they were knee-deep in the swirling sea and he was freezing cold.

'Hold on to me,' Claudia shouted over the wind.

'I am,' he yelled back.

She shone the flashlight toward some rocks.

'Over there,' she said. 'Hurry, the tide – it's still coming in.'

This was more frightening than his incarceration.

They fought their way through the breaking waves to the rocks. By the time they reached them, they were soaked through and numb with cold.

Claudia was as agile as a gazelle. She leaped onto the rocks, then leaned behind her and grabbed Lennie's hand, helping him up.

As he started to clamber over the sharp-edged clusters, a jagged piece ripped his foot. 'Shit!' he exclaimed, his foot dripping blood.

'Come on!' Claudia encouraged.

Finally they reached the bottom of a rugged cliff.

Lennie looked up and his stomach turned. Climbing it was a daunting prospect.

'Follow me,' Claudia urged.

He did as she said, and they began slowly clawing their way up the side of the cliff, clinging to vines and trees until, after a few feet, they reached a rocky, man-made path.

Lennie almost slipped and fell a couple of times. The nightmare was getting worse. If it hadn't been for Claudia's strength and bravery, he'd have had no chance.

When they got to the top, they both collapsed onto the ground.

After a few minutes Lennie got up and took the flashlight from her, shining it on the sea below.

Realization hit hard. He'd been buried somewhere within the bowels of the earth. Hidden in a place nobody could ever find. It was a miracle he'd survived, and it was only thanks to Claudia.

'You must hurry, Lennie,' she said anxiously. 'Be safe. Take the path to the right and keep moving fast.'

'How am I ever going to thank you, Claudia?'

'You don't have to,' she said. 'Go home to your wife and children. Be happy, Lennie.'

And before he could say anything, she kissed him softly on the lips, and slipped off in the other direction, vanishing into the darkness.

Once more he was all alone.

Chapter Sixty-five

SATURDAY MORNING was one of those beautiful days – the kind of day that makes everybody aware of why they live in LA, in spite of earthquakes, riots, floods and fires. This day was what LA was all about – crystal clear blue skies, balmy sunshine, a city surrounded by palm trees, grassy hills, lush greenery and magnificent mountains.

Lucky couldn't sleep. She got up early and wandered onto her bedroom terrace, gazing out at the ocean. After a few minutes she decided to jog along the seashore. She put on shorts and a T-shirt, ran downstairs and set off along the shoreline.

Half an hour later she found herself below Alex's house. She stood still, jogging in place, wondering what he was doing.

A steep stone stairway led up the bluff to where his house stood. She considered visiting him. It was early, maybe he was still asleep, or perhaps Tin Lee had stayed the night.

What the hell? The gate to the bottom of the stairs was unlocked – surely it was a sign that he wouldn't mind visitors.

She headed up the stone steps, taking them two at a time until she was out of breath.

She stopped for a moment. *What are you doing?* she

thought. *Why are you encouraging him? You pushed him away and he went. Now what are you trying to do? Get him back?*

No way. I simply like his company and conversation. It doesn't have to be sexual. What's wrong with having a platonic male friend?

Platonic. Bullshit. You like him.

Wrong.

Yeah, sure.

At the top of the steps was another gate, she threw the catch and stepped onto his property.

Alex was sitting out on his terrace, surrounded by a laptop computer, his script, newspapers, a pot of coffee, orange juice, toast and cereal.

'Hey—' she waved, heading toward him. 'Surprise visitor.'

He glanced up, startled. 'Lucky,' he said, breaking into a big smile. 'What a *nice* surprise.'

'Jogged down the beach and happened to find myself outside your house,' she said casually. 'Is that coffee for one or can I get a cup, too?'

'Sit down. I'll call my housekeeper.' He pressed a buzzer and a moody-looking Japanese woman appeared. 'One more cup, Yuki.'

Lucky flopped into a chair beside him stretching out her long, tanned legs.

'Didn't know you were so athletic,' he remarked, delighted she was visiting. As soon as he'd drawn back, she'd come to him.

She laughed. 'I'm not. I needed to release a whole bunch of pent-up tension.'

'I can think of better ways to do that,' he said, putting down his script.

Yuki returned with another cup and filled it with coffee. Lucky took a sip. 'I can't wait to get back to the studio on

Monday,' she said, removing her sunglasses and placing them on the table.

'And I can't wait to start *Gangsters*,' Alex said. 'I have more fun making my movies than at any other time.'

'That's because it's your escape.'

'You're right,' he said wryly. 'Sometimes I wonder what I'm escaping from. I have no relationship with my mother, no wife, no children, in fact, no connections at all.'

'Making movies is your life,' Lucky pointed out. 'The actors and the crew are your family.'

'Yeah, right again,' he said, biting into a thin slice of toast. 'Y'know, I'm one of the few directors who actually *likes* actors. I worked with a producer once, who came up to me after I'd had lunch with the talent, and said, in a pissed-off voice, "You gonna eat with the actors?" as if they were some form of repellent underlife.'

'I like actors, too,' Lucky said. 'In fact, I married one. Thing is – I see them as slightly damaged and incredibly needy.'

'You see everybody as damaged,' he remarked. 'You should've been a psychoanalyst.'

'I would have been good,' she said, stealing a piece of his toast.

'So,' he said, 'are you going to tell me what happened with the French hooker?'

'Well . . . she assured me she never slept with Lennie.'

'Oh.'

'I believe her. She had no reason to lie. She thought she was getting paid to set Lennie up for a magazine. Actually she was surprised he didn't succumb to her charms, and, let me tell you, her charms are plenty. She's gorgeous.'

He regarded her curiously. 'How did you find this out?'

'I flew her in as a birthday present for Johnny Romano.'

Lucky never failed to amaze him. 'You did *what*?'

'Johnny owed me a favor, so he went along with it.'

'Is she a luscious blond?'

'That's right.'

'Thought I recognized her. He brought her with him to the reading. Didn't you see her?'

'No, Johnny was gone by the time I got there.'

'She was definitely with him.'

Lucky grinned. 'They must've clicked. Trust Johnny to fall for a hooker. Daniella was supposed to fly back to Paris the next morning.'

'Guess she didn't.'

'How's your mother?' Lucky asked, pouring more coffee.

'Haven't spoken to her lately.'

'Why not?'

'When you and I talked the other day, you made me see things more clearly. You're right – if I don't choose to see her it shouldn't make me feel guilty.'

'*Now* you're getting it.'

'Dominique wasn't exactly the greatest mother in the world,' he added, thinking about his fucked-up childhood.

'Understanding people's weaknesses is the key to a healthy relationship,' Lucky said wisely. 'Accept her for what she is, and she'll cease bothering you.'

'Her latest ploy was to push Tin Lee on me. The result was she pushed her right out of my life.'

'Tin Lee seemed sweet,' Lucky said, helping herself to more toast. 'And she obviously adores you.'

'Yes, she's *very* sweet and patient. However, according to my shrink, whom I haven't seen in six months, there was a reason I only went out with Oriental women.'

'Oh, yes. What reason was that?'

'It doesn't matter, because you came into my life and made me realize there's nothing wrong with a good old American.'

She threw him a quizzical look. 'Old?'

He laughed. 'You know what I mean.'

'In that case I'm flattered.'

They sat in companionable silence for a few minutes. 'What about you, Lucky, how are you feeling?'

She picked up her sunglasses and put them back on, hiding behind the dark lenses. 'Pretty lousy about us. I slept with you to get even with Lennie. Now I find out I had nothing to get even about.'

He was getting fed up with her excuses – it didn't make him feel good. 'You weren't planning on becoming a nun, were you?' he asked, a touch sharply.

She refused to get mad. 'It was too soon, Alex,' she said quietly.

He stood up, changing the subject. 'What are you doing today?'

She shrugged vaguely. 'No plans. How about you?'

'I'll work on my script, maybe go down to the gym, do a little kick boxing. I used to be into that on a regular basis.'

'I'd love to try it.'

'Come with me.'

'I wouldn't mind.'

'I'll pick you up in an hour.'

She jumped up. 'I've got a better idea – drive me home and wait. I don't feel like jogging all the way back.'

He shook his head disapprovingly. 'Low stamina.'

'You can say that again.'

They looked at each other and burst out laughing.

☆　☆　☆

Venus woke up, reached out and was ridiculously pleased to discover Cooper asleep beside her. She rolled over, snuggling cozily against his broad back. 'Y'know,' she murmured, 'you're a great lover . . . but did anybody ever tell you you're a great cuddle, too?'

'Can you believe this?' he said sleepily, turning around and holding her warm body close.

'What?' she asked, delightfully comfortable.

'You've got me off other women. I'm cured! It's like getting a drunk off booze!'

'One drink and I'll shoot your balls off,' she threatened jokingly.

He struggled to sit up. 'You've been spending too much time with Lucky,' he said disapprovingly. 'You're beginning to sound just like her.'

'Wouldn't mind that, I think Lucky's great.'

'So do I. Only her language is out of control.'

'Coop! For a world-famous womanizer, there are times when you can be such a prude!'

'Women should be seen and not swear.'

'Veree funny.' She threw her leg over him, cuddling even closer. 'You know what I'd like?' she murmured.

'What, baby?' he said, stroking her platinum hair.

'That's it,' she said triumphantly. 'I'd like to have a baby – *our* baby.'

'*You* were the one who always said—'

'I know,' she interrupted. 'I said I didn't want to. But I've been thinking. After I've finished *Gangsters*, let's get pregnant.'

'It might be nice,' he said, unsurely.

'Nice!' she exclaimed, sitting up. 'Cooper, get *with* it. You and I will have the cutest little babies in the world!'

'Are we talking baby or babies?' he asked.

'I was thinking one or two might do it.'

'Oh, one or two, huh?' he said, playfully grabbing her breasts. 'And when the baby is feasting on *these*, what am I supposed to do?'

'You'll take turns.'

'I want my turn now,' he said, putting a nipple in his mouth and sucking vigorously.

The intercom buzzed. 'You get it, Coop,' she said, extracting herself.

'It's your house.'

'*Our* house,' she corrected, reaching for a robe. 'From where I sit you've definitely moved back in.'

'Wise woman,' he said, picking up the phone. 'Yeah?'

'Oh . . . uh, Mr Turner . . . Miss Venus's brother is here. He says it's urgent he sees her.'

'It's your brother,' Cooper said, covering the mouthpiece. 'When did Emilio creep back into town?'

'What does he want?' she asked, frowning.

'The guard said it's urgent.'

'Will you see him with me?'

'Prepare yourself. I'm likely to throw his fat ass out.'

'That's *exactly* what Emilio needs – somebody to boot him out of my life forever.'

☆　☆　☆

Santo awoke with a nagging toothache. He informed his mother, expecting her to be sympathetic. She was not.

'I'm in agony,' he whined, rubbing his cheek.

She called the dentist and made an emergency appointment.

'Drive me there, Mom?'

'No,' she answered brusquely. 'It's time you learned what punishment is. When you treat *me* with respect, I'll treat *you* the same way.'

Stupid old hag. How could he respect her when she was married to a loser jerk like George?

'So you won't take me?' he said accusingly.

'No, Santo,' she replied, not even looking at him.

Screw her. At least it gave him an opportunity to get out of the house.

He ran upstairs, grabbed his jacket and a printout of the letter he'd composed to Venus last night. He'd spent three hours hunched over the computer, trying to decide exactly what to say. In the end it was short and to the point.

His mother buzzed on the house intercom, telling him he had to leave immediately as the dentist was coming into his office especially to see him.

He checked his closet to make sure it was locked, then hurried back downstairs.

''Bye,' he yelled, passing the open door to the breakfast room.

Nobody answered.

Fuck 'em. One of these days he'd *force* them to pay attention.

☆　☆　☆

George removed his spectacles, peered through the window and watched Santo drive off. 'What does he do all day?' he asked.

'Works on his computer,' Donna replied.

'At what?'

'I've never asked him,' she said, sipping her coffee.

'It's obvious he needs help.'

'I know.'

George nodded to himself. 'I'll find out the name of a capable psychiatrist.'

Donna wasn't sure if she liked that idea – Santo talking to a stranger, revealing family business. For now she decided to agree with George. But when she came back from Sicily she'd make her own decision.

'Oh, yes,' she said. 'I almost forgot to tell you. One of my brothers called. My father is sick, I have to make a trip to Sicily. I thought I'd leave Monday. It's his heart.'

'Should I come with you?'

'No, you stay here and watch the business.'

'If you're sure . . .'

'Yes, I'm sure.' A pause. 'By the way,' she added casually, 'did you happen to take something from my safe?'

'I wouldn't dream of going to your safe, Donna. Why? Is something missing?'

'Not missing . . . misplaced. I'm sure I'll find it.'

George picked up the newspaper and started reading.

'I'll be upstairs,' Donna said.

If George hadn't invaded her safe, who had? Could it have been Santo? Could *he* have taken the photos and the tape?

No. He didn't even know she *had* a safe.

Still . . . it wouldn't hurt to check out his room.

☆   ☆   ☆

As soon as Santo left the dentist's office, he drove over to Venus Maria's house, cruising past a couple of times before parking across the street. He sat in his car watching the house for a few minutes.

The guard's station was close to the entrance of the property. He could see a middle-aged man sitting inside the small wooden structure reading a magazine and eating an apple.

Very alert. Venus should get herself better security. This jerk was useless.

He knew a place around the back of the property where he could sneak onto the grounds without anyone spotting him. It was risky during the day, but so what? He'd do it, anyway, because it was about time the whore knew who she was dealing with. Once she read his letter, she'd realize he'd busted her cheating ass.

Venus deserved to be punished just as he'd been punished.

And who better to do it than him?

☆   ☆   ☆

Santo's room was certainly tidier than it had been the other night. For a teenage boy he was really quite neat – there were no horrible posters of half-naked women on the walls, no dirty clothes lying around the floor, no drugs, thank God!

Donna sat on the edge of his bed thinking about her other three children who'd all left home. She didn't want Santo leaving too. Deep down he was still her baby, her sweet little boy. The truth was he was all she had, and she loved him.

She wondered if George was forcing her to be too hard on him. He said they had to be tough, but not if it was going to drive Santo away. The last thing she wanted was to lose her son.

She noticed he'd left his computer on. She crossed the room to switch it off.

There was a message printed on the screen. She bent to look.

> Whore.
> Cunt.
> You lick everybody's cock.
> I fucking hate you.

Oh, my God! Who was this message for?

Was it meant for her?

A cold chill swept over her.

Santo, her own flesh and blood, had finally turned against her.

Chapter Sixty-six

'WHY DO YOU keep on bothering me?' Venus demanded.

Emilio glared at her accusingly. 'You could be nicer to me,' he said defensively. 'I *am* your brother.'

Didn't he *ever* get it? 'No, Emilio, you're not,' she said, her temper heating up. 'When you sold me out to the media, you *ceased* being my brother.'

'I'm gonna have ta write a book,' he said, his expression turning crafty because he knew she'd hate that more than anything.

'Go ahead and write it – there's nothing else you can say about me that will hurt me any more than the things you've already told the press.'

'How about leaving your sister alone?' Cooper suggested, joining in.

'How about butting out?' Emilio replied nastily.

'Get smart with me, Emilio, and you're heading for a broken leg.'

'You *threatening* me, Cooper?' Emilio asked disdainfully. ''Cause that'll make *really* good copy.'

'I gave you a thousand bucks last time – what do you want now?' Venus wailed.

'I blew it.'

'On what?'

'Had a bad night . . . got mugged.'

'Mugged my ass.'

'It happens to people in LA all the time.'

'I wish I hadn't given you the money,' Venus said. 'I felt sorry for you, now I realize nothing helps. This time I'm leaving instructions that you *do not* get in here again.'

'Listen to your sister,' Cooper said. 'Do yourself a favor and stay away.'

'You rich bastards make me puke,' Emilio sneered. 'You got no fuckin' clue what it's like bein' me.'

'Deal with him, Cooper, I've had it,' Venus said, exasperated.

Cooper grabbed Emilio's arm.

Emilio pulled roughly away. 'Don't fuckin' touch me, man,' he snarled. 'I'm leavin'.' He marched out, slamming the door behind him.

'Jesus!' Cooper said. 'Are you *sure* you have the same parents?'

'Unfortunately, yes.'

'He's a dumb prick.'

'The worst kind.'

'Well, let's not spoil our day.'

'Whatever you say . . . husband.'

Cooper smiled, lazily pulling her toward him. 'Come here, wife.'

She smiled back. 'You don't have to ask twice.'

☆　☆　☆

Emilio stood outside the front door, burning up. Why *should* he leave – simply to please them? They treated him like a piece of shit. As her brother surely he deserved more?

He glared at his beat-up old rental-car parked in the driveway. She had three frigging cars sitting in her garage. A

Mercedes, a Corvette and a jeep. Would it kill her to give one to him?

He made his way around the side of the house, contemplating climbing up to her bedroom and relieving her of some of her jewelry. She had plenty – she wouldn't miss a diamond bracelet or two.

Just as he was edging around the back of the house, he noticed a fat boy lurking in the bushes acting suspiciously.

'Hey—' Emilio called out. 'What d'ya think you're doin'?'

Santo took one look at Emilio and started to run.

Emilio saw his chance to be a hero. Without thinking of the consequences, he raced off in pursuit, tackling Santo to the ground when they were only a few yards from the surrounding wall.

Santo struggled ferociously, but even though Emilio was not as fit as he should have been he was able to keep him pinned down. He sat on top of the fat boy yelling for assistance.

A neighbor's dog started to bark. A maid darted out of the kitchen door, saw what was going on and scurried back into the house to summon help. A few seconds later Cooper emerged, followed by Venus.

'What's happening?' Venus shrieked.

'Caught this asshole sneakin' around,' Emilio puffed, out of breath. 'I'm lookin' out for you, little sis.'

Cooper grabbed his cellphone and called for the guard. 'What are you doing here?' he said, walking over to Santo.

'Got lost,' Santo mumbled. 'Didn't know this was private property.'

'Lost? You had to have climbed the wall to have gotten in,' Venus said angrily. Then she noticed the envelope clutched in his hand. She took a closer look, immediately recognizing the scrawly writing on the front. 'Oh, God!' she exclaimed. 'It's you, isn't it? You're the sick little fuck who's been writing me all those filthy letters.'

'What letters?' Cooper said.

'Porno letters,' she said, snatching the envelope out of Santo's hand.

The guard ran up, gun drawn.

'You're too late,' Emilio said, shooting an *I-saved-your-butt* look at his sister. 'Good thing *I* was around.'

Venus began scanning the letter. 'Read *this*!' she said, handing it to Cooper.

He studied the letter, then took another look at Santo sprawled on the ground. 'Wait a minute,' he said. 'Aren't you the Landsmans' son? Weren't you at the Stollis' house? What the *fuck* are you doing here?'

☆　☆　☆

Lucky and Alex were in the gym, practicing kick boxing. 'Where did you learn to do this?' Lucky asked, her eyes shining, face flushed.

'Is this great or what?' Alex said enthusiastically. 'Learned it in Vietnam – one of the few good things I got out of that place.'

'Wow!' she exclaimed. 'It sure beats the treadmill.'

'That's why I do it.'

'I'm sweating.'

'Let's go home and take a shower.'

'Alex,' she said, frowning. 'Please, remember what I said – just friends.'

'Hey, I didn't mean together.' He shook his finger at her. 'You and your dirty mind, Miz Santangelo.'

She laughed. Being with Alex made her feel good. 'Drop me home. I've a ton of paperwork to go over.'

'Can we have a platonic dinner tonight?'

'Nope.'

'How about lunch, then? I'll buy you a hot dog.'

'I don't eat hot dogs.'

'You're an American, aren't you?'

'Have you any idea what they put in them?'

'Don't tell me.' He groaned. 'Can I interest you in a pasta salad?'

'A pasta salad – are you *crazy*?' she exclaimed. 'I have Italian blood. Let's go get a big dish of spaghetti Bolognaise. Then we'll both go home and work – good plan?'

'You in your house, me in mine?'

'What's wrong with that?'

'Can I ask you a question?'

'Go ahead.'

He stared at her. 'When *will* you be ready for a relationship?'

She took her time before replying. 'That's not a question I can answer right now,' she said at last. 'But when I can, you'll be the first to know.'

☆　☆　☆

'I beg your pardon?' George said into the phone, his plain face reddening.

'Who is it?' Donna asked impatiently.

'We'll be right there,' George said, slamming down the receiver, which was unlike him. 'Well,' he said, shaking his head as if he didn't believe what he'd just heard. 'That letter you were telling me about on Santo's computer was not meant for you.'

'How do you know?'

'Apparently he's been writing porno letters to the singer

550

Venus Maria. He's been caught on her grounds, trying to deliver his latest effort.'

'No!' Donna said, shocked.

'Oh, yes,' George replied. 'We'd better get over there before they call the police.'

☆　☆　☆

'I've got a surprise,' Nona said. 'We're taking a cab to Times Square.'

'My billboard is up!' Brigette said excitedly.

'Yup.'

'Does Isaac know?'

'He's probably been gaping at it ever since it appeared!'

'Should I call him?' she asked eagerly.

'Don't start that again,' Nona warned. 'Isaac is not for you.'

'Okay, okay, he's history.'

They went downstairs, hailed a cab and fifteen minutes later they were there.

Nona paid the cab while Brigette leaped out shrieking with delight. 'Oh, my God!' she said. 'It's fantastic!'

'You look incredible!' Nona said, joining her on the sidewalk. 'Boy, is that asshole Michel Guy gonna be sorry he blew your career!'

They stared up at the giant billboard of Brigette and Isaac clad in nothing but tight blue jeans and big wide smiles.

A camera crew from *Entertainment Tonight* passed by and began to film it.

Nona nudged Brigette. 'If they only knew you're standing right here . . . I think I should tell them.'

'No way,' Brigette said, panicking. 'I look awful.'

'You don't, you look fantastic. Let's start the publicity

machine rolling. Girl, prepare yourself – 'cause you're going to be the biggest.' Nona sauntered over to the camera crew. 'Excuse me,' she said. 'Are you shooting the Jeans billboard?'

The cameraman turned to her. 'Yeah, it's a hot campaign. There's sure to be a lot of talk about this one.'

'What do you think of the model?'

'She's a beauty.'

'I'm Nona, her manager. And she's standing right over there. Her name's Brigette Brown. Remember it – she's going to be the next big supermodel.'

The cameraman couldn't believe his luck. 'Can we talk to her?'

'Absolutely,' Nona said. 'Come this way.'

☆ ☆ ☆

They stopped for lunch at a little Italian restaurant situated on the beach. Lucky ordered the spaghetti she craved, and Alex went for a steak. They shared a bottle of red wine.

'I'm real happy everything worked out for you,' Alex said, pouring her more wine. 'No more trouble from Donna Landsman.'

'Funny,' Lucky said reflectively. 'I never think of her as Donna Landsman. She'll always be a Bonnatti to me.'

'Get over it, Lucky.'

She looked at him intently. 'No, Alex, you don't understand. She'll *never* go away, not unless I do something about it.'

'You did something about it – you got your studio back.'

'Donna's Sicilian. There's no way she'll quit.'

'What else can she possibly do?'

'Anything she feels like,' Lucky said grimly.

'You can't live the rest of your life surrounded by guards.'

'I don't intend to.'

'What *do* you intend to do?'

She gazed out at the sea for a moment, watching a blond boy surf the waves. 'The Santangelos solve things their own way,' she said at last. 'We've always had to.'

'Forget about taking the law into your own hands,' Alex said. 'You got away with it once, twice would be pushing it. And I'm telling you now, I am *not* visiting you in a jail cell. No way.'

'Trust me, I know what I'm doing.'

'No, *you* trust *me*,' he said forcefully. 'When I was in Vietnam, I had experiences that haunt me to this day. Don't even think about doing anything you'll regret.'

She took a sip of red wine. 'Hey, Alex, you're a writer,' she said lightly. 'You should be loving this.'

'Lucky,' he said seriously. 'Make me a promise that whatever you decide, you'll discuss it with me first.'

'I have a policy,' she said. 'I refuse to make promises I'm not sure I can keep.'

He looked at her for a long moment, wondering how far she was prepared to go.

No, she wouldn't do anything drastic. She was no longer the wild girl who'd shot Enzio Bonnatti. She was a woman with responsibilities, who wouldn't be foolish enough to do anything that might put her family in jeopardy.

'Just remember,' he said, 'you have three young children. Do anything dumb, and you could go to jail for the rest of your life. I don't think you'd want to do that to your kids – not after they've lost Lennie.'

She sighed. 'Time to take me home, Alex. I've a lot of thinking to do.'

He drove her home and dropped her off. 'Are you jogging in the morning?' he asked, as they stood at the door.

'Maybe,' she said vaguely.

'Coffee. Same time. Same place.' He kissed her lightly on the cheek, willing her to invite him in.

She didn't. She walked into her house without looking back.

Miss Cool. Only this time she'd come to him. At least that was progress.

Lucky clicked on her answering machine. There were a couple of hang-ups, a message from Venus and another one from Boogie.

She did not feel like returning calls.

She went upstairs to the bedroom, and threw open the terrace doors so she could smell and hear the sea.

This room reminded her of Lennie so much.

Lennie . . . Her love . . . Her life . . .

And while Donna Landsman lived she would never be able to erase the pain.

Chapter Sixty-seven

DONNA AND George got in the Rolls and hurriedly drove to Venus's house.

'Thank God she called us instead of the police,' Donna said, imagining the consequences if it had been otherwise.

George agreed. 'You're going to have to do something about Santo,' he said. 'He needs to be sent away to a different environment – somewhere he'll get discipline.'

'I know,' Donna admitted, reluctantly.

The guard met them at the gate. Venus was pacing around outside with Cooper, not looking pleased.

'Where is he?' Donna asked.

'In the guard-house,' Cooper replied.

Donna peered through its glass window: Santo was huddled in a corner, his head down on his knees.

Venus was quite civilized about the incident. 'I'm only glad it's not some freako,' she said. 'Do me a big favor, make sure there's no more letters.'

'Don't worry,' George said. 'You have my word Santo will never bother you again.'

'Get him out of here, and we'll forget it,' Cooper said, anxious to be rid of the problem as quickly as possible.

Santo could hear them talking about him as if he didn't exist. It filled him with rage.

Then Venus sent for her assistant, who appeared with copies of all his letters neatly filed in a manila folder. Shit! His mother was going to see his freaking letters!

'Take a look at these,' Cooper said, handing the folder to George. 'My suggestion is you get the boy to a shrink fast. He needs help.'

'We appreciate you not calling the police,' George said.

'I couldn't take the publicity,' Venus replied, rolling her eyes.

The guard shepherded Santo into the Rolls. He slouched down in the back of the car.

Donna turned around, glaring balefully at her son. She was repulsed. For the first time she saw him as he really was: a mirror image of Santino.

Face it, she told herself, *Santo is exactly like Santino. A vile, sex-crazed pig.*

'You sicken me,' she said savagely. 'You're a disgusting low-life pervert, just like your father. You even look like him.'

'My father was a great man,' Santo managed, hating her. 'George isn't good enough to wipe his ass.'

'You shut your filthy little mouth,' Donna said, coldly furious. 'I'll deal with you when we get home.'

☆ ☆ ☆

Venus removed a carton of orange juice from the fridge. 'Some sick wacko!' she exclaimed, shaking her platinum curls. 'Did you read the letters?'

'Glanced at them,' Cooper replied. 'Pour me some, too, hon.'

'Good thing I caught him,' Emilio said, reminding them of his presence.

'Yeah ... really,' Venus said, handing Cooper a glass of juice.

'It wasn't easy,' Emilio boasted. 'I coulda walked away.'

'We appreciate your quick action, Emilio,' Cooper said.

'He coulda had a gun.'

'We know.'

Emilio basked in his moment of glory. 'So, y'see, little sis, I'm always lookin' out for you.'

'Don't worry,' she said briskly. 'You'll get a check. This time you deserve it.' She reached for the phone. 'I'm calling Johnny Romano, he has the best security in town.'

'Good idea,' Emilio said, strutting around the kitchen, wondering how generous she'd be.

'Isn't that like shutting the gate after the rabid dog has gotten out?' Cooper remarked sagely.

Venus sighed. 'It'll make me feel better.'

She spoke to Johnny, telling him what had taken place.

'Daniella and I are takin' a trip to Vegas,' Johnny said. 'I'll send a couple of my guys over. They'll put together a new security team for you. In fact, I'll have 'em bring the dogs.'

'Thanks, Johnny, I appreciate it.'

'You know,' Cooper said thoughtfully. 'In my whole career I never had to have security.'

'That's 'cause you were fast on your feet.'

'I guess we live in different times now.'

'It only takes one maniac,' Emilio said helpfully, thrilled to be part of the family again.

'He's right,' Venus agreed, shivering. 'Santo happened to be Donna Landsman's son, but it could've been some crazed out-of-town freako—'

'With a gun,' Emilio added quickly.

'Don't worry, Venus,' Cooper said. 'I'm here to protect you.'

She put her arms around his neck and hugged him tightly. 'Wow, Coop, I never knew you were so macho!'

☆ ☆ ☆

Johnny put down the phone. 'That was Venus,' he said.

'Who?' Daniella questioned, licking her pouty lips.

Johnny looked at her quizzically. 'You gotta have heard of Venus Maria.'

'No.'

'She's a big star. She's in *Gangsters* with me. You met her yesterday.'

'Oh, yes.'

'Hey, we'd better get movin'. I got a little surprise waitin' for you in Vegas. You'll love it.'

'What surprise, Johnny?'

He grinned. 'You'll see.'

☆ ☆ ☆

Lucky sat in her study, attempting to work. She was happy to see that in the short time Mickey had been at Panther, he'd not done too much damage. She noted he'd canceled several of her movies in development, and made deals with a group of producers she didn't approve of. Nothing that couldn't be fixed. Monday morning she'd reinstate her team, and go over everything more thoroughly. One thing she knew for sure – it was great to have her studio back.

What are you going to do about Donna? an inner voice screamed in her head. *What are you going to do?*

Could she risk taking no action?

Impossible. Donna was too dangerous an enemy. She was as evil as her late husband, Santino. There had to be a resolution of some kind.

She murdered Lennie, the voice continued. *Set him up, then had him killed. She put a hit on Gino, and tried to ruin Brigette. And as if that wasn't enough, she took your studio. Morton Sharkey and Sara Durbon are dead because of Donna. Is your plan to sit around and let her get away with everything, or are you going to resolve the situation?*

Lucky stood up and began walking up and down the room. Her head was spinning, she didn't know what to do. She knew that if she was so inclined she could put a hit out on Donna – Boogie would arrange it in a minute. But that wasn't the Santangelo way. The Santangelo way was retribution.

And yet something was holding her back. Alex had been right. She couldn't afford to do anything that might have dire consequences.

She had a desperate craving for a joint. She went to her stash in the drawer and lit up. Then she wandered restlessly around the house, unsettled and edgy.

She missed her children, but there was no way she could bring them home while Donna was still at large.

When are you going to do something about her?

I can't. I'm not the same person. Alex is right – I have responsibilities.

Oh, get a fucking life! You're a Santangelo, you can do it.

I'm not sure anymore . . .

Oh, yes you are. You know exactly what you have to do.

☆　☆　☆

They sat outside at the Ivy. 'This is a nice surprise,' Dominique said, patting her short black wig. 'The two of us, dining together. Where's Tin Lee tonight?'

'Stop pushing Tin Lee on me,' Alex said irritably. 'She's one of the reasons I wanted to see you by myself.'

'Why?'

'I felt it was time we talked.'

'About what, Alex?'

'About the way you treat me.'

'I treat you very nicely.'

'No, you don't. I'm forty-seven, as you constantly remind me, and I have no intention of listening to your non-stop criticisms anymore. If you keep it up, I'll stop seeing you.'

She looked at him with displeasure. 'Alex! I'm your mother. How can you be so cruel?'

'When my father died, you turned away from me, sent me off to military academy. You knew I was unhappy, yet you let me rot there until I was old enough to get out. It was torture.'

'You needed the discipline, Alex.'

'No!' he said, almost shouting. 'What I needed was a loving mother who cared.'

'I cared.'

'Bullshit,' he said harshly. 'You were out with a different man every night.'

'No, Alex, I—'

'I went to Vietnam,' he interrupted. 'You never wrote. And when I lived in New York all those years – did you ever try to find me?'

'It wasn't easy—'

'No,' he continued, relieved to be saying what had been on his mind for so long. 'The only time you've been half-way civil to me is since I became successful.'

'Nonsense.'

'If I'd turned out to be a bum, you wouldn't bother seeing me at all.'

'That's untrue,' Dominique objected.

'I'm not taking your shit anymore,' he said angrily. 'It's time you realized that it's *my* life. No more guilt trips.'

He waited for her to start screaming and yelling.

She didn't. She merely looked at him and said, 'This is the first time you've reminded me of your father. Gordon was a son of a bitch, but he was a strong man and in spite of all his faults, I suppose I loved him.'

'So, Mom,' he said carefully, sensing an opening, 'do we have an understanding?'

Dominique nodded. 'I'll try my best.'

☆　☆　☆

Venus and Cooper entered Spago like the stars they were. A sudden silence fell over the room as everyone checked them out.

Venus squeezed her husband's hand. It felt so good being back with Cooper, they belonged together. 'Gotta feeling we're making an impression,' she whispered.

'You *always* make an impression,' he replied, amused by the attention they were receiving.

'This'll give the tabloids something to think about,' she said, laughing. 'Did you catch the latest headline?'

'Wasn't I supposed to be screwing an alien?' he said sardonically. 'And you were busy having sex with three NBA players – simultaneously. Hmm . . . difficult . . .' he grinned. 'However, knowing how talented you are . . .'

She giggled. 'It's amazing what they can make up and get away with.'

'That's 'cause nobody has the time to sue.'

'Honey,' she squeezed his hand again, 'I love you so much.'

'You, too, baby.'

They sat at a corner table for two and ordered the duck pizza, a specialty of the house.

Wolfgang Puck came running over to greet them. 'You two back together?' he said, beaming.

'Where else would we be?' Venus replied, smiling sweetly.

The waiter brought over a complimentary bottle of champagne. They toasted each other, clinking glasses the old-fashioned way.

'You're so handsome,' Venus said admiringly. Even though Cooper had been a movie star for many years, she knew he could never get enough compliments. It was part of his insecurity, a side of him she loved.

He pulled a face. 'Used to be, I'm turning into an old man. I ran a couple of weeks ago – couldn't walk properly for a week!'

'So *that's* why you wanted to get back together,' she teased. 'You figure your playboy days are over.'

He laughed. 'Yeah, *right.*'

Venus sipped her champagne. 'Don't look now,' she said, 'but guess who Charlie Dollar just walked in with?'

'Do I get a clue?'

'One of your old girlfriends.'

'Honey, they were all nothing compared to you. I was going through a mid-life crisis, a dying man seeing if he could still get it up!'

'You sweet-talker you.'

'Well, aren't you going to tell me who it is? Or do I have to turn around?'

'Since you're so interested, it's Leslie Kane.'

'Leslie and Charlie, huh?'

'Jealous?'

'Insanely so,' he joked, taking a surreptitious look. 'At least she's with Charlie and not that deadbeat from the other night.'

'Feeling protective?'

'I didn't treat her very nicely.'

'My heart breaks.'

'Where's your compassion? Leslie's not a bad girl.'

'Don't push it, Coop,' Venus said, losing her sense of humor. 'She's an ex-hooker who was fucking my husband.'

He threw up his hands. 'Okay, okay – I get the message.'

Venus waved at Charlie. 'As long as we understand each other,' she said succinctly.

'Whatever you want,' Cooper said, not about to screw things up again.

Venus sipped her champagne. 'Lucky never called back,' she said. 'I wanted to tell her about my number-one fan – dear little Santo Landsman. She'll freak!'

'Maybe it's not such a good idea to spread it around,' Cooper said, thinking of the repercussions.

'Telling Lucky is hardly spreading it around.'

'Think about it first.'

'Whatever you say, darling.' She leaned across the table with a wicked expression. 'Now, tell me the truth, I've been *dying* to ask.'

'What?'

'Exactly how far *did* you get with Veronica the guy?'

'Venus!'

'Yes?' she said innocently.

'I'm gonna have to spank you if you keep this up.'

'Oooh, Coop, how exciting! *When?*'

He shook his head. 'You really are incorrigible.'

She grinned. 'Tell me about it!'

Chapter Sixty-eight

 THEY'D TAKEN out his computer, but they hadn't gotten into his closet.

'What do you have in there?' Donna demanded, angrily pacing around his room. 'More filth?'

He knew it was only a matter of time before his stupid mother managed to get into it. She'd already searched his room and discovered a couple of joints hidden in his underwear drawer which, of course, she'd confiscated. She'd yelled some more when she couldn't open his closet and demanded the key.

He'd told her he'd lost it.

She didn't believe him. 'Tomorrow morning I'll have a locksmith here,' she threatened.

If she ever found his stash of Venus memorabilia and porno magazines she'd go berserk. He had to smuggle his suitcase out of the house until things cooled down. Maybe if he locked it in the trunk of his car it would be safe.

He scowled. 'I dunno what you're getting so mad about,' he said. 'I wrote to Venus Maria as a joke – somebody at school dared me.'

Donna glared at him imperiously, like he was the worst piece of shit in the world. 'Who would dare you to write such vile pornography?'

He shrugged, wishing they'd both get the frig out of his room. 'One of the guys. It's no big deal.'

'It's a very big deal,' George interrupted, puffed up with his own importance. 'The trouble with you, Santo, is that you take no responsibility. You expect everything to be easy. Well, this time you've gone too far.'

Who voted that creep could have a say in his life? If it wasn't for George trying to show he had balls, everything would've been okay by now.

'You're to stay in your room until we decide what to do with you,' Donna said, throwing in a contemptuous look for good measure.

We? What the fuck was she bringing George into it for? He had no say in his life.

The two of them marched out. A couple of tired old fools.

Santo went into his bathroom. He was sick of being bossed around.

Peering at himself in the mirror above the sink he slicked back his hair with gel. Yes, with the hair off his face he did look like his father. He was proud he bore such a strong resemblance to Santino. *He* was a true Bonnatti.

He went back into the bedroom, opened his desk drawer, and took out the wedding photograph he kept of his father and mother. Santino and Donatella. The prince and the peasant. She couldn't even speak English when his dad married her. Santo knew all about her past, in spite of the airs and graces she put on.

Santino Bonnatti had been a fine man – Santo remembered him well. His dad had bought him expensive clothes, taken him out to ball games and movies, and sometimes to fancy restaurants. The two of them had always done things together.

Sometimes Donatella had tried to tag along. Santino

wouldn't allow it. 'Ya gotta know one thing about women,' his father had taught him. 'Keep 'em at home slavin' in the kitchen where they belong.'

Yes, well . . . his mother hadn't stayed at home, had she? She'd changed her appearance with plastic surgery, lost a ton of weight and turned into a monster. It was like she'd been waiting for Santino to die so she could undergo a transformation and marry his freaking feeble-minded accountant.

Now he fully understood why his father had always kept girlfriends.

Oh, yes, he knew about the girlfriends too. He even remembered the last one's name – Eden Antonio, a horny blond. Santino had called Eden a business associate, but Santo knew his dad was screwing the ass off her.

It was in the house Santino had bought for Eden that he'd been shot. Boom! Just like that he'd gotten his freaking head blown off.

If Santino was alive, he wouldn't be locked in his room now.

If Santino had caught him with a girl, he wouldn't have been punished.

If Santino had found out about the letters, he wouldn't have thought it was so disgusting.

No. Santino would have laughed. 'Leave the boy alone,' he'd have said to Donna. 'Get off his fuckin' case.'

Many times he'd heard Santino say those words to her. She'd rushed off into the kitchen muttering Sicilian curses under her breath, later returning to the living room to scream insults at her husband in broken English.

Why was his father dead and not his mother? It wasn't right. It wasn't the way it should be.

He unlocked his closet, hastily removing the suitcase filled with his Venus collection. Had to smuggle it out to his car, lock it in the trunk, then maybe in a couple of days he'd get the opportunity to ask Mohammed to look after it for him.

In the meantime, he hid it under his bed where she'd already looked.

That done, he suddenly remembered his gun. His twelve-gauge semi-automatic Magnum shotgun. Shit! If she found that, she'd really have a nervous breakdown.

The shotgun was propped in his closet cleverly hidden behind a bunch of winter clothes. She'd have to search to find it but, knowing his mother, she'd do just that.

Maybe he'd hide the gun in his car, too. Yeah, for now that was the safest plan.

As soon as they were asleep, he'd make a couple of trips to his car. First he'd take the suitcase, then the shotgun.

He quickly hauled it out of the closet, shoving it under the bed next to the suitcase.

All he had to do now was wait for them to retire for the night.

☆ ☆ ☆

Donna never drank, it did not suit her to lose control. Tonight she was so distressed by Santo's behavior and the happenings of the last few days, that she told her houseman to fix her a vodka martini.

One turned into two, then three.

By the time she sat down to dinner with George she was swaying slightly and more than a little belligerent.

'Why are you drinking?' George asked, a disapproving note in his voice.

Ha! Like she had to explain herself to George. She'd had

enough of him trying to assert himself. It was time to put him back in his place where he belonged. 'None of your business,' she snapped.

'I know it's upsetting, dear,' George said, attempting to soothe her.

'You have no idea how upsetting it is,' Donna replied bitterly, picking up a glass of red wine and draining it just to spite him. 'No idea at all.'

After dinner, George announced he had work to attend to. 'There're some papers you must sign before you leave,' he said.

Was this her lot in life? Men placed documents in front of her and she signed them.

She had the houseman fix her another martini and carried it up to her bedroom. For the last two years she and George had maintained separate rooms. It suited her that way: when she wanted sex – which was less and less often – she summoned him. He had no choice in the matter.

She went into her bathroom, stripped off her clothes and inspected herself in the mirror.

All the liposuction in the world could not bring her flesh back to the way it had been when she was a young girl in Sicily. A young girl . . . pursued by Furio . . . the belle of her village. She turned sideways. Not bad. Since she'd lost all that weight, she liked to admire her body, although it was wasted on George – he was no longer the lover he'd been when they were first married. She'd thought that having control of a Hollywood studio might lead to more exciting relationships. A movie star wouldn't be bad. Lucky had a movie star, why shouldn't she?

The room was spinning. She wasn't used to drinking. She wasn't used to losing either.

She ran a hot bubble bath, sat in the tub, martini glass

balanced on the side, then stretched out and reached for the phone.

☆　☆　☆

The phone rang. Lucky picked up. A woman's voice, thinly disguised, very drunk – ''S that you, *bitch*?'

'Who's this?'

'You . . . think . . . you're so goddamn . . . clever.'

Lucky tried to stay calm. 'Donna?'

'You think you're . . . Miss Fucking . . . Smart-ass.'

Her voice cold. 'What do you want?'

'You notta so smart, *bitch*,' Donna said, weaving in and out of her former accent. 'Your precious Lennie he's a dead now. You had a chance to save him, but no . . . You were too busy with your studio to figure he might still be alive. Ha! You gotta Panther now, I hope you're happy. This isn't the end . . . This is . . . just the beginning.'

The line went dead.

What was Donna talking about? A chance to save Lennie? There'd been no chance – he'd died in that car crash, nobody could have survived.

Unless he hadn't been in the car . . .

But he *was* in the car. The doorman had seen him drive off.

They'd recovered the body of the driver. Why hadn't they found Lennie?

Lucky's mind began racing. Was there something she'd missed?

Screw Donna Landsman. Now she was trying to mess with her brain.

She went upstairs to her bedroom, unlocked the drawer beside her bed and took out her gun.

Back downstairs.

Another joint.

Several long drags, then she walked outside and sat down, cradling the gun on her lap.

Very soon she'd have to make a decision.

Very soon . . .

Chapter Sixty-nine

 DONNA SNORED loudly. Santo put his head against her bedroom door, listening intently. From the sound of her she wouldn't surface until morning, which only left George to avoid.

He crept downstairs, angling himself so he could see into the library. George was busy poring over a stack of papers. If he moved quickly, he could sneak downstairs with his suitcase and gun, and hide them safely in his car before George noticed.

He hurried back upstairs, dragging the suitcase out from under his bed. It was heavy, filled not only with his Venus stuff, but his collection of porno magazines, too.

He snuck past his mother's room – her snoring still loud and clear.

Stealthily he started down the stairs, lugging the heavy suitcase behind him. It pained him that he couldn't keep his collection near him, but the cow had given him no choice.

On the other hand, what did he care about Venus anymore? She was the slut who'd exposed him, shown his letters to other people and humiliated him. Didn't she realize they were personal? That the private love messages the letters contained were supposed to be between them?

She'd taken their love and made it into something public and dirty. He hated her now.

Half-way down the stairs he tripped and fell. The suitcase burst open, and videos, posters, photos and magazines came tumbling out.

George emerged from the library and stood at the bottom of the stairs glaring up at him. 'Where do you think *you're* going?' he said.

'Where the fuck I want,' Santo snarled, lumbering to his feet.

Donna appeared at the top of the stairs and switched on the light. 'Whatta going on?' she screeched. 'Whatta you doing?'

She sounded like the old Donatella. And she looked like a crazy woman, with her hair standing on end, and smeared makeup. She wore a diaphanous nightgown with nothing underneath. It was not a pretty sight.

'Whatta you got in the suitcase?' she demanded, swaying slightly. 'You running away like your sisters? The whores, *puttane.*'

'My sisters aren't whores,' Santo said, thinking that they'd made the smart choice and gotten out while they could. 'They ran to get away from you. You try to control everyone. Well, you can't control me.'

'Oh, yes, I can,' Donna said, unsteadily making her way down the stairs. 'You're only sixteen. You're mine, you hear me – *mine!*'

He tried to avert his eyes because he could see right through her nightgown.

She stooped down, picking up one of his porno magazines and throwing it in his face. 'You're sick!' she yelled. 'That's what you are – sick! Justa like your father.'

'I'm glad I'm like him,' he yelled back. 'I *want* to be like him.'

'You can get out,' Donna shouted, holding onto the banisters. 'I don'ta care anymore. *GET OUT!*'

'I'm going,' he said, frantically picking up his stuff and attempting to jam it back in the suitcase.

'Leave,' she shouted. 'And don'ta think you're taking your car. You go in the clothes you stand up in – nothing else. I've put up with you long enough.'

'Put up with *me*?' he yelled, outraged at her unfairness. '*I'm* the one who's put up with you.'

'I mean it,' Donna shrieked. 'You're notta welcome here, Santo. You're fat and ugly. You're lazy. You're scum like your father. DIRTY, FILTHY SCUM. You leave tonight.'

Santo looked at George, who stood silently at the bottom of the stairs. There was a twisted expression of triumph on the older man's face. 'You heard your mother,' George said, with a great deal of satisfaction. 'Pack your things and get out.'

☆　☆　☆

Lucky was completely calm. She went back upstairs, took a shower, pulled her hair back into a ponytail, and dressed in a simple black turtle-neck, black jeans and boots. Then she stuck her gun in the waistband of her jeans and left the house.

Donna was playing mind games, and she wasn't going to take it anymore.

She got into her Ferrari and drove fast, heading in the direction of Donna's house.

Heading for revenge.

☆　☆　☆

Santino dragged the suitcase back to his room. A red film of fury swam before his eyes – little dancing devils encouraging him to do bad things.

Fat. She'd never called him fat before. Ugly. No way. She'd always told him he was handsome.

YOU'RE DIRTY, FILTHY SCUM LIKE YOUR FATHER.

She wasn't fit to shine Santino's shoes.

Without really thinking about it, he took the loaded shotgun from under the bed.

Fuck them! Fuck the two of them. They deserved exactly what they were about to get.

He ran out into the hall and burst into his mother's bedroom.

She was half-way across the room. She turned when she heard him come in. 'Whatta you doing—'

Before she could finish the sentence, he lifted the twelve-gauge shotgun, aiming it at her stomach. Then he pulled the trigger.

The blast almost blew her apart. Blood and gore splattered everywhere as she fell to the ground.

A blissful feeling of peace descended over him. As if in a trance, he walked closer, put the gun to her head and let off another shot.

Then he walked out of the room.

George stood transfixed at the bottom of the stairs with a horrified expression, staring up, too shocked to move.

He was easy pickings.

Easy.

Chapter Seventy

 LENNIE KEPT moving all night, sticking close to the mountains above the sea, eventually finding himself on a coastal road that led down to isolated beaches.

After a while the land began to get very flat, surrounded by uneven clusters of rocks and a few trees. Forgetting about his aching ankle and cut foot, he concentrated on reaching a safe haven.

Several hours later dawn began to break. He collapsed at the base of a tall tree, ravenously stuffing chunks of the bread he'd saved into his mouth. It tasted better than a gourmet meal.

He groped in his pockets. He had Claudia's flashlight and map, which he'd consulted from time to time; about six hundred dollars in crumpled American money; a credit card, which was probably canceled by now; his passport and several thousand dollars in traveler's checks. It was fortunate he'd always carried his passport and money on him when out of America – even more fortunate his captors hadn't discovered the money which he'd kept hidden in the cave.

He'd abandoned the idea of getting to an American Embassy. If he did that he'd have to tell his story, and there'd be questions and major publicity. Plus he didn't want Claudia getting into trouble.

His new plan was to get home as fast as possible. Home to America and Lucky and his children, that's all he wanted.

As the light came up he found himself heading into a picturesque valley. Goddamn it, he *had* to be safe now – he'd been walking all night.

You're free, he told himself as he trudged along. *Free, free, free*. It was a heady feeling.

A short while later he reached the outskirts of a town, and started seeing people. He didn't stop to ask for help, just kept on going.

A schoolchild pointed at him; a mangy dog ran up and growled; an ancient old crone, dressed all in black, watched him pass and crossed herself. Human contact – it was strangely comforting.

Eventually he came upon a small train station. The old man behind the ticket counter looked at him oddly, and told him there'd be a train in an hour. He purchased a ticket to Palermo, then went into a small market next door and bought bread, cheese and some kind of cooked sausage. Outside the sun was shining. He sat on a bench and tried to eat slowly, relishing every mouthful.

By the time the train arrived he was completely exhausted. Settling in a window seat, he slept fitfully until he arrived in the big city.

In Palermo he found a tourist shop and purchased a shirt, trousers and shoes, which he put on in a back room the girl in the shop let him use. Staring in the mirror he was shocked. It was the first time he'd seen his reflection since his capture. He was thin and gaunt with a rough beard and long wild hair. One good thing – nobody would ever recognize him. At least he could remain anonymous until he was safely home.

The shop girl spoke a little English. He asked if there was a barber shop around, and she directed him to a place five minutes away.

He went there immediately and got rid of the matted beard and long hair. It was a big improvement, although he still looked like shit.

He felt completely alone in the world, but it was a satisfying feeling. Once more he was in control of his own destiny.

Within an hour he caught a ferry service to Naples, and from there he took another train into Rome, where he went straight to the airport, using his traveler's checks to buy a cheap ticket to Los Angeles. There was a flight leaving in one hour. He bought some magazines and a cheap pair of sunglasses just in case he *was* recognized.

It wasn't until he was sitting on the plane heading home, that he felt completely safe.

Chapter Seventy-one

SANTO'S MIND was a movie. And he was the macho action hero.

He'd killed them. Donna and George. He'd killed the bad guys, and it was a good thing. How many people got to realize their dreams?

Now the deed was completed, he couldn't decide what to do next. There was blood everywhere – some of it had splashed on his clothes. Should he clear up the mess? Donatella wouldn't like blood all over her house – she'd be really pissed.

Someone murdered my mother. An intruder. Yes. That's what had happened. An intruder broke in and killed poor George and Donna.

Too bad.

Now, the question was, why had they been so brutally murdered?

Simple. Venus Maria was the reason. Now she had to be punished, too.

He walked into his mother's bedroom and stood over her for a moment, staring unblinkingly at her ungainly body sprawled on the floor in a pool of dark red blood. Her nightgown was crumpled and bloody. She didn't look neat.

He went to her dresser, took a pair of scissors and returned to her side. Then he carefully cut the offending nightdress off her body, arranging her limbs in a more symmetrical fashion.

Satisfied, he went downstairs and inspected George's body, crumpled at the bottom of the stairs.

Santo walked around him several times, trying not to get blood on his sneakers.

George's mouth was open, so were his eyes.

Too bad they couldn't be together. Mommy and Step-daddy, side by side.

Life wasn't perfect.

After a while, Santo took his shotgun and went outside to his car.

Carefully placing the gun on the floor, he set off toward Venus Maria's house. This time nothing would stand in his way.

☆ ☆ ☆

As Lucky drove toward the Landsmans' mansion, a car raced toward her, speeding in the opposite direction. She swerved to the side of the road, narrowly avoiding a head-on collision. She caught a quick glimpse of the driver and recognized the Landsmans' son.

She parked on the street outside the gates, and sat in her car for a minute.

It was one thing to rationalize, think sensibly, and imagine people would get punished properly. It never happened that way, and she knew what she had to do. Finally she had no choice. If she didn't take care of it, Donna would never leave the Santangelos in peace.

Donna Landsman, formerly Bonnatti, had killed Lennie.

Never fuck with a Santangelo.

Lucky got out of her car and walked around the property until she found an unlocked side gate. It was a sign.

She slipped through the gate, noting that the big house was in darkness.

Moving swiftly and silently she circled the house and was surprised to find the front door ajar. Another sign?

She entered tentatively.

Sprawled at the bottom of the stairs lay George Landsman – his head practically blown off.

Lucky's heart began to pound in her chest. He was dead. The man was dead. Oh, God, somebody had gotten here before her.

She backed away, nervously touching her gun tucked in her jeans. Then she edged past George's body, and headed upstairs. There was an eerie silence in the house. She flashed on the memory of Santo driving past at high speed, his face a white blur. Was he running from the killer? Or was *he* responsible?

She shivered. The master bedroom door was open. She edged into the room, holding her breath.

There was Donna lying in the middle of the floor, naked and spread-eagled, laid out for all to see.

Poetic justice.

Slowly Lucky backed out of the room, ran downstairs and left the house.

By the time she reached her car she was shaking.

Donna Landsman would never bother anyone again.

☆ ☆ ☆

Santo was on a mission. Nobody could stop him now. He knew Venus Maria was responsible for everything, there was no doubt about it.

She'd killed his mother.

She'd murdered Donna.

George was dead because of her.

She was a tramp bitch who deserved everything she was about to get.

Her guards were useless, and her stupid brother must have left by now.

This time he'd get her good, no more love letters. She'd betrayed him. Let's see if she liked the shotgun better than the letters.

His gun gave him power.

His gun enabled him to shoot his way out of any situation.

He was Sylvester Stallone, Clint Eastwood, Chuck Norris. He was the quintessential American hero.

He drew up to the guard's station in his car.

'Yeah?' The man half opened the security window and peered at him suspiciously. 'What can I do for you?'

Without a word Santo lifted the gun and blasted him in the face.

Pow! The guard dropped without a sound, blood splashing on the window.

Just like in the movies, Santo thought gleefully.

Laughing to himself, he drove toward the house.

☆ ☆ ☆

Venus sighed luxuriously – a long drawn-out sigh of pure pleasure. Cooper made love to her like nobody else. From the tips of his fingers to his versatile tongue, he was a master-lover, transporting her to the land of ecstasy, giving her orgasms the like of which she'd never experienced before.

He'd made her come twice – each time she'd screamed aloud with utter abandonment as the climax sent her into shuddering paroxysms of rapture.

'Turn over,' he said.

'No more,' she said.

'Turn over.'

'I can't take it.'

'Do it!'

She rolled onto her stomach. He parted her legs and began licking the soft flesh of her inner thighs. Her head was buried in the sheets. She couldn't see him, only feel his burning touch. It was impossible that he could make her come again so soon.

Absolutely impossible.

And yet ... the feeling began to sweep over her. The incredible mind-blowing build-up of a storm waiting to break ...

☆ ☆ ☆

Santo parked his car outside the mansion.

This mission felt good.

This mission was going to give him the clout and recognition he'd yearned for all his life.

No longer was he a sixteen-year-old fat kid. He was Santo Bonnatti. He was a big man just like his dad. AND NOBODY COULD STOP HIM!

He got out of the car, and stood in front of the tramp's house, and raised his gun, and shot the fucking lock right out of the fucking door.

☆ ☆ ☆

Venus thought she heard a gunshot, but she was too close to bliss to care.

'Honey ...' she murmured. Then the thought was lost as she climaxed with an earth-shattering shudder of pure sensual lust.

She screamed her pleasure – loud, abandoned, piercing screams.

As Santo started to enter the house, he didn't notice the three dogs racing in his direction.

It was only when their vicious teeth sank into his flesh, tearing it away from the bone, that he began to scream – loud, abandoned, piercing screams.

He screamed until everything went a deadly black.

And then it was over.

Chapter Seventy-two

ALEX SLEPT WELL for the first time in months. No sleeping pills, no Valium – he put his head on the pillow, falling into a deep, relaxed sleep.

In the morning he awoke refreshed, rolled over in bed and, as was his habit, reached for the TV clicker.

The set was tuned into HBO, where he'd left it the night before. There was a bad movie on about a drug deal gone wrong. Corny shit.

He had a positive feeling he was getting his life together at last. He'd told his mother something he should have got into years ago. Now if she'd only get off his case and leave him alone.

He clicked to the next station. Another movie. Another piece of mindless violence.

The clicker was power. He moved on to a fitness show, watching for a few mindless minutes, trying to decide if he should order the piece of equipment guaranteed to give you unbelievable abs. Maybe not. Who had the time? Or the inclination.

The next channel was all news. A serious black newscaster was in the middle of a breaking story: 'Early this morning, the bodies of millionaire corporate raider Donna Landsman and her financial adviser husband, George Landsman, were discovered shot to death in their six-million-dollar mansion in

Bel Air. The grisly discovery was made by a maid who immediately summoned the police.'

Alex sat bolt upright. *Oh, God, Lucky, what did you do?*

He grabbed the phone. She answered immediately. 'Lucky,' he said, his voice low and distressed. 'I just saw the news.'

'Good morning, Alex,' she said cheerfully, as if there was nothing wrong.

'*Why*, Lucky? *Why* did you do it?' he said urgently.

'I didn't,' she replied calmly. 'It wasn't me.'

'Oh, come on.'

'I promise you, Alex, I had nothing to do with it.'

'So you're saying it was a convenient coincidence? That somebody else wanted her dead?'

'Get off my case, Alex,' she said sharply. 'If you don't believe me that's your problem – not mine.'

'I'm coming over.'

Her voice was firm. 'No, please don't.'

'Yes,' he said insistently.

She didn't want to see him, he was trying to get too close too fast. It was time to step back again. 'Look,' she said patiently, 'I'll call you later.'

'Make sure you do,' he said sternly, irritating her even more. 'We have to talk.'

'I will.'

Alex jumped out of bed and went into the bathroom. Jesus! What had she done? His mind began buzzing. She'd need help, the best lawyers . . .

Whatever happened, he'd be there for her.

☆ ☆ ☆

Lucky went downstairs to the kitchen and switched on the coffee machine. Life made strange turns, sometimes too strange to follow. Were the Santangelos finally free of the Bonnattis?

Oh, God, she hoped so. The feud had taken enough lives.

Last night, when she'd gotten home, she'd called Gino in Palm Springs, asking if he was responsible in any way. He'd assured her he wasn't. Gino wouldn't lie. Besides, she'd *seen* the assassin, Santo, Donna's son, fleeing from the scene of the crime in his car, almost colliding head-on with her. She wondered how long it would take the cops to figure it out.

Alex didn't believe she'd had nothing to do with the murders. She couldn't blame him, after all – she'd told him she was going to do something, and now it had happened. Why would he think she was innocent?

At last she could bring her children home. It was a sweet feeling of relief to know they were finally safe and that they'd all be together again soon.

The coffee was bubbling. She took a mug from the shelf, pouring herself a cup.

'Hey—'

Her imagination was playing tricks. She thought she'd heard Lennie's voice.

'Hey – *you*.'

She turned around, startled. Lennie was standing behind her, smiling. 'Missed me?' he said. ''Cause I sure as hell missed you.'

She stared at him speechless, utterly stunned. 'Oh – my – God! Lennie . . .' she gasped at last.

'That's me,' he said flippantly.

She was floating, dizzy, confused. This couldn't be happening. Yet it was. And Lennie was here . . . her Lennie . . . her love . . .

'You're alive!' she cried out. 'Where did you come from? Oh . . . my . . . God! LENNIE!'

He grabbed her, hugging her fiercely to him as if he would

never let her go. 'Lucky ... Lucky ... I dreamt of this moment – it's the only thing that kept me sane.'

She leaned back in his arms, softly touching his face, marveling that he was actually there. 'Lennie ...' she murmured, her eyes filling with tears. 'Oh, God, Lennie ... What *happened* to you?'

'It's a long story, sweetheart, a very long story. All you have to know for now is that I love you, I'm here, and I promise you this – we will *never* be separated again.'

EPILOGUE

 # EPILOGUE
One Year Later

THE EXTRAVAGANT première of Alex Woods'
Gangsters was a major Hollywood event. Everybody
who was anybody was invited, and if they weren't,
they left town or pretended to.

The venue was Mann's Chinese Theater on Hollywood
Boulevard. A red carpet stretched down to the curb, a
luxurious welcoming mat for all the famous guests to parade
down. Kleig lights, strategically placed, lit up the sky for miles
around.

The excited crowds surrounded the theater, police barri-
cades holding them back from mobbing the stars as they
arrived.

A long line of limousines snaked around for at least ten
blocks. TV camera crews were alert, ready and lined up, as
were the *paparazzi*. Manic publicists grabbed the stars as they
got out of their limos, leading them down the line of media
people.

It was a major event.

☆　☆　☆

Abe Panther, settled comfortably in the back of his limo,
winked at Inga Irving. 'This is the first time I've left the
house in years,' he said, puffing on a fat cigar.

'You'll do anything for Lucky,' Inga remarked indulgently. 'She calls, you run.'

'Lucky's like the granddaughter I never had,' Abe mused. 'She's a ballsy broad, the kind we used to have in Hollywood in the good old days. I like that in a woman.'

Inga nodded, she'd finally grown to accept Abe's fondness for Lucky.

Inga had dressed for the occasion. Lucky had paid her generously for her shares, and she'd invested in a few good pieces of jewelry which she'd told Abe were fake. The man was in his nineties, and he still hung onto his money like a hooker on a bad night.

Abe leaned forward, wheezing. 'Got something for you,' he said gruffly, groping in the pocket of his 1945 tuxedo, which still fit him perfectly. 'Since we've been married a year or two, I started thinking there's no gettin' rid of you.' More wheezing as he handed her a leather ring box.

She opened it and gasped. Sparkling up at her was a magnificent eight-karat diamond ring.

'No, Abe,' she said, her normally stoic face breaking into a wide smile. 'There's certainly no getting rid of me.'

Abe cackled. 'That's exactly what I thought.'

☆ ☆ ☆

Abigaile and Mickey Stolli, along with Tabitha and her date – Risk Mace, a long-haired, heavily tattooed rocker – were sitting in the limo behind Abe.

Tabitha had changed from an out-of-control punk to a Hollywood princess. She'd dropped out of her exclusive Swiss boarding school, informing her father she wished to become an actress. Mickey had gotten her an agent, who in turn had arranged for her to audition for a small part on a TV sitcom.

To everyone's surprise she'd gotten the role, the audience had taken to her, and within six months Tabitha was a major TV star.

Mickey was proud. Who would have thought that his daughter would become a role model for teenage girls all over America?

He puffed on his cigar and thought, *Hmm ... I didn't do a bad job raising my kid. At least she's making her own money.*

Abigaile sat back and thought, *Why is Tabitha wasting her time with this strange-looking rock 'n' roller? Why doesn't she find herself a decent studio executive – someone who has a chance to rise to the top and make lots of money?*

Abigaile was ignorant of the fact that Risk was a millionaire several times over. Had she known, she might have regarded him in a different light.

Tabitha was bored. She couldn't imagine why she'd agreed to come to this première with her parents. It was such a lame thing to do. Risk must think she was a total dweeb. Her father had insisted – he wanted the cachet of arriving at the première with his famous daughter on his arm. Mickey had to attend the première on account of the fact that Johnny Romano was due to star in his first independent movie. Yes, Mickey Stolli, ex-studio head, was venturing into indie-prod, land of the failed studio executive.

Tabitha hoped there might be a role for her – she really wanted to break into movies.

☆ ☆ ☆

Leslie Kane stepped out of a long white stretch limo in front of the theater, and the crowds went wild. Then her date got out behind her, and when everyone saw who it was, the screams and excitement reached fever pitch.

The *paparazzi* and TV crews launched into frenzied action as three publicists moved in to escort the two stars down the line.

Charlie Dollar and Leslie Kane – the good girl and the rogue – what a dynamite combination!

They both had the routine down pat. Charlie with his trademark dark glasses and maniacal grin; Leslie making sure the photographers only caught her good angles, not that she had any bad ones – early on she'd learned not to let them shoot low, or up her skirt when she got out of a car.

She hung on to Charlie's arm and smiled.

He waved to the crowds who screamed their appreciation.

Leslie Kane and Charlie Dollar – a new front-page sensation.

☆ ☆ ☆

Ron Machio was excited for his best friend, he'd seen a rough cut of *Gangsters*, and knew how sensational Venus was in it – certainly the performance of her career.

Anthony, in his new tuxedo, pressed down the black side window.

'Don't do that,' Ron said, fussily. 'The fans can see in.'

'I *want* everybody to notice me in a limo,' Anthony said proudly. 'Can you imagine? If we're on TV in London, they'll know *I'm* a star, too.'

'You're not a star,' Ron said. 'You're still Venus's assistant.'

'I'm living with *you*,' Anthony said tartly. 'That *makes* me a star.'

A slow smile spread across Ron's face. 'You say the nicest things.'

Sitting across from them, Emilio scowled. Why did he have to get stuck in a car with the gay brigade?

He supposed it was better than not getting invited at all. Still . . . didn't he deserve his own limo?

Since he'd caught that crazed intruder on Venus's property, she'd been almost nice to him. And in return he'd quit selling stories and worked for her as a part-time assistant. Thank God he'd caught Santo that first time – if he hadn't, Venus wouldn't have called Johnny Romano and borrowed his dogs, and without the dogs on her property that night, she might not be here today . . .

So really, it was all thanks to him. Not that anybody appreciated it.

Occasionally, when Venus and Cooper took him to dinner at Hamburger Hamlet, they acted like they were doing him a big favor. This pissed him off – wasn't he good enough to accompany them to any of the fancy restaurants they frequented?

When Venus had invited him to her première, he'd said, 'How'll I get there?'

'You'll go with Anthony and Ron,' she'd replied. 'They'll make sure you behave.'

'But, little sis,' he'd objected, 'I thought I could take a date and get my *own* limo!'

'No, Emilio,' she'd said firmly. 'I don't trust you. You'll go with them.'

And that had been that.

☆　☆　☆

Brigette peered out of the window. 'Get an eyeful of the crowds,' she exclaimed. 'Wow! Amazing!'

'Stay cool,' Nona said. 'Remember – you're a star, too.'

Zandino beamed and nodded agreeably. They'd gotten married six months ago. Now Nona was five months pregnant and they were both incredibly happy.

Brigette couldn't keep still. 'I'm really glad Lucky and Lennie invited us,' she said. 'This is *sooo* cool.'

'Maybe you'll meet the hunk of your dreams,' Nona said. 'There's a lot of cute guys in Hollywood.'

'The hunk of my dreams does not exist,' Brigette said wistfully. '*Especially* in Hollywood. In fact, I'm beginning to think he doesn't exist at all.'

'You're a star, Brigette – a supermodel – you never know who'll come chasing after you, hot for your gorgeous young bod. Sean Penn. Emilio Estevez. Who would you like?'

Brigette grinned. 'Dunno. But if I see him, I'll be sure to let you know!'

Their limo drew to a stop outside the theater. 'Out!' Nona said. 'Be a star!'

'You're so bossy.'

'You'd be uncontrollable if I wasn't.'

'Ha! Betcha no one will know who I am.'

'Ten bucks. You're on.'

Brigette stepped out of the car, breathed deeply and faced the crowds.

'BRIGETTE! BRIGETTE! BRIGETTE!'

They were chanting her name. She was stunned! And a little bit thrilled.

A handsome young publicist grabbed her arm, preparing to escort her along the media walk.

'You owe me ten bucks,' Nona whispered, somewhere behind her.

She smiled, and faced the press.

☆ ☆ ☆

Johnny Romano and his bride of one year, Daniella, sauntered down the red carpet with Daniella's nine-year-old daughter clutching Johnny's hand. They made a lovely-looking family. Johnny so dark and sexy; Daniella so blond and beautiful; and the little girl a mirror image of her mother.

The press considered their story incredibly romantic. Daniella, a French journalist, had come to LA to interview Johnny for a magazine. One interview and they were in love, he'd sent for her daughter, married her, and now they were the perfect Hollywood couple.

Daniella was content.

Johnny had never been so happy.

It really was a love match.

☆ ☆ ☆

'You look gorgeous,' Cooper said.

'No way,' Venus replied, pulling a disgusted face. 'I'm fat.'

'Not fat. Pregnant. There's a big difference.'

'I should be looking all sleek and sexy,' she worried. 'My fans expect it. I should be wearing something outrageous.'

'Your performance in the movie is outrageous. Everyone who's seen it says you're a dead cert for a nomination, including me.'

She stared at him anxiously. 'Do you *really* think so, Coop? You're not just saying that to make me happy?'

He smiled knowingly. 'I have other ways of making you happy.'

'Yeah, witness this,' she said, ruefully patting her swollen belly.

He put his hand over hers. 'I love you so much,' he said. 'Never thought it would happen to me.'

'And to think we nearly blew it.' She sighed.

'Well, we didn't.'

'I know. One night with Veronica and you came running back to me! I should thank him/her – whatever.'

'Ha ha! Very amusing.'

'Did I tell you that you look fantastically handsome tonight?'

'Thank you,' he said, smiling at his adorable pregnant wife. She always knew how to make him feel like a king.

☆   ☆   ☆

Alex was tired, but it was a good tired. He'd finished cutting the movie six weeks earlier, and since that time they'd had several test runs which had surpassed everyone's expectations – word of mouth was phenomenal.

He knew that *Gangsters* was the movie he'd win an Oscar for. And two of his principal actors – Venus and Johnny – would definitely get nominated. He felt fulfilled and satisfied.

He was also thrilled for Lucky. She'd had faith in the movie *and* him – now it was pay-off time for Panther.

He thought about Lucky for a moment. He'd always have a special feeling for her, but since Lennie's return he'd drawn back because she'd made it quite clear that she loved Lennie and would always put him first.

The nice thing was that the three of them had become good friends. Lennie was a great guy – Alex not only liked him, he respected him too.

Dominique sat opposite her son in the limo with her date – a tango-dancing stockbroker she'd met at a club on Wilshire. He was a pleasant man, older and quite dapper.

Lately Dominique was a changed woman – no more criticisms. He wondered how long it would last.

Tonight he was escorting Lili and France. They'd both worked hard on the movie, and deserved a treat.

He reflected that now *Gangsters* was finished and launched, it was time to get his personal life back on track. Who knew what was out there?

He planned on taking a vacation – traveling to Italy and finding out.

Maybe there was a wildly beautiful, unpredictable dark-haired woman waiting for him somewhere . . .

Maybe . . .

☆   ☆   ☆

'Well, sweetheart,' Lucky said, her black eyes sparkling, 'this is it – the première of *Gangsters*. I'm kinda buzzed.'

'You should be,' Lennie replied. 'You put in plenty of time to make sure everything went smoothly.'

'Thanks,' she said, thinking about what an amazing year it had been, and how fortunate she was to have Lennie back.

'You look so goddamn beautiful tonight,' he said, squeezing her hand. 'Sometimes I wake up in the morning and I can't believe I'm safely home in bed next to you.'

'I can't believe it either,' she said, marveling at how things had turned out. 'It seems incredible.'

'How did we both get through it?' he questioned, shaking his head.

'Somehow we did, we're together and we're here.'

'Every moment I was away, you were in my thoughts. You kept me alive.'

'And you were in mine,' she said softly. 'Even though you didn't phone, you didn't write.'

'My wife the comedian,' he said wryly.

'That used to be *your* job,' she pointed out.

'Oh, no,' he said. 'I've had the acting-performing bit – no more in front of the camera for me.'

She knew it was going to be a hard job persuading him to resume his career. Since his return he'd become reclusive, preferring to stay at home with the children rather than go out in public. It didn't bother her, but she knew – for his own sake – she had to do something to get him involved in the real world again. Right now he was happy doing nothing. Eventually he'd realize it wasn't enough.

'So, your friend Alex must be happy about tonight,' Lennie remarked. 'Y'know, when you first introduced us, I wasn't sure about him.'

'Really?' she said, her tone noncommittal.

'Yeah, but he's a nice guy. I like him.'

'I'm glad, because Alex was a very good friend to me while you were gone.'

He threw her a look, his green eyes probing hers. 'Is that all he was?'

She didn't hesitate. 'Yes, that's all.'

'He's got a major crush on you.'

'No way.'

'Oh, yes.'

They were silent for a few minutes as their limo edged its way toward the theater.

'And Claudia?' Lucky asked, breaking the silence. 'You've told me what she did for you . . . Was *she* just a friend?'

'Of course,' he said quickly.

'So maybe one day we'll go visit her.'

'Maybe . . .'

'Anyway,' Lucky said, 'I'm looking forward to tonight, and then – I've got a big surprise for you.'

'What?'

'Guess.'

'With you I wouldn't have a chance. You give unpredictable a whole new meaning.'

'I'm taking a six-month leave of absence from the studio.'

He sat up straight. 'You're doing *what*?'

'You heard. We're going on a trip around the world . . . you, me, the kids. No work, just play. I think we deserve it.'

'Sweetheart, you don't have to do this for me—'

'It's for us,' she interrupted, staring at him intently. 'And when we get back you can decide what you want to do.'

'Y'know,' he said thoughtfully. 'I've been thinking ... I wouldn't mind getting into directing ...'

'Have I got a studio for you!'

'You're a funny lady tonight.'

She grinned, her black eyes sparkling. 'Whatever makes you happy.'

'*You* make me happy, you always have. You're the most special woman in the world, and I love you more than I can ever put into words.'

'Love you, too, Lennie,' she said softly. 'And I always will.'

They smiled at each other and squeezed hands, and it was as if they'd never been apart.

Dangerous Kiss

Acknowledgements

I would like to thank the wonderful team at Macmillan for their dedication and enthusiasm every time they publish one of my books. I would particularly like to thank all the sales force and the great group of people I get to work with:

Ian S. Chapman, Arabella Stein, Clare Harington, Elizabeth Bond, Katie Roberts, Nadya Kooznetzoff, Morven Knowles, Jacqui Graham, Chris Gibson, Annie Griffiths, Mark Richmond, Liz Davis, Tess Tattersall, Matt Smith, Neil Lang, Annika Roojun, Fiona Carpenter, Lucy Hale, Vivienne Nelson, Michael Halden, Julie Wright, Dan Ruffino, Jeannine Fowler, Andrew Wright, David Adamson, Fiona Killeen, Gabrielle Dawwas, John Lee, John Neild, John Talbot, Kate Hales, Keith Southgate, Keren Western, Norman Taylor, Phil Trump, Robert Ferrari, Sally Ferrari, Steve Shrubsole, William Taylor Gill, Kay Charlton, Ray Theobald, Alison Muirden, Karen Schoenemann and Ray Fidler.

I would also like to thank Andrew Nurnberg and everyone at Andrew Nurnberg Associates for selling my books worldwide with such class and style:

Beryl Cutayar, Paola Marchese, Vicky Mark and Christine Regan.

Jackie
xx

P.S. And a big thank-you to my loyal and dedicated readers.

BOOK ONE
Los Angeles

Chapter One

'TAKE IT!' the young white girl urged, thrusting the gun at the sixteen-year-old black youth, who immediately backed away.

'No!' he said fervently. 'My old man would bust my ass.'

The girl, clad in a mini-skirt and tight tank top, had long legs, a big bosom, a pointed face, hazel eyes heavily outlined in black, and unevenly cropped dark hair. She stared at the boy scornfully. 'Chicken!' she jeered, in a scathing voice. 'Daddy's little baby chickee boy.'

'No way!' he grumbled, pissed that she would talk to him that way. He was tall and gangly with large ears that stuck out, and big brown eyes.

'Oh, yes,' she taunted. 'Way!'

On impulse he snatched the gun out of her hands, sticking it down the front of his pants with a macho grunt. 'Satisfied?'

The girl nodded, hazel eyes gleaming. She was eighteen, but looked older. 'Let's go,' she said authoritatively. It was obvious who was in charge.

'Go like where?' he asked, wishing she could be a bit nicer. She was always so short with him.

'To have a blast,' she answered airily. 'Y'know, cruise around, get shit-faced. We'll take your car.'

His father had recently bought him a black jeep for his sixteenth birthday. It was also a present to celebrate their return to LA after a year and a half of living in New York.

3

'I dunno . . .' he said hesitantly, remembering that tonight he was supposed to have an early dinner with his dad, but thinking that the idea of getting shit-faced with her seemed much more appealing. 'An' why we need a gun?' he added.

The girl didn't answer, she simply made chicken noises as she sauntered towards the door.

The boy followed, his eyes glued to her legs. He had a hard-on, and he knew that if he played it right, tonight might be the night he scored.

Chapter Two

LUCKY SANTANGELO Golden stood up behind her enormous art-deco desk in her office at Panther Studios, then she stretched and yawned. It had been a long hard day, and she was beyond tired. However, the day was not over yet because tonight she was being honoured at the Beverly Hilton Hotel for her work towards raising money for AIDS research.

As owner and head of Panther Studios, Lucky was in an extremely high profile position, so she had no choice but to accept the limelight gracefully.

The problem was that she was not looking forward to being the centre of attention. It wasn't as if she'd *asked* to be honoured – the evening had been thrust upon her, making it impossible to refuse.

She reached for a candy bar, nibbled hungrily on the sweet chocolate. *Nothing like a sugar rush to get me through the next few hours,* she thought ruefully. Michael Caine's famous Hollywood quote kept running through her head: 'In a town with no honour, how come everyone's always being honoured?' *Yeah, right on, Michael!* she thought, with a wry grin. *But how does one avoid it?*

Lucky was a slender, long-limbed woman with an abundance of shoulder-length jet curls, dangerous black-opal eyes, full, sensual lips and a deep olive skin. Hers was an exotic beauty mixed with a fierce intelligence. A brilliant businesswoman, she'd been running Panther Studios for eight years, making it one of the most respected and successful studios in Hollywood. Lucky had a knack for greenlighting all the right movies and picking up others for distribution, which always did well. 'You're Lucky in more ways than one,' Lennie was forever telling her. 'You can do anything.'

Lennie Golden, her husband. Whenever she thought about him her face brightened. Lennie was the love of her life. Tall, sexy, funny – yet, most of all, he was her soulmate, and she planned on staying with him for ever, because they were truly destined to be together and after two previous marriages she was finally totally happy. Lennie and their children – seven-year-old Gino, named after her father, and adorable eight-year-old Maria – satisfied her completely.

And then there was her fifteen-year-old son Bobby from her marriage to the late shipping magnate Dimitri Stanislopoulos. Bobby was so handsome and adult-looking – over six feet tall and extremely athletic. And there was Bobby's niece, Brigette, whom Lucky considered her godchild. Brigette lived in New York where she was a supermodel. Not that she needed the money because she was one of the richest young women in the world, having inherited a Greek shipping fortune from her grandfather, Dimitri, and her mother, Olympia, who'd died tragically of a drug overdose.

Tonight, Steven Berkeley, Lucky's half-brother, was picking Lucky up, because Lennie was on location downtown, directing Steven's wife, Mary Lou, in a romantic comedy. Lennie had once been an extremely successful comedian and movie star, but since his kidnapping ordeal several years ago he'd given up performing in front of the camera. Now he concentrated solely on writing and directing.

The movie he was shooting with Mary Lou – a talented and successful actress – was not for Panther. Both he and Lucky had decided not to provide any opportunity for snide rumours of nepotism. 'If I'm doing this, I'll do it on my own,' he'd said. And, of course, he'd succeeded, just as she'd known he would.

Tonight she was going to make an announcement at the end of her speech – an announcement that would blow everyone away. She hadn't even told Lennie about it – he would be as surprised as everyone else and, she hoped, pleased. Only her father, Gino, knew what she was planning to say. Feisty old Gino, eighty-seven now, but still a man to be looked up to and admired.

Lucky adored Gino with a fierce passion; they'd been through so much together – including many years when they hadn't spoken at all. Now their closeness was legendary, and Lucky always went to him first when it came to making decisions. Gino was the smartest man she knew, although she hadn't always felt that way about him.

Oh, God! What a checkered past they shared – from the time he'd married her off to a senator's son when she was barely sixteen, to the years they hadn't spoken while he was out of America as a tax exile and she'd taken over his Las Vegas hotel empire.

Gino Santangelo was a self-made man who had power, charisma, and quite a way with women. Women adored Gino, they always had. Even now he still knew how to charm and flatter. Lucky remembered her adopted uncle, Costa, telling her all about the infamous Gino when he was a young man. 'His nickname was Gino the Ram,' Costa had confided, with an envious chuckle. 'That's 'cause he could have any woman he wanted, an' did. That is, until he met your dear mother, God rest her soul.'

Maria. Her mother. So beautiful and pure. Taken from her when she was a child. Brutally murdered by the Bonnatti family.

Lucky would never forget the day she'd run downstairs to

find her mother floating on a raft in the family swimming-pool. She was five years old, and the memory had stayed with her for ever – as vivid as the day it happened. She'd sat by the side of the pool staring at her exquisite mother, spread-eagled on the raft in the centre of the pool. 'Mama,' she'd murmured quietly. And then her voice had risen to a scream, as she'd realized her mother was no longer with her. 'MAMA! MAMA! MAMA!'

Discovering her mother's body at such a young age had coloured her entire life. After the tragedy, Gino had become so protective of her and her brother, Dario, that living at home in Bel Air was like being shut away in a maximum security prison. When she'd finally been sent abroad to a boarding-school in Switzerland, she'd immediately rebelled and turned into a wild child, running away with her best friend, Olympia Stanislopoulos, to a villa in the South of France where they'd wreaked havoc and partied non-stop. Oh, yes, those were crazy times. Her first taste of freedom, and she'd lived every minute of it, until a sour-faced Gino had tracked her down. Shortly after that he'd decided she would be better off married than careening around on the loose. So he'd made a deal with Senator Peter Richmond to marry her off to his son, the extraordinarily unsexy Craven. What a trap *that* had turned out to be.

When she thought about it, Lucky realized that her life had been a series of incredible highs and lows. The highs were so utterly amazing: her three beautiful, healthy children; her marriage to Lennie; the success of running a major Hollywood studio; not to mention her earlier achievements in Vegas and Atlantic City where she'd built hotels.

The lows were too dreadful to contemplate. First, the murder of her mother, then the brutal killing of her brother, Dario, and her beloved Marco getting shot in Las Vegas.

Three devastating tragedies, for which she'd extracted her own form of revenge.

But she had survived. Gino had taught her that survival was everything, and she'd learned the lesson well.

The intercom on her desk buzzed, and her assistant informed her that Venus Maria was on the line. She hurried to pick up. Not only was Venus Maria an adored and controversial superstar, she was also Lucky's best girlfriend.

'What's up?' Lucky asked, flopping down in the leather chair behind her desk.

'Good question,' Venus replied. 'Here's the major problem – I have nothing to wear tonight.'

'*Boring.*'

'I know you're not into fashion like I am, but I'll be photographed from here to Puerto Rico, and you *know* I can't look ordinary.'

Lucky laughed: Venus was such a drama queen. 'You? Ordinary? *Never!*'

'Nobody understands,' Venus grumbled. 'The expectations are enormous.'

'*What* expectations?' Lucky asked, picking up a pen and doodling on a pad.

'I'm a superstar, dear,' Venus announced, tongue in cheek. 'A superstar who's supposed to alter her look daily. I mean – for Chrissake – how many times can I change the colour of my hair?'

'What colour is it now?'

'Platinum.'

'Then wear a black wig. Clone me – we can go as twins.'

'You're no help,' Venus wailed. 'I need assistance.'

The *last* thing Venus needed was assistance. She was one of the most together and talented women Lucky had ever met. At thirty-three, Venus was not only a major movie star, she was also a video and recording superstar, with legions of fans who worshipped her every move. Everything she did still made headlines, even though she'd been doing it for over a decade.

Several years ago she'd married Cooper Turner, the ageing but still extremely attractive movie star. After a shaky start, their marriage had taken, and they now had a five-year-old daughter named Chyna. In addition to the joy of a daughter, Venus Maria's career was going great. Ever since being Oscar-nominated for her cameo role in Alex Woods's *Gangsters*, she'd been able to pick and choose her roles.

'It's not that simple,' Lucky had replied. 'You have to keep trying. Pick a goal and go for it.'

'I guess that's what *you* did,' Venus had said. 'I mean, considering you started off with a father who hated you and—'

'Gino *never* hated me,' Lucky had interrupted.

'Well, you told me he always put you down 'cause you were a woman and he wanted his son to run his empire, right?'

'Ah, yes,' Lucky had said. 'But I soon changed his mind.'

'That's it,' Venus had said. 'You *got* what you wanted. Now I'm going for what *I* want.'

Lucky listened as Venus carried on about what her look for the evening ahead should be. She knew that her friend already had her entire outfit planned, but Venus liked affirmation.

'And what are *you* wearing?' Venus asked, when she finally stopped talking about herself.

'Valentino,' Lucky said. 'Red. It's Lennie's favourite colour on me.'

'Hmm . . .' Venus said. 'Sounds sexy.' A pause. Then – 'Is Alex coming?'

'Of course,' Lucky said matter-of-factly. 'We're all sitting together.'

Venus couldn't keep the purr out of her voice. 'How does Lennie feel about *that*?'

'Will you get off it?' Lucky said, irritated that Venus was always trying to make a big deal out of her and Alex when there was absolutely nothing going on. 'You *know* Alex and Lennie are good friends.'

'Yes, but—'

'No buts,' Lucky interrupted briskly. 'Take your fertile imagination and go write another song!'

As soon as she hung up, she opened her desk drawer and took out the scribbled speech she planned on giving. She studied it for a few minutes, changing a word or two.

One final read-through and she was satisfied.

Tonight she was going to shock the socks off everyone in Hollywood.

But, hey – shocking people – wasn't that what her life was all about?

Chapter Three

'FANTASTIC! UNBELIEVABLE! More! More! Give me the lips! Those delectable lips!' Fredo Carbanado crooned encouragement, his expressive Italian eyes flashing signals of deep lust as they appeared above his camera. 'I get off on those luscious lips. More! *Bellissima!* More!'

Brigette moved her body sensuously in front of the camera, giving him the exact poses he wanted. She was blonde and curvaceous, with luminous peaches-and-cream skin, enormous blue eyes fringed with the longest lashes, and full pouty lips. Devastatingly pretty and sexy in a child-woman way, her huge appeal had to do with a distinct air of vulnerability.

'Can it, Fredo,' she scolded, adjusting the top of her revealing coffee-coloured lace slip. 'How many times must I tell you? I do *not* need to hear the riff. Save it for some new little bimbette who'll get off on your phoney bullshit.'

Fredo frowned, forever puzzled that Brigette didn't fall for him like all the other models.

'Brigette!' he said sadly, lowering his camera and pulling a disappointed face. 'Why you always so *mean?*'

'I'm not mean,' she retorted. 'Merely honest.'

'No, you *mean*,' Fredo said, scowling. 'Mean and ornery.'

'Thanks!' she said tartly.

'But, Fredo, he knows what you need,' the Italian photographer said, nodding knowingly.

'And what might that be?'

'A man!' Fredo announced triumphantly.

'Ha!' Brigette said, shifting her provocative pose. 'What makes you think I'm into *men*? Maybe *women* do it for me.'

'Hallelujah!' exclaimed Fanny, her black lesbian makeup artist, stepping forward. 'I'm here! All ya gotta do is *say* the word!'

Brigette giggled. 'Just f–ing with Mr Charm,' she said sweetly.

'As if I didn't know,' Fanny retorted, touching up Brigette's full lips with a sable brush. 'You have *no* idea *what* you are missin'. Women got it goin', girl!'

'Can we turn up the music,' Brigette requested. 'I so *love* Montell Jordan.'

'Who doesn't?' said Fanny. 'If I was ever considering changin' tracks, *that*'d be the man who'd do it for me!'

'And if *I* made a switch,' Brigette retorted, toying with all of them, 'I'd definitely go for k.d. lang. Saw her at a benefit last week, she has, like, this *insane* sexual aura. It's almost as if she's Elvis or something.'

'Dyke alert!' screeched Masters, her hair stylist, a skeletal man dressed in a one-piece yellow jumpsuit with spiked hair to match.

'Get *out*!' said Brigette, giggling again.

She loved the camaraderie of working on a shoot. These people were her family – even if Fredo *was* the lech of all time. He was a star photographer, and for that reason she would never dream of succumbing to his somewhat suspect charms, because Fredo could have anyone – and usually did. He went through models at an alarming rate, loving and leaving them like a regular Don Juan.

Brigette watched him as he danced around behind his camera. Fredo missed being handsome on account of an exceptionally large nose, small eyes and alarmingly bushy eyebrows. He was also very short, which didn't seem to faze him because most of his conquests towered over him. Her best friend, Lina, had given her a strong warning. 'Stay away from Fredo,' Lina had said, rolling her saffron-coloured eyes in a knowing fashion. 'That boy fucks an' tells. *And* in spite of all 'is boastin', 'e's got a tiny little dick! So, girlfriend, you do *not* wanna go there.'

Lina was an incredibly exotic-looking black girl from the East End of London. At twenty-six she was a year older than Brigette, but in spite of their very different backgrounds, over the last eighteen months they had become good friends. Brigette had recently purchased an apartment in Lina's building, so now they were neighbours on Central Park South.

The fashion industry regarded them as supermodels. The very word 'supermodel' sent them both into paroxysms of uncontrollable laughter.

'Supermodel, my arse!' Lina would exclaim. 'They should catch me in the mornin' with me curlers in! *Not* a pretty sight!'

'I can vouch for that,' Brigette would reply.

Lina's turn. 'An' 'ow about *you* with no makeup? You look like a bloody albino caught in some bloke's headlights!'

Unlike Brigette, Lina went through men at an alarming rate. Rock stars were her favourites, but she wasn't averse to any man as long as he was extremely rich and bought her lavish presents. Lina *loved* receiving presents.

The other thing she loved was trying to fix Brigette up, but Brigette shied away from all involvements. She had a checkered history with men – as far as she was concerned they were all trouble. First boyfriend, young actor Tim Wealth. She'd been an innocent teenager with a crush; he'd been an ambitious man with an agenda. And he'd gotten himself beaten up and murdered – all because of his connection to her.

Next there was the frightening encounter with the Santangelos' arch enemy, Santino Bonnatti, who'd tried to sexually molest both her and her uncle, Bobby, when they were both kids. She'd shot Santino with his own gun. Lucky had tried to take the blame, but Brigette had made sure the truth came out. The judge had pronounced it a clear case of self-defence, and ordered her to check in with a probation officer once a month for a year. After that it was over.

Then there was Paul Webster. She'd had a crush on Paul for a long time, right up until she got engaged to the wealthy son of one of her grandfather's business rivals. When Paul finally came running, she'd decided a career was more important than any man, so she'd broken her engagement and concentrated on making it as a model. Unfortunately, one of the first people she'd hooked up with in the modelling world was Michel Guy, a top agent who'd turned out to be a sick pervert, forcing her to perform scenes with other girls, then blackmailing her with the photos. Once again Lucky had come to her rescue. Brigette loved and admired Lucky. She was her self-appointed godmother and a true friend.

Since her disastrous experience with Michel Guy, Brigette had put men on the back burner, suspicious of their intent. And, apart from a brief affair with fellow model Isaac, that was it as far as involvements were concerned.

'Doncha miss *sex*?' Lina was forever demanding, after another night of passion with one of her retinue of ardent – sometimes married – rock stars.

'Not at all,' was Brigette's airy reply. 'I'm waiting for the right guy, *then* I'll make up for it.'

Truth was she was wary of any serious involvement. To her, men spelled disaster and danger.

Occasionally she dated. Not that she enjoyed the dating game – it was always the same dance. Dinner at a hot new restaurant; drinks at a happening new club; the inevitable grope; and then, as soon as they moved in for the kill, *she* moved on.

Safe and never sorry, Brigette had found it was the only way to go.

'What you and Lina do tonight?' Fredo asked, snapping away.

'Why?' Brigette retorted, changing poses as fast as he clicked his shutter.

''Cause I got a cousin—' he began.

'No!' she interrupted firmly.

'From England.'

She raised an eyebrow. 'An *English* cousin?'

'Carlo's Italian, like me. He work in London.'

'And *you* promised to fix him up with a couple of hot young models, right?'

'It's not like that, *cara*.'

'I bet!'

'Carlo is engaged.'

'Even better,' Brigette said, shaking her head vigorously. 'Last fling before the wedding. I think not.'

'So suspicious,' Fredo grumbled. 'I thought we could have nice dinner, the four of us. Just friends.'

'The only thing *you*'re just friends with is your cat,' Brigette said tartly. 'And there's been rumours about *that* . . .'

Fanny and Masters, listening on the sidelines, shrieked with laughter. They loved seeing Fredo rejected, it was *so* unusual.

Later, when the photo session was finished and Brigette was on her way out of his studio, Fredo stopped her by the door. 'Please!' he wailed. 'I *must* impress my cousin. He's what you Americans call a prick.'

'Wonderful!' Brigette said crisply. 'Now you want us to have dinner with a *nasty* guy. This is getting better every minute.'

'Brigette,' Fredo pleaded, 'for me. It make me look good. One big favour.'

She sighed. Suddenly Fredo the ladykiller appeared needy, and since she was a sucker for anyone in trouble, she immediately felt sorry for him. 'Okay, I'll ask Lina,' she said, sure that Lina had a date with bigger and better, while *she* had a date with a double cheese pizza and an *Absolutely Fabulous* marathon on the Comedy channel.

Fredo kissed her hand. He was still so Italian, in spite of having lived in America for many years. 'You are special woman,' he crooned. 'My little American rose.'

'I'm not *your* anything,' she retorted crisply, and quickly skipped out of the studio.

☆ ☆ ☆

'Don't!' commanded Lina.

'What?' said Flick Fonda, a married rock star with a penchant for gorgeous black women.

'Don't touch me feet!' Lina warned, rolling away from her latest victim.

'Why?' he asked, crawling across the bed after her. 'You ticklish?'

'No,' she said crossly. 'Me feet are very sensitive – stay away!'

'As long as that's *all* I gotta stay away from,' Flick said, with a ribald laugh.

Lina tossed back her long straight black hair, inherited from her half Spanish mother, and turned onto her stomach. She had hoped for Superman. What she'd got was an ageing rock star with no technique. She was bored with Flick. He was just another conquest and not that exciting between the sheets.

The trouble with rock stars was that they were sated with

women – all they really wanted to do was lie back and get their dicks sucked. Not that she was averse to such activity, but she did expect it to be reciprocal, and rock stars *never* cared to return the favour.

She stretched languorously. 'Gotta go,' she said.

'Why?' he said, lecherously eyeing her smooth black skin. 'I have all night. My wife thinks I'm in Cleveland.'

'Then she's an idiot,' Lina said, jumping off the bed in his sumptuous hotel suite. She'd met Flick's wife once at a fashion show. Pamela Fonda was an ex-model who'd given him three kids in a pathetic attempt to keep him home. Trouble was, there was no one who could keep Flick home. The man craved constant action. He was a Hall of Fame rocker with a wandering cock and macho attitude.

'Where you goin'?' Flick whined, not used to women leaving unless he ordered them to.

'Meeting my girlfriend,' Lina said, plucking her skimpy Azzedine Alaïa dress off the floor and shimmying her slender body into it.

'Whyn't I take you both to dinner?' Flick suggested, watching her as she dressed.

'Sorry,' Lina said, stepping into her scarlet Diego Della Valle exceptionally high heels. 'We already got arrangements.'

Flick stretched his sinewy body across the bed. He was naked, very white and quite hairless, apart from a full pubic bush of fuzzy orange. He was also hard again. Quite impressive for an almost-fifty non-stop raver, Lina thought. Shame he didn't know what to do with it.

He caught Lina looking. 'See anything you might wanna hang around for?' he asked, with a self-satisfied smirk.

'Nope,' she said. 'Can't be late for me best friend.' And before he could stop her she beat a hasty retreat.

She stood in the elevator on her way down to the lobby trying to ignore an elderly couple who were blatantly staring at her. The woman began nudging her husband to make sure he recognized the famous supermodel.

Lina was used to the scrutiny; in fact, there were times she got off on it. Tonight wasn't one of them, however. She began staring back at the man, licking her full lips suggestively, poking out her extra long tongue. He blushed a dull red.

Oh, yes, this was slightly different from the life she'd led in England where she'd been a hairdresser's apprentice and treated like crap because she was young and had no money and lived in a one-room dump with her waitress mother, her Jamaican father having taken off shortly after she was born. What a bastard *he* was. Not that she'd ever met him, although one of these days – if he ever realized she was his daughter – he'd probably come crawling back to bask in the fame and glory.

Fuck him if he did. She didn't need a dad: she'd done very nicely without one.

Everything changed when she was discovered by the aunt of a modelling agent who insisted she go see her niece. Even though Lina was only seventeen at the time, the niece, recognizing enormous potential, had signed her on the spot.

After that it was all go, a dizzying ride to the top with plenty of adventures along the way.

She'd moved to America permanently five years ago, although most of her time was spent travelling the world. From Paris to Milan to the Bahamas, Lina was always in demand, always the centre of attention.

Downstairs she slipped the doorman ten bucks to get her a cab and fished a small cellphone from her oversized Prada purse. 'Brig,' she said, when her friend answered, 'what we doin' tonight? It just so 'appens I'm free.'

Chapter Four

HANGING OUT in his trailer during a late lunchbreak, Lennie Golden leaned over and grabbed a bottle of beer from his portable fridge, swigging heartily until the bottle was almost empty. Lennie was tall and lanky with dirty-blond hair and ocean-green eyes. He was extremely attractive in an edgy, offhand way, with a dark humour and sometimes acerbic wit. Age agreed with him: at forty-five, women found him more attractive than ever.

Lennie liked being alone in his trailer where he could concentrate on his work, especially as he was writing an original script and was well into it. His laptop was laid out ready for action, so it was annoying that soon it would be time to put on black tie – which he hated – and get his ass in gear. He wasn't into big-time Hollywood events, but since tonight it was Lucky who was being honoured, there was no getting out of it.

Lucky Santangelo Golden, his wife – the most beautiful woman in the world *and* the smartest. He often thought how fortunate he was to have her, especially a few years ago when he'd spent several soul-destroying months as the victim of a horrible kidnapping plot, trapped and manacled in an underground cave in Sicily. He'd sat out those interminable months dreaming of his escape and of returning to Lucky and his children. Thank God his prayers had been answered.

Now he was safe and settled and things had never been better.

Looking back on his nightmare, it all seemed surreal – as if it had happened to someone else. If it hadn't been for Claudia, the Sicilian girl who'd answered his prayers and helped him escape . . .

A second assistant hammered on his trailer door, interrupting his thoughts. 'Ready on the set, Mr G.'

'I'll be right there,' he responded, shutting down his laptop, banishing the vision of Claudia with her big, soulful eyes, long tanned legs and smooth skin.

Skin like silk . . .

He'd never told Lucky what really happened, how he'd managed to secure his escape from the underground prison he'd been trapped in. He'd never told her and he never would. It was the one thing he kept from his wife because he didn't want to hurt her.

Lucky would not believe he'd had no choice. It was his secret, and he planned on keeping it.

He turned off his laptop, left his trailer and headed for the street location nearby, greeting Buddy, his black cinematographer, with a friendly high five on the way.

'Whass up, man?' Buddy said, falling into step beside him. 'No food today?'

'Saving myself for the plastic chicken tonight,' he answered, with a wry grin.

'Yeah!' Buddy said forcefully. 'Bin there!'

They both laughed.

☆ ☆ ☆

Mary Lou Berkeley was feeling nostalgic. It was a week away from her ninth wedding anniversary and she couldn't help thinking about how she and Steven had first met. Of course,

21

what she *should* be thinking about was her role in Lennie's movie, especially the upcoming scene. But reminiscing about Steven was irresistible. *He* was irresistible, and thankfully she still loved him as much as when they'd first gotten together. They were a perfect fit, and they always would be.

Mary Lou was a glowingly pretty curvaceous black woman of thirty-one, with huge brown eyes, shoulder-length black curls and a totally captivating smile.

The day she'd met Steven had been traumatic, to say the least. She'd been eighteen at the time, a TV star and full of her own importance. It had *not* been love at first sight. She'd walked into his office at the prestigious New York law firm of Myerson, Laker and Brandon, accompanied by her mother, her manager aunt, and her edgy white boyfriend. Some entourage.

But Steven had been pleasant and reassuring, managing to persuade everyone else to wait outside while she told him her story. And what a sorry story it was. Rashly she'd allowed her then boyfriend to take nude pictures of her when she was fifteen – nothing hard-core, simply some fun stuff they'd gotten into together while fooling around. Recently, cashing in on her TV fame in a family sitcom, the old boyfriend had sold the offending photos to a skin magazine, they'd been published, and now Mary Lou was determined to sue.

Steven warned her that suing a magazine was not easy: there would be depositions, endless questions and all the pressures of negative publicity. 'I can handle it,' she'd said, full of the confidence of youth. 'I want to see those scummy rats pay for what they've done to me.'

'Okay,' Steven had said. 'If that's what you want, we'll go for it.'

Finally, almost three years later, they'd gone to court. Her appearance went well. She was poised and articulate and the jury fell in love with her – especially when she smiled. They loved her so much that on the final day they awarded her sixteen million dollars in damages.

Mary Lou was elated and triumphant. So was Steven. They went out to dinner to celebrate, and before long the innocent celebration turned into something more.

One thing about Mary Lou – when she wanted something, she was determined. And apart from suing the magazine, she had her big brown eyes firmly fixed on Steven – even though he was over twenty years her senior.

Later that night they ended up in bed. It was warm and exciting and it made Steven feel guilty as hell. She was too young. He was too old. As far as he was concerned it was a no-win situation.

'This relationship is not going to work,' he told her sternly.

'Sure,' she answered cheerfully. 'I have a *great* idea. Let's make it not work together.'

All she had to do was smile and he was lost. A week later she moved into his house.

Mary Lou gave him the personal happiness he'd been lacking for so long. His life had fallen apart for a while when his mother, Carrie, had revealed that she wasn't sure who his father was. Mary Lou helped him to get his head straight, and to stop obsessing about his past and concentrate on his work as a lawyer.

Then came the second magazine incident. The publisher of the magazine Mary Lou had sued published a ten-page spread of extremely explicit photos, claiming they were of Mary Lou. They weren't. They were clever fakes with *her* face superimposed on a porno star's body. Unfortunately, the magazine hit the stands before anyone could stop it.

When Mary Lou saw the magazine, she was so distraught that she attempted suicide. Fortunately Steven managed to rush her to the hospital in time.

Mary Lou was released a week later and Steven knew for sure that he couldn't live without her. They were married shortly after.

Marriage saved both of them. For Steven it was finding someone who cared about him above all else. And for Mary Lou it was the security and love she'd always craved.

Within a few months she was pregnant, eventually giving birth to a beautiful baby girl they named Carioca Jade. Carioca was now eight. Looks-wise she was the image of her mother. Smarts-wise she wanted to be a lawyer, exactly like Daddy.

Mary Lou was a sensational mother. In spite of a successful career she always managed to put Steven and Carioca first, making them feel like the two most important human beings on the planet.

It had been Steven's idea to move to LA when they'd returned to the States after a two-year stay in England, where he'd studied English law, played golf and generally done nothing except enjoy spending time with his wife and daughter. 'Settling in LA will make it easier for you to get back into the business,' he'd told Mary Lou. Besides, he didn't want to live in New York again, and he had the urge to spend some time with his half-sister, Lucky, and his father, Gino. It had taken him a lifetime to find out that he had a family, and when he did it was a strange, overwhelming feeling. Lucky had accepted him immediately, but it had taken Gino a while to fully realize he had fathered a black son, the result of a long-ago one-night affair with Carrie, Steven's mother.

When Steven told his friend and partner, Jerry Myerson, that he wanted to settle in LA, Jerry had been understanding as usual. He'd suggested that they open a West Coast branch of Myerson, Laker and Brandon. Steven liked the idea, so did Mary Lou.

Fortunately Steven had been proven right: re-locating to LA was great for Mary Lou's career. She started getting the movie roles she'd been missing out on while living in Europe. And after taking on two junior partners, Steven's new law firm took off. It was an excellent move for both of them.

'They're ready for you on the set, Miz Berkeley,' said a second assistant director knocking on the open door of her trailer.

'Oh, right,' Mary Lou said, jumping back to the present. 'I'm on my way.'

Chapter Five

ZIPPING ALONG the Pacific Coast Highway in her red Ferrari, vintage Marvin Gaye blasting on her CD player, Lucky felt pretty good about everything. All she hoped was that she was making the right decision. Gino seemed to think she was.

'You gotta do what you feel in your gut,' he'd told her. 'So if you feel it, do it!'

Well, she'd find out soon enough when she got everyone's reaction to her announcement – especially Lennie's.

It was too late now, but it occurred to her that maybe she *should* have told him first. The problem was that Lennie had a way of analysing things, and she didn't want him analysing her decision, she simply wanted to do it.

At the beach-house everyone was assembled in the big, comfortable kitchen overlooking the ocean. There were little Gino and Maria with their cheerful black nanny, CeeCee, and Bobby – who was so damn good-looking, a taller version of his grandfather, Gino.

'Hi, Mom,' Bobby said. 'Wait'll you see my Armani tux. You're gonna freak.'

'I'm sure,' Lucky said drily. 'Who told you you could go to Armani?'

'Grandad,' Bobby said, chewing on a carrot stick.

'Gino spoils you,' Lucky said.

'Yeah,' Bobby said, laughing. 'And don't I love it!'

Lucky had agreed that Bobby could come to the event tonight. However, she did not want little Gino and Maria coming too, they were too young. She had no intention of raising them as Hollywood kids: she'd seen enough of those brats with no manners and a Porsche at sixteen.

CeeCee, who'd been with the family since Bobby was born, was busy serving the younger children rice and beans.

'Mmm . . .' Lucky said, hovering over the table. 'That looks yummy.'

'Where's Daddy?' Maria asked. 'He promised we could jog along the beach.' Maria was a pretty child, with enormous green eyes and wispy blonde hair. She looked a lot like Lennie, while little Gino favoured Lucky in the looks department.

'Daddy's working,' Lucky explained. 'He'll jog with you this weekend. How's that?'

'I'm going to my friend's this weekend,' Maria announced. 'She's having a big, big birthday party.'

'You're deserting us for a whole weekend?' Lucky said, pulling a sad face.

'You *told* me I could go, Mama,' Maria said seriously. 'You *promised*.'

Lucky smiled. 'I know,' she said, remembering how she had been at eight. She'd had no mother to watch over her, only the gloomy walls of the Bel Air house, with Gino keeping guard. 'I'm going upstairs to get ready for tonight,' she said, 'and when I come down, I want to see all this food eaten up. *And* I want to see pyjamas on bodies, and two small people ready to give me big hugs and kisses.'

Little Gino giggled. She bent over and gave him a hug before hurrying upstairs to her bedroom, where Ned, her hair-stylist, was waiting patiently. She usually fixed her hair herself, but since tonight was such an important event, she'd decided that she'd better make a special effort.

Ned appeared quite agitated.

'What's up?' Lucky asked.

'You make me nervous,' he complained. 'You're always in such a rush.'

'Especially today,' she said, causing him to become even more agitated. 'I've got to be dressed, made up and in the limo by five thirty.'

'Okay, into the chair,' Ned said, clapping his hands together. 'How are we doing your hair?'

'Up. Something sophisticated.'

'You mean something that's completely not you?'

'Ha ha!' Lucky said. 'I can look like a grown-up for once, can't I?'

'Of course,' Ned said. 'Only do *not* nag. Nagging gives me heart palpitations.'

'You've got twenty minutes,' she said, glancing at her watch. 'I can't sit still for longer than that.'

'Oh, God,' he groaned. 'Give me a movie star any day. At least they'll stare at themselves in the mirror for hours and not utter a word.'

Ned fixed her hair in record time. She thanked him, paid him and hustled him out. As soon as he was gone, she raced into the shower, making sure to angle her head back so that she didn't ruin Ned's do. Then she quickly towelled herself dry and sprayed herself all over with Lennie's favourite scent. Next she applied her makeup, and slid into a long slinky red Valentino, with spaghetti straps, plunging neckline, and a slit to the top of her thigh. The dress was very revealing; fortunately she was slender enough to carry it off.

She stared at herself in the mirror. *I look like a real grown-up now*, she thought with a smile.

Lucky Santangelo. Little Lucky Saint, as they'd called her at school so that her real identity was never revealed, and it would not be known that she was connected to the notorious

Gino Santangelo – the Las Vegas hotel tycoon with the somewhat shady past.

Gino. Daddy. What memories they shared. Nobody could ever break the bond between them. Not one single person.

She remembered how at nineteen she had pleaded with him to let her take over the family business. But no, Gino had never entertained the idea, until finally she'd proved to him that there was no stopping her.

'Girls gotta get married and have babies.' That's what he used to say to her.

'Not *this* girl,' she'd replied, full of steely determination. 'I'm a Santangelo – just like you. I can do anything.' And in the end she'd won.

She opened her safe, removing the diamond hoop earrings Lennie had given her on her fortieth birthday. Then she added a wide diamond and emerald bracelet, a present from Gino, and she was ready to go. It was exactly five twenty.

Downstairs Bobby was showing off his new tux to his siblings.

'Why can't we come, too?' Maria complained, adorable in Snoopy pyjamas.

'Because this is not a children's event,' Lucky explained. 'It's strictly for adults.'

'Then why's Bobby going?' little Gino asked.

'Because he's taller than all of us,' Lucky said, thinking this was rather a good answer. 'Is the limo here?' she asked Bobby.

'Yeah, Mom, it just arrived.'

'Then let's go,' she said, kissing Maria and little Gino.

☆ ☆ ☆

'Honey,' Steven said, frantically rummaging through his top drawer, the phone balanced precariously against his ear, 'I can't find my bow-tie.'

'Steven,' Mary Lou said, 'how can you call me when I'm on the set? You just blew a take.' She was speaking into her cellphone, trying to edge away from her co-star, who could not believe she'd left her phone on while they were in the middle of a scene.

'Sorry, sweetheart,' Steven said, 'but this is an emergency. Lucky's gonna be here any moment.'

'Your tie is on your dresser where I put it this morning. I *told* you where it was before I left.'

'Oh, yeah, right,' he said, suddenly remembering.

'You drive me crazy, Steven,' she said crossly.

'Good crazy?'

A quiet giggle. 'Well, *of course* good crazy.'

He put on his real low-down sexy-soul-singer voice. 'Later tonight, I'll *really* getcha outta your mind.'

'Oooh, baby, baby . . .'

Now they both giggled, secure in the knowledge that they were still crazy about each other, and that the sex got better as each year of marriage passed.

'Mary Lou,' Lennie yelled from behind the camera, 'we'd like to get out of here sometime this year. Is that okay with you?'

'Sorry, Lennie,' she said guiltily. And then into the phone. 'See you soon, lover. There's somethin' special I have to tell you.'

'What?' he asked, hoping she hadn't signed for another movie without telling him, because in his mind they both needed a nice long vacation.

'You'll see,' she said provocatively, and clicked off her phone.

'Can we get back to work now?' Lennie enquired.

'You got it,' Mary Lou said, smiled her captivating smile, and nobody could stay mad at her.

Chapter Six

CRUISING AROUND getting shit-faced was not exactly what the boy had imagined they'd do. He'd kind of pictured sex in the back of his jeep, or at least a blow-job. But no: the girl – who was extremely bossy – had her own agenda.

She'd always pushed him around, ever since they were kids. It was do this, do that, and usually, because he was in awe of her, and she was two years older than he was, he obliged.

But he resented her big time.

He also lusted after her with a permanent hard-on.

He was sure that if he could have sex with her, just once, it would break the hold she had over him. Meanwhile, she kept on telling him what to do.

They drove to a supermarket, where she purchased a couple of six-packs of beer. She looked much older than her eighteen years and, besides, she knew the checkout clerk, so the dude didn't bother carding her; he was too busy staring at her tits.

In the parking lot she opened two cans of beer and thrust one at him. 'Last one to finish is a pussy,' she said, immediately lifting the can to her lips.

He was up to the challenge, conveniently forgetting his dad's words when he'd handed him the keys to the jeep: 'Now you gotta promise me, son – you will never drink and drive.'

'Yeah, Dad,' he'd said. 'You got my word on that.'

The beer was ice cold and tasted good. Not only that, but he beat her to emptying the can, a minor triumph.

'Not bad,' she said grudgingly.

'Where we goin' now?' he asked.

'Dunno,' she said.

'How about a movie?'

'Waste of time,' she said disdainfully, fiddling with one of several stud earrings attached to her left ear. 'Movies are for morons who got nothin' better t' do.' She knew he was crazy about her, and used it. 'Let's go steal something,' she suggested, as if it was the most normal thing in the world.

'Why'd we wanna do that?' he asked, pulling on his ear – a habit he had when he was nervous.

'Kind of an initiation,' she answered casually. 'If you wanna stay tight with me, you gotta do stuff that'll make me believe you're committed to our friendship.'

'Committed?' he said, wondering if committed meant an eventual blow-job.

'It's easy. All we gotta do is go by the CD store an' see how many you can score.'

'Why don't I pay?' he said logically. 'My dad picks up my credit-card bill.'

'What's the matter?' she jeered mockingly. 'Daddy's precious little boy don't wanna mess with trouble?'

'That's crap.'

'What did Daddy do?' she continued, in her mocking tone. 'Keep you locked in the house in New York? I would've thought living in the city would've given you balls.'

'I got balls,' he said, suddenly angry.

'Naw . . . you're a daddy's boy.'

'No way.' And as if to prove her wrong, he opened another can of beer and took a few hearty gulps.

'Oh,' she said. 'Mr Macho, huh?'

'You don't know anything about me really,' he said.

'I know everything about you,' she answered quickly. 'Bet you've never had sex.'

The fact that she knew he was still a virgin threw him. 'That's crap,' he said, quickly denying it.

'Good,' she said. 'I like a guy who can get it up an' keep it that way.'

He swigged more beer. Did that mean that later she'd allow him to prove it?

The first can of beer had made him more relaxed; the second one was helping with the job. 'Okay, let's do it,' he said, swallowing a burp. 'Bet I can score more CDs than you.'

'That's what I like to hear,' she said, pleased. 'Want me to drive?'

'No,' he said. 'I'm cool.'

And they set off.

Chapter Seven

THINGS WERE moving slower than Lennie had anticipated, and on top of everything else they would soon be losing light. He'd promised he would get to Lucky's event as soon as he could, but the way it was going, he and Mary Lou would definitely be late arrivals.

No good obsessing. Two more set-ups, and they could finally wrap this particular location. Especially as everyone was cooperating by working as fast as possible.

The good news was that Mary Lou was a pleasure to work with. Some actresses were divas, bitching and complaining about every little thing. Not Mary Lou. She had it down. She was pretty and talented, but above all she was nice, and the entire crew adored her.

Buddy had a major crush, which Lennie found amusing to observe, because usually Buddy was Mr Stud, a true ladies' man with a happening wardrobe and an Eddie Murphy swagger.

'She's married, you know,' Lennie remarked, strolling over to Buddy while they were setting the lights for the second to last shot.

'Hey, man, I know that,' Buddy said, hardly able to take his eyes off Mary Lou, who was sitting in her chair chatting with one of the grips. 'And I also know if she wasn't—'

'Hey, hey,' Lennie interrupted. 'She's *married* to my brother-in-law.'

'Fortunate guy,' Buddy said.

'He sure is,' Lennie answered. 'Good fortune runs in the family. My wife . . . well, what can I tell you about my wife?'

'I've seen her,' Buddy said. 'You don't have to say a word. But, let me ask you, isn't it kinda difficult being married to a woman like Lucky?'

'Why difficult?'

''Cause she's running a studio, man, making all kinds of big decisions. The woman's a real power player in Hollywood, and, uh . . .'

Lennie shook his head and laughed. 'You think my wife running a studio threatens my ego?'

'Naw, didn't mean that.'

'Oh, c'mon, that's exactly what you meant.'

'No, man,' Buddy insisted. 'All I'm thinkin' is that *I* couldn't do it.'

'Do what?'

'Be with a woman who got all the attention.'

'I *had* the attention,' Lennie said. 'When I was acting in movies the attention never stopped. Hot and cold running women. Phone numbers stuffed in my pocket. Naked pictures in the mail. Believe me, I much prefer it this way.'

'That's cool,' Buddy said.

'Right,' Lennie agreed. 'Now, keep your eyes off Mrs Berkeley an' let's get it going here.'

☆　☆　☆

Gino Santangelo was dressed and ready to go. It didn't take much preparation to get ready when you were eighty-seven years old. Christ! He looked in the mirror and saw this old, grey-haired man, and he thought, *When the fuck did this happen?*

In his mind he still felt about forty. Forty and ready for

action. Only the action wasn't so easy to come by when you were his age. There were aches and pains to contend with. A stiffness in his joints. Getting up to go to the john a thousand times a night. Growing old was a bitch, but it sure as hell beat out the alternative.

He went to the bar in his Wilshire apartment and poured himself a hefty slug of Jack Daniel's. *Two inches of Jack Daniel's a day keeps the doctor away* – that was his motto, and he was sticking to it.

He thought about Lucky, his crazy daughter – she was strong, smart, and knew all the right moves. In fact, she was him in a dress. What a girl!

He was *so* goddamn proud of her, which is why he'd flown from his home in Palm Springs to attend this special evening honouring her. His wife, Paige, had been planning on coming with him, only Paige had gotten the flu at the last minute and stayed in Palm Springs. Paige was a good woman. They'd been married several years and got along fine, even though she was over thirty years younger than he was. He liked her spirit, not to mention her sexy pocket-Venus body, which *still* turned him on. Not that he was as into sex as he once was. But at least he could still get it up on occasion – much to his doctor's amazement. 'You're eighty-seven, Gino,' his doctor had told him last week. 'When is it going to stop?'

'Never, Doc.' He'd laughed. 'That's the secret.'

Gino had never really gotten over his first wife and one true love, Maria. Her murder had shattered his life, and changed him for ever. Even now, all these years later, he still lived surrounded by high security. He often begged Lucky to do the same, but she ignored him. She didn't realize the Santangelos had enemies out there going back many years. Between them, he and Lucky had dealt with the Bonnatti family in a vendetta that had lasted several decades. Now, with the demise of Donatella Bonnatti, the last of the clan – that particular feud was over. But there were others who'd always harboured a grudge.

Gino worried about Lucky. Sure, she was independent and feisty, but she was still a woman, and no woman could ever be as strong as a man.

Not that he'd dare tell her that. Lucky would bust his chops if he ever voiced such a thought.

He grinned, downing the Jack Daniel's in one fell swoop. His daughter, Miss Balls of Fire, the original feminist. And tonight she was being honoured. Tonight she was the most important person in Hollywood. *His daughter*. It was some thrill.

The intercom buzzed and the doorman informed him there was a limo waiting downstairs.

'I'll be right there,' Gino said.

And he wished his precious Maria were alive to see this memorable day.

☆ ☆ ☆

Meanwhile, in his house on Sunset Plaza Drive, Steven found his tie, put it on, stared at himself in the mirror, decided he didn't look too bad for a guy in his fifties, and, with a smile on his face, thought about Mary Lou and their conversation.

Steven was extremely modest, having no idea that he gave handsome a whole new meaning. He was six feet three inches tall with a killer body. His skin was the colour of rich milk chocolate, his black curly hair only slightly touched with grey, and his eyes were an unfathomable deep green. Mary Lou spent hours telling him he was the most handsome man she'd ever seen. This from an actress who mixed with perfect specimens every day. 'You're just prejudiced,' he told her.

'You bet your ass I am,' she answered, with the sweetest smile in the world.

Steven figured he was a pretty lucky guy. He had a wife he adored, who adored him back; the cutest little daughter in the world, and a whole new family. Lucky was the greatest: she treated him as if they'd grown up together. 'When my brother, Dario, was murdered,' she'd told him, 'I never imagined anyone could replace him. Then *you* came along, and I'm so grateful to have you in my life, Steven.'

Gino had finally accepted him too. 'Gotta tell you,' he'd growled one day, 'never thought I'd have myself a black kid.'

'Yeah, well,' Steven had responded, 'never thought *I*'d have myself a white Italian father.'

'Guess we both got unlucky,' Gino had joked, and then he'd hugged Steven.

Sometimes the three of them went out for dinner. To Steven, those nights were the best of times, special evenings that he treasured.

He never thought about his past – the dark days when he was married to ZeeZee, a crazy, exotic dancer; or being raised by Carrie, his mother, who once worked in a whorehouse; and then there were the interminable years of never knowing who his real father was.

He had good friends too. Jerry Myerson had always come through for him, even when he was at his most miserable and a real pain in the ass.

Now he was content, he had everything he'd ever wanted and it was a satisfying feeling.

His eight-year-old daughter came into the room. She was the image of Mary Lou, with her sweet smile, light brown skin, and cascades of curly hair.

'Anyone ever told you you look *exactly* like your mom?' Steven said.

'Daddy, *you* look *sooo* handsome,' Carioca Jade said, peering up at him.

'Why, thank you.'

'You're welcome, Daddy.'

His daughter was growing up so fast. Surely it was about time they considered having another child? He'd been meaning to talk to Mary Lou about it. He wanted a son. A boy he could go to ball games with and teach many things – not that he didn't adore his daughter, she made every day worthwhile, but a son . . . Well, it was his dream.

'Where's Mommy?' Carioca Jade demanded, tilting her head on one side.

'On location, sweetheart,' he answered. 'She asked me to tell you to be a good girl and be sure and do your homework.'

Jennifer, their English au pair, appeared. 'Everything all right, Mr Berkeley?' she asked crisply, shades of Mary Poppins.

'Everything's fine, Jen,' he said. 'You've got the number of my cellphone if you need me. I guess we'll be home around midnight.'

'Don't worry about a thing, Mr Berkeley. Come along, Carrie, let's get into that homework.'

'Daddy, can't I watch TV and do my homework later?' Carioca pleaded, all big eyes and quivering lower lip.

'No way.'

'Why?'

''Cause education is everything. And don't you ever forget it.'

'O*kay*, Daddy,' Carioca said reluctantly. 'I get it.'

'I'll see you in the morning, sweetheart,' he said, giving her a hug and a kiss. Then he walked out the door just as the limo drew up in front of the house. The driver jumped out and opened the car door.

'Hey,' Steven said, ducking inside.

'Hey,' Lucky answered. And they grinned at each other.

'Evening, Steven,' Gino said.

'Hey – Gino, Bobby. Everyone's lookin' mighty good,' Steven said. 'This must be a special occasion.'

'Let's go,' Lucky said impatiently. 'This is going to be a big night, and now that I'm committed, I do not intend to miss one single moment.'

Chapter Eight

'IT'S BABE alert big time!' Lina said.

'What?' Brigette said.

'*Look* at 'im,' Lina said admiringly, staring at Fredo's cousin as they headed to their table on their way back from the ladies' room where they'd gone to touch up their makeup and discuss the situation. 'He's definitely the shit!'

Brigette took another look. True. Carlo Vittorio Vitti *was* handsome in an arrogant way: he was tall, with dark blond hair, piercing ice-blue eyes, designer stubble and a slender body. He was wearing a grey pinstriped suit and casual black silk T-shirt. She figured him to be in his early thirties.

In spite of her afternoon session with Flick, Lina was in lust at first sight. '*And* 'e's got a title,' she said, fully impressed. 'Fredo told me 'e's a count. My mum would 'ave a fit if she knew I was out with a real live count!'

Brigette wasn't really listening. She was too busy regretting eschewing pizza and *Ab Fab* for a night on the town. This was not her idea of a good time. Fredo was all over her like a particularly annoying rash, and his arrogant cousin had barely said a word. What did she need this for?

Lina was definitely after the cousin. Brigette couldn't care less: she merely wanted to go home.

'I'm gonna fuck 'im tonight!' Lina announced, licking her full, glossy lips in a predatory way. '*Oh*, yeah!'

'He's engaged,' Brigette pointed out, idly wondering to whom.

'Ha!' Lina snorted. 'Engaged means *nothing*.'

Brigette nodded as if she agreed, although actually she didn't.

'Just lookin' at 'im makes me dead horny,' Lina continued. 'Know what I mean?'

Brigette nodded again, as if she knew exactly what Lina meant when, actually, she didn't get it at all. It had been several years since she'd slept with a man. Sometimes she thought her libido had died and drifted off to heaven. Now she felt no desire at all. *Nada*. None. It was quite obvious she was a freak of nature.

Sometimes she wondered how her friendship with Lina survived. Because of their great camaraderie, she tried not to let the fact that Lina was man hungry get in the way of their friendship. The truth was that she understood exactly where Lina was coming from. Both of them had grown up with no father around, so Lina was always chasing the strong masculine image, whereas Brigette did the opposite and shied away from men altogether. They were so different, yet they had fun together and plenty of laughs, especially when they travelled around the world on their various assignments. Location shoots were the best. Brigette was especially looking forward to flying to the Bahamas where they were doing a major shoot for *Sports World International* magazine. Last year she'd been on the cover. This year she knew that Lina was after the coveted spot and she was rooting for her to get it.

Back at the table Fredo had ordered a bottle of Cristal. He was so delighted they'd agreed to have dinner with him that he hadn't stopped beaming all night. 'Well, my beauties,' he said enthusiastically, 'what club shall we visit next?'

'You choose,' Lina said, flashing a seductive smile at

Carlo, who, much to her annoyance, failed to respond. Lina was used to men falling all over her and she did not appreciate indifference.

'I want to go home,' Brigette announced, causing both Lina and Fredo to glare at her.

'It's much too early,' Lina snapped, shaking her head in an exasperated fashion. 'It's time for dancin'.' She turned to Fredo. 'I should *never* 'ave warned 'er about you.'

'What you mean?' Fredo said, bushy eyebrows shooting up. 'You warn her about *me*?'

'Yeah,' Lina said, with a wicked grin. 'I told 'er you're a real fuck-an'-run merchant. *That*'s why you've never got anywhere with 'er.'

'Thanks,' Fredo said huffily. 'Now I must show her my true personality.'

'She's seen your true personality all right,' Lina said slyly. 'An', believe me, *that*'s all she wants to see.'

While Lina and Fredo were bantering back and forth, Brigette took the polite route and leaned towards Carlo. 'Fredo told me you live in London,' she said. 'That must be interesting.'

He fixed her with his piercing blue eyes. 'You are very beautiful,' he said in a low voice – so low that neither of the other two heard.

'Excuse me?' Brigette said, taken aback.

'I think you understand me,' he said.

She glanced quickly at Lina. Her friend would not be happy if she thought Carlo was coming on to someone else. 'Well, uh . . . thanks,' she said, slightly flustered. 'It's my job to look good in front of the camera.'

'I'm not talking about your photographs,' Carlo said smoothly.

For a moment she felt uncomfortable under the scrutiny of his probing eyes. 'Well,' she said, lifting her champagne glass and making a big show of including the others, 'I'd like to propose a toast. Here's to Carlo and his fiancée. What a pity she's not here.'

Lina shot her a deadly look for mentioning that her new object of lust was engaged.

'*What* fiancée?' Carlo asked, as if he had no idea what she was talking about.

'Fredo told us you were engaged,' Lina said, shooting Fredo a look that said, Well, is he or isn't he?

'Me? I think not,' Carlo said, with a fleeting smile. 'It is over.'

'You didn't mention it was over to me,' Fredo said accusingly.

'You did not ask,' Carlo replied, freezing him out.

Lina immediately moved in, snuggling close to Carlo. 'Not engaged, huh?' she said happily. 'Nor am I. That makes us a cosy couple, don't it?'

Carlo smiled politely, but his eyes remained on Brigette.

Chapter Nine

'WHERE THE hell are they?' Lucky muttered, pulling on the sleeve of Steven's jacket so she could take a peek at his watch.

'It's only eight,' Steven said, calm as usual. 'They'll be here in time for your speech.'

'Yeah, honey,' Gino joined in. 'You gotta learn t' relax. Lookit me.'

'I guess it's easy when you're eighty-seven,' she murmured drily.

'My kid,' Gino said, with a wide smile. 'Always with the smart answers.'

'Wonder where I inherited *that* from,' she drawled.

They'd just sat down after a long cocktail hour. Bobby was hovering at the next table, desperately trying to make conversation with the perky young star of a TV sitcom as he strutted proudly in his first tux. He was certainly good-looking, with his mother's striking colouring and his deceased father's charisma. Dimitri had been a major charmer.

Lucky nudged Gino. 'Was that you at fifteen?' she asked, watching her son as he attempted to put a move on the eighteen-year-old sitcom star.

Gino checked out his grandson and roared with laughter. 'When *I* was his age,' he said, 'I was screwin' my way around the block.'

And so was I, Lucky wanted to say, but she didn't; Gino wasn't too fond of remembering his daughter in her wild days. He'd married her off at sixteen to curb her out-of-control behaviour. Big deal. She'd soon gotten out of *that* fiasco, and the moment Gino took off for Europe on an extended tax exile, she'd moved back to Vegas and taken over the family business with a vengeance.

'Is that how you got your nickname, Gino the Ram?' she asked innocently, pretending she didn't know he hated that tag from so long ago.

'I always knew how t' treat a woman,' Gino said indignantly. 'Treat a lady like a whore an' a whore like a lady. Works every time.'

'Now don't you be teaching my son sexist crap like that,' Lucky scolded sternly.

'Bullshit!' Gino spat. 'The sooner he learns, the better off he'll be. For his sixteenth birthday I'm takin' him to Vegas an' buyin' him the best-lookin' hooker in town.'

'No, you're not.'

'Yes, I am.'

'The last thing I need is my son getting your antiquated take on women.'

Gino roared with laughter. 'I never had no complaints, kiddo.'

'Shove it up your ass, Gino.'

They did not have the traditional father–daughter relationship.

Steven returned to the table. 'What are you two up to?' he asked.

'I'm listening to Gino blow wind,' Lucky said, feigning an exaggerated yawn.

'That's nice,' Steven said, shaking his head. 'When you two get together it's exactly like being back in high school.'

'I can't help it if he's stuck in a time warp,' Lucky said, laughing.

'Time warp, my ass,' Gino interjected. 'I'm tellin' you the way it is with men and women. It's about time you understood.'

'Hold that thought,' Steven said. 'Here comes Alex and his date.'

Lucky glanced up at the approaching couple. 'And what exotic little number is Alex with tonight?' she asked casually.

'What do you care?' Steven asked. 'It's you he wants.'

'Nonsense,' Lucky said, knowing that Steven, along with Venus, was absolutely correct. Alex Woods *did* have a thing about her, and she was strongly attracted to him, too, but not enough that she would ever betray Lennie – except, of course, that one time when Lennie had been gone for months and she'd thought he was dead. It was a secret she kept close to her heart, because it was better Lennie never knew. Instead of lovers, she and Alex had become best friends, a friendship they shared with Lennie, although he was not as close to Alex as she was.

Alex Woods. Writer. Director. A man who did everything his way and usually got away with it because he *was* Alex Woods, and in the great Hollywood tradition he was one of those characters who stood alone. Alex was shining brilliance in a sea of mediocrity, a true original talent like Martin Scorsese, Woody Allen and Oliver Stone.

'Lucky,' Alex said, bearing down on her. At fifty-one he was still a dangerous-looking man: darkly brooding, with compelling eyes, heavy eyebrows and a strong jawline. He was tall and fit, due to vigorous daily workouts. His hair was longish, curling just above the back of his collar, and he always wore black. Tonight he was in a black tuxedo with matching shirt and no tie. Alex enjoyed making statements.

His date was Asian. *Big surprise*, Lucky thought. The girl was petite and in her twenties. Lucky hadn't seen this one before. It was rare that any of them lasted longer than six weeks. She often joked with Alex that he had an assembly line that churned out Asian women on a regular basis.

'Hi, Alex,' she said warmly, standing up to greet him.

He let out an admiring whistle. 'Spectacular!' he said, checking out the floor-length red Valentino that skimmed her slender body, plunging at the back to reveal almost everything. 'Sometimes,' Alex said, 'I almost forget how dazzlingly beautiful you actually are.'

'Compliments,' she said, smiling. 'You must want something.'

'Oh, yeah,' he said, smiling back. 'That shouldn't surprise you.'

'Stop it, Alex,' she said sharply, not in the mood to deal with his heavy flirting, which he indulged in whenever Lennie wasn't around. 'Introduce me to your date.'

'Pia,' he said, pulling the girl forward.

'Hi, Pia,' Lucky said, checking her out.

'Hi, Lucky,' Pia said, not quite as submissive as his usual type.

Thank God! Lucky thought. Dealing with Alex's never-ending procession of girlfriends was exhausting. Recently she'd told him that she couldn't do it any more. 'Do what?' he'd asked innocently.

'Well,' she'd said, 'when the four of us go out to dinner, you and Lennie have a fine old time talking about everyone and everything, while *I*'m stuck making polite conversation with your date.'

'So?' he'd said.

'So,' she'd answered, '*you* get to fuck 'em. *I*'ve got to talk to them!'

Alex had roared with laughter.

Lucky smiled at the memory.

'Where's Lennie?' Alex asked, looking around.

'Working,' Lucky explained. 'He'll be here shortly.'

'Shame!' Alex said.

'Will you *stop*?' Lucky said.

'Never,' Alex said.

There was a sudden commotion and turning of heads as Venus Maria made her way to the table, accompanied by her extremely smart movie-star husband, Cooper Turner.

Venus was huffing and puffing, all platinum hair, luscious cleavage, and glossy lids and lips. 'Jesus!' she exclaimed, finally reaching the table. 'It took us twenty-five minutes to negotiate the press line. The things one does for friends!'

'What did they ask you?' Lucky said.

'What *didn't* they ask me?' Venus replied. 'Am I pregnant again? How's my marriage? Do I consider Madonna competition? If I was single would I date Brad Pitt? The usual crap.'

'No, I mean what did they ask you about *me*? This *is* my evening, remember?'

'I thought you hated publicity.'

'I do.'

'So I tried not to mention you – except to say that next to Sherry Lansing you're probably the smartest woman in Hollywood, and that under your amazing guidance Panther makes the best movies. Lucky Santangelo is the queen of equal sexuality, I said. How's *that* for a killer quote?'

Lucky grinned and kissed Cooper, who was his usual smooth self. Before marrying Venus he'd been the number-one playboy in Hollywood. Now he was Mr Married and revelling in it. Fatherhood suited him, and had certainly calmed him down. Chyna, their five-year-old daughter, was the pride of both their lives.

'Hi, Alex,' Venus said, kissing the director on both cheeks. 'When am I going to star in your next movie?'

It had become a joke between the two of them that since she'd been nominated for her small role in his film, *Gangsters*, he'd never asked her to work for him again.

'Dunno . . .' he said hesitantly. 'Can you play a flat-chested psycho with a penchant for cutting off men's balls?'

'My dream!' Venus squealed, her animated face lighting up. 'You won't find another actress more suited to the role!'

'Well . . .' Alex said thoughtfully. 'Would you be prepared to shoot a test?'

'Hmm . . .' she said, pretending to think about it. 'I guess it would depend on whose balls you wanted me to chop!'

Everyone laughed.

Lucky looked around. *At least I'm surrounded by friends*, she thought. *People who genuinely love me. And that's a good thing considering the announcement I'm about to make concerns all of them in one way or the other.*

She wished Lennie would hurry up and arrive. He was all she needed to make the evening complete.

Chapter Ten

FINALLY LENNIE said the magic words: 'Cut. Print. That's a wrap, everyone.'

'Thank goodness,' Mary Lou said, rushing to her trailer, unbuttoning the suit she'd worn in the scene on her way.

Terri, one of the wardrobe assistants, ran behind her. 'Can I help?' Terri asked. She was black, overweight and out of breath, but full of enthusiasm. Like everyone else on the set, she adored Mary Lou and would do anything for her.

'Yes!' Mary Lou said. 'I need to be ready, like, an hour ago!'

'You got it,' Terri said. 'I'm here to assist.'

'How's that little brother of yours?' Mary Lou asked, as they reached her trailer.

'Doin' okay, thanks,' Terri answered, marvelling that Mary Lou even remembered her confiding about her sixteen-year-old brother, who'd recently been arrested for vandalism. 'They gave him three months probation.'

'That should teach him a lesson.'

'My *mama* taught him a lesson,' Terry said, rolling her eyes. 'She paddled his ass so fine he couldn't sit down for a week!'

'Good,' Mary Lou said. 'Now he'll think twice next time he plans on getting out of line.'

'Ain't *that* the truth,' Terri said, hanging up Mary Lou's skirt after she stepped out of it.

'Y' know,' Mary Lou said, opening the small fridge where she'd hidden her heart-shaped diamond earrings and necklace – anniversary gifts from Steven, 'if you like, I can arrange for my husband to see him, give him some advice about how *not* to get into trouble.'

Terri's expression perked up. 'Really?'

'Steven's great with kids. He occasionally talks to boys at a school in Compton – helps them with career tips, that kind of thing. They think he's the greatest.'

'I bet.'

'Sometimes we have a few of them over for a barbecue. Steven knows how to motivate. He makes them *want* to get an education and do well.'

'Sounds like exactly what my little brother needs,' Terri said, carefully removing Mary Lou's shimmering white evening gown from its protective plastic covering.

'I'll arrange it,' Mary Lou said, unhooking her bra and reaching for her dress.

'You're so slim,' Terri said enviously, watching as Mary Lou navigated her way into the slinky gown.

'It's called hardly ever eating!' Mary Lou said ruefully. 'In my job you *have* to be thin. I'd much sooner be pigging out on fried chicken and grits. But I figure one of these days – way, way in the future – that's what I'll do. Right now it's important I keep my figure.'

'Look at me,' Terri said, with a helpless shrug. 'I'm eighty pounds overweight.'

'Make a goal,' Mary Lou said. 'Promise yourself you'll lose four pounds a month. Take it slow and easy, and in less than two years you'll be down to the weight you want.'

Terri laughed at the thought. 'I can't do that.'

'Yes, you can,' Mary Lou said. 'We can do anything we set our minds to.'

'Gee, I wish *that* was true,' Terri said wistfully.

'Do I look all right?' Mary Lou asked.

'Fine as silk,' Terri said, with a sigh, zipping the back of her dress.

'Thanks,' Mary Lou said, quickly applying a thin coat of lip-gloss. 'Now, I promise I won't forget about your brother. I'll talk to Steven tonight.'

'You're the best,' Terri said.

'No, I'm not,' Mary Lou said. 'It's just that I understand when someone needs guidance. One day I'll tell you how Steven and I first met. Boy! Did I need guidance then! Actually, it's quite a story.'

'Tell me now,' Terri pleaded.

'No time now,' Mary Lou said, laughing. 'Sit with me at lunch tomorrow and I'll reveal everything. Oh, yes, and tomorrow you're starting your diet – right?'

'If you say so.'

There was a knock on the trailer door, followed by Lennie calling out, 'You ready?'

'Just about,' she said, quickly putting on her spike-heeled silver shoes as Terri opened the trailer door.

'Let's get going,' Lennie said. 'If I don't make it in time for her speech, Lucky will kill me.' He took her arm and helped her down the steps.

''Bye, Terri,' Mary Lou said, waving.

'Don't *you* look something?' Lennie remarked, as they made their way to his car.

'Like my dress?' Mary Lou asked, doing a little twirl for him.

'Love it,' he said. 'But you'd better prepare yourself – Steven'll have a heart-attack when he sees you. He's too old to have a wife who looks like you.'

'Great!' Mary Lou said. 'Don't tell *him* that, he's already experiencing a mid-life crisis.'

'Steven is?'

'He thinks he's getting fat and boring.'

'C'*mon*. Mr Handsome?'

Mary Lou giggled. 'I told him he can turn into the fattest, most boring man in the world, and I'll *still* love him.'

'What a woman!'

'He's the best.'

'So are you.'

'Thank you, Lennie. I appreciate that.'

'Hey,' Lennie said, as they trekked down the street. 'I'm afraid it didn't occur to me to hire a limo for tonight. I prefer driving myself. But what with you looking so outrageous, I realize I should've gotten us a car.'

'Don't be silly,' Mary Lou said. 'I'm happy as long as we get there. And the sooner the better.' She smiled softly. 'Y' know, it's so funny: Steven and I have been married almost nine years, yet when I'm away from him, I *still* miss him. Even if it's only for a day.'

'I know what you mean,' Lennie said. 'Sometimes I look around at all the miserable marriages in this town – people playing musical beds and getting divorced – and I think how happy I am with Lucky. She's my everything. Yes, I'm into working, but coming home to her at the end of the day makes it all worthwhile.'

'That's how I feel,' Mary Lou said, wide-eyed. 'We're exactly alike.'

'Yeah, except you're a *little* bit younger than me,' Lennie said.

'Just a tiny bit,' she said, smiling.

Buddy caught up with them on their way to Lennie's car. 'Baby, you look *hot*!' he said to Mary Lou, checking her out admiringly.

'Why, thank you, Buddy,' she said, well aware of his respectful crush. 'Coming from you that's a real compliment.'

'What's *that* mean, coming from me?' Buddy said, putting on the charm big time.

'Well,' Mary Lou said, 'everyone *knows* you're the campus superstud.'

'Yeah?' he said, preening. 'I got myself a reputation, have I?'

'Let me see, Buddy,' she said, pretending to think about it. 'Since we've been making this movie I've observed at least *three* different girls visiting you on the set.'

'My sisters,' Buddy said, grinning.

She grinned back. 'Your sisters, my ass!'

'And a fine ass it is, too, if I may say so.'

'C'*mon*,' Lennie said, opening the passenger door of his Porsche and hustling Mary Lou inside. 'You two can flirt tomorrow. Right now we gotta get going.'

She settled into the front seat, fastened her seatbelt, and gave a little wave to Buddy who hovered by the car.

'Does your husband know how lucky he is?' Buddy said as Lennie ran around and started the car.

'I hope so,' she said, blowing him a kiss.

'Baby,' Buddy sighed, 'if you *ever* decide you want bigger and better, I am *waiting*!'

'There's no such thing as bigger and better than my Steven,' Mary Lou said. 'Sorry to disappoint you.'

'Oh, baby, baby,' Buddy said, shaking his head. '*You* are something else.'

The Porsche took off. Mary Lou closed the window and grinned. 'I hope he makes me look good on screen.'

'Buddy's the best,' Lennie said. 'And, considering he has a thing about you, *you* will look sensational.'

'It's so much fun to be making a movie with you, Lennie,'

she said. 'I never imagined we'd work together, and now it's even better than I thought it would be.'

'Hey – you're a pleasure to work with.'

'Coming from you that's a big compliment.'

'I'm bummed we had to run so late tonight,' Lennie said, adjusting his rear-view mirror. 'D'you think Lucky will be pissed?'

'Lucky *never* gets pissed at you.'

'Oh, yeah?' he said, knowing his wife. 'It's almost eight thirty. By the time we get there it'll be past nine. Trust me, *tonight* she will be pissed.'

Chapter Eleven

THE BOY threw himself into the jeep, adrenalin coursing through his veins, vision blurred. The girl wasn't far behind, giggling insanely.

'How many didja get?' she asked, falling into the passenger seat.

'Four,' he said, heart pumping wildly.

'Chicken,' she said. 'I got six. We'd better get outta here before they send a guard after us.'

The boy didn't need to be told twice. He started the jeep and they roared out of the parking lot, practically colliding with a blue Toyota driven by an elderly man who shook his fist at them.

The girl reached for a beer, cracked one open and handed it to him. He was already drunk, but who cared? He felt like he could do anything. He wasn't stuck in the house, he was out and free. Freedom was a good thing. Freedom ruled!

The girl knew how to enjoy herself, she always had. When they'd been small and growing up together she'd always taken the initiative, shown him the way to go. Sometimes she'd even stood up for him.

'Let's see what you got,' the girl said, fumbling in his pockets.

'Didn't know I was supposed to choose. Grabbed anything I could.'

'Crap,' the girl said, disgusted. 'You're supposed to get stuff we want.' She pulled a CD out of his pocket. 'Celine Dion!' she exclaimed. 'Who listens to her?'

'I told you,' the boy said, embarrassed. 'Wasn't looking.'

'Dunce!' the girl said, reaching under her sweater and pulling out a CD of Ice T. 'Put this on.'

He slipped the disc into the player, and throbbing loud rap filled the jeep.

The girl began moving her body to the beat, then she reached in her pocket for a cigarette, lit up, took a drag and handed it to him.

'Don't smoke,' he mumbled.

'You're such a wuss,' she muttered. 'New York sure didn't wise you up.'

'I smoked grass there,' he boasted.

'Ooooh!' she said mockingly. 'What a *bad motherfucker* you are. How about coke – you ever done that?'

He shook his head. His dad was against drugs, having once been a major user of anything he could get his hands on.

'Wanna try?' she suggested. 'I got some, y'know.'

'Where'd you score coke?' he asked.

'Don't you worry 'bout that,' she said, with a sly smile. 'I can score anything I want. I got friends in all the wrong places.'

Chapter Twelve

'WHERE'S THAT husband of yours?' Gino asked.

'I wish I knew,' Lucky replied, tight-lipped as she wondered the same thing herself.

'Has he left the location yet?' Venus asked, leaning into their conversation.

'Yes,' Lucky said. 'I called the production trailer. He and Mary Lou took off ten minutes ago.'

'Where were they shooting?'

'Downtown. It'll take them at least half an hour to get here.'

'Not the way Lennie drives,' Steven interjected. 'I hope Mary Lou remembers to buckle her seatbelt.'

'Are you accusing Lennie of being a bad driver?' Lucky sniffed.

'He's a road warrior,' Steven said, sounding amused. 'Thinks he's the only one out there.'

'He's a defensive driver,' Lucky explained, 'and certainly better than you, Steven. *You* drive like an old lady, huddled over the wheel like it's gonna jump up and bite your ass!'

'*Whaaat?*'

'Seriously,' Lucky said. 'What shall I do? My speech is already half an hour late, but I refuse to give it without Lennie being here.'

'Why?' Steven asked.

'Because I can't, that's why.'

'He must've heard it? Didn't you rehearse?'

'No. It's a surprise. Okay?'

'Well, maybe you could read it to him later. Y' know, like when you're in bed.'

'Brilliant bad idea,' she drawled sarcastically.

'Don't get uptight. Go tell the organizers to delay it.'

'They're already on my case. My speech was supposed to be *before* dinner. After dinner there's entertainment.'

'Why don't you tell 'em to serve dinner, and by the time it's finished Lennie will be here and you can make your speech.'

'Oh, great!' Lucky said. 'When everyone's stuffed and complacent, *I* get up.'

'Hey, listen, it's your problem, not mine. If I were you, I'd give it now.'

'No, Steven. I'm going to wait, okay?'

'Whatever you want.'

Right, she thought. *The story of my life. I've always done whatever I want.*

She was mad at Lennie. Oh, sure, he was shooting a movie, but he *was* the director, so if he'd planned it right he could've wrapped early.

She got up and went to talk to the organizers, stopping at several tables along the way, greeting friends and acquaintances in the movie business. Oh, yes, they were all nice to her now because she owned and ran a movie studio. But when she wasn't in the movie business, would it be true what they said? That in Hollywood, if you didn't have a hit, people crossed the street to avoid you?

Maybe, maybe not. She couldn't care less, because she'd always walked her own road. Lucky was not conventional in any way. Perhaps that was why she and Venus were such good friends.

The organizers threw a fit when she told them her plan. She stood firm. They finally agreed. Since she was the star of the evening they had no choice.

Alex joined her as she made her way back to their table. 'Husband running late, huh?' he said, taking her arm in a proprietary fashion.

'Hey – nobody knows better than you what it's like when you're in production,' she said coolly.

'True,' he said. 'But if it was *me*, and I knew it was your evening, I would've wrapped early.'

Alex was voicing her thoughts, and it aggravated her. He had an uncanny way of tuning into what she was thinking. 'How's your mother?' she asked, knowing exactly how to set his teeth on edge. Alex had an extremely domineering mother, the French-born Dominique, who up until the last few years had ruled his life with an iron fist, or at least tried to.

'Fine,' he said noncommittally.

'Still interfering in your life?' Lucky asked.

'You've got it wrong,' Alex said calmly. 'She gave that up a while ago.'

'Hmm . . .' Lucky said disbelievingly. 'One of these days you'll admit it. You know you're always trying to please her.'

'I hardly ever see her any more,' he said.

'Have it your way,' she said. 'I've no desire to get into your personal business. And perhaps you'll do me the same favour.'

'I *like* Lennie,' he objected. 'Just because he's acting like a rude jerk tonight, I don't hold it against him.'

'He's *not* acting like a jerk,' Lucky countered, furious at his criticism. 'He'll be here any moment.'

'Okay, okay. In the meantime allow me to escort you back to the table so you don't have to stop and talk to every asshole who grabs you.'

'Thanks, Alex. I'm sure this will make the gossip columns very happy.'

'What do you mean?'

'Lucky Santangelo Golden being escorted across the ball-room by bad-boy director Alex Woods.'

Alex laughed. 'Big fucking deal.'

'Where's Pia?' Lucky enquired. 'And where exactly did you come up with this one?'

'You seem to be under the impression that I only date bimbos and actresses,' Alex said. 'Well, let me tell you, this one's a very capable lawyer.'

'She is?' Lucky said, trying to keep the amusement out of her voice.

'What's the matter with you?' Alex said irritably. 'Don't you think an attractive woman can function as a lawyer?'

'Sure I do. And if this one's so smart, maybe she'll last longer than five minutes.'

'You can be such a bitch.'

'I can be a good friend, too. Never forget that, Alex.'

'There *is* something I'll never forget.'

'What?' she said, before she could stop herself.

'Remember that one special night long ago and far away?'

'No, Alex, I do not remember it. We both promised we would forget it ever happened. And if you *ever* tell Lennie, I will personally slice your balls off with a blunt knife. Do you get the picture?'

'Yes, ma'am,' he said, thinking that only Lucky could come up with such a descriptive phrase.

'It's *not* funny,' she said sternly. 'I am quite serious, so quit with the shit-eating grin and let's go back to the table where I'll try to be nice to Mia or Pia, or whatever her name is.'

'If I didn't know you better,' Alex said, fixing her with a quizzical look, 'I'd think you were jealous of all my girl-friends.'

'I told you the problem, Alex. *I*'ve got to talk to them; *you* get to fuck 'em.'

'Hey,' he said, straight-faced. 'You think it's *fun* for me? One blow-job and they expect me to return the compliment.'

She shook her head. 'You're absolutely incorrigible.'

'Thanks,' he said, with a big crocodile grin. 'I love it when you talk dirty!'

Chapter Thirteen

THE WHITE *girl took the black boy into a restroom at a gas station. She locked the door and laid out the white powder next to the basin, then she snorted it with a rolled dollar bill, carefully showing him how to do the same.*

'I'm not gonna get sick, am I?' he asked, feeling like a dumb ass. 'Or maybe it'll turn me into an addict?'

'You're really whacked,' she said, running a hand through her short dark hair. 'Snort the coke for fuck's sake and shut up.'

He was drunk enough to do as she said. Drunk and horny. Tonight he was definitely getting lucky. After all, he'd done everything she'd told him to do – stolen the CDs, driven around with her in the jeep, played music and had a blast. Obviously she wanted to be with him. Why else would they be spending all this time together?

The coke tickled his nose. He began to sneeze.

'For Chrissakes, don't sneeze in this direction,' she said irritably. 'You'll blow it away.'

'Where'd you get it anyway?'

'Why do you keep on asking me that? I've got my suppliers.'

'You do this often?'

'Don't you worry about it,' she said secretively. 'I do what I do.'

After a few minutes he began to feel pretty damn good. Maybe it was because he was drunk, but the coke must be helping too, because as each moment passed he felt better and better. Shit! He could do anything. Anything she asked him to. He could jump off a fucking mountain if that's what was gonna get him laid.

Why did he have this fixation on her?

Because she'd always been there. Always in his face. Always challenging him. And when his dad was doing drugs and sliding into one of his manic rages, she'd been there to rescue him.

They left the restroom and got back into the jeep. 'I'll drive,' she said, shoving him over. 'You're too wasted.'

'No, I'm not,' he argued.

'Yes, you are,' she said, getting behind the wheel as he slumped back into the passenger seat. 'You're fuckin' out of it.'

Maybe she was right. Everything was rolling around in circles in front of his eyes. It was like being on a high-speed rollercoaster ride.

Zoomin' up.

Zoomin' down.

Zoomin' in a big wide old circle.

Shit! He didn't care about anything at all. He was one happy guy.

Chapter Fourteen

'YOU KNOW what's nice?' Mary Lou said, gently touching Lennie's arm.

'No, what's nice?' Lennie said, staring straight ahead as he drove the Porsche fast, anxious to get to Lucky's event as soon as possible.

'The fact that you and I are brother-in-law and sister-in-law. Family.'

'Yep,' Lennie agreed. 'That *is* nice.'

'And the other thing,' Mary Lou continued, 'is Carioca and Maria being cousins and all, *and* the same age. The two of them are so cute together. Have you ever watched them? They play Barbie dolls for hours on end. And the thing I like about it is that Carioca is so politically correct. She's got the black Barbie, Maria's got the white Barbie, and they kind of share the Ken doll. It's so adorable. I love it that they're so close.'

'I know,' Lennie said. 'The thing I love is that they're growing up with no prejudices at all, because they understand that whatever colour your skin is, everyone's the same.'

'*Very* profound, Lennie.'

'Y' know,' he said thoughtfully, 'my mom was a total racist – only she didn't know it. She'd make all these rude comments when I was a kid, and I never really understood what she meant until I got smart enough to realize. Course, I never blamed her, she didn't know any better.'

'Your mother lives in Florida now, huh?'

'*Finally* she moved out of California. She met a ninety-year-old retired gangster who took her to Miami. I see her once a year when she comes out here to spend Christmas with the kids.'

'Is that an ordeal?' Mary Lou asked.

'Not really,' Lennie said. 'Alice has mellowed as she's gotten older. Years ago she used to be something else. My dad was a comedian in Vegas and Mom was a stripper – Alice the Swizzle. We were quite a family!'

'Wow!' Mary Lou exclaimed. 'Your mom was a stripper. Didn't that give you hang-ups with women?'

'Not really. I guess it could've, though. Never thought about it.'

'I love how you and Lucky first met,' Mary Lou said, sighing. 'It's *so* romantic, what with you both being married to other people and all.'

'Well, you know the story. Things worked themselves out. *She* left her husband and I split up with my wife. Then Lucky and I got together, and neither of us has ever looked back.'

'You're a great couple,' Mary Lou pronounced.

'Same goes for you and Steven.'

Mary Lou grinned, totally happy. 'I know.'

Chapter Fifteen

INSTEAD OF leaving as she wanted to, Brigette allowed Lina to talk her into making a round of the clubs. Lina insisted, although Brigette would have been much happier at home, in bed, watching TV.

Fredo continued to pay her plenty of attention, but she tuned him out. She was too busy thinking about the men in her life and how dangerous they'd all turned out to be. Sometimes, when she was alone, her thoughts drifted to Tim Wealth and how he'd lost his life because of her. His gaunt face haunted her. Oh, sure, he'd taken advantage of her youth and treated her badly, but he hadn't deserved to die for it.

Tim Wealth was her recurring nightmare.

Lina kept on pleading with Carlo to dance with her. 'I do not dance,' he said politely, dismissing her with an elegant wave of his hand.

'Then I guess I'll 'ave to make do with you, Fredo,' Lina said, jumping up, her long lean body already moving to the beat. 'Let's go show 'em how it's done,' she said, dragging him on to the crowded dance floor.

Brigette stared straight ahead, her mind still on Tim.

'What are you thinking?' Carlo asked, sliding along the banquette, getting uncomfortably close.

She noticed that he had hardly any accent at all, and she

wondered where he'd learned English. Lina was right, he *was* a babe, only she was totally uninterested.

'Oh . . . stuff,' she replied vaguely, sipping more champagne because he made her nervous.

'You are different from other girls,' he remarked.

'What "other girls" did you have in mind?' she asked flippantly.

'Every time I come to New York, Fredo attempts to impress me with his model friends. They are usually quite stupid. Beautiful but dumb.'

'Now that's a myth,' Brigette said, annoyed that he would lump every model into the same category. 'All models are *not* dumb.'

'I can see that now,' Carlo said, his probing ice blue eyes making her more and more uncomfortable.

She took another gulp of champagne. 'Uh . . . I'm quite tired,' she said. 'Would you mind if I took a cab home?'

'It's still early,' Carlo pointed out. 'Besides, I cannot allow you to go home alone. A gentleman would never do that.'

'Nobody minds,' she said, feeling suddenly hot and flustered.

'*I* do,' he said, putting his hand on her arm.

His touch made her even more nervous. She edged away. 'Y' know,' she said, struggling to stay sober, 'Lina really likes you.'

'I like her too,' he answered mildly. 'That doesn't mean I have to be with her, does it?'

And then his eyes were all over her again, and she didn't know what to do. For the first time in a long while she felt a slight flicker of something. Was it attraction? Fear? Too much champagne? She wasn't quite sure.

She stood up from the table, swaying slightly because she was not used to drinking so much. 'I absolutely have to go,' she said, feeling dizzy and lightheaded. 'Please say good night to everyone for me.'

He stood also. He was much taller than she, and he had extremely broad shoulders. He smelt of some masculine scent that she found quite intoxicating.

'I will escort you home and come back,' he said.

'I told you, it's not necessary,' she said, panicking slightly as the room began to spin.

'I will be most insulted if you don't allow me to do this.'

Who cares? she wanted to scream. *Who cares if I insult you?*

'Come,' he said, taking her arm. 'I will have the maître d' inform our friends that I shall return shortly.'

What could she do? Lina and Fredo were on the dance floor, lost in a sea of gyrating bodies. And she knew if she didn't get out of there fast she might faint.

'Okay,' she said at last, knowing she should have said no, absolutely not, but somehow or other, Carlo had managed to penetrate her defences.

They got into a cab outside the club and rode in silence to her apartment. She closed her eyes and almost fell asleep. When they arrived she leaned across the seat and attempted to shake his hand. 'Thanks for bringing me home. Good night.'

'An Italian gentleman would *never* allow a lady to go up to her apartment alone,' he said. 'I will escort you to your door.'

'No, please,' she protested, getting out of the cab. 'I'm perfectly safe.'

But he was already right behind her.

They walked into the building together, past the night porter, into the elevator and up to her apartment. She fumbled in her purse for her key, found it, and couldn't fit it in the lock.

Very gently he removed the key from her trembling hands

and inserted it himself. Before she knew it he was in the apartment with her.

Why are my hands shaking? she thought, furious with herself. *Why am I allowing him to cross the line?*

She hit a light switch. Her apartment was all pale beige and marble, with huge Moroccan pillows scattered across the floor, oversized coffee tables, Tiffany lamps and real art on the walls.

'You have a most interesting style, Brigette,' he said. 'May I fix us a drink?'

'I'm sorry,' she said quickly, feeling even more disoriented and dizzy. 'I can't let you stay. Lina's waiting for you, so's Fredo. You've got to get back to the club.'

And she turned away.

Her mistake. He grabbed her from behind, surprising her completely, turning her towards him, crushing his mouth down on hers so hard that she could barely breathe.

She struggled to get free, but as she did so a strange thing happened – her body reacted in such a way that she found herself unable to resist. It was almost as if she were powerless.

'Why are you doing this?' she managed.

'Because we both want me to,' he said, and immediately began kissing her again.

This was crazy. She'd held out all this time, and now suddenly here was this stranger, this Italian who lived in London, and he was kissing her, and she was incapable of fighting him off.

Too much Cristal. No more drinking for you, young lady.

'Carlo, you've got to go,' she said, finally summoning the strength to push him away.

'Why?' he said calmly. 'Are you married?'

'No, of course not.'

'Engaged?'

'No.'

'Do you have a boyfriend?'

'I don't.'

'Then what is stopping us? Are you a lesbian?'

'That's ridiculous . . .'

He thrust his strong hands into her long blonde hair and concentrated on her mouth.

She tried to pull back, but her body wouldn't let her. Besides, everything was spinning again . . .

'Brigette,' he murmured, between deep, soulful kisses. 'Ah, my sweet, adorable Brigette . . .'

Chapter Sixteen

IT WAS past nine and dinner was finished.

'You've got to make your speech without Lennie here,' Steven urged. 'It's getting too late to wait any longer.'

'Where *are* they?' Lucky demanded, impatiently drumming her fingers on the table. 'They left the location an hour ago. It doesn't take *that* long at this time of night.'

'I don't know, Lucky, but you *have* to make your speech. You can't do it after the entertainment – half the people will have left by that time.'

'All right, Steven, don't nag,' she said irritably, signalling one of the organizers. 'I'm ready,' she said briskly. 'Let's get going.'

'Good,' said the man, relieved. 'I'll see if I can find Mr Dollar. He's making the introduction.'

'Charlie Dollar is introducing me?' she said, unable to conceal her amusement. 'Whose brilliant idea was *that*?'

'It was supposed to be a surprise, but uh . . . due to the delay we had to keep him in the back. I hope he's still here.'

'You mean you left old Charlie alone with a bottle of Scotch. *That* was daring!'

'If you'll wait a few moments I'll try to locate him.'

Charlie Dollar was one of Lucky's favourite people. He was a fifty-something movie star with stoned eyes, and an off-the-wall, irreverent attitude. Women loved him in spite of his generous gut, slightly receding hairline and penchant for eighteen-year-old beauty queens. He'd won an Oscar for his last movie, and kept it propped against the door of his guest toilet. Typical Charlie.

When they found him he was stoned and drunk – nothing unusual for Charlie. He swayed his way on to the podium with his usual shit-eating grin, trademark tinted shades, and a glass of Scotch in one hand, which nobody had managed to extract. He immediately began speaking.

Lucky listened with a smile as he extolled her virtues, ending up with, 'An' now . . . I wanna introduce you to one of the greatest broads in this town. She's a friend. She's a beauty. An' I love her. May I present – Lucky Santangelo.'

The audience responded to his introduction with enthusiasm, leaping to their feet and applauding heartily. Charlie was a popular number.

Lucky took a deep breath as she made her way up to the podium. She'd learned her speech, doing away with any prompters. The only disappointment was that Lennie wasn't there to hear it.

The audience were quiet as she reached the microphone, patiently waiting to hear what she had to say. She took another deep breath and started off slowly, telling them how delighted she was to be there and how satisfying it was to have helped raise so much money for Aids awareness and research. Then she related a story about two very young brothers she'd met who both had the AIDS virus, inherited from their mother who'd been infected by a blood transfusion. The two boys had convinced Lucky to become involved. 'Mark and Matthew are no longer with us,' she said quietly, 'but I do know they'd be happy to see the progress being made to find a cure.' The audience applauded. 'On a personal note,' Lucky continued, 'I have decided, after a great deal of thought, to step down as head of Panther Studios.'

This was a bombshell. The audience gasped.

'Many movies and a lot of fun later, I feel the time has come to move on and explore other things. And while I'll miss the non-stop action in Hollywood, I've decided to concentrate on my husband and family. Oh, yes, and maybe write a book about all of you.' Another gasp from the audience. 'Seriously,' Lucky continued, 'if I *do* decide I'm capable of writing a book, it'll be dedicated to women and how to make it in what is still mainly a man's world. I feel if *I* did it, anyone can. So . . . I guess there's nothing else to say except keep up the good work for AIDS research. Good night and thank you. I leave you with good thoughts and may the best studio win.'

Charlie was waiting to escort her off the podium. 'You're freakin' unbelievable!' he muttered.

'I am?'

'Walkin' away from a studio when you're kickin' prime ass.'

'I'm bored.'

'Bored?'

'Movie stars are boring.'

He raised an incredulous eyebrow. 'You talkin' to me?'

'No. You, Venus and Cooper are the only exceptions.'

'*Sheeit!*'

'What?'

'You're crazier than me. An' that ain't easy.'

Then the press were coming at her, cameras and tape recorders on red alert; a babble of voices and questions.

She was cool and polite. 'I've said all that I'm going to say,' she murmured, moving forward, somehow making it back to her table where everyone wanted an explanation.

'Why?' Venus demanded.

'When?' Cooper questioned.

'Mom,' Bobby complained, thinking of all the benefits he'd miss out on, 'your decision sucks.'

'Thanks, Bobby,' she said evenly, 'but here's the thing of it, it's *my* decision, not yours.'

'Congratulations, kiddo,' Gino said, beaming. 'You make an old man proud.'

'Is Lennie here?' she asked anxiously.

'Not yet.'

'Then I guess he doesn't know,' she said, disappointed that he still hadn't shown up. She hoped nobody would tell him on his way in – that would really go down well.

Now she was regretting that she hadn't discussed it with him first because, knowing Lennie, if he heard it elsewhere, he'd be pissed – maybe even hurt.

She'd been thinking about doing it for months. Being the head of a studio took up too much time and energy. There were always decisions to be made, producers and agents on her case trying to sell her this movie, that star. Problems with back-end, development, giant egos, distribution. Since she'd taken over at Panther she'd turned the studio around, which is exactly what she'd planned on doing. She'd made several movies she was extremely proud of, movies that portrayed women as strong, independent, sexually equal beings who could achieve anything they set their minds to. And in this day of ageism and sexism, that was quite something.

Now all she wanted to do was nothing for a while.

Maybe she *would* write a book, it could be a challenge, and she *always* had relished challenges.

Perhaps Lennie would help her.

No. Bad idea. She didn't need any help.

She glanced across the table to see how Alex was taking the news. He appeared to be deep in conversation with Pia, which Lucky knew meant he was ignoring her on purpose, probably because he was pissed she hadn't confided in him.

Jeez! How many people did she have to check in with before she made a move?

She slid into her seat beside Gino, just as the David Foster-produced show commenced. The MC was the adorable and very funny Howie Mandel, who was set to introduce talented singer and producer, Baby Face, the scintillating Natalie Cole, and finally Price Washington, the superstar comedian. Quite a line-up.

Lucky settled back to enjoy the entertainment.

Chapter Seventeen

FUCK, SHE drove fast! The boy had a strong urge to throw up, his stomach couldn't take it. But he managed to control the feeling, because barfing all over her would not be a cool move, and tonight he was determined to make her realize he was cool – in spite of all her criticisms.

He'd been away in New York for eighteen months, back for ten days, and this was the first time she'd taken any notice of him. Bitch! But he'd get her attention tonight. Oh, yeah! He'd get her attention big time.

'Where we goin' now?' he asked.

'Cruisin',' she replied vaguely. 'Lookin' for an opportunity.'

'An opportunity for what?'

'For whatever comes along, jerk,' she said, throwing him a disdainful look.

He had no clue what she was talking about. But who cared? This was good. He was with her. He'd forgotten all about his controlling father, who was more than likely pissed that he hadn't turned up for their early dinner. So what? He didn't have to do anything he didn't want to. And that included graduating high school and going on to college. His dad had never attended college, so why did he have to? His plan was to get out and enjoy himself, not be stuck in some boring classroom learning useless crap for several more years.

The girl raced the jeep towards a yellow light, trying to make *it. Too late. The light turned red and she pulled up with a sharp jerk.*

It occurred to him that maybe he should fasten his seatbelt. But no, she'd think he was stupid if he did that. Stupid and afraid.

'I gotta take a piss,' he mumbled, feeling the urge.

'What?' she said.

'Gotta go t' the john.'

'Jesus H,' the girl said excitedly. 'Take a look at the diamonds on that bitch in the car next to us.'

Now he knew for sure he had to take a leak immediately. There was no waiting.

'Take a look,' the girl repeated, speaking low and fast.

He leaned across her, peering into the neighbouring car. He saw a pretty black woman sitting in the passenger seat of a silver Porsche. She had on a low-cut dress, diamond necklace and sparkling earrings.

'So?' he said.

'So,' the girl said, looking around and observing they were the only two vehicles on the street. 'We're gonna take 'em.'

'Take 'em where?' he asked blankly.

'You're so fucking stupid,' she spat in disgust. 'We're gonna take her necklace and earrings an' make ourselves big bucks.'

'No way,' he scoffed, sure she was joking.

'Wanna get your dick sucked?' she said.

His eyes bugged. 'Huh?'

'You heard. 'Cause if you're chicken, I ain't doin' it.'

Jesus! She was serious. 'Sure,' he said quickly, before she changed her mind.

'Then all you gotta do is wave the gun at them, an' order the bitch to give you her stuff.'

'You're crazy,' he said, swallowing hard. 'I can't do that.'

'Okay, okay, we'll both *do it,' she said. 'There's no one*

around, we're alone on the street. C'mon, asshole, if we don't act now we won't get another opportunity.'

He couldn't think straight. His mind was totally fogged out and he wanted to pee more than anything else. But, still, the fact that she'd offered to suck his dick . . .

Suddenly the girl hit the accelerator, swerving the jeep in front of the stationary Porsche, blocking it. 'Move!' she yelled, opening the door. 'Gimme the fucking gun.'

Blindly he groped for the gun stuck in his belt, and thrust it at her. She jumped out of the jeep and ran around to the passenger side of the Porsche, waving the gun in the air. He trailed behind her.

Chapter Eighteen

'OH, SWEET Jesus!' Mary Lou exclaimed. 'Lennie – look!'

He didn't have to look, he'd already seen. And before he could take any kind of action, a skinny girl with cropped dark hair had pulled open Mary Lou's door and was brandishing a gun in her face. Behind her hovered a black teenage boy who seemed to be having trouble keeping his balance.

'Gimme your fuckin' necklace!' shrieked the girl at Mary Lou. 'An' your earrings and rings. Give 'em to me *now*, bitch – or I'll blow your fuckin' head off!'

Jesus! Lennie could not believe this was happening to them. 'Hand her your jewellery,' he said to Mary Lou, speaking in a reasonable, calm voice, desperately trying to figure a way out.

'No!' Mary Lou said stubbornly. 'Steven gave me these things. I'm not giving them to her.'

'Take off the fuckin' jewellery, bitch!' the girl yelled.

'You don't want to do this,' Mary Lou said, exhibiting great bravery in the face of a dangerous situation.

The boy, stationed behind the girl, didn't move.

Lennie's mind was racing. He kept a gun in the glove compartment of his car, but there was no way he could reach across Mary Lou and grab it. The best thing to do was simply comply with their wishes.

The girl waving the gun was flushed and edgy. 'You'd

better do it, cunt,' she said, in a low, angry voice. ''Cause I'm gettin' impatient.'

'For God's sake, give it to her *now*,' Lennie urged Mary Lou.

Reluctantly Mary Lou reached up, attempting to unclasp her necklace. Her hands were shaking so much that she couldn't quite get it undone.

In the distance, Lennie heard the sound of a police siren.

The girl heard it too, which started to freak her out. 'Gimme the fucking shit!' she shouted excitedly, reaching over, grasping Mary Lou's necklace and yanking it off her neck. The boy standing behind her still hadn't moved. 'Take it, asshole!' the girl screamed, thrusting the necklace at him. He stuffed it in his pocket.

'Now the earrings,' the girl snarled, as the sound of the police siren grew nearer.

'No,' Mary Lou said. 'You've got my necklace. Take it and go.'

'You dumb bitch!' the girl shrieked, whacking Mary Lou across the face with her gun.

That was it for Lennie. He threw himself across Mary Lou, grappling to reach his own gun stashed in the glove compartment.

The girl saw what he was trying to do and completely lost it. 'Fuck you!' she bellowed. 'Fuck all of you!' And with that she raised her gun, took a step away and fired, hitting Mary Lou in the chest.

The explosion was so loud that the boy jumped back a couple of paces and pissed himself.

Lennie was in shock. It was like he was caught in the middle of a slow-motion nightmare. All he could think of was that at any moment he'd open his eyes and it would all be a bad dream.

But he saw Mary Lou's blood soaking the front of her

gown, and he knew with a feeling of dread that this was no dream, this was the real thing.

'You've shot her,' the boy cried out in a panic. 'You've fucking shot her.'

'*We*'ve shot her,' the girl yelled back. 'An' the dumb cunt deserved it.' Then she reached forward, snatching the earrings from Mary Lou's ears and began going for her rings.

Lennie roared into action, struggling to grab the girl and stop her. Cold-bloodedly she fired again, the bullet catching him in the shoulder.

He fell back, groaning with a sudden onslaught of sharp pain.

'Let's get outta here,' yelled the girl, and the two of them began running back to the jeep.

Somehow or other Lennie managed to hoist himself up, frantically trying to catch a glimpse of their licence plate.

The numbers danced before his eyes. Then he slumped back in his seat and passed out.

Chapter Nineteen

BRIGETTE STIRRED, almost awake, but not quite. She'd been dreaming – vivid sensual dreams about love and passion. She rolled over and opened her eyes with a start. The room was dark. Reaching for her bedside clock, she pressed the top button to illuminate the time. It was just before one a.m.

She tried to collect her thoughts because the last few hours were a complete blur. Dinner with Lina, Fredo and his cousin. A club or two, and after that – nothing.

Hmm . . . she thought. *Aren't I a bit young for short-term memory loss?*

She stepped out of bed and padded into the kitchen to get a glass of water, suddenly realizing she was completely naked.

She *never* slept naked. Had she been drinking?

She couldn't remember.

She poured a glass of water and drank it down in several large gulps, quenching a raging thirst. Then she started going over the events of the evening one more time. She remembered the restaurant where they'd had dinner, drinking champagne, dropping by a couple of clubs. She had a vague memory of Lina and Fredo heading for the dance floor, and Carlo talking to her. After that it was all one big blank.

Oh, God! Am I losing my mind?

She gulped down another glass of water, satiating her

incredible thirst. Then she went back into her bedroom, put on a robe and sat on the edge of the bed desperately trying to recall at least something.

Had she gotten sick? Drunk? What the hell had happened?

This was ridiculous. She couldn't remember a thing. *Someone must have brought me home*, she thought. *Maybe Lina.*

She wondered if Lina was home. Probably not. When Lina didn't have to work the next day she was into partying all night and sleeping until past noon the following day.

Brigette tried her number. No response. She kept trying until the service picked up. Then she left a message for Lina to call her.

She felt . . . different. Her breasts were tender, and when she parted her robe she discovered bruises on the insides of both her thighs.

If I didn't know better, I'd think I'd been making love, she thought. But that was impossible.

And yet . . . she felt as if she'd had sex.

Her mouth was so dry she needed more water. She ran back to the kitchen, panicking slightly. Something had happened and she wasn't sure what.

Fredo would know. She hurriedly dialled his number. He mumbled hello.

'This is Brigette,' she said urgently.

'I'm asleep.'

'Sorry, but I need to talk to you.'

'You and Carlo deserted us,' he said, between yawns. 'Lina is very furious.'

'I . . . I left with Carlo?' she questioned, her stomach sinking.

'We go dance, come back, you're both gone.' Fredo snorted his annoyance. 'Why you wake me at this time? Call Lina.'

'She's not home.'

'Maybe she found Carlo,' he said slyly. 'If you let him free, I'm sure she would've taken him into *her* bed.'

'Y' know, Fredo,' Brigette said irritably. 'It's not *all* about sex.'

'Ah, my sweet little naïve one.' And he hung up.

So, Fredo seemed to think that Carlo had escorted her home. Maybe so, easy enough to find out. She buzzed downstairs to the night porter. 'What time did I get in?' she asked.

'Must've been around eleven, Miss Brigette.'

'Was I . . . uh . . . was I with someone?'

'A gentleman.'

An inward groan. 'How long was he in my apartment?'

'About an hour.'

Oh, God! Here was the deal. She must have been drunk, had sex with Carlo, and couldn't remember. *Totally* humiliating.

Yet how was it possible? She'd had too much to drink before and never completely blanked out.

It occurred to her, with a feeling of deep dismay, that she might have been drugged. Some of the models had been talking lately about a dangerous new pill doing the rounds. Rhohipnels – known on the street as ruffies. Apparently the pills were colourless and odourless, and guys were slipping them in girls' drinks so they could take advantage of them. One of the effects of the drug was total memory loss.

Could Carlo possibly have done this to her?

She buzzed the front desk again to find out if Lina was home. The porter informed her that, no, Lina was still out.

She didn't know what to do next. She had no proof, although maybe if she went to a doctor they could take a blood test and find out for sure if she'd been drugged.

No. The humiliation wasn't worth it.

She ran a bath, collapsed into the soapy bubbles, and lay there thinking. She was rich, pretty and successful – yet every time she ventured out and let her guard down, something happened.

I'm cursed, she thought grimly. *Exactly like my mom.* Her mother, the heiress Olympia Stanislopoulos, with everything to live for, had died in a seedy hotel room with her current addiction – Flash, a drugged-out rock star.

I don't want to be like my mom, she thought, shivering uncontrollably. *I don't want to end up the way Olympia did.*

She wanted to call Lucky in the worst way. Then she remembered that Lucky was out at an event honouring her in LA. And, anyway, every time she got into trouble she couldn't go running to her godmother.

You are not a child any more, she told herself sternly. *You have to learn to deal with things.*

But how could she deal with this when she wasn't even sure what had happened?

She got into bed, huddled beneath the covers, and eventually fell into a fitful sleep.

Chapter Twenty

THE SCREAMING sound of an ambulance's siren awoke Lennie with a jolt. He was about to get up and shut the bedroom window because the noise was so goddamn loud when he realized he was not in his own bed: he was *in* the ambulance.

Christ! was his first thought. *What the hell am I doing in an ambulance?*

He must've made a noise, more like a groan, because a medic appeared beside him, carefully lifted his head an inch or two and fed him a few sips of water.

'What happened?' he managed.

'You were shot,' said the medic, a cheerful-looking ginger-haired man. 'Took a bullet in the shoulder.'

'Jesus!' he mumbled, trying to get his mind around this startling fact of life. 'How?'

'Attempted car-jacking. You must've given 'em a fight.'

Car-jacked. Car-jacked. Slowly it started to come back. A girl yelling, waving a gun. Mary Lou clinging on to her necklace. A black boy standing silently in the background.

Fuck! The girl had shot him. She'd pointed a gun and shot him! It didn't seem possible.

'Where's Mary Lou?' he asked weakly, noticing a throbbing pain in his shoulder.

The medic turned away for a minute. 'She your wife?'

'No . . . my . . . sister-in-law.' He groaned, suddenly remembering. 'Oh, God, she was shot, too. How's she doing?'

'The police will need to talk to you.'

'Why?'

'Find out what happened.'

'Lemme see Mary Lou,' he said, thinking how pissed Lucky would be when she heard. She was always warning him to be more careful. 'Havta call my wife,' he said, closing his eyes. 'Gotta tell her . . .'

Suddenly everything began to spin, and he didn't feel so great. This could be because he'd never been shot before.

It was not a good feeling.

☆ ☆ ☆

'Something's wrong,' Lucky said, suddenly sitting up very straight.

'Shh . . .' Gino said gruffly, nudging her to shut up. 'I like this Baby Face, the guy's got a voice.'

'I know something's wrong,' Lucky said sharply. 'I'm calling home.'

'You can't walk out while the man's singing.'

'I can do whatever I want, Gino,' she whispered fiercely, leaving the table and making her way to the back of the crowded ballroom.

Steven came after her. 'What's going on?' he asked.

'I . . . I don't know, Steven. I've got this weird feeling something's wrong.'

He sighed. 'You and your weird feelings.'

'I have to call home, see if the children are okay.'

'You know they are,' he said, producing his cellphone anyway. 'You shouldn't've walked away from the table,' he added. 'It's your night, Lucky, everyone is watching you. And Baby Face is in the middle of a song.'

'What are you? My keeper?' she snapped, in no frame of mind to have either Gino or Steven telling her what to do.

'*You*'re in a good mood,' he said.

'That's because I need to know where Lennie and Mary Lou are. This isn't like him, and it's certainly not like your wife – she's *always* concerned about getting everywhere on time.'

'I'll call my house,' he said, punching out his number. Jennifer answered and assured him all was quiet. He handed the phone to Lucky. 'Your turn.'

She took the small phone and reached CeeCee. 'Everything okay?'

'Of course,' CeeCee said. 'Why?'

'It's late and Lennie hasn't gotten here. I thought he might have called.'

'I'm sure he would've been in touch if anything was wrong.'

'So you haven't heard from him?' Lucky said, turning her back on a hovering photographer.

'Wait a minute,' CeeCee said. 'The other line's ringing. Shall I get it?'

'Yes,' Lucky said abruptly. Sometimes she experienced hunches, feelings that enveloped her, feelings she couldn't explain. She had one now. It was like a black cloud hovering overhead, and she *knew* something bad was about to happen.

A few moments later CeeCee came back on the line. 'It . . . it's about Lennie,' she said, sounding upset.

Lucky felt a cold chill. 'Yes?' she said, fearing the worst.

'He . . . he was shot in a robbery. They've taken him to Cedars.'

'Oh, my God!' Lucky said.

Steven grabbed her arm. 'What?' he demanded.

'Lennie's been shot. He's at Cedars.'

'What about Mary Lou?' Steven asked urgently. 'Was she with him?'

'CeeCee,' Lucky said, desperately trying to stay calm, 'was Mary Lou with him?'

'They . . . they didn't say.'

'What *did* they say? Is it bad? Is he going to be okay?' WILL HE LIVE? screamed silently in her head.

'He's being taken to emergency.'

'Stay with the children,' Lucky said, trying to think straight and not panic. 'Do *not* tell them. I'm on my way to the hospital.' She clicked off the phone. 'I don't believe this,' she said, shaking her head. 'I *knew* something was wrong. I fucking *knew* it.'

'Where's Mary Lou?' Steven said.

'Probably looking after him, you know how she is.'

Steven nodded, praying that this was the case.

'Let's go,' Lucky said.

'What about Gino?'

'Go back to the table, say I'm not feeling well, and tell Gino to take Bobby home after the show. Hurry. I'll get the limo and meet you in front.'

Oh God, that feeling in the pit of her stomach never lied. How many times had she begged Lennie not to drive the Porsche in bad areas of town? He'd laughed at her. 'You're such a panicker,' he'd said. 'Always worrying something's going to happen.'

'I'm smart, Lennie,' she'd answered. 'And if *you*'re smart you can stop stuff from happening.'

'Yeah, yeah, sure.' He'd laughed. 'Miss Know-it-all.'

'You think getting mugged is planned, Lennie? It doesn't happen that way. Crime is a spur-of-the-moment thing, you've *always* got to be on the alert. Gino taught me that.'

'I'm careful,' he'd assured her.

'No, you're not. You're in a world of your own – always thinking about the script you're working on, your movie . . .'

And so they'd argued. And now this had happened.

She hurried out of the hotel and into the limo. Steven joined her a few moments later.

'Let's go, driver,' Lucky said. 'And break records. We need to be there like now!'

Chapter Twenty-one

'YOU'RE A right little bitch,' Lina said, her face contorted in anger, not at all her usual friendly self.

Brigette stood at Lina's door, makeup-less, clad in leggings and a baggy sweatshirt. She looked miserable.

Lina, heading for a major hangover and clutching a short scarlet robe around her, resembled the wild woman of Borneo. Her black hair was standing on end and her skin was all blotchy. Without her immaculate makeup she was certainly not the exotic, feline supermodel featured in all the fashion magazines.

'Let me in,' Brigette insisted, shoving past her. 'Something happened.'

'You bet your skinny arse something 'appened,' Lina said crossly. 'You *knew* perfectly well *I* fancied Carlo, yet *you* ran off with 'im. You can't do that to a girlfriend an' expect t' get away with it.'

Brigette marched into the kitchen, shaking her head. 'You don't understand,' she said.

'Sure I do,' Lina said, following her. 'I understand plenty. And now I want to go t' bed an' get some sleep, so piss off.'

'No, no – you *don't* understand,' Brigette assured her, sitting down at the kitchen table and putting her head in her hands. 'I was drugged.'

Lina stopped short. 'You were *what?*'

'I think Carlo slipped a pill into my drink.'

'What kind of pill?' Lina said suspiciously.

'You know, ruffies. Whatever those stupid drugs are that guys give girls so they can rape them.'

'C'*mon*,' Lina said disbelievingly. 'Carlo doesn't 'ave to drug anybody for sex. Look at 'im – 'e's a babe, 'e can 'ave whoever 'e wants. He could've 'ad *me* if *you* hadn't dragged 'im off.'

'You don't get it,' Brigette said excitedly, sitting up straight and banging her fist on the table. 'I *didn't* drag him off. I don't remember anything.'

'Not *anything*?' Lina said cautiously.

'I don't remember coming home, or leaving the club – nothing. I woke up just now, and I'm covered in bruises.' A long pause – then, 'I *know* somebody made love to me.'

'Shit!' Lina said, frowning.

'There's no way I'd take a guy from you,' Brigette continued earnestly. 'I swore off sex ages ago. *You* know that. I don't even *like* sex.'

Lina nodded. 'I'll pour us a brandy an' get Fredo over here.'

'We can't tell him,' Brigette said, panicking. 'We can't tell anybody.'

'If Carlo did what you *think* he did,' Lina raged, 'then 'e's a right bastard, an' I'll personally kick his scummy balls all the way to Italy an' back! But first we gotta find 'im, an' that's where Fredo makes 'imself useful.'

'This is the most embarrassing thing that's ever happened to me,' Brigette wailed.

'No, it's not,' Lina said firmly. 'Remember Michel Guy? *That* was the most embarrassing. *This* is something you can deal with.'

'How?' Brigette asked, feeling powerless. 'I don't even know where he's staying.'

'I told you,' Lina said, attempting to smother a yawn. 'Fredo will know.'

'You must think I'm such an idiot.'

'Revenge, baby,' Lina said, nodding vigorously. 'Think about *that*.'

'I don't know . . .' Brigette said unsurely.

'Oh, yes,' Lina's eyes were gleaming at the thought, 'I'm *really* into revenge.'

'You are?'

'It's the only way, ain't it?'

'Maybe . . .' Brigette said, thinking that Lucky always said the same thing.

'Stop worrying,' Lina said. 'We're gonna get the wop bastard, or *I'm* not a bleedin' supermodel!'

By the time Fredo put in a reluctant appearance, Lina had slipped into a T-shirt and ripped jeans, hidden her unruly hair beneath a Chicago Bears baseball cap, and added Dolce & Gabbana oblique shades.

'Where's your freakin' cousin?' she demanded, before he was half-way through the door.

'Excuse me?' Fredo said, wondering what his handsome cousin had done now.

'Where's the bastard stayin'?' Lina shouted.

Fredo gave a vague shrug. 'I don't know. He leaves in the morning. And why you get me out of bed?'

'Ha!' Lina said, outraged. 'Where's 'e goin'?'

'Why you so mad?' Fredo asked. 'And what's the matter with *you*?' he said, glancing at Brigette, who was now sitting on the couch in the living room, her knees pulled up to her chin.

'I'll tell you why we're mad,' Lina said furiously. ''E bleedin' raped her, didn't 'e?'

'Don't be ridiculous,' Fredo said, his bushy eyebrows shadowing his eyes with a deep frown.

'It's not ridiculous,' Brigette said flatly. 'I'm sure Carlo must've slipped a pill in my drink.'

'I do not believe this,' Fredo said, blinking rapidly. Actually, he believed it only too well.

'You'd better,' Lina said angrily, ''cause she's gonna bleedin' sue 'im. An'—'

'No, I'm not,' Brigette interrupted.

'Yes, you are,' Lina said, silencing her with a stony stare.

Fredo didn't know what to say, so he remained silent, figuring that was the safest way to play it. All he wanted to do was go home and get into bed. Lina was scary when she was angry.

'So . . . the scumbag is goin' back to England and his fiancée, I suppose,' Lina sneered disparagingly. 'There *is* a fiancée, isn't there?'

'As far as I know,' Fredo said, gesturing vaguely.

'Who *is* this asshole anyway?' Lina demanded. 'And why'd you drag *us* out with him?'

'Yes,' Brigette said, joining in. 'You said he was a prick, so why did you introduce us?'

'Sorry,' Fredo said, throwing up his hands. 'Carlo and I, we grew up together in Roma.'

'How come?' Lina said.

'When my mother died, I was sent to live with Carlo's family. His father is my mother's brother,' Fredo explained. 'Carlo was always the handsome one. Me, I was looked upon as merely the stupid cousin. So when I came to America and make the big success, I was finally able to impress him. Every time Carlo visits, I introduce him to beautiful models. This way *I* am the important one now.'

'He's a bastard,' Lina said shortly. ''E fuckin' raped 'er, an' you'd better do somethin' about it.'

'I told you,' Fredo said. 'Carlo leaves tomorrow, and I don't know where to reach him.'

'You know what,' Brigette said, suddenly jumping to her feet. 'Let's forget about it. I never want to see him again, or hear his name mentioned. Okay, Fredo? Lina?'

'You're gonna let it drop?' Lina said in disgust. 'Do nothing?'

'Yes,' Brigette said, making up her mind. 'As far as I'm concerned, it's over.'

'If Carlo did what you say he did, then I am very sorry,' Fredo said, thinking that what Brigette claimed was probably true, because Carlo had never been a man to be trusted.

'So you should be,' Lina muttered ominously.

By the time Fredo left, Brigette felt a lot calmer. She went back to her own apartment and took a shower, frantically scrubbing her skin, wondering what kind of advantage Carlo had taken of her while she was passed out.

Then she decided it was better that she didn't know. And she got back into bed and tried to sleep. Early in the morning she and Lina were leaving on a photo shoot to the Bahamas. She'd soak up the sun, enjoy posing for the photographs, and forget all about her ordeal.

If there was one thing Lucky had taught her it was always move on, never get dragged down by the past.

And that's exactly what she planned on doing. She was moving on.

Chapter Twenty-two

DETECTIVE JOHNSON stood beside Lennie's bed. He was a tall, awkward-looking man in his forties, with an austere Marine crew-cut, and heavy steel-rimmed glasses. He stared down at Lennie, slightly uncomfortable because he knew Lennie Golden was famous, and that would make this case all the more difficult. Before long the press would be swarming, especially if Mary Lou Berkeley died – which right at this moment seemed to be a possibility. A team of doctors was working on her in the operating room, but right now it didn't look too good.

'They came at us out of a dark-coloured jeep,' Lennie said. 'Two of them, a girl and a boy.'

'How old?' Detective Johnson asked, making copious notes in a looseleaf notebook.

'Teenagers. Seventeen, eighteen. I dunno,' Lennie said, shifting uncomfortably. 'Has somebody contacted my wife?'

'She's on her way.'

'How's Mary Lou doing?'

'Holding on.'

'Shit!' He groaned. 'How serious is she?'

'We're . . . hopeful,' the detective said, clearing his throat. 'Uh . . . Mr Golden, I know this isn't the ideal time, but the sooner I get the facts . . .'

'Yeah, yeah, of course,' Lennie said, still in semi-shock.

'Two teenagers,' Detective Johnson said, prompting him. 'White? Black? Asian?'

'Uh . . . the girl was white. She was the one waving the gun at us. In fact, she was the one doing all the talking.'

'Talking?'

'Y' know, she was demanding Mary Lou's jewellery. Threatening to blow her fucking head off if she didn't give it up. That kind of movie-speech stuff.' He laughed bitterly. 'I couldn't write it if I tried.'

'And the boy was—'

'Black. Didn't say a word. Kind of hung behind her like he wasn't into it.'

'That's unusual.'

'*She* was definitely in charge.'

'And so?'

'So Mary Lou reached up to take off her necklace, and the clasp got stuck or something. That's when the girl leaned in and dragged it off her neck.'

'Yes?' Detective Johnson encouraged.

'It's . . . it's kind of a blur after that. We heard a police siren in the distance. The girl wanted Mary Lou's earrings and she wouldn't give them up. I guess she felt brave 'cause the siren sounded like it was getting nearer.'

'Is that when the girl shot her?'

'No. She hit Mary Lou across the face with her gun, and I kinda lost it—'

'Lost it?'

'I tried to reach *my* gun, which was in the glove compartment. Then she shot Mary Lou, just like that. In cold fucking blood.'

'What did the boy do?'

'Nothing. He was standing behind her. She shoved the necklace at him and he put it in his pocket.'

'And then?'

'She started ripping the earrings out of Mary Lou's ears, so I went for her. That's when she shot me. After she fired the gun, they ran . . .'

'Back to the jeep?'

'Yeah . . .'

'Did you get the licence-plate number?'

'Don't remember it,' Lennie mumbled, feeling dizzy.

'Anything would help.'

'I – I can't be sure.'

'Excuse me, Officer,' said a stern-faced nurse, moving close and taking hold of Lennie's wrist to check his pulse. 'It's time for you to go.'

Detective Johnson nodded. 'Get some rest,' he said to Lennie. 'It'll help. I'll come back in the morning. When I do, I'd like you to take a look through some books and talk to our sketch artist.'

'Sure,' Lennie said.

'Thanks, Mr Golden.'

'When can I see Mary Lou?'

'Someone will let you know.'

'Jesus!' Lennie sighed. 'This is surreal. Like it never really happened.'

'Common reaction,' Detective Johnson said. 'I'll be back tomorrow.'

'Not too early,' the nurse said snippily. 'This patient needs his rest.'

☆ ☆ ☆

Lucky raced into the hospital, Steven right behind her. Reception directed them to the intensive care unit.

Travelling up in the elevator neither of them said a word. Lucky was praying that Lennie would be okay, and Steven was too busy wondering why Mary Lou hadn't called. She had the number of his cellphone, which she knew he always kept on, so he couldn't understand why he hadn't heard from her.

They got out of the elevator and hurried down the corridor to the nurses' station.

'Lennie Golden,' Lucky said, to a tall, thin, black nurse.

'Mr Golden's been moved out of Intensive Care into a private room,' the nurse said. 'He's doing fine.' She stepped out from behind the desk. 'Please follow me.'

Steven put his hand on her arm. 'Where's Mary Lou Berkeley?' he demanded. 'She was with Mr Golden when he was shot.'

The nurse glanced at him. 'And you are . . .?'

'Her husband.'

'Uh . . . Mr Berkeley, you should speak to Dr Feldman.'

'Who's Dr Feldman?'

'He's looking after your wife.'

He felt his stomach drop. 'So she *was* hurt?'

'If you wait right here I'll page the doctor,' the nurse said. 'Mrs Golden, you can come with me.'

Lucky quickly kissed Steven on the cheek. 'I'm sure she's fine,' she said encouragingly. 'I'll see Lennie, then I'll come find you.'

'Right,' Steven said, attempting to keep it together, although inside he was petrified. What if something bad had happened to his precious Mary Lou? What if she'd been shot too?

No. It was impossible. He was thinking the worst when everything was going to be okay.

The power of positive thinking. It worked every time.

☆ ☆ ☆

Lucky hovered over Lennie's bed. He looked pale and shaken, but very much alive. He winked at her.

'Oh, God, Lennie!' She sighed, grabbing his hand and squeezing it tightly. 'You've got to stop pulling these stunts. I can't take it any more.'

He grimaced. 'We got held up by a couple of kids. They came out of nowhere.'

'I don't want to say I told you so, but for Chrissakes get rid of that fucking Porsche.'

'My wife the nag,' he said, summoning a weak grin.

'What happened to Mary Lou?' Lucky asked. 'Where is she?' From the look on Lennie's face, she knew it was not good news. 'Oh, God.' She groaned. 'How bad is it?'

'Dunno,' he said. 'Can't seem to get any information.'

'Damn,' Lucky said. 'Now that I know you're okay, I'd better go find out.'

☆ ☆ ☆

Dr Feldman looked Steven straight in the eye and said, 'I'm not going to lie to you, Mr Berkeley. Your wife has suffered serious damage from the bullet, which is lodged extremely close to her heart. She's lost a tremendous amount of blood, and I'm sorry to tell you that she's also lost the baby.'

'What?' Steven said blankly.

Dr Feldman cleared his throat and looked uncomfortable. 'You *did* know that your wife was pregnant?'

'I . . . I didn't.'

'She was in the early stages . . . no more than two months.'

'Can I see her?' he asked, his mind in turmoil.

'She's very weak, Mr Berkeley.'

'Can I see her?' he repeated forcefully. 'I want to see her *now*.'

'Certainly,' the doctor said, taking a step back.

Steven followed the man down the corridor to Intensive Care. The doctor was droning on about the bullet being lodged in a place they hadn't been able to get to. And since she was in such a weakened state they were not going to try again until she'd had a blood transfusion. However, this would have to take place soon, because the bullet was blocking certain functions and it was essential they remove it, otherwise . . .

Mary Lou was in a semi-conscious state. Her beautiful big brown eyes flickered when she saw Steven, and she made a vain attempt at a smile.

'Baby,' he whispered, bending over her. 'My sweet, sweet baby.'

'I'm sorry . . .' she murmured. 'Wasn't my fault . . .'

'Nobody said it was,' Steven said, brushing a lock of hair off her forehead.

'You do know that I love you,' she said very softly.

'Yes. I do know that, baby.'

'If only . . .'

'If only *what*?' he said, leaning closer.

And she opened her eyes very wide and gazed into his. 'Take . . . care . . . of . . . Carioca.'

Then she began to convulse, and as Steven screamed for help, she quietly slid away.

By the time Lucky reached them, Mary Lou was gone.

Chapter Twenty-three

EARLY IN the morning Brigette and Lina shared a limo to the airport, both hiding behind oversized dark glasses – the supermodel staple. Lina attempted to bring up the subject of Carlo, but Brigette shushed her with a finger to her lips. 'I don't care to discuss it,' she reminded her friend. 'Whatever happened is over. Please don't make me sorry I told you.'

'Ha!' sniffed Lina. 'If you can't tell *me*, who can you tell? We're friends – remember?'

'The only reason I told you was because I didn't want you thinking I'd chased after him when I knew *you* were interested.'

'I probably 'ad a narrow escape,' Lina mused. 'Rape ain't my cuppa tea.'

'Me neither,' agreed Brigette, wondering how Lina could be so insensitive, but forgiving her anyway. 'Let's make a pact that we'll never mention it again.'

'Cool with me,' Lina said.

Brigette felt a lot calmer. She'd made up her mind to put the Carlo incident firmly in the past where it belonged.

'I'm looking forward to seein' a bit of sunshine,' Lina remarked, staring out of the limo window at the windy New York gloom. 'Growin' up in England, it bloody rained every day. Bleedin' rain drove me bonkers.'

'Ever thought of living in LA?' Brigette ventured.

'Nah,' Lina said, with a wild chuckle. 'I'd be dead within a year. All those temptations. You *do* know that me willpower's non-existent!'

'Like there aren't temptations in New York?' Brigette said.

'I'd get carried away in LA,' Lina explained. 'Anyway, when I'm a movie star I'll 'ave to spend more time there.'

'You should meet Lucky,' Brigette remarked. 'She's got a kick-ass attitude you'd love.'

'I bet.'

'I wish I could be more like her.' Brigette sighed. 'She's got it together. Career, husband, kids. Lucky has it all.'

'Who's she married to?'

'Lennie Golden – he *used* to be my stepdad.'

'Sounds complicated.'

'I suppose it is – *was*. You see, he was married to my mom for a short while – who happened to be Lucky's best friend.'

The limo entered the private part of the airport. They were flying to the Bahamas on a chartered plane, courtesy of *Sports World International*, who were organizing the photo shoot for their once-a-year sportswear issue. This year they had six girls going to the Bahamas, accompanied by Sheila Margolis, the *Sports World International* den mother. Also along was their star photographer, Chris Marshall.

'I'm totally into Chris.' Lina sighed. 'Wish he wasn't married.'

'Since when did that make any difference to you?' Brigette remarked.

'It does when 'is wife comes on the trip,' Lina said, lighting a cigarette. 'Remember? The old bag was there last year.'

'Maybe this year you'll get lucky.'

'Yeah,' Lina said ruefully. 'Lucky or unlucky – depending 'ow you look at it.'

'What does *that* mean?'

'I could go for him big time,' Lina said, eyes lighting up at the thought. 'We come from the same background an' all. He was born, like, five minutes away from me. We got history.'

The limo drove across the tarmac to the plane, where Sheila Margolis waited to greet them. Sheila organized the shoot, watched every detail, and kept a beady eye on everyone. She was plump, friendly and well liked. The girls never crossed Sheila – they wouldn't dare. She was the one who made sure they weren't out partying all night, got their sleep and had plenty of energy for the gruelling shoot under the hot Bahamian sun. For six days she kept them under control, and on the last night everyone partied – including Sheila, who last year had been discovered at seven a.m. emerging from the room of a black basketball star, much to Lina's chagrin, because Lina had wanted him for herself, and couldn't imagine what he'd seen in the hardly glamorous Sheila.

'Hi, Sheil,' said Brigette, emerging from the limo and kissing Sheila on both cheeks.

'Hello, darlings,' Sheila greeted them, beaming.

Lina kissed her too. 'Where's Chris?' she asked casually.

'Already aboard,' Sheila said, adding a succinct, 'and keep your hands to yourself, Lina, dear. His wife's not with him this trip.'

'*Ooooh*,' Lina said, with a wicked laugh. 'There *is* a God.'

As they stood talking to Sheila, another limo drew up, and out got Annik Velderfon, the famous Dutch model. Annik was tall and wide-shouldered with a magnificent sweep of long blonde hair and a toothy smile. 'Hello, girls,' she said.

'Hello, Annik,' they chorused.

Annik began conferring with her driver, who was busy unloading her matching Vuitton luggage.

'She's got about as much personality as a dead salmon!' Lina muttered.

'Now, now,' chided Brigette, stifling a giggle.

'C'mon,' Lina said. 'Let's grab the best seats.'

Chris stood up when he saw them coming. Chris was English, a Rod Stewart clone but younger, with a cheeky smile and plenty of attitude. ''Ello, ladies,' he said, his thick Cockney accent matching Lina's. 'Fancy an 'orrible time?'

''Ello, darling,' said Lina, swooping in for a big intimate hug. 'I hear you left wifey-pie at home.'

'The old bird's pregnant,' Chris announced, stopping Lina in her tracks.

'Oh, that's just great!' she said, with a disappointed grimace. 'I s'pose that means you're off limits again.'

'Sorry, darlin',' Chris said, chuckling. 'The butler did it!'

'Who else is coming today?' Brigette asked.

'There's you,' Chris said. 'Lina, Annik, Suzi, and . . . oh, yeah . . . Kyra.'

'Good, I like Kyra,' Lina said. 'She's got balls – just like me!'

'Where d'you keep 'em?' Chris asked, with a cheeky wink.

'Wouldn't *you* like to know?' Lina answered, with a flirty smile.

And so it starts, thought Brigette.

'I forgot,' Chris said. 'Didi Hamilton's on this trip too.'

'Shit!' Lina said, pulling a disgusted face. 'The poor man's me.'

'Don't be like that, darlin',' Chris said. 'Didi looks nothing like you.'

'She's black, isn't she?'

'You tellin' me all black girls look alike?'

'Only in the dark,' Lina deadpanned. She was quite jealous of Didi who, at nineteen, was seven years younger than her, very skinny, with exceptionally large boobs – which Lina had tried to convince everyone were silicone-enhanced.

'She's the road version of you,' Brigette whispered. 'No style.'

'Thanks a lot. I don't need a freakin' road version of me on this trip,' Lina grumbled, sulking.

They found seats and settled in.

Kyra Kattleman arrived next. Kyra was Australian, over six feet tall, with a mane of reddish brown hair, a surfer's body, big extra white teeth, and a high, squeaky voice. She'd recently married a fellow model. 'I'm exhausted!' she said, flopping into a seat. 'Anyone got illicit drugs? I need a boost.'

'Who doesn't?' grumbled Lina.

Sheila Margolis bustled aboard. 'Somebody's missing,' she said, looking around and frowning.

'Didi's late,' Chris said.

'As usual,' Lina added.

'No, not Didi, someone else,' Sheila said.

'Suzi,' Kyra said. 'I spoke to her last night.'

'Suzi's always on time,' Sheila said, worrying.

'She probably got held up in traffic,' Lina said. 'It's a bitch getting here at this time.'

Most of the girls were secretly envious of Suzi, who'd recently starred in a Hollywood movie and was currently engaged to a sexy movie star.

'Suzi's a wanker's dream,' Lina had once said about her. 'Totally non-threatening. They can come all over her an' she'll never complain!'

Suzi arrived two minutes later, apologizing for not being on time. She brought flowers for Sheila, a rare photography book for Chris, and home-made cookies for everyone else.

'If I didn't know 'er better, I'd swear she was kissing arse,' Lina whispered.

'No,' Brigette said. 'She's just thoughtful.'

'Bitch!' Lina said.

After Suzi's arrival, they all sat for another twenty minutes before Didi put in an appearance.

Didi sauntered on to the plane as if she had no idea she'd kept them all waiting, infuriating Lina. Naturally she had twice as much luggage as everyone else, so they had to wait even longer while it was loaded aboard.

'You're late,' Lina snapped. 'Don't worry about keeping us all sitting around like a bunch of spare pricks at a wedding.'

'You're always in such a bad mood,' Didi said, blowing finger kisses at Chris. 'Going through the menopause?'

'*What* did you say?' Lina demanded, furious. 'I'm twenty-six, for Chrissakes.'

'Oh . . . sorry,' Didi said, all girlish innocence. 'You seem so much older.'

The two black supermodels glared at each other.

This is going to be fun, Brigette thought.

Lina fastened her seatbelt, seething. 'I'm not goin' on another fucking location with that cow!' she muttered ominously. 'This is *it*.'

'Ignore her,' Brigette said.

'She's always effing with me. Did you *hear* what she said?'

'Everyone knows she's only trying to piss you off,' Brigette said, trying to calm her down.

'I don't 'ave to take her shit,' Lina said broodingly. 'Who needs to be in stupid *Sports World International*? I'm gonna bleedin' *kill* if she gets the cover an' I don't.'

'She won't,' Brigette said reassuringly.

'Easy for *you* to say, you made the cover last year. I've *never* been on the bleedin' cover, 'ave I? Guess I'm too black.'

The plane began taxiing down the runway.

Brigette leaned back in her seat and closed her eyes. Every day she thought the same thing. *This is the start of a whole new life.* But where was her life taking her? The only time she seemed to be living was in front of a camera. And a press-clipping book of magazine covers and fashion layouts would not keep her warm at night.

She was never going to find a man she could trust, one who would treat her nicely. They'd all proved themselves to be untrustworthy time and time again. And yet she'd like nothing better than to meet the right one. Settle down, have a family. Be normal.

Oh, well . . . she had her career, and for now that would just have to do.

☆ ☆ ☆

One thing Brigette loved was the excitement of being on location, hanging out in a place that completely took over her life. When she got up in the morning she didn't have to make any decisions. There were people to do her makeup, style her hair, choose the outfits she was to wear that day. Everything was taken care of.

Then there was the camaraderie with all the other girls. Brigette got along with everyone. Supermodels – a rare and exotic breed. Leggy girls with slim bodies, manes of shiny hair, luminous skin, gorgeous smiles, and plenty of attitude.

Early in the morning, Brigette and Lina took a long power jog along the beach before raiding the hotel room where all the clothes for the upcoming shoot were kept. Today they were starting off with a group shot, so naturally Lina had decided to outshine everyone. She sorted through the hanging racks of outfits, finally picking an outrageous leopard thong bikini with matching sarong skirt. 'This'll do,' she said, stripping off her shorts and tank top and putting on the sexy bikini. 'Think Chris'll like me in this?'

Brigette shrugged. 'Dunno and don't care.'

'Ha! Thanks for your support,' Lina said, prancing like a thoroughbred horse waiting at the gate.

'You know I support you,' Brigette said patiently, 'only it beats me why you have this sick desire to sleep with married guys. What's the kick in *that*?'

'Knowing they want me more than anybody else,' Lina said, licking her full lips. 'And that sometimes they can 'ave me, an' sometimes they can't.'

'Don't you ever think about their wives? And what you're doing to them?'

'What am *I* doing if the wife don't know about it?' Lina said defiantly.

'How would *you* like it if it was your husband sleeping with some beautiful model?' Brigette asked, attempting to reason with her, although she knew it was useless.

'Wise up, Brig,' Lina said, with a casual shrug. 'I couldn't care less. What kind of idiot expects any man to be faithful?'

'You don't think it's possible?'

'Men are dogs, baby,' Lina pronounced, with a knowledgeable nod. 'Offer 'em a blow-job an' they're yours. It don't matter who it is. Politicians, movie stars, the man in the street. Trust me, they're all the bleedin' same.'

'You honestly believe that?'

'Yeah. An' if you don't, then you're naïve,' she said, barely smothering a huge yawn. 'But, then, of course, I'm forgetting – you *are* naïve. For a girl who's gonna inherit all kinds of money, you're *way* not street smart. When *do* you get it all?'

'I have enough now to keep me very happy,' Brigette said, reluctant to discuss her money, because she hated any reference to her role as an heiress.

'Yeah, but don't you score, like, billions of dollars or something?' Lina enquired, pushing it.

'When I'm thirty,' Brigette said, thinking that she wasn't looking forward to that day for a variety of reasons. Big money brought big problems.

'Hmm . . . you'd better not let that little piece of information out the bag,' Lina said, offering advice, ''cause if you do, guys'll be storming your life.'

'You think that's the only reason men would be after me?' Brigette asked, slightly irritated.

'Don't get shirty,' Lina said, yawning again. 'Y' know what I mean. You're gorgeous anyway. You can have whoever you want, money or no money.'

'Trouble is,' Brigette said wistfully, 'there's nobody I want.'

'Oh, that's right, I forgot, you're Miss Particular,' Lina said, still posing in front of the mirror. 'The good thing is you an' I get along so well 'cause we appeal to different types. You all blonde an' bubbly, and me – like some exotic prowling black panther.' She giggled at her own description. 'D'you think men find me . . . dangerous?'

'You scare the crap out of them, Lina,' Brigette said crisply.

'Scare the crap out of who?' Kyra asked, entering the room.

'Lina scares men,' Brigette said. 'She's got that predatory look.'

'You mean that carefully cultivated eat-shit-and-die look?' Kyra said, tossing back her luxuriant mane of hair as she approached the clothes rack. 'It sure works wonders on the runway.'

'Secret of me success!' Lina giggled. 'Let's see now . . . It got me four rock stars, one moody film star, a tennis player, two billionaires—'

'Enough!' Kyra shouted, in her high-pitched, squeaky voice. 'You're making me jealous. Before I got married I only had *one* rock star, and he was a dud in bed.'

'Who was that?' Lina enquired.

'Flick Fonda.'

'Bingo!' Lina screamed triumphantly. '*I* just 'ad 'im! You'd think with his studly reputation, an' all that gyrating on stage, he would've been a major performer.'

'Big dick. Has no clue what t' do with it,' Kyra said matter-of-factly.

'Right!' Lina yelled her agreement. 'Calls it 'is joystick. An' the only one to get any joy is *'im*!'

'Since you're always complaining about rock stars,' Brigette said, joining in. 'Why sleep with them?'

'There's too many women around waiting to service 'em,' Lina said. 'Same reason most models are boring fucks.'

'Excuse *me*,' huffed Kyra, quite insulted.

'Beauty's not always a good thing,' Lina continued. 'When *I*'m with a bloke, I give it me all!'

'So I've heard,' Kyra said, with an insinuating giggle.

'*Especially* if they buy me presents,' Lina added, tapping one of her diamond-stud earrings.

'What *is* this thing you've got with presents?' Brigette said, genuinely puzzled. 'You can afford to buy yourself anything.'

'I know,' Lina said airily. 'Think it's 'cause I was deprived as a child, or some such crap.'

Sheila bustled into the room followed by Didi and Annik. 'Brigette, dear,' she said, 'can I talk to you a moment? It's . . . personal.'

Lina raised an eyebrow. 'Personal?' she said, as if she was entitled to know everything that happened to Brigette.

'Come with me, dear,' Sheila said, leaving the room.

Brigette followed. 'What's up, Sheil?' she asked.

'We uh . . . had a call from your godmother, Lucky Santangelo.'

'You did?' Brigette said, surprised.

'She tried to reach you at your apartment, but of course you'd left,' Sheila went on. 'Then she contacted the agency, and they got in touch with me here.'

'What is it?'

'There's been an unfortunate accident, dear. And Lucky wanted to be sure you heard about it before it's all over the news.'

'Is Lucky all right?' Brigette asked, her stomach doing a crazy somersault.

'She's fine,' Sheila replied, pausing for a moment. 'It's simply that . . . well, Lennie Golden and his sister-in-law, Mary Lou, were the victims of an attempted car-jacking.'

'Oh, God!' Brigette gasped. 'Are *they* all right?'

'Lucky would like you to call her.'

A car-jacking, Brigette thought. *One of the reasons not to live in California.*

She rushed back to her room and immediately placed a call to Lucky.

'Be here Monday,' Lucky said quietly. 'I'm sorry to tell you this.'

'What?' Brigette demanded, filled with foreboding.

'Uh . . . Mary Lou is dead. I know she'd want you at her funeral.'

Brigette hung up the phone in shock, too startled to cry, too numb to do anything.

Poor Steven. Poor little Carioca.

And there was absolutely nothing she could do.

BOOK TWO
Six Weeks Later

Chapter Twenty-four

'DINNER IS served, Mr Washington.'

'Thanks, Irena,' Price Washington replied, strolling into the formal dining room of his Hancock Park mansion and sitting down at the long table set for two. 'Didja call Teddy?'

'He's coming,' Irena said, unfolding a pristine linen napkin and placing it on his lap.

Price Washington was a superstar comedian. Tall, rangy and very black, he was not exactly handsome, but with his gleaming shaved head, full lips and heavily lidded bedroom eyes, he had a look plenty of women found irresistible.

At thirty-eight and currently single, Price was at his peak. His on-the-edge HBO comedy specials were legend, and his in-person performances were always sold out months in advance. Recently he'd starred in a television sitcom that had made him even more famous, and soon he was set to embark on a movie career, which people in the business seemed to think would surpass even Eddie Murphy's raging success.

Irena Kopistani had been his housekeeper for over nineteen years. She was a thin, austere white woman of forty-eight, exactly ten years older than Price. Quite attractive, she was five feet six, with pointed features and straight brown hair, usually worn back in a bun. He'd hired her when he was nineteen years old and out of his mind on drugs. She'd arrived for an interview at his recently purchased Hancock

Park mansion, and he'd said, 'Start today,' even though he had no idea what he was doing or who he was doing it to.

At the time, Irena had recently immigrated to America from her native Russia, so she was happy to land any job, especially as she had no references. She moved into the maid's quarters above the garage, and tried to make order out of the chaos that was Price's life.

Over the years she'd succeeded. Now Price could not contemplate being without her. Irena kept him straight. She watched over him with a steely eye. She was always on his side, ready to defend and protect. He'd missed her while he'd been making his sitcom in New York, but somebody had to stay in LA and take care of the house, and there was nobody he trusted more than her.

Sometimes Price couldn't help marvelling at how his life had turned out. Born in the Watts area of LA to a mother who already had three children by three different men, he was raised in abject poverty with no father. His mom had been a real ballsy woman, who by sheer force of will had kept him out of the gangs. And how had she done that? She'd slapped him around so hard that he still had the scars to prove it. She hadn't taken any shit, his mom.

Unfortunately she'd died before he'd achieved any kind of success. When he was fourteen she'd gotten hit by a sniper's bullet crossing the street, and he'd been sent to live with a cousin.

Losing his mother was his one big regret, because she would have derived so much pleasure from his fame and success. Not to mention his grand mansion where she would've had a fine old time.

Not that he didn't enjoy it himself. Once he'd gotten past the drug years it was all a fantasy. Although getting married so young and fathering a son probably had been a mistake.

He loved Teddy, but Price was still only thirty-eight, and the responsibility of raising a sixteen-year-old hung heavy.

The trouble with Teddy was that he took everything for granted. He had no clue what it was like growing up on welfare with rats running over your feet while you slept, and having to endure the constant struggle to get enough to eat. Teddy had it too easy. Problem was he was too young to realize his good fortune.

Price knew that God had smiled on him. He had money, fame, happiness – well, not really happiness, because he wasn't exactly ecstatic living by himself in his big old mansion with nobody to keep him warm at night. But he figured that *one* day he'd find the right woman.

He'd been married twice. Both wives had taken up residence in his Hancock Park mansion. Both had tried to force him to fire Irena. He'd stood firm.

Ginee and Olivia. Two witches.

Ginee, black and beautiful, and stoned out of her mind most of the time. He'd lived with her on and off for several years, then made the mistake of marrying her when she'd gotten pregnant with Teddy.

And Olivia. White, blonde and stacked – a ten-month mistake that had cost him dearly.

He knew he had a thing about beautiful women. And he also knew it was about time he got over that particular addiction.

Teddy, dressed in baggy, falling-down pants and an over-sized hooded Tommy Hilfiger sweatshirt, slouched into the room. Price scrutinized his son. Lately he had a feeling that something was going on with the boy, although he couldn't figure out what. A few weeks ago Teddy had arrived home way past his curfew and totally wasted. Price had punished him by not allowing him to leave his room for a week except to attend school. Since that time, Teddy had turned moody and difficult, and he'd developed a real smart mouth.

Irena had agreed with his punishment of Teddy. She understood how difficult it was raising a teenager. She had a daughter, Mila, who'd been born in America. Price didn't see much of the girl, who kept to herself. What he did see, he didn't like. Mila had a bad attitude. She'd been brought up in their household as part of the family, but every time he ran into her she still struck him as an outsider. He discouraged Teddy from hanging with Mila. She was bad news – Price recognized the type.

Teddy flopped into a chair.

'How'd you do at school today?' Price asked, rubbing the bridge of his nose.

'All right,' Teddy said.

Price often wondered if he spent enough time with the boy. Hey, if he wasn't working so hard maybe they could spend more time together, but work came first. It had to. Work paid the bills and kept him straight. Irena, with a little help from his shrink, had taught him that the high he got from working was a better buzz than the one he got from doing drugs.

'Y' know,' Price said, trying to get a dialogue going, 'a good education's everything.'

'You keep on telling me that,' Teddy muttered, his eyes looking everywhere except at his father. 'Only *you* don't get it. I don't *wanna* go to college.'

'No, *you*'re the dumb shit who doesn't get it,' Price said warningly. 'You're goin' whether *you* want to or not. If *I*'d had the opportunity to attend college, I would've considered myself the luckiest dude around. But no, Teddy, *I* hadda bust my ass workin'. *I* was out in the street pimping girls when I was fourteen. How d'you think *I* made it? Sheer guts an' ambition, nothing more. I didn't have no education. You're gonna have that advantage.'

'Don' want it,' Teddy said, scowling.

'You know somethin'? You're an ungrateful little prick,' Price snapped, wishing he could whack his son like his mom used to do to him.

Somehow he controlled himself: his shrink had warned him never to get physical with Teddy, she'd assured him that repeating patterns never worked.

Jesus! Raising a kid today was a bitch. It didn't matter that he was famous, that he knew what went on out there in the real world. Okay, so he was Price Washington, big fucking star. But he was well aware of how it was for other black men. They still had to struggle with the racism that was rampant in every large city across America, and anyone who denied it was living in an unreal world.

'Listen to me, son,' he said, attempting to be patient. 'Education's *it*. If you have knowledge, you got the shit.'

'How much education did *you* need to get up on stage and say motherfucker fifty times a night?' Teddy said, glaring resentfully at his famous dad.

Price slammed his fist on the table. 'Don't you have no goddamn respect, fool?' he shouted. 'I'm your father, for God's sake. Gettin' up on stage is what I do. That's how I make money to put food on this table.'

'I don't give a crap,' Teddy muttered.

'You don't give a crap,' Price repeated, his voice rising menacingly. Goddamn it, he wanted to whack this kid so bad. 'I thought takin' you with me to New York might've done you some good. Forget about it. Since we're back, you're worse than ever.'

'That's 'cause you won't let me do what I wanna do,' Teddy said, staring at the tablecloth.

'Uh-huh, and what exactly *is* it that you wanna do? Sit around the house all day watchin' videos? Or maybe join a gang? You can do that. Go downtown, hang with the dudes in Compton, get yourself shot. That's what black guys are *supposed* to do, right?' He sighed, thoroughly disgusted. 'The young black men of America are killing each other, an' I've given *you* a life like you can't believe, an' all *you* do is hand *me* shit.'

'Why don't you ever let me see my mother?' Teddy demanded.

''Cause she's a whore,' Price said, not prepared to discuss it.

'She used to say that 'bout you.'

'That's not smart, boy,' Price said furiously. 'She's a whore who fucked other men in *my* bed. An' when I divorced her she didn't want you. Are you listenin' to me? She signed a paper *sayin'* she didn't want you.'

'You paid her.'

'Sure I did. An' the whore took the money an' walked.' Price didn't know what to say next. What could he say to a sixteen-year-old kid who thought he knew it all? Since he'd decided never to beat him, all he could do was encourage him. And that's what he was trying to do, encourage the dumb little shit to get himself an education. As for wanting to see his mom, what kind of garbage was *that*? Ginee hadn't seen Teddy in twelve years. And, knowing Ginee, she didn't give a damn.

Irena entered the room, her thin face impassive. Irena never interfered between him and his son. She'd tried once, and he'd told her to stay out of family business. Irena knew her place. She was his housekeeper. She organized the workforce that cleaned his house, ironed his shirts, washed his shorts, folded his socks. Irena bought the groceries, drove the car, ran errands, that's what Irena did. And she was good at it.

Both of his wives had hated her. They'd resented that he'd allowed her kid to be raised on the premises, even though Irena and Mila lived above the garage in the back. It was *his* prerogative if he wanted someone living there, someone who took care of everything when he wasn't around. And Irena was a good cook, too, although some of the Russian shit she dished up didn't exactly appeal to his palate. Over the years he'd trained her not to cook that way. Simple foods were what he liked: steaks, fried chicken, salads. Now she had it down.

'Don't forget,' he said to Irena, 'tomorrow night the guys are comin' by for poker. Pick up some of that Jewish shit – y'know, smoked salmon, bagels, all of that crap. They like it.'

'Yes, Mr Washington,' she said, serving him from a heaping platter of grilled lamb chops, mashed potatoes and green beans.

When she reached Teddy, he pushed his plate away. 'Not hungry,' he mumbled. 'Don't wanna eat.'

'If I didn't know any better, I'd swear you was doin' drugs,' Price said, staring at him accusingly.

'*You* should know,' Teddy countered, remembering the many years his dad had been a total addict.

'I'm gettin' damn sick of your mouth,' Price said, narrowing his eyes.

'And I'm sick of *you* telling me what to do,' Teddy said sullenly.

That was it. Price had had enough. 'You're not hungry?' he roared, getting up from the table and throwing down his napkin. 'Then go to your room, an' don't let me catch a glimpse of your smart ass again tonight.'

Teddy shoved his chair away from the table and slouched out of the dining room.

Price looked at Irena. She returned his look.

'Kids,' he said, with a helpless shrug, sitting down again.

'I know what you mean, Mr Washington,' she agreed.

He reached out his hand. 'C'mere a minute.' She took his hand and moved closer. 'You miss me while I was gone?' he asked, his voice softening.

'Yes, Mr Washington,' she said. 'The house was very quiet.'

'Yeah?' he said, reaching up and touching her left breast, fingering the nipple in a familiar fashion. 'You must've missed me plenty, huh?'

She took a step back, her face expressionless. 'Yes, Mr Washington.'

He chuckled. 'Okay, sweetcakes, maybe later tonight you'll tell me exactly how *much* you missed me.'

Irena kept the same stoic expression. 'Yes, Mr Washington.'

☆ ☆ ☆

Upstairs, Teddy paced around his room like a rat on a treadmill. Ever since that fateful night six weeks ago, he couldn't get the horrible scenario out of his head.

Two people sitting in a car. Two people not doing any harm to anyone.

And Mila. Blowing the woman away. Grabbing her jewellery and running.

Blood. Teddy kept on seeing the blood soaking the pretty black woman's white gown.

Jesus! And she was a sister too, which made it even worse.

Mila had told him to forget about it. Once they were back in the jeep she'd started yelling about how it was an accident and nobody's fault. But he *knew* the horrible truth. It had been no accident. Mila had brutally shot two people, and the woman had died.

The next day it was all over the news on account of the two people she'd shot being famous. Maybe his father even knew them! That thought really freaked him.

'We're gonna get caught,' he'd told Mila. 'They're gonna find us.'

'They can't,' she'd answered, staring him down. 'There were no witnesses.'

'They'll find us,' he'd repeated. 'The gun – where'd you get it?'

'It doesn't matter.'

'They could put a trace on it.'

'How? They don't *have* the goddamn gun.'

'Where'd you hide it?'

'You think I'm stupid?' she'd sneered. 'I got rid of it.'

'What about her jewellery?'

'Don't worry, when the time comes you'll get your share of the money.' And she'd glared at him with a savage look in her eyes. 'Don't *ever* open your mouth, Teddy Washington. 'Cause if you do, I swear I'll kill you.'

He lived in fear. Fear of his father finding out, and fear of Mila and her threats.

If she was capable of shooting two people, then she was certainly capable of killing him.

Teddy had nowhere to turn.

Chapter Twenty-five

THE UNREAL tragedy had affected all of them. The days drifted into weeks and Lucky was glad she'd made the decision to leave Panther because it gave her time to spend with Lennie and Steven, both of whom desperately needed her – especially Steven, who was totally devastated by the death of his wife.

She'd placed people she trusted in positions of power at Panther. Since her departure there was not one person running the studio, there were three. Which meant that no decisions could be made without all three of them consulting each other, and since she was on the board, it meant that she was still very much involved. She certainly didn't want the studio being less of a power simply because she'd left. After all, she hadn't sold Panther, she'd merely stepped down as studio head, and this way gave her an option if she ever chose to resume control. She'd decided that if in a year she was no longer interested, then she'd sell. She'd make that decision when the time came.

Carioca Jade was staying at their house, comforted by her cousin Maria. The two little girls were inseparable, sleeping in the same room and spending all their time together. *Thank God they have each other*, Lucky thought, remembering how she and her brother, Dario, had clung together when their mother was murdered.

Physically Lennie had recovered quickly. His gunshot had been a surface wound and not that bad. It was the shock of losing Mary Lou that he couldn't seem to get over. 'There's nothing you could've done,' Lucky kept assuring him.

'I shouldn't've gone for my gun,' he said, going over it time and again. 'It was a mistake that cost Mary Lou her life. It's like the worst fucking nightmare in the world.'

Lucky didn't know what to say. He was right, it *was* a nightmare, one they were both trapped in.

Orpheus Studios had shut down production on Lennie's movie until they could recast Mary Lou's role. It might not even get recast because it would put the film way over budget. Lennie had vowed not to return as director. 'I refuse to direct it with another actress,' he'd said. 'Let them get somebody else.'

She'd noticed that he didn't want to leave the house, which is exactly what had happened after his kidnapping. The only time he went out was to take long solitary walks along the beach. He never asked her to go with him, and she didn't volunteer, because she knew he preferred being alone.

He'd hardly mentioned her decision to leave the studio. 'I *wanted* to tell you,' she'd explained, 'but then I thought it would be better to surprise you.'

'It's a surprise all right,' he'd said. And that had been his only comment on the subject. She knew he was pissed.

Now she was at home with him every day, and for the first time in their marriage things between them were strained. They weren't even making love, and she didn't know what she could do to make the situation better.

She understood that he was suffused with guilt, but he had to get over it sometime.

Steven was in a complete depression. Like Lennie, he blamed himself. '*I* should have gone to the location and picked her up,' he kept on saying. 'It was my mistake. I thought she'd be safe with Lennie.'

They both called Detective Johnson on a daily basis. 'We're not the kind of people who can sit back and do nothing,' Lucky informed the detective. 'We expect action.'

Detective Johnson assured them he was doing his best. He'd interviewed Lennie several times to go over things. Unfortunately, Lennie could only remember so much. And, try as he might, he could not recall the licence-plate number of the jeep.

'We've got it down to about six thousand black jeeps registered in California,' the detective told them. 'That's if the jeep *was* black. It could've been dark green or blue, even brown.'

'That's encouraging,' Lucky said, unimpressed with his so-called detective work. 'How do you plan on finding the right one?'

'We're working on it, Miss.'

'Don't call me Miss.'

'Sorry, *Miz* Santangelo.'

Lennie spent many hours with a police sketch artist and who'd come up with a computer likeness of the two suspects. 'She doesn't look any older than Bobby,' Lucky said, staring at the girl's picture. 'To think that teenagers with guns can snuff out a life just like that. There should be a law against it.'

'There *is* a law against it,' Lennie said grimly. 'If you carry a gun, you're supposed to have a licence.'

Lucky decided it might be good for Lennie to get out of Los Angeles for a while. 'How about a trip to New York?' she suggested. 'Remember? The early days – you and me in my apartment?'

'And my big old loft,' he said, with the glimmer of a smile. 'The one you made me sell.'

'I could try to buy it back.'

'Don't be silly.'

'Y'know, Lennie,' she said. 'I keep on flashing back on the night you were shot. Going to the event and you not being there, then hearing about the shooting. Losing Mary Lou is bad enough, but if I'd lost you . . . I wouldn't have been able to go on.'

'Yes, you would,' he said. 'You're a survivor. You've survived a lot of shit in your life.'

'So have you, Lennie, and believe me, we'll survive this together. It's like being robbed – somebody breaks in your house, takes your things and runs off into the night. If you caught 'em, you'd feel a hell of a lot better.'

A few days later she contacted Detective Johnson. 'I've been thinking,' she said. 'How about if we hire our own detective agency to help you with this investigation? I'm sure you're short on man-power.'

'I'd have no objections.'

'Would you co-operate?'

'Of course.'

'Then I'll do it. Oh, yes, and I want to post a reward for information.'

'Sometimes that can be helpful. Sometimes not.'

'Let's try it,' Lucky said.

Fuck the system, she thought. One way or another, they were going to catch the killers.

And a reward of one hundred thousand dollars might be the answer.

Chapter Twenty-six

BRIGETTE HAD been back from LA for a month when she announced, 'I'm taking off for a few weeks.'

'And where are you goin'?' Lina asked, sitting cross-legged on the floor of her apartment, painting her toenails in complicated zebra stripes.

They were having a girl's night in, with Alanis Morissette on the stereo, and a large, half-eaten pepperoni pizza on the table.

'I promised Lucky I'd go to Europe with her,' Brigette said vaguely, not wanting to get too specific.

'Sounds good t' me,' Lina said. ''Ow's Lucky doing?'

'*She*'s okay. Steven's a wreck.'

'It must be awful,' Lina said, taking a swig from a can of Diet Coke.

'It is. You should see him, it's like he's in a permanent daze. And Lennie isn't doing much better 'cause he blames himself. Thinks he could've done something to stop it.'

'Could he?' Lina asked, still painting.

'Not according to Lucky. They had this crazy girl waving a gun in their faces. Can you imagine what it must've been like? They were totally trapped.'

'I'd *freak* if I 'ad a gun in *my* face,' Lina said. 'I'd, like, lose it big time.'

'So would I,' Brigette agreed.

'An' especially it bein' a girl an' all,' Lina added. 'That's like a double whammy – y' know, it's *really* messin' with his machismo.'

'I know,' Brigette agreed.

'They got any leads on who did it?'

'Lennie doesn't remember much.'

'Talk about fate,' Lina said, picking up the remote and clicking on the TV *sans* sound. 'One moment you're sitting in your car, the next you're lying there – dead.'

'Mary Lou was such a sweetheart,' Brigette said. 'Kind and thoughtful. Always nice to everyone. You should've *seen* the turn-out at her funeral.'

'I used to watch her on that sitcom she did years ago,' Lina said, flipping channels.

'The saddest thing of all is that Steven and Mary Lou were *so* happy together.' Brigette sighed. 'And then there's little Carioca, she's only eight, and now she's got no mother. It's a tragedy.'

'Terrible,' Lina said. ''Ow old were you when *your* mum died?'

'Fifteen,' Brigette answered flatly. 'I was better off than Lucky – she was five when she found *her* mother floating in the family swimming-pool, murdered.'

'*My* mum drives me insane,' Lina said, holding out her foot and admiring her freshly painted toenails. 'Although I s'pose I shouldn't complain.'

'I'd have liked nothing better than to have known my mother properly,' Brigette said wistfully, remembering the few good times. 'You should make the most of yours.'

'Fifteen's not that young,' Lina remarked. 'At least you got to spend time with her.'

'Not really,' Brigette said pensively. 'Olympia was never around when I needed her.'

'Where was she?'

'Where was she?' Brigette repeated, recalling the blonde bombshell who'd never wanted to miss a thing. 'Good question. London, Paris, Rome, Buenos Aires. Olympia was the original jet-setter – always flying somewhere for a happening party or a new lover. She had boyfriends, husbands and too much money. I was shunted away to a boarding school in Connecticut which I hated.'

'*Quelle* drag.'

'It certainly was.'

'You can 'ave *my* mum if you like,' Lina joked. 'The old bag keeps on threatenin' to visit.'

'What's wrong with that?'

'She's a colossal pain in the butt.'

'I don't understand. How can you have a problem with her when she doesn't even live here?'

'She 'ad me when she was fifteen,' Lina explained. 'She's forty now, an' still a looker.'

'You should be proud of her then.'

'No, no, you don't get it,' Lina said excitedly. 'The thing that pisses me off most is that sometimes she bloody imagines she's *me*!'

'What does *that* mean?'

'Well, she does all these modelling jobs for magazines an' the English papers. An' the copy always reads Lina's mum this an' Lina's mum that, an' isn't she lovely – just like her famous daughter. That kind of crap drives me bonkers.'

'You shouldn't begrudge her,' Brigette said, wishing that she still had a mother, someone she could trust and confide in. 'She's only trying to emulate you. It's flattering.'

'It is?' Lina said.

'Anyway,' Brigette said, reaching for a second slice of pizza, 'I called the agency and got out of the Milan shows.'

'You did *what*?' Lina wailed. 'Milan's such an adventure. All those horny Italians with their dicks 'anging out!'

'It's more important that I spend time with Lucky.'

'You mean she's taking off and leaving Lennie behind?' Lina said, standing up and stretching.

'He's not exactly in a travelling mood.'

'Poor bastard.'

'So,' Brigette said, 'I'll fly to Europe with Lucky, then probably head back to LA for a while.'

'I'm learning to shoot when *I* get to LA,' Lina announced. 'Which might be sooner than you think, 'cause *I* got an audition for a role in the new Charlie Dollar flick.'

'You have?'

'*Not* that I usually audition,' Lina said quickly. ''Owever, according to my agent, the studio is after a name actress, an' Charlie wants *me*! So, if it comes off, I'll fly out to LA for a couple of days an' meet the man 'imself.'

'I saw him at Lucky's while I was there,' Brigette said. 'He's kind of a weird and wonderful character.'

'Oooh!' Lina said, licking her lips. 'I get off on weird!'

'You can't possibly sleep with him,' Brigette admonished. 'He's almost sixty.'

'So?' Lina said with a mischievous grin. 'I've 'ad older.'

Brigette couldn't help laughing. 'You're incorrigible,' she said.

'I'll take that as a compliment,' Lina replied.

'Well,' Brigette said, jumping up, 'I guess this is a wrap.'

'*When* are you leaving?' Lina asked, following her to the door.

'Tomorrow.'

'I can't believe it!' Lina exclaimed. 'You almost sneaked off without telling me.'

'I just told you.'

'Hmm . . .' Lina said, considering it. 'Maybe I should come with you.'

'Maybe you shouldn't,' Brigette said, grabbing her purse from the hall table. 'You're expected in Milan.'

'I don't *havta* go,' Lina said. 'I can tell 'em to go fuck 'emselves if I want. Then I'll go see Charlie early.'

'The thing is,' Brigette said, 'much as I love your company, I *should* spend time with Lucky by myself.'

'Okay, okay,' Lina said huffily. 'You don't havta draw me a picture.'

They hugged each other, making fervent promises to keep in touch. Both of them knew they wouldn't. Life in the modelling world was always frenetic, they'd meet again soon enough.

Brigette returned to her apartment, put on the Smashing Pumpkins' *Siamese Dream* CD, then began packing, throwing clothes into a suitcase without much thought because her mind was elsewhere.

She was not telling Lina the truth. The truth was painful and very private.

Lucky had no plans to travel to Europe, but *she* did.

She was going to London.

She was confronting Carlo.

And maybe – just maybe – she'd tell him she was pregnant.

Chapter Twenty-seven

LUCKY'S FRIENDS rallied. Venus was particularly concerned. 'Are you *sure* you know what you're doing?' she said, while they were having lunch at Le Dôme one day.

'Absolutely sure,' Lucky replied, munching a Chinese chicken salad.

'But you've given away your power base in this town,' Venus said, dazzling in a skin-tight snakeskin dress.

Lucky stared at her platinum blonde friend with a quizzical expression. 'Who needs a power base? *I* certainly don't.'

'Yes, you do,' Venus said excitedly. 'You have to realize, you were like Superwoman in this town. You could get anybody you wanted to come to a party, meet anyone in the world. Owning a Hollywood studio is like being the fucking President, for Chrissakes.'

'Not quite the same,' Lucky said, with a wan smile. 'However, I get the analogy. Besides, you're forgetting, I still *own* the place.'

Venus downed a quick shot of vodka. She never drank when she was with Cooper, because since the birth of their child he had liked to view her as virginal. 'Have you spoken to Alex?' she asked, picking up her sunglasses.

'No,' Lucky said slowly. '*Should* I have?'

'I thought you two were best friends.'

'You and *I* are best friends,' Lucky said patiently, knowing exactly where Venus was going. 'Alex is just, you know . . . someone Lennie and I pal around with.'

'Ha!' Venus exclaimed. 'Don't give *me* that crap. You like him, I *know* you do.'

'I'm married to Lennie,' Lucky said evenly. 'There's no other man that even remotely interests me.'

'God, you're good,' Venus said admiringly. 'You've even got yourself convinced.'

'What *are* you talking about?'

Venus nodded knowingly. 'Everyone sees the chemistry between you and Alex.'

'The only people Alex has chemistry with are his never-ending supply of Asian beauties,' Lucky said, wishing Venus would get off the subject. 'He doesn't like American women. Haven't you noticed?'

'That's true,' Venus agreed. 'Only *you*'re the exception.'

'Can we drop it?' Lucky said, starting to get irritated. 'I haven't heard from him. He's probably feeling left out that I didn't discuss this whole studio thing with him. But, hey, since when do I have to do things by committee?'

'You don't. Although usually with friends you tell them stuff. *Especially* before they read it in the newspapers, or hear about it at an intimate dinner for five hundred people.'

'So you think he's pissed with me?'

'As a matter of fact, I do.'

'You're wrong, Venus. He's been to see Lennie a couple of times.'

'And?'

'And what?' she said, exasperated. 'Will you stop making a meal out of this.'

'Speaking of food,' Venus said, knowing when to move on, 'Cooper and I are planning an anniversary party. We'd like you and Lennie to come.'

'When is it?'

'Next week.'

'We might be in New York.'

'What are you doing there?'

'I thought a change of scenery would be good for Lennie. He's still depressed. It's difficult – how would you feel?'

'Like shit.'

'Right. And there's nothing I can do,' Lucky said, shrugging helplessly. 'He's in the same mood he was in after the kidnapping – moody and withdrawn. It took me months to get him to communicate last time. Now this.'

'How is he with the kids?'

'Quiet. They don't get it. I have to keep telling them Daddy's got a headache. Christ! You'd think it was *him* who'd lost his wife.'

'What are you going to do?'

'I'd like to get him to a shrink. Not that I believe in them, but somebody's got to help him.'

'I have a great shrink,' Venus said, her face brightening.

'Of course you do.'

'She got me through that whole stalker drama a few years ago. I'll give you her number.'

Lucky nodded. 'Sounds like a plan.'

Venus waved at John Paul DeJoria and his exquisite wife, Eloise, as they entered the restaurant. 'He owns all those Paul Mitchell hair products,' Venus said. '*Love* their stuff.'

'I've got to go,' Lucky said. 'I'm meeting the kids.'

Venus nodded. 'Think I'll join Eloise and John Paul.'

☆ ☆ ☆

Later that day Lucky collected Maria, Carioca and little Gino from school, then took them to the Hard Rock, where she ordered them double chocolate milkshakes and burgers with everything on. The kids were totally excited, chattering to each other as they stuffed their mouths.

Lucky watched them. Playing mom full-time was a whole new experience, and although she adored her children, she wasn't sure family outings were a permanent staple for her. She needed action and excitement. She needed to be doing something creative. And for the first time she had doubts about leaving Panther.

She sat in the restaurant observing the passing crowd. *Somewhere out there is the person who shot Mary Lou and Lennie*, she thought. *And one day soon they'll be found and punished. That's for sure.*

She was determined they'd be caught. And when they were, she expected to see justice.

And if she didn't . . .

Well, there was always Santangelo justice.

And Santangelo justice was something Lucky would not hesitate to use.

Chapter Twenty-eight

BRIGETTE SAT in a first-class seat on a British Airways flight to London. She could have watched a movie, or read a magazine, but she chose to do neither, because all she could think about was confronting Carlo.

The fact that she was pregnant had confirmed her worst fears. If she and Carlo had made love and she'd been a willing participant, she would have remembered it. But she didn't. And that was proof enough that he'd drugged her.

Brigette did not believe in abortion. Once, when she and her mother were having a fight, Olympia had told her that she'd tried to get rid of her before she was born. Brigette knew she could never do that to her unborn baby. It wasn't right, and she wished her mother had never shared that story with her.

It wasn't as if she was running to Carlo, saying, 'Oh, I'm pregnant, please give me the money to get an abortion.' She had a fortune of her own, she needed nothing from him. All she wanted to do was look into his eyes and find out what the lying scum had to say for himself.

A few days earlier she'd gone over to Fredo's studio, and while he was busy on the phone she'd checked out his Rolodex, found Carlo's address and phone number in London and copied them down. Once she'd done that she'd felt more in control of the situation.

She hadn't told Lina, because Lina would have relished every moment and probably begged to join in.

What am I going to say to Carlo when I catch up with him? she thought. *Who knows? When I see him I'll come up with something.*

Suddenly she flashed back on the night Santino Bonnatti had kidnapped her and Bobby, sexually abusing them both. How had she dealt with *that* drama?

She'd reached for a gun and blown him away.

She shuddered at the memory.

Revenge is sweet. Lucky had taught her that. It was a lesson she'd learned well.

She leaned back in her seat and closed her eyes. Soon she'd be there, ready to deal with anything.

☆ ☆ ☆

Heathrow airport was crowded as usual. Special Services met her as she alighted from the plane and whisked her through Customs. Outside the airport a car and driver were waiting to take her to the Dorchester, her favourite hotel. In fact, under different circumstances, London was her favourite city.

After a short drive into town, she checked into the Dorchester, ordered room service, ate in front of the television, then climbed into bed and slept for fourteen hours. Brigette knew how to beat jet lag better than anyone.

She awoke at eight a.m. refreshed and ready to face anything.

The first thing she did was call Lucky in LA. Lucky wanted to know what she was doing in London. 'Work,' she said vaguely. 'I might go on to Milan.'

'Take care,' Lucky said. 'And don't forget to have fun.'

'I always do.'

'Keep in touch.'

whisper. 'Brigette doesn't like people knowing,' he said. 'But the truth is, she's a Stanislopoulos.'

'Of the Stanislopoulos fortune?' Carlo enquired, perking up considerably.

'Yes,' Fredo replied. 'Eventually she will inherit everything. But don't mention that you know.'

'Of course not,' Carlo said smoothly. And as Brigette made her way back to the table, he saw his future.

Carlo was not a foolish man. At thirty-one, he'd been around and knew women very well. Because of his title and elegant looks, women were constantly throwing themselves at him – just like the black girl with Brigette, he could have her any time he wanted. He considered most women to be worthless whores, cheap *puttane* not worth a second glance.

However, as soon as he learned who Brigette was, he made a plan. And because he was in New York for only two days, his plan had to be executed quickly. In his pocket he kept a packet of little white pills, using them when he couldn't be bothered courting a girl all night. One dropped in her drink, and she was his. Not that he needed to drug his conquests, but it was so much easier this way, and did not involve conversation and false declarations of love.

Instinctively he knew that Brigette was not the kind of girl to jump into bed on a first meeting, so shortly before they left the club, he slipped half a pill into her drink. When they reached her apartment she was in an extremely relaxed state, and it was easy to make love to her.

He left before she awoke. He knew exactly what he was doing, using just half a pill. He wanted her to remember this one night of passion. He wanted her to fret and wonder why he hadn't called.

If she was like every other girl he'd slept with, she'd be

waiting by the phone, holding her breath until she heard from him.

Mission accomplished, he flew back to London and his fiancée. But his mind was full of Brigette and what a match they would make.

Calculatingly he decided to give it three months, then he'd return to New York and sweep Brigette up into his arms like a conquering hero. By that time she'd be easy pickings.

In the meantime he needed capital, so he worked on his fiancée, persuading her to buy an antique diamond pin she didn't need, and pocketing the hefty commission he got from the dealer. He then asked her for a short-term loan, explaining that money he was expecting from Italy had inexplicably been held up.

She would do anything for him, this unattractive thirty-three-year-old heiress who still lived at home with her equally unattractive parents.

Unfortunately for her, she wasn't rich enough. Why have her when he could have a beauty who was due to inherit the world?

Chapter Twenty-nine

BASICALLY TEDDY was living his life in fear. Nothing new about that, because the truth was he'd always been a fearful kid – ever since his mother had taken off when he was only four years old.

'Goodbye, Teddy,' she'd said, drunk and full of venom, her luggage stacked in the front hall. 'See if *you* can get along with this whoremongering bastard who calls himself your father!'

Nice words for a four-year-old to remember his mother by.

After that there had been a series of nannies, who never stayed long because they couldn't stand being around Irena, who made their lives miserable.

And then, when he was just eight, along came Price's wife number two – a blonde with a huge bosom and a habit of hugging Teddy too close. She was forever whispering in his ear that he should live his life like a white boy and forget about being black. She told him about racism and hate and that he didn't want to get called a nigger, so maybe he should try bleaching his skin like Michael Jackson.

When Price heard what she'd been filling his son's head with, he'd gone berserk and informed her she was the world's biggest idiot. A few months later she was history.

At an early age, Teddy became used to treading carefully.

And since his dad was always on the road doing stand-up, Teddy's only real companion was Mila. He looked up to her because she was two years older than him and tough. But she never let him get close, always treating him with a mixture of disdain and disinterest.

Now this terrible thing had happened, bonding them together for ever. And he was scared.

He drove his jeep reluctantly, taking it out of the garage only when absolutely necessary. He started leaving the house later and later, riding the bus to school. Every day he expected the cops to turn up at their front door and arrest both of them.

'What's wrong with your car?' Irena asked, because Irena was a witch – she never missed a thing.

''S making a weird noise,' he lied, wishing she'd butt out for once.

She immediately told their night-time guard, who informed him in front of his father that he'd checked out the jeep, and there was absolutely nothing wrong with it.

'I bought you the goddamn car two months ago,' Price complained. 'If there's somethin' wrong with it, why didn'cha tell me? We could've sent it back.'

'Thought I heard a rattle,' Teddy muttered. 'Nothin' serious.'

'Serious enough for you to start ridin' the bus,' Price said.

'I *like* taking the bus,' Teddy said truculently. 'That's the only way I get t' meet real people.'

'Y' know, Teddy,' Price said, staring at him accusingly, 'if I *ever* catch you doin' drugs, I'll whack your ass so bad you won't be able to sit down for a week. You listenin' to me, fool?'

'Yeah, Dad, I hear you.'

'You'd better,' Price said ominously.

Teddy's main priority was staying out of Mila's way, which

was easier since she'd gotten a job at a local burger joint and was no longer in school. Whenever their paths crossed, she glared at him with a scary malevolent look in her eyes. He was a witness to her crime, and she *knew* that he *knew* she was guilty, and that it wasn't his fault.

Occasionally she sidled close enough to make a few threats. 'Remember what I told you, fuck-face. Don't open that puny dumb mouth of yours, 'cause if you *ever* say anything, I'll kill you. You can depend on that.'

He didn't know what to do. He would've liked to have gotten it all out in the open, gone to the cops and confessed everything. The only problem was that if Mila didn't do it first, his father would most certainly kill him. Price's rage would be unbearable.

He spent hours trying to figure out how it had happened. Where had Mila gotten the gun? And the biggest question of all, why had she used it? The two people in the car weren't doing anything to them, they hadn't even put up a real fight.

Every day he pored over the newspapers, trying to find out anything he could about the two victims. One thing he knew for sure: Lennie Golden had recovered, Mary Lou Berkeley was dead.

He studied Mary Lou's pictures in the newspapers and magazines, clipping everything he could about her and hiding it under his mattress for further review. She was so pretty. What had she done to deserve Mila blowing her away?

His school grades suffered. He couldn't sleep at night and couldn't concentrate during the day. He knew that any moment his dad was likely to get on his case, so to ease the tension he started smoking a little weed he scored from a boy at school. At least it took his mind off the horror of what had taken place.

It didn't take long for Price to catch on. One day Teddy arrived home to find him standing in his room. 'What the *fuck* is this?' Price demanded, holding up a couple of half-smoked joints that Teddy had hidden in his closet.

'C'mon, Dad,' Teddy whined. ''S better than mainlining heroin or gettin' into crack – like *you* used to.'

'What *I* used to do has nothin' the fuck t' do with *you*,' Price yelled, eyes bulging. 'Don't look at me to be your example in life, 'cause I ain't no shinin' angel.'

'Never said you were,' Teddy muttered.

And outside his room he saw Mila flit by, ever watchful.

He knew she was listening, spying on him to see if he'd weaken.

He had a plan.

He was going to take off.

It was the only answer.

☆ ☆ ☆

Mila Kopistani did not know who her father was, but she had her suspicions. Irena, her mother, refused to discuss it. All she'd managed to get out of her was that her father was a Russian ex-boyfriend who'd visited America, knocked Irena up, and then returned to his homeland. Mila didn't believe her for a moment: there had to be more to it than that.

Growing up, she hadn't thought about it that much. However, once she reached school age and the other girls started questioning her, she'd grown curious. At first, she'd thought her father might be Irena's boss, Price Washington. But no. He was black and she was white, so she'd abandoned that idea. Then she'd considered Father McBain, the priest at the local church. He and her mom seemed pretty damn friendly. 'Impossible,' one of her girlfriends informed her. 'Priests aren't allowed to do it. He can't be your dad.'

Another dead end.

Desperately, Mila tried to discover the truth. Whenever

Irena left the house, Mila searched through her things but couldn't find anything worth shit.

Mother and daughter did not have a warm and wonderful relationship. Irena was a cold woman, who ran the house with a rigid hand. Two maids came in daily, and she bossed them about as if she were a queen. She treated the gardener, the pool man and any other workers who came to the house the same way. Nobody liked her except Price, and Mila was sure he only put up with her 'cause she was his faithful work slave. She often wondered if they were sleeping together. Sometimes she thought yes, sometimes no. If they *were* sleeping together, they certainly kept it a secret.

Mila had hated Price's two wives. Ginee, the first one, was as bad a druggie as he was at one time. And his second wife, a bimbo blonde, was a joke. A *Playboy* centrefold with fake tits, cascades of dyed blonde ringlets, and a big stupid smile. Mila had spent many an amusing day pinning the bimbo's naked photographs up all over the school, much to Teddy's embarrassment and humiliation.

Mila had always toyed with Teddy, teased and taunted him. Why not? He was a male, wasn't he? He had a father. She didn't. It wasn't fair.

Everyone at school knew she was only the housekeeper's daughter. It irked her that she had no standing while Teddy had a famous dad. Sometimes she made him pay for it. Unfortunately, he was too dumb to understand that she wasn't his friend, that she actually loathed him. And she loathed her mother too, because Irena had never had any time for her. Her mother always put Price Washington first, like he was a fucking king and they should all bow down to him.

When Mila had taken Teddy out with her that other night, her intention had been to get him drunk and mess with his head. She certainly hadn't *meant* to kill anyone, although she had to admit it was a wild feeling. Snuffing out a life had given her a jolt of tremendous power. Price had lorded it over her and Irena all those years, yet she'd produced a gun and managed to end somebody's life, just like that.

She could do it to *him* if she wanted. She had her own kind of power now.

She wouldn't mind shooting Price.

Shooting him or fucking him.

She couldn't decide which would be the worse punishment.

She'd never attempted to turn her mother's boss on, although she knew she could if she tried. Men chased after her all the time, especially at work where she got several propositions a day. She was young, and well aware how to flaunt it. Tight little tank tops, short clingy skirts – all the better to show off her long legs and big bosom. Her cropped dark hair brought out her hazel eyes, and she piled on the makeup when she wanted to look her most alluring.

Men were always checking her out. A few of them had even gotten lucky. Nobody she gave ten cents about, though: she was saving herself for the one who would take her away from being the housekeeper's daughter.

She never wanted to end up like her mom – some rich, famous asshole's work slave. Mila was after money and power. *She* wanted to be the mistress of the house. *She* wanted to have it all. Sometimes she looked at Teddy and saw him as her future. That's if nothing better came along. If she and Teddy got married when they were older, eventually Teddy would inherit all his father's money which meant he'd be rich because Price Washington must have stashed away a bundle. But marrying Teddy would be her last resort. He was never going to change. Even when he was twenty he'd still be a weak loser.

Right now she was worried about him opening his mouth and spilling everything. It was just the kind of dumb thing he was likely to do.

It occurred to her that being mean to him was not helping her case. So she decided to go in the opposite direction and lure him in. A little sex would go a long way towards keeping him on her side. Sex would make him realize where his *real* loyalties lay.

Yeah. Maybe she'd give him a taste of what he was always lusting after. That way she'd have him totally hooked.

Either that or she'd shut his mouth permanently.

Mila could not make up her mind which would be better.

Chapter Thirty

LUCKY TOOK out a full page ad in the *LA Times*, offering a hundred-thousand-dollar reward for information concerning the hold-up and Mary Lou's murder. She also had posters printed and pasted all over the city, concentrating on the mid-Wilshire area, where the crime had taken place. And on either side of the reward sign were the computer-generated images of the two suspects the police sketch artist had come up with.

Detective Johnson warned her they'd be dealing with a lot of cranks and crazies. 'People crawl out of the sewers when they smell money,' he said.

'So be it,' Lucky said. 'Let 'em come. I've got a hunch that, for a hundred grand, we're about to get some answers.'

'I don't usually condone doing this,' Detective Johnson said. 'Makes people greedy. Gives us a lot of extra work, too.'

'Hey,' Lucky said restlessly, 'if it gets results, what do you care?'

She went home to Lennie, who was in his usual blue funk, sitting upstairs in the master bedroom flipping channels with the remote. 'It's a good job I love you,' she said, flopping down on the couch next to him, wondering when he was going to snap out of it.

'Huh?' he said, still changing channels.

'I said,' she repeated, 'that it's a good job I love you.'

'What's *that* supposed to mean?' he said, staring at the TV. 'You had enough?'

'Enough of what?'

'Me.'

'I want the *real* you back, Lennie,' she said softly. 'Is that a major felony?'

'I can't help the way I feel.'

'You should see somebody.'

'Who?'

'There's this woman – she's a shrink and, uh . . . it'd be a good idea for you to talk to someone, and get it all out.'

'Fuck!' he said, standing up. 'You *know* I don't believe in that crap.'

'Nor do I, but I think you need it.'

'How come *you* don't?' he said belligerently.

''Cause I'm not the one sitting around the house sulking,' she answered, not happy with the way this was going.

'Sulking?' he repeated, furious. 'I was with a woman who got blown away, and you think I'm *sulking*. What the fuck is wrong with you, Lucky?' And with that he marched out of the room.

She shook her head. This was getting ridiculous. Lennie's anger was out of control, and there seemed to be nothing she could do.

She went downstairs to the family room, where the kids were excitedly getting ready to visit Gino and Paige in Palm Springs for the weekend. Carioca was going with them. Bobby was not. He finally had a date with the sitcom star he'd been lusting after. And then in the morning he was flying to Greece to spend time with some of Dimitri's relatives.

'Where are you taking her?' Lucky enquired, playing good mom, although Lennie had deeply disturbed her with his non-stop bad mood.

'Dunno,' Bobby said. 'Can I borrow your Ferrari?'

'Are you insane?' Lucky said, trying to decide if now was the time to give him a lecture on safe sex and the use of condoms. 'You're not borrowing my Ferrari. You've got your jeep.'

'Everyone has a jeep.' Bobby groaned. 'Why couldn't I have gotten a Porsche?'

'So you could've been held up like Lennie?'

He shrugged. 'I feel stupid taking a girl like her out in a jeep. She's, like, a big TV star, Mom.'

'Bobby!' Lucky said forcefully. 'I hope you're not turning into a Hollywood kid. A jeep is cool, so don't give me any more of your crap.' Now it was her turn to march out of the room. In the background she heard Maria imitating her. 'Don't give me any more of your crap, Bobby,' squeaked Maria, before dissolving into fits of giggles with Carioca.

Lucky couldn't help smiling. Maria reminded her of herself when she was a kid, feisty and bold, never afraid of anything.

After seeing them off, she looked for Lennie and found him standing on the deck overlooking the ocean. Sliding open the heavy glass doors she went and stood beside him. 'Don't let's fight,' she said, putting her hand on his arm. 'Fighting doesn't help anybody – especially Steven. He's coming for dinner tonight.'

'No, no, I can't see him,' Lennie said, panicking. 'Every time I see him it makes me feel worse.'

'That's pretty damn selfish. Steven's all by himself. Remember – he lost his *wife*?'

'Fuck!' Lennie shouted. 'I can't do this any more.'

'Do what?'

'Any of this shit. I'm taking a drive.'

She almost stopped him, but didn't. She'd never been the clinging type.

On the other hand, she wasn't about to sit around waiting

for him to come home so he could scream at her some more. If she wasn't so goddamn understanding, she'd be screaming back.

She called Steven at his office. 'Would you mind if we switched to a restaurant tonight?' she said. 'Just the two of us?'

'I'd like that,' Steven said. 'How come?'

'The kids have gone to Palm Springs, and Lennie's not feeling great. So how about you and I go to La Scala and tell each other our problems?'

'You got problems, Lucky?'

'Not as big as yours, Steven. I'll pick you up at the office.'

An hour later they sat in a cosy booth in La Scala, eating spaghetti and chopped salads.

Lucky stared at her half-brother intently. 'Steven,' she said, placing her hand over his, 'I want you to know how much I love you and that I truly feel your pain. I wish there was something I could do, but obviously there isn't.'

'I love you too,' Steven said. 'But loving you doesn't bring back Mary Lou.'

'The reason Lennie isn't here,' Lucky continued, 'is because he's consumed with guilt. I'm trying to help him get over it, but it's not easy.'

'Lennie has nothing to feel guilty about.'

'I keep on telling him that.'

'Should I talk to him?'

'No. He's a big boy, he'll have to figure it out on his own.'

'If you change your mind, just say the word. I can talk to him.'

'Let's see how it goes. The important thing is how are *you* doing?'

'I have good days, mostly bad nights.' He gave a hollow laugh. 'I'm getting through it.'

'It's not easy.'

'Tell me.' He picked up a piece of bread and tore it into pieces. 'How's Carioca?'

'Sensational. When do you want her back?'

'She's better off with you, Lucky. She has such a good time being with your kids. What can she do with me? Sit in the house by herself?'

'You're her father,' Lucky said quietly. 'She loves you.'

'I *know* that. But if you could keep her a little longer . . .'

'I will, only you've got to remember that it's tough for her, too. The last thing you want is for her to feel abandoned. Believe me, I know what that's like.' She paused while the waiter refilled their wine glasses. 'I'll never forget the day I discovered my mother floating on that raft in the swimming-pool . . .' For a moment her black eyes clouded over. 'Everything stopped. You can't imagine . . .' Another pause. 'Maybe you can.'

'When I think about what you went through, Lucky, it gives me the strength to keep going.'

'I still miss her,' Lucky whispered softly. 'The pain never goes away, it's always there, it simply gets pushed into the background.'

Steven squeezed her hand. 'Love you, sis.'

She managed a wan smile. 'You too, bro.'

By the time she returned to the house, Lennie was in bed asleep. She hovered beside their bed for a moment, wondering if he was faking it. Since he didn't stir, she decided he wasn't.

This is what marriage is all about, she thought. *For better or worse*. Right now it was for worse, and she had to get him better. If they could only find the attackers, she was sure that would help Lennie feel good again.

Tomorrow she'd badger Detective Johnson, something he was getting used to because she did it every day. And she couldn't care less if he was getting sick of her, since she was convinced that unless she kept bothering him, this case would never get solved.

She went into her bathroom and slipped into black silk pyjamas. Tonight sex with her husband, the love of her life, might be nice. And there was no reason why they shouldn't make love. By withholding himself sexually, Lennie was punishing *her*, and she didn't appreciate it one bit.

She climbed into bed and snuggled up behind him.

He groaned in his sleep and moved away.

This was a first.

Lucky had always been under the impression that she had the perfect marriage. Maybe she was wrong.

She closed her eyes, attempting to sleep. But sleep was a long time coming, and by the time she did drop off she was hurt and angry.

Lennie better get his act together or, as far as she was concerned, they were heading for serious problems.

Chapter Thirty-one

BRIGETTE HAD breakfast in the living room of her hotel suite with Horace Otley, a short, sweaty-palmed man in his mid-forties, who looked like an out-of-work hack for one of the tabloids. However, Horace was not an out-of-work hack. Horace was probably the best private detective in England.

Brigette had hired him two weeks ago from America.

'It'll cost you,' Horace had told her over the phone.

'I don't care,' she'd answered. 'Privacy is my main issue. I'll want you to sign an agreement that you'll never reveal anything about this investigation.'

Horace had agreed, so she'd had one of her lawyers draw up a paper and fax it to him. Horace signed and faxed it back. After that she'd faxed him Carlo's full name and where he worked, and requested every bit of information Horace could come up with. Now here they were, finally getting together.

'It's nice to meet you, Mr Otley,' Brigette said politely.

He bobbed his head, quite startled to be faced with such a gorgeous female, and a famous one too. Naturally he recognized her, and so he should, considering she'd appeared on magazine covers the world over.

'I didn't realize who you were when you hired me,' he said, thinking that he couldn't wait to tell his life partner,

Will, about *this*. Will would *cream* when he heard who Horace was dealing with.

'That's all right,' she said. 'Now perhaps you understand my need for privacy.'

'I protect *every* client's privacy,' Horace said pompously. 'Every one of them is just as important to me, whoever they might be.'

'That's nice to know, Mr Otley. Would you care to order breakfast?'

He put on a pair of wire-rimmed spectacles and perused the menu, deciding on toast, eggs, bacon, sausages and grilled tomatoes.

'Sounds good to me,' she said, calling room service and ordering the same.

Soon she was picking at her food while Horace stuffed his into his mouth as if he hadn't eaten in weeks. 'I've got every bit of information you could possibly need,' he said, between mouthfuls.

'Excellent,' she said, sipping orange juice.

'Carlo Vittorio Vitti. *Count* Carlo Vittorio Vitti – you did know he has a title?'

She nodded.

'Yes, he's a count,' Horace said, 'although the family has no money.'

'Are you sure?'

'His parents reside in Italy, in a run-down palace outside Rome. They're down to two servants and a chauffeur. Both parents are alcoholics.'

'Sounds like a pleasant family.'

'Carlo was sent to London eighteen months ago.'

'How come?'

'There was a big disgrace in Italy.'

'What was it?'

'Carlo was seeing a twenty-year-old married woman,

whose eighty-year-old husband was found asphyxiated in his own garage. The suspicion fell on Carlo.'

'Why? *Did* he do it?'

'There was talk . . . scandal. Before the police acted, his father sent him here to London, which, from what I can ascertain, he hates. He's looking for a rich woman. He's found *one*, but she's not his ideal. However, they *are* engaged.'

'So he *is* engaged?'

'She's a dog,' Horace said, chewing on a piece of bacon. 'Need I say more?'

'That's not a very nice thing to say, Mr Otley,' Brigette scolded. 'A woman might not be the best-looking in the world, but she can have a lovely personality.'

'This one doesn't.'

'How do you know?'

'I have my sources,' he said smugly.

'What about photos?'

'Yes. I have some with me.' He bent down, fishing in a battered leather briefcase, producing an eight-by-ten manila envelope from which he slid several pictures.

Brigette inspected the photos. There was Carlo, undeniably handsome in a blue blazer and grey pants, standing with his arm around a short, plumpish woman who was not at all attractive.

'Is *this* his fiancée?' she asked, hardly able to hide her surprise.

'That's her,' Horace said.

'Hmmm . . . well, I suppose he could've done better.'

'Not money-wise,' Horace said, with an odd little chuckle. 'There aren't that many good-looking heiresses around.'

Brigette pushed away her plate and got up from the table. 'What else can you tell me about him?'

'He's a loner, his father pays his bills, keeps him on a

short leash because, as I said before, they're low on cash. From what I understand, Carlo is waiting to return to Rome when the scandal dies down. Either that or he'll marry this Englishwoman, especially if her father makes him an offer he can't refuse regarding the family business.'

'What's her name?'

'Fiona Lewyllen Wharton. She's heiress to a paper empire.'

'Is there a lot of money?'

'Enough to keep Carlo happy although, from what I hear, *she* doesn't.'

'Why do you say that?'

'Fiona never stays over at his apartment, nor he at her family home – she still lives with her parents in a house in Eaton Square. But he has been known to send for high-class call-girls at midnight. They visit his apartment, stay an hour, and leave.'

'Really?' Brigette said.

And in her mind she was already forming a plan.

Chapter Thirty-two

'WE'RE GETTING inundated,' Detective Johnson said.

'Anything worthwhile?' Lucky asked, not at all satisfied with the way the investigation was progressing, but trying not to blow her cool.

'We're sifting.'

While he was sifting, Lucky had her own team of detectives going from house to house, questioning all jeep owners within a five-mile radius of the hold-up, showing the sketch artist's rendition of the two suspects. If only Lennie could remember at least one of the numbers on the licence-plate. But he couldn't, his mind was a blank.

With the children safely in Palm Springs at their grandfather's house, and Bobby away in Greece, Lucky made a concentrated effort to spend more time with Lennie, hoping she could persuade him to visit Venus' shrink.

Getting him to agree was impossible: he refused to even consider it.

She held her temper and attempted to go along with whatever he wanted to do. Eventually, she knew, he would return to being the man she loved.

'That's okay, Lucky,' he said, when one day she offered to accompany him on one of his marathon walks along the beach. 'Truth is, I'd sooner be alone.'

'You would?' she said, somewhat uptight.

He didn't seem to notice her reaction. 'Uh huh,' he said evenly.

'If that's the way you feel . . .'

'I'm allowed to feel, aren't I?' he snapped.

'Keep it up, Lennie,' she said, her patience faltering. 'You can be alone permanently if that's what turns you on.'

'Is that what you *want*?' he countered. ''Cause if so, it's easy enough to arrange.'

She'd been trying to avoid a fight, but obviously Lennie was heading in that direction – in fact, he seemed determined to get into an argument.

'You're acting like a jerk,' she said. 'Nothing ever pleases you.'

'Can I help it if I prefer to be by myself?'

No, she told herself, staring at him. *I will not get into a fight with this man who I love. I refuse to. And he will not goad me into it.*

'Have you given any thought to New York?' she asked casually. 'We could go for a long weekend and *try* to have fun?'

'Fun?' he said, shaking his head in disbelief. 'Mary Lou's ten feet under and *you* want to have fun?'

'Jesus, Lennie,' she snapped, 'you're really pushing.'

'*I*'m pushing?'

'This feeling sorry for yourself shit has to stop. How long do you think we can take it?'

'Who's we?'

'Me, the kids, anybody who tries to get close to you. You've shut off, Lennie. Just like you did after the kidnapping.'

'I'm sorry if Mary Lou getting killed is inconveniencing everyone,' he said stiffly. 'The timing was wrong, huh? You decided to dump the studio and sit around having *fun*, but unfortunately things haven't worked out the way you planned. And while we're on that subject, it would've been nice if you'd discussed leaving the studio with me *before* you announced it to the world. Do *I* make major decisions without including you?'

'So *that*'s what you're burning up about?'

'No, I'm merely saying I remember once before you made a major decision without asking me – and that was to *buy* the goddamn studio in the first place.'

'Let's not fight, Lennie.'

'Why? You've been following me around for the last six weeks looking for a fight.'

'You are so full of shit!' she responded, outraged that he should be this unfair. '*You*'re the one who's looking for a fight.'

'No. *I*'m the one who merely wants to be left alone. Is that too much to ask?'

'Yes, Lennie, it is,' she said angrily. 'You have a life, a family, and a wife. Do you know that we haven't made love in nearly two months?'

'Ah, so that's what this is all about – sex.'

'It's not sex, Lennie. It's about being together and loving someone.'

'I should've known you would have focused on the sex.'

She stared at him as if he were a stranger, because that's the way he was acting. 'If you could remember the goddamn licence-plate number, perhaps we could catch the killers and get on with our lives,' she said, needling him.

'You think I'm forgetting on purpose?' he said, furious.

'No. But you say you thought you saw it, and yet you can't even remember the first letter.'

'That's not my fault.'

'Y' know, Lennie – I don't care to be around you when you're like this.'

'I think I should move out for a couple of days,' he said.

'Get my head straight without you, since I'm making you so miserable.'

'Move out and what?' she challenged.

'Get laid, get drunk,' he said, waving a verbal red flag. 'Who the fuck knows? I'm fed up with you watching every move I make. You're a very controlling woman. Maybe what I need is some freedom.'

'Screw freedom,' she said vehemently. 'We're married. Being married is togetherness. If it's freedom you want, then let's get a divorce.'

She could hardly believe the words had come out of her mouth. She loved Lennie, they'd been through so much together, yet if he was going to behave like an asshole, she wasn't about to take it.

'Fine with me,' he said, just like that.

Did nine years of marriage mean nothing to him? Was he simply prepared to walk? This situation was getting out of control. But, hey, she'd never been the little woman sitting at home waiting to take crap from some man. She was Lucky Santangelo, and she lived life by *her* rules. If he was so anxious to go, let him.

'I'm outta here,' Lennie said. 'I'll call in a few days when you've calmed down.'

'When *I*'ve calmed down?' she said. 'You've got it wrong, Lennie.'

'No. I can see what's happening here. I'm caught in a trap with you. I'm in prison.'

'*You*'re the one who never wants to leave the beach,' she said heatedly. '*You*'re the one who sits in the house every day. If it's a prison, it's yours – not mine.'

'So what is it you *want* me to do, Lucky? Go out with your Hollywood friends – Venus, Charlie Dollar and that group? They're not my kind of people.'

'Since *when*? You love Venus, and you've always got along great with Charlie.'

'How come you're not mentioning your close friend, Alex, who's only nice to me 'cause he's got a hot nut for you? *And* everyone knows it.'

'Now you're really talking crap.'

'You know it's true. Anyway,' he said abruptly, 'I don't want to discuss it any more. I'm leaving.'

'Go ahead,' she said coldly.

And he did. He went upstairs, threw some clothes in a bag, walked downstairs and out of the house.

Lucky shook her head in disbelief. She loved this man. She'd loved him from the moment they'd met in Las Vegas and had an erotic first encounter. And when they'd re-met a year later, she was married to Dimitri and he to Dimitri's daughter, Olympia. What a tangled web. But they'd loved each other – fiercely, passionately. They'd had two children together, and now he'd walked out. Impossible.

What was she going to do now? Cry?

No fucking way. She was a Santangelo. Santangelos didn't cry.

Besides, as soon as Lennie got his head straight, he'd realize what a mistake he'd made and come running back.

And if he didn't?

Well . . . much as she loved him, Lucky Santangelo was a survivor. And she would go on – with or without Lennie by her side.

Chapter Thirty-three

BY CHANCE Brigette ran into Kyra Kattleman in the health spa at the Dorchester. It was a fortuitous meeting as she'd been thinking about who she could have lunch with, and there was Kyra wearing a bright orange leotard, lifting weights with effortless ease, looking every inch the superjock supermodel she was.

'What are *you* doing here?' they both said at once.

'I'm on my way to Milan,' Kyra said, in her incongruous squeaky voice. 'Is that where you're headed?'

'No, actually I have business here,' Brigette explained. 'I ducked out of Milan this year.'

'I'm doing the Valentino show,' Kyra said casually. 'Dear Val says he can't live without me. I'm his favourite.'

'You sound like Lina,' Brigette said, laughing. 'By the way, what are you doing for lunch today?'

'Nothing,' Kyra said, with a casual shrug. 'I was planning a bit of shopping 'cause I'm leaving in the morning.'

'Then let's go to Le Caprice,' Brigette suggested. 'I hear it's fun.'

'I *love* Le Caprice,' Kyra said enthusiastically. 'And we can do the shopping thing after.'

The last thing Brigette felt like doing was going shopping, but she needed Kyra so she rallied. 'Where did you have in mind?' she asked.

'Harvey Nichols – it's *such* a great store, makes Blooming-dale's look sick.'

'Sure,' Brigette said. 'I'll get us a reservation for lunch. Let's meet in the lobby at noon.'

'Aren't you working out?'

'Of course,' Brigette said, heading for the nearest Stair-master. Working out was boring, but if she wanted to keep a great body it was absolutely necessary. Olympia had verged on the plump side; she would never allow that to happen to her.

Things were falling into position nicely. Lunch at Le Caprice with Kyra and, according to Horace, Carlo would definitely be there.

Good. She didn't plan on wasting a moment.

☆　☆　☆

It was raining in New York as Lina made a wild dash for the airport. Early that morning her agent had called to inform her that Charlie Dollar was leaving for Africa on location, and that the only time he could meet with her was within the next twenty-four hours.

'Don't worry,' Lina had said. 'I'll make it.'

Since her assistant was out sick, she'd called American Airlines, booked herself on a flight, and now she was in a cab on her way to the airport. She glanced at the script her agent had sent over, scanning the role she was supposed to audition for.

The cab driver hit a pot-hole, and she abandoned the idea of reading until she was on the flight.

An hour later she was settled in her seat on the plane, and once more began leafing through the script. The part she was up for was Zoe, the girl next door to Teal – Charlie's character. Zoe's description in the script was of a beautiful, exotic model.

Hmm, that shouldn't be too hard, she thought, reading through Zoe's scenes. In the first scene Zoe heads out of her apartment on the way to the laundry room, bumps into Teal, and a mild flirtation ensues. In a later scene they end up in bed together. *Nudity required,* Lina thought. So what? She'd paraded up and down enough runways in see-through crap – everyone knew what she looked like without clothes, and it was pretty damn spectacular. Besides, all the big actresses were stripping off in the movies, she wouldn't be an exception. No body doubles for Lina: she was prepared to go all the way, *especially* if she was in bed with Charlie Dollar. He had that Sean Connery/Jack Nicholson thing going for him. He was an oldie but a goodie!

The role of Zoe was small, which was a drag. After all, in the modelling world Lina was a major star. But her agent had pointed out that unless she had film on herself, she'd never get a chance. And a flashy role in a Charlie Dollar movie could be it.

She wondered if she should call Brigette's godmother, Lucky, when she got to LA. Then she remembered, Lucky was in London with Brigette. Shame. She'd like to have met her.

The businessman sitting next to her was desperate to make conversation, he kept shooting her knowing looks. She foiled him by hiding behind a Stephen King paperback, which she had no intention of reading, but knew it offered good protection.

She hadn't remembered to order a limo at LAX, so it was into another cab and on to the Bel Air Hotel, where she was greeted by fellow Brit Frank Bowling, the manager, who always looked after her. He gave her a room near the pool, and she unpacked the few things she'd brought with her.

As soon as she was settled she called the LA branch of her agency. 'I'm here,' she announced to Max Steele, her LA agent, whom she'd never met.

'Great, Lina,' Max said, sounding overly friendly. 'Wanna have dinner?'

'No thanks,' she said crisply. 'What I *would* like to know is when I'm supposed to meet Charlie Dollar.'

'I'll set it up,' Max said. 'I might even get good old Charlie to come to dinner.'

'What *is* this?' she asked, slightly irritated. 'A social event or a bleedin' audition?'

Max laughed. 'Don't get upset. It's an audition. This is the way we do things in LA. I'll get right back to you.'

She hung up the phone. One of the disadvantages of being a world-famous supermodel was that everyone wanted to be seen with her. *Especially* agents. They thought it raised their profile. *And that's not the only thing it raises*, she thought, with a ribald chuckle.

Of course, Max Steele might be incredibly attractive, and if he was, she'd be missing out. *Better check him out over drinks*, she thought. Because if she liked him, they might end up in bed. Lina excelled at sex, it was her favourite pastime, and lately she'd been going through a dry spell. Nobody since Flick Fonda, and *he* had been a total waste of time and energy.

Sometimes, when she was feeling very bad, she imagined what it would be like to be a porno star. Oh, God, what a kick – showing off her goods in front of the world! Naughty, naughty!

Not that she'd ever consider it. It was merely one of her erotic fantasies – of which she had many.

☆ ☆ ☆

Kyra talked too much in her loud, squeaky voice. Brigette wished she'd shut up as they entered the exclusive London restaurant. Jeremy, the man who ran the place, gave them a big greeting, ushering them to a prime table against the wall. Brigette made sure *not* to look around. She didn't want to catch Carlo's eye if he was already there: she wanted *him* to come to *her*.

Kyra ordered a martini and immediately began talking about her husband, a fellow model she'd married a few months ago. 'He's meeting me in Milan,' she squeaked. '*I* got him the job. Calvin wanted him in New York, but I insisted he come to Milan. He's *sooo* hunky. A real man.'

'I know,' Brigette said. 'I've worked with him.' Actually, she'd always thought he was gay.

'Can you imagine what kind of children we'll have?' Kyra said dreamily. 'Do you *know* how cute they'll look?'

Hmm, Brigette thought. *Kyra's about as modest as Lina.* 'I'm sure they'll be very beautiful,' she said.

'I'll get pregnant in two years,' Kyra announced. 'Then I'll give birth in Australia, because my mum would like that.'

'She must be very proud of you.'

'Oh, yes, all my family are. I'm a national treasure in Australia. Me and Elle MacPherson and Rachel Hunter – we're *totally* famous. Not like here where there's supermodels all over the place. Cindy, Suzi, Naomi, *you*. Lina, Didi—'

'You'd better not let Lina hear you call Didi a super-model,' Brigette interrupted.

'Why? Is she jealous of her?'

'I'd say there's a touch of rivalry. And, besides, Didi hasn't been working that long, she doesn't deserve the title.'

'She's still pretty famous,' Kyra remarked. 'It's those great big tits on that skinny little bod. Guys cream over her.'

'She's famous because she hired a PR,' Brigette pointed out.

'*I* have a PR,' Kyra said, as if it was a given. 'Don't you?'

'No,' Brigette said. 'Publicity is the *last* thing I need.' And out of the corner of her eye she observed Carlo enter the restaurant.

Good, she thought. *Let the games begin*.

Chapter Thirty-four

TEDDY SPOTTED the posters first. How could he miss them? How could anyone miss them? They were everywhere. Big freaking posters with a hundred-thousand-dollar reward printed in huge letters right in the middle. Naturally everyone stopped when they saw that. And then they read the smaller print, and when Teddy read it, his stomach did a double somersault.

ANYONE WITH INFORMATION
CONCERNING A CAR-JACKING
ROBBERY ON 1 SEPTEMBER
AT THE CORNER OF WILSHIRE
AND LANGTON WILL BE ELIGIBLE
TO COLLECT A REWARD OF ONE
HUNDRED THOUSAND DOLLARS

The reward announcement was bad enough. But there were also pictures – supposedly of him and Mila. Not that the sketches looked like either of them, but there were certain similarities. Mila's narrow eyes and sharp nose. His wide forehead and cropped hair.

He immediately ran to the burger joint where Mila worked and told her what was going on.

She freaked out. 'You'd better keep your mouth shut,'

she warned. 'Nobody knows we did it. There are no witnesses. They don't have the number of the jeep, so we're safe. Remember – keep your fucking mouth *shut*, Teddy.'

But even as she uttered those words, her mind was zooming in a million different directions. A hundred thousand dollars. Boy, what she couldn't do with a hundred thousand dollars!

Teddy, meanwhile, was making his own plans. It was definitely time to run: things were getting too hot. Any moment the cops could come knocking at the door, and when his father discovered he'd been involved in a murder . . . Well, it didn't bear thinking about. He shuddered at the memory of that horrible night. If his dad ever found out he would definitely kill him. Price was a maniac when he lost his temper. He expected his son to be perfect.

Teddy decided he'd better get to his mother's fast. He knew she lived in an apartment on Wilshire, and even though he'd had no contact with her in years, he was sure that when he arrived at her door she wouldn't turn him away. He'd make up a story that Price was back on drugs and beating the crap out of him: that way she'd *have* to take him in.

Saturday afternoon he put on his best rapper outfit – baggy pants swaddling his hips, a hooded oversize sweatshirt and high-top Nikes – then attempted to sneak out.

Price was lounging on the couch in the den watching football on TV. 'Wanna catch some plays with me?' he called, as Teddy tried to sidle past.

'Gotta see some friends, Dad,' Teddy said, in a low voice.

'What time you comin' back?'

'Later.'

'Later,' Price repeated, tossing pretzels into his mouth. 'Now, don't you go smokin' no weed with any of your friends. 'Cause I'll know, an' I'll whack the shit outta you. Got it, boy?'

'Yes, Dad,' he said, moving towards the back door.

As he walked out to the garage, Mila appeared from the kitchen, wearing a tight T-shirt with no bra, and a short fake red leather skirt. She'd dyed her dark hair a startling shade of white blonde and cut it even shorter so that it looked like a crew-cut. He knew why.

'Where you goin', Teddy?' she asked.

He couldn't take his eyes off her nipples, they were sticking out under her T-shirt, demanding attention.

She saw him looking and stuck them out even further.

'Gonna hang with some friends,' he mumbled, not about to confide in *her* – she'd be the last one he'd tell.

'Shame,' she said, chewing on a hang-nail. 'Thought we'd do something today.'

She'd hardly spoken to him since the night of the murder, except to warn him of the dire consequences if he opened his mouth. 'Like what?' he ventured, frightened of her, yet at the same time drawn to her.

'Dunno,' she said, with a casual shrug. 'Take a drive, catch a movie.'

'Not me,' he said, shaking his head. 'Not after the last time.'

'Shit, man,' she said scornfully. 'That's never gonna happen again. I don't even have a gun.'

He didn't believe her, but her nipples were beckoning and he was beginning to weaken. 'You sure?'

'Course I am,' she said, thrusting her tits in his face. 'Besides, you an' I never get t' spend any time together since I'm workin'. Don't you think we should talk?' He nodded. 'You like my hair?' she added.

''S okay,' he said.

'How about it?' she said, moving even closer. 'Can we do something together?'

'S'pose I could meet the guys later,' he said.

'That's my Teddy,' she said, giving him a playful punch on the chin. 'Let's go see *The Bodyguard*.'

'Who's in that?' he asked suspiciously.

'Kevin.'

'Kevin who?'

'Kevin Costner, dunce!'

'Who wants to see *him*?'

'*I* do. Anyway, you can jerk off over Whitney Houston. She's in it, too.'

'Okay,' he said, unable to resist.

'Okay,' she mimicked, teasing him. 'I'll go get a sweater.'

He waited patiently, hoping she'd come back soon. He could always go to his mother's in the morning. If he had a chance to be with Mila, he didn't want to blow it, even though she still scared the crap out of him.

She emerged a few minutes later, a blue sweater tied casually around her narrow waist. 'Let's go,' she said bossily.

He looked at her long legs, then at her tits. 'I'll drive,' he mumbled.

For once she didn't argue.

☆ ☆ ☆

Irena took her boss lunch on a tray. Price was lounging in front of the TV in a tracksuit with no underwear. Irena was well aware that on weekends he never wore underwear, it was one of his little idiosyncrasies.

'Okay, hon,' he said, indicating the coffee table in front of him. 'Put it there.'

'Yes, Mr Washington,' she said.

He glanced up at her briefly, his heavily lidded eyes immediately swivelling back to the TV. 'Teddy's out. Where's Mila?'

'She went with him,' Irena said. 'They're seeing a movie.'

'Nice t' see the kids gettin' along,' he remarked, although he would have preferred Teddy not to hang out with Mila – he still considered the girl a bad influence.

'They should,' Irena said. 'They were raised together.'

'Right,' he said, splaying his legs in front of him.

She couldn't help noticing that he had a semi hard-on, quite obvious in his tracksuit pants.

'Sit down here for a minute,' he said, patting the space next to him. 'Watch the game with me.'

'I have things to do, Mr Washington.'

'I got things for you to do, too,' he said, pulling her down beside him.

Irena was tense. Price Washington was her boss, but he was also, when he felt like it, her lover. Well, not exactly her lover. A more apt description would be that she was his sex slave.

She hated herself for doing everything he asked. She hated herself for being there whenever he felt like getting serviced and none of his girlfriends was around. She knew she was a fool to oblige him. But the sad fact was . . . she loved him.

Price Washington had taken her in when she'd had nothing, just the one small suitcase of possessions that was all she'd brought with her when she'd fled Moscow, where her life had been unbearable. Thank God for the man in the American Embassy who'd befriended her and helped her get an exit visa in her dead cousin's name. They would never have let her out of the country, a convicted prostitute and felon who'd done jail time for killing her pimp, an unspeakable monster who'd grabbed every rouble she'd ever made, and amused himself by carving his name on her buttocks. She'd been lucky and escaped. And when she'd arrived in America, Price Washington was there for her. She would always be grateful.

'Eat your lunch, Mr Washington,' she said stiffly.

'Quit with the Mr Washington shit,' he said, taking her hand and placing it on his crotch. 'There's nobody around.'

She knew exactly what he expected her to do. She was supposed to rub it a little, make it hard, take it out, suck it, put it back and go away. The routine never varied.

'I have work to do,' she said.

'Work this,' he said, moving her hand up and down.

In a way she supposed she should be flattered. Price Washington had many girlfriends, and any one of them would have been only too happy to sit in front of the TV with him all day doing whatever he wanted. But Price enjoyed watching football alone. He liked making his phone bets, hollering at the players on the TV screen, and snacking on a variety of junk foods. Maybe he even liked having *her* around. She didn't know. He never told her.

Once in a while he summoned her to his room late at night when Mila and Teddy were asleep. There were times he even touched her, but not very often. Once, when Teddy was away at summer camp, and Mila was staying with a girlfriend, she'd spent the night in his bed, naked and in total abandon. It had been the most memorable night of her life. After it was over he'd never mentioned it again.

When he'd first started coming on to her it had been in his drug days, those lazy, hazy days when he had no idea what he was doing. She'd dismissed his attentions at first. But even after he was stone cold sober and absolutely straight, he continued from time to time to call on her services.

There weren't any other men in Irena's life. She lived for Price, he was all she cared about.

Of course, there was her daughter, Mila. But Irena was well aware what a devious little bitch Mila could be. There was nothing she could do about it. She'd given up trying.

Although if she was truthful with herself, she'd admit that she'd never really tried in the first place.

Her most fervent hope was that Mila would find a man, get married and go away. And then when Teddy left, she'd finally be alone with Price, and maybe, just maybe, he'd realize she was the only woman who genuinely cared about him.

☆ ☆ ☆

To Teddy's amazement, Mila snuggled close in the cinema. He couldn't believe it. This was something he'd dreamed about ever since he'd hit puberty, yet he was still scared of her. He couldn't help thinking of her firing the gun . . . killing Mary Lou. At the same time he wanted to grab a feel of those perky little tits and touch those hot sexy thighs. He wanted to shove his johnson at her and have her caress it.

He'd never touched a girl – he was way behind the other dudes in his class, who'd all been making out while he'd been shut in a boys-only school in New York, thanks to Price, who thought that would force him to concentrate on his work.

Price did not want him getting into any of the things that he'd done. Endless women, wild sex, drugs, and booze. Price wanted him to be perfect. And that was impossible.

'Wanna touch my tits?' Mila whispered seductively in his ear.

'Wh-what?' he stammered, sure he hadn't heard correctly.

'Do you?' she encouraged, moving even closer.

'C-can I?'

'Christ, Teddy,' she said forcefully. 'You're such a loser. For God's sake, go for it.' And with that, she grabbed his hand and shoved it up her T-shirt.

Feeling her hard, pointed nipples, he nearly came in his pants. Her tits were the best thing he'd ever felt.

Was this sex? He had a giant hard-on – which was nothing new because he got hard every time he looked at a girlie magazine. Only this was the real thing, this was Mila, and his heart was pounding.

Her hand crept down to stroke his erection. 'Oooh, aren't *you* a big boy?' she said, licking her lips with a snake-like pink tongue. 'My little Teddy – what a surprise!'

They were sitting in the back row, her choice. Whitney Houston and Kevin Costner were emoting on the screen, but who cared? Teddy certainly didn't. Right now he didn't care about anything except his interaction with Mila – the object of his lust.

She snaked her hand down the front of his pants. Flesh upon flesh. He thought he'd died and gone to heaven. Then, without warning, he felt himself squirting all over her hand.

'Ha!' she exclaimed. 'That was quick. Now you belong to me. Did you know that, Teddy? You always belong to the first woman you have.'

'But – but I haven't had you,' he stammered.

'That's okay,' she said, matter-of-factly. 'We're just starting. We got plenty of time.'

Chapter Thirty-five

'I HAVEN'T heard from you in a while.'

'Who's this?'

'You're kidding, right?'

Lucky sighed and held the phone tight. 'Hi, Alex,' she said. 'Your timing is impeccable.'

'What does *that* mean?'

'It means that twenty minutes ago Lennie and I had a big fight and he walked.'

'Walked?'

'You heard it here first.'

'Jesus! This isn't right.'

'Tell me about it. I'm sitting in an empty house with nobody to punch in the face.'

'If it's a face you want, you can have mine.'

'I'm angry and frustrated.'

'Sounds healthy.'

'Are you alone?'

'I could be in ten minutes. Why?'

'Thought I might come over and vent.'

'Want me to drive to your house and collect you?'

'I'm still capable of driving, thankyouverymuch.'

'I'll get out the vodka.'

'I'll see you in ten.'

What am I doing? she thought. *Running to Alex at the first sign of trouble. This is insane.*

And, yet, why shouldn't she go to Alex? Whether Lennie liked it or not, he *was* her best friend. And she couldn't burden Steven: he had enough to cope with.

Besides, her relationship with Alex was absolutely platonic.

Of course, there was that one wild night five years ago . . . but that had been a one-off they'd both agreed to forget about. And, anyway, Alex only went for Asian women, and she was in love with Lennie. There was absolutely no chemistry between her and Alex. Absolutely none.

Before leaving, she called Palm Springs to talk to her children. Instead she got Gino, who informed her they were all eating dinner. 'Everything okay with you, kid?' Gino asked.

'Of course. Why?'

'Somethin' in your voice.'

Oh, he knew her very well indeed, her father. He was a canny old man. 'Don't be silly,' she said lightly. 'I'm enjoying the break.'

'We'll keep the kids as long as you want,' he said. 'They're havin' a good time.'

'Thanks, Gino. And please thank Paige for me.'

Five minutes later she was in her Ferrari on her way to Alex's house. He lived further along the Pacific Coast Highway, in a Richard Meier-designed modern masterpiece. They were neighbours in a way, although neither of them ever dropped by.

He was standing at his front door, waiting for her. 'This is a nice surprise,' he said. 'Sorry to hear that you're so pissed off.'

'Right,' she said, getting out of her Ferrari. 'And so would you be.'

'I'll tell you what the plan is,' he said, holding her arm. 'We'll take my car, 'cause I hate your driving.'

'Take your car where?'

'We're going up the canyon to the Saddlebag Inn, where we will have a leisurely dinner, during which you can tell me everything.'

'I wasn't planning on dinner,' she said, gesturing at her outfit. 'I mean, look at me – I'm in jeans and a sweater.'

'Lucky, I don't know how to tell you this – but you're the most beautiful woman I've ever seen.'

'You're prejudiced, Alex, 'cause I'm your best friend.'

'Could be. But since you're also the smartest woman I know, we won't argue. Here's the deal. My fridge is empty and we both need to eat.'

'I'm not hungry.'

'You'd better be. I was planning a wild night of tantric sex with Pia, but since you've ruined *that* little scenario, let's go satisfy me in some other way.'

She couldn't help smiling. 'Hmm . . . just because I'm not into tantric sex . . .'

'Ha ha!' Alex said. 'I'm amused.'

'I aim to please.'

'Stop carrying on,' he said, 'and get in my car.'

'God, you're bossy,' she grumbled. 'I'd forgotten what it was like being around you.'

'I'm a director,' he said briskly. 'That's the way we are.'

She climbed into his Mercedes and they set off.

As they drove up the canyon, she started laughing.

'Glad to see I've brought a smile back to your face,' he said, glancing over at her. 'Care to share the joke?'

'I'm remembering,' she said.

'What?'

'The last drive we took under adverse circumstances.'

'You mean that drive when we were *supposed* to go see Gino in Palm Springs?'

'That's the one,' she said. 'I was in a freaked-out state

'cause that's when I thought Lennie was dead. But instead it turned out he'd been kidnapped. Only we didn't know that, right?'

'Sounds like a plot from one of my movies.'

'I hope not.'

'If I remember correctly you were *so* wasted. And we ended up in a sleazy bar with some crazy stripper – what was her name?'

'Driving Miss Daisy,' Lucky said, chuckling as she remembered the outrageous black stripper they'd somehow gotten attached to.

'Right,' Alex said, laughing too. 'You insisted I give her a job.'

'And you wouldn't,' Lucky said.

'God!' Alex said, smiling at the memory. 'That was some night. You were totally out of it.'

'And I suppose *you* were stone cold sober.'

'As a matter of fact I was,' he said. 'Had to be. One of us needed to be in control.'

'Sure,' she said.

'Then we had wild sex in that Norman Bates motel in the middle of nowhere,' he reminded her. 'And in the morning you were gone.'

Lucky stopped laughing. 'Alex,' she said, her face serious, 'you were never supposed to mention that. I *was* drunk. I didn't know what I was doing.'

'Never thought I'd hear *you* come up with an excuse like that,' he said, shaking his head.

'It's not an excuse, it's a fact. For all I know we didn't even *have* sex. You probably passed out.'

'Thanks a lot.'

'Did you?'

'What?'

'Pass out?'

'If it makes you feel better.'

They drove in silence for a few minutes, then Alex said, 'You ever tell Lennie?'

'Of course not.'

'Then why does he hate me?'

'He doesn't hate you.'

'Sure he does.'

'That's not true. We're all friends.'

'We *were* all friends for about two months after he reappeared, then suddenly his attitude changed. You must've noticed.'

'He likes you, Alex.'

'Bullshit! I think he knows.'

'There's no way he could possibly know,' she said. 'I never told him.'

'Anyway, what was he doing all that time he was held captive in a cave – jerking off?'

'That's not a very nice thing to say.'

'What about the girl who rescued him?'

'Nothing happened between them.'

'How do *you* know?'

'Because he told me and I trust him.'

'Okay, if *you* believe it, *I*'ll believe it.'

'Can we quit this conversation, Alex.'

'Yes, Lucky, whatever you say.'

☆ ☆ ☆

Once Lennie was out of the house and in his car, he realized he had nowhere to go. He also realized that Lucky was right, he *was* taking his lousy mood out on her, and any sane person knew that it wasn't her fault.

She'd mentioned divorce. How could she mention divorce at a time like this? The very fact that she'd done so angered him. Christ – didn't she understand what he was going through?

Yes, a little voice whispered in his head. *She understands all right. You're behaving like an asshole, and it's gone on too long.*

Cool down, that's what he had to do. Cool down and get his head together. Go home, apologize, and resume normal life. Because whatever he did could not bring Mary Lou back.

In the meantime, he drove around aimlessly, finally deciding to check into the Sunset Marquis for the night. Being by himself for one night wasn't such a bad idea. After all, he'd endured months of solitary confinement when he'd been kidnapped.

It had taken him a while when he'd got back from that ordeal to face life again. Now this: the setback he'd been praying wouldn't happen.

Mary Lou's image kept dancing before his eyes. So pretty and sweet and talented. What if he'd gone for his gun immediately? What if he'd thrown open his car door and fought with the attackers?

What if, what if, what if . . . The words kept going through his head, driving him insane.

Perhaps tomorrow he'd feel better. He wasn't going home until he did. Lucky deserved better.

☆ ☆ ☆

Alex allowed her to talk. They sat outside at a table for two, and Lucky let fly with all her problems.

'Maybe I made a mistake giving up my job at the studio,' she said, reflecting on the situation. 'It wasn't that I didn't enjoy what I was doing, I simply felt my responsibility was to spend more time with Lennie and my kids.'

'Do you miss being at Panther?' Alex asked.

'I *think* I do,' she said uncertainly. 'It was hard work, but that's what I enjoy. I've always worked hard. When I was in my twenties I was building hotels in Vegas and Atlantic City. Gino taught me the work ethic, y' know. Get out there and do it – and do it good.'

'If you miss it, you can always go back. After all, you still own the studio.'

'I'd feel kind of stupid going back so soon. I have to give the people I've put in charge a chance.'

'Then what's your plan? You'll go nuts sitting around doing nothing.'

She nodded, picking up her wine-glass. 'You're right.'

'I have an idea,' he said.

'What?'

'Why don't you produce a movie? It's a whole different deal from sitting in an office, fighting off agents and producers. Produce your own movie, Lucky,' he urged. 'Something you feel passionate about.'

'I never thought of that.'

'You'd enjoy the challenge. Besides, you're in the perfect position. You don't have to go through the shit of getting a studio to put up the money. You can greenlight your own project, then produce it.'

'I'm not experienced enough.'

'How about taking on a project with me?'

She laughed drily. 'That would go down well with Lennie.'

'So now you're going to live your life worrying about what Lennie thinks, huh? Where's that independent spirit of yours?'

'Lennie *is* my husband, Alex.'

'I know that, but surely you don't have to ask his permission?'

'To tell you the truth, I think you're right – he *is* a little bit jealous of you. So if we undertook a project together, that might put him over the top.'

Alex shrugged. 'Just an idea.'

'Thanks for the thought anyway,' she said. 'We'd probably drive each other crazy, because I'm *very* opinionated. And so are you.'

'*You*'re opinionated?' Alex said, his lethal crocodile grin coming at her full force. 'Wow! I'd never have guessed.'

Lucky couldn't help smiling back. 'Let's talk about *you* for a while. How's your mother?'

'Dominique's fine. Since she married the opera singer, she leaves me alone.'

'That's nice to know. You must feel good about that.'

'Stop sounding like a shrink.'

'I'd have made an excellent shrink.'

'You'd have made an excellent anything.'

'You always make me feel good, Alex.' She took another sip of wine. 'By the way, how's your love life?'

'You *know* about my love life, Lucky,' he said ruefully. 'They come, they go. *I* come, they go.'

'Alex, Alex, why don't you find a nice girl and settle down?'

'Now you sound like my mother.'

She laughed softly. 'First your shrink, then your mother. Which do you choose?'

'If I had a choice,' he said slowly, 'you'd be a free woman.' A long meaningful pause. 'And you'd be with me.'

Chapter Thirty-six

'DON'T LOOK now,' Kyra said, speaking out of the corner of her mouth. 'There's a guy sitting at the table to our left who hasn't taken his eyes off me.'

'Really?' Brigette said.

'Yeah,' Kyra said. 'He keeps on staring at me. Of course, I'm used to it.'

Here we go again, Brigette thought. *Kyra and Lina are exactly alike. Apart from the colour of their skin and their accents. Mega egos!*

'I should tell him I'm married, put the poor bloke out of his misery,' Kyra said, fluffing out her hair.

'Why don't you do that?' Brigette said.

'I will when he comes over.'

'What makes you think he's coming over?'

''Cause he's getting up now. He's on his way. And, baby, he's *major* cute!'

Brigette picked up her glass of Evian water and took a sip. Kyra was in for a surprise when she saw whom he was really coming over to see.

A moment later, tall and handsome Carlo stood in front of their table. 'Brigette!' he exclaimed. 'How nice to see you. *What* are you doing in London?'

She glanced up as if she was utterly surprised. 'Excuse me?' she said politely. 'Do I know you?'

'Do you know me?' he said with a laugh. 'I am Carlo.'

'Carlo?' she said vaguely. 'Oh . . . *Fredo*'s Carlo. How *are* you?'

His expression told her he couldn't believe she didn't recognize him.

Kyra, meanwhile, was trying to get introduced. 'Friend of yours?' she asked, giving Brigette a sharp nudge.

'Oh, yes, uh . . . Carlo . . . sorry . . .'

'Count Carlo Vittorio Vitti,' he said, kissing Kyra's hand. 'And you are?'

'Oh, come on,' Kyra said, bursting with laughter. 'You don't know who I am?'

'No, I'm sorry – should I?'

'The rest of the world certainly does,' Kyra said, slightly put out. 'I'm Kyra Kattleman.'

'Kyra Kattleman.' He repeated her name, rolling it over his tongue. 'Are you an actress?'

'Oh, Lordy, where do *you* live?' Kyra said, unamused by his total lack of recognition.

Brigette was quite enjoying the exchange.

'So, Brigette,' Carlo said, 'what are *you* doing here in London?'

'Visiting friends,' she answered casually.

'And Fredo didn't ask you to call me?'

'No. Actually, I haven't worked with Fredo lately. It's nice to bump into you though.'

He stared at her, noting that she was even more lovely during the day. Skin like peaches and cream, soft honey-blonde curls, and an exquisite mouth, pouty and inviting. He remembered making love to her, *he* remembered it well. Only she probably didn't recall the details. One of the disadvantages of the little white pills.

'Where are you staying?' he asked.

'The Dorchester.'

'So am I,' Kyra said, joining in. 'Leaving tomorrow for Milan. It's fashion week. Valentino can't do his show without me.'

'Ah,' Carlo said. 'So you are a model?'

'Not *a* model,' Kyra said, fluttering her long lashes. 'A *super*model. You've heard that word, I'm sure.'

'Ah, yes . . . Naomi Campbell.'

Kyra frowned. 'Why does everyone say Naomi Campbell. There *are* other supermodels, you know. Cindy, me, Kate Moss . . .'

'Brigette,' he said, turning his attention back to the woman who was one day to be his wife, 'are you free for dinner tonight?'

She smiled sweetly. 'As a matter of fact,' a pause, 'I'm not.'

'That *is* a shame.'

'Yes, isn't it?'

'How long will you be staying in London?'

'A few days. Depending on what my friends want to do.'

He wondered if they were male or female friends. It would not do to have a rival enter the picture; he hadn't counted on that. According to Fredo, Brigette was a loner who did not go out a lot. Now all of a sudden she was here in London with a group of friends. This wasn't the way he'd planned it.

'How about dinner tomorrow night?' he suggested.

'Mmm . . .' she said. 'I think I'm busy.'

This was ridiculous. Women never turned him down. 'Perhaps you can change your plans?'

'I could try. Why don't you give me a call.'

'I will,' he said, lifting her hand to his lips. 'You look as beautiful as ever.' He lowered his voice. 'You *do* remember our night in New York?'

'Of course,' she said cheerfully. 'You, me, Lina and Fredo. We went dancing, didn't we? Had a great time.'

Now he was in a quandary. Was it possible that she did *not* remember anything at all about him making love to her? Damn! He'd only given her half a pill, she was supposed to be wondering why he hadn't called her. And here she was sitting in London without a care in the world.

'I will call you later, Brigette,' he said. 'We will talk.' He nodded briefly in Kyra's direction. 'A pleasure.'

'The pleasure was all mine,' Kyra said, adding a succinct, 'By the way, I'm married, so *I* can't have dinner with you either.'

'I'm glad you told me that.'

'Well!' Kyra said, as he walked away from the table. '*Told* you he was staring at me. Good job he knew you, so he had a legitimate excuse to come over.'

Brigette nodded. Things were working out just fine. Soon she would get her revenge on Carlo for taking advantage of her. It was a good feeling.

☆ ☆ ☆

Lina considered Max Steele a babe, which meant that more than likely she'd fuck him later. That's if Charlie Dollar didn't materialize. If she had a choice between an agent and a star, she'd take the star every time. Law of the jungle.

Max was a partner in IAA, International Artists Agency, a very hot place to be. He was partners with Freddie Leon, the super-agent. She was a bit miffed that Freddie himself hadn't chosen to handle her but, from what she'd heard, Max was almost as good.

He met her at the bar in the Peninsula, and they got along straight away.

'Is Charlie coming?' she asked, crossing her long legs and lighting a cigarette.

Max's eyes were popping. 'Baby, one look at you and he'll be coming all the way to Africa!'

'You're a cute one, huh?' she said, blowing smoke in his direction.

'There's only one cute one here,' Max said with a sly smile. 'And it certainly ain't me.'

She continued checking him out. Max Steele was not movie-star handsome, but he had an abundance of boyish charm, a full head of curly brown hair, an in-shape body, and plenty of charisma.

'So who's the director?' she asked, sipping a rum and Coke through a straw.

'A friend of mine,' Max said, with a wink. 'But you don't have to worry about the director. If Charlie likes you, we're in.'

'Who does the studio want for the part?' she asked, anxious to find out who she was up against.

'They're after a name,' Max said. 'They're pushing for Angela or Lela, even Whitney.'

'Don't be daft,' Lina said, snorting with laughter. 'It's not a big enough part for Whitney. And she *certainly* wouldn't take her clothes off. Bobby would *never* put up with it.'

'You'd be surprised,' Max said. 'Roles for black actresses are not that easy to find.'

'Oh, it's a *racist* thing in Hollywood, is it?' she said, cocking her head to one side.

'It's always been a racist thing in Hollywood,' Max replied, thinking that this girl was a total knock-out.

'Really?'

'You're far more stunning than your photographs.'

She giggled. 'Yeah, like I haven't heard *that* line before.'

'It's not a line,' he said indignantly. 'I'm an agent, I have to be truthful with my clients. If you looked like shit I'd tell you.'

'Sure you would,' she said sanguinely. 'An' the Pope goes rollerskatin' up my arse.'

'Oh,' Max said. 'Charlie's going to *love* you.'

☆ ☆ ☆

Brigette accompanied Kyra on her shopping trip to Harvey Nichols. She even bought a few things herself – some cool Police shades, a soft pink cashmere sweater and a long silk scarf.

'*Told* you this was a great store,' Kyra boasted, as if she was personally responsible for the array of tempting goods.

Brigette nodded.

'Y' know,' Kyra announced, completely oblivious to the fact that Carlo had only had eyes for Brigette, 'if I wasn't married, I would've gone out with that bloke at lunch.'

'Why?' Brigette questioned.

'*Why?*' Kyra answered, surprised that Brigette would even ask. ''Cause he's a babe. And he's got that count thingy going for him.'

He's a bastard, Brigette wanted to say. *He drugged and raped me, and he's going to pay for it.*

But she didn't say a word.

This was her game now, and she would play it her way.

Chapter Thirty-seven

TWO THINGS struck Lennie when he awoke. One, he wasn't in his own bed; and two, several numbers were jumping around in his head.

Was it possible that he was finally remembering the licence plate?

He groped for a notepad and quickly jotted down the numbers – three of them. Not enough, but better than nothing. Then he called his wife.

Lucky answered, sounding sleepy.

'It's me,' he said, very upbeat as if nothing was going on. 'We should talk.'

'That's what I've been trying to do for the last six weeks,' she said, waking up with a start.

'Okay, okay,' he said. 'I admit it's my fault. No need to get belligerent, I'm trying to be nice here.'

'*You*'re trying to be nice?' she responded hotly, struggling to sit up. 'Wasn't it *you* who walked out last night?'

'I know, honey,' he said soothingly, 'and I got a feeling it was a good thing 'cause it gave us space. And guess what?'

'What?' She sighed, thrown by his sudden change of mood.

'I came up with a couple of numbers that I'm sure were part of the licence plate.'

'Have you called Detective Johnson?'

'Not yet.'

'What're you waiting for?'

'To speak to you first. Can we meet for breakfast, or shall I come home right now?'

'No, Lennie,' she said sternly, not about to forgive him so fast. 'You walked out last night. You're right, we both need space.'

'But I miss you, baby.'

She felt herself beginning to weaken, Lennie had that effect on her. 'I miss you, too,' she said quietly.

'I'll be there in twenty minutes.'

'No,' she said quickly. 'I'll meet you for breakfast.'

'If that's what you want.'

'Yes. Where are you?'

'At the Sunset Marquis. Hurry.'

'As soon as I'm dressed. In the meantime call Detective Johnson.'

Thoughtfully she put down the phone. Maybe Lennie was right, one night apart and he realized how wrong he was. Thank God! Because she couldn't stand fighting with him, it drove her crazy.

Before she could get out of bed the phone rang again. She grabbed it. 'Okay, okay – I'm on my way,' she said.

'You are?' Alex said.

'Oh – it's you.'

'Oh, it's me. Does that indicate that you've heard from your husband.'

'What're you? A psychic?'

'Kind of.'

'Okay, you're right. He called, wants to meet. And I must say he sounds a whole lot better.'

'I couldn't be happier,' Alex drawled sarcastically.

'Don't be a prick. Be happy for me.'

'I prefer it when you're separated.'

'It didn't even last twenty-four hours.'

'Shame.'

'Quit being such a smartass.'

'And she continues to entice me with her masterful use of the English language.'

'Anyway, Alex, thanks for last night, you helped as usual. Talking to you is the best.'

'You know I'm *always* here for you, Lucky.'

'And it's much appreciated. Oh, yes, and the good news is that I won't be bothering you again. You're free. You can call up Mia or Pia, or whatever her name is, and get into that tantric-sex thing you mentioned.' A meaningful pause. 'By the way, is it worth it?'

He gave a dry laugh. 'When you're ready to find out, let me know.'

'Oh, and, Alex,' she added casually, 'not that it's a big secret or anything, but I'd sooner not piss Lennie off, so let's keep last night's dinner between us.'

'Damn! And I was gonna call the *Enquirer*.'

She hung up smiling, and dressed quickly. She was excited at the thought of seeing Lennie, it was almost as if she was embarking on a date with him.

Before leaving the house she called Steven. 'How's my favourite brother today?' she asked cheerfully.

'Still here,' Steven said. 'I was thinking of driving down to Palm Springs to visit the kids.'

'Sounds like a great idea to me.'

'Want to come?'

'I would, but it seems like I only just got rid of them. And actually . . . I was planning a romantic weekend alone with Lennie.'

'Think I'll call Gino, tell him I'm on my way.'

'By the way, before I forget, Venus and Cooper are having an anniversary party on Monday. They wanted me to ask if you'd drop by.'

'Thanks anyway, but I'll pass.'

She had hoped he'd say yes. As far as she knew he'd gone nowhere since Mary Lou's death. 'Isn't it time you got out?'

'Lucky,' he answered slowly, 'it hasn't been long enough.'

'I know you need time, Steven, but eventually you'll have to meet other women.'

'No,' he said fiercely, 'I had enough women before Mary Lou. She *was* my life, my prize. I'll never be able to replace her. And I have no desire to do so.'

'That's how you feel now, but don't forget that old cliché, time heals everything.'

'It doesn't heal, it covers up.'

'Whatever you say,' she said, backing off, because the worst thing she could do was push him. 'Have a good drive to Palm Springs. Kiss my babies for me, and hug Carioca.'

'I will.'

'Uh . . . Steven, maybe when you leave Palm Springs you should take her home with you, spend time together. Y' know, daddy and daughter, that kind of deal.'

'She likes staying with you, Lucky.'

'And we love having her, but she can't stay here for ever, because that's not good for either of you.'

'Okay,' he said impatiently. 'I get it.'

He knew she was right, his daughter should be with him. But he didn't need it shoved in his face. It was difficult enough getting through each day. And the sad thing was that every time he looked at Carioca she reminded him of Mary Lou.

'By the way, I have excellent news,' Lucky added.

'What?'

'Lennie came up with a couple of numbers from the licence-plate.'

'That *is* good news.'

'I kind of threw him out last night, and I guess sitting alone in a hotel room gave him time to think.'

'You threw Lennie out?'

'It was a mutual deal. I told you before, he's having a lot of trouble with this.'

'We both are, Lucky,' Steven said grimly. 'We both are.'

☆ ☆ ☆

When Lucky walked in Lennie was sitting at a table near the hotel pool. He jumped up and waved. She waved back, dodging her way around palm trees to reach him.

'Hello, you,' he said, holding out his arms, half an embrace, half a gesture of apology.

'Hello you, too,' she said, falling into them. He gave her a long, lingering soul kiss. 'Wow!' she said, backing off and gasping for breath. 'Where did you come up with *that*?'

'You're my wife, aren't you? I'm entitled.'

'Hmm . . .' she said, thinking that he looked more relaxed than he had in weeks. 'Did you call the detective?'

'I did.'

'And?'

'He told me it's a big help.'

'This ain't bad,' she said, looking around, checking out the small hotel.

'I figured if I was taking off I may as well do it in style,' he said. 'This hotel is full of horny models and English rock stars. Better vibe than the fancier places.'

Lucky regarded him with a quizzical expression. 'Okay,' she joked. 'I'll take the rock stars – you can stick with the horny models.'

He scratched his chin. 'Wanna see my room?'

'Is it worth seeing?'

'You tell me,' he said, taking her by the hand and leading her along the side of the pool to one of the bungalows.

Inside the room the shades were drawn, the bed rumpled. 'So . . .' she said casually. 'Did you get laid and drunk?'

'Oh, yeah, sure,' he said, gesturing across the room. 'Can't you see all the signs? Empty bottles, women's panties, drug paraphernalia.'

'Lennie, Lennie,' she said, shaking her head and smiling. 'What am I going to do with you?'

'What're *you* gonna do with *me*?' he said, perplexed. 'The question is, what am *I* gonna do with *you*?'

She sighed. 'Don't let's get into that game again.'

'What game?'

'Repeating everything.'

'Okay,' he said. 'Let me tell you what happened. I woke up this morning, and it was like I was struck by a ray of light. I *saw* the jeep driving away. I *saw* the licence plate, and those numbers came to me. If I keep thinking about it, I'll come up with the rest of them. You're right. When those murderers are caught, I'm gonna feel totally different.'

'Revenge has always worked for me,' Lucky said. 'Lock 'em up and throw away the key.'

'I want to help make it happen,' Lennie said. 'I want my day in court.'

Lucky sat down on the edge of the bed, testing the mattress. 'Nice room,' she said, 'but now I'd like you to come home.'

'I'm ready.'

'This is good, 'cause I sent the kids away so we could have a romantic weekend.'

He came over and stood in front of her. 'I'm sorry for

walking out and acting like a jerk. I kind of got stir crazy, and took it out on you.'

She reached up and touched his cheek. 'And I'm sorry I didn't tell you about the studio. You're right, Lennie, I was wrong. I did it to you once before and you went crazy – I remember that now.' A long beat. 'Y' see, I thought I'd surprise you. Then after, I realized we should've discussed it.'

'Right.'

'But you know me, I have a thing about making my own decisions. Thing is, I've never *had* to answer to anyone.'

'Do you know?' he said. 'We've been married nine years.'

'I know that.'

'And right now I feel as if we've been married nine minutes.'

'Me, too.'

'I know I haven't been much fun to be around lately, but believe me, I'll make it up to you.'

'Promise?'

'You got it. Anything you want.'

'Anything?' she teased.

'You,' he said, smiling, 'are such a turn-on.'

'I am?' she said, toying with his zipper. 'Tell me more, Lennie.'

'Well, all I have to do is look at you . . .'

'And?'

'. . . and Elvis is back in town.'

She burst out laughing. 'Such a way with words!'

'Remember our first hotel room?' he said.

'How could I ever forget?' she said, laughing. 'Vegas.'

'And you walked out on me.'

'That's 'cause you thought I was a hooker.'

'You acted like one.'

'Thanks a lot,' she said indignantly. 'I was single. I saw something I liked and went for it. What's wrong with *that*?'

'You always lived your life like a man, didn't you?'

'Seems to me men have always known how to have a good time.'

'And you, my little darling, have always had a good time, too.'

'And you, my little sweetheart,' she countered, 'were never exactly a virgin. In fact ... the word *stud* comes to mind. You and your never-ending parade of blondes.'

Now they were both laughing as she pulled him down on the bed beside her.

'Lucky, Lucky,' he sighed, 'I love you more than anything in the world.'

'You too,' she whispered.

'And I *never* want to hear the word divorce come out of your mouth again.'

'I promise.'

'You do?'

'I do.'

And then they were kissing, and soon they were caught up in passion and love and everything nice.

Lennie was back, and it felt indescribably good.

Chapter Thirty-eight

AT BRIGETTE'S request, Horace Otley came up with a detailed report of Fiona Lewyllen Wharton's movements. According to Horace's report, Fiona worked at an art gallery off Bond Street, and every Saturday morning she had a standing appointment at a nearby hairdresser's with a stylist named Edward.

Brigette made an appointment for herself. It wasn't difficult because once she announced who she was the salon were so thrilled to accommodate her that they would have cancelled anybody. As it happened, she made her appointment fifteen minutes before Fiona was due to appear.

Carlo had called her several times since bumping into her at lunch. She'd instructed the hotel switchboard to inform him that she was not available, which she knew must be driving him crazy. Carlo was not a man used to being turned down.

The one thing Brigette didn't think about was being pregnant. She pushed the thought out of her mind – it was too disturbing. Right now she had to concentrate on dealing with Carlo.

She arrived at the hairdressing salon on time. There were several stylists working hard, and a few assistants who couldn't help staring at her.

Edward was a sweet-faced, fair-haired boy who could

hardly believe his luck. 'My goodness, who recommended me?' he gasped. 'I'm so *flattered*.'

'Someone at the hotel,' Brigette answered vaguely. 'I was told you're good with long hair.'

'Oh, you've got beautiful hair,' he exclaimed, picking up a strand. 'Absolutely fab. And what would her loveliness like me to do to it today?'

'A wash and blow-dry would be great.'

'Certainly. And may I take this opportunity to tell you that we're all big fans of yours here?'

Fiona Lewyllen Wharton entered the salon a few minutes later. She was a plump brunette, not quite as homely as she looked in her photographs, but hardly a beauty. She wore an unflattering tweed suit, patterned tights and comfortable pumps. Her legs were sturdy.

Brigette was sitting in Edward's chair getting her hair blow-dried.

'Are you running late, Edward?' Fiona enquired, in a louder-than-usual voice.

'No,' Edward answered, flitting around Brigette with his blow-dryer. 'By the time you're washed I'll be ready for you.'

Brigette met Fiona's eyes in the mirror. 'I'm *sorry*,' she said. 'I do hope I haven't taken your appointment.'

Fiona frowned and glanced at Edward, who looked embarrassed. 'I crammed Brigette in,' he explained quickly. 'She's a big New York model, and uh . . . we wanted to accommodate her. You don't mind, do you?'

'You mean she's taken my appointment?' Fiona said, obviously not pleased.

'No, no, she was here earlier. You'll only have to wait five minutes.'

'It doesn't matter,' Fiona said. 'However, I do have somewhere special to go tonight.'

'Wish I did.' Brigette sighed wistfully. 'I'm in London for such a short time, and I hardly know anybody.'

'Can't imagine you sitting home knitting socks, dear,' Edward said boldly.

Fiona emitted a horsy laugh. 'Weren't you on the cover of *Vogue* last month?' she asked, peering at Brigette in the mirror. 'Mummy takes it.'

'That was me,' Brigette said.

'You must be terribly famous in America.'

'She's terribly famous everywhere,' Edward pointed out.

'And what do *you* do?' Brigette asked politely.

'Oh, me – I work in an art gallery.'

'What kind of art do you sell?'

'Old masters,' Fiona said airily, as if it was the only thing any art gallery could possibly sell.

'How fascinating,' Brigette said. 'Do tell me all about it.'

Fiona's eyes lit up, it wasn't every day a famous New York model wanted to know about *her*.

By the time Edward had finished blow-drying Brigette's long hair, she and Fiona were fast friends. Brigette had a way of bringing people out, getting them to speak about themselves. It was probably why she was so popular with Lina and the other girls. She never talked about herself, always listened.

Fiona was quite flattered. 'I have a super idea,' she said, full of enthusiasm. 'Why don't you come over to Daddy's tonight? Every Saturday we have a little soirée. Daddy calls it our salon. Mummy calls it Daddy's liquorice all-sorts.'

'That's an English candy,' Edward said, *sotto voce*.

'We invite fifteen or twenty interesting people,' Fiona continued. 'Sometimes they're politicians, and once we had Fergie – she's charming, quite amusing, too. Will you come?'

Brigette glanced at Edward, who nodded encouragingly.

'Well, I . . . I don't know,' she said. 'I mean . . . I hardly like to intrude.'

'Daddy will be delighted to have you,' Fiona said, with another horsy laugh.

'Then I'd love to come,' Brigette said. 'That's very kind of you.'

'I'll write down the address,' Fiona said. 'About seven thirty. Cocktail attire.'

Brigette nodded. 'Seven thirty it is.'

☆ ☆ ☆

Dinner at Morton's. A good table near the front of the room against the wall. Max Steele was showing off.

'Where's Charlie?' Lina asked, as they were finishing their main course of delicious swordfish.

'He'll be here,' Max said confidently. 'Charlie's got a reputation for running late. In fact, if I didn't want to avoid insulting you, I'd say he runs on black time.'

'Black time?' Lina said, pushing a piece of fish across her plate.

'Well, y' know,' Max said easily, picking up a French fry with his fingers, 'black people do things by their own clock.'

'Are you a racist?' she asked sharply, like he'd admit it if he was.

'That's the second time you've mentioned the word racist,' Max said, throwing his hands in the air. 'I'm sitting here with *you*, aren't I?'

'Bloody 'ell,' Lina said indignantly. 'You should be so *lucky* to be sitting 'ere with me. Men give their right balls to sit with me.'

'Modest,' Max said. 'I like that in a woman. If you can act, we'll own the world.'

''Course I can act,' Lina said, like it was a given. 'What

206

do you *think* I'm doing when I'm poncing up and down those stupid runways. *That*'s acting. I put on my drop-dead-you-morons face, an' give 'em what they want.'

'And what is it they want?'

'They wanna see girls who look better than everyone else. You've gotta admit it, Max, right now models are a lot more glam than all those scrungy actresses up on the screen. Who've *you* got to write 'ome about? Holly Hunter and Meryl Streep. Ha! Great actresses, but not exactly drop dead gorgeous. It's the models who 'ave all the glamour today.'

'I disagree,' Max said. 'How about Julia Roberts and Michelle Pfeiffer?'

'Okay, I'll give you them, only that's about it.'

'Can't wait to see you and Charlie together,' he said. 'This'll be some combination!'

'If he ever bleedin' turns up,' Lina said huffily.

'He will,' Max said confidently.

Half an hour later Charlie ambled in, wearing one of his favourite Hawaiian shirts, baggy white pants, dark shades and his usual shit-eating grin. 'Hey,' he said, slapping Max on the back, 'what's goin' on in Agent Land?'

'Hey,' Max said, standing up, 'meet Lina.'

Lina gave Charlie a long, penetrating look.

'Quite an eyeful!' Charlie said. 'Five feet ten and—'

'Eleven,' she interrupted.

'Dark hair and big . . . eyes. Just my type.'

Lina narrowed her cat like eyes. 'Hmm . . . let me see. Fifty-something, chubby, an' ever so talented.' She grinned. 'Just my type, too.'

'Okay, doll,' Charlie said, nodding. 'I can see you and I are gonna get along like a gang of hookers at a sailors' convention in Puerto Rico.'

'I've been wanting to meet you,' she said, hoping she didn't sound too much like a fan. 'I think you're smashing.'

'Smashing, huh?' Charlie said, raising an extravagant eyebrow. 'In that case, I'm gonna join you good people.'

And with that he pulled out a chair and sat down.

☆ ☆ ☆

The Lewyllen Whartons lived in a luxurious, well-appointed five-storey townhouse in Eaton Square. A butler answered the door and ushered Brigette in.

She looked around for Fiona, who came running over to greet her. 'Welcome,' Fiona said, as if they were old friends. 'I'm so glad you're here.'

'It was nice of you to invite me,' Brigette said.

'Come,' Fiona said, leading Brigette into the formal living room to meet her parents.

Editha, her mother, was a small, wispy blonde woman, and Leopold, her father, was large, bald and blustery.

'This is my new friend, Brigette,' Fiona announced proudly. 'She's a top model, you know. She was on the cover of American *Vogue* last month.'

'How nice,' Editha said, completely unimpressed as she turned away to talk to someone else.

Brigette couldn't help noticing that Leopold was giving her a different kind of look – the kind of look that made her feel as if she was standing naked in front of him. 'Delighted to welcome you, dear,' he said. 'Fiona, introduce your friend to some of the other guests.'

'I'm delighted to be here,' Brigette said. 'It's so nice of you to invite me.'

'Any friend of Fiona's is a friend of ours,' Leopold said, not even attempting to shift his gaze from her breasts.

She had chosen to wear a simple black Isaac Mizrahi dress, not too low-cut, just enough to attract the attention of every man in the room. Fiona was in fussy brown velvet with a long skirt and wide sleeves, a most unfortunate choice, Brigette thought.

'You *have* to meet my fiancé first,' Fiona said, taking her arm and pulling her across the room. 'He's over here. He's an Italian count, you know. We're getting married next year.'

'How wonderful,' Brigette murmured, feeling her heart start to beat rapidly.

Carlo had his back to them as they approached. He was busy talking to a distinguished-looking man and a somewhat bored redhead.

Fiona tapped him on the shoulder. 'Darling, I'd like you to meet my new friend, Brigette.'

Carlo turned around. Their eyes met. He stared at her for a second or two before saying, 'A pleasure to meet you, Brigette.'

'Oh,' she responded, not letting him get away with a thing, 'Carlo – it's you!'

'Me?' he said, trying to warn her with his eyes that he would prefer it if they did not acknowledge knowing each other.

'Brigette,' she insisted. '*You* remember – I bumped into you at lunch the other day, and you reminded me of that fantastic night we spent together in New York.'

Fiona looked from one to the other, confused. 'Do you two *know* each other?' she asked, her expression sagging.

Carlo shrugged. 'Brigette must be mistaking me for some-one else,' he said coolly. 'We have never met.'

'No mistake,' Brigette said, nailing him – although this was only the beginning. 'You're Count Carlo Vittorio Vitti, Fredo's cousin. You came up to me in Le Caprice the other day. Surely you can't have forgotten?'

Carlo gritted his teeth. What a bad coincidence *this* was. 'Ah, yes,' he said stiffly. 'Of course. Brigette. *Now* I remem-ber. You were with my cousin, Fredo.' He turned quickly to

Fiona. 'I told you about that dinner for twenty people I went to with Fredo in New York. Brigette was one of the guests.'

'Oh,' Fiona said unsurely. 'I don't remember.'

'Small world,' Brigette said, feeling bad because she hadn't expected to like Fiona. And not only did she like her, she felt sorry for her, too.

Still . . . it was better that Fiona discovered what a two-timing rapist-scumbag-rat her fiancé actually was before she went ahead and married him.

'This is a beautiful house, Fiona,' Brigette said. 'Would you mind if I took a look around?'

'Not at all,' Fiona said.

And Brigette turned and walked away, leaving Carlo to explain the situation to his fiancée.

Chapter Thirty-nine

'HOLD THIS,' Mila said, throwing the gun at Teddy.

He caught it, a look of abject amazement on his face. 'You told me you'd gotten rid of it,' he said, thoroughly alarmed.

'I was going to, then I figured it was safer to wait,' Mila explained, giving him a sly sideways glance.

He tossed the gun on to the middle of her bed. 'You gotta get it outta here,' he said, panicking. 'What if the cops come and search?'

'You're so right,' she agreed. 'I will.'

They had just returned from the movies, and Mila had smuggled him out to her room in the back. 'Irena's watching TV,' she'd said. 'The old crow never comes in here anyway. This is *my* place, an' she knows it.'

He looked around her room, sparsely furnished with just the essentials and bare walls. A tattered red scarf was draped over one lamp, while another faded one hung half-way across the window. Her clothes were piled on a chair, with her shoes in an untidy jumble underneath.

Teddy thought of his own cosy room – walls covered in posters, piles of books everywhere, a large-screen TV; and an Apple computer. Not to mention a stack of CDs and videos, and a radical new stereo. He had everything, while she had nothing. Suddenly he felt incredibly guilty.

'I'm thirsty,' she said. 'Wanna sneak down to the pool bar an' get us a couple of beers?'

'Okay,' he said. 'But you gotta promise you'll dump the gun.'

'I will,' she said guilelessly.

He left her room and hurried to the pool bar, hoping he wouldn't bump into the dreaded Irena.

When he came back the gun was gone. 'What didja do with it?' he asked, handing her a bottle of beer.

'Put it somewhere safe,' she said mysteriously. 'I'll get it out of here tomorrow.'

'Promise?'

'You got it, Teddy.'

Teddy drank from his bottle of beer, surreptitiously edging closer to her. They were a couple now: nothing and no one could come between them.

'I'm tired,' she said, yawning in his face. 'I need sleep.'

'Don't you want me to stay?' he asked, disappointed.

'You've had enough excitement for one day,' she said, yawning again.

'Stop talkin' to me as if I'm a kid,' he said, annoyed that she still treated him with no respect. 'I've proved to you I'm not.'

'Okay, okay,' she said, stifling yet another yawn. 'Don't get your stones in a twist, there's always tomorrow.' As she spoke, she hustled him towards the door, finally shoving him out.

As soon as he was gone, she opened the drawer where she'd hidden the gun, carefully wrapped in a small towel. Teddy was the dumbest shit alive. He had no clue that he'd gotten his prints all over it.

'Oh, Teddy, Teddy,' she murmured. 'When are you gonna wise up?'

☆ ☆ ☆

Price had a choice: he could stay home and relax, or he could call one of three women he was currently dating.

He thought about them for a moment. There was the actress, black and extremely beautiful in a kind of uptight way. She'd recently gone through a very public divorce, and all the tabloids were telling tales and calling her a maniac. She was sweet as pie to him, but he didn't want to get involved with *another* maniac – his first wife was quite enough.

Then there was the very famous white actress, older and hungry. He had a strong suspicion she was only dating him because he was black.

The third prospect was Krissie, an ex-*Penthouse* Pet with a body to die for. Unfortunately she was irredeemably stupid. Recently interviewed on TV as to what her favourite beauty aid was, she'd fluttered her long eyelashes and said, 'I simply can't *live* without my eyelash curlers.' A brain she wasn't, although he had to admit that she used those eyelashes to good effect when giving him a masterful blow-job.

Still, staying home seemed like the best idea of all. He'd have Irena cook him up some fried chicken and her special potatoes, then he'd get into bed and watch a movie. In a few days he was due to play Vegas, and that was hectic time. He got so hyped up after a performance that the only way he could calm down was to be with a woman. Sex was his last drug of choice – that and an occasional joint. Especially after a live performance.

He wondered if Teddy was home. If he was, they could eat together. Price prided himself on being a good father. He kept a watchful eye on Teddy and didn't let him get up to much. Thank God the only thing Teddy seemed to have gotten into was smoking a little grass. No big deal.

Price wandered into the kitchen, where Irena was busy cleaning out a cupboard. 'What're you doing?' he asked.

'The maids are never thorough enough for me,' she said, scrubbing out the cupboard with a stiff wire brush, exerting herself well beyond the call of duty.

'Isn't that what *they* get paid for?' he remarked.

'Yes, Mr Washington. However, I prefer to see that everything is perfect.'

One thing about Irena, she kept a spotless house. She also had a very nice ass, which he sometimes took advantage of. She didn't object. In fact, she seemed disappointed if he *didn't* pay her attention.

As far as Price was concerned, Irena Kopistani was one lucky White Russian. She lived under his roof, serviced him whenever he felt like it, *and* got paid. Other women would pay *him* for the privilege.

Plus he knew he was a great boss. He'd never complained when she'd gotten pregnant and had a kid, never badgered her with questions about who the father was. He'd noticed that no man ever came around to visit, which didn't bother him at all. Who needed some strange dude sniffing around? He liked the fact that she was all his, available whenever he wanted.

Once a year he raised her salary, which kept her happy, because one thing he knew for sure, he couldn't manage without her.

'Think I'm gonna be eating at home tonight,' he said. 'Where's Teddy?'

'I have no idea,' she said.

'Is he back from the movies?'

'I don't know,' she said, still scrubbing.

'Y' know, sometimes you could talk a little more,' he said. 'You're not exactly the most communicative person in the world.'

She stopped her work and looked up at him. *I'm your sex slave*, she wanted to say. *You use me in every way. Now you want me to talk too?* But she didn't say a word. 'I will buzz Teddy in his room,' she said, moving over to the intercom.

At that moment, Teddy entered the kitchen.

'Hey, boy,' Price said, pleased to see him, 'how was the movie?'

'Pretty cool,' Teddy said, wishing his father would stop calling him 'boy'. He wasn't a kid any more, he'd proved that today.

'Whaddya see?'

'*The Bodyguard.*'

'Whitney Houston, huh? Now *there*'s a body I wouldn't mind guarding!'

'Didja ever meet her, Dad?' Teddy asked, just to be polite because, after his mind-blowing experiences with Mila, the last thing on his mind was Whitney Houston.

'Run into her and Bobby at a couple of events,' Price said casually. 'What're you up to for dinner?'

'Nothing,' Teddy said, unable to think of a quick enough excuse.

'So we'll do the father-son thing. You'll eat with me.'

'Yes, Dad,' Teddy said glumly, trapped.

'I'll send Irena out to rent a video. Anything you wanna see?'

'I got homework,' Teddy said. After dinner he planned to go to his room and think about what had taken place that afternoon. Mila allowing him to touch her tits. Coming in his pants. Jeez! Just thinking about it got him horny. For the time being, running away was put on a back-burner.

'Dining room, seven o'clock,' Price announced. 'Try to be on time for once.'

'Sure, Dad,' Teddy said, making a fast exit.

As soon as Teddy was gone Price began rubbing his crotch. Irena might not be as foxy as his trio of girlfriends, but she sure gave a hell of a blow-job. So maybe later, when everyone was asleep, he'd buzz her to come up to his room. He might even fuck her, give her the thrill of her life.

The truth of the matter was that he enjoyed sex with Irena more than with any of his transient dates. And wasn't *that* something to admit?

Only to himself, of course.

Irena was his guilty secret, and that's the way it had to stay.

Chapter Forty

THEY SPENT the morning making love in Lennie's hotel room.

'This is totally wild and wonderful,' Lucky said, rolling across the bed and stretching luxuriously. 'We should do it more often. I gotta tell you – hotels are dead sexy.'

'They certainly are,' Lennie agreed, stroking her thigh.

She laughed softly.

'What's up?' he asked. 'Did I say something funny?'

'I feel like I'm cheating on my husband.'

'If I ever find you cheating on your husband, you're a dead woman,' he said, mock-threateningly.

Running her fingers lightly across his chest, she leaned close to his ear and whispered, 'Would you kill me, Lennie? Would you really do that?'

'Believe me,' he said sternly, 'you don't wanna try it.'

'Then you'd better remember it's mutual.'

'Right,' he said, laughing. 'Knowing you, you'd cut off my dick and keep it in a jar by the bed.'

'No, I wouldn't,' she said, laughing back. 'I'd drop it down the waste-disposal.'

'You're a dangerous woman,' he said, shuddering.

'Never said I wasn't.'

'I'm starving,' he said, sitting up. 'Shall we order room service?'

'I was thinking that maybe we should go home.'

'Why? I'm perfectly happy here.'

'You are?'

'I get off on hotel living. It's impersonal, kind of like a time-suspension deal.'

'Yes, well, don't forget, we've got three kids to think about. You're a family man, Lennie. Mr Married.'

'Ouch!'

'Is it that painful?'

'Not when I'm with you.'

'What do you want to eat?' she asked, climbing out of bed, searching for a menu.

He lay back, watching her slender body as she crossed the room, naked and still as beautiful as the first time he'd seen her. 'I'll have an omelette.'

'An *omelette*?' she exclaimed, running a hand through her unruly black hair. 'What kind of girly food is *that*? *I* need a hamburger.'

'That's 'cause *you*'ve got a voracious appetite,' he pointed out. 'In every way.'

'Then aren't *you* the fortunate one?' she said, finding a menu on the desk and hurrying back to bed.

'That's me,' he said, grinning.

'That's you,' she agreed, straddling him and pinning his shoulders to the bed, thinking that it was so damn good to have him back. He'd been missing since the hold-up. Now here he was, the Lennie she knew and loved.

For a moment her thoughts turned to Alex. She'd enjoyed being with him last night, but they were just friends. Nobody could ever come between her and Lennie. They were truly bound together.

'When you were kidnapped,' she said casually, 'what did you think about every day?'

He regarded her quizzically. 'You're asking me five years later?'

'You must have thought of *something* – you can't have just sat there, staring at walls.'

'I thought about *you*, Lucky,' he said, his face serious. 'You and the kids and coming home. That's *all* I thought about.'

'And the girl who helped you escape – what was her name?'

'Uh . . . I don't remember.'

'Yes, you do.'

'I think it was Claudia.'

'Ah, yes . . . Claudia.' A long beat. 'Did you have any . . . feelings for her? I mean, there you were, trapped in a cave, and she was your only human contact.'

'Why are you asking me this now?'

'Sometimes I get to thinking about it,' she said slowly. 'I was alone here, I thought you were dead . . .'

'What are you getting at?'

'I simply wondered if anything happened between the two of you.'

He shook his head. 'Now I know you're crazy.'

'Was she pretty?'

'*What?*'

'Well, was she?'

'If it'll make you happy, she was a dog,' he lied.

'Shame,' she murmured.

'C'mon, Lucky,' he said sharply. 'It's bad memories, and I do not care to talk about it any more.'

'Okay, okay, I understand,' she said, kissing him fervently. 'Pass me the phone. I'll do the ordering.'

☆ ☆ ☆

Alex Woods did not call Pia. The truth was that any woman paled in comparison to Lucky Santangelo, so even though he was prepping a new movie, and that was *all* he should have been thinking about, his thoughts lingered on Lucky. Ever since that one wild night in the desert he'd known she was the woman for him. And yet he'd had to stand by, an observer, as she welcomed Lennie home; he'd had to watch their relationship flourish. He'd also been a guest at their house many times, had seen Lucky in every situation – as boss of Panther Studios, mother of her three children, god-mother to Brigette. She was a remarkable woman, and as far as he was concerned she could do anything.

He'd really meant it when he'd suggested she should produce a movie. In fact, he'd welcome her savvy and know-how on any one of his projects.

In his heart he knew that Lennie would never allow it, because Lennie was well aware of how he, Alex, felt about Lucky. It was a man thing: instinctively you knew when another man was checking out your woman.

Not that Alex didn't like Lennie, he considered him an okay guy. But not okay enough for Lucky. He, Alex Woods, was the man she should really be with.

Alex had never married nor had children. His mother, the formidable Dominique, continually berated him for that. 'You *should* be married,' she often scolded. 'It's not normal for a man of your age to be alone.'

Hey, he wanted to say, you're *not fucking normal. You're the one who sent me to military school and treated me like a piece of shit all my life. That is, until I finally made it. Then, all of a sudden, I was your son again and you wanted everyone to know it.*

But he never said anything. She was getting old. She was married now and not such a domineering presence, thank God!

One thing he knew for sure: he certainly wasn't looking for a woman who reminded him of dear old Mama.

He often thought with wry amusement about his first encounter with Lucky. The movie he was involved with at the time – *Gangsters* – was in turn-around, and Freddie Leon, his agent, had suggested they run it over to Panther Studios, where Lucky had recently taken over. He'd walked into her office and been faced with this indescribably powerful and beautiful woman. Tall and slender, with a tangle of jet curls framing an incredible face, dangerous black eyes and a seductive smile.

The meeting had gone well, except that just as he was about to leave she'd stopped him at the door and said, 'I'm aware that Paramount passed on your movie because of the graphic violence, and I'm not asking you to tone it down. However, about the sex – the script makes it clear several of the actresses are naked in certain scenes, yet it seems our hero and his friends remain modestly covered.'

'What's the problem?' he'd asked, genuinely not getting it.

'This is an equal opportunity studio,' she'd said. 'If the females take it off, so do the guys.' He'd stared at her like she was a crazy woman. 'Let me put it this way, Mr Woods,' she'd added. 'If we get to see tits and ass, we get to see dick. And I'm *not* talking Dick Clark.'

He'd left her office outraged, complaining to Freddie all the way to his car. Freddie had laughed at him, so had his two Asian assistants – Lili, a softly pretty Chinese woman who'd been with him for ever, and France, who'd since departed.

Yes, Lucky Santangelo had managed to shock him, something that few women had been able to do. And yet, he'd fallen in love with her then and there.

He'd never forget the one magical night they'd spent

together. Never. No woman could ever live up to Lucky. She was the woman he'd been searching for all his life, and when things seemed to be on track and moving along at a good pace, Lennie had come back into the picture, returning from the dead so to speak.

So now Lucky was his friend. But he wanted more than that.

He wanted her to be his everything.

☆ ☆ ☆

They returned home around six. Lucky hurried straight to the answering-machine, where there was a message from Detective Johnson acknowledging the licence-plate information. She listened to his message, then clicked off the machine. 'Let's hope they can finally get some action going,' she said. 'Those guys are useless.'

'You think?'

'I *know*. They should've made an arrest long ago.'

'Can you believe how quiet it is here without the kids running around?' Lennie remarked.

'It sure is,' she agreed.

'Kind of like old times, huh?' he said, throwing himself down on the couch and smiling lazily. 'And, my darling wife, I have a great idea.'

'Wanna share it?'

'Well . . . how about you take off your clothes, and walk around naked?'

'I don't believe you!'

'C'mon, Lucky, humour me.'

'You're such a little voyeur,' she said. 'No way am I parading around like a hooker.'

He grinned. 'I love it when you turn prudish.'

'Okay, okay, here's the action,' she said, happy to see

a smile on his face. 'I'll take *my* clothes off if you do the same.'

'It's a deal!' he said, leaping up and immediately starting to unbutton his shirt.

Lucky smiled and began humming stripper music. After a few moments, when he was down to his underwear, she collapsed in fits of laughter. 'You'll never make it as a male stripper,' she gasped. 'Sorry!'

'Why not?' he said indignantly, flexing his muscles while macho posing in his jockey shorts. 'I've got moves you haven't even seen.'

'And I don't want to.'

'I'm insulted.'

'Go back to acting, Lennie,' she said, choking with laughter. 'You're such an actor in real life.'

'Come here, woman,' he said, holding out his arms. 'There's something wrong with this picture. I'm down to my Calvins, and you're still fully dressed.' She ran into his arms and he hugged her to him, crushing his mouth down on hers. 'I've missed you so much,' he said. 'You gotta forgive me for behaving like an asshole. I think I'm out of it now. Normal life will resume.'

'It doesn't matter,' she whispered. 'I love you anyway. I always have and I always will.'

'You do realize how precious time is?' he said, holding her close. 'One moment we're here, the next gone. I've decided I don't want you out of my sight ever again.'

'It's you and me, babe,' she murmured. 'We're destined to be together for ever. Soulmates.'

'Soulmates,' he repeated. 'You don't have to tell me twice.'

Chapter Forty-one

BRIGETTE EXPLORED the house, talked to some of the guests, endured Leopold Lewyllen Wharton peering down her neckline, and found herself seated next to him at dinner, an elderly Member of Parliament on her other side. She'd never been so bored and restless. But, as she reminded herself, she wasn't in London to enjoy herself, she was here to make sure Carlo paid for what he'd done.

There were three tables, each seating ten people, so it wasn't until after dessert, when she got up to go to the ladies' room, that she bumped into Carlo again.

He caught up with her outside the dining room. 'What are you doing here?' he demanded.

'Excuse me?' she said innocently, noticing that he seemed disturbed. *Good*.

'Why did you tell Fiona we knew each other?' he continued, the expression on his handsome face quite agitated.

'I wasn't aware it was a secret, Carlo,' she said coolly. '*Is* it a secret?'

'Well . . .' He obviously didn't know what to say. 'Because of what happened between us . . .'

She fixed him with her big blue eyes. 'What *did* happen between us?'

'Surely you remember?'

'No. Why don't you tell me?'

'We made love, Brigette,' he said, lowering his voice. 'And, if I may say so, you enjoyed it a great deal.'

'Oh, God!' she said, pretending to be upset. 'I had no idea you really were engaged. What'll Fiona *say* when you tell her?'

He took a step back. 'I am not planning on telling her.'

'You *have* to,' she said, widening her eyes.

'I do not *have* to do anything,' Carlo answered churlishly. Maybe it was her imagination, or did she see a bead of sweat on his perfect brow?

'Oh dear, I must have had too much to drink,' she apologized, fanning herself with her hand. 'Champagne's my downfall. Although I seem to recall that at the dinner in New York, you told us all that you *weren't* engaged.'

'True,' he said quickly. 'Fiona and I had broken our engagement for a few days.'

'How convenient.'

'Believe me, Brigette,' he said, ignoring her stab at sarcasm, 'it is best to say nothing.'

'Why?' she said, staring at him.

'Meet me for lunch tomorrow and we will discuss it.'

'You mean the three of us will have lunch?' she asked, still playing the innocent – albeit a sexy one in her low-cut dress.

'No,' he said sharply. 'Just you and me.'

'Well . . .' she said, pretending to consider it. 'If you think it will help . . .'

'In the meantime,' he said, in a stern voice, 'do *not* mention the night we spent together in New York.'

'How can I mention it,' she asked ingenuously, 'when I don't even remember it?'

He leaned closer, sure that soon they would be a couple, and with her kind of money behind him he would rule the world. 'You're still as lovely as you were that one magical night, Brigette,' he whispered. 'I will remind you of things we did together. You will want to do them again.'

'I can't sleep with a man who is already taken,' she said primly. 'If you wish to see me again, then you must break your engagement immediately.'

'I know,' he said. 'The moment I met you, I realized it was over between Fiona and me. I am an Italian count. *You*, my sweet Brigette, will be my contessa.'

'There's something I don't understand,' she said, frowning.

'What, my darling?'

'If we had such a wonderful time in New York – and I'm sure we did, although I'll have to take your word for it – how come you didn't call me?'

'It's complicated,' he said. 'Fiona's father has been discussing my joining his company.'

'Really?'

'Tomorrow I will explain everything.' A pause, while he gave her the benefit of a long, lingering look. 'You *will* meet me, won't you?'

She nodded her agreement, knowing that soon she would have Count Carlo Vittorio Vitti *exactly* where she wanted him.

☆ ☆ ☆

'I love you,' Lina said.

'*What?*' Charlie managed, his eyebrows shooting up in alarm.

'I always say that,' Lina said, shrieking with hysterical laughter. 'I get off on seeing the panic rise.' She rolled off Charlie, stretching out one of her long arms to grab a cigarette from the bedside table. 'Course, I never mean it.'

'Shitcakes!' Charlie exclaimed, shaking his head in bewilderment. 'You really do dance your own tango.'

'Takes two, don't it?' she said, lighting up.

He regarded her with a certain amount of puzzlement. 'You're very . . . energetic.'

'Oooh,' she said mockingly, flinging back a curtain of long, straight black hair. 'Tired you out, 'ave I?'

'I'm a movie star, baby,' he deadpanned. 'Movie stars never get tired or go to the bathroom. Surely you knew that?'

'I'm a supermodel, darlin',' she said, handing him her cigarette for a drag. 'We never get tired either. We always gotta look gorgeous an' be nice to people.'

'How convenient for you,' he said drily.

'Screw being nice,' Lina said vehemently. 'Sometimes I wanna kick 'em in the 'ead. Specially some of those bitches who call themselves fashion editors. They're the worst.'

'You're forthright,' Charlie said. 'I like that in a supermodel.'

'No point in beating around the bush, is there?' she said. 'I'm a little Cockney girl from London who made good. Now I wanna make even better.'

'Ambition. Another admirable quality.'

'So,' she said, giving him a penetrating stare, 'am I gonna be in your movie or not?'

He blew lazy smoke rings in her direction. 'Is that why you fucked me?'

'No,' she said, taking back her cigarette. 'I fucked you 'cause you was there.'

Even Charlie was puzzled by that one. 'Explain?'

She giggled. 'Me mum would have a freaking fit if she knew I was in bed with Charlie Dollar. She *loves* you, thinks you're the best thing since a bit of toast and marmalade.'

'How about Grandma?' Charlie drawled sardonically. 'She love me, too?'

Once again Lina shrieked with laughter. 'You're funny,' she said. 'I thought all you American movie stars 'ad no sense of humour.'

'Depends on which American movie stars you've been sleeping with.'

Lina stretched languorously. 'I love sex, don't you? 'S better than a sleeping pill any day.'

'You're not planning on spending the night in big bad Charlie's bed, are you?' he asked, worried at the thought. 'I have a sometime girlfriend who's likely to walk in on us and shoot you dead. She's a devil with a gun.'

'It's usually the wife I'm watching out for,' Lina remarked, completely unconcerned.

'Sorry,' Charlie said. 'I'm all out of those at the moment.'

Lina kneeled up on the bed, hugging a pillow to her chest. 'Do you think Max is pissed?'

'About what?'

'About me coming home with you.'

'Not Max – he's used to it,' Charlie said, opening his bedside drawer. 'Here's the deal. You've got an agent on one side and a movie star on the other. Who do *you* think's gonna get the girl?'

'He's kind of cute,' Lina mused.

'You wanna fuck him, too?' Charlie enquired, taking out a plastic bag and a neat stack of cigarette papers.

'Why?' she said boldly. 'You into threesomes? 'Cause if you are, we can call him up, see if he'll give us ten per cent of his dick!'

Charlie roared with laughter. 'I have here some very fine grass,' he said, starting to roll a joint. 'That's, of course, if you're interested.'

Lina grinned. '*Now* you tell me.'

Chapter Forty-two

'Is Steven coming?' Venus Maria asked.

'He's not,' Lucky said. 'I invited him, but he feels it's too soon.'

They were talking in the gym of Venus's ultra-modern house in the Hollywood Hills. Lately Venus had been on Lucky's case about working out with her. 'I hate exercise,' Lucky had said. 'It's boring.'

'You're not twenty any more,' Venus had pointed out. 'You *have* to work out – unless you want to turn into a fat slob.'

'Ha!' Lucky had replied. 'All you want is company in your quest for perfection!'

Now they were sitting on a bench in their workout clothes, waiting for Sven, Venus's personal trainer.

'You've gotta tell Steven that it's never too soon to get back into life,' Venus said briskly. 'Look at me after that horrible experience with the stalker at my house. I was back doing things immediately.'

'Yes,' Lucky said, 'but that was only a stalker. This is the murder of Steven's wife we're talking about. And, of course, he's broken up about the baby – who wouldn't be? He didn't even know Mary Lou was pregnant. I can understand why he doesn't want to go out.'

'Maybe *I* should go talk to him myself,' Venus decided. 'He's always liked me.'

'No,' Lucky corrected. '*You*'ve always liked *him*. If you didn't have Cooper, I'm sure Steven would've been a contender.'

'He *is* gorgeous,' Venus admitted. 'Didn't you tell me that when you first met, and you had no clue he was your half-brother, you had kind of a big flirtation?'

Lucky chuckled at the memory. Nineteen seventy-seven. The big New York power outage, and her and Steven trapped in an elevator together. Pure fate. Neither of them had had any idea they were related. 'It could have been a lot more than a flirtation,' she said, 'but Steven's always been so straight. Apart from when he was married to that Puerto Rican maniac.'

'Can you imagine,' Venus said, 'if anything had happened between you and him?'

'No, I can't,' Lucky said briskly, reaching for a cigarette. 'Mind if I smoke?'

'You know I do,' Venus retorted. 'Anyway, I thought you gave it up.'

'I give it up, then I do it again,' Lucky said, gesturing helplessly. 'It's kind of a see-saw deal.'

'Smoking is bad for you,' Venus said sternly.

'You're becoming *such* a boring health nut,' Lucky replied, lighting up and taking a long, deep drag. 'You've even got Cooper working out, and *he* was the run-around stud of all time.'

'Ha!' Venus exclaimed. 'How about Lennie? In his movie-star days he didn't exactly keep it zipped up.'

'Ah . . . but he wasn't Cooper Turner,' Lucky responded, with a mischievous grin. 'Cooper's legendary in this town. Him and Warren Beatty.'

'I suppose he is,' Venus said, smiling proudly. 'Of course,' she added, after a thoughtful pause, '*I* wasn't exactly hiding in a convent.'

'True,' Lucky agreed. 'Miss If-it-moves-I'll-fuck-it!'

'I like being married though,' Venus said, stretching her arms in the air. 'It's . . . comfortable.'

'That's 'cause you're never peering out of your marriage to see what you're missing,' Lucky said wisely. 'You and I both experienced everything, so did our husbands. Which means we never missed a thing.'

'Been there, done that,' Venus said, with a crazed giggle.

'There should be a law against getting married too young,' Lucky said. 'Thirty for women. Thirty-five for men. Seems reasonable to me.'

'According to Gino,' Venus said. 'You were so wild he *had* to marry you off at sixteen. The other night he was telling *insane* stories about you.'

'Here's the thing about Gino,' Lucky said, stubbing out her cigarette after two drags. 'Never believe a word he says. Gino likes to embellish.'

'Seems you had almost as much fun as me.'

'*Nobody* had as much fun as you,' Lucky remarked drily. 'You *invented* the word party!'

'Hmm . . .' Venus said, savouring the fond memories. 'Sometimes I miss being single . . .'

'Do you really?'

'Nope. But it sounds good.'

Sven arrived, cutting short their conversation. He was a tall well-built Swede with muscles to spare. 'Ladies,' he said, with what Lucky considered to be an evil sneer. 'Are we ready to be tortured?'

'No,' Lucky said irritably, 'I'm ready for another cigarette. I had a hard weekend.'

'How hard?' Venus asked provocatively.

'Hard enough,' Lucky replied, smiling. 'Lennie has returned to the land of the living. And how!'

'I'm glad to hear it.'

'So am I.'

'After we've worked out,' Venus said, 'I think I'll call Steven. In fact, I might even visit him at his office.'

'*That*'ll cause a riot,' Lucky said. 'You – walking into the law offices.'

'Steven represented me on a couple of things,' Venus said. 'They're used to me.'

Lucky shook her head. 'Nobody's used to you, Venus. You're an original.'

'That is true,' Sven said, flexing his considerable muscles. 'Now, ladies, enough time wasted. Let us get to work!'

☆ ☆ ☆

Steven was gazing out of his Century City office window, when his secretary announced that Venus Maria was there to see him.

'Does she have an appointment?' he asked.

'No, Mr Berkeley. She said she'll only take five minutes of your time.'

'Okay.' He nodded, knowing that if Venus was on the premises there was no getting rid of her. 'Show her in.'

Venus entered his office in a body-hugging Claude Montana purple dress, platinum hair in a straight bob, huge black shades obscuring her eyes. 'I'm here,' she announced.

'I can see that,' he said, getting a whiff of her exotic perfume.

'I'm a walking, talking personal invitation,' she said, with a seductive smile.

'For?'

'Our party tonight,' she said, removing her sunglasses. 'You're coming,' she added, perching on the edge of his desk.

'Venus,' he said patiently, 'I explained it to Lucky. It's too soon.'

'You'll bring Carioca,' she said, matter-of-factly, as if it was a done deal. 'There'll be a special kiddies' table. Chyna has personally requested Carioca's presence. You're not going to deprive your daughter, are you?'

'Stop making it difficult for me,' he said.

'I'm not making it *that* difficult, Steven. I want you there. Anyway . . . I'll be hurt if you don't come.'

'Well . . .'

'Good,' she said, getting off his desk and undulating her way to the door. 'We'll expect you both at seven.'

☆ ☆ ☆

On her way back to the beach Lucky stopped by the police station. She paced impatiently around Detective Johnson's office, waiting for him to put in an appearance.

He arrived a few minutes later, styrofoam cup of coffee in one hand, the traditional jelly doughnut in the other.

'I do hope I'm not disturbing your breakfast,' she said sarcastically, annoyed because in spite of everyone's efforts there were still no results.

'Glad you're here,' he said, not meaning it. Lucky Santangelo was on his case day and night. The woman was slowly driving him nuts. 'The plate numbers are a help,' he said, taking a swig of coffee. 'We're narrowing down the list.'

'How about the reward?' she asked. 'What's going on with that?'

'We're snowed under with false information,' he said, settling behind his desk and clearing off a stack of papers so he could put his coffee down. 'There was one interesting phone call, though.'

'From?'

He paused, took a bite of his doughnut. 'A girl claiming she knows who did it.'

'What makes this phone call different?'

'She had details other people wouldn't know.'

'Like what?' Lucky said, staring at him.

'Well,' he said, a dribble of jam making its way down his chin, 'she knew exactly how the car was positioned, the dress Mary Lou had on . . .'

'Are you bringing her in?'

'She told me she could give us the shooter, but first she wants to make sure she gets the reward. I informed her that's not the way things work.'

'How did you leave it?'

'She'll call again.'

Lucky attempted to curb her anger. 'You mean you had her on the phone and you let her go?'

'We tried putting a trace on her call, but by that time she'd hung up.'

'Did you get her name . . . anything?'

'No. But we'll hear from her again,' Detective Johnson said confidently. 'She wants the money.'

Lucky was furious. What kind of detective work was *that*? People were just plain incompetent, including the police – *especially* the police.

She drove to the beach breaking speed records, checking in on her car phone with the private detective firm she'd hired. They were also useless. In spite of plenty of time and unlimited money they'd come up with nothing.

The house was quiet when she arrived home; the children weren't due back from Gino's until later.

'Lennie,' she called out, throwing down her purse.

'In here,' he yelled.

She went into his office and was delighted to find him

234

positioned in front of his computer – an excellent sign, considering he hadn't gone near it since the shooting.

Walking up behind him, she began massaging his shoulders. 'Working on something good?' she asked.

'I'm planning a film about violence,' he announced. 'Random violence on the streets today. What do you think?'

'Terrific idea.'

'Yeah,' he said, nodding vigorously. 'Y' know, one of the things that struck me most about what went down was the unbelievable hate in the girl's voice. How did she get like that? What made her learn to take off on total strangers? It's something worth exploring.'

'I'm so happy to see you working again,' Lucky said, kissing the back of his neck.

'How about *you*?' he said, turning around. 'What are *your* plans now that you've given up the studio?'

'It's not that I've given it up,' she explained. 'It's simply that I'm not interested in doing that any more. Eight years running a studio, dealing with everyone's egos on a daily basis. It's a goddamn lifetime, and frankly I've had it.'

'I know you, Lucky,' he said. 'You'll never be happy sitting around doing nothing.'

'I do have kind of an idea . . .' she said, wandering over to the window and gazing out at the ocean.

'Tell me,' he said.

She turned around and faced him. 'I was thinking I might produce a movie.'

He laughed derisively. '*You* don't know anything about producing.'

'I ran Panther for *eight* years,' she said, frowning. 'I know plenty.'

'Physically producing a movie is completely different from sitting in an office greenlighting other people's projects,' he pointed out.

'Are you saying I *can't* do it?' she said, narrowing her eyes.

'You can do anything you set your mind to, as long as you realize it's not as easy as it seems.'

She hated it when Lennie tried to tell her what to do, but since she was on a mission to make him feel better about himself she held back a snappy retort. 'Hey,' she said, being nice, 'how about *you* write me a movie and *I*'ll produce it?'

'Oh, no,' he said, shaking his head like it was the worst idea he'd ever heard. 'Working together, the two of us – bad, bad idea.'

'Why?' she said, trying to stay reasonable even though he was beginning to irritate the hell out of her.

'Because I hate every producer I've ever worked with,' he said shortly. 'They try to cast people I don't want. They're always trying to cut my budget – not to mention screwing with my actors. They get in my way. No, no, no, let's not get into *that*.'

'Then how would you feel if I produced a movie with someone else?' she asked, thinking of Alex.

'Hey, that's your decision.'

It was always her decision until he didn't like it. Lennie was difficult that way. 'I'm trying to discuss things with you, see how *you* feel about it,' she said calmly.

'Whatever you want, sweetheart.'

'You're *sure*?'

'Absolutely. Oh, and, Lucky,' he said, giving her a little more attention, 'thanks for this weekend. It was beyond great.'

'Yes, it was,' she said, smiling at the memories of wild hotel sex. 'When we're good, we're *very, very* good.'

He began to laugh. 'And when we're bad, we're a freaking *mess*.'

She laughed too. 'No, *you*'re a mess.'

'No, *you* are.'

'No, *you*,' she countered, playfully punching him on the chin.

'I'm hungry,' he said. 'Think you can fix me one of your great tuna sandwiches?'

'What am I? The cook?' she said, exasperated.

'You *do* know that in most civilized countries wives fix husbands lunch?'

'Screw you!' she said affectionately. 'Make your own sandwich.'

'Love you, too,' he said, grinning. 'Easy on the mayonnaise.'

'Lennie!'

'Please?'

'Okay,' she said grudgingly. 'Just this once.'

'Thanks, babe,' he said, turning back to his computer.

And, as much as she loved her husband, Lucky knew that being a homebody was not for her.

Chapter Forty-three

LUNCH WITH Carlo, and Brigette thought that she played him pretty smoothly as they sat side by side in San Lorenzo, a fashionable Italian restaurant in Knightsbridge.

What are you doing?

Getting my revenge. Just as Lucky taught me. Because revenge is sweet. And then I'll worry about being pregnant.

Carlo was continuing with his well-worn line about how the moment he'd set eyes on her he'd known his engagement was a sham and that he would have to end it immediately. He wasn't exactly smooth, corny was more like it.

But she pretended to fall for it, all the while watching him carefully, wondering how such an attractive man could be such a rat.

'Fiona seems nice,' she said carefully. 'However, if you're sure this is the way you feel . . .'

'When I returned to London after meeting you,' he said, 'I knew I must finish with Fiona and move to New York.'

'But first you had to break your engagement,' she said, twirling spaghetti around her fork.

'I'll do it now.'

'What about her father and the business you were discussing?'

'It is not important.'

She picked up her wine-glass and took a sip. 'Will you tell her what happened between us in New York?'

'That is not a good idea,' he said, thinking that it was an extremely bad idea. What if, by some fluke, things didn't work out with Brigette? He had to have Fiona to fall back on. And her father. *And* her father's money. 'When do you leave?' he asked.

'Tomorrow.'

'Then tonight I shall come to your hotel, and we will make it a night to remember.'

Oh, yes, Brigette thought. *We certainly will.*

☆ ☆ ☆

Breakfast at the Bel Air Hotel in the dining room.

'You got the part,' Max Steele said, as Lina sashayed in and sat down, causing most people to stare. In a town filled with stars, Lina still stood out.

'I know,' she answered, with a wicked grin. 'All eight inches!'

Max spluttered out a mouthful of coffee. 'So it's true about Charlie?'

'For an old man, 'e rocks,' she said, winking roguishly.

Max took another gulp of coffee. 'Don't *ever* let Charlie hear you call him old.'

'Why?'

'Ego. It's big.'

'Just like his—'

'Okay, okay,' Max interrupted. 'I don't need details. The good thing is he thinks you're perfect for his movie. Doesn't even want to see you on video.'

'I can finally say it, Max,' she said, with a Cheshire-cat grin. 'I slept with a star an' got a role in 'is film.'

'It doesn't make any difference whether you slept with

him or not,' Max assured her. 'It's a done deal. He likes you.'

'What about money?' Lina asked, making eye-contact with a hovering waiter who was undeniably cute.

'Leave that to me. It won't be a lot but, at this stage in your career, exposure is more important than money.'

'I'll 'ave to trust *you* on that,' Lina said, abandoning her mild flirtation with the waiter and concentrating once more on Max.

'Tomorrow you'll meet with the wardrobe people,' he said. 'My assistant will set a time.'

'It'll 'ave t' be early,' she said, gulping back a yawn, ''cause I'm flying to Milan in the evening.'

'What a life!' Max said admiringly.

'It beats packin' plastic raincoats, which was my first job. We called 'em the wankers' special!'

'*I* started in the mail room at William Morris,' Max said.

'Didn't we do well!' she said, with another Cheshire-cat grin.

Max signalled for a refill of coffee. 'Charlie's leaving this afternoon,' he said. 'You got to him just in time.'

Lina picked up a muffin and took a healthy bite. 'I always 'ad great timing,' she said, favouring the waiter with another quick glance. He *was* quite delicious in an early-Brad-Pitt sort of way. If only she had a few moments to spare . . .

'I believe it,' Max said.

'So tell me, Max,' Lina said, a predatory look in her saffron eyes, 'what are you an' I doin' tonight?'

'You don't believe in sitting around, do you?' he said. He'd been around Hollywood for years, but this girl was something else.

'Why waste a great opportunity?' she said, with another wicked grin. 'Unless, of course, you're busy . . . or scared of comparisons . . .'

'*Me?*'

'*You.*'

'Got a hunch I can handle any comparison you have to offer,' he boasted.

'Oooh, good. I'm gonna get lucky twice, huh?'

'If you feel like it,' he said, 'there's a party tonight you might enjoy.'

'I *love* parties. Who's giving it?'

'Venus Maria and Cooper Turner. They're celebrating their anniversary.'

'I met Cooper when 'e was single,' Lina said. 'Chased me all over Paris 'e did.'

'Did he catch you?'

She rolled her eyes mysteriously, remembering a long drunken night of great sex. 'Wouldn't *you* like t' know.'

'You'd better not remind him of it.'

'I'm a big fan of Venus Maria,' she said. 'Used to dress up like 'er when I was a kid.'

'How old *are* you?' Max asked, waving at a fellow agent who was breakfasting with Demi Moore.

'Twenty-six.' She pulled a miserable face. 'That's old, ain't it?'

'Twenty-six is not particularly old,' he said. 'Only don't go telling people in Hollywood you admired them when you were a kid – it's the worst thing you can do. This is Ego City, everyone wants to be perceived as young.'

'I wrote Venus a fan letter once,' she admitted.

'I repeat,' Max said sternly, '*don't* tell her.'

''Ow old is she, anyway?'

'Only a few years older than you and, trust me, she would *not* appreciate you informing her that you used to admire her when you were a kid.'

'Girls say that to me all the time,' Lina said, fidgeting restlessly.

'How do *you* like it?'

''S okay if they're twelve!' she said, blowing a kiss at Frank Bowling, who was hovering at the door with a group of Arab dignitaries. 'Gotta go shopping,' she said, pushing her chair away from the table. 'Must buy something knockout for tonight. Will the party be jammed with movie stars?'

'Who do you want to meet?' he asked, amused.

'Let me see now . . . Hmm . . . I've always fancied Robert De Niro. 'Course, I *love* Denzel too. An' I wouldn't kick Jack Nicholson out of bed.'

'Into older men, huh?'

'Experience an' stamina. Turns *me* on every time.'

'Didn't you say tonight was *my* night? You're not dumping me for a movie star, are you?'

'Well . . .'

He clicked his fingers for the check. 'You're quite an operator, Lina.'

A final grin as she headed towards the door. 'So I've been told.'

☆ ☆ ☆

The scene was set. Soft music, candlelight, and Brigette in a silver slip dress that left nothing to the imagination.

Carlo was exactly on time, which was good, because she'd counted on him being prompt. He called from the lobby, and she asked him to come straight up to her suite.

He arrived at the door a few minutes later.

Pity he's such a bastard, she thought, as she let him in, *because he is extraordinarily handsome, in an arrogant kind of way. And under other circumstances . . .*

He brought her red roses, naturally. No imagination.

She took the sweet-smelling blooms from him and placed

them on the hall table. 'How lovely!' she exclaimed. 'I'll call the maid to put them in a vase.'

'You look exquisite,' he said, touching her arm.

'I ordered champagne,' she said. 'Will you open it?'

He followed her into the living room where the bottle was sitting in an ice-bucket on the table. 'Ah . . . Cristal,' he said, picking it up. 'Excellent choice.'

'And there's caviar over there.'

'Brigette,' he said admiringly, 'for an American girl, you are very sophisticated.'

Yes, she thought. *So sophisticated that I fell for your little trick of slipping a knock-out pill in my drink. How clever is that?*

She couldn't help wondering why he had to drug women, anyway, since he could probably take his pick. He was tall, blond and handsome with a title – what more could any man possibly need? Lina would've jumped into bed with him in a flash. So would a hundred other girls.

'How long have you lived in London?' she asked, moving over to the fireplace.

'Eighteen months,' he answered, popping the champagne cork. 'I do not like it here, the English are too cold. I'm Italian. We Italians are more warm-blooded.' He gave her one of his long, lingering looks, obviously a Carlo speciality. 'You know what I mean?'

'I hope I'll find out tonight,' she murmured seductively.

He continued to look at her with lust in his eyes. Not only was this delicious blonde due to become one of the richest women in the world, she was also one of the most desirable.

He revelled in the thought that soon she would be all his. *He* would be in control of the Stanislopoulos fortune. He, Carlo, who'd never been in control of anything in his entire life, would be in charge of a billion-dollar fortune. Watch people kiss his ass when *that* happened.

'Come over here, my little angel,' he said, beckoning her towards him.

She walked over and allowed him to kiss her. He had a most insistent tongue that darted in and out of her mouth in a practised way as his hands began moving over her body, coming to rest on her breasts.

After a few moments she gently pushed him away. 'I'd like to make a toast,' she said, slightly out of breath.

'Please, allow *me*,' he said, moving over to the champagne bottle, filling two glasses, and handing one to her. 'To the most beautiful girl in the world,' he said, raising his glass to her.

Another corny line. Didn't he have anything original to say?

They clinked glasses, and he twisted his arm through hers as they drank.

Better make sure he doesn't slip another pill in my drink. Got to watch him every moment.

'You must miss Italy,' she said, taking a small sip of champagne.

'I do,' he said. 'Only it seems that when I am with you, I do not miss anything.'

Oh, God, his lines were getting cornier all the time.

He moved in to kiss her again. Over his shoulder she glanced at her watch, this had to be timed perfectly. 'Shall we go in the other room?' she suggested.

'It will be my pleasure,' he said, delighted that the evening was progressing so well.

'Come,' she said, taking his hand and leading him into the bedroom, where – very slowly – she stepped out of her silver dress, revealing that all she had on underneath was a flesh-coloured thong.

'*Bellissima!*' he murmured, thinking this was moving faster than he'd anticipated. 'So beautiful!'

'Take off your clothes, Carlo,' she said invitingly.

He didn't need asking twice. Without further ado he quickly threw everything off until he stood before her in his black briefs, erection bulging.

She lay back on the bed, and he got on top of her. Even though she felt incredibly vulnerable, she knew that any moment now she was going to feel triumphant, because any moment now revenge would be hers.

As he started to kiss her again, the doorbell rang.

Saved by the bell! Timing was everything.

'Ignore it,' he commanded.

'It'll be the maid to arrange the flowers,' she said, struggling to sit up.

'She'll come back later.'

'No, get it – please, darling. Those roses are so beautiful, let's have them in here while we make love.'

Hey, if he can be corny, so can I.

'Very well,' he said, reluctantly getting up. Clad only in his underwear, he went to the door and opened it.

It wasn't the maid, it was Fiona.

'Carlo?' she said, her eyes widening with shock and surprise as she took in his lack of clothes and saw past him to the bed. 'Carlo. I don't understand . . .'

Next to her stood her father. 'Carlo!' Leopold bellowed, immediately understanding. 'What the bloody hell is going on here?'

Brigette knelt on the bed, holding up the sheet to cover herself. 'I . . . I'm so sorry, Fiona,' she said, meaning it, because she had nothing against the poor girl. 'I . . . I thought Carlo had told you about us.'

Fiona was in shock. 'You cow!' she exclaimed, her eyes

filling with tears. 'You unbearable little cow!' And with that she turned and ran off down the corridor.

Leopold glared at Carlo. 'I will *ruin* you in this town,' he roared, before turning and chasing after his distressed daughter.

Carlo shook his head, obviously stunned. 'This is impossible,' he said, a dull red flush covering his face. 'How could they possibly know I was here?'

'Maybe they had you followed,' Brigette said, surprised that her feeling of triumph was so hollow. 'You were breaking it off anyway, you shouldn't feel *too* bad.'

'I never expected her to find out like this,' he said. 'Never.'

'You have to go,' Brigette said, getting off the bed and slipping on her dress.

'Why would I go?' he said, puzzled.

'Because I'm too upset for you to stay.'

'Don't be ridiculous.'

'I have feelings, Carlo. What happened is very disturbing.'

'We will sit quietly and talk about this,' he said, taking her arm.

'No,' she said, shaking free and going into the living room.

'Brigette,' he said, right behind her, 'you are leaving tomorrow, we must talk.'

'I don't think so,' she said, finally turning to face him.

'What do you mean?'

'Here's the deal, Carlo,' she said, savouring every word because this was the moment she'd been waiting for and standing up to him felt good. 'You just got yourself set up.'

His ice blue eyes clouded over. 'Excuse me?'

'*I* invited Fiona and her father here,' she announced triumphantly. 'I know what you did to me in New York. You drugged me so you could sleep with me. And, if you thought

I was going to sit back and take that kind of behaviour, then you picked the wrong girl.'

His face darkened with fury as her words sank in. 'You set me up?'

'Yes.'

'You set *me*, Carlo Vittorio Vitti, up?' he repeated.

'Yes, Carlo, I did,' she said. 'Now kindly put your clothes on and get out. And *never* try to contact me again. This game is over.'

'You fucking American bitch!' he snarled, and without warning, swung his arm back and hit her so hard across the face that she stumbled and almost fell.

She could not believe that he'd struck her. It was totally unexpected.

He went to hit her again.

'Stop it!' she yelled. She hadn't reckoned on his violent temper. 'You'd better get out of here before I call Security.'

'Shut the fuck up, American bitch!' he screamed, his handsome face a twisted mask of fury.

She backed away, suddenly scared.

He went after her, grabbed her in a lock from behind, placed his hand over her mouth and slapped her again. Then he dragged her into the bedroom and threw her down on the bed.

'One word out of your mouth and I'll kill you,' he threatened, a wild look in his eyes. 'Nobody treats Carlo this way and gets away with it. Do you hear me, bitch? Nobody. DO YOU HEAR ME?'

Chapter Forty-four

PRICE DID not go for conventional, he preferred his look to be more cutting edge: for Venus and Cooper's party he chose a black tuxedo with a black shirt, and instead of a satin stripe down the sides of his pants, the stripe was black leather. With his bald head and smooth, dark-chocolate skin, he knew that he looked pretty damn hot. And he felt good too, for that afternoon his agent had sent over the final contracts for his first starring role in a movie. Price Washington: soon to add movie star to his long list of achievements.

He was psyched.

His date for the evening, whom he'd be picking up shortly, was Krissie, the no-brain model. He'd decided to take her because she was the best-looking armpiece of all, and as long as she kept her mouth shut he'd be the envy of every man there.

He checked himself out in the mirror one more time, rubbed a touch of oil on his head to make it gleam, and doused himself in Christian Dior's Eau Sauvage. Finally ready, he went downstairs.

As usual, Irena was busy in the kitchen. 'I'm leaving now,' he said.

She didn't turn around, which irritated him. The woman had spent the night in his bed, the least she could do was pay him some attention and tell him how fine he looked.

But no. She was too goddamn busy polishing a silver coffee jug.

'I said, I'm leaving now,' he repeated.

This time she turned her head. He threw out his arms expecting a compliment. 'Like the outfit?'

'You look nice, Mr Washington,' she said, her face impassive as usual.

Nice? Fuck that shit. 'Yeah, well, a man's gotta try,' he said.

You smell like a whorehouse, she wanted to say, but she bit her lip. It wouldn't do to be truthful, there were certain boundaries she never dared cross.

Mila wandered into the kitchen and let forth a low wolf whistle. 'Wow, Mr W – lookin' *good*!'

He nodded in her direction. Truth was he couldn't stand the girl: everything she said was insincere. He reminded himself to tell Teddy he didn't want him hanging with her now that they were back in LA. Lately he'd noticed Teddy sniffing around the girl again, and it was best to discourage him before it went any further. Now that Mila had a job, there was no reason for him to spend any more time with her.

Mila threw him a cold hint of a smile. 'Going somewhere special, Mr W?'

Irena shot her daughter a look. She did not approve of her talking to the boss.

'A party,' Price said.

'Someone famous?' Mila persisted.

Irena shot her another furious look.

'Venus Maria and Cooper Turner's,' Price said, annoyed with himself for bothering to reply.

'Oooh, big stars,' Mila said, a faintly mocking tone in her voice. 'Maybe I should give you my autograph book.'

Maybe I should give you a sharp slap across the face, he

249

thought. And what was with the badly dyed blonde hair? 'Where's Teddy?' he asked abruptly.

Mila shrugged. 'Dunno.'

'In his room,' Irena said.

Price went to the bottom of the stairs and called his son. 'Teddy!'

Teddy appeared at the top of the stairs. 'Whass up, Dad?'

'I'm leavin' now. You home tonight?'

Teddy nodded, noticing that Mila was downstairs. If they could only get rid of Irena, they'd have the house to themselves and maybe they could take up where they'd left off.

'So . . . uh . . . behave yourself,' Price said, waiting for a comment on how he looked. Teddy didn't say a word. 'See you later, then,' Price said, walking out to the garage and getting into his black Ferrari – a recent purchase.

Settling behind the wheel, he started the car and set off to pick up Miss No Brains.

☆ ☆ ☆

'It's rude to question Mr Washington about where he's going,' Irena said, glaring at her daughter. 'You're fortunate he allows you to stay here now that you're grown.'

'Aren't *I* the lucky one?' Mila said sarcastically. 'Suppose I should learn to kiss his big black ass – like you.'

Irena's eyes signalled anger. '*What* did you say?'

'Nothing,' Mila murmured, beating a quick retreat. She never stopped hating her mother. Hating her for many reasons, the main one being that Irena had never been truthful about the identity of Mila's father. She did not believe it was some old boyfriend from Russia. If that was the case, then why couldn't she know his identity?

Irena was full of lies and mystery about her life in Russia before coming to America. She'd informed Mila that her entire family had perished in a train wreck. According to Irena, there were just the two of them. Oh, yes, and Mr Big Star Price Washington and his wimpy son, the jerk with the pussy balls. Mila hated Teddy, too.

For the last few days she'd been trying to figure out a way she could nail Teddy for the shooting *and* pick up the reward. One hundred thousand dollars. An astronomical amount. A fortune. The entrée to a new, much improved life. She'd called the cops to make sure the reward existed, now all she had to do was figure out a way to claim it.

It was a tricky problem, of course, because *she'd* been the shooter and, apart from Teddy – who didn't matter – there was only one other person who could finger her and that was Lennie Golden, the survivor. So even though she had Teddy's prints on the gun, Lennie Golden would identify *her*, and that simply couldn't happen.

How to stop it? That was the question.

She'd finally come up with an off-the-wall solution.

Kill Lennie Golden.

Oh, yes, and how was she supposed to do that?

For one hundred thousand dollars, she'd come up with something.

Chapter Forty-five

THE HOLLYWOOD Hills mansion of Venus Maria and Cooper Turner was alive with lights and hidden security as the guests began arriving. There was also plenty of security on show – guards at the gate holding clipboards with lists of invited guests, off-duty cops with dogs patrolling the enormous grounds, a few chosen detectives who mingled looking like guests.

No press. Cooper had been adamant about that, and over the six years they'd been married, Venus had learned to go along with what he wanted. It made life so much easier. After all, she was married to a catch, a confirmed playboy bachelor whom everyone had assured her would *never* get married.

Oh, yes? She'd soon changed *that* misconception. And, after a shaky start, they were now as happy as two people could be, living in the Hollywood fish-bowl. Because it *was* a fish-bowl. Everything Venus and Cooper did was scrutinized and written about. Once a month the tabloids came out with scandalous stories about how Cooper had fallen in love with his current co-star, or how Venus was sleeping with the latest stud around town. It made a change from the reports that she was supposedly suffering from anorexia, bulimia, or having a nervous breakdown. Or the stories that Cooper had been caught with three strippers in Tijuana –

that is, when he wasn't conducting a secret affair with Madonna, Venus's biggest rival.

All the outlandish headlines were pure fantasy, of course. They'd settled for laughing about them – suing cost too much and took too long.

For their party, Venus had chosen to wear a gold strapless dress that skimmed her incredible body like a second skin. She worked hard at keeping the best body in town; it was a tough daily grind, but worth it.

Cooper was in his bathroom putting the finishing touches to his bow-tie when she walked up behind him. He studied her reflection in the mirror. 'You look great, baby,' he said.

'So do you,' she answered, knowing that Cooper got off on compliments as much as any woman did. After all, he was an actor and, however famous, all actors were insecure and needed constant reassurance.

'Thanks,' he said. 'Are we ready to go downstairs?'

'If you think it's cool to be the first guests at our own party.'

'I do,' he said. 'Oh, and before we go, I've got a little something for you.'

'Not *now*, Cooper,' she said, with a dirty laugh. '*Please*. You're insatiable. We'll do it later.'

'Get your mind out of my pants,' he joked.

'Why? I like it there!'

He reached in his pocket and handed her a small leather jewellery box. She opened it. Inside nestled a perfect square-cut emerald and diamond ring.

'Happy anniversary,' he said.

'Wow!' she exclaimed, taking it out of the box. 'It's fantastic!'

'Does it fit?'

She slid the ring on her finger. 'Perfectly.'

'Then, my sweetheart,' he said, taking her arm, 'let us go downstairs and enjoy our party.'

☆ ☆ ☆

'You're late,' Lucky said crisply, looking strikingly beautiful in a black Richard Tyler evening suit with nothing underneath.

'I don't even know why I'm here,' Steven said.

'You're here because Carioca wants to go to the party, and therefore it'll be fun for you. It also means you can leave early.'

'Isn't she staying the night with you?'

'*No*, Steven. Tonight Carioca is going home with you. I don't know how many times I have to tell you this but your little girl lost her mother, and it would be tragic if she lost her father, too. By the way, you look extremely handsome.'

'Thanks,' he said dourly. 'I don't feel it.'

'Can I fix you a drink before we go?' she asked, walking over to the bar.

'No,' he said. 'Where are the girls?'

'Upstairs, finishing getting dressed,' she answered, pouring herself a shot of vodka. 'You should see how excited they are. I'm so glad you changed your mind and decided to come.'

'Venus sat in my office and changed it for me.'

'You should be very flattered that she went to all that trouble.'

'Yeah, it was nice of her to bother.'

'Your friends all love you, Steven. Never forget that.'

Before he could answer, Lennie entered the room. 'Good to see you, Steven,' he said.

Steven nodded. 'You too, Lennie.'

Lucky knew how strained things had been between them, but she was hopeful that tonight would change everything.

A few minutes later, Maria and Carioca came running downstairs, all dressed up and extremely giggly.

'You two little monkeys look fantastic!' Lucky said, grabbing her Nikon camera. 'Come on, get together. Photo time!'

Maria threw an arm around Carioca's shoulders, stuck out her leg and tilted her head, posing like a *Vogue* model.

I'm going to have my hands full with this one, Lucky thought. *She's exactly like I was at her age. A true mind of her own.*

'Steven,' she instructed, 'get in the photo. Stand between the girls.'

'No photos,' he said, shaking his head.

'Come on, it's an adorable picture.'

'Yes, c'mon, Daddy,' Carioca pleaded. 'Please! Please! Please!'

'Uncle Steven, do it!' Maria commanded.

Reluctantly Steven obliged. Lucky took the shot.

'Okay,' she said. 'Enough. It's time to party!'

☆ ☆ ☆

'I'm overdressed, aren't I?' Lina said, sounding unsure for once.

'You look sensational,' Max answered, helping her into his Maserati.

'No, I went too far,' she said, wishing she'd chosen the sleek, black Versace instead of the shocking pink Betsey Johnson.

'Lina, you're gonna knock everybody on their *ass*!'

'You think so?'

'I know so,' he said, throwing her a sideways glance. Personally he thought she'd gone over the top with her dress. It was a shocking pink number, with ruffles and frills, short in the front and long in the back. She resembled an overdressed bridesmaid. Fortunately he knew enough about women not to voice his opinion.

'Can I tell people I'm in the new Charlie Dollar movie?' she asked, extracting a pot of lip gloss from her purse.

'No. Never mention anything until a deal is signed.'

'Got it,' she said, dabbing more gloss on her lips with her finger.

'What do you care anyway?' Max said. 'Everybody knows who you are. It's the year of the supermodel – and, baby, you're it!'

She grinned happily. 'That's true.'

'I spoke to Charlie before he left,' Max said, steering his Maserati into the fast lane.

'Oh, yeah,' Lina said casually. 'Mention me, did 'e?'

'Thinks you're enchanting.'

'Enchanting, huh?' she said, with a pleased smile.

'You *do* know he has a girlfriend?'

'Yes. He mumbled something about her busting in an' shooting me.'

'Don't think she wouldn't,' Max said, imagining the headlines. 'Dahlia's a tough lady, and I *mean* lady. She's not one of those pretty little things he takes to bed on occasion.'

'Who is she?' Lina asked curiously.

'Dahlia Summers is a serious actress. She and Charlie have been on and off for years. They have a two-year-old son together, Sport.'

'That's 'is name?'

'Chosen by Charlie himself.'

'Figures. Anyway,' she added, 'I wasn't planning on *marrying* him.'

Max laughed. 'I'm relieved to hear that, 'cause *I*'m not into sleeping with married women.'

'What makes you think you're sleeping with me tonight?' she said, teasing him with a slow, sexy look.

'Because . . . you remind me of myself. We're both predators. We both get off on stalking the prey.'

'Yes?' she said.

'Yes,' he said.

Lina smiled. For an agent Max Steele was pretty damn smart. And she liked that in a man. Brains and a great butt. Two major assets.

Tonight, if he kept up the dialogue, Mr Max Steele might get extraordinarily lucky.

Chapter Forty-six

SLOWLY BRIGETTE regained consciousness. As she began to come to and remembered what had happened, she was gripped with fear.

She was lying on the bed in the bedroom of her hotel suite, with Carlo hovering over her holding a damp towel to her forehead. He was fully dressed. She wasn't. 'You fainted,' he said.

'I didn't faint,' she managed, wincing with pain because it felt as if someone had hit her across the face with a sledgehammer.

'Yes, you did,' he said, in a soothing voice, his patrician features calm and composed. 'I was worried about you.'

This was unbelievable! He'd beaten her into unconsciousness and now he was sitting on the edge of the bed acting as if nothing had happened.

She attempted to move.

'Stay where you are,' he said. 'We don't want you fainting again, *cara*.'

Oh, God! This was crazy. He'd beaten her up and now he was acting like a concerned boyfriend.

She lay very still, trying to collect her thoughts. What would Lucky do? Probably shoot his balls off and run. Lucky lived by her own rules.

She reached up and touched her face, her cheek felt tender

and swollen where he'd hit her. Maybe she was marked for life. Should she start screaming? Or now that he seemed calm, should she simply work on getting him out of there? Some night of revenge this was turning out to be.

'Carlo,' she said, in a cool, even tone, 'I think it would be best if you left.'

'Why?' he said, frowning.

Why? Was he kidding? Didn't he know what he'd done?

'Because I'm tired and I want to sleep. We can talk in the morning.'

'I can't leave you, Brigette,' he said. 'I never want to leave you again.'

'I know,' she said, playing along with this bizarre game. 'I feel the same way. But right now I'm exhausted.'

'I hit you, didn't I?' he said.

'Well . . . yes.'

'I didn't mean to,' he said, 'but you made me so mad.' He got up and began pacing around the room. 'You treated me badly, Brigette. I can't stand it when people treat me badly.'

She was smart enough not to get into it with him. She did not want him losing control again, he was obviously unbalanced.

'I'm sorry if you think I treated you badly,' she said slowly.

'You accused me of things,' he said heatedly. 'Things that are not true.'

'Maybe I was mistaken,' she said, struggling to sit up.

Without warning, he leaned over and hugged her. She felt his shoulders begin to shake. Oh, God! He was actually crying.

'Brigette,' he sobbed, 'you must forgive me. Sometimes I don't know what I do. Please – forgive me.'

'I need to sleep, Carlo,' she said, asserting herself.

'No, no, I can't be alone,' he said. 'Come home with me to my apartment.'

'That's impossible.'

'Why?'

'Because I'm uh . . . expecting some important phone calls,' she said, thinking fast. 'If I'm not here, people will worry.'

'You can phone *them*.'

'Well . . . yes.'

'Put some things in a bag and come with me.'

'No, Carlo, I can't.'

His eyes flashed sudden danger. 'Yes, Brigette, you can, and you will.'

'Okay,' she said, forming a plan. Once they were in the lobby she would be able to scream for help and escape from him. 'If you really want me to.'

'I do,' he said, helping her off the bed. 'I have to make this up to you, my angel.'

She grabbed her dress from the foot of the bed and slipped into it. The bastard must have taken it off her when she was out. She wondered what else he'd done . . .

She was desperate to peek in a mirror, see how damaged her face was. 'I need to use the bathroom,' she said.

'I'll come with you.'

'No, Carlo. You wait outside.'

'I don't trust you, Brigette.'

'Trust me to what?' she said lightly, although inside she was shaking. Why did she always find herself in these impossible situations. Why? Why? Why?

Her legs felt weak as he escorted her to the bathroom. He came in with her and stood by the door, blocking the wall phone.

'Go,' he said. 'Hurry.'

'I don't need to go now,' she said, trying to catch a glimpse of herself in the mirror.

He blocked her there too.

They returned to the bedroom. He went to the closet and flung it open.

'What are you doing?' she asked, wondering if she could make a run for it.

No. Impossible. He was between her and the door, and she didn't care to risk being beaten again.

'You need something to cover you,' he said, pulling out a long purple Armani scarf. 'Put that over your head. Where are your sunglasses?'

'It's dark outside,' she said.

'I know,' he said. 'Now, where are they?'

She pointed to a drawer. He opened it and found the opaque glasses.

Do something, a voice screamed in her head. *Get the fuck away from him.*

How can I? He's got me trapped.

He searched through the closet, found her long raincoat and handed it to her. She put it on.

'We're leaving,' he said, taking her arm. 'Is there anything you wish to bring?'

She shook her head, no, thinking that the moment they hit the lobby she would be free. It wasn't as if he had a gun on her or anything. And he could hardly beat her up in front of people.

He went to the door, opened it a few inches, and peered out. 'Okay,' he said, 'let's go.'

The long corridor was empty.

Damn! She had hoped to see a maid or a room-service waiter, someone who could help her.

Carlo gripped her arm firmly as they headed for the

elevators. When they got there, he bypassed them and headed through another door.

'Where are we going?' she asked, starting to panic.

'The service entrance,' he said.

She stopped abruptly. 'No!' she said. 'Take me back to my room.'

'If that's what you want, my angel.'

And then he socked her so hard on the jaw that once more she fell into a deep hole, and everything faded to black.

Chapter Forty-seven

LUCKY CIRCLED the party searching for Venus and Cooper. People kept trying to stop her and talk but, over the years she'd spent in Hollywood in a position of power, she had become extremely adept at moving on. Lennie had vanished into the throng of guests, Maria holding tightly on to his hand. Steven and Carioca had gone with them.

An overly familiar hand on her shoulder. 'What's going on, Lucky?'

She spun around, coming face to face with Alex. 'What's going on with *you*, Alex?' she retorted, not even sure if she was glad to see him because he was becoming a complication she didn't need.

'How was the rest of your weekend?' he asked.

'Pretty good,' she said noncommittally. 'And yours?'

'It would have been better if—'

'Now don't start, Alex,' she interrupted, giving him a warning look, for she knew exactly what he was about to say.

'I take it the reconciliation went well.'

'It wasn't a reconciliation. We were only apart one night.'

'Yeah, but that one night could be the start of something.'

'Don't get your hopes up.'

His eyes searched the room. 'Where *is* the missing husband?'

'He's here. And the good news is he's getting back to work.'

'Doing what?'

'Writing a script about violence,' she said, extracting a cigarette from her purse.

'Violence isn't Lennie's genre,' Alex said, producing a light. 'He's known for comedy.'

'Well, now he wants to write something more serious,' she said, drawing deeply on her cigarette.

'Really?' Alex said, holding her eyes with a more than best-friends look.

'Yes, really,' she answered, wishing he wasn't so damn attractive.

'Let's go to the bar,' he suggested, taking her arm.

'I was actually looking for Venus. Have you seen her?'

He gestured across the room. 'She's in the middle of those ten guys over there.'

'Guess she's enjoying *that*.'

'I'm sure she is,' Alex agreed.

'Are you ever going to put her in another movie?'

'If I find the right project.'

'I know it's what she wants. She loved working with you.'

'Venus is a very underrated actress,' he said, steering Lucky to the bar. 'What'll you have?'

'Vodka martini.'

'Make that two,' he instructed the barman.

'Didn't figure you for a martini drinker,' she remarked.

'I'm not. But tequila always gets us in trouble, remember?'

He was determined to bring up the past, and she was equally determined to bury it. 'No, I don't,' she said shortly.

The bartender expertly mixed their drinks and handed over two chilled martinis.

'Did you give any thought to that discussion we had?' Alex enquired, as he led her over to a quiet corner.

'What discussion was that?' she asked, sipping her drink.

'The one about you producing.'

'Haven't had time to think about it,' she lied, because she wasn't about to tell him that Lennie had been less than enthusiastic.

'How about the *three* of us working together?' he suggested. 'You, me and Venus? What a combination that'd be. We could *really* kick ass.'

'You're very persistent.'

'That's 'cause it's not much fun seeing you out of work. You're not the housewife type.'

She couldn't help smiling. 'You sound like Lennie. I had to make him a sandwich today because he informed me that's what stay-at-home wives do.'

'Bet you loved *that*.'

She rolled her eyes. 'You can imagine.'

'I've got a couple of interesting things in development,' Alex said. 'How about I send you the scripts, see what you think?'

'Are they good?'

'No, Lucky,' he deadpanned. 'I only develop projects that stink.'

'Okay,' she said, laughing. Hey – if Lennie didn't want to work with her, how could he possibly object to her doing something with Alex?

Only she knew that he would. No doubt on *that* score.

☆ ☆ ☆

'That's Dahlia,' Max said, nudging Lina, who was gobbling small toast squares loaded with caviar from the hors d'oeuvres table.

'Where?' Lina said, continuing to stuff her mouth.

'Over there. The woman in the green dress.'

'Oooh!' Lina said, checking out a tall, thin woman in her forties with a sweep of long dark hair and prominent features. 'Scary!'

'She's actually very nice,' Max said. 'If Charlie was smart, he'd marry her.'

'And she's, like, got no clue 'e fucks around?'

'I'm sure she knows. But Dahlia's a wise woman, she chooses to ignore it.'

'What's so wise about *that*?' Lina asked, cramming more caviar into her mouth.

'As long as no one threatens her territory, she's happy.'

'What's 'er territory?'

'The public Charlie,' Max explained. 'The one that goes to benefits, award ceremonies, industry events and sits at the top tables. Dahlia is *always* his date on those occasions.'

Damn! Lina thought. *There goes my chance of being photographed with him.* She'd envisaged walking into a première with Charlie, arm in arm, flashbulbs popping and everyone oohing and aahing. Her mum would've creamed over *that*.

'Hold the eating for a minute,' Max instructed. 'My partner, Freddie Leon, is on his way over. Be nice. Freddie takes care of most of the major talent in this town.'

'Am I supposed to be impressed?'

'Yes. And do *not* come on to him. Freddie is very happily married.'

'Sure,' Lina snorted disbelievingly. 'Aren't they all!'

'Hey there, Freddie,' Max said, as his partner approached. 'I want you to meet Lina, she's with the agency.'

'Hello, Lina,' Freddie said. He was a poker-faced man with flat brown eyes and an expressionless demeanour.

'Guess I'm with your better 'alf,' Lina said cheerfully. ''Ope 'e's as good as you.'

'Max'll look after you,' Freddie said smoothly. 'I hear we've got you into the new Charlie Dollar film. Congratulations.'

'I'm not supposed to say anything until it's signed.'

'That's all right,' he said. 'We represent you.'

'Oh, yes, so you do,' she said, attempting a quick flirt.

Freddie was unresponsive. 'Pleasure to meet you, Lina,' he said, and quickly moved on.

'He's a cold one,' Lina remarked, returning to the caviar.

'That's Freddie,' Max said, with a glimmer of a smile. 'There's one thing you have to remember in this town. *Never* cross Freddie Leon.'

'I wasn't planning to. Oh, Christ!' she said. 'Look who's comin' our way *now*!'

'Who?'

'Flick Fonda.'

'You know Flick?' Max said, wondering who the legendary rock star's agent was, and if Flick was stealable. 'I've never met him. Introduce me.'

'He's with that boring wife of 'is,' Lina said, pulling a disgusted face. 'Quick, let's make a run for it!'

'Don't be crazy,' Max said. 'It's too late anyway.'

'Hello, darlin',' Flick said, bearing down on them, looking suitably rock star-ish in sprayed-on leather pants and a floppy white shirt, diamond studs in both ears. 'How ya doin'?'

'Nice to see you, Flick,' Lina said, giving him a perfunctory kiss on each cheek, leaving full lipstick imprints. 'You know Max Steele, the agent? *My* agent, actually.'

'Hello, Max,' Flick said, bloodshot eyes checking out the room to see if there were any women he'd missed out on.

'My pleasure, Flick,' Max said, suddenly oozing bullshit agent charm. 'I'm a big, big fan.'

'Always happy to hear that,' Flick said. 'That'll sell me a

few more CDs, huh? This is my wife, Pamela. Pammy, say hello to everyone.'

Pamela stepped forward, an angry expression on her long-suffering face. Once a beauty, she was now suspicious of every woman her husband talked to, and considering he'd been to bed with most of them, her suspicions were usually justified.

'Hi, Pam,' Lina said, with a lackadaisical wave. ''Aven't run into *you* in a while.'

'I see *you* everywhere,' Pamela retorted. 'Aren't you frightened of overexposure?'

'Nah,' Lina replied, tossing back her long black hair while giving Flick 'the look'. 'The more you give 'em, the more they want. Right, Flick?'

Flick, sensing trouble ahead, grabbed his wife's hand and said, 'C'mon, darlin', I spy Rod and Rachel. Let's go say hello.'

'Nice dress,' Pamela said, unable to resist a parting shot. 'Left over from Mardi Gras?'

'What a cow!' Lina muttered, as the two of them moved off.

'I see his wife is a fan,' Max remarked.

'Can't win 'em all.' Lina sniffed, once again returning her attention to the caviar.

☆ ☆ ☆

Miss No Brains wore a dress that had to be seen to be believed. Price had wanted to be the envy of every man there, but the dress Krissie almost had on was ridiculous. The orange material was cut down to the cheeks of her ass in the back, plunged all the way to Cuba in the front, and up the sides were see-through zigzags revealing even more skin.

Price was embarrassed. She looked like she belonged on

the cover of an X-rated video. 'Krissie,' he'd said, when he'd picked her up, 'you wearing that?'

'Price,' she'd retorted, quite sassy for a dumb blonde, 'you wearing *that*?'

Their evening did not get off to a great start.

As soon as they arrived at the party, Price found a corner couch, placed Krissie there with a drink and took off, assuring her he'd be right back. No way was he cruising around with *her* by his side.

Truth was, he hadn't needed to bring a date, the party was full of glamorous women of all shapes and sizes. He even spotted supermodel Lina across the room – someone he *definitely* wanted to meet, although the dress she had on was another disaster. What was wrong with these women tonight? One big party and their clothes sense ricocheted out of control.

He searched around for Venus. They'd been friends for a while, ever since they'd gotten together at a couple of charity events. He'd taken Teddy to her last concert at the Hollywood Bowl, and Teddy had loved it, even though the only music he claimed to be into was gangsta rap.

'Price,' Venus said, sneaking up behind him, 'don't tell me *you*'re responsible for bringing the tart in the orange dress?'

'Shh, girl,' he said, holding a finger to his lips, 'she's a mistake.'

'I was under the impression you had better taste,' Venus said tartly.

'I do,' he said.

'We'll have to find someone to palm her off on.'

'Like who?'

'There's a bunch of Cooper's old producer friends here,' Venus said. 'I'm sure one of them would be thrilled to get a quick grope in the back of a limo.'

'Arrange it,' Price begged. 'I need help.'

'You certainly do,' Venus said, pursing her luscious lips, looking every inch the superstar.

'Oh, yeah,' Price added. 'On the way in I got an eyeful of that model, Lina. She's unfuckin' believable! You gonna set me up?'

'Any time, baby. You're a star, it's arrangeable.'

'I love it when you talk up to me!'

'How's about down and dirty?' she said, mildly coming on to him.

'Don't even go there.'

'If you insist. Now, how's that cute little son of yours?'

'Kid's doin' okay,' Price said.

'I bet half your girlfriends are younger than him,' Venus said, grabbing a glass of champagne from an attentive waiter. 'Anyway, no need to sweat it – the two of you look like brothers.'

'Will you *stop*, woman?' he said, loving every compliment that came his way.

'Let's go find that little model babe,' she said, linking her arm through his. 'I haven't met her myself yet. Gotta hunch she's here with Max Steele.' A sly laugh. 'Rumour has it that Max hangs out at airports picking off the girls as they leave the plane!'

Price winked. 'Sounds like my kinda guy!'

☆ ☆ ☆

Venus and Cooper's five-year-old daughter, Chyna, was holding court at her own table. She was precocious, but in a likeable way. She wanted to act, just like Mommy and Daddy, and had already appeared in one of Cooper's movies.

'Daddy, Daddy, I gotta go to the bathroom,' Carioca announced, pulling on her father's sleeve.

Steven, who was busy wishing he wasn't there, was only too happy to take her. He felt completely out of place and couldn't wait to go home.

'I'm coming back,' Carioca informed Chyna.

'Hurry!' Chyna said, bouncing up and down in her seat. 'Gonna have big huge cake!'

Steven led his daughter through the crowded room. He hardly knew any of the guests, which didn't bother him at all because he wasn't interested in the movie crowd. Carioca clung to his hand, a mirror image of her mother.

'Daddy,' she said, her pretty little face twisted into a serious expression.

'Yes, baby-girl?' he asked, sad because she would never see her mother again, and that wasn't right.

'I'm glad you came to Palm Springs. It was so so *fun*! *This* is fun. And, Daddy, I am *not* a baby.'

'Okay, big girl.'

'Daddy, now that Mommy's not here, can we do stuff together?'

'Of course we can, honey,' he said, squeezing her hand.

'I like staying at Lucky's, but being with you is *best*!'

'That's nice to know, Carrie,' he said, using his mother's name as her nickname, 'and I promise you, we'll spend a lot more time together.'

When they reached the guest bathroom it was occupied. Carioca waited outside, hopping from one foot to the other. 'Daddy, Daddy, I *gotta* go *now*!' she squealed.

'Okay, honey,' he answered, tapping on the bathroom door. 'Can you hurry it up?' he called out. 'I've got a desperate child out here.'

A few seconds later the door was flung open, and there stood a vision in a shocking pink dress. 'Sorry,' Lina said, staring directly at him. 'Was I in there too long?'

'Uh, no, that's okay,' he said, somewhat taken aback by

the woman's exotic beauty. 'My little girl here was getting out of control.'

'Daddy!' Carioca scolded. 'I wasn't *desperate*. I just gotta *go*.'

'That's what I meant, honeybun.'

'It's all yours, cutie,' Lina said, patting Carioca on the shoulder. 'In you go.'

Carioca raced into the bathroom, pushing the door shut behind her. Lina turned to Steven with a dazzling smile. He was the best-looking man she'd seen in a long while – giving new meaning to the phrase 'Black is beautiful'. 'Your little girl's adorable. What's 'er name?'

'Carioca.'

'Now *that*'s what I call a name,' she said, staring at this incredibly handsome man, wondering if he was an actor. Then it suddenly occurred to her who he was. 'Hey, wait a minute,' she exclaimed. 'You must be Steven.'

'Do I know you?' he asked politely.

'I'm Lina.'

He frowned, embarrassed because it seemed she expected him to know who she was and he didn't. 'Lina?' he questioned.

'Don't you recognize me?' she said, almost teasingly.

'Should I?' he asked tentatively.

'I'm Brigette's friend,' she said, as if that would explain everything. 'Y' know, Lucky's goddaughter, Brigette Stanis-lopoulos? God, that's a mouthful, wonder 'ow she struggled through childhood with a name like *that*.'

'Of course . . .' Steven said. 'Brigette's a model in New York. What do *you* do?'

Lina started to laugh. 'You honestly *don't* recognize me, do you?'

'I'm really bad at recognizing people. Are you an actress? My wife was an actress.'

'I was ever so sorry to 'ear about your wife,' Lina said, suddenly serious. 'Brigette told me 'ow beautiful the funeral was.'

'Thank you.'

'Your wife was lovely,' Lina continued, talking too fast, but quite mesmerized by this delicious-looking man. 'I used to watch 'er on TV. It's difficult to find words, but I'm really, really sorry for you. Um . . . I mean, y' know, for your loss.'

'I appreciate it,' he said.

'That's okay.'

'So, where *is* Brigette tonight?'

'In London with Lucky,' Lina said, imagining this green-eyed man without his clothes.

'She can't be,' he said. 'Lucky's here with me.'

'You mean she's back?'

'She hasn't been anywhere.'

'Hmm . . . Brigette must've been telling little white lies. Maybe she got herself a fellow and didn't want me to know.'

'Are you two close?'

'Best mates. We live in the same building in New York. By the way, for your information we're *both* models.'

'Interesting.'

'You're a lawyer, right?'

'Guilty.'

'I'd love to *meet* Lucky. Will you introduce me?'

'When I can find her. Who are you here with?'

'My agent. It's strictly business. Actually,' she said, leaning towards him, 'can you keep a secret?'

'Lawyers are good at keeping secrets.'

'I flew out to LA to see Charlie Dollar. Now I'm gonna be in his new movie. My agent said I mustn't tell anyone.'

'Your secret's safe with me,' he said, intrigued by this exotic creature with the oddball accent. 'Then you *are* an actress?'

'Model slash actress.'

'An *English* model slash actress, right?'

''Ow did you guess?'

'Beats me,' he said, smiling.

She giggled. 'Gotta take some speech lessons if I'm gonna be a movie star.'

'I think you sound charming.'

'Thanks.'

'I lived in London for a couple of years,' Steven said.

'Really? Whereabouts?'

'Hampstead.'

'Very posh.'

Carioca emerged from the bathroom. 'Come along, Daddy,' she said impatiently, tugging on his sleeve. 'We gotta go now.'

'Okay, sweetie.'

'See you later,' Lina said, giving him a lingering look.

'It was nice meeting you,' Steven said.

'You too. Brigette 'as talked about you a lot.' A pause. 'Although she forgot to tell me 'ow handsome you are.'

'No need to flatter me,' he said, half smiling.

'I know that,' she said, uncharacteristically shy.

'Daddy, come *on*!' Carioca said crossly, pulling his arm.

'Uh, if I find Lucky I'll let her know you want to meet her,' he said.

Lina dazzled him with a smile. 'Thanks.'

☆ ☆ ☆

'Are we having fun?' Lucky said, finally locating Lennie, who was sitting at the kiddies' table next to Maria.

'The kids are having a great time,' he said. 'We've had balloons, a magician, watched a clown show. What've *you* been doing?'

274

'Circulating. Missing you.'

He pulled her close. 'Come here, wife.'

'Yes, husband.'

'Can we go home soon?'

'I can't desert Venus so early.'

'Then would you mind if I took Maria home and sent the limo back for you?'

'Well . . .'

'Please, babe, I'm not feeling social yet. I just want to be . . . you know, at home.'

'If that's what you want,' she said, sighing, 'but I *have* to stay.'

'Understood.'

'Okay, but when you go, do *not* say goodbye. There's nothing worse than guests saying goodbye too early. Slip out quietly, and I'll be home as soon as I can.'

'You're the best.'

'No, Lennie,' she said, mock-serious. 'I am *not* making you another sandwich.'

'It wasn't a sandwich I had in mind.'

'Later, you sex-crazed homebody!'

'Love you, babe.'

'You, too.'

'Sure you'll be all right without me?'

'Somehow I think I'll manage.'

And she kissed Maria, hugged her husband and slipped back into the heart of the party.

Chapter Forty-eight

AND SO the nightmare continued. Once more Brigette regained consciousness, and this time she found herself in a strange bed in a dark, unfamiliar room. The drapes were pulled tightly over the windows, and when she got unsteadily out of bed and tried the door, she discovered it was locked.

It came to her in a horrible flash – Carlo had kidnapped her.

She felt as if she were caught in the middle of some insane TV soap opera. This kind of thing didn't happen in real life, it simply didn't.

I will not panic, she told herself. *I will stay calm and talk myself out of this mess.*

But there was no one to talk to. Carlo was not around.

She got up and went to the window, pulling back the drapes. The window overlooked an alley and was probably ten or eleven storeys up, too dangerous to attempt an escape.

'Damn!' she muttered. Now her jaw hurt, too, where he'd hit her. Gingerly she opened and closed her mouth, finding that, fortunately, nothing seemed to be broken.

She returned to the door and tried it again. Still locked. She rattled the handle and yelled his name.

Nobody came.

After a while she went back to the bed and lay down. There was no point in using up all her energy. She felt like crying, but she didn't. She'd shed too many tears in the past to keep on repeating the same old pattern.

Instead she began chanting a mantra in her head.

You will be strong.

You will survive.

You will be strong.

You will survive.

And eventually she drifted off into a fitful sleep.

She awoke a few hours later to an even worse nightmare. Standing over her were Carlo and a strange man. The man was in his thirties, tall and gangly, with tufts of hair growing out of his ears, and long, greasy sideburns. He was dressed in brown pants and a stained sweatshirt. A small gold ring protruded from one of his nostrils.

Carlo was holding her down, while the stranger was tightening a leather belt around her left arm, searching for a big fat vein. In his other hand he held a syringe.

The horror of what they were about to do struck her too late. As she began to scream, the man plunged the needle into her arm.

'You sure this is what the bitch wants?' she heard him say.

'Yes,' Carlo replied, 'but it doesn't matter, does it? You're getting paid. That's all that should concern you.'

And then everything started spinning, and a wave of euphoria came over her.

She lay quietly watching the shadows on the ceiling, feeling kind of peaceful and happy.

And soon she drifted off into a long drug-induced sleep.

Chapter Forty-nine

IRENA HAD gone to bed early, and since Price was at a party, Teddy realized that he and Mila had the house to themselves.

He found her in the kitchen watching a game show on television. 'Whass up?' he said.

'Nothing,' she answered, not in the mood to hang with him. He was boring, and she had too much on her mind to bother with him.

But he was all over her and, since she couldn't risk him turning against her at this crucial stage, she let him have a quick grope or two. Then they went upstairs to his room where she unzipped his pants and took it out for some air.

He was certainly well hung – better than her current boyfriend at work: he had a long, thin johnson that didn't get her off at all. It was a shame. Teddy had the equipment, not the brains.

She wondered if he took after his father in the goodies department. Hmm . . . maybe she should give Mr W a test drive, simply to prove that she could.

In the meantime, she'd keep Teddy happy and try to work out how she was going to eliminate Lennie Golden. One hundred thousand dollars was the jackpot she'd been dreaming of all her life. One way or another it was going to be hers.

She pushed Teddy down on his bed and gave him a little mouth action. When he was satisfied, she told him she wanted to see Price's room.

'He gets mad if I go in there,' Teddy said nervously. 'My dad's got a thing about privacy.'

'Crap!' Mila said. 'Like, you can't show *me*?'

Teddy was ready to show Mila anything she wanted. She had taken him to heaven and back, and even though she hadn't let him touch her *there*, he felt like a man at last. And for once he'd stopped thinking about that fateful night. Mila was right, he had to forget about it and move on.

Price's bedroom was a fantasy of deep brown leather and black lacquer furniture. Masculine and sexy, one of LA's top designers had put it together. The platform bed was positioned in front of a large-screen TV. And it was covered in a luxurious fur throw. Mila flopped on to it, grabbed the remote and clicked on the TV.

'Better not mess with anything,' Teddy warned.

'Oooh, is this you?' Mila said, picking up a silver frame next to the bed and staring at a picture of a cute little four-year-old boy balanced on Price's shoulders.

'Don't touch,' he said, attempting to grab it from her.

She wouldn't give it up. He fell across the bed on top of her, and before he realized what was happening, she was unzipping his pants again and pulling up her skirt.

Man! He was on his freaking father's bed and she wanted him to do it to her! This was *so* bad it was good. Especially since he was hard as a bat and ready for the home run.

She began wriggling out of her panties. 'You ever done this before, Teddy?'

'Sure,' he gasped.

'Liar,' she jeered. 'I know you haven't.'

It didn't matter what came out of her mouth, because once he got an eyeful of the mound of black hair between her legs, he wanted in. The fact that they were on his dad's bed in his very private bedroom made it all the more forbidden and exciting.

Her skirt was bunched up around her waist, her panties around her ankles. She kicked them across the room and spread her legs. 'If you're gonna do it, get started,' she said.

He knew he should wear a rubber, take precautions just as his dad had warned him to do if he ever had sex. But what was one more risk? This was happening now, and nothing was going to stop him.

He rolled on top of her, dipping into a sticky, welcoming paradise. And then he was brought up short by the resounding buzz of the front gate.

Both of them froze. Teddy's pride and joy shrivelled like a collapsible umbrella.

'Shit!' Mila said. 'The buzzer's gonna wake my mom and she'll come nosying around. *You*'d better get it fast.'

Teddy crawled across the bed, grabbing the phone and pressing the button that connected him to the gate. 'Who's there?' he yelled, shouting, because the thought of Irena catching him with his pants down, rolling around with *her* daughter in the middle of his dad's bed, was enough to panic anyone.

'The police,' said a disembodied voice. 'We'd like to talk to the owner of the black jeep.'

Chapter Fifty

'*FINALLY!*' LINA exclaimed, tapping Lucky on the shoulder.

'Excuse me?' Lucky said, turning around.

'I'm Lina. Brigette never stops talking about you. Says you're the greatest thing since fried bread.'

'Fried bread?!' Lucky said, amused at the girl's off-the-wall accent. 'Is that English flattery?'

''Spect she's told you all about me,' Lina said confidently. 'Only you mustn't believe a word. She's a raging liar!'

'Actually,' Lucky said, recognizing the famous model, but not remembering Brigette ever mentioning her, 'she's always spoken very highly of you.'

'I must admit I'm confused,' Lina said. 'Brigette told me she was going to London with you, only when I spoke to Steven earlier, 'e said you weren't with her. So I don't get it.'

'She told *me* she was flying to Milan,' Lucky said.

'No, no, she cancelled out Italy,' Lina said, 'which kind of pissed me off, 'cause we always go there together. Y' know, run riot on the runways, 'ave a wild time.'

'Hmmm . . . I wonder what she's up to,' Lucky mused. 'Maybe I should give her a call.'

'Could be she's got herself a secret boyfriend,' Lina said. 'Although if she 'as, I'm pissed she didn't confide in me.'

'Does she tell you everything?' Lucky asked, amused.

'Usually. Only I guess she didn't want me knowing about this one.'

'I was under the impression that Brigette had given up on dating for a while – at least, that's what she told me last time we spoke.'

'Well, yes. Then she had that 'orrible experience in New York.'

'What horrible experience?'

'Uh-oh,' Lina said, clapping a hand over her mouth. 'I'm givin' away secrets.'

'Too late now, keep going.'

'Some jerk slipped a pill in her drink – y' know, one of those date rape drugs. And Brig is under the impression that the bastard might've raped her. I promised not to tell anyone – especially *you* – 'cause Brig says she always 'as to run to you to get 'er out of trouble.'

'When did this happen?' Lucky asked, frowning.

'A coupla months ago,' Lina said. 'She was furious, but she got over it. Me – I would've chopped off 'is ding-dong with a blunt knife!'

Lucky couldn't help smiling. 'Lina, Lina, you're my kind of girl.'

Lina grinned back. 'That's what Brig always says.'

'So who is this guy?' Lucky asked.

'Some Italian arsehole we 'ad dinner with. I mean 'e was an attractive bloke – I would 'ave given 'im one in a flash. It beats me why 'e 'ad t' do it.'

'Men are a problem for Brigette. She's always had bad luck with them,' Lucky said. 'I'm sure you've heard things.'

'Yeah. Brutal,' Lina said. 'Thought *I*'d met every prick in town until I 'eard *her* war stories.'

'What are you doing in LA?' Lucky asked.

'Actually, I'm leaving tomorrow, going to Milan for fashion week. I came out here to meet with Charlie Dollar for his new film.'

'Charlie's a good guy,' Lucky said. 'You'll love him.'

'I know,' Lina said, with a secretive smirk.

'You do?'

'Well,' Lina said. 'I know 'e's great in the sack. I've already 'ad 'im.'

'I advise you not to advertise,' Lucky said drily. 'Charlie has a very steady relationship with Dahlia.'

'Guess I'm not being exactly discreet,' Lina admitted. 'It's just that it was *sooo* exciting. Me mum loves him.'

'Here comes Venus,' Lucky said. 'Have you two met?'

'No. I've met Cooper, though,' Lina said, refraining from adding that she'd had him, too. Somehow she didn't think Lucky would appreciate the information, even though it had been way before he married the blonde superstar.

'Venus,' Lucky said, 'this is Lina. She's a good friend of Brigette's.'

'Of *course* I know who Lina is,' Venus said. 'Watched you kick ass in Paris at the Chanel show. You *killed* 'em on the catwalk. Loved it!'

'Thanks,' Lina said, quite intimidated for once.

'Oh, and this is Price Washington,' Venus added, as Lucky drifted off. 'He's been dying to meet you all night.'

''Ello, Price,' Lina said, giving him the lowering-of-the-eyes look. Sexy and demure. An unbeatable combination.

'Hey—' Price said, checking her out and liking what he saw. 'Noticed your African safari in *Vogue* last month. Those were *some* pictures.'

'What were *you* doing reading *Vogue*?' she teased.

'One of my girlfriends left it at the house.'

'*One* of your girlfriends?' she said, flirting outrageously. ''Ow many d'you 'ave?'

'A guy's gotta go for variety, huh?'

'Oh, so *that*'s what you're into?'

'Could be.'

'Lordy, Lordy,' Venus said, fanning herself with her hand. 'Lust is in the air. I'm tracking down my husband. See you all later.'

☆ ☆ ☆

Somehow or other, Max Steele found himself deep in conversation with Price Washington's girlfriend, Krissie. He was unamused at getting trapped.

'So, you see,' Krissie said, huge breasts jiggling with indignation, 'after I did the *Playboy* shoot, I thought it was all going to happen. Everybody *told* me it would. I mean, if you do the full spread, you expect results – right?'

'Right,' he said, searching for an escape.

'Now I've got this agent who tells me I have to be *seen*. He chose this dress for me 'cause he wanted everyone to notice me tonight. But Price is not being very nice to me. He should be nicer to me, wouldn't you say?' Max nodded. 'And I know you're a very important agent, 'cause someone told me. So I hope you don't mind me coming up and talking to you, but I need a new agent, and I think you'd be the man for me.'

'Have you had any film experience?' he asked, still looking around for someone to rescue him.

'No, except I did do a kind of . . . Well, it was really *soft* core. And if Traci Lords can make it in legit movies, *anybody* can, don't you think?'

'Traci Lords is a passable actress,' Max said. 'She did pornos when she was a teenager. After that she studied her craft and now she's not bad.'

284

'I can study my craft, too,' Krissie said excitedly, forty-inch double Ds heaving with emotion.

Christ! Max thought. *Where's Lina when I need her?*

☆ ☆ ☆

Lina was sharing a joint with Price Washington on the terrace. And although he was black and a star and very sexy, she couldn't help wondering what had happened to Steven Berkeley – him being one of the best-looking men she'd ever seen, black *or* white. And he was nice with it: he hadn't even come on to her, although she'd certainly given him every opportunity.

She was dying to ask Brigette more about him, but who knew where Brigette had run off to, the secretive little brat? Lina hated being left out. If Brigette had a boyfriend, she wanted to know about it, and how.

In the meantime, here she was in LA, surrounded by eligible black men – and that was quite unusual, because she usually only came across white dudes. White, rich and horny. The story of Lina, supermodel.

It wasn't that she didn't like men of colour, it was simply that she never got to meet any. There were a couple of gorgeous black models she often ran into on the circuit – both gay. And she'd briefly dated rapper Big TMF, who'd treated her like some hot little honey on a star trip. *Thank you, no.* Especially when all he'd wanted her to do was go down on him while he listened to his own CDs! What a cheek!

'So, Lina,' Price said, taking a healthy drag on the joint before handing it back to her, 'how long are you in LA?'

'Only a few more hours,' she said.

'Goin' to spend them with me?' he said, giving her the heavy-lidded sexy stare for which he was famous.

'You don't believe in wastin' time, do you?' she said archly.

'My mama taught me a moment wasted is a moment lost.'

Another city. Another night. And he might have been in with a chance. But LA was getting too crowded. Lina wanted to go back to her hotel and think about Steven. And she also had to let Max down. Gently, of course. After all, he *was* her agent.

'Sorry,' she said to Price, with a dazzling smile. 'Me dance card is full.'

☆ ☆ ☆

Lina's story about Brigette had worried Lucky. Basically Brigette was sweet and vulnerable, not the kind of girl to get caught up in the whole modelling scene of parties, drugs and money. Fortunately she'd made it to the top fast, like lightning in fact. And that had saved her from the seamier side of the business. Lucky knew all about the predatory men who preyed on gorgeous young girls with endless ambition; the agents who pursued them with phoney promises; and the designers who used them until they were finished.

Brigette had yearned for a career, something she could achieve on her own and, like an answered prayer, it had come to her, for if Brigette had nothing except her vast inheritance, it would have destroyed her. As it was, Lucky could weep when she thought of all the things Brigette had suffered through.

Early in the morning, she decided she'd call Brigette's agent and find out exactly where she was and who she was with. If Brigette needed any kind of help, she'd be there.

Glancing across the room, she observed Alex talking with Pia. This one was lasting longer than the others, perhaps because she was a smart girl, a lawyer.

Why are you thinking about Alex, she asked herself, *when you should be getting home to Lennie and your children?*

Ah ... domesticity. She loved and adored her family, but sometimes the thought of freedom was so damn tempting!

Maybe Alex was the wise one. No family. No ties. Only his work – about which he was passionate – and the occasional lover.

Ah, yes, but Alex would never feel the whispered kiss of a child, a baby's soft warm cuddle, or hear a little voice calling, 'Daddy, I love you,' in the middle of the night.

She took another look at him. Damn! He was whispering in Pia's ear.

Wasn't it about time he traded her in?

☆ ☆ ☆

'Good night, Steven,' Venus said, kissing him on both cheeks. 'I hope you're glad you came.'

Carioca was asleep in his arms, her innocent little face pressed tightly against his shoulder. '*Somebody* had a great time,' he said, with a trace of a smile.

'Good,' Venus said. 'We want to see more of you.'

'You will,' he said, thinking of Brigette's friend with the appalling dress and crazy accent. There was something about her . . .

'We'll call you next week,' Venus said. 'I'll set something up with Lucky and Lennie.'

He nodded. 'I'd like that.'

☆ ☆ ☆

And so the party wound down, and everyone went home. Venus grinned at Cooper and said, 'It was a *huge* success.'

Cooper agreed, and they went upstairs and made love under the stars in the Jacuzzi on their bedroom terrace.

And somewhere in a far-off tree, a paparazzo, balancing precariously on a high branch, took unbelievably intimate pictures with his telephoto lens.

And the caterers left.

And most of the security left.

And soon it would be just another balmy day in Hollywood.

BOOK THREE
Two Months Later

Chapter Fifty-one

TEDDY HAD left it too late to run. Too freakin' late. The last few weeks had been his worst nightmare come true, starting with two detectives turning up at the house, *questioning* him about the jeep – with Mila skulking upstairs in his bedroom, frightened to come down in case they recognized her from the computer likeness.

They'd questioned him for ten minutes before Irena had appeared, bundled into a long brown robe, her face scrubbed of makeup. 'What going on?' she demanded, glaring at everyone in a most unfriendly way.

For once, Teddy was thrilled to see her.

'We're investigating an incident involving a jeep with several of the same licence-plate numbers as the jeep registered to this address,' Detective Johnson said.

Irena pulled herself up to her full five feet six inches. 'Do you realize whose house this is?' she asked imperiously.

'Excuse me, ma'am,' the second detective, a heavy-set Hispanic man, enquired, 'who are *you*?'

'Who am *I*?' Irena said, putting on a good show of indignation. '*I* am Mr Price Washington's personal assistant, and I am sure Mr Washington's lawyer would be most disturbed if he knew you were speaking to Mr Washington's *son* without him present. You must leave immediately.'

Teddy was impressed. Irena could kick it *good*.

'Thank you, ma'am,' Detective Johnson replied, recognizing a pain in the ass when it stared him in the face. He was well aware that dealing with so-called celebrities was always trouble, and this uptight woman was definitely on protection duty. 'Hopefully we won't need to bother you again.'

'What was *that* about?' Irena asked, as soon as the two detectives had left.

Teddy shrugged, attempting to appear unconcerned, although inside he was shaking. 'Dunno. Somethin' about a jeep involved in a robbery.'

'There are thousands of jeeps in Los Angeles,' Irena said crossly. 'Why they come here?'

Teddy shrugged again and turned away. He didn't want her to see his face, which probably had 'Guilty' written all over it. 'Beats me,' he said.

'Where's Mila?' Irena snapped.

'Haven't seen her,' Teddy lied.

'Do not answer the door again,' Irena said sternly. 'It is *my* job to look after this house. *My* job, not yours.' She shot him a suspicious look. 'You have something to hide, Teddy?'

'Don't be stupid,' he mumbled.

Once rid of Irena, Teddy raced upstairs where he and Mila conferred way into the night.

'Whatever happens,' Mila insisted, her pointed face agitated and angry, 'deny everything. Understand, Teddy? Or, I promise you, you'll regret it big time.'

A week later the same two detectives were back. This time they requested to see the jeep.

Once again, Irena stonewalled them.

'How about we come back with a search warrant?' Detective Johnson said, with a weary sigh. He'd spent too much time and energy on this case. All he wanted to do was solve it so he could get the Santangelo woman off his back. She

292

was bugging the shit out of him, completely unaware of the many other homicides that needed solving.

'Yes,' Irena said, glaring at him. 'Perhaps that's what you should do.'

'If that's what the miserable witch wants,' Detective Johnson muttered to his partner as the two men returned to their car, 'that's what she'll get.'

The more he thought about it, the more he was convinced that the jumpy black kid they'd talked to a week ago looked a lot like the artist's rendition of one of the suspects. That, combined with the jeep having some of the same numbers, was giving him cause to think they may have hit pay dirt.

Twenty-four hours later they returned with a warrant to inspect the jeep.

Irena, who on principle detested the police, almost panicked. Price was in Vegas and she didn't wish to bother him with such nonsense, so she made the two detectives wait at the door while she contacted Price's lawyer, who yelled at her for not alerting him the first time they'd come to the house.

'*Podonki!*' she snapped, reverting to her mother tongue as she slammed down the phone. Police. Lawyers. All figures of authority made her sick. They thought they could march in anywhere and do whatever they wanted. But not in Price Washington's house they couldn't. Not while she was there to protect him.

The detectives with their precious warrant were out of luck, because Teddy was not home, so the jeep wasn't there.

'When will he be back?' the Hispanic detective asked.

'I not know,' she said, guarding the front door like a sentinel.

'We'll wait,' Detective Johnson said.

'Outside,' she said.

'What was your name again?' he said.

'Irena Kopistani,' she said. And felt fear, because if anyone discovered her true identity it was quite possible she would be deported, considering she'd entered the country under an assumed identity.

'Miss Kopistano,' Detective Johnson said, mispronouncing her name, 'do either of these people look familiar to you?' He held up the two computer-generated photographs.

Irena's stomach flipped. The girl in the photo resembled Mila. And the boy could certainly be Teddy.

'No,' she said, staring straight ahead.

'No?' Detective Johnson said, observing that her pinched face had flushed a dull red. 'Doesn't the boy look like that kid we spoke to the other day?'

'No,' Irena repeated.

'That boy was Price Washington's son, right?'

She nodded, reluctant to tell them anything.

'Does he have a white girlfriend?'

'Excuse me?'

'A white girlfriend,' Detective Johnson repeated, wondering what kind of bee she had up *her* ass, because she was definitely suffering an attack of the guilts.

'No,' Irena said flatly.

'Where are you from, Miss Koposta?'

Her face was stony. 'Do I have to answer your questions?'

Oh, yeah, she *definitely* had something to hide. 'It's up to you,' he answered mildly, playing good cop.

She threw him a filthy look. 'By *law* do I have to answer them?'

Detective Johnson's gut feeling told him he'd come across a vein of gold. He'd got a search warrant for the jeep, now he was turning around and getting one for the house. Pronto. This old bag knew more than she was saying.

Forty-eight hours later they were back with a warrant to search the house.

This time the surly housekeeper couldn't stop them. She got on the phone to Price Washington's lawyer again, but it was too late: they were all over the house, concentrating on Teddy's room. And when they picked up his mattress and discovered the many press clippings about the murder and Mary Lou Berkeley Detective Johnson knew for sure that this was it. They had suspect number one. And his experience told him that, once Teddy Washington was in custody, the boy would give it up within the first few hours, and they would have the name of his partner in crime.

☆ ☆ ☆

'Who's the girl?' Detective Johnson asked, waving the computer likeness of Mila in front of Teddy's face.

'Dunno,' he mumbled, terrified, because when Price found out he'd been arrested and hauled down to the police station, his life would turn to pure garbage.

'No good protecting her,' Detective Johnson said, ''cause the moment we get her in custody she'll give you up like the school tramp on prom night. And you seem like a nice kid – in fact, from what I understand you didn't participate.' He gave Teddy a moment to think about *that*. Then he said, 'Of course, being there makes you an accessory, and a sharp lawyer can turn this case around, and before you know it, you'll find yourself doing time for murder. Ever seen those prison movies, Teddy?' He paused to let that sink in. ''Cause if you have, then you know what goes on inside. So I strongly suggest you co-operate and tell us who the girl is, 'cause we'll find out anyway. An' if you're trying to protect her, it'll blow up in your face.'

Teddy shuddered. Murder. *He* hadn't murdered anyone, he'd just been along for the ride – that was all. And if they *did* find Mila, she'd *tell* them he was innocent, then they'd *have* to let him go. Yeah. Mila knew the truth better than anyone.

'So . . .' Detective Johnson continued. 'Who is she? And where can we find her?'

Teddy kept his silence, but they found her anyway. They discovered that Irena had a daughter, and when they saw her and noted her resemblance to the computer photo, she was arrested at her place of work in front of everyone.

Mila did not go to the police station quietly, she informed anyone who would listen that Teddy had *forced* her to go on the ride that fateful night; that he'd plied her with cocaine and booze; that he'd been carrying his father's gun, and that *he*'d shot Mary Lou. 'He raped me, too,' she added, for good measure, frustrated and angry that she hadn't been able to find anyone prepared to put a hit on Lennie Golden, therefore she had not been able to claim the reward. Now she was in deep shit and what the hell could she do about it? Exactly nothing.

Detective Johnson sat her down in the interrogation room and questioned her for three long hours.

She stuck to her story.

'Teddy says it was *you* who fired the gun,' he said, regarding her carefully. 'He says it was *you* calling all the shots.'

'Liar!' she snapped.

'Wanna tell us about it?'

'Teddy's in denial,' she said stubbornly. 'He's not thinking straight. I *told* you, *he* did the shooting. What would *I* be doing with his dad's gun?'

'Why didn't you come forward after it happened?'

'I was scared,' she lied, lowering her eyes. 'Teddy threatened to kill me if I talked.'

Detective Johnson sighed. Nothing was ever simple.

By the time Price Washington's lawyer arrived, both Mila and Teddy were locked away for the night. Teddy in juvenile hall, and Mila in jail.

'Too late for bail. Come back tomorrow morning,' Detective Johnson said, hardly looking at the Beverly Hills lawyer, whom he disliked on sight.

Howard Greenspan, a smooth-looking man with a tan, a two-thousand-dollar suit and plenty of attitude, bristled. 'Price Washington won't like this,' he warned.

'I said tomorrow,' Detective Johnson repeated, refusing to be intimidated by the fat-cat lawyer in his expensive suit, reeking of costly aftershave.

'Mr Washington has friends in high places.'

'Congratulations,' Detective Johnson growled.

The two men locked eyeballs.

'What's the charge?' Howard demanded.

'Accessory to murder,' Detective Johnson said.

Howard G. Greenspan nodded. Price was out of town anyway. He'd spring Teddy in the morning, and then they'd see who had the clout in this town.

Chapter Fifty-two

As soon as Lucky received word of the two arrests, she felt a deep sense of satisfaction. Lennie felt it too. 'This is exactly what I needed, closure,' he said. 'I'll never forget the hate in that girl's voice, or the cold-blooded way she went ahead and shot Mary Lou like it didn't mean a goddamn thing. When I see her put away for life that'll do it for me.'

'This is California,' Lucky pointed out. 'She might not get life.'

'By the time *I* get out of the witness box,' he said fiercely, 'it'll be life.'

Lucky nodded, although she wasn't so sure. California law was a strange and laughable thing. Criminal justice, more often than not, meant 'justice' for the criminal.

Steven felt the same way. 'When it comes to the trial we have to be there every day,' he said. 'It's *imperative* that the jury sees the victim's family as a united and ever present unit.'

'I'm in,' Lennie said.

'Me too,' Lucky said.

Although she was happy about the arrests, she was still worried about Brigette, who was due to arrive in LA any day. After talking to Lina at Venus' party, she'd immediately called Brigette's agent in New York, who'd informed her the agency had no idea where Brigette was. So Lucky had tracked her down to the Dorchester in London, where the reception desk confirmed that Brigette had been staying there but had checked out and left no forwarding address. Lucky was alarmed. It wasn't like Brigette to take off without telling anyone her whereabouts. 'I'm flying to London,' she'd informed Lennie. 'I've got a feeling something's wrong.'

'You're crazy,' Lennie had said. 'Brigette's a grown woman grabbing some privacy, you can't begrudge her that.'

'Brigette's an heiress,' Lucky had reminded him, 'due to inherit a billion-dollar fortune. *Someone* has to look out for her.'

Before she'd made up her mind whether to go or not, they'd received a postcard from Brigette with no return address, saying she'd met someone special and would be travelling around Europe for a while.

This did not satisfy Lucky, although Lennie seemed to think it was okay. 'Hey, listen,' he'd said, 'the kid's had all those bad experiences with guys. She wants to have fun. I'm glad she's found herself a guy.'

'Yes, but who is he?' Lucky had said, worried. 'For all we know he could be some fortune hunter in it for her money.'

They heard from her again the next week. Another postcard. 'Touring around Tuscany, having a fantastic time! Love Brigette.'

And so it went on for the next few weeks, Brigette communicating by postcards with no return address, until finally she'd phoned.

'Where have you *been?*' Lucky had demanded. 'And who's this guy you're with?'

'Take it easy,' Brigette had said. 'I'm having a great time travelling around Europe. I'll get in touch again soon.'

In the meantime, while Lennie worked on his computer all day, Lucky busied herself reading the scripts sent over from Alex's office. After several duds, she'd found one she liked in particular, a sharp romantic comedy about a very rich divorcee and a sexy male stripper, kind of a *Pretty Woman* in reverse. After reading it through twice, she'd messengered it to Venus, who'd immediately fallen in love with the female lead. 'I've got to play her,' Venus had said. 'She's me in another life.'

Lucky called Alex to tell him, and two days later the three of them had sat down over lunch at the Grill to discuss it. Venus wanted several changes, Lucky had her own ideas and Alex was simply delighted that he and Lucky might get a chance to work together.

'Have you told Lennie?' he'd asked, over coffee.

'No,' Lucky said, waving at James Woods as he sauntered out of the restaurant with a pretty teenager. Probably his niece. Or maybe not. Who could tell with actors? 'I'll tell him when we're closer to a deal.'

Alex had smiled his lazy crocodile smile. 'Really?' he'd said, liking the fact that Lennie wasn't in on this.

'No big thing, Alex,' Lucky had said crossly. 'Lennie won't mind.' But, deep down, she'd known that he would.

After thinking it over, she'd decided not to tell Lennie until the deal was set because the thought of producing a film *and* working with her two best friends was too exciting a prospect even to contemplate giving up.

A few weeks after Brigette's phone call, they'd received a glossy ten by eight wedding photo of her with a tall, hand-some, blond man. Brigette had scrawled across it in her own handwriting, 'COUNT AND COUNTESS CARLO VITTORIO VITTI!!'

Lucky had raced straight into Lennie's study. 'You're not going to believe this one,' she'd said, waving the photo in front of him. 'She *married* the guy. No pre-nup, nothing. This is insanity!'

'Still no address?' Lennie had asked, checking out the photo.

'Nope. I can't believe it, we don't even know who he is. If it had been up to me I would've tracked her down weeks ago and found out all about him.'

'I hate to keep telling you, sweetheart,' Lennie had said, more interested in getting back to his computer than anything else, 'it's none of our business.'

Oh, yes, it is, Lucky had thought. *Somebody has to look out for her. And I guess that somebody is going to be me.*

She'd immediately phoned Lina, who'd just checked into the Bel Air Hotel ready to start shooting her movie with Charlie Dollar.

Lina had no idea what Brigette was up to either. Like Lucky and Lennie, she'd received the occasional postcard with no real information.

'Did Brigette send you a photo?' Lucky asked.

'No . . . but I've been in Paris for the collections,' Lina explained. 'Flew directly to LA.'

'Do you happen to be free for lunch?'

'For you, Lucky. Yes.'

'Good. It's important that we talk.'

☆ ☆ ☆

They met in the garden of the Bel Air Hotel, a leafy paradise with attentive waiters and delicious food. Lucky sat down, ordered a Perrier, lit a cigarette, and as soon as Lina arrived, got straight to the point. 'She married the guy.'

'*What?*' Lina exclaimed. 'Who *is* 'e?'

'See if *you* know him,' Lucky said, handing her the photo. 'This arrived today.'

'Bleedin' 'ell!' Lina squealed, peering at the photo. 'It's the Italian bloke she thought raped her.'

Lucky stubbed out her cigarette. 'You've *got* to be kidding?'

'No, that's 'im all right,' Lina said, still studying the photograph.

'Obviously she must have been mistaken about the rape.'

'Obviously,' Lina agreed. 'Oh, boy . . . ain't love grand? I know 'is cousin – shall I talk to 'im, see what 'e knows?'

'Good idea,' Lucky said. 'Maybe at the same time you can find out where she is.'

As soon as she got back to her room, Lina called Fredo, who was as shocked as everyone else.

'I will telephone Italy and get back to you,' he'd promised.

'Not a word about the whole drugged-drink thing,' Lina said. 'It can't 'ave happened if she's married 'im, can it?'

'I understand,' Fredo said, obviously anxious to get off the phone and find out the real story.

He phoned back twenty minutes later. 'It is true,' he said, in shock. 'They were married at the Palace.'

'Are Brigette an' Carlo still there?' Lina asked.

'No. They left on a honeymoon.'

Lina reported in to Lucky, who immediately decided she'd better have Count Carlo Vittorio Vitti investigated. She contacted the private detective agency she used, and they immediately went to work.

Finally, Brigette phoned. 'We're coming to LA,' she announced over the phone from Portofino. 'Carlo wants to meet everyone.'

'And about time!' Lucky exclaimed. 'I'm so mad at you for running off the way you did and marrying in secret. I wanted to be at your wedding. So did Lennie and the kids. Not to mention you not conferring with your lawyers before you did it. Brigette, you have to realize, you are *not* an ordinary girl, you have big responsibilities. As soon as you get here, we must sit down and go over everything.'

'You're not my mother, Lucky,' Brigette said, in a flat voice. 'I'm aware of my responsibilities, so is Carlo. In fact, *he*'s the one who wants to meet with my lawyers. We're stopping in New York on our way to LA.'

Lucky was shocked at Brigette's unfriendly tone. 'What's the matter with you?'

'I resent being told what to do.'

'I'm merely pointing out that you'll be inheriting a vast amount of money, and you have to be careful.'

'I *know*,' Brigette said impatiently. 'Carlo and I will be there next week. We're staying at the Four Seasons.'

'We'd like to throw a party for you,' Lucky said. 'So we can all celebrate.'

'I . . . I don't know,' Brigette answered tentatively. 'I'll have to check with Carlo.'

'Does Carlo make all your decisions now?' Lucky asked, unable to keep a sharp edge out of her voice.

'No, Lucky, he doesn't,' Brigette snapped. 'Why would you think that?'

'The way you're talking . . .'

'Anyway, you'll like him. He's a count, very handsome. And Italian. Gino will be pleased about that.'

'There's more to a person than good looks.'

'Don't be mad at me, Lucky,' Brigette pleaded, suddenly sounding like her old self. 'I can't stand it when you're mad at me.'

'What about your career?' Lucky said, knowing how much Brigette's success meant to her. 'Your agent's not exactly thrilled about you running off. You'd better call in and tell her where you are.'

'Carlo doesn't want me to work,' Brigette said.

'*What?*'

'He says it's not necessary.'

'Why? Is he jealous?' Silence. 'Oh, God! Don't tell me you've married a *jealous* Italian, the worst kind.'

'He loves me,' Brigette said. 'That's all that matters, isn't it?'

How naïve and sweet. Typical Brigette. Her judgement of men was irreparably damaged; she always trusted the wrong ones.

Lucky hung up, hoping and praying that Brigette hadn't got caught up in another bad scene.

Shortly after their conversation, the detective agency delivered a report on Carlo. According to their research he was from a good but impoverished family, had been a playboy around Rome before going to London to work in a bank, and had been engaged to an English heiress. They had parted abruptly on a sour note shortly after he met Brigette.

Lucky feared the worst, that he'd homed in on Brigette for her money.

Not that her goddaughter wasn't beautiful – she was totally gorgeous *and* sweet *and* successful. But Lucky's gut instinct told her it was the Stanislopoulos fortune Carlo was after. And control. Italian men got off on control.

Oh, well, soon Brigette would be in LA, and there was nothing Lucky could do now except simply wait and see.

And watch . . . very, very carefully.

Chapter Fifty-three

'SURELY YOU are not wearing that?' Carlo said, his voice filled with criticism. They were standing in the living room of Brigette's New York apartment.

'What's wrong with it?' she asked, smoothing down the waistline of her long-sleeved dress.

'Makes you look fat.'

'I *am* fat,' she said flatly. 'I'm almost four months pregnant.'

Actually, she wasn't fat at all, she was painfully thin. Only her stomach protruded. The heroin Carlo had been feeding her on a regular basis had sucked the energy out of her. She was still beautiful, but not the glowing beauty she'd been two months ago. Now she was deathly pale, with sunken cheeks and huge, bright blue staring eyes. She personified the currently popular heroin-chic look – but in her case it had become the real thing.

'I'll change,' she said dully, realizing that whatever she changed into she had better keep her arms covered. The tell-tale tracks were becoming a problem. 'If you're sure you don't like this dress.'

'I suggest that you do change,' Carlo said, sipping a martini as he continued staring at her critically. 'Now that you are a contessa, Brigette, I would appreciate it if you would make an effort to look the part. Right now you look like a *puttana*.'

Sometimes he could be mean and cruel, other times kind and loving. She was never sure *what* sort of mood he'd be in.

There were moments she considered him to be the most wonderful man in the world. Other times she hated him with a deep, dark loathing.

Despite the mood, however, whatever he said, she did. It wasn't worth upsetting him: his temper tantrums were too violent to endure.

She sighed. Carlo was her life. He supplied the drugs that kept her happy, and the insidious heroin was all she cared about. She'd never known such euphoria, such a feeling of peace and joy each time after she shot up. Every trouble she'd ever experienced vanished – it was as if she were floating on a gossamer cloud of pure pleasure. She lived for the shots that Carlo's acquaintance had taught her to administer to herself.

The events of the last couple of months were more or less a blur. She vaguely remembered Carlo taking her to his apartment in London, where she'd been injected with drugs on a twice-daily basis, until eventually she'd been unable to function without them. And by the time he'd told her she was free to go, she'd had no desire to go anywhere. Carlo was the keeper of her heroin supply, and she had no intention of trying to stop using it, since it was the first time she'd felt free and alive and totally happy. Especially when Carlo made love to her, which he did frequently.

She depended on Carlo for everything, conveniently forgetting that it was he who'd forced her into such a position, because when he was sure she was truly hooked, he'd lured her with his charm, constantly telling her how much he adored her, making love to her with a fiery passion that left her breathless.

After a while they'd said goodbye to London and started travelling around Europe. Carlo was with her day and night, never letting her out of his sight.

One morning, after a night of passionate lovemaking, he'd informed her they should get married, for surely it was as obvious to her as it was to him that they were destined to be together for ever. Somehow she'd agreed, and later that day he'd driven her to his parents' palace outside Rome, where a priest had performed the simple ceremony in the garden, with only Carlo's family and a few servants present.

She was too out of it to understand what she was getting into. Besides, it seemed like the right thing to do, for Carlo was constantly telling her that he loved her more than any man had ever loved her before, so why *shouldn't* they be married?

After the brief ceremony they'd stayed in Rome only one night, then they'd set off on a honeymoon trip around Europe.

When they'd arrived at the first hotel, Carlo had handed her one of her chequebooks, instructing her to pre-sign dozens of cheques. 'I'm waiting for some money from England,' he'd said vaguely. 'In the meantime . . .'

She didn't care, money meant nothing to her.

A week later Carlo informed her that he thought it was best if she gave up her modelling career. She agreed readily. Who gave a damn about work? All *she* cared about was getting high.

One night in Paris they bumped into Kyra Kattleman at a disco. 'Oh my God!' Kyra squeaked, in her incongruous baby voice. 'I hardly recognized you, Brig. You must've lost thirty pounds.'

'This is my husband,' Brigette said, a blank expression on her face. 'Count Carlo Vittorio Vitti.'

'I know you!' Kyra exclaimed. '*You*'re the guy from the restaurant in London. You two got *married*! Way cool. Are you doing the Paris shows this year?'

Brigette had shaken her head. 'Not me. I've given up working.'

'Wow!' Kyra exclaimed. 'Maybe that's what I should do.'

After a while, Carlo decided they should go to America and meet with her lawyers. 'I must see exactly how your money is handled,' he told her. 'How do we know they're looking after it properly? I am the only one who has your best interests at heart, Brigette, the only person you can trust. All your life you've had people leeching off you. Now *I* will oversee everything.'

'My lawyers handle my trust and all of my investments,' she'd said. 'I'm sure they do a good job.'

'It might be prudent for you to give me power of attorney,' he'd suggested. 'That way I can make *sure* nobody steals from you.'

So far New York had been a nightmare. Her team of lawyers were concerned and angry that Carlo was attempting to interfere and take over. They'd tried to pull her aside and warn her that giving any kind of control to her husband was not a good idea. But Carlo had made sure they did not get her alone for more than a few brief moments.

'I liked it better in Europe,' she complained to Carlo, 'where people left us alone.'

'I know, *cara*,' he answered, in one of his caring moods, 'but we must get this settled so you and I can enjoy our lives. I was thinking that we should buy a house outside Rome. You could live there quietly with the baby, while I travel and take care of business. Would that please you, my sweet?'

As long as I have what I need every day, she wanted to say. But she didn't. She merely smiled, high as usual.

Sometimes she thought about the moment she'd told him

she was pregnant. At first he'd been furious. 'Whose baby is it?' he'd demanded. 'What bastard did this to you? Slut! Whore! Who did you sleep with?'

'It's *your* baby, Carlo,' she'd assured him. 'I haven't slept with anyone else. It happened that night in New York.'

When he'd realized she was speaking the truth, he was pleased. 'It had better be a boy,' he kept on repeating. 'A boy who looks like me.'

Doctors were not on her agenda. She was scared to have the test that would tell her the sex of the baby. She was also smart enough to know that doctors would try to stop the drugs that allowed her to get through each day.

Carlo had found a doctor in New York who did not ask awkward questions. They went to see him together and, after examining her, the doctor warned her that she had to give up drugs, otherwise her baby would be born addicted.

'Oh, yes, Doctor,' she'd lied sweetly. 'I intend to.'

'I can help you,' he'd said. 'There's a methadone programme we can put you on. You have to do this, Brigette.'

'I'll be back,' she'd said. 'Maybe then.'

'You've got to get off that shit soon,' Carlo had said, when they left the man's office. 'It would not do for our baby to be born addicted.'

'You got me on it,' she'd pointed out. 'I don't want to stop.'

'Of course not,' he'd spat in disgust. 'Because deep down you're a drug whore – exactly like your mother.'

She knew she should never have confided in him about Olympia, but in moments of intimacy she'd told him everything because when he was in a loving mood there was no one as sweet as her Carlo.

Now they were preparing to go out to dinner with Fredo, something she had no desire to do. She fumbled through her closet, muttering to herself. She hated it when Carlo was mad at her. All she asked for was peace and harmony and to be left alone. And to have her drugs.

After a while she pulled out a simple black Calvin Klein dress and a tuxedo jacket that hid her slightly protruding stomach. She changed quickly, pinning up her long blonde hair and adding jet drop earrings. The result was stunning.

When she returned to the living room, Carlo grunted his approval. 'That's better,' he said.

Fredo met them at Coco Pazzo with red roses and champagne on ice. He was with Lina's favourite model, Didi, who stared at Brigette rudely and said, 'What in hell happened to *you*? You're positively *skinny*!'

Fredo gave Didi a sharp nudge in the ribs, and she shut up. He, too, was wondering what had happened to the once glowing Brigette. She was pale and agitated and far too thin. She was still a knock-out, but in a different way.

Whereas Carlo, in an expensive Brioni suit with flashing gold and sapphire cufflinks that matched his piercing blue eyes, was even more handsome, if that was possible.

Fredo was not happy. Brigette was a true prize in every way, and somehow or other Carlo had won her. Fredo remembered going over to Lina's apartment the morning after the dinner they'd all had together. Brigette had accused Carlo of rape. Now she was married to him. It didn't make sense.

He wondered what Lina had to say about it, and if she'd seen them together.

As the evening progressed, Fredo noticed that Brigette did not seem like her normal self. If he hadn't known better, he would've sworn she was on drugs. But no, not Brigette – the girl he knew wouldn't so much as pop an aspirin.

After dinner he suggested they all go on to a club. Carlo said no, explaining that they were leaving for LA in the morning and had to be up early. Brigette said nothing, her expression dreamy.

'Have you seen Lina?' Fredo asked.

'Haven't had time to call her,' Brigette answered vaguely. And that was that.

The next morning they were on a plane to LA. Brigette leafed through a copy of *Vanity Fair*. Her latest fear was facing Lucky.

'Who is this Lucky woman anyway?' Carlo said irritably. 'She's not your mother or a blood relative. Why are you so influenced by her?'

'She's my godmother,' Brigette answered, watching the pretty stewardess flirt with Carlo as she leaned over and served him another drink. 'Lucky was married to my grandfather.'

'Ha!' Carlo said. 'She must be some gold-digger.'

'She's not,' Brigette said simply. 'Lucky's wonderful. I'm sure you'll get along with her.'

'*I*'ll be the judge of that,' Carlo said ominously.

She didn't like his tone. It would be impossible if he started trouble with Lucky, she simply couldn't stand it. 'Lucky's very smart, Carlo,' she said, 'so please, *don't* upset her.'

'Are you telling *me* not to upset *her*?' he said imperiously. 'I suggest you tell *her* not to upset *me*, otherwise I will make sure that you never see her again.'

Brigette was silent. She'd learned that when Carlo had a certain look in his eye, it was best to stay quiet.

☆ ☆ ☆

Shooting a movie with Charlie Dollar was like one long enjoyable party. Lina could not get over how much fun it was. She'd had two acting jobs before, both of them absolutely boring. Now here was Charlie, racing around the set, laughing, joking, encouraging everyone to do their best work. And when the cameras started to roll, his performance was so right-on that the entire crew was totally mesmerized. Charlie Dollar always delivered.

'How was Africa?' she asked, one day between takes.

He threw her one of his famous quizzical looks. '*You*'re asking *me*?'

She rubbed the tip of her nose and laughed. 'I might be black, but we're not *all* out of Africa. I'm from London, as a matter of fact. The Elephant and Castle, if that means anything to you.'

'I got a yen for English girls,' Charlie ruminated, with a beatific smile. 'Spent several months in London making a flick. Hung my hat at Tramp every night. Had myself many a page-three beauty.'

'I'd hardly call 'em beauties,' Lina snorted. 'More like scrubbers.'

'Scrubbers?' Charlie said, with a wild chuckle. 'Now *that*'s a word.'

'It's what we call 'em.'

'And it means?'

'Some cheapo bimbo babe who'll flash her tits an' sleep with anybody.'

'You wouldn't be calling *me* anybody, would you?'

Lina wagged a long finger at him. 'You'd better watch out, Charlie. Those little dolly birds'll sell their story to a newspaper soon as look at you!'

'Thanks for the warning. In the future I'll make sure I give them something juicy to write about.'

On the days that Dahlia visited the set, Charlie acted like a different person. It was as if one moment he was a naughty schoolboy up to no good, and then Mommy arrived, and he immediately turned into the opposite.

'Gee!' Lina exclaimed, after one of Dahlia's surprise appearances. 'Has *she* got your balls in a vice! Must be dead painful.'

'Dahlia's a lady,' Charlie said sonorously. 'And a talented one at that.'

'Do you two fuck?' Lina asked boldly.

'We did,' Charlie said. 'Hence, our son, Sport. However, now I have too much respect for Dahlia to give her the old one two three.'

'Oh, I see. You got a Madonna-complex thing going, huh?'

'You think you're very smart, Lina, don't you?'

'I *am* smart.'

'I suppose you are,' Charlie said, nodding to himself. 'You agree with my shrink. According to him, there is absolutely nothing wrong with a healthy Madonna complex. Y' see, my dear little English girl, I can't get it up for somebody I respect.'

'Guess that says a lot about me,' Lina said, getting in a quick dig.

'We did the dirty deed once,' Charlie said. 'And please take note that I have *not* invited you into my trailer since we've been shooting.'

'*Oooh*, should I be insulted?' she drawled sarcastically.

'Depends on your insult threshold.'

'I was going to ask you,' Lina said, changing track. 'Lucky's throwing a party for her goddaughter, Brigette, my friend. Can you take me?'

'If Dahlia's out of town.'

'The party's in two days'.'

'Hmm . . . I do believe Dahlia will be visiting her father on location in Arizona at that time.'

'How convenient,' Lina said, well pleased. 'So now you've got *no* excuse.'

Charlie executed an extravagant bow. 'Delighted, my dear.'

Chapter Fifty-four

WHEN PRICE returned from several weeks on the road and discovered that his son had been arrested and actually spent the night in juvenile hall, he flew into a foul rage.

'What the *fuck* am I payin' you a retainer for?' he yelled at his lawyer, as he paced furiously around his living room. 'How come nobody contacted me? Why did you allow *my* son to spend the night locked up? You should've sprung him immediately.'

'They couldn't set bail until the next morning,' Howard explained, trying to placate one of his most high-profile clients. 'Teddy had to appear before a judge and, believe me, it wasn't easy springing him without you there. I had to call in some very big favours.'

'What the fuck is this anyway?' Price steamed, getting even angrier. 'I wanna know *why* they arrested him.' An ominous pause, then, 'Could it be 'cause he happens t' be *black*?'

'Calm down, Price,' Howard said, using his best soothing voice. 'The cops have an idea it was Teddy's jeep used in the Mary Lou Berkeley shooting.'

'What kind of bullshit is *that*?' Price yelled. 'That murder happened months ago.'

'There's a girl involved, too,' Howard continued. 'The daughter of your housekeeper.'

'Mila?'

'Yes. She was arrested with Teddy. Since she's eighteen they took her to jail. It seems Lennie Golden identified her as the shooter, but *she*'s telling the cops it was Teddy who did it. And here's the bad news. Apparently he used *your* gun.'

Price's eyes bulged. '*My* fucking gun?' he said, outraged.

'I suggest you check out where you keep it, see if it's still there.'

'*My* fucking gun?' Price repeated. 'Man, this is some bad joke.' He marched over to the bar and poured himself a hefty shot of Scotch. 'Where's Teddy now?'

'Out, in your custody. I figured school's the safest place for him to be – so that's where he is. I instructed him to continue to conduct his life as if nothing is happening.'

'Have the press gotten hold of this?' Price demanded.

'Not yet,' Howard replied, wondering if Price was going to offer *him* a drink. Not that he wanted one, but it was damn bad manners not to make the offer. 'It's only a matter of time.'

'Jesus!' Price said, slamming his glass down on the coffee table. 'I go away for a few fuckin' weeks, and come back to *this* shit storm. Who'd believe it?'

'Believe it,' Howard said. 'In my opinion they have a case.'

'Yeah? What kinda case?'

'Lennie Golden came up with the licence plate of the jeep. It's Teddy's jeep, no doubt about it.'

'Then it must've bin stolen.'

'Unfortunately not. The description of the two perpetrators matches Mila and Teddy. Besides, she's talking.'

'*Who*'s talkin'?'

'Mila. As I mentioned before, she's told the police Teddy did it. She's also said that he forced her along for the ride.

Oh, yes, and she's accusing him of plying her with drugs and raping her.'

'Rape? Are you shittin' me?'

'This is most unfortunate, Price,' Howard continued. 'When the tabloids get hold of it, you won't like it.'

'What does Teddy say?'

'That it was all her.'

'Shit!' Price exclaimed. 'Where *is* the bitch?'

'I told you, she's in jail. I didn't imagine you'd want me posting her bail, considering what's going on.'

'Right,' Price said, thinking of Irena and what must be going through *her* head. She hadn't mentioned a word to him when he'd gotten home an hour ago. She'd merely said his lawyer had to see him immediately, so he'd instructed her to call Howard and tell him to get over to the house. Now this.

'What's the plan?' he said.

'I've already arranged an appointment with one of the best criminal defence attorneys in the state,' Howard said. 'He's prepared to meet with you and Teddy tomorrow. I figured that would give you a chance to talk to Teddy first, hear his side of it.'

'Can't *wait* to do that,' Price fumed. 'I don't get it – I gave the dumb shit everythin' *I* never had, an' what does he do? Pisses all over me. Like I need *this*.'

'I have a suggestion,' Howard said.

'What?'

'Bring his mother in on this as soon as possible. When we go before a jury it'll mean a lot. A boy with a concerned mother sitting in court is a more sympathetic figure than one without.'

'You *gotta* be taggin' my ass!' Price yelled. 'Ginee's an out-and-out coke whore.'

'When did you last see her?'

'What the fuck does *that* matter?'

'Maybe she's straightened out.'

'Not Ginee,' he said grimly.

'So we'll clean up her image for the occasion,' Howard said. 'Dress her in sensible clothes. Pull her hair back, instruct her not to wear makeup.'

'Ha!' Price exclaimed. 'Ginee wouldn't go t' the fuckin' john without stickin' on false eyelashes. Besides, she don't give a shit about Teddy. She hasn't seen him in years.'

'We'll see what your criminal attorney has to say. In the meantime I recommend that you start thinking about it.'

'Maybe *you* should start thinking about *this*,' Price said, almost spitting his fury. 'Your job is gettin' my boy off, an' keepin' the press outta my goddamn face.'

As soon as Howard left, Price summoned Irena into the living room. They exchanged a long, silent look.

'Why didn't you tell me?' he said, at last.

Irena's expression was pure stone. 'I don't understand what is going on,' she said. 'Mila is in jail – I must have money to bail her out.'

'Have you heard what she's saying?'

'Nobody's told me anything.'

'She's tellin' anyone who'll listen that *Teddy* shot the woman.'

'This is difficult to believe,' Irena said.

'Then why the fuck believe it?' Price shouted. 'The witness says it was *Mila* who pulled the trigger. You understand what I'm tellin' you? *She* had the fuckin' gun, an' *she* shot Mary Lou Berkeley.' A vein throbbed in his temple. 'Now she's tryin' t' shift the blame to Teddy.'

'Mila doesn't own a gun,' Irena said.

'Nor does Teddy,' Price shouted. 'But *I* do. And, according to your fuckin' kid, it's *my* gun they used.'

'Where is your gun?'

'Like *you* don't know,' Price sneered. 'You know where I keep everythin', from my grass to my rubbers. You know more about what goes on in this fuckin' house than *I* do. Now go check an' see if my gun is where it should be.'

Irena let out a long, deep sigh. 'I already have,' she said. 'It is not there.'

'Jesus!' Price yelled, punching his fist in the air.

'Mila could not have taken it. I do not allow her free access to the main house.'

'Mila has all the access she wants. She wanders around here whenever I'm out. I *know* she's been in my bedroom.'

'I would never let Mila do that.'

'This is shit!' Price said, thinking aloud. 'An' it'll affect me 'cause it'll be all over the fuckin' tabloids. An' it won't be about Teddy or Mila, it'll be about *me*, Price Washington, the black superstar with the big bad drug habit.' He marched back to the bar and poured himself another shot. 'Thank God Mary Lou was black,' he said, still thinking aloud. 'If she'd bin a white chick, Teddy's black ass would be fuckin' *lynched*!'

'What about Mila?' Irena said. 'She needs a lawyer.'

'Fuck Mila,' Price snapped. 'I gotta speak to Teddy. Go to the school an' bring the fool home. We'll talk about Mila later, after I've heard Teddy's story.'

☆ ☆ ☆

Teddy arrived back at the house with a lead weight in his stomach – or, at least, that's how it felt. Price was home, so he knew he could expect the worst.

The sad truth was that Mila had betrayed him. Not only had she betrayed him, but she was coming out with a bunch of damaging lies. He was confused and frightened. How was he going to convince people that *she* was the killer, not him?

Howard Greenspan had warned him to talk to no one about the case, so he hadn't. Now he was forced to face his father alone.

Price was in the living room drinking a large tumbler of Scotch, which Teddy knew was a bad sign: since cleaning up his drug addiction, Price rarely drank unless he was under pressure.

'Hi, Dad,' Teddy managed, as he sidled into the room.

Price greeted his son calmly. 'Sit down, Teddy,' he said.

'Yes, Dad,' he muttered, finding a place on the couch.

There was an uncomfortable silence, finally broken by Price who stood in front of his son, glaring at him accusingly. 'Now I want you t' give it to me straight, boy,' Price said. 'An' don'tcha go handin' me no bullshit story. You understand what I'm sayin' here?'

Teddy was flooded with shame. His dad had trusted him and he'd let him down. 'Mila did it,' he blurted. 'I didn't do nothin'. It was horrible, Dad.'

'So horrible you couldn't go to the cops an' tell 'em everything?' Price demanded. ''Cause if you'd done that, you wouldn't be in this mess today.'

'I know,' Teddy muttered.

'You'd better tell me, boy, what the fuck happened here?'

Teddy began to relate his miserable story. All about how he and Mila had gone for a drive, stolen CDs, drunk beer, snorted coke. And when he came to the bit about Mary Lou, he suddenly lost it and could barely speak.

Price turned away from him. 'Mila grabbed her jewellery, an' *you* put it in your pocket,' he said, in a low, angry voice. 'Is that what I'm hearin'?'

Teddy nodded, too ashamed to look his father in the eye.

'Where's the jewellery now?'

'Mila's got it.'

'And where the fuck's my gun?'

'Didn't know it was your gun,' Teddy mumbled. 'She must've taken it.'

'Jesus!' Price said. 'This is a tough one.' A long beat. '*I*'m gonna believe you, 'cause *I* know what kinda girl Mila is. But whaddya think the jury's gonna do, you bein' a black boy an' all, an' she bein' a white girl? That's one big mark against you. An' if Mila gets herself a smart lawyer, they'll dress her up like Little Mary Sunshine, an' make *you* out to be this bad motherfuckin' black asshole influencing this innocent white girl – feedin' her drugs an' shit. *Rapin'* her. You *do* know that's what she's sayin'?'

Teddy's eyes bugged. 'That I raped her?'

'Right on.'

'No way, Dad,' he shouted indignantly. 'She *wanted* me to do it to her. She was all over me.'

'So 'cause she was comin' on to you, you couldn't help fuckin' the little bitch? That your story?'

Teddy nodded miserably.

'Oh, I get it,' Price said sarcastically. 'You go out with her, she screws with your head, *shoots* somebody. Then later you find you gotta fuck her for good measure. That the way this went down?'

Teddy stared at the floor. 'I . . . I . . . thought she liked me,' he muttered. 'Didn't know it was gonna turn into this.'

'You didn't know, huh?' Price said harshly. 'You were with her when she *killed* somebody, boy. You stood back and *watched* it happen. An' you never came to me, never went to the cops. Are you fuckin' *insane*?' He marched back to the bar and refilled his glass. Then he came back and stood in front of Teddy, his eyes glittering with anger. 'I raised you to be a good upstandin' citizen, an' whaddya do? You shit all over everythin' I taught you. Fool!' He shook his bald head disparagingly. 'I can't save you, Teddy. I'll get you the best lawyers I can, but I can't save you. An' don't think *I'm* not gonna be dragged through the mud. Oh, yeah, they're gonna rake it up about me – Price Washington, ex drug addict. Let's hope it don't reflect on my career. Let's get down an' pray you haven't fucked *that* up, too.'

'I'm sorry, Dad . . .'

' "Sorry" don't cut it, boy. You'd better get your black ass up to your room an' stay there, 'cause I can't stomach lookin' at you no more.'

'I gotta talk to Mila,' Teddy said desperately. 'I know I can get her to tell the truth.'

Price gave a hollow laugh. 'Stupid, too, huh?'

Irena, who'd been listening outside the door, took a step back. She felt the same way Price did. She'd given Mila everything she could, and the girl had betrayed her. Mila was a bad girl, she'd bring Irena down, for how could Mr Washington keep her as his housekeeper if Mila and Teddy were up against each other?

If only she could persuade Price to bail her daughter out, then maybe she could talk some sense into her, because if Mila confessed everything, then Teddy would be free.

Irena waited until Teddy pushed past her and ran upstairs to his room, then she knocked tentatively on the door. Price did not answer.

Very slowly she opened the door and peered inside.

Price was sitting at the table, his head buried in his hands. She could be mistaken, but she thought he might be sobbing.

This was no time to disturb him. Very slowly she backed out of the room and closed the door.

Tomorrow she would ask him about Mila.

Chapter Fifty-five

LUCKY SUGGESTED to Brigette that they get together before the party, but her goddaughter demurred, saying she had a thousand things to take care of. Lucky had asked her whom she wanted invited, and all Brigette said was, 'I'd love to see Gino and the kids, I don't care about anybody else.'

'Fine,' Lucky said. 'I'll put together a list of interesting people.' She didn't mention that Lina was in town; she thought it would be a nice surprise.

Lucky fervently hoped she was wrong about Brigette's new husband, that maybe he'd turn out to be a great guy. She reasoned that if he was making Brigette happy, that was all that mattered. Although, when she'd spoken to Brigette's lawyers in New York, they'd seemed to think that Carlo was on a mission to take control of Brigette's fortune, and they were quite disturbed. 'As you know, Lucky,' one of the lawyers had told her, 'the way things are set up, nobody can touch the bulk of Brigette's inheritance until she's thirty. That means it's secure for another five years.'

'Perfect,' Lucky had said. 'Because if the marriage lasts five years, then it proves she's really in love. And if it doesn't she'll be well rid of him.'

After she'd finished dressing for the party, Lucky had the barman fix her a vodka martini before she strolled casually into Lennie's study. She'd decided that now was as good a time as any to tell him she was producing a movie with Alex. Although he knew she'd been reading scripts, he wasn't aware of where they'd been coming from.

'Hey, babe,' she said, standing behind him, 'time to get dressed. Guests will be arriving soon.'

He was barely able to drag his eyes away from his computer, but eventually he did. 'Don't *you* look beautiful?' he said, letting out a long, low whistle as he checked her out. 'Love your hair that way.'

She'd worn her hair long and wild and curly, the way she knew he preferred it. And she'd slithered into a long red dress, his favourite colour.

'Sweetheart,' she said, massaging his shoulders, 'remember I told you I'm looking to produce a movie?'

'Uh-huh.'

'Well . . . I think I've found the right property,' she said, continuing to knead his back. 'And here's the good news. I've got my co-producer, my director, *and* my star. So I'm considering making an announcement in the trades next week. Naturally I wanted you to hear it first.'

'Sounds good to me,' he said. 'How come you haven't mentioned it before?'

She stopped massaging his shoulders and perched on the edge of his desk. 'Because you've been so totally immersed in your script that I didn't want to disturb you.'

'Yeah, I do get kinda carried away,' he said, smiling ruefully. 'I like what I'm working on. It's a different deal from anything I've done before. Of course, I'll probably never get a studio to put up the money. And since you're not at Panther any more . . .' A big grin. 'Hey, maybe you can slide in a good word for me.'

'If you're very nice to me, maybe I will,' she said, smiling back at him.

'So,' he said, switching off his computer. 'Tell me about *your* movie. What's the story?'

'It's kind of an edgy black comedy with a feminist twist. And, uh . . . Venus has agreed to star in it.'

'Venus, huh? The two of you together will be a trip. Who's the brave man who's agreed to direct this project?'

A short pause before she gave him the zinger. 'Alex,' she said casually.

'Alex,' he repeated, the smile sliding from his face.

'That's right,' she said, speaking fast. 'It was one of the scripts he had in development, and he thought it might be a good vehicle for Venus. So, since he knew I wanted to work with her, he sent it my way.'

'Alex Woods is going to direct your movie,' Lennie said slowly. 'Is that what I'm hearing here?'

'You don't sound thrilled.'

'Should I be?'

'Why not? If I'm doing this, it has to be with the best, and you *know* Alex is one of the most talented directors in town.'

'Alex Woods is a raving egomaniac,' Lennie said sourly. 'He does everything *his* way. You'll be at each other's throats before you can turn around.'

'I think I can handle him,' she said, annoyed that Lennie didn't trust her judgement.

'Yeah,' Lennie said. 'I'm sure you can.'

'What does *that* mean?' she said, her black eyes giving forth major danger signals.

'I'm not happy about you working with Alex.'

'Why?'

'Hey – news flash – the man has a gigantic crush on you.'

'Lennie,' she said, curbing her anger, 'Alex was very good to me when you were kidnapped. He was always there for me whenever I needed support. I love him as a friend, nothing more, so please don't spoil this for me because of some petty jealousy.'

'What would you do if I said I *didn't* want you working with him?' Lennie said, getting up abruptly.

'I don't like people telling me what I can and can't do.'

'Uh huh, that figures,' he said, walking into their bedroom.

'Are you mad at me?' she said, following him.

'I'd better take a shower or I'll be late for the party.'

'I repeat, are you mad at me?'

He headed into his bathroom. 'I'm not mad, Lucky. You can do what you want. You always have and I guess you always will.'

And before she could say anything else, he slammed the bathroom door in her face.

Why do I have to go through this? she thought, angry and frustrated. *I don't want to have to ask for permission to do anything. I love Lennie. I'm faithful to him. What more can he possibly want?*

And yet, deep down, she knew that if the situation was reversed she'd probably be pissed, too.

☆ ☆ ☆

Steven stood in front of his bathroom mirror, shaving carefully. He was in a reflective mood. Two people being arrested for Mary Lou's murder had brought back every detail of that fateful night. And now that they'd caught the perpetrators, there would be a trial ahead, which meant that the publicity machine would start again, wrecking his privacy, bringing back all the painful memories.

It was going to be difficult to forget and move on when the story of Mary Lou's senseless murder would be all over the news media every day. And, of course, it would be, all the more so because the boy they'd arrested was the son of Price Washington.

Steven was well aware that he would have to be there during the trial, sitting in the front row of the court-room every day. He'd told Lucky it was important they present a united front along with Mary Lou's family, who were still totally devastated. Carioca would have to be there too.

God! How could he possibly put his little daughter through such a painful process? Yes, her presence would definitely sway the jury, but there was no way he wanted her to hear the details of that awful night.

Life without Mary Lou did not get any easier. He'd tried to compensate by throwing himself into his heavy caseload of work, but nothing took away the loneliness he felt. At night, in bed, there was nobody lying next to him, nobody to fight over the remote control with; nobody to share a hot dog or a tunafish sandwich with on a Saturday afternoon while he sat in front of the TV watching football. Nobody . . . nobody . . . nobody.

And the sad fact was that he didn't want anybody. Because there wasn't a woman in the world who could possibly replace Mary Lou.

'I'm very, very happy, Daddy,' Carioca Jade announced, bouncing into his bathroom, all dressed up in her best party dress.

'Why's that, honeybunch?' Steven asked, glancing down at his daughter.

'I'm happy 'cause we're going to a party and *I*'m your date.' She tilted her head, gazing up at him, her big brown eyes filled with love. 'Can I *always* be your date, Daddy?'

'You always *are*,' Steven assured her. '*You* are the most important girl in my life.'

'*I* get to spend the night with Maria,' Carioca said.

'Yeah, you haven't done that in a while.'

'She's great, Daddy,' Carioca said seriously. 'She's like my sister.'

He finished shaving and put down his razor. 'She's your sister all right. And don't you two girls go getting into any trouble.'

'CeeCee's taking us to Disneyland tomorrow,' Carioca informed him.

'Disneyland, huh?' he said, reaching for a clean white shirt.

'Daddy?'

'Yes, honey.'

'Where's Mommy?'

He felt the pain as he always did whenever she mentioned Mary Lou. 'You know where she is,' he said quietly. 'Mommy's sleeping with God.'

'Does God have a very big bed?'

'Yes, he does. And all his favourite children curl up in it every night.'

'I wish Mommy could come home now,' Carioca said, her lower lip trembling. 'I wish she could sleep in *our* bed with you.'

'We'd both like that, but it's not going to happen. Mommy was taken because she's so special. You know that, baby, I've told you before.'

Carioca gave a big sigh. 'I know, I know. Sometimes I get sad, though, 'cause I miss Mommy so much.'

'Yes, honey,' he said, sadly. 'Everyone does.'

'Everyone,' Carioca repeated. 'Everyone in the world.'

'And who looks pretty tonight?' Steven asked, quickly changing the subject.

'Me!' she said, giggling.

'And why is that?'

''Cause *I* get to see Brigette,' Carioca said. 'An' *she*'s really pretty.'

'Not as pretty as you.'

'Silly Daddy,' Carioca said, beaming.

Steven reached for his watch. 'I'd better get a move on,' he said. 'We're picking up my friend at the Beverly Hills Hotel, and we shouldn't be late.'

'Who?'

'Uncle Jerry, my partner from New York.'

'Will he have a present for me?'

'I'll be *very* surprised if he doesn't.'

'Okay, Daddy, but hurry *up*!'

'I gotta finish getting dressed first.'

'Okay, I'll wait.'

☆ ☆ ☆

'I'm, like, *so* honoured!' Lina exclaimed, dazzlingly sleek and sexy in a bias-cut Versace burnt-sienna silk dress.

'You are?' Charlie said, eyebrows shooting up above his tinted glasses as they strolled through the gardens of the Bel Air Hotel.

'Well, of course,' she said, linking her arm cosily through his. 'The great Charlie Dollar picking up little old me. I'm flattered.'

'The doll is flattered,' Charlie said, as if addressing an audience. 'I'm ten degrees away from a freakin' heart attack, and *she*'s flattered.'

'Are you sick?'

'Only mentally.'

'Charlie,' she giggled, 'stop teasing me.'

'What I'm trying to tell you, kiddo, is that I'm an old fart movie star who could drop at any moment.' He sighed despairingly. 'I'm freakin' *old*.'

'Not too old for me,' she said quickly. 'Or anyone else you fancy.'

'I'm thinkin' of marryin' Dahlia,' he said mournfully. 'She's under the impression it's time we walked that thin red line to Dullsville.'

'Oh,' Lina said, not even trying to hide her disappointment. 'Does that mean I shouldn't try seducing you tonight?'

'I'm *thinkin'* of marryin' her,' he said, with an affable grin. 'Not *doin'* it.'

'So sex *is* a possibility?' she teased.

A raunchy chuckle. 'Thought you only slept with me t' get the part?'

'I did. But the sex was *sooo* good, I've decided I want more.'

'Sassy *and* smart,' he said, raising his glasses for a moment. 'I like that in a woman.'

'I *do* 'ave an ego, you know,' Lina said, quite indignant. 'Since we've been making the movie, you 'aven't looked twice in my direction – 'cept as a friend.'

'It's safer being friends with me,' Charlie said. 'I might be carrying all kinds of unspeakable diseases.'

'This is a twist!' Lina exclaimed. 'Usually it's *me* beatin' 'em off with a stick!'

He threw her a quizzical look. 'Are you by any chance chasing me, my dear?'

'Well,' she answered cheekily, 'I wouldn't mind another slice.'

'You English girls,' he said, with a wild chuckle. 'You and your funny language.'

'What's *wrong* with our language?'

'Nothing that a nice fat joint won't cure. Follow me,' he said, leading her down a path to the serene lake where several magnificent swans made their home.

'Oooh,' she said, '*now* you're talking. Got any coke?'

'Don't do coke,' he answered calmly, as if it was a perfectly normal question – which, in the film and modelling worlds, it was. 'A joint takes the edge off, makes me nice and mellow.'

'A joint'll do,' she said.

'You don't wanna get into that whole coke scene,' he lectured. 'Snorting it up your pretty little nose – it ain't lady-like.'

'Ha!' Lina said. 'Lady-like is the *last* thing I am!'

'I never argue with a female,' Charlie said, producing a joint from his pocket and lighting up.

'Good!' Lina said, accepting a toke.

Then they strolled companionably by the side of the lake, sharing the cigarette, taking turns inhaling deeply.

When they were finished, Charlie said, '*Now* I'm ready to party.'

'So am I,' Lina said, winking at him. 'Ready to rock 'n' roll the night away!'

Chapter Fifty-six

'YOU LOOK like shit,' Carlo said, inspecting Brigette in an arrogant way. 'Surely you can pull yourself together better than this?'

Lately he never had a good word to say. When they were first together he'd often told her how beautiful she was, especially after they'd made love and were lying relaxed in each other's arms. Now, whenever he opened his mouth, it was to spew forth criticism.

'I can't help being pregnant,' she said defensively. 'Clothes don't hang on me the way they used to.'

'You're an embarrassment,' he grumbled, his handsome face full of disdain.

'I'm doing my best,' she said, fighting back tears, although she really couldn't care less *what* she looked like. All she cared about was the comfort of drugs.

'I can assure you,' he said pointedly, 'your best is not good enough.'

'Carlo,' she said restlessly, 'before we go tonight I need . . . a shot.' She glared at him accusingly. 'You promised you'd get me something.'

'I told you, Brigette,' he said irritably, 'you have to stop depending on that stuff so much.'

'*You* introduced me to it and I like the feeling, so don't try to cut me off because you'll . . . you'll regret it.'

'Are you threatening me?' he said, turning on her.

'Yes,' she answered bravely. 'I am.'

'You're nothing but an uppity bitch!' he said. And before she saw it coming he slapped her hard across the face.

It had been a while since he'd hit her, so she was taken by surprise. She fell back on the bed and before she could stop herself, started crying, engulfed in her own pitiful misery. 'Can't you see I need something?' she sobbed. 'And you'd better give it to me, or I'm not going anywhere tonight.'

'Whiny bitch,' Carlo sneered. 'And to think that *I*, Carlo Vittorio Vitti, married someone like you. It seems impossible.'

'You begged me to marry you,' she cried.

'Don't make me regret it,' he said warningly. 'Now that you are my wife, it is about time you started living up to the title I've bestowed on you. *Not* that you deserve it.'

'Just get me something,' she moaned.

He marched out of the room. Brigette lay on the bed, pulling her knees up and hugging them to her stomach.

I have a baby growing inside me, she thought. *And what am I doing? I'm feeding it heroin, not eating properly, allowing this man to beat me. And yet . . . I don't care, because all I crave is the drugs.*

And she knew she was spiralling downwards, but there was absolutely no way she could stop herself.

☆ ☆ ☆

Gino had flown in from Palm Springs accompanied by his wife, Paige.

'Whatever you're doing to him, it works,' Lucky said, drawing her stepmother to one side. 'He looks sensational.'

'Gino is in excellent health,' Paige said briskly. She was quite a woman, with her mass of red hair, compact curves, and genuine love for her much older husband. 'He's planning a European tour for us next year. I told him I can't keep up with him.'

Lucky smiled. 'Yeah, my old man's something, isn't he?'

'He certainly is,' Paige agreed. 'And I wouldn't trade him for Mel Gibson!'

Lucky knew that her father and Paige had a chequered past. At one point in their relationship, before they were married, Gino had caught Paige with another woman – the other woman being Susan Martino, his wife at the time. That particular incident had nearly been the end, but somehow or other they'd got through it, and now they were happy in their Palm Springs house, playing golf and poker, and hanging out with their friends.

'Where's Lennie?' Paige asked. 'I haven't seen him.'

'Sulking somewhere,' Lucky said, with a shrug.

'Oh?' Paige said. 'Anything you want to talk about?'

'Not really,' Lucky said offhandedly. 'It's just that I can't be told what to do. It drives me crazy, and Lennie knows it.'

'Hmmm . . .' Paige said knowingly. 'You're exactly like your father. You look like him, you sound like him, you *are* him.'

'I'll take that as a compliment,' Lucky said, grinning. 'Although I'm not too sure about the looking like him.'

'Tell me, dear,' Paige said, always one for a quick gossip, 'what *exactly* is Lennie sulking about?'

'Oh, something stupid,' Lucky said casually, not wanting to make a big deal out of it. 'I'm planning on producing a movie with Alex Woods, and Lennie's under the mistaken impression that Alex will immediately jump my bones. It's quite ridiculous.'

'Well, won't he?' Page drawled, giving her another knowing look.

'Don't *you* start,' Lucky said, with a weary sigh. 'Alex and I are the best of friends. Can't anyone understand that?'

'Maybe you protest too much,' Paige ventured.

'*What?*' Lucky said.

'Nothing,' Paige said, suddenly distracted as she glanced over towards the bar. 'I've got to go rescue your father. He still attracts the women. Look at that silicone blonde draping herself all over him. It's disgusting what these girls will do to get a man.'

'He's eighty-seven, for God's sake!' Lucky exclaimed, quite amused. 'You can't possibly be *jealous.*'

'I've always found it prudent to keep a beady eye on my territory,' Paige said, smoothing down her short dress. 'If you're smart, Lucky, you'll do the same.'

'Right,' Lucky murmured, irritated because Lennie had not yet emerged to join the party, and she hated having to greet all the guests by herself. God! He could be a pain. And yet, she understood him, because in some ways they were exactly alike. Stubborn, stubborn, stubborn.

Still, there was no way she was giving in to him. She'd never objected when he was an actor and had to perform steamy love scenes with sexy actresses. After all, it wasn't as if she was planning a love scene with Alex. They were simply going to work together as friends. What was wrong with that?

Just as she was thinking about him, she spotted Alex coming through the door accompanied by Pia. *Hmm . . .* Lucky thought. *This one is definitely lasting longer than any of the others.*

'Hi, Pia,' she said, lukewarm as the girl came towards her. 'Welcome to our house.'

'We've driven past it on many occasions,' Pia said, pretty and petite in a Vera Wang cocktail dress, her shiny black hair worn in a straight, shoulder-length bob with a fringe. 'Alex always points it out. Last time I said to him, "Alex, if you tell me one more time this is Lucky Santangelo's house, I'll throw myself out of the car screaming." '

'Very funny,' Lucky said. 'I guess Alex feels I'm some kind of a tourist attraction.'

'Leave out the tourist and you've got it,' Pia said succinctly, her almond-shaped eyes never leaving Lucky's face.

Oh, God, what *was* this? Pick-on-Lucky-and-Alex Night? Did *everyone* think they were all set to have a raging affair?

'Where's the happy couple?' Alex asked, walking up to join them. 'I brought them a wedding present.'

'That's nice of you,' Lucky said.

'This *is* their wedding celebration, isn't it?'

'I suppose so. What did you get them?'

'A set of knives.'

'Excuse me?'

'One of those wooden block things where you keep ten lethal knives. It's my standard wedding gift. I figure one of these days somebody'll turn around and stab their partner, then *I* can take the credit. Maybe even make the movie.'

'Alex,' Lucky said, shaking her head and smiling, 'you *do* know you're a little off.'

'You only just realizing that?' he questioned.

Pia studied both of them then, seemingly bored by their conversation, she wandered off to the bar.

'What's up with *this* long-lasting romance?' Lucky asked, nodding after the pretty Asian woman.

'Jealous?' Alex said, grinning.

'*Pleeze!*' Lucky responded scornfully.

'I like it when you get into my love life.'

'Who's getting into your love life?' she said, unamused that he should think she cared.

'You are.'

'Don't flatter yourself, Alex,' she said coolly. 'Oh, and by the way, not a word to Lennie about our movie.'

'How come?'

'Because . . . well, I kind of mentioned it to him earlier and he's not exactly dancing.'

'That's pretty stupid,' he said, plucking a canapé from a tray held by a passing waiter.

'I know, but do me a favour and don't bring it up. Unless, of course, he does. In which case, sort of dismiss it. Tell him it's one of many movies you're involved with, and you probably won't be able to spend much time on it.'

Alex gave her a long, sardonic look. 'Never thought I'd hear *you* talking like this.'

'Like what?' she asked irritably.

'A nervous married woman.'

'Bullshit.'

'Truth.'

'It's merely polite in a marriage to keep your partner happy.'

'Oh, really?' he said, teasing her. 'The only things *I*'ve heard about marriage is that once you sign those papers, sex goes out the window.'

'I can assure you, Alex,' she said haughtily, 'that is *not* the case with *my* marriage.'

'I can assure *you*, Lucky,' he said, still grinning because he loved it when he could get to her, 'I believe you.'

They locked eyeballs, challenging each other.

'Where the hell's Brigette?' Lucky said, breaking the look and glancing at her watch. 'I throw a party in her honour and she's not even here.'

'Have you met the husband?'

'I wanted to take them for a quiet dinner last night. However, she informed me they were busy. I have a gut feeling he's going to be a money-hungry prick.'

'What's worse?' Alex asked. 'A plain prick, or a money-hungry one?'

She laughed. 'A prick is a prick is a prick.'

'So eloquent.'

'But of course.'

'I love you,' he said lightly.

'Right back at you,' she said, without taking a beat.

Chapter Fifty-seven

MUCH AS he hated doing it, Price contacted his ex-wife, Ginee, with an eye to bringing her into the loop before the press jumped on the story.

'We have a crisis with Teddy,' he said, over the phone. 'I need to see you immediately.'

'Who's this?' Ginee wanted to know – as if she didn't.

It crossed his mind to say, 'Hey, this is the dude who's been paying you all that alimony you sure as hell don't deserve for the last twelve years.' But he held back: he needed something from her, so the deal was to play it like a gentleman. Not that Ginee was any kind of lady – she was a coked-out nightmare, always had been. He'd married her when he was equally out of his head, and the moment he'd stopped doing drugs he'd realized his mistake. By that time they had a kid – Teddy – and a nightmare of a marriage.

Extracting Ginee from his life had taken a long time, for she had not gone without a vicious, dragged-out battle. And when he'd married his second wife – the ten-month mistake – even though it was four years later, Ginee had *really* freaked.

He'd been paying ever since.

'Don't fuck with me,' he said sharply. 'This happens t' be important shit concernin' both of us. Can you come over?'

'Why should *I* come there?' she sneered.

''Cause it's about *your* son.'

'Oh,' she said sarcastically. 'Do you mean the son *you* insisted on having custody of? *That* son?'

Once a bitch always a bitch. 'Quit breakin' my balls, Ginee.' He sighed, hating the fact that he had to talk to her again after all these years.

Her voice curled with sarcasm. 'Still got 'em, have you?'

With great difficulty he kept his cool. 'If it's easier for you, I'll come there.'

'Have your ass here in ten minutes,' she said shortly. 'I havta go out.' And, true to form, she hung up without waiting for his answer.

Swearing to himself, he grabbed a jacket and hurried out to his car, because if he knew Ginee she wouldn't wait.

On the drive over to her apartment on Wilshire he listened to some vintage Al Green, attempting to get his head in a better place. Nothing worked. By the time he got there he was ready to explode. He needed a joint and a drink. And he needed them like an hour ago.

Ginee met him at the door clutching a miniature French poodle in her arms. The surprise was that his once gorgeous ex-wife must have piled on over a hundred pounds. She was now a big fat mama with dyed strawberry blonde hair and an even more belligerent attitude than he remembered.

Mountains of flesh came towards him, clad in patterned leggings and a purple knit top. Huge jiggling breasts, wobbly thighs, and incongruously thin calves balanced on red patent hooker heels. What a sight!

He pretended not to notice her tremendous weight gain. She knew that he did and it infuriated her. 'S'pose you think I put on a pound or two,' she said, challenging him to say yes.

A pound or two! Was the woman nuts? She was a walking, talking mountain for Chrissakes.

'Can I come in?' he said.

'Ha!' she snorted. 'Too goddamn famous to stand out in the corridor.' She spun around, and he followed her mammoth ass into the apartment.

Her taste level was the same as when they'd parted company. Pink, pink, and more pink. Oversized pink couches, fancy pink cushions and rugs – even a large shell-shaped pink coffee table. Above the fireplace hung an enormous oil painting of a much thinner Ginee wearing a diaphanous gown and leaning on a grand piano. The outrageously vulgar portrait dominated the room.

'You, Price Washington, are a mothafuckin' bastard,' she announced, before he had time to take a breath. 'You ruined my goddamn life, my gorgeous figure, my everything!'

Bad-assed, foul-mouthed drama queen. Nothing had changed about Ginee – except her weight.

'Teddy's in trouble,' he said dourly, sitting down on one of her overstuffed pink couches.

'What kinda trouble?' she demanded, heavy false eyelashes fluttering above her small eyes like a series of trapped birds.

'He's bin involved in a shooting.'

'I knew you could never be a decent father to that poor boy,' she shrieked. 'You got him runnin' around in gangs shootin' people. It ain't right!'

'He's not in a gang.'

'Then what in hell was it? A drive-by?'

'Ginee, I repeat, he is *not* in a gang. This has to do with some girl gettin' hold of him an' leadin' him astray.'

'*What* girl?' she asked suspiciously.

'Mila.'

'Who's she?'

'My housekeeper's daughter.'

'*Jeez!*' Ginee exclaimed. '*That* Russian witch. I coulda told you her brat would turn out no good. You shoulda fired her skinny ass years ago.'

'Well, I didn't,' he answered patiently. 'An' it's not Irena's fault.'

'Nothin' was *ever* that cow's fault,' Ginee muttered, double chins quivering with indignation as the dog struggled to escape from her suffocating embrace. 'She musta bin blowin' you stupid with all the shit you let *her* get away with.'

He focused on the reason he was there. 'Can we concentrate on Teddy?' he said gruffly.

'Sure, honey,' she replied, with a sugary smile. 'All you gotta do is tell me what you want, an' then I'll tell *you* exactly how much it's gonna cost you.'

Money. Oh, yeah, he'd almost forgotten: with Ginee, nothing was ever free.

Chapter Fifty-eight

CARLO GAVE Brigette what she needed, and after a while she felt ready to face the world. She changed her dress, touched up her makeup, piled her hair on top of her head, and after she'd done all that, they left for the party.

'*Now* you look like my adorable Brigette,' Carlo said, taking her hand in his and squeezing it reassuringly as they walked outside to the waiting limo. 'Come, my darling, you must be looking forward to showing me off to all your friends.'

When he was nice it was almost as if she imagined his bad moods. She smiled dreamily. Everything was peaceful. Everything was good . . . except that soon she would have to face Lucky and, much as she loved her, in a way she was dreading it, because Lucky was the only person who could see right into the depths of her soul.

You're a big girl, a voice said in her head. *Lucky doesn't control you. You control your own destiny.*

No, another voice argued. *Carlo controls everything you do. You are completely under his influence.*

'Carlo,' she said, settling into the plush leather seat in the back of the limo.

'Yes, my dear?'

'I want you to promise me that you'll be nice to Lucky. It's important to me. She and Lennie, their kids and Gino are my only family.'

'Brigette, Brigette,' Carlo said, shaking his head in a pitying way. '*I* am your family now. You've told me how you were treated when you were growing up. You had a mother who was never around. Your father was long gone, and you were raised by a series of nannies. *I* am the one who will look after you now, Brigette. *I* am closest to you. This Lucky woman is nothing more than a friend.'

'She's my godmother, Carlo.'

'That means nothing – trust me. She will see you are fine with me, and if she doesn't,' he gestured with his hands, 'too bad.'

'Promise you'll be nice,' Brigette said anxiously, dreading the evening ahead.

'Of course, my contessa, I am nice to everyone.' And he smiled his superior smile and patted her reassuringly on the knee.

☆ ☆ ☆

Lennie finally put in an appearance. By the time he did, Lucky was simmering. First of all, Brigette was unforgivably late for her own party, and Lennie, leaving Lucky to cope with all the guests by herself, had infuriated her.

'Nice of you to join us,' she hissed, as he passed by. 'Sure it's not too much trouble?'

'I've had it with you making all your own decisions without including me,' he said, in a low, angry voice. 'We're *married*, in case you forgot.'

'I *told* you, Lennie, I do not require permission to do what I want.' And she turned her back on him and hurried over to the bar, where Gino was surrounded by an admiring group listening to him tell tales of his early days in Vegas.

'Everyone having a good time?' she asked, falsely cheerful. It was almost nine o'clock. The party had started at seven thirty. The caterers kept badgering her about what time she wanted them to serve dinner. Normally she would've had them start at nine, but since the guest of honour had not yet arrived, she instructed them to try to hold off.

'Where's Brigette?' Gino demanded. 'I'm waitin' to see the kid.'

'She'll be here any minute,' Lucky assured him, thinking that it wasn't like Brigette to be so rude.

Lina strolled over, hand in hand with Charlie Dollar. They looked like a couple.

'Well, well, well,' Lucky said. 'What's this? A new you two?'

Charlie chuckled. 'Do *not* tell Dahlia,' he said, like a naughty little boy caught sneaking candy.

'As if I would,' Lucky said.

'Lina's in my movie,' Charlie explained. 'And she's pretty damn sensational.'

'Oooh!' Lina squealed, thrilled. 'Do you really think so?'

'Wouldn't say it if I didn't, doll.'

Lucky shook her head. 'Charlie, Charlie . . .' she murmured.

'Yes?' he said, with a big, wide, shit-eating grin.

She shook her head again. 'Nothing.' It was no use warning Charlie that Dahlia would not be pleased if he was photographed with Lina. Dahlia suffered the little unknowns who shared his bed for a night or two, but there was no way she'd accept Lina, who was far too high-profile.

'So, where's Brig?' Lina asked. 'I'm dyin' t' see 'er.'

'*You* tell *me*,' Lucky said.

'Hmm . . . she's not usually late,' Lina said. 'Did you tell 'er *I* was 'ere?'

'No, you're the big surprise.'

'I think you'll find *Carlo* is the big surprise,' Lina said, rolling her eyes. 'Can't wait to see 'im again. He's absolutely gorgeous, if you like that type, but I gotta feelin' 'e's a bit of a bastard. I dunno . . . you'd better form your own opinion.'

'Oh, I will,' Lucky said. 'I certainly will.'

☆ ☆ ☆

Steven's partner, Jerry Myerson, was delighted to be in Los Angeles – even more delighted to be at a genuine Hollywood party filled with glamorous women. Recently divorced for the third time, Jerry was acting like a horny teenager let loose in the girls' locker room. Steven was embarrassed: age did not slow good old Jerry down – he was after action with a vengeance.

'Who's that?' he kept asking, every time an attractive woman walked by.

'Hey, slow down,' Steven said, thinking there was nothing worse than a fifty-something divorced man with a permanent hard-on. 'You've got the rest of the night in front of you.'

'Jesus!' Jerry exclaimed. 'How can you live here? The women are too fucking much.'

'You get used to it,' Steven said calmly.

'Nothing fazes you, does it?' Jerry said, winking at an over-endowed redhead. 'But, then, pussy has never been your burning passion.'

Steven threw him a cold look. He did not think it appropriate that Jerry was discussing women with him so soon after Mary Lou's death.

Carioca had run off to play with Maria. He wished she hadn't, he would sooner have spent the evening with his daughter rather than talking about women with Jerry. Sure, Jerry was his friend and partner, but he didn't need this crap.

'Holy shit!' Jerry exclaimed, eyes popping. 'Now *that*'s what I call a sexy broad.'

'You're giving away your age,' Steven remarked. 'Broad is not a politically correct term any more.'

'Who gives a shit?' Jerry said. 'Look at her – it's that supermodel, Lina. What a body!'

The name sounded vaguely familiar. Steven followed Jerry's rapt gaze, and immediately recognized the girl Jerry was staring at. He'd met her at Venus's party when he'd been standing outside the guest bathroom with Carioca.

'Yes, that *is* Lina,' he said.

'Don't tell me you fucking know her?' Jerry asked, practically salivating.

'Sure, I know her,' Steven answered casually.

'I think she's with Charlie Dollar,' Jerry said. 'Jesus! You can't turn around here without bumping into a star.'

'That's Hollywood for you,' Steven said.

'So if you know her, introduce me,' Jerry said, gulping straight bourbon.

'I'm not about to go over there and interrupt her.'

'You don't have to,' Jerry said, smoothing back his reddish hair. 'She's on her way over here.'

And before Jerry could say another word, Lina was upon them. ''Ello,' she said, with a huge smile directed at Steven. 'Fancy bumping into *you* again.'

Jerry edged forward, dying to be introduced, while Lina gave Steven the famous Hollywood kiss on each cheek. She smelt exotic and womanly. For a moment Steven thought about Mary Lou and the way she'd smelt – sweet like spring flowers. It was a painful memory.

Lina was obviously waiting for him to say something. 'Uh . . . nice to see you again,' he managed. Jerry gave him a sharp dig in the ribs, his somewhat bloodshot eyes begging for an introduction. 'This is my friend and partner, Jerry Myerson, he's visiting from New York.'

'Hi, Jerry,' Lina said, without much interest.

'I'm a big fan,' Jerry said, standing tall. 'Big big fan.'

'Thanks,' Lina said casually, barely looking at him.

'Saw your photos in a *Victoria's Secret* catalog. My God, they were sensational. You're the best.'

Steven threw him a why-don't-you-shut-up? look, but Jerry was on a roll and kept going. Steven moved away: he'd spotted Venus across the room and was anxious to talk to her.

'You're a bad boy, Steven,' Venus scolded, when he came over. 'You never answer my phone calls.'

'Sorry,' he said. 'I've been so busy at the office, then on weekends Carioca and I usually take off.'

'I'm glad to hear you're spending more time with her,' Venus said, licking her succulent bright red lips. 'You should bring her over to spend the night with Chyna.'

'Can we talk about Price Washington and his son?'

'God!' she said. 'When Lucky told me the boy was involved, I was completely shocked.'

'It'll hit the news any moment,' Steven said. 'I don't see how they can keep it quiet much longer.'

'Oh, yeah, the tabs'll go all the way with this one.'

'Do you *know* his son?'

'Met him once. Price brought him to one of my concerts. He seemed like a nice enough kid.'

'Did he look like a gang member?'

'A gang member? No, why would you say that?'

'I'm confused. Lennie insists it was the girl who pulled the trigger, while the boy stood there watching. Which makes him an accessory. But what I'm hearing from Lucky is that the girl's accusing *him* of doing the shooting.'

'I feel sorry for Price,' Venus said. 'He's a nice guy. This must be such a downer for him. Can you imagine?'

'It might be bad for him,' Steven said harshly, 'but think about what happened to Mary Lou . . .'

'I know, Steven,' Venus said softly. 'We all know.'

Chapter Fifty-nine

THE WOMAN was young and voluptuous, perhaps in her mid-twenties, and although quite beautiful in a raw and natural way, she was cheaply dressed and nervous-looking. Hanging on to her hand was a five-year-old child – a boy – with dirty-blond hair and green eyes.

The two of them hovered across the street from the valet parking area of Lucky and Lennie's house at the beach. Nobody took any notice of them – if anybody *had* noticed them, they would have dismissed them as a couple of fans trying to get a glimpse of the parade of famous people arriving at the house in the Malibu Colony.

The boy was tired and hungry, he kept indicating to his mother that he wanted a drink. She shushed him. She was tired and hungry herself, for it had been a long day and she had not expected to get to the house and find a big party in progress.

They'd arrived that afternoon on a flight from Rome. Neither of them had ever been on a plane before, and the boy had been sick, throwing up all over her dress. She'd cleaned up as well as she could, but she knew she was not looking her best.

It had taken a while to get through Customs, until eventually she'd convinced the official sitting behind his high desk that they were staying with her aunt in Bel Air and would only be in the country for a few weeks.

He'd nodded and stamped their passports, imagining what it would be like to make love to such an earthy-looking woman. Her smouldering eyes alone would keep him happy for the rest of the day.

She'd felt lost at the airport – it was so big and crowded and noisy. Her son had clung to her leg while she'd tried to discover how they could get to a place called Malibu. She'd had no idea if it was near or far. Fortunately, her English was passable and her looks so appealing that she was able to find out the cheapest way to get there by asking around.

A friendly black porter had given them a lift into the city, dropping them off on Wilshire. From there they'd got on a bus to Santa Monica.

Once off the bus, she'd stopped at a fast-food place and bought a hamburger, which she and her son had shared, then they'd got on another bus, which took them along the Pacific Coast Highway.

As the bus progressed, she'd gazed out of the window, filled with wonderment at the odd array of houses lining the edge of the ocean and the tall cliffs towering over the other side of the road. Her stomach was churning with the daring of this adventure she had embarked on – an adventure she had dreamed about for five years.

America. She was in America.

The thought made her weak with excitement.

Chapter Sixty

'HI, LUCKY,' Brigette said, finally arriving at the house.

'And about time too!' Lucky exclaimed. 'I was beginning to think you'd flown back to Europe!'

It was meant as a joke, but Brigette didn't seem to get it. Neither did she apologize for arriving so late, which pissed Lucky off.

'This is my husband, Carlo,' Brigette said, her normally exuberant tone strangely flat.

'Where's my hug?' Lucky said, sussing out the situation. She'd immediately observed that Brigette was thin and jumpy, with blank eyes and a slack expression, whereas Carlo, a tall, good-looking man with arrogant features and long, blondish hair, was glowing with health.

Brigette gave her a perfunctory hug.

You're too damn skinny, Lucky immediately wanted to say. But she didn't, since obviously this was neither the time nor the place. 'Nice to meet you, Carlo,' she said, with a pleasant smile. 'We've all been looking forward to this.'

He took her hand, brought it to his lips and gave it one of those barely there kisses.

A bullshit artist, she thought. *I can recognize 'em a mile off. A bullshit artist, wearing a five-thousand-dollar suit and a twenty-thousand-dollar Patek Philippe watch. Damn! He was spending pretty good.*

'Where's Bobby?' Brigette asked.

Lucky took another close look at her goddaughter. The once vivacious and adorable Brigette was a shadow of her former self. Something was definitely not right.

'He's gone to see your mutual relatives in Greece,' she said. 'Something you might think about doing in the future.'

'Maybe,' Brigette said vaguely.

'We have no plans to visit Greece,' Carlo said.

Who asked you? Lucky thought, as she looked around for Lennie. Where was he now? She couldn't wait to get *his* take on the situation.

'So,' she said cheerily, 'what's with the sneaking off and getting married bit? You *know* we would have given you a sensational wedding. Everyone's disappointed.'

'Brigette and I did not require one of those lavish Hollywood weddings,' Carlo said, with a touch of disdain. 'We preferred to be married at the palace. It has been in my family for hundreds of years.'

'How nice,' Lucky said, with an edge. 'If we'd known, we would've flown over.'

'Sorry,' Brigette said, a touch sheepishly. 'We didn't plan it . . . we just did it.'

'And what exactly is it that you *do*, Carlo?' Lucky asked.

'Investments,' he replied, staring at the exotically beautiful dark-haired woman with the dangerous black eyes. She was not to be charmed, he knew that instinctively. He had to tread carefully with this one.

'Sounds interesting,' Lucky said, deciding that he was an arrogant prick.

'It is,' he replied.

By the time Lennie came over, there was simmering animosity in the air. 'Lennie, meet Carlo, Brigette's husband,' Lucky said.

'Congratulations,' Lennie said, sweeping Brigette up in a big bear hug. 'How's my favourite golden girl?'

'Married.' She giggled, feeling somewhat light-headed.

'Oh, yeah, we know that,' he said, with an affectionate grin.

'Where's Maria and little Gino?' she enquired.

'They've gone to bed,' Lucky said, 'but Steven's around somewhere. And I know big Gino is longing to see you, so why don't we go find him?'

'I'll be right back,' Brigette said to Carlo.

'I'll come with you,' he said quickly.

'I think she's safe with me,' Lucky interrupted, leading Brigette away from her husband. 'So,' she said, as soon as they were out of earshot, 'how *are* you?'

'I'm fine, Lucky. I told you on the phone.'

'You look a little pale to me.'

'I do?' Brigette said, filled with guilt, because if Lucky knew the real truth . . .

'Yes, you do.'

'Too much travelling,' Brigette explained. 'I have *major* jet lag. It's a killer.'

'How about just you and I have lunch tomorrow?' Lucky suggested. 'That way we'll get to talk.'

'We can talk now.'

'Not with your husband hovering a foot away,' Lucky said. 'I *know* what Italian men are like – possessive isn't the word for it!'

'Carlo's not possessive,' Brigette said, springing to his defence.

'Oh, yes, he is,' Lucky said. 'I can tell.'

'No, he's *not*,' Brigette repeated.

'Ah, there's Gino,' Lucky said, refusing to argue with her goddaughter. 'Eighty-seven and still kicking butt.'

Gino jumped to his feet as they approached. 'Hey, kiddo!' he said to Brigette, tapping his cheek for a kiss. 'You went an' got yourself married, huh? An' I was lookin' forward to bein' best man.'

Brigette kissed him on both cheeks, she'd always had special feelings for Gino. 'You're my best man anyway,' she said, adding a warm hug.

'Yeah, yeah, sure,' he said, chuckling. 'Betcha say that to all the guys.'

'Of course I don't.'

Suddenly Lina crept up behind Brigette, placing her hands over Brigette's eyes. 'Surprise!' she yelled.

'Oh, wow!' Brigette said, wriggling free. 'What are *you* doing here?'

'*Bitch!*' Lina said, with a happy grin. 'How come you ran off an' got hitched without me? I thought we were planning a *double* wedding?'

'Sorry!' Brigette said, laughing.

'An' *look* at you,' Lina added. 'You must've dropped twenty bleedin' pounds. What's up with *that*?'

'It's the new me,' Brigette explained. 'I decided it was time to dump my puppy fat.'

'Puppy fat, my ass,' Lina shrieked. 'You're thinner than a stick. Jeez, what's your agent gonna say?'

'Nothing, because I've given up work.'

'*You've* given up work?' Lina exclaimed. '*You?*'

'Yes, me.'

'I don't get it. Why? Are you pregnant?'

She hadn't planned on telling anyone, but this seemed like the perfect opportunity. She took a long deep breath and plunged right in. 'As a matter of fact I am.'

Once again Lucky was shocked. If Brigette was pregnant, how come she didn't look more healthy?

'How pregnant are you?' she asked quickly.

'Only a couple of months,' Brigette replied vaguely.

'Way t' go, girl!' Lina hooted, obviously delighted for her friend. 'Bags I'll be the godmother. Y' know, the *black* godmother. I like it!'

'So do I,' Brigette said, and suddenly she felt like bursting into tears. She didn't know why, but seeing her friends and family seemed to bring back only good memories. Carlo had kept her isolated for so long that she'd forgotten what it was like to be with people she genuinely loved.

I'm doing heroin, she thought. *I'm in a drugged-out haze most of the time. That's how he keeps me under control. I've got to get away from him. He's sucking the life out of me.*

Oh, God, what had happened to her? Was she repeating her mother's pattern?

Before she could think about it any further, Carlo strolled over, placing a possessive arm around her shoulders.

'Well,' Lina said, wagging a finger at him, 'aren't *you* the sneaky one? *Daddy!*'

'Ah,' Carlo said, with a satisfied smirk. 'So Brigette has told you.'

'It's fantastic news!' Lina said enthusiastically. 'Does Fredo know? He'll freak!'

'No, this is the first time we have told anyone,' Carlo said. 'It is indeed wonderful news. I wanted Brigette to share it with the people she is close to.'

Lucky watched him as he spoke. There was something very devious and cold within those icy blue eyes, something she didn't trust. Abruptly she walked away and sought out Lennie to ask him what he thought.

'It's not good,' Lennie said, frowning.

'Why do you say that?'

'I gotta tell you, Lucky, I think she's doing drugs.'

'You mean smoking a joint? What?'

'No. She's on something. Take a look at her eyes. Then notice how thin she is. This isn't our Brigette.'

'Well, here's the big news,' Lucky said, hoping Lennie was wrong. 'She just announced she's pregnant.'

'You'd better have a serious talk with her.'

'We're having lunch tomorrow. I'll find out everything.'

'That's good.'

'What's your take on *him*?' Lucky asked.

'He's not exactly Mr Warmth. What do *you* think?'

'A good-looking con man with a big dick,' she said flatly. 'I can smell 'em at twenty feet.'

Lennie nodded. 'So, Lucky,' he said, trying to appear casual, but obviously bothered, 'have you made a decision about Alex?'

'What decision?' she asked innocently, although she knew exactly what he meant.

'You're not doing the movie with him, right?' he said, obviously uptight.

'Why are you on about Alex?' she said, exasperated. 'We're friends, that's all.'

'Friends, my ass.'

'Don't push me in a corner, Lennie. If I say we're friends, you'd better believe me.'

'Who's pushing? I'm merely asking you not to work with him.'

'That's totally unreasonable,' she said angrily. 'I have a project I want to do, and it happens to be attached to Alex. Big fucking deal. Get over it, Lennie.'

'So you're telling me that, if there's a choice here,' he responded heatedly, 'you'd choose Alex?'

'Are you *forcing* me to make a choice?'

'Jesus! You're *really* starting to piss me off.'

'Oh, like you're not pissing *me* off?'

'I never do anything to piss you off. I'm the perfect faithful husband, and I ask you one little thing—'

'Lennie, can we talk about this later? Now's hardly the time.'

'Whatever,' he said. 'As usual, it's *you* calling all the shots.'

☆ ☆ ☆

Over dinner Brigette was quite animated. Lucky had surrounded her with the people she was closest to, including Lina, who was all over Steven.

Watching the action, Lucky noticed that the more lively Brigette became, the more withdrawn Carlo seemed to be. She made an attempt to engage him in conversation. 'Where are you two planning to live?' she asked.

'Perhaps we buy a house outside Rome,' he answered restlessly, one eye on Brigette.

'Wouldn't that be lonely for Brigette?' Lucky said. 'Y' know, her being in a strange country where she doesn't speak the language. Stuck outside the city with a baby to look after.'

'Brigette does not need people around her,' Carlo said shortly.

'I think it's very touching that you seem to know so much about her, when in point of fact you've only known each other for – what? Three months?'

'Lucky,' he said, fixing her with a malevolent gaze, 'I realize you have Brigette's best interests at heart, but it is time for you to let go. She is *not* your daughter. She is *my* wife. And I will see that she is happy.'

'I'm sure you will,' Lucky murmured. 'There's only one small thing – she doesn't *look* happy.'

'You are ridiculous,' Carlo snapped. 'And rude.'

'Really?' Lucky said, thinking what a pompous asshole he

was. 'I was Brigette's mother's closest friend, and since Olympia is no longer with us, I look out for Brigette. So you'd better treat her right, Carlo, otherwise you'll have *me* to answer to.'

'Is that a threat?' he said, arching an aristocratic eyebrow.

'No threat, Carlo,' Lucky replied calmly. 'I'm merely telling you the way it is. You might have had her to yourself for the last few months, but in future I shall be watching what's going on. Oh, and by the way, I spoke to Brigette's lawyers in New York. There's no necessity for you to interfere in the way her trust is being run. She does not inherit the bulk of her estate for another five years, so I suggest you lie back. In five years, if you're still married, then I'm sure Brigette will be only too happy for you to take over.'

'I resent the way you talk to me.' He bristled, livid that she would have such nerve.

'I'm sorry, Carlo, but that's the way it is. So here's what I suggest.' Her black eyes hardened. 'Get used to it.'

☆ ☆ ☆

'What kind of music are you into?' Lina asked, toying with the stem of her champagne glass as they sat at one of the round dining-tables set out next to the pool.

'Al Green, the Temptations, Aretha. Y' know, classic soul,' Steven said. 'How 'bout you?'

'Soul's cool,' she said quickly. 'Keith Sweat, Jamiroquai . . .'

He smiled. 'You like to dance, don't you?'

'How can you tell?'

''Cause you've been jiggling around in your chair all night.'

She grinned. 'I have?'

'You have.'

She took a sip of champagne. 'Y' know, Steven, you're a *really* nice guy.'

'What makes you say that?'

'Well, I mean, take that friend of yours, Jerry whatever his name is, the one from New York. Every time I speak to him the guy is leering all over me like I'm naked or something. But you, you're just a regular guy. And you *could* be a prick, 'cause you're major good-looking.'

'Don't say that,' he mumbled, embarrassed. 'I'm not an actor. No need to build *my* ego.'

'You're better-looking than any actor I've ever seen,' she said, meaning it. 'You've got that Denzel Washington charisma thing going.'

He roared with laughter.

'An' you got great teeth,' she added with a cheeky grin.

'Y' know,' he said thoughtfully, 'this is the first time I've laughed since Mary Lou died.'

'I told you when I met you before 'ow sorry I was to 'ear about your wife,' Lina said. 'It must've been tough for you.'

'It's beyond tough, it's impossible. Nobody realizes what it's like unless they've lost somebody close to them,' he said gravely. 'There are mornings you barely make it out of bed. All you want to do is pull the covers over your head and stay there for ever. It's the nightmare that never goes away.'

'I can imagine,' she murmured sympathetically.

'Sometimes, when I walk into my house, I almost expect to find her waiting for me.'

'I'm sorry, Steven. What else can I say?'

'Thank you, Lina. I hope you never have to go through it.'

☆ ☆ ☆

'We're leaving,' Alex told Lucky shortly after dinner was finished.

'Why so early?' she asked, disappointed.

'You know parties aren't my favourite thing,' he said. 'Let's meet tomorrow and talk about the script.'

She hesitated a moment. 'Uh . . . I'm having a slight problem with Lennie.'

'What problem?' Alex said, giving her a penetrating look.

'He doesn't want me to do it.'

'That's crazy!'

'I know. And I'll work it out. But in the meantime, don't call me, I'll call you.'

'What does *that* mean?'

'It means I'm playing good little wife.'

'Bullshit!'

'I promise I'll get back to you in the next couple of days.'

'Are you saying we might *not* work together?'

'Of course we will. I simply have to handle it my way.'

'You know, Lucky,' he said, staring at her intently, 'I'm only going to tell you once—'

'Oh,' she said, challenging him with her eyes. 'What are you going to tell me, Alex?'

'Sure you love Lennie, and he's a great guy. But he's too moody for you. You need somebody more in sync with your lifestyle.'

'Somebody like you, I suppose.'

'You could do worse.'

'Only one problem.'

'And what would that be?'

'I'm a nice Italian American girl – well, actually, leave off the nice. But here's the thing. It's a well-known fact that you only go for Asians.'

'You kill me, Lucky. Call me when you've sorted things out with your husband.'

'Bet on it.'

☆ ☆ ☆

'So tell me, Princess, am I getting the royal English dump?' Charlie enquired, not sounding too disappointed because he already had his eye on a replacement – a scrubbed-faced TV star with big boobs and trouble in her eyes.

'What?' Lina said, all girlish innocence.

'You've been talking to that lawyer dude all night. The old fart movie star is beginning to feel like a spare prick at a wedding.'

'Oh, Charlie,' she giggled, leaning back in her chair, 'can I help it if I'm in lust?'

'So I *am* getting the good old English dump?' he said triumphantly.

'No,' Lina insisted. 'Me and 'im were just 'aving a very interesting conversation about the environment, that's all.'

'Like, *you* know about the environment.' Charlie snorted.

'I do,' she said indignantly. 'I used to walk in the park in London when I was a kid. I love trees and stuff like that.'

Charlie squinted at her. 'I'm not used to getting the old heave-ho, doll.'

'You've got a girlfriend, Charlie,' she pointed out. 'You're hardly marriage material.'

'Is that what you're looking for? To get hitched 'cause Brigette did the dastardly deed?'

'Not at all,' she said, glancing across the table at Steven, who was now conferring with his friend from New York. 'You've got to admit, 'e *is* cute. *And* – 'ere's the biggie – 'e's *my* bleedin' colour. We match.'

Charlie jumped on that one. 'Ha!' he said. 'Are you tellin' me I'm too white for you? Is that your current complaint?'

'You're *scary* white, Charlie. Don't you ever go in the sun?'

'Sunbathing's for movie stars who've got nothing else to do.'

Lina clinked her wine-glass with his. 'Anyway, it's not like 'e's asked me out or anything.'

'Oh,' Charlie said. 'And if he did? What would that make me? Second choice?'

She giggled again. 'Better than not being in the running at all, huh?'

☆ ☆ ☆

Pia was waiting for Alex by the door. 'Sorry, honey,' he said. 'Had to take care of business.'

'You like Lucky Santangelo, don't you?' she said, as they walked out to the parking area.

'She happens to be my best friend,' he replied, handing his ticket to the valet.

'No,' Pia said softly. 'I mean you like her as a man likes a woman.'

'Where do you come up with this crap?' he said, irritated that she knew so much.

'A woman's intuition.'

'I'm with *you*, aren't I?' he said, thinking of what he would do to her later in bed.

'If you had a choice, Alex . . .' she murmured.

'You're full of shit.'

'Am I?' she said. Then, because she was smart, she briskly changed the subject. 'See those two people across the street? They were here when we arrived. They look like gypsies. A child shouldn't be out this late at night.'

'Maybe they're lost,' Alex said, hardly glancing over.

'Do people get lost on the Pacific Coast Highway, and wander down to the Malibu Colony?'

'If you're so concerned, go ask them.'

'I think I will,' she said, crossing the narrow road. The woman stood up from the kerb as Pia approached. 'Excuse me,' Pia said. 'I couldn't help being concerned, seeing you out here all night with your child. Are you all right?'

The woman nodded, clutching her thin sweater across her dress. 'I – I wait to see Mr Golden,' she said tentatively. 'Is he in house?'

'Yes,' Pia said. 'Would you like me to ask someone to fetch him?'

'Please,' the woman said, shivering.

Pia returned to Alex. 'She's apparently waiting to see Lennie Golden.'

'Is she a fan?'

'I hardly think so. She's quite beautiful, and speaks English with an Italian accent.'

'Maybe *I* should talk to her,' he said, 'see what she wants.'

'Go ahead.'

He walked across the road.

The woman stared at him as he approached. He took a good look back and was quite startled by her smouldering beauty. She reminded him of a young Sophia Loren in the movie *Two Women*. Full breasts, long legs, ample hips and a swirl of long, wavy chestnut hair. He wondered if she was an actress – she was certainly lovely enough in a very raw, womanly way.

'You're waiting to see Lennie Golden, right?'

'That is right,' she said, her lilting accented voice barely more than a whisper. 'If I can see him, it would be good.'

'Do you *know* Mr Golden?'

'Five years ago . . . we knew each other in Sicily.'

'You did, huh?'

She nodded.

'What's your name?'

'Claudia. I think he remember me.'

'Oh, yes, Claudia,' Alex said, as it all came together. 'I've got a feeling he'll remember you very well indeed.'

Chapter Sixty-one

'I WISH TO leave,' Carlo said imperiously. 'I wish to leave soon.'

'We can't,' Brigette answered. 'The party's for me, and I'm having a nice time.'

'If *I* say I want to go,' Carlo snapped, 'then we will leave. That Lucky Santangelo woman is a bitch. Make the most of her tonight, Brigette, for I will not allow you to see her again.'

'Don't tell me that, Carlo,' Brigette said, starting to get distressed. 'I love Lucky. I'll see her whenever I want.'

'If we were at the hotel now,' he said ominously, 'you would not dare talk to me like that.'

It was at that exact moment that she realized how desperately she needed help, and right now she was in the only place she was likely to get it.

Perhaps Carlo realized it too, for he was certainly anxious to get her out of there.

Her mind was running in different directions. She had to tell someone what was going on. Maybe Lina. Yes, that was it – tell Lina, who'd alert Lucky, who would come once more to her rescue.

But how could she ask Lucky for help again? She was supposed to be all grown-up. She had a career, a baby growing inside her, and a husband.

No, she couldn't humiliate herself again.

And yet . . . she knew she had to escape, or was she doomed to be under Carlo's evil spell for ever?

'I have to go to the bathroom,' she said.

'Do so,' he said. 'Then we must leave. You will tell them you are not feeling well.'

Her blue eyes searched the party for Lina.

Gotta tell her, gotta tell her, gotta tell her, she thought.

But Lina was nowhere to be seen. Damn!

Outside the bathroom, she ran into Lennie.

'How's my favourite ex-stepdaughter?' he asked.

'I'm great, Lennie,' she said, still looking around for Lina.

'Enjoying the party?'

'It's great.'

'So . . .' he said. 'Little Brigette is having a baby.'

'I certainly am.'

'I was thinking how sad it is that Olympia isn't here to see it – she would have been very proud of you.'

'She would?' Brigette said, reacting immediately. 'My mother never noticed anything I did. I was simply there, Lennie. I was a child accessory.'

'That's where you're wrong, sweetheart,' he said, watching her closely. 'Olympia was *always* talking about you.'

'How could she?' Brigette said. 'She never even *knew* me.'

'You know, Brig, in her own way, she loved you very much. I *know*,' he added. 'I was married to her.'

'Well . . . I suppose she might have been excited about the baby,' Brigette admitted. 'Although she would've hated being called Grandma, right?'

'Oh, yeah,' he said. 'She would've hated *that*.' They both laughed at the thought. 'So, tell me,' he continued. 'How *is* married life?'

'Wonderful,' Brigette said, falsely cheerful.

'You like it, huh?'

'Of course I do. Carlo's very . . .' She searched for the right word. 'Uh . . . special.'

'Wanna snort some coke?'

'Excuse me?' she said, startled, her eyes widening.

'Y' know,' he said casually. 'You an' me – do a little of the white stuff?'

Now she was really disturbed. 'Lennie, what *are* you *talking* about?' she asked agitatedly.

'I know it's what you like to do, Brig,' he said gently. 'I can see it in your eyes.'

'You're wrong,' she said, flushing a dull red. 'Why would you even think that?'

''Cause I used to be into that whole scene.'

'I resent you assuming such a thing.'

'Take a look in the mirror, sweetheart. It's written all over your face.'

'How can you say that?' she mumbled, close to tears.

'Because I'm right. And, since you're pregnant, I was figuring you might need some help.' He took a long beat. 'Is Carlo involved?'

She shook her head. 'Carlo doesn't do drugs.'

'Then why do you?'

Her eyes filled with tears. She wanted to tell him everything, but Lennie wasn't Lucky, he would not be able to save her. 'I don't understand why you're saying such things to me,' she cried, pushing past him into the bathroom, slamming the door behind her.

She stood in front of the marble sink staring hopelessly into the mirror. Blonde Brigette with the huge blue eyes and pathetic little face.

Brigette Stanislopoulos – heiress.

Brigette – supermodel.

Lennie was right: all anyone had to do was look at her and they could see she was nothing but a drug addict.

She was disgusted with herself. Why *was* she doing drugs?

Because Carlo had hooked her up. Gotten her addicted so that she couldn't stop.

Then she'd embarked on a relationship with him – which, if she was truthful with herself, was totally sick.

Sometimes he loved her.

Sometimes he treated her as if he hated her.

Mostly he controlled her.

How had she ever gotten into such a mess? This made all the other dramas in her life pale in comparison.

'Lucky, Lucky, please save me,' she murmured.

No, a voice answered in her head. *You cannot run to Lucky every time. No! This time you must do it by yourself.*

She splashed water on her face and touched up her makeup. Then she stood up very straight.

I can handle it, she told herself. *I can handle anything.*

☆ ☆ ☆

'Steven, can I spend the night with you?' Lina murmured provocatively.

'What?' he said, not sure he'd heard correctly.

'It's not that I'm forward or anything,' she said, in a low husky voice, 'it's just that I really want to be with you.'

He took a long, steady beat. 'I thought you came with Charlie Dollar?' he said at last.

'I did. But I'd sooner be with you.'

He was silent. He hadn't felt like this in a long time. The excitement of something new. That pounding-heart thing. Sweaty palms. A feeling of recklessness.

And yet it was ridiculous. He wasn't a young stud looking to get laid. He was a fifty-something widower with a pain in his soul that was too deep ever to go away.

And then there was Lina . . . so indescribably lovely. Skin

with a dark satin sheen, long luscious black hair, a mouth to die for . . .

Who could blame him if he fell?

'Well, can I?' she asked insistently.

'I . . . uh . . . don't know.' *Yeah, right. Sound like the biggest fool in the world.*

'*What* don't you know?' she asked, leaning into him. And there came that smell again. Warm, exotic, intoxicating.

'I don't know if it's the right thing to do.'

'There is no *right* thing, Steven. We're here, Mary Lou's gone. She wouldn't want you turnin' into a monk or anything.'

No. Mary Lou wouldn't want that. She'd expect him to start living again as soon as possible. And why not? He was so goddamn lonely he could die.

'If you . . . would like to,' he finally managed.

'Course I would, otherwise I wouldn't've asked.'

'Then . . . all right.'

'All right, 'e says,' Lina crowed, with a big grin. 'Don'tcha know that most men would cut off their right ball for a night with me?'

She was not very modest, but that was okay – he wasn't planning on spending the rest of his life with her. Just one night of pure, unadulterated pleasure. He deserved that, didn't he?

☆ ☆ ☆

'I told her I thought she's doing drugs,' Lennie offered, catching Lucky on her way out of the dining room.

'What?' Lucky said. 'Why did you do that? I'm seeing her for lunch tomorrow, now you've probably frightened her off.'

'I did it in a very laid-back way.'

'How laid-back can it be when you tell somebody you think they're doing drugs?' Lucky said, exasperated. 'What was her reaction?'

'Naturally she denied it.'

'You should've asked me first.'

'I needed your permission?'

'No . . . but—'

'Why does everything have to be a fight with us?' he said angrily. 'Why is it always a fucking battle?'

'There's no battle. It's you. I thought you'd recovered from the whole shooting incident, but I guess I was wrong.'

'Incident?' he said, outraged. 'Is that how you regard it? A fucking *incident*?'

'You know what I mean, Lennie,' she responded, regretting her choice of words.

'Anyway,' he said stiffly, 'I thought I should warn you.'

'Where is she now?'

'In the bathroom.'

'I'll try to catch her when she comes out, make sure she's not freaked.'

'I'm sure you can do it, Lucky. Let's face it, you always get your own way.'

'I'm getting a little tired of your snide remarks.'

'And *I'm* getting tired of always jumping to your tune.'

'Hey, if you don't like it . . .'

They locked eyeballs, both angry, both refusing to back down.

'. . . I know what I can do,' Lennie said, finishing the sentence for her.

'Fuck you, Lennie. Just fuck you!'

'Thanks. Now I know how you really feel.'

☆ ☆ ☆

'It's like this,' Steven said.

'Like what?' Jerry replied.

'Well . . .' Steven said, frantically trying to think of a good enough excuse. 'You'll have to get a ride back to your hotel. There's plenty of people who'll be driving to town. Or you can call a cab.'

'Are you shitting me?' Jerry said. 'Why would I need a ride?'

'Because uh . . . I have to leave soon, and I know you want to hang out.'

'Of course I do. It's a Hollywood party, isn't it? There's broads a-plenty, and I don't plan on missing a thing.'

'Exactly,' Steven said. 'I have to meet with the district attorney early in the morning, she's trying to get the case put on an accelerated schedule, so I'm sure you'll understand if I split.'

'You can't stay for another hour?' Jerry said, sounding disappointed.

'You'll get along fine without me,' Steven assured him.

'What am I supposed to do? Walk up to somebody and request a ride?'

'Ask Gino. You know him.'

'Gino's eighty-seven years old. He'll be staggering out of here any moment.'

'Don't bet on it. He's a Santangelo.'

'I forgot about the freaking Santangelos,' Jerry said, raising his bushy eyebrows. 'They can walk on water, right?'

'Only Lucky,' Steven said, straight-faced.

'Yeah, yeah,' Jerry said. 'Okay, get lost, leave your friend here all by himself. See if I care.'

☆ ☆ ☆

While Steven was talking to Jerry, Lucky grabbed Lina. 'What do you think?' she asked.

'I think I'm leaving any moment with *the* most gorgeous man,' Lina said breathlessly, perfectly happy.

'I'm not talking about your sex life,' Lucky said. 'And, anyway, since when was Charlie Dollar so gorgeous?'

'Not Charlie,' Lina said. 'Steven.'

'*My* Steven?'

'Oh, yeah, *your* Steven. I forgot – he's your half-bro, right?'

'Exactly.'

'I don't quite get it,' Lina said, cocking her head on one side. ''Ow come 'e's black an' you're white?'

'Steven's mother was a beautiful black society woman with whom Gino had an affair many years ago,' Lucky explained. 'It took Steven a long time to track down his family roots, and when he did – we stuck.'

'Holy cow!' Lina exclaimed. 'Life's always stranger than fiction, in't it?'

'You could say that. Especially *this* situation. Now, what's your take on Brigette's husband?'

'What's yours?' Lina countered.

'I think he's after her money,' Lucky said bluntly. 'Can't you see that?'

'I wasn't exactly looking, but now that you mention it I can't help remembering what happened in New York when she thought 'e raped her.'

'Lennie thinks she might be into drugs.'

'Who? Brig?' Lina hooted. 'She won't even smoke a joint!'

'Things change.'

'All I know is that when we girls used to get together on a shoot, y' know, when everyone was doin' blow an' 'aving fun, Brig *never* got involved. Although, now that you mention it, she *does* look kind of zonked tonight.'

'We're having lunch tomorrow. Can you come?'

'If I'm not on call.'

'Good,' Lucky said. 'I've got a hunch Brigette needs us.'

☆ ☆ ☆

Brigette ventured out of the bathroom, hoping not to bump into Lennie again. He'd unnerved her with his accurate assessment of what she was doing. How did he know?

She wished she could shoot up right now. She needed the feeling of peace and calm it gave her.

Occasionally, in moments of lucidity, she thought about quitting. Only, when she was straight she felt so empty and alone – it was as if she was nobody, nothing, like she didn't even exist. And that Carlo was the only man who would have her because she was so worthless.

Ah, Carlo . . . when he was nice, he was very, very nice . . .

And when he was bad, he was horrid.

'Hey,' Lina said, racing up to her. 'We 'aven't 'ad a chance to get together all night.'

'Oh, hi,' Brigette said.

'Did you get an eyeful of Steven?' Lina said excitedly. 'What a babe!'

'I certainly noticed you lusting after him all through dinner.'

'Was it that obvious?' Lina said, delighted.

'Very.'

'Anyway,' Lina confided, 'he and I are making a discreet exit. And since *you* an' I 'aven't had any time together, I'm coming to lunch tomorrow. I've *sooo* much to tell you. You must've heard I'm making a movie with Charlie Dollar? Is that cool or *what*?'

'I'd love to see you, Lina,' Brigette said wistfully. 'I miss you.'

'You, too, sweetie. I miss working with you, 'aving you

disapprove of all the things I get up to. An' I *certainly* miss not telling you all the good stuff. Have I got gossip!'

'I guess I was busy getting married.' Brigette sighed.

'Do you love 'im?' Lina asked. 'Do you really, really love 'im? 'Cause if you don't, get out now, girl. Make a run for it.'

'Of course I love him,' she said defensively.

'He 'asn't got you doing stuff you don't want to, 'as he?'

'What do you mean?'

'You seem kind of – I dunno . . . distracted.'

'I'm not distracted, I'm pregnant.'

'Yeah, well, I guess that'll do it every time.'

Brigette nodded.

'I'm outta here,' Lina said. 'Lucky will set a time and place so I'll see you tomorrow.' She gave Brigette a big hug. 'It's cool about the baby, but listen to me, girl, you *gotta* put on a pound or two.'

'I will,' Brigette promised.

'God!' Lina said. 'Now I gotta deal with dear old Charlie.'

'I shouldn't think he'll mind too much,' Brigette said, gesturing towards the terrace. 'He's making out with that TV actress by the pool.'

'What am I gonna *do* with that boy?' Lina said, rolling her eyes. 'He's, like, *unbelievable*. Oh, well,' she added, 'at least I don't have to say goodbye to him.' And with that she made her way to the front door, where Steven was waiting.

They walked outside, almost bumping into Alex, who was entering the house accompanied by a young woman and a small boy.

'Seen Lennie?' Alex asked.

Lina shook her head. 'He's around somewhere.'

'Thanks,' he said. 'Wait here,' he instructed the woman, stationing her by the door. She stood very still, the small boy clinging to her skirt while her huge eyes darted nervously around the spacious hallway.

'Don't move,' Alex warned. 'I'll be right back.'

He found Lennie drinking at the bar. 'There's somebody here to see you,' he said.

'Who?' Lennie said dourly.

'Come with me and check it out.'

'Y' know, Alex,' Lennie said aggressively, 'I want you to stay away from my wife. I know what's going on, and I don't fucking like it.'

'Well,' Alex said, 'it's not really *your* decision whether I see Lucky or not. It's hers.'

'Fuck you,' Lennie said. 'You're the cause of nothing but trouble between us.'

'I thought you and I were friends,' Alex said.

'That's the way Lucky would like it,' Lennie responded, half drunk. 'But I *know* what you're trying to do.'

'Yeah, well, maybe you'd like to see what *you*'ve been doing. Follow me.'

'What the fuck is this shit?' Lennie muttered belligerently.

Spotting Lucky, Alex waved her over. 'You might want to be along for this,' he said.

'For what?' she asked.

'You'll see.'

The two of them followed Alex to the front door.

Claudia was standing where he'd left her, the child still clinging to her dress. When she saw Lennie, her face brightened. 'Lennie!' she exclaimed excitedly. 'I have prayed for this moment so long.'

'Claudia?' he said, hardly able to believe she was standing in front of him.

'Yes, it is me,' she said.

'Jesus!' he said. 'What are you *doing* here?'

'I came to America to find you,' she said. 'And now that I have, I am the happiest woman in the world.'

Chapter Sixty-two

'I SUPPOSE YOU are satisfied,' Carlo said, his face grim.

Brigette slid along the leather seat in the back of the limo, moving as far away from him as she could. She sensed the mood he was in and did not care to be the recipient of his anger.

'The party was nice,' she said noncommittally.

'Nice for *you*,' he said, steaming. '*You* did not have to sit around and be insulted by that bitch!'

'What bitch?' she asked, with a sigh, for now it would start, the nagging and the screaming and the cold-blooded fury that somehow he'd been slighted.

'Lucky Santangelo.'

'She's not a bitch, Carlo,' Brigette said patiently. 'She's merely looking out for me.'

'Do you *realize* how badly she insulted me?' he said, his voice becoming loud and accusing.

'No, what did she do?'

He reached up and pressed the switch for the tinted privacy glass, cutting them off from the driver. 'She implied that I, Count Carlo Vittorio Vitti, am after your money.' A glowering pause. 'I do not need your money, Brigette, I have plenty of my own. My family goes back hundreds of years. Who are *you*? You're nothing.'

'My grandfather was a very well-respected Greek billionaire,' she pointed out. 'He was a friend of kings and presidents.'

'Pity that your mother turned out to be such a piece-of-shit whore,' Carlo sneered.

'Don't say that,' she cried out. 'My mother might have had her problems, but she was *not* a whore.'

'I abhor your attitude,' he said. 'Try to behave like the wife of a count. I gave you that honour, and you spit on it.'

'Perhaps getting married was a mistake,' she ventured bravely.

'*My* mistake,' he said harshly.

'Then what shall we do about it?' she said, trying to keep her composure.

The thought crossed his mind that if they were to divorce, he would certainly be able to claim millions. But why claim millions when he could control an unbelievable fortune?

'You used to be such a beauty,' he said spitefully. 'Now look at you.'

'What do you want from me, Carlo?' She sighed, tired and dispirited. 'What do you really want?'

'For you to respect me as a proper wife should.'

'I try,' she said wearily.

'Tonight you did nothing to support me.'

'What do you mean?'

'You *allowed* that Santangelo bitch to insult me.'

'I have no idea what she said.'

'I can assure you, Brigette, I will *never* allow you to see her again.'

And he determined that as soon as they got back to the hotel, he would call the airlines and book them on an early-morning flight to Europe, away from the people who dared to threaten his future.

☆ ☆ ☆

'Slow down,' Steven said.

'What?' Lina said, half-way out of her Versace dress.

'You're moving too fast.'

'For what?' she asked, genuinely confused.

'For me.'

'I thought—'

'Don't think. Slow it down.'

Lina was puzzled. The first thing guys wanted to do was to get her out of her clothes. So what was with Steven and his request for her to slow down? She knew what she was doing. Oh, yes, and so she should, she'd been doing it since she was fourteen.

They'd walked into his house five minutes ago. 'Would you like a drink?' he'd asked.

'Champagne,' she'd answered. And when he'd gone over to the small bar in the corner of the living room, she'd started to remove her dress, thinking he'd be totally turned on. Instead of which he was asking her to slow down. Talk about being embarrassed!

She quickly pulled the top of her dress up, insecure for once.

'I have no champagne,' Steven said, still at the bar. 'Only white wine.'

'That'll do,' she said, feeling awkward, for she really liked this man, and now he probably thought she was the world's worst tramp out for a quick fuck.

He poured her a glass of wine, took a Diet Coke for himself, came over and sat beside her on the couch.

'Lina,' he said gently.

'Yes, Steven?' she said, switching from wild party girl to demure good listener.

'Always let the guy set the pace.'

'Huh?'

'You're young, famous, extremely sexy – not to mention beautiful. I'm sure you're rich, too. So, lay back.'

'I don't think—'

'Listen to me,' he interrupted. 'When was your last serious relationship?'

Her mind started racing, ticking off a list of conquests that included rich playboys, rock stars, media moguls, sports personalities, trust-fund babes – she'd had 'em all.

'I'm not into getting serious,' she said defensively. 'Doesn't interest me.'

'Why?'

Why? Why? Why? Good question. She was twenty-six years old and the longest time she'd spent with any one man was a seven-week fling with an extremely wealthy New York business tycoon who'd used her to irritate his wife, a jaded society woman who was busy screwing their Puerto Rican chauffeur.

'Me mum was always by herself,' she said at last, 'an' she did all right. Brought me up, didn't she? No bloody man 'anging round *'er* neck tellin' 'er what t'do.'

'A relationship is not telling someone what to do,' Steven explained. 'A relationship is being with someone you love, having fun together, caring through good times and bad.'

'Oh,' she said, wondering how she was going to get him into bed, because the more he talked, the more she wanted him. And getting everything she wanted was one of the main perks of being a supermodel.

'All I'm saying,' Steven continued, 'is take it easy.'

'Yes, Steven,' she said obediently, and waited for him to kiss her.

☆ ☆ ☆

'Claudia, what are you *doing* here?' Lennie said, in total shock.

Claudia smiled at him, a dazzling smile filled with warmth and raw love. 'You said if I ever needed anything . . .' she murmured, her words trailing off as Lucky stepped forward and stared at Lennie questioningly.

'Uh . . . sweetheart,' he said, highly uncomfortable because who in a million years would imagine that this situation could occur? 'This is Claudia. She's the uh . . . person who helped me escape when I was kidnapped. I uh . . . guess I owe her my life.'

'I guess you do,' Lucky said, checking out the curvaceous combination of Salma Hayek and a young Sophia Loren. Lennie had failed to mention how gorgeous his rescuer was. In fact, when questioned, he'd mumbled something about her being a dog.

'This is my *wife*, Claudia,' Lennie said, with a strong emphasis on wife.

'Oh.' Claudia's face clouded over with disappointment – something Lucky did not miss.

Neither did Alex, who was still standing there, an avid observer.

'Where did you come from?' Lennie asked, noting her somewhat exhausted appearance.

'Italy,' she said.

'Italy?' Lucky repeated. 'You mean you arrived today?'

Claudia nodded. 'This is so,' she said. 'We arrive by plane from Roma. Then a kind man drove us to a place where we could get a bus to come here. All I had was your address, Lennie. I was hoping you would still be here. It has been five years . . .'

'I know,' he said, utterly confused. 'So you got on a plane and came here – with the hope of finding me?'

Her eyes shone with sincerity. 'You told me if I ever needed help . . .' she said again.

'Well, yeah, but you should've called or something.'

'Is this your son?' Lucky asked, gesturing towards the little boy. 'He looks exhausted.'

'Yes,' Claudia said. 'He is tired and very hungry.'

'What's his name?' Lucky asked, feeling sorry for the child, who hadn't uttered a word.

Claudia glanced at Lennie, before dropping her gaze to the floor. 'Leonardo,' she murmured.

'Leonardo,' Lucky repeated. And then, even though she knew the answer just by looking at the boy, she couldn't help asking the question, 'Who's his father?'

Claudia's eyes met Lennie's. 'He is *our* son, Lennie,' she said, her voice barely more than a whisper. 'Leonardo is the reason I am here.'

'Oh, God!' Lucky cried, turning to her husband. 'Your *son*?'

'I – I don't know anything about this,' Lennie muttered, shocked and surprised.

Lucky's expression was icy. 'Why don't we go somewhere where Claudia can explain properly, without half the party listening?' she said coldly, shooting Alex a look. 'Good night, Alex,' she added abruptly.

'Hey, it's not my fault,' Alex said, shrugging. 'She was hanging around outside asking for Lennie. I was only doing my good deed for the day.'

Lucky turned on her heel, furious that on top of everything Alex was a witness to her humiliation. 'Bring Claudia into the library,' she said to Lennie.

Once they were settled in the library, Claudia started to talk, her words directed at Lennie. 'The day we made love I became pregnant,' she said, clasping her hands together.

'After you escaped, my brothers and the rest of my family became very angry. When they discovered it was *I* who helped you I was beaten. Then later, when my baby started to show, I was sent to live with relatives in a distant village.' She hesitated for a moment, overcome with emotion. 'They said I was a disgrace to my family. After my son was born, nobody would talk to me, so one day we fled to Roma, where I got a job. But the money was not enough to make things work. After years of hardship, I realized my son should be with his father, so I brought Leonardo to you, Lennie, in America, where I know he will be well looked after.'

Lennie swallowed hard as the world he knew crumbled around him. He had a child he hadn't been aware of until now. A son. And he knew it would change everything.

Yes, it was true, he *had* made love to Claudia – once. He should've told Lucky as soon as he'd gotten home, asked for her forgiveness.

But he hadn't. He'd figured it was something she need never find out.

Wrong. Because if he knew Lucky at all, he knew that she would never forgive him. Never.

He'd lied to her about another woman, and in her eyes that was about as bad as it could get.

Chapter Sixty-three

WHEN THE news hit, it exploded with a vengeance, becoming the lead news story on all three TV networks. Not to mention headlines in the *LA Times* and *USA Today*, even making the third page of the *New York Times*. The tabloids came out in force with a slew of lurid stories about Price's former drug addiction and Mary Lou's long ago nude photos – as if either of those things had anything to do with the murder.

Price Washington had not realized what big news he was. *Fuck!* This was not the way he'd wanted to make the headlines. If his mother knew – Teddy's grandma – she'd climb out of her grave and beat up on both of them.

Outside his house, news crews and reporters gathered, clamouring for a quote or a soundbite.

This was shit! He forbade Teddy to leave the premises. 'An' don't look out any windows,' he added. 'They're everywhere with their goddamn cameras.'

Mila was still in jail, even though Irena had begged Price to put up bail if it was granted.

'No fuckin' way,' he'd growled. 'She's the one that got Teddy into this shit storm. Let her stay there.'

'If I can see her, I'll make her tell the truth,' she'd said.

'Yeah, sure,' Price had answered disbelievingly. 'You'll let your daughter take the rap so Teddy can go free? Not on my time. You'd better pack your bags an' split, Irena, it's over.'

'I cannot understand how, after all these years, you would tell me to go,' she'd said, in a muffled voice.

'What the fuck am I *supposed* to do?' he'd yelled, filled with frustration. 'How can I keep you with what's goin' on?'

Irena had gone to her room and brooded.

☆ ☆ ☆

The day the news broke, Howard Greenspan smuggled Ginee in through the back of the house for a reunion with her son. Once inside, she strutted her enormous bulk around the living room like she owned it, which of course she once had – in a way. 'Place is lookin' good,' she said grudgingly, fingering the plush velvet-covered couch. 'I see you re-decorated.'

'Be careful what you say to Teddy,' Price warned, hating the fact that she was back in his house, her very presence invading his personal space. 'He's real down.'

'Shit! *I*'m down,' Ginee announced, double chins quivering. '*I*'m the goddamn *mother* of the criminal. You think *that*'s the kinda reputation gonna get me the best table in a restaurant?'

'We made a bargain, Ginee,' Price said evenly. 'You keep your side of it and I'll keep mine.'

'Now, now,' Howard said, playing good lawyer. 'It's important that you two get along, *especially* in front of the boy.'

Price nodded his agreement.

'Price an' I always get along good,' Ginee said, sticking out her mammoth bosom. 'An' I got the cheques to prove it!'

Price glared at her. He was trying to stay calm, even

though he was heading for a black funk. His agent had been on the phone that morning claiming the studio wanted to push the start date back on his upcoming movie. 'What kinda bullshit is *that*?' he'd screamed.

'It's a stalling technique,' his agent had explained. 'They're waiting to see which way the case'll go before committing. If you attract the public's sympathy, it'll mean big box office. If you don't, it's disaster time, so they're hedging.'

'Fuck the studio,' Price had steamed.

'Yeah,' his agent had said. 'Like I haven't heard *that* before.'

'What does a girl havta do t' get a drink around here?' Ginee asked coyly.

Price buzzed Irena, who arrived instantly, as if she'd been listening outside the door.

'Christ!' Ginee said, her lip curling in disgust when she saw Irena. '*You*'re still here. What a freakin' joke *that* is.'

Irena avoided eye contact, although it didn't cause her grief to notice that Ginee had put on a hundred pounds.

'Get me a black coffee with a shot of Sambuca,' Ginee ordered, then turning to Howard she added – 'This Teddy crap is upsetting. I gotta get me a lift.'

Howard nodded, wondering how on earth Price had ever been married to this large piece of blubber.

Irena glided from the room. The only lift Ginee needed was around her face.

☆ ☆ ☆

Teddy combed his hair yet again and pulled a pose in the mirror. He had a definite look. Oh, yeah, Will Smith mixed with a touch of Tiger Woods.

Today he was seeing his mom for the first time in twelve

years, and his stomach was turning upside down with fear and anticipation. Would she still love him with all this shit going on? Had she *ever* loved him? Was it true what his father said about her? *Was* she a whore?

Price had taken him to one side last night and warned him, 'Your mom's put on a few pounds. Don't mention it, 'cause she could get nasty.'

Did that mean she was *fat*? It didn't bother Teddy if she was. What *did* bother him was that she hadn't wanted to see him in all these years.

Still . . . seeing her now was better than nothing, because he sure as hell couldn't communicate with his dad. Price's fury was a scary thing.

The news was full of Mary Lou again. Her picture stared out at him from the front of every newspaper. That heart-shaped face and sweet, sweet smile reminding him of that fateful night. Every image of her filled him with grief, self-loathing and a fearsome guilt.

He hated himself all over again. Hated Mila even more. She was a witch. *She*'d done it. *She*'d shot down Mary Lou like a dog. And he'd stood and watched. Done nothing to stop her.

He deserved to be punished – even if it meant being locked away with gang-bangers and thieves and murderers. He deserved the worst.

His dad was right, he should've gone to the cops when he'd had a chance.

But he hadn't. Now it was time to pay the price.

☆ ☆ ☆

Locked away with a bunch of other females, Mila didn't like it one bit. She especially didn't like the unflattering uniform and the prison guards who seemed incapable of cracking a smile. Bunch of ugly old dykes. She'd be out before they could screw with *her*.

On her second night in jail she got into a verbal battle with a puny brunette, and ended up beating the crap out of the girl. Twenty-four hours in solitary confinement went a long way to raising her status with the bad-ass contingent.

Shortly after she got out of solitary she bonded with her cell-mate, Maybelline Browning. Maybelline was slight and pretty with a baby face and quite an appealing overbite.

'What did *you* do?' Maybelline asked, chewing on a strand of her own wispy pale red hair, a disgusting habit Mila soon got used to watching.

'Shot some black bitch who was getting in my way,' Mila replied, full of bravado. 'How 'bout you?'

'Stabbed my step-grandma with a bread-knife while she was sleeping,' Maybelline said, an angelic smile on her baby face. 'Unfortunately the old cunt didn't die. But that's okay, I'll get her another time. Me or my brother will finish her off.'

'Did your brother help you last time?'

'No. Duke was away, otherwise the miserable old cow would've been dead meat.'

'What did she do to piss you off?' Mila asked curiously.

'Stayed alive after my grand-daddy died. Bitch!'

Mila appreciated Maybelline's style, although her street smarts warned her that Maybelline was a girl to be careful around.

As the days passed, Mila waited for Irena to arrange bail. It didn't happen.

She also waited for Price's expensive Beverly Hills attorney to arrive. That didn't happen either. Instead, a court-appointed public defender came to see her. Willard Hocksmith, a seedy-looking jerk with yellow teeth and bad breath. He was dressed in a mud-brown suit and a frayed-at-the-collar white shirt. She didn't trust him on sight.

'I want out,' she said, glaring at him balefully, as if it was *his* fault she was locked up. 'I didn't do it. Teddy Washington did it. And I can prove it.'

'How?'

'You'll see.'

'Give me whatever you can.'

'When the time is right.'

'I'll see what I can do,' he said. And then she didn't hear from him.

As the days passed, a deep fury started to build within her. It appeared that everyone was against her – even her own mother, who had not come to see her. Surely Irena realized IT WASN'T HER FAULT.

She didn't care, because they'd all pay, Teddy and Price *and* Irena. She had her secret weapon. She had Price Washington's gun with Teddy's prints on. It was hidden away and she didn't want to mention it until she was sure it would get into the right hands. Because cops could be bought, and it would be easy enough for Price to pay someone off.

So she would wait. Until the right moment.

And then, oh, yes, by the time she was finished, they'd all pay big time. Every single one of them.

☆ ☆ ☆

'Say hello t' your mom,' Price growled, lurking by the door, rubbing his bald head – a sure sign that he was uptight.

Teddy stood in the doorway, frozen for a moment. What was he supposed to do? Run towards her yelling, 'Mommy! Mommy!'

Who was this woman anyway? Nobody *he* remembered.

This woman was huge. A mountain. A mountain he had no desire to hug.

'How ya doin', Teddy?' she asked, chewing gum like a cow chewing the cud, lipstick smeared liberally across her front teeth.

'Okay,' he mumbled, unable to match this woman with the picture he had of his mother holding him on her lap when he was two years old. The woman in the picture was a beauty. This other woman was a big fat freak with clown makeup.

'We'll leave you two alone,' Howard said, steering Price out of the room and shutting the door behind them.

There was an awkward silence.

'Got yourself into some trouble, huh, kid?' Ginee said at last, picking up one of Price's TV awards and examining it.

'Guess so,' he said, staring at the carpet, focusing on her low-cut-at-the-front red shoes, from which her toes bulged like a row of fat black maggots.

'It's your fuckin' father's fault,' she said, putting the award down with a bang. 'Bad fuckin' genes. Guess you inherited 'em.' She sighed and fluttered her hand in front of her face. Her painted nails were so long that they curved under at the tips. He wondered how she ever did anything with nails of that length. 'So you wanna tell me about it?' she continued. 'This girl grabbed you by the short an' hairies an' you got all hot 'n' horny, that it?'

'She . . . she influenced me,' Teddy said carefully.

'Course she did,' Ginee said, plopping her heavy frame on to the couch. The springs creaked. 'Any sixteen-year-old hot-rod with a hard-on is gonna get himself influenced by some little honey. Anyway,' she added, twirling one of her large gold earrings, 'here's the thing – ya gotta learn to think with your brain, not your ding-dong. Get it?'

He was embarrassed that she was talking to him this way.

Was that how mothers talked to their sons? He had no point of reference.

'I suppose Price has told you the DA's gonna prosecute,' she continued. 'Which means *I*'ll havta be in court every day, sittin' there bored outta my goddamn skull. Course, your father's compensatin' me – an' so he should.'

'How come I never saw you all these years, Mom?' Teddy asked, determined to get some answers. 'Didn't you *wanna* see me?'

'Oh, *pul-ease*. Don't go givin' me that poor-little-boy-lost bit,' she said, irritated. 'Your daddy wouldn't *let* me see you. Only thing *he*'s got on his poor excuse for a mind is makin' money an' gettin' laid.' She tapped her long nails on the table. 'He's a *bad* mothafucker. Paid me to skedaddle, so I went. Couldn't fight him in court.'

'Why?' Teddy wanted to ask. But he didn't.

'You could've come to visit me if you'd wanted,' she added lamely.

'Didn't think you'd see me,' he muttered.

'Anyway, it's old news,' she said, yawning, bored by having to deal with her son after all these years. 'An' I'm gonna havta buy myself a whole new wardrobe.' She glanced at her watch, embedded deep in the folds of her fleshy wrist. 'So *I* gotta get goin',' she said, hauling her massive bulk off the couch, happy to be on her way. 'See ya in court, Teddy-bear.'

Was that it? Was this the meeting he'd dreamed about?

His father was right about her. She was a money-hungry whore with her bright red lipstick, fake eyelashes and mag-goty toes.

At least his dad seemed to care about him. This woman didn't give a rat's ass.

BOOK FOUR
Six Weeks Later

Chapter Sixty-four

'SO WHAT do *you* think?' Alex said.

They were sitting around a big conference table at his offices. Alex and several of his assistants, Venus with her production partner, Sylvia – a gay woman with plenty of attitude – and Lucky, who'd come to the meeting by herself.

'Are you talking to me?' Lucky said, suddenly realizing that everyone was looking at her.

'No,' Alex said sarcastically. 'I'm talking to the fucking man in the moon.'

Her lips tightened. Alex sure turned into a different person when he was working. 'Sorry, Alex,' she said coolly. 'I must have lost my concentration for a moment.' She threw him a long hard look. 'No crime? Right?'

Everyone at the table sensed the tension. 'Hey,' Alex said, 'either you're into this meeting or you're not.'

'I'm into it,' she said, glaring at him.

This was the first production meeting on their movie, working title *Seduction*. Everything had come together fast, Lucky had worked hard to make sure of that. So had Alex. Between the two of them they'd made it happen.

Six weeks had passed since Claudia's arrival on her doorstep. Claudia – armed with Lennie's child.

Naturally, once the story was out, she and Lennie had become involved in a big battle. He'd lied to her, told her nothing had gone on between him and the Sicilian girl. And now, five years later, here she was with his goddamn kid.

'Why weren't you truthful with me?' she'd demanded, hurt and angry.

'I was fighting for my life,' he'd answered, obviously as shocked as she was. 'Claudia was my only way out.'

'I see,' she'd responded coldly. 'You were *forced* to fuck her to get out of there – is that it?'

'Oh, God! Try to understand, Lucky.'

'Maybe I'd be more understanding if you'd told me,' she'd said unsmilingly. 'Why didn't you *fucking tell me*?'

'It didn't seem important enough to risk hurting you.'

'And I suppose some Sicilian hooker turning up with your kid – that *doesn't* hurt me?'

'Claudia's not a hooker,' he'd said curtly.

That's all she'd needed, Lennie defending the girl. 'You know, Lennie,' she'd said icily. 'As far as I'm concerned, you can take off and check into a hotel with your new family. Because I don't care to have either of them anywhere near my children.'

'You're not being fair,' he'd argued. 'I'm trying to tell you, I didn't know anything about the boy.'

'Hey, now you do. *You* fucked her, take the consequences.'

She knew she was being hard-nosed about it, but the one thing she refused to accept was lying, and he'd lied about the most important thing of all. Fidelity.

Maybe she'd have been more forgiving if he'd told her the truth when he'd first gotten back from his ordeal. But he hadn't. He'd insisted that nothing had happened between him and the girl.

Timing was everything. She could kill him. Kill the cheating son-of-a-bitch. He'd ruined their lives.

The day after the party Alex had called, wanting to know

everything. She'd refused to discuss it with him or anyone else. It was private.

On top of everything, the court case was coming up and Steven was getting real edgy. The DA had put it on an accelerated schedule on account of all the publicity. This was good, it meant they could get it over and done with.

The other thing on Lucky's mind was Brigette. By the time she'd called the hotel the day after the party, she'd been informed that Count and Countess Vitti had checked out, news that stunned her. She'd immediately called Lina, who knew nothing.

'As soon as I can get away, I'm tracking them down,' she'd said to Lina. 'That bastard has her under some kind of spell and I'm *breaking* that spell – along with his fucking Italian balls.'

Most nights she lay in bed, filled with unrest and confusion about Lennie, remembering the time she'd caught her second husband, Dimitri, with his former lover, flamboyant opera star Francesca Fern. That was shortly before Lucky had had her second encounter with Lennie in the South of France. After that memorable day everything had changed. Their passion was on fire. Nothing and no one could stop their affair.

Alex called a break in the meeting. Grabbing Lucky by the arm, he pulled her roughly to one side. 'Are you planning to concentrate on this project or not?' he demanded. 'I can't work with someone whose mind is elsewhere.'

'I'm *here*, aren't I?' she said stubbornly.

'*You*'re here, your mind isn't.'

'Oh, please, Alex. Sometimes you talk such crap.'

'Producing a movie has to become your life,' he lectured. 'Can you allow that to happen, Lucky? Or are you going to spend all your time brooding about Lennie and his new-found kid?'

'I don't brood,' she answered coldly. 'Lennie's history. We had a few good years together, now he's free to go his way and I'll go mine.'

'You're not very forgiving,' Alex said. 'So he screwed the girl. So what?'

'You don't get it.'

'Did you tell him about us?' Alex said, lowering his voice.

'I've asked you never to mention that,' she said, furious that he was bringing it up.

'I know. But you can't deny it happened.'

'I thought Lennie was dead,' she said flatly. 'It didn't count.'

'Listen,' he said. 'I'd like nothing better than for you to dump the guy, but you gotta think about it carefully 'cause I don't want you dumping him then wishing you hadn't.'

'I hate to tell you this, Alex,' she said, thoroughly fed up with him, 'but what I choose to do has absolutely *nothing* to do with you.'

'Yes,' he said forcefully, 'it does. Because if you're available, so am I.'

'Meaning?'

'You and I should be together. That's where we belong.'

She knew he was mad that the only contact she'd had with him since her split with Lennie was business-related. But, hey, the last thing she needed was an involvement. Besides, he was still with Pia.

Venus came over with Sylvia, interrupting them. 'Y' know,' Sylvia said, somewhat officiously, 'there's still some changes Venus requires in the script.'

'Yes,' Venus agreed. 'The scene where my character's in the swimming-pool. Why does it take place in a pool? A sauna's sexier.'

'Pools are over,' Sylvia added, in case they hadn't got the message.

'You've got to get it visually,' Alex said, irritated that he had to explain. 'I'm not using just any fucking pool. I see a black-bottomed infinity pool perched precariously on the edge of a mountain. That way there's a real element of danger. The audience doesn't know if he's going to push her over the side or not. They simply have an uneasy feeling that he *might*.'

'Or that *she* might,' Venus interrupted. 'I plan to play her as a dangerous woman.'

'I can go with that.'

'Dangerous like Lucky,' Venus said, teasing him, because she knew how he felt about her friend. 'Lucky's my role model, you know.'

'Really?' Alex said.

'Uh-huh,' Venus said. 'Lucky taught me everything about being a real strong woman. And believe me, Alex, some of it would blow even *your* mind.'

'Nothing would blow *my* mind, Venus,' he said shortly. 'I've seen it all and done it all. I'm a weary warrior.'

'And a poetic one, too,' she said slyly.

'Can we get back to work?' Lucky questioned. 'There are decisions to be made.'

☆ ☆ ☆

Living in a large hotel suite at the Chateau Marmont with Claudia and Leonardo was freaking Lennie out. He hadn't touched Claudia since she'd reappeared in his life, wasn't even tempted. She was unsophisticated and vulnerable, almost childlike in a way. And she was so grateful for every little thing he did.

He slept in one bedroom, Claudia and Leonardo in another.

All he could think about was getting back with Lucky.

The problem was that his strong-willed wife refused to have anything to do with him. As far as she was concerned, she'd thrown him out and that was that.

'I have to see the kids,' he'd told her over the phone.

'Get a court order,' she'd replied curtly.

'Is that what you want me to do?'

'Yes.'

Lucky could be a hard woman.

He'd driven to Palm Springs and appealed to Gino. Gino had shrugged and said, 'Hey, you think I can tell my daughter anythin'? She's a Santangelo, for Chrissakes. She does whatever she wants t' do.'

Lennie knew what *that* meant. Lucky made all her own decisions, and whether they were right or wrong, she followed them through to the end.

Claudia, meanwhile, was filled with wonderment at her new surroundings. She ran around the hotel suite touching the furnishings, inspecting the kitchen, staring at the television. America was all new and exciting to her, and she was entranced.

Lennie soon found out that Leonardo had a problem. The boy was hearing-impaired. Claudia's eyes had filled with tears when she'd revealed that such was her brothers' anger at her for betraying the family, that while Leonardo was growing up, he'd endured numerous beatings. 'They punished him for what I did,' she'd explained.

Lennie was filled with guilt. If he hadn't slept with her she'd have led a completely different life.

But he *had* slept with her. Temptation had gotten the better of him, and he'd made love to her and given her a child. Now he had to take the responsibility.

As each day passed, Claudia was there to smile and comfort him, never uttering a cross word. And Leonardo seemed like a good kid. He didn't speak English; in fact, he barely spoke at all because of his hearing problem.

Lennie often found himself staring at the boy. Leonardo had ocean-green eyes and longish dirty-blond hair. Lennie found the resemblance to him at the same age unmistakable.

He was looking to rent a house to put them both in. He'd also fixed Leonardo appointments with some first-rate doctors, to find out if there was anything they could do. In the meantime, he kept working on his script, but it was not easy to concentrate, especially with the court case coming up in which he would be the key witness.

The media had run with the story as everyone knew they would. Along with Lucky and Mary Lou and Gino, he was also a favourite of the tabloids. Lennie Golden: former movie star, former comedian, son of Jack Golden and a Las Vegas stripper. Once married to the fabulously wealthy heiress, Olympia Stanislopoulos, who'd died of a drug overdose in a hotel room with Flash, a famous rock star. They dragged it all up. Pictures too. Lennie's life flashed before him.

Lucky was also getting her fair share of unwanted publicity. According to the press, she was the gangster's daughter who'd made good. The studio head with the shady past. The woman who'd killed a man and pleaded self-defence.

He knew she must be devastated by all the publicity. Lucky's preference was for staying *out* of the spotlight. He wished he was with her so he could protect her from all this crap. But every time he called and tried to see her, she wanted nothing to do with him.

The last time he'd called she'd been quite even-tempered. 'I understand that you didn't know she was pregnant, Lennie,' she'd said calmly, 'but I'm afraid you betrayed me, so therefore I feel I can never trust you again. And if I can't trust you, I can't be with you. So, please, stop calling.'

Lucky's logic. Sometimes it defied reality.

He'd heard she was forging ahead with her movie with Alex, and that drove him crazy. All Alex wanted was an opportunity to get close to her, then the bastard would move in and cement the deal. Alex was not to be trusted.

Lennie called him up one night when he'd had too much vodka, and Claudia and Leonardo were asleep in the other room. 'Stay away from my wife,' he warned.

'Aren't you separated?' Alex said.

'Stay away from my wife,' he repeated.

'Go fuck yourself,' Alex said.

This situation made Lennie even more uneasy. What was he supposed to do? How was he going to win her back?

The day before he was due to appear in court, he decided to take them both to Disneyland. The day trip was as much for him as for them. He desperately needed to chill out, put things in perspective.

Claudia was excited, Leonardo too. First he took them to the Gap, where they fell in love with everything.

Their excitement made Lennie feel good. If only Lucky could accept the situation. Claudia was a beauty, but she meant nothing to him. He'd clung to her in a time of fear and desperation. She'd been his only hope.

Why couldn't Lucky understand?

Chapter Sixty-five

MILA MADE a short court appearance where, due to the severity of the charge against her, she was refused bail. The public defender in his mud-brown suit tried to argue on her behalf, but the judge dismissed him with a wave of his hand.

Irena, sitting in the front row, was unable to help, even though she'd gone to the bank and withdrawn every penny of her precious savings to assist her daughter in case they allowed bail.

It was probably just as well that they didn't, for if she'd been allowed to take Mila home, Price would more than likely have kept his threat and thrown them both out. As things stood now, he hadn't mentioned again her leaving.

Mila spotted Irena and bounced a quick look off her. Why wasn't her mother doing anything to get her out? Teddy was free because of his rich fucking daddy. She was locked up because her mother had no damn clout. It wasn't fair.

Irena was torn between wanting to help her daughter and being loyal to the love of her life. For although she'd never told him, Price *was* the love of her life.

Often, from the age of four, Mila had demanded to know who her father was. Irena had always lied, making up some story about an old boyfriend from Russia.

It was not the truth. The truth was too awful for anyone to hear. The truth was Irena's dirty little secret.

She would never forget that fateful night. Price and Ginee were upstairs in the bedroom, stoned out of their minds . . .

They'd kept on buzzing the kitchen with outrageous demands, summoning her, telling her what to do, bossing her around. This was between house calls from two different drug-dealers.

Ginee was Price's girlfriend then, an extraordinarily beautiful woman, with waist-length hair and a devastatingly sexy body.

Irena was in awe of the beautiful black woman, but at the same time she loathed her. She loathed the fact that she and Price were both out of their heads on drugs all the time, and that Ginee was the one who encouraged him to get wasted.

This one particular night they were both completely out of control, and on a twenty-four-hour binge. The third time they summoned Irena to the room, Ginee staggered out of bed wearing nothing at all, waved her inside and locked the bedroom door behind her.

Irena, who was twenty-nine at the time, and quite well versed in the ways of the world, having been a prostitute in Russia for several years, did not think anything of it. However, when Ginee refused to let her out, she began to be concerned. There she was, trapped in a room with her employer and his girlfriend, both naked, laughing, joking and stoned, and she was their prisoner.

'Tell us about Russia,' Ginee said, sprawling on the bed, legs spread. 'You ever get fucked in the good ole mother country? You ever taken it up the ass?'

Price was lying on the bed snorting, smoking, mainlining. He was not really listening to any of this. It was Ginee's idea to torment her.

'I'm sorry?' Irena said, staring at the woman with loathing in her eyes.

'Cut the crap, Irena, we're all girls together,' Ginee said. 'You ever get *laid*? You look like you never get any. You look *real* uptight.'

Price surfaced from his drug haze long enough to say, 'Hey, babe, what's goin' on here? Thought we was gettin' another girl for tonight. You promised me.'

'Irena was supposed t' arrange it,' Ginee slurred, 'but seems she got a soft spot for you herself, Pricey hon. She wants your *fine* black body. An' your fine black ass. Oh, yeah, an' that *fine oversized* black cock.'

Irena backed towards the door, immediately realizing that she couldn't get out because Ginee had taken the key.

'Step outta your clothes, honey,' Ginee instructed. 'An' stop bein' so goddamn uptight. You *know* you're *creamin'* for some action.'

Irena glanced over at Price to see what *he* wanted her to do.

'Yeah, yeah, go ahead,' he mumbled, his eyes glazing over. 'Chill out.'

'Mebbe she needs a drink,' Ginee suggested. 'Loosen up, for Chrissakes, you're not a bad lookin' fox. Take it all off an' chug a little drinkie.'

Irena shook her head, which infuriated Ginee. 'Whassamatta? You too good for us? You come over from freakin' Moscow or wherever, an' now you're too freakin' *good* for us? You wanna work for this guy, you better get with it. Anyway, 's too late to find us another girl. You're it, hon.'

And with that, Ginee pounced, pulling at Irena's clothes like a madwoman.

Irena didn't know whether to fight back or not. She needed to keep her job, losing it was unthinkable. Would it be such a terrible hardship to sleep with Price? Not if Ginee wasn't around.

Ginee had already ripped off her bra and sweater, now she was dragging on her skirt. Irena did nothing to stop her.

Price attempted to sit up. 'Hey, babe, nice tits,' he said, reaching for them. 'Real nice.'

She decided that if she was going to do it, she may as well make it memorable. She reached up, removing the pin that held her hair in a tight bun. It came tumbling down around her shoulders. Long brown wavy hair complementing her thin face and porcelain skin – a complete contrast to Ginee, whose skin had a dark black sheen.

Then she picked up the vodka bottle beside the bed and took a long swig, thinking, *Why not? Why shouldn't I have some fun? It isn't like I haven't done this before.*

Then she was into it. And Ginee was pawing her, hungry hands everywhere, and Price was watching them, cheering the two women on.

As the night continued, she allowed herself to be used by both of them, soon realizing that the thrill of making love to Price was something she'd dreamed about since coming to work for him.

Later, when Ginee and Price fell into a drug-induced sleep, she'd found the key, let herself out, gone back to her room, and hugged herself to sleep, comforting herself because she knew that nobody would remember except her. Tomorrow she'd be just the housekeeper again, someone for Ginee to boss around.

Six weeks later she discovered she was pregnant. She didn't tell anyone because she *wanted* to have his baby. If she had his baby, he'd *have* to take notice of her.

While she waited to give birth, she made up a story, told him she was pregnant by an old boyfriend, and Price allowed her to stay on. 'You wanna have a kid, go ahead,' he said, in spite of Ginee's extremely vocal objections. Ginee kept insisting that he fire her. Price refused.

When she gave birth, the baby was white, which shocked her, because since arriving in America, Price was the only man she'd slept with.

Because of the baby's skin colour, she knew there was no way she could convince Price he was the father, and yet she also knew that, without a doubt, he was.

She had no choice but to keep her silence. If she said anything, nobody would believe her, and Ginee would force him to get rid of her.

Eighteen months later *Ginee* became pregnant, and because of this she managed to nag Price into marrying her. A few months after that Ginee gave birth to Teddy. It took four tumultuous years for Price to decide he'd had enough. He divorced Ginee, which as far as Irena was concerned was a good thing: she was convinced that if Price didn't clean up his excessive drugging and drinking, he'd be finished.

She'd never told anyone the identity of Mila's real father.

Today there were DNA tests that were extremely accurate. If Mila and Price were tested, they'd be able to tell without a doubt whose daughter she was.

But how could she reveal the truth to him now? How could she tell him, when she suspected that Teddy had been sleeping with his own half-sister?

Oh, God, what was she going to do?

For a brief moment she thought about confiding in Price's lawyer, but instinctively she knew Howard Greenspan would be no help.

There must be somebody out there who could advise her. But until she found them, the only thing she could do was keep her silence.

Chapter Sixty-six

BRIGETTE TOSSED and turned in her sleep before waking with a start, her cheeks flushed.

She was experiencing the same old nightmare – the nightmare that had haunted her for years.

Tim Wealth.

Smiling.

Happy.

Saying, 'How ya doin', little girl?'

His dead body lying in his apartment, while Santino Bonnatti stripped off her clothes and did his degrading deeds, abusing her and Bobby.

The gun.

Santino's gun.

Lying on the table.

Santino, molesting Bobby, his filthy face a smirking mask.

It was up to her to stop him . . .

She'd crawled across the bed, reaching the weapon, Bobby's screams of terror spurring her on.

With shaking hands she'd picked up the gun.

Santino's gun.

She'd pointed it at him. Squeezed the trigger.

Santino. Blood splattering everywhere. Surprise and fury spilling from every pore.

She'd pulled the trigger two more times, and he had fallen to the floor without another word.

The memories of that fateful day floated around her brain in vivid technicolour and terrifying detail. Now she had an extension to the nightmare.

Locked in a room.

Carlo and another man coming at her with a syringe.

Days.

Weeks.

Maybe even months.

The pure rush of heaven as the heroin hit her system.

Oh, God! What had happened to her? She was pregnant and desperate to get off heroin. But there was no way she could do it by herself. She needed help.

While they were in America she'd planned on telling Lucky, but Carlo had rushed her out of the country before she'd had a chance. She'd argued with him all the way to the airport to no avail. He'd hustled her on a plane to Europe, far away from anyone who could help her. And when they'd arrived in Rome, he'd taken her straight to his parents' palace outside the city, where they'd moved into a suite of rooms at the back. He'd kept her away from everyone, although occasionally she bumped into his mother, a granite-faced woman who looked upon her with disapproval.

What a cruel and thoughtless son-of-a-bitch Carlo was. He'd raped her, forced a powerful addiction on her, and trapped her into marriage. Now he thought he had her exactly where he wanted her. And maybe he did.

She knew that, for the baby's sake, she had to do something about her three-times-a-day habit.

She remembered the doctor in New York who'd told her he could help her, something about putting her on a methadone programme.

'I have to quit,' she told Carlo. 'I know it'll be tough, but

I must do it for our baby's sake. I need help. I'm not strong enough to do it on my own.'

'I cannot send you to a clinic,' Carlo grumbled. 'People would know, and they would blame me. If this comes out you would be an embarrassment to the entire family.'

'Carlo,' she said, pleading with him, 'you *have* to get me help. How about that doctor in New York? He can put me in a methadone programme like he said. Can we go back to him?'

It occurred to him that if Brigette was *not* hooked on heroin, she might try to leave him. But then he thought, How could she? They were married, she was pregnant. There was no way she could leave him now, so he might as well help her, because who needed a drug addict for a wife? Especially as one day she would be the mother of his child.

'You are right,' he said. 'I will think of a plan.'

She nodded, relieved. She was prepared to go through anything to get straight.

A few days later he told her to pack a small suitcase and be ready to leave in an hour.

'Where are we going?' she asked.

'To get the help you asked for,' he said.

She was flooded with relief, hopeful that they were returning to New York.

Instead he drove her to the family hunting lodge several hours away in the middle of sparsely populated countryside.

It was a large, overgrown place, deserted and unused because the Vitti family did not have the money for its upkeep.

'Where are we?' Brigette asked, when they arrived. 'This doesn't look like a clinic.'

'That's because it isn't,' Carlo said, unloading canned foods and bottled water into the kitchen. 'You will be fine here.'

'Is there a nurse coming? A doctor?'

'Of course,' he said, his face expressionless. 'I have everything arranged.'

'When will they arrive?'

'I have to meet them tomorrow, bring them here myself. This place is too isolated for them to find without me to guide them. There is no other house for thirty miles.'

She looked at him with hope in her eyes, anxious for the well-being of her baby. 'Are you sure this will work?'

'Yes, Brigette. You wanted help, and I am giving it to you.'

'Thank you, Carlo,' she whispered. 'Thank you so very much.'

Chapter Sixty-seven

THE FIRST day of the trial, Steven was up at five thirty a.m. After taking a shower he called Lina in the Caribbean where she was working on a modelling job.

'Hello, you,' she said affectionately, taking the call in her room. 'This is telepathy. I was just about to pick up the phone, only I thought it was too early in LA and you'd be snoring.'

'You know I don't snore,' he said, delighted to hear her quirky voice.

'I've 'eard a peep or two,' she said, laughing.

'What were you going to say to me?'

'Oh, y' know, wish you good luck an' all. An' tell you I'm on a plane out of here and back to LA this afternoon.'

'That's great,' he said. 'Only you *do* know that you can't come to court with me. The publicity on this trial is outrageous. If they even get a sniff that you and I are seeing each other . . .'

'Right,' she agreed. 'I 'aven't told a soul.'

'Somebody showed me one of the tabloids last week,' he said casually, trying not to sound as if he cared. 'You and Charlie Dollar walking around the lake at the Bel Air Hotel smoking grass. How do they get those pictures?'

'Some schmuck lurkin' in the bushes with a telephoto lens,' she said, matter-of-factly. 'Anyway, that was before you. I've got a new motto now.'

'And what would that be?'

'BS. An' I *don't* mean bullshit.' She giggled. 'BS stands for Before Steven. Nothing mattered Before Steven.'

'You're a very impulsive woman.' A beat. 'When are you coming?'

'Now, if I could,' she said with a dirty laugh.

'Don't talk like that, Lina,' he admonished.

'Oh, yeah, right. That's how I *used* to talk BS.' She giggled again. 'You're really a big old handsome prude, aren't you?'

'Enough with the big.'

'You should be flattered. I was referring to your dick!'

'Have you got the key I gave you?' he said, choosing to ignore her ribald comment.

'I wear it around my neck when I sleep. It sort of reminds me of you.'

'She's a romantic too.'

'Aren't *you*?'

'I used to be.' He sighed.

'Do you realize I 'aven't even *looked* at another guy since you an' I got together? It's the first time I'm not into eyeballing other men.'

'That's encouraging.'

''Ow about you?'

'I *never* look at other guys,' he said, mock-serious.

'Glad you 'aven't lost your sense of humour.'

'I'll probably lose it today, sitting there staring at that girl's face. Jesus! I'm going to be facing the person who murdered my wife – shot her for no reason. What kind of monster *is* she?'

'At least they caught her. That's *gotta* make you feel good.'

'Nothing's good about this whole mess, Lina. Except now, when I wake up in the morning, I thank God I found you. You've managed to put a little bit of happiness back in my life.'

''Ave you told Carioca I'm comin' t' stay?' she asked curiously, because above all else she wanted his daughter to like her.

'Yes. She's excited. Thinks you're the best thing since fried chicken.'

'*Oooh*, did I ever tell you I can *make* fried chicken?' Lina said proudly, for she was not known for her culinary skills. 'I was 'anging with this rap star, and 'e was, like, into cooking. So he taught me.'

'I do not care to hear what any other man taught you – okay?'

'Okay,' she said, laughing. 'See you tonight. Keep the bed warm. Oh, and, Steven, don't forget, I'll be thinking of you.'

He hung up with a thoughtful expression. He hadn't intended to embark on an affair so soon after Mary Lou's death, but Lina was something else. She was unique, and once he'd calmed her down, and got her to realize that liking somebody did not mean immediately jumping into bed with them, then they'd been able to take the time to get to know each other.

They'd gone out on three dates before anything had happened. On their second date he'd presented her with an AIDS test certificate, and asked if she'd mind doing the same. 'Bloody 'ell,' she'd commented, all haughty and pissed off. 'Nobody ever asked me t' do *that* before.'

'Which is exactly why I'm asking you,' he'd said. 'I have responsibilities. A wonderful little daughter. Not that I'm casting any doubts, Lina, but you don't exactly come across like a vestal virgin.'

'Ooh,' she'd said, grinning, liking him too much to stay angry. 'What's a vestal virgin?'

She made him smile, which was a good thing. And once

Carioca got used to seeing another woman around the house, she was crazy about her, too. Not that Lina had moved in, she stayed with them when she was in LA. Most of the time she travelled around the world on modelling assignments.

When they'd first got together, he'd reasoned with her exactly the same way he'd reasoned with Mary Lou at the beginning of *their* relationship. 'There's a big age difference,' he'd warned her. 'You live a different kind of lifestyle. I have a young daughter, responsibilities. We're not a good match.'

She'd held his face in her hands and kissed him very, very slowly, her tongue snaking in and out of his mouth. And suddenly none of the differences had mattered.

He reached for the phone and called Lucky. 'Should I pick you up?' he asked.

'No, I'm taking my own car,' she answered, as she finished getting dressed. 'At lunch recess I'm planning to drive over to the production offices. We start principal photography in a few weeks, I need to see what's going on.'

'What will you do when you see Lennie?'

'Don't worry,' she said calmly. 'I'm sure we'll be polite to each other.'

'That's a relief.'

'The thing I'm really pissed about is the way everyone's being dragged through the tabloids,' she said, putting on a pair of silver hoop earrings. 'Jesus, Steven, I've *tried* to live in a very private way, now they're digging up any kind of dirt simply to sell papers. They're vultures.'

'Mary Lou realized that,' Steven said. 'She's an innocent victim, and look at all the trash they're writing about her.'

'Yes, *and* they're dredging up crap about Gino being a former Mafia boss – which is total bullshit. And me shooting Enzio Bonnatti all those years ago. It was self-defence for Chrissakes. What does it have to do with anything?'

'Self-defence?' Steven questioned, his tone quizzical. 'I was there – remember?'

'Hey,' Lucky said indignantly. 'He tried to rape me. He deserved what he got.'

'And it had nothing to do with the fact that he was the man who ordered a hit on your mother, brother and boyfriend?'

'Steven,' she said, her black eyes glittering dangerously as she cradled the phone under her chin, 'Enzio Bonnatti got his. Santangelo justice works its own way.'

'So I found out.'

'Well, you should know, you were the DA at the time. Talk about fate.'

'Right. I'll never forget *that* day.'

'Neither will I, Steven.' She sighed. 'Neither will I.'

Chapter Sixty-eight

FLANKED BY his publicist, bodyguard and lawyer, Price attempted to enter the courthouse. The media, gathered outside, flew into a frenzy. This was *the* story of the moment, and they were out to capture every single detail. Several helicopters hovered overhead as the press rushed Price. 'We have no comment,' Howard said, as the bodyguard pushed a path through the crush.

Teddy had been smuggled into the courtroom earlier. Price had not wanted his son subjected to the glare of the media. As it was, Price had read things about himself that even *he* couldn't begin to believe.

Howard had suggested that Ginee arrive with him. 'No way,' Price had argued. 'I'm not gettin' photographed with that greedy user.'

'It's good for your image,' Howard had said. 'She's a big fat mama. Every fat woman across America will identify with her.'

'Bullshit,' Price had responded. 'Nobody wants to identify themselves with Ginee. They all wanna look like Whitney Houston. I am *not* being photographed with her. Don't even think about it.'

'You have to sit next to her in the courtroom,' Howard had pointed out.

'Fine. I'll do that. Shit! I'm payin' her to be there.'

The criminal defence attorney they'd hired, Mason Dimaggio, was one of the best in Los Angeles. Price was more than satisfied. A large, imposing man with florid features, Mason was a character. He was always a sartorial delight in a three-piece, pinstriped suit, and a large cowboy hat. The suit and the hat made for an incongruous combination, but Mason seemed to know what he was doing, and he had an impeccable reputation. He'd gotten off twin sisters who'd shot their uncle just so they could borrow the uncle's Ferrari for the night. He'd also pleaded the case of a female serial killer, who'd murdered three rich old husbands. Somehow or other, he'd made it look like they'd asked for it, and his client had walked.

'Don't worry about a thing,' Mason had informed Price at their first meeting. 'It'll cost you, but I can assure you your boy will be walking.'

'The sooner this is over and done with, the better,' he'd responded.

'We got the case on an accelerated schedule,' Mason had said with an expansive smile. 'Can't do more than that.'

'What about the girl?'

'Mila Kopistani has a court-appointed lawyer. He takes care of *her*, and *I* take care of Teddy.' A confident smile. 'Now, I ask you, Mr Washington, who do *you* think will come out of this smelling like Madonna on a good day?'

☆ ☆ ☆

Teddy knew he must look like the geek of all time. They had him in some kind of Brooks Brothers button-down white shirt and a dark blue suit. They'd also insisted that he get a real short haircut. And Mason Dimaggio had forced him to wear glasses, giving him the studious, serious image they were obviously going for.

'When you're on that witness stand,' Mason had informed him, in his loud, booming voice, 'you make sure you talk nicely at all times. No jive talk, no slang.' A long meaningful pause. 'And no black talk.'

'What's black talk?' Teddy had asked rudely, not sure if he liked the overbearing, bossy attorney.

'I think you know what I mean,' Mason had answered. 'If you listen to me at all times, you'll walk away, Teddy, and the girl will stay in jail. But you start screwing with what I tell you, boy, and it could be *you* who ends up in jail. Remember, initially their sympathy will be with her.'

'Why's it gonna be with her?' he'd asked. '*She*'s the one who did it.'

'That's what *you* say. And, fortunately, so does Lennie Golden. But it's just you and him against this poor little white girl who'll come into court looking as innocent as apple pie. And never forget – you're black and this is America.'

Teddy, who'd never experienced racism, had no real idea what Mason was getting at. But he was prepared to obey him, because Price had impressed upon him that he was fighting for his life, and therefore he realized the seriousness of the situation.

There were times, though, when he couldn't help wondering what was going through Mila's head. She'd been locked up in jail for a while. Was she frightened like he was? Or was she braving it out in her usual sassy way? He'd been dying to ask Irena how she was doing, but Price had forbidden him to talk to Irena about anything.

'I really shouldn't keep her,' Price had griped, 'but my life would fall apart without her.'

After his one meeting with his mother, Teddy had expected her to call, or at least ask to see him again before they landed up in court. She didn't do either. That one visit was it.

Out of the corner of his eye he saw Price enter the courtroom. He was grateful his father was there, for he knew what an ordeal it must be for him to brave the photographers and news crews milling around outside.

Shortly after Price arrived, Ginee made her own flamboyant entrance. She had ignored Mason and Howard's advice about how she should look, and was all done up in a leopardskin jumpsuit, an outfit that emphasized every one of her overly ample curves. Over it she wore a shaggy red shawl, huge red plastic earrings, and a this-is-my-moment-in-the-sun smile on her overly made-up face.

Teddy heard Mason mutter curses under his breath. Then Mason and Howard huddled in a furious discussion.

Oblivious to the fuss her entrance had caused, Ginee settled in next to Price. 'I was gonna bring my little doggy,' she confided to her uninterested ex-husband, 'only some dunce told me dogs aren't allowed in here. Asshole!'

Price threw her a glare. 'Didn't the lawyers instruct you to dress down?'

'You think I wanna look like some kinda *skank* for all those photographers outside?' she countered. 'This could be a big moment for my career.'

'*What* career?'

'You're not the only one with a goddamn career, Price. After we split I took up singing. An' I have quite a voice.'

'Singing?' he said, choking back his amazement. 'You can't even carry a tune.'

'That's what *you* think,' she replied smugly. 'Truth is, I got a real Diana Ross thing goin', an' plenty of people know it.'

'The whole point of you being here,' Price said, curbing his irritation, 'is to give Teddy a united family image. Right now you look like you wandered in off Hollywood Boulevard.'

'Screw you!' Ginee snapped. 'I'm here, ain't I?'

'You're here 'cause I'm *payin'* you to be here,' he muttered. 'Dress down tomorrow, or don't bother comin'.'

'Screw you!' she repeated.

Price clenched his jaw. Last night he'd heard from his agent that his upcoming movie had been put on hold indefinitely. Fuck the movies! Who needed to be a movie star? He made his living with on-the-edge comedy. There should be plenty of material from this little adventure by the time they were finished.

☆ ☆ ☆

Sitting in the van on the way to the courthouse, Mila was thinking about Maybelline and what they'd agreed.

'Consider this,' Maybelline had said a few days earlier. 'You got one witness *saw* you do it. And then you got Teddy. Now, if that one witness wasn't around, who've you got? Just Teddy. It'll be you against him. White girl, black boy. Who do *you* think'll win?'

'I thought of that,' Mila said. 'When they posted the big reward, I was planning on hiring someone to put a hit on Lennie Golden. My bad luck I left it too late.'

'You should've known me then,' Maybelline said slyly. 'I could've helped out.'

'Yeah, well, now there's no more reward.'

'You got money?' Maybelline asked, sucking on her hair.

'Me? I'm broke.'

'Can you get any?'

'What do you mean?'

'Your mom works for Price Washington. His house is probably full of stuff. He must have a safe filled with jewellery and cash. Y' know black dudes always keep a lotta cash around, it's kind of their thing 'cause they're raised in the ghetto with no money.'

'There *is* plenty of stuff around the house,' Mila said, thinking about it. 'Price has an expensive watch collection and, yeah, there's a safe in his dressing room.'

'Well, then,' Maybelline said. 'So if you were free, you could get your hands on plenty. Y' know, steal his crap an' make a run for it. Hang out in Mexico until everything cools down.'

'Right,' Mila agreed.

'Or, even better, you could draw *me* a map of the house and tell me how to work the alarm. And you could share with me exactly where the safe is.'

'So you could—'

'Have someone break in.'

'What would be in it for me?'

'I've got this great plan,' Maybelline said. 'My brother will whack Lennie Golden for you.'

There was a short silence while Mila digested this information.

'It'd be cool,' Maybelline continued. 'My brother knows what he's doing.' Another pause. 'You into it?'

Mila's mind was spinning. Only Lennie Golden could finger her. Teddy didn't count. She nodded wordlessly, excited and sick all at the same time.

'I'll ask Duke,' Maybelline said, as casually as if she was asking him to stop by the supermarket. 'He'll go down to the courthouse when the trial starts, follow Lennie home an' blow him away. It's that simple.'

'I like it,' Mila said, a chill coursing through her veins. 'Do you think your brother will do it?'

'Why not? He's got nothing else going for him right now. And Duke'll do anything for me. Did I tell you we're twins?'

'No, you didn't tell me that.'

'We think alike, look alike. This'll be a blast.'

And then, because it seemed that Maybelline was the only

person on her side, she told her about the gun with Teddy's prints on it.

'What?' Maybelline said, eyes bugging. 'You've got evidence like that and you haven't told your lawyer?'

'I don't trust him,' Mila said. 'But if Duke can get the gun, and keep it until I'm sure, that'd work for me.'

'Oh, yes,' Maybelline said, deciding that this current scenario could work in their favour. 'He can do that. All you've got to do is tell me where it's hidden . . .'

So Mila had told her. Then she'd drawn a map of the house, pinpointing the alarm system and the safe. She'd also given Maybelline the alarm code.

Now, sitting in the van on her way to court, she wasn't sure if Maybelline wasn't all talk.

Maybe.

Maybe not.

She'd soon see.

Chapter Sixty-nine

BRIGETTE THOUGHT she was going insane. She'd never known a feeling like this in her life. It was as if her entire body had been taken over by a million demons, and every inch of her screamed aloud for relief.

Carlo had left her in the middle of nowhere. A pregnant woman hooked on heroin.

'I'll be back in a few hours with a doctor and a nurse,' he'd promised, the day after they'd arrived at the lodge.

'Why are you leaving me?' she'd asked, nervous about being by herself in the deserted house with no heating or electricity.

'Because, as I told you before, I have to bring them here myself. This place is impossible to find.'

Now it was a week later and she'd gone through a living hell.

At first she'd been calm, not realizing what lay ahead. She'd wandered around the ramshackle house, and after a while she'd curled up on a bed and tried to take a nap.

When she awoke she was horrified to find it was early morning and Carlo had still not returned. She'd immediately panicked, for she had already begun to crave the drugs that saw her through each day.

She felt nauseous – nothing new about that, for it was the

same feeling she experienced every morning before getting her first shot.

Later in the day the pains started to come. Shooting pains that racked her body, followed by excruciating cramps, diarrhoea, sweating and even more nausea.

By the next day she was screaming aloud, even though there was nobody around to hear her.

Weak and faint, her skin crawling, she'd yelled curses at Carlo for failing to return, realizing the bastard had tricked her. There was no doctor or nurse on their way to help her through this. She was on her own.

As each day passed, she'd wanted to die. But because of the baby growing inside her, she'd forced herself to stay sane.

On the fourth day, racked with agonizing cramps, weak and dehydrated, she'd begun to haemorrhage. Hours later she'd lost the baby.

The pain of the miscarriage was indescribable. Dazed and bloodied, she'd lain on the floor, too weak to move, and thought she was dying. In fact, death would've been a welcome relief.

After a long while she'd managed to crawl into the kitchen and grab a bottle of water to take a few sips.

I will live, she vowed. *I will survive*.

And after that she'd slowly started to regain her strength and sanity.

The baby was a boy. She'd buried him under an olive tree in the garden and said a little prayer.

She wondered how many days or weeks Carlo would leave her alone in the lodge. He'd probably checked into it, discovered how long it would take before she was even vaguely normal.

Allowing her to go through this withdrawal by herself was the lowest thing he could have done.

What if she'd died? Would it matter to him?

No. Why should it? He was her legal husband, and as such he'd inherit plenty.

That's when she started thinking that maybe he had no intention of ever coming back.

Then she thought, *No, he's too smart to do that. He might be accused of murder.*

One thing she knew above all else, Carlo was capable of anything. And it was imperative that she get away from him, otherwise her life was over.

Chapter Seventy

LUCKY ARRIVED outside the courthouse to be greeted by a blinding barrage of flashbulbs. To her horror she was becoming the tabloids' favourite. Journalists were digging into her life like maggots feasting on a rotting carcass.

Their latest story was all about her teenage marriage to Craven Richmond, son of Senator Peter Richmond. Since Craven himself was now a senator in Washington, Lucky could just imagine his embarrassment at this revelation. Not to mention hers – Craven was a major jerk.

She had nothing to hide. She'd always lived her life in a very upfront, honest way. Unlike Lennie, who was really pissing her off with the way he was carrying on. It was driving her crazy that he'd set up housekeeping with the Sicilian girl in the Chateau Marmont. She had her spies, she knew exactly what was going on, and it didn't please her.

What was Lennie *thinking*? This was no way to win her back. Claudia had come looking for him. Did that mean he'd had to move in with her?

Was he sleeping with the girl? Lucky couldn't believe he'd be so blatant.

He kept on calling, insisting that he wanted her back.

If he wanted her back so badly, why didn't he get rid of Claudia? He could give her money, and put her on a plane back to Italy where she and the kid belonged.

Then, of course, there was the Sicilian girl's identity to take into consideration. Lucky had found out that she was Donatella Bonnatti's niece, which made her part of the Bonnatti family. Surely Lennie *realized* this? Wasn't that enough to tell him *something*?

Now Lennie had a son who was connected to the Bonnattis. It didn't bear thinking about.

Their own children missed him, they asked about him every day. Lucky had told them he was on location, and that they'd have to get used to the fact that daddy wasn't coming home any time in the near future.

She wanted a divorce. She'd made up her mind. There was no going back, she was too hurt by his behaviour.

Alex was being a real pain. He kept trying to remind her that they'd slept together once. How often did she have to tell him that at the time she'd truly believed Lennie was dead? Plus the fact that she'd been completely drunk and barely remembered the entire episode.

Alex was causing other problems. On the movie he was treating her like someone he could boss around. If this was how he behaved when involved in production, it was no wonder he had such a terrible reputation for being an ogre on the set.

Alex Woods. Troubled genius. Well, he needn't try his little Star Director tricks with her, because she refused to take it.

Casting on *Seduction* was in full swing, and although she hated missing a moment of the action, Steven needed her support in court, and naturally she was there for him.

She also had Brigette on her mind. There was something very troubling about her situation. Why had she and Carlo left LA so abruptly? What was the deal with the way Brigette looked?

After thinking it over, Lucky had contacted her former

bodyguard, Boogie, who now lived on a farm in Oregon, and persuaded him to track down Brigette and find out exactly what was going on. 'It's important, Boog,' she'd said, luring him out of retirement. 'You have to take care of it for me.'

Over the years Boogie had been a friend and confidant and she trusted him implicitly. He'd left for Europe several days ago.

Her handsome brother was waiting when she arrived.

'Hey, babe,' she said, kissing him on the cheek. 'Are we holding up?'

Steven nodded. 'We're holding up.'

Lately she'd noticed a new ease about him, which made her think he might have a woman in his life. It was just a hunch, because he certainly hadn't said a word. 'Don't rush into anything,' she wanted to warn him. 'Take your time.'

But who was she to give lectures on relationships?

☆ ☆ ☆

The deputy DA was a woman, Penelope McKay, early forties, attractive and business-like. Steven liked her, because although she presented a cool, calm exterior he knew her to be a tough one.

She nodded at Steven when he entered the court room. He nodded back. He knew he would not be called as a witness today because the first day of the trial was a settling-in period when both sides presented their opening statements.

He noticed Mary Lou's family sitting together in the middle of the courtroom, her mother, aunt and various cousins. He hadn't brought Carioca with him, because although he knew it was a good move as far as the jury was concerned, it was also bad for Carioca. He didn't want her exposed to the media circus this early on. In fact, he was seriously considering not bringing her at all.

Jury selection had taken place the previous week. There were two sets of jurors, one for Mila and one for Teddy. Steven took a seat near the front, and waited for them to file in so he could check them out. He had an eye for jurors: experience usually told him which way they'd go.

Penelope McKay had informed him that they'd selected an interesting mixed group. Teddy's jury was a perfect balance of six men and six women. Three of the women were black, as were two of the men. There was also an Asian woman and two Hispanic men. The rest of the jurors were white. Mila's jury was mostly women, with only two men included.

Steven was well aware that when it was his time to get on the witness stand he should play to the women. He didn't fool himself: his appeal to the opposite sex had been one of his greatest assets as a successful lawyer. Women always fell for his looks. At first he'd tried not to use it – it had seemed like a cheap ploy – but now, he thought, *what the hell*? Jerry had taught him to go with what he had, and he planned to.

Before the judge arrived, Steven got up and went over to Mary Lou's family, greeting them all. Her mother had tears in her eyes. 'Why?' she said to Steven, desperately clutching a framed photo of Mary Lou on her lap. 'Why?'

It was a question he had asked himself on many a sleepless night.

☆ ☆ ☆

When Mila was brought into the courtroom there was a hush. Everyone wanted to get a look at the girl at the centre of this drama. She was dressed in a plain white blouse, below-the-knee blue skirt and penny loafers. Her hair, recently white blonde, was back to its natural shade of brown. She wore little makeup and no jewellery. Her expression was as demure as she could make it.

Maybelline had given her advice on how to come across. 'I know it's a drag,' she'd said, 'but you gotta play to the stupid jury. Get their sympathy.'

So Mila had followed her advice, although she'd have preferred to tell them all to go fuck themselves. Mila did not care to be judged by anyone.

Her narrow eyes raked the courtroom. Bunch of wankers come to watch.

Willard Hocksmith, her lawyer, touched her arm. His suit smelt of mothballs, he gave her the creeps. 'What?' she snapped, pulling away.

'Put a pleasant expression on your face,' Willard whispered, his bad breath disgusting her.

'Why?' she whispered back. 'They all hate me. I'll never get a fair trial.'

She didn't look at Teddy, even though he was only a few feet away.

Teddy. What a pathetic dork.

Soon she'd finish him off for good.

☆ ☆ ☆

Penelope McKay had attitude and style, all of which impressed Lucky, and she listened carefully as the deputy DA presented the case for the prosecution.

As Penelope spoke, Lucky inspected the jurors. Steven had taught her plenty about reading people's faces, and she was good at it. She imagined being one of them, sitting in their place and listening to the case. Who would have their sympathy? Teddy Washington, rich son of a famous super-star? Mila Kopistani, an ordinary-looking girl of Russian descent, arrogant and pinch-faced?

Or Mary Lou Berkeley, a gorgeous young black actress murdered in her prime, and Lennie Golden, also shot?

Lucky studied the defendants. Teddy, the boy, looked scared shitless. And Mila Kopistani, yes, definitely guilty. Lucky didn't need to sit through the trial to realize *that*. Lennie's word was enough. He'd told her all about the hate in the girl's voice and the way she'd lifted her gun and shot Mary Lou without giving it a second thought.

Lucky did not feel sorry for either of them. Play with guns and you get hurt. This girl had shot Mary Lou in cold blood, and for that she deserved to be locked away for a long, long time.

And if she wasn't . . .

Santangelo justice was not a bad thing.

Chapter Seventy-one

DUKE BROWNING was twenty-five and a psychopath. Baby-faced, of medium height, slim and well dressed in grey pants and a preppie sweater, he sat in a stolen car across the street from Price Washington's house, watching and waiting.

He observed Price's exit early in the morning, thinking to himself that this was one stylish dude. Black guys, when they possessed style, had it going for them. As far as Duke was concerned, black guys had always known how to have a better time than their white brothers. They were better dancers, better dressers and, from what his ladyfriends had told him, certainly better in the sack.

Duke reached in his pocket, removing a small bottle of Binaca spray. He opened his mouth and took a couple of hits. Keeping fresh was important to Duke. He sweetened his breath every hour, and carried a toothbrush, which he always tried to use after meals. First thing every morning he took a shower; if he happened to be home at lunch, he jumped in another time; before going out at night, shower number three; and finally, before bed, one last wash-down.

Cleanliness was next to godliness. Duke Browning knew that only too well.

Shortly after Price left his house, a woman appeared. Obviously the Russian housekeeper: he'd had a description of her from his sister.

Poor Maybelline, stuck in jail awaiting trial. At least she seemed to be making the best of it. *Making connections,* that's what Grandpa Harry had always taught them. *Making connections,* according to Grandpa Harry, was the most important thing a man or a woman could do.

Grandpa Harry had been a highly respected con man, and fortunately he'd done very well at it. He'd taught Duke and his sister a thing or two when they were growing up. Oh, yes, Duke and Maybelline had had quite an education.

Their parents had been killed in a car crash when they were eight. A somewhat eccentric couple, they'd named *him* after the famous jazz musician Duke Ellington, and Maybelline after a makeup company. She wasn't thrilled with her name. He loved his.

After the demise of their parents, they'd been sent to live with Grandpa Harry, the only sour note being Harry's second wife, step-grandma Renee, a bitch on roller skates with an insatiable appetite for money. Maybelline loathed Renee, and Renee loathed her back.

Since Harry's unfortunate death – he'd died choking on a piece of undercooked liver – they'd all lived together in a rambling Hollywood Hills house, left to the three of them by Harry.

Not any more. Maybelline had ruined that cushy set-up with her vicious, unpredictable moods. One day he'd have to teach her how to control that nasty little temper. It got her into more trouble . . .

Duke was sad that his sister was languishing in jail. He missed her. They'd done everything together. Of course, if Maybelline had exhibited more sense she would've waited for *him* before stabbing Renee with the stupid bread-knife. What a *dumb* thing to do. What was she *thinking*?

If he'd been there – instead of doing time in Florida for a series of rapes – he would have come up with a far better way to get rid of Renee. And he certainly wouldn't've gotten caught.

He waited five minutes after the Russian woman's departure before alighting from the car and slowly crossing the street. Then he strolled casually up to the front door and rang the bell.

Consuella answered. Consuella was Hispanic and pretty with a round ass and big belly.

'Good morning,' Duke said politely, flashing a phoney identification card. 'I'm from the DA's office. I've been sent to collect some items from Teddy Washington's room. Is it all right if I come in? Or would you prefer me to return later?'

Consuella regarded the well-dressed, nice-looking man and decided it was perfectly okay to let him in. After all, if he was from the DA's office, what could be wrong about it?

'Come in, please,' she said, holding open the front door.

And Duke entered the house. An invited guest.

Chapter Seventy-two

LUCKY SPENT the entire morning in court. As soon as they called lunch recess, she hurried off to join the group at Alex's production office.

When she arrived, his Asian assistant, Lili, stopped her outside the conference room. 'They've already seen seventeen actors this morning,' Lili confided, 'every one of them quite gorgeous. Right now they have a young TV actor in there.'

'Has Alex liked any of them?' Lucky asked.

'No,' Lili replied. 'However, Venus is perfectly happy. At the last moment she decided to come in and read with all of them.'

'Hmm . . . I wonder how Cooper will feel about *that*,' Lucky said, thinking of Venus's movie star husband, who had a definite jealous streak.

'Not too happy,' Lili said, with an enigmatic smile.

Lucky snuck into the conference room and took a seat next to Mary, the casting director, with whom Alex had worked on five movies and whom he trusted implicitly. Venus was reading through a scene with a young, good-looking actor.

Alex glanced up. 'Everything okay?' he mouthed.

She nodded.

When the TV actor had done his stuff, and everyone had

told him how excellent he was, and Mary had said that they'd contact his agent, Alex stood up and announced, 'Time for a break. I've got actor phobia. They're all too goddamn eager.'

'Interesting morning?' Lucky asked.

'You missed it,' he said, giving her a quick kiss on the cheek.

'Oh, boy, did you miss it!' Venus said, joining in. 'There sure are some hot and horny guys in this town. I can't wait to get home and tell Cooper how old and decrepit he is!'

'That'll be good for your marriage,' Lucky remarked drily, groping in her purse for a cigarette.

'It'll do him good to know about all the studly competition floating about.'

'Competition? Or great butts?'

Alex shook his head. 'You girls! Is this the way you talk about guys?'

'Yes, when we're being *clean*,' Venus said, fluffing out her platinum hair.

'Was there anyone *really* exciting?' Lucky asked.

'A couple of possibles,' Alex said. 'Nobody special. How about you, Venus? See anything big in the talent department?'

'I thought that Jack Something guy was kind of great. He had intense eyes and great shoulders.'

'Too old,' Alex said, dismissing him instantly.

'Oh, right,' Venus responded sarcastically. 'He must've been all of twenty-five, *definitely* too old.'

'Hey, c'mon, you know what I mean. The character in the script is twenty. Kind of a young Richard Gere.'

Sylvia put in her two cents. 'I liked the second actor we saw today,' she said. 'He had a lot of sexual energy.'

'Bad skin,' Venus said. 'I saw a guy on TV the other night. He had a small role in one of those sitcoms but, boy, he really buzzed the screen.'

'So tell Mary, and she'll get him in,' Alex said.

'Dunno his name,' Venus said vaguely.

'Find out what show it was and when it aired. Mary'll do the rest. All it takes is a little detective work.' A beat. 'Now, can I take you ladies to lunch?'

'Oh, wow, Alex, you're getting so formal,' Venus said, teasing him. 'Lucky shows up and all of a sudden you turn into Mr Nice.'

'Something wrong with that?' he said, putting his arm around Lucky's shoulders. 'How was it?' he asked.

'Pretty harrowing,' she said. 'I didn't see Lennie. They're keeping him outside because he's their key witness. Steven was there, of course. And all of Mary Lou's family.' She took a long drag on her cigarette. 'You know what really blew my mind?'

'What?'

'Watching that girl. Her name's Mila Kopistani. She's a bad one.'

'Nothing wrong with bad girls,' Alex said, being flippant.

'Don't even joke about it,' Lucky snapped, her eyes flashing. 'You know exactly what I mean.'

The three of them went to lunch at Alex's favourite Chinese restaurant around the corner. He invited Sylvia to join them, but she informed him she was meeting her girlfriend.

'Don't you think it looks a little odd, your production associate being a dyke?' he mentioned to Venus as they settled into a corner booth.

'You know, Alex,' Venus said, dazzling the hovering proprietor with her famous smile, 'for someone so hip, you really are an old-fashioned guy.'

'People might think you're gay,' he said, ordering three large bottles of Evian for the table.

'Why would they think that?'

'Well, if *I* had a fag by my side at all times—'

'You probably have and you don't even know it,' Venus said. 'And I might remind you that *fag* is not a politically correct term.'

'I can see you two are getting along great,' Lucky interrupted. 'What am I? The outsider.'

'No, as a matter of fact,' Alex said. 'Venus and I have discussed it.'

'Discussed what?'

'We want to do an intervention.'

'Excuse me?' she said, frowning.

'An intervention,' Alex repeated, wondering why he'd allowed Venus to talk him into this.

'I hate to tell you guys this, but I hardly ever drink,' Lucky said, thinking they'd both gone a little bit crazy.

'It's not *about* your drinking,' Venus said, leaning across the table. 'It's about your marital status.'

'My marital status is nobody's business but mine,' Lucky said irritably.

Alex summoned a waiter and quickly ordered an obscene amount of food.

'Don't we get a choice?' Lucky asked.

'I know what's good here,' he said.

'So you're saying our tastes don't count?'

'What do you want that I haven't ordered?'

'Seaweed.'

'Seaweed?'

'Yes.'

'The lady wants an order of seaweed,' he said to the waiter, who added it to the order pad and departed. Alex turned back to Lucky. 'Venus knows how I feel about you,' he said. 'She's your best friend, so I'm sure there're no secrets between you. In fact, you probably even told her about that one crazy night.'

'*What* one crazy night?' Venus asked, jumping in.

'He doesn't know what he's talking about,' Lucky said, throwing him an angry shut-the-fuck-up look.

'Anyway, here's the thing,' Alex continued. 'Venus and I have been talking and, for your own peace of mind, we've decided that you've got to give Lennie another chance.'

She couldn't believe these words were coming out of *Alex*'s mouth. 'Excuse me?' she said.

'Yes,' Venus said, joining in. 'You and Lennie are fantastic together. Everyone knows it.'

'The jerk made a mistake,' Alex said. 'Which is understandable, because the poor bastard was trapped in a fucking cave for three months with no chance of escape, and along came this girl who gave him an opportunity to get out.'

'He was lonely and frightened,' Venus continued, 'so he went for it. He's destroyed, Lucky. All he wants is a chance to get you back.'

'If he wants me back so much, how come he's living in a hotel with that – that woman?'

'He's there because of his kid,' Alex said. 'People make mistakes. How did he know she'd get knocked up? The kid is deaf or something, Lennie's trying to help.'

'He's renting a house for them to live in,' Venus added. 'He spoke to Cooper the other night and told him. He certainly doesn't want to live with them himself.'

'Then why is he?'

'They're in a huge suite at the Chateau Marmont, separate bedrooms.'

'It's not that I'm jealous of her,' Lucky explained, feeling like a fool, because maybe if she was honest with herself she'd admit that she *was* jealous. 'I mean, look at her, she's just some kind of peasant girl.'

'Now, now,' Venus admonished, 'don't get bitchy. It doesn't suit you.'

'Yeah,' Alex said. 'You're usually so supportive of women, it's not like you to put them down.'

'I guess I'm upset.' Lucky sighed. 'You know, her being Bonnatti's niece and all.'

'She's not *really* Bonnatti's niece,' Venus said.

'Think about it,' Alex said. 'Donatella was married to Santino, so Claudia's only his niece by marriage. It's not as if she has Bonnatti blood running through her veins.'

'She got him out of that cave,' Venus said. 'If she hadn't, you'd probably never have seen him again.'

'And y' know, Lucky,' Alex said, 'I'm the *last* person who wants to see you back with Lennie, but you gotta give the guy a break. If you don't, you could spend the rest of your life regretting it. And that I do *not* want to see.'

'I don't know . . .' she said unsurely.

'Go back to him, Lucky, before it's too late,' Venus urged.

'Yes,' Alex said. 'Take him back, and although it pains me to say so, it could be the right thing for you to do.'

Chapter Seventy-three

PERHAPS THE first day in court was the worst. Teddy didn't know. All he knew was that every eye was on him. It was quite unnerving. He saw his dad sitting near the front, and his mom next to him. He noticed people, probably journalists, scribbling in notebooks, and a handsome man whom he recognized from the pictures in the newspapers as Mary Lou's husband.

'Try to sit very still,' Mason whispered in his ear. 'And don't make eye contact with any of the jurors. It's too early to try to win them over.'

So he sat and listened as both sides presented their opening statements, listened to Mason Dimaggio talk about him as if he wasn't even there. Occasionally he glanced over at Mila. She refused to acknowledge his presence, her expression blank as she stared straight ahead.

Late in the afternoon, when he was allowed to leave, there was no escaping the media onslaught. The TV news cameras and reporters made a frantic dash in his direction, yelling his name, thrusting microphones under his nose. Fortunately the judge had refused to allow TV cameras in the courtroom, so it was only outside that he was set upon.

His father had slipped out a few minutes earlier. 'It'll be less of a party that way,' Price had said.

Yeah, sure, Teddy had thought. *Like the press is going to ignore Mr Major Star.*

Ginee was hanging around outside, waiting for him to emerge. As soon as she saw him, she grabbed his arm and clung to it, urging him to pose for pictures with her.

'No,' Howard said brusquely. He and Mason had discussed it earlier, and they'd decided that in view of Ginee's unsuitable appearance, they should keep Teddy well away from her. She was not the comforting mother figure they'd envisioned.

'Dad said I mustn't pose for pictures,' Teddy mumbled, shaking his head.

'Oh, *c'mon*,' Ginee crowed, basking in the limelight. 'I'm your *mommy*, for Chrissakes. C'mere an' cuddle up for a photo op. It'll make all the front pages.'

Teddy backed away. The press, sensing dissension, began to yell. 'C'mon, Teddy, let's have a picture with your mom. Teddy! Teddy! This way, this way. Smile! Wave! *Do* something.'

Howard hustled him through the rabid throng, leaving Ginee to pose all by herself.

She was happy. She was a woman *finally* getting what she wanted after all these years of being shoved in the background.

Eat your heart out, Price Washington. I'm a star, too.

And she beamed for the cameras.

☆ ☆ ☆

While Ginee posed, Irena sidled quietly from the court, unnoticed. She'd slipped out of the house directly after Price, leaving Consuella in charge. She and Price had not discussed the case, it was such an awkward situation, and at this point in the proceedings it was probably just as well not to get into it.

When she'd entered the courtroom she'd made sure Price had not seen her sitting at the back. Even if he spotted her, there was no way she was going to miss being there, she was just as entitled as anyone else to watch what happened.

Mila had not noticed her either, so all day long she'd sat there, staring at her and Price's daughter, thinking to herself that maybe she was mistaken, because there was nothing to remind anyone of Price in Mila's looks. In fact, she was the image of Irena at the same age.

The truth was, it didn't matter who Mila looked like, she *was* Price Washington's daughter. That was a fact.

As Irena left the courtroom she was more confused than ever because apparently Mila had been saying such terrible things – accusing Teddy of plying her with drugs and raping her. If it came out that she was his half-sister, the scandal would be too much for anyone to bear. It would also cast Irena into the spotlight, which she feared because of her nefarious past.

Besides, she could never do it to Price.

She could never ruin his career.

Because if she revealed the truth – the scandal surely would.

☆ ☆ ☆

Steven needed a drink. On the way home he had a strong desire to stop at a bar, but he knew that if he did one drink would not be enough.

Being in court all day had left him numb. Listening to the two sides present their opening statements had completely stunned him. He'd known what had happened to Mary Lou, but hearing it in so many words was beyond his comprehension. And the Russian girl sitting there, her pointed face blank and expressionless. No remorse there.

He'd wanted to stand up, go over and beat her senseless. She'd taken away the love of his life, and he hated her for it. He, who'd always been so liberal, wanted to see her die for what she'd done.

God, what was happening to him? He drove home filled with a mix of emotions.

It wasn't until he got into the house and Carioca ran to greet him, throwing herself into his arms, that he started to feel even slightly normal.

'Hey, cutie,' he said, hugging her close.

'How was it today, Daddy?' Carioca asked, all big eyes and sticky hands, for she was in the middle of eating a peanut butter and jelly sandwich.

'Not much fun,' Steven said, glancing over at his English au pair, Jennifer. She was a bright girl, and nice too. He was fortunate that she'd been there for him and Carioca all the way.

'You know, Jen, I've got an idea,' he said.

'Yes, Mr Berkeley?'

'How about you take Carioca to London for a few weeks? You know, just while the case is going on.'

'Sounds like a brilliant idea to me,' Jennifer said cheerfully. 'Carioca will love London. We can stay with my parents in St John's Wood. When would you like us to go?'

'As soon as possible,' he said, grateful that Jennifer was so together.

'Super! I'll organize it.'

'Hey, cutie,' he said to his daughter, 'what d'*you* think?'

'Do I get to ride on a plane?' Carioca asked excitedly.

'You certainly do.'

'Then I wanna do it, Daddy. It'll be *cool*!'

When Carioca went off to bed, Steven wandered into the den, put on the television, and fell asleep in his favourite leather chair. The next thing he knew, Lina was standing behind him with her hands over his eyes.

'Surprise, surprise,' she said. 'It's your trusty FedEx lady delivering a package from the Bahamas.'

'Oh, baby,' he said, pulling her around the chair and on to his lap. 'You're a sight for very tired old eyes.'

'Was it tough today?' she asked, settling on his knee and cuddling up.

'It was.'

'Wish I could've been there with you.'

'I know.'

'Listen to *this*,' she said. 'I've cancelled all my gigs for the next two weeks. This girl ain't goin' nowhere!'

'You can't do that because of me.'

'Already done,' she said firmly. 'I want you to 'ave someone t' come 'ome to.'

He couldn't believe how sweet she was. To look at her, most people would imagine she ate guys up and spat 'em out. Maybe she did that to other men. To him she was an angel. A very sexy angel who'd come along to help him through this painful ordeal.

'How did the shoot go?' he asked.

'Same old boring thongs.'

He summoned a smile. '*You* might find them boring.'

'Can you imagine if your mate from New York, Jerry whatsisname, was there?' she said, with a ribald laugh. ''E'd 'ave bin drooling from 'ere to Sin City.'

'You got *his* number.'

'You eaten anything?' she asked, climbing off his knee.

'I'm not hungry.'

'*I* am,' she said forcefully. 'They served *the* most disgusting 'amburger on the plane. I refused to 'ave anythin' t' do with it.'

'Not a Fatburger, huh?'

''Ow about we go out somewhere cosy an' grab a bite?' she suggested.

'This is LA, Lina,' he said, standing up and stretching. 'There's nowhere cosy. Besides, you'll be spotted everywhere we go.'

'Then let's send out,' she said. 'I'm 'appy to stay right 'ere.'

'I don't want to turn you into a hermit.'

'We can stay 'ome as much as you want until this is over. That 'ardly makes us 'ermits.'

'You're very sweet.'

'Ooooh.' She giggled. 'Never been called sweet before.'

'There's always a first with you, isn't there?'

'Yup. An' you're my first soul brother. An' you know what, Steven?'

'What?'

'I like it.'

'So do I, sweetheart, so do I.'

Somehow Lina always managed to make him a little less sad.

Chapter Seventy-four

BY THE time Lennie left the courtroom to go home, he had the headache from hell. Being in a small, stuffy room all day, not knowing what was going on, except for occasional reports from Brett, the other deputy DA who was working the case with Penelope McKay, did not make for a pleasant day.

He felt totally out of it and alone, especially as he knew Lucky was in there somewhere. He hadn't seen her in weeks, and the truth was that he needed her. She might be gone from his life for now, but he was determined that it was only on a temporary basis. There had to be some way of winning her back. Only how?

Flowers didn't work with Lucky. She wasn't into roses and heartfelt speeches, so how could he prove to her that he loved her above all else? How could he make it up to her?

He'd sat in the little room for hours, developing a major headache, trying to work things out.

Shortly before he left, he'd called the hotel and spoken to Claudia. 'What's going on?'

'A lady phoned,' she'd said. 'I am to tell you she's found the perfect house.'

'Good. Call her back, say I'll go see it tonight.'

He wondered how Claudia would manage without him once he had settled them in a house. He'd been thinking about *buying* her the house as opposed to renting: it was the least he could do under the circumstances.

Yes. He'd buy them a house, find her a job – if that's what she wanted – and hopefully get the kid some help with his hearing difficulties. What more could she expect from him?

There was no way he could abandon them. He'd ruined her life, and she'd *saved* his. Why couldn't Lucky understand that?

'Do you think I'll be called tomorrow?' he asked Brett before leaving.

'No,' the young man said. 'It'll take a few days. There's a huge amount of interest in this case, so both sides will take their time. You're our star witness. We're saving you.'

'How are the lawyers on the other side?'

'Naturally Teddy Washington has the *crème de la crème*, Mason Dimaggio. And the girl, Mila, she's stuck with an ambulance-chaser.'

'Is that good or bad?'

'The good news is that they're up against each other. The bad news is that it could work against us.'

'How come?'

'We might end up with one of the juries being split.'

'What do *you* think?'

'It's a tough call. Mary Lou was a public figure with a clean reputation. You're famous. In my experience, celebrities usually come out on top. Unless you're Kim Basinger and the opposing lawyer gets the jury to turn against you. I think we're in pretty good shape.'

Lennie was able to leave before the session was over. He'd parked several blocks away on purpose, so he ducked out of a back entrance and strode down the street, managing to avoid the crowds of media people milling around out front.

His mind was buzzing. If he could only put this case behind him, he could concentrate on getting Lucky back.

☆ ☆ ☆

The press might have missed Lennie Golden's exit through the back, but Duke Browning didn't. He'd known exactly where Lennie would emerge. Duke had a knack for getting inside people's heads and figuring out what they'd do. Lennie Golden would leave by the back entrance, and he would leave early. That was a fact.

Duke had spent a most enjoyable day, even finding time for a midday shower – not in his own home, but sometimes one had to make do with what was available.

He was in a different car from the one he'd stolen that morning. Now, instead of a 1990 Ford, he was in a '92 green Chevy. He pressed a cassette into the tape deck to see what kind of musical taste his latest victim had. Joe Cocker. Duke was not pleased, his preference was classical.

He sat in the car allowing Lennie to get ahead of him as he walked along the street. Duke idled the engine, barely keeping up.

When Lennie finally reached his car, Duke pulled the Chevy into the kerb, stopped the car and emptied the centre ashtray out on to the road. If there was one thing he could not abide, it was the smell of stale smoke.

As soon as Lennie set off, Duke slid into the traffic behind him, humming softly to himself. The sound of his own voice pleased him far more than the annoying rasp of Joe Cocker.

This was an interesting assignment. Maybelline had come up trumps – she knew how he liked his juices tickled. And this morning he'd had more than his juices tickled.

He would never forget the look on the maid's face when he'd turned on her. She was so trusting, so secure that he was a good person simply because he'd flashed some phoney ID that she'd hardly bothered looking at.

Why were these women so dumb? They deserved everything they got for not having plain common sense. They should all learn from his sister.

Nobody was more street smart than Maybelline. Which made it so irritating that she'd got herself caught. And not only caught, she hadn't even finished the job. Step-grandma Renee was alive and well and living in *their* house.

He would have to take care of it himself at a later date. Now was not the time because it wouldn't do to draw suspicion, considering he'd only recently been released from a Florida jail.

Yes, he mused. *A little time, a good alibi, and then he could go in and finish Renee off.*

A truck slid between his car and Lennie's, annoying him. He honked his horn. The truck driver gave him the finger.

Ah! If only he had more time, the man behind the wheel would regret that little move. Duke did not appreciate rude gestures. Too bad that he had other things on his mind.

He was considering whether he should hit Lennie Golden now, or wait until he got out of his car. An interesting choice.

Or maybe he wouldn't even do it today, because sometimes watching and waiting was the most fun of all.

Prolonged foreplay.

Prolonged foreplay to . . . murder.

Chapter Seventy-five

PRICE COULDN'T find his key so he rang the doorbell, expecting Irena to answer immediately. She didn't, which annoyed him.

He had to do something about Irena. Keeping her on as his housekeeper was a big problem, considering that his son was in court accused of being an accessory to a murder, with Mila right next to him, pointing an accusing finger in the boy's direction.

The fact that Irena was still living in his house wasn't right. 'You've got to fire her,' Howard had told him repeatedly.

'You don't get it,' Price had answered. 'She organizes everything I do.'

'So you'll get somebody else to iron your shirts,' Howard had said sarcastically. 'It's imperative you fire her, Price. If the press finds out . . .'

'Yeah, yeah, I will,' he'd promised.

But deep down he had no intention of doing so. Irena was part of his life, he couldn't manage without her. Over the years she'd done so much for him, including helping him to conquer a fierce drug addiction, then keeping him more or less straight. The truth was that he owed her.

He rang the doorbell again, waiting impatiently for a response. Nobody came.

Goddamn Irena! The press could be here any minute, and he wanted to get safely inside before they arrived. He rang a third time. Still no answer. He searched his pockets, finally coming up with the elusive key. He let himself in quickly.

The first thing he noticed as he entered the house was a strange smell – kind of a musky, pungent odour.

'Irena!' he called out. 'Where the hell are you?'

Throwing off his jacket, he started upstairs. Things were turning to shit. He had a son being tried for murder, an ex-wife who was the joke of the century, and his career was going to pot. Plus he had no time to work on new material, and his movie had been put on hold. Fuck! What else could go wrong?

What was it with kids today? Didn't they have any con-science? He'd raised Teddy so carefully, giving him all the guidance he'd never had himself. And even if Teddy *hadn't* pulled the trigger, he'd been there, watching, while that little Russian witch had blown Mary Lou Berkeley away. And Teddy, the dumb shit, hadn't done a thing to stop her.

Price shook his head. Right now he needed some pleasure. He needed to get high.

One joint. Was that such a terrible thing? One joint and a woman.

Hey – not a bad idea. One joint, one woman, and a good steak dinner. He'd take the fortunate lady to Dan Tana's.

Yes. That's exactly what he needed. One long night of mindless sex.

Naturally Krissie came to mind. He hadn't spoken to her since he'd dumped her at Venus's party, but she was the sort of woman who was always available to a star. And he wouldn't mind burying his head in those huge silicone boobs and forgetting about everything.

He walked into his bedroom and was startled to see that his bed was unmade. Then he heard the sound of running water coming from the bathroom. It sounded like someone was in there taking a shower.

'Irena!' he called out again. 'You there?'

No answer.

The smell he'd detected in the hall was even stronger now, a weird mix of scents.

God! he thought. *Don't tell me a fan has broken in and is taking a shower in my bathroom.* Stranger things had happened.

Tentatively he entered his bathroom. The shower was indeed running, but the cubicle was empty, the etched-glass door swinging open, water starting to spill out on to the marble floor.

Every bottle of aftershave he possessed was open and lying around the black porcelain sink, the contents splashed all over the room. And sitting in the middle of the bathroom floor, tied to a stool, was Consuella – her mouth taped, hands and ankles bound to the chair. She was naked.

He stared at her.

She stared back at him, a hysterical whimper emerging from the back of her throat.

'Jesus!' he yelled. 'What the *fuck* . . .'

Then he called 911.

☆ ☆ ☆

Lucky was confused, she, who was usually so together. Lunch with Alex and Venus had thrown her. She wasn't an idiot, she was well aware how Alex felt about her, and even though he was still with Pia, she knew he'd drop his girlfriend in a minute if she gave him any encouragement at all. So the fact that even *Alex* was trying to persuade her to take Lennie back made her think about it very carefully.

On her way home she called Gino from the car. 'How'ya doin', old man?' she asked.

'Who the fuck you callin' old man?' he grumbled, feisty as ever.

'The kids are coming to stay with you again this weekend,' she informed him. 'I'm starting to think they're spending more time with you than with me.'

'And *I'm* startin' to think you should let 'em see their father,' he responded gruffly.

Why was everyone ganging up on her at the same time?

'Has Lennie been phoning you?' she asked suspiciously.

'You gotta let him see the kids, Lucky,' Gino said. 'It ain't fair.'

'Why?' she demanded, more than a little irritated.

''Cause if you don't, he'll get a fuckin' lawyer to make *sure* he does. Tell him he can drive to Palm Springs this weekend.'

'You mean you'd have Lennie stay at the house?' she said furiously. 'Maybe he should bring the Bonnatti girl? Would you like that too?'

'Don't get cunty with me, kiddo. He can come an' stay, an' if he wants he can bring the other kid.'

'Fuck you, Gino!' she yelled, and slammed down the phone, almost rear-ending a truck.

What was going on here? Didn't anyone *get* it? Didn't anyone understand how Lennie had betrayed her?

She was mad as hell. Yet . . . she knew she wasn't being fair to little Gino and Maria. They *should* see their father, she had no right to deprive them of that.

Feeling guilty, she called Gino back. 'Okay,' she said guardedly. 'If you want to see him so much, *you* call him. He's shacked up at the Chateau Marmont with the Sicilian. Invite him down, I don't care. But you'd better not invite her.'

'Calm down,' Gino said. 'It don't suit you to be hysterical.'

'And it doesn't suit *you* to be on his side,' she retorted sharply. 'And, for the record – I am *not* hysterical.'

'Hey, what's right is right.'

'I hear you, Gino. And if you think what Lennie did was right, then your opinion is *crap*!'

'Well, anyway, kid,' he said, ignoring her outburst, 'I'm lookin' forward to seeing the little ones. An' since it's okay with you, I'll give Lennie a buzz.'

'I repeat. As long as he doesn't drag along that – that woman.'

'Okay, okay, I got the message. Is it all right with you if he brings the kid?'

'Why not?' she drawled sarcastically. 'You can all have a nice time with the little Bonnatti brat. I'm sure it'll be wonderful.'

She slammed down the phone again, immediately regretting she'd told Gino it was okay. How could she allow little Gino and Maria to meet Leonardo, or whatever the stupid boy's name was? They might even *like* him. This was impossible.

She imagined the situation in reverse. What if *she*'d got pregnant after her one night with Alex? What if *she*'d said to Lennie, 'Oh, here's a little Alex Woods junior for you.' Would he have accepted *that*? No freaking way! He didn't like Alex as it was.

Ha! He *should* like Alex. Alex was the one trying to persuade her to take him back.

God, she was so furious! And, on top of everything else, she'd had to sit in court all day listening to the lawyers' opening statements, and watching the girl with the thin pointed face and the black boy with his rich fat-cat white

Beverly Hills lawyers, who were so sure they were going to get him off just because his daddy was a famous person.

If it was up to her, she would've hauled Mila Kopistani and Teddy Washington outside, and given them both a taste of what they'd given Mary Lou.

She called her service. There were several messages, the most important one from Boogie in Rome. She had no desire to hear more bad news but, then again, she needed to know what was going on with Brigette.

She called him back, even though it was three in the morning in Italy.

'Hey,' Boogie answered, sounding alert. 'Knew it was you.'

'How did you know that?'

'Other people are thoughtful, Lucky. They'd wait until six at least.'

'Don't criticize me, Boog.' She sighed. 'I've had it with criticism today. What have you found out?'

'It's not good, not bad.'

'Tell me.'

'Carlo flew back here with Brigette and took her to live at the family home – some kind of rundown palace just outside Rome. They holed up there for a while, and when I went looking for them, Carlo's mother, who barely speaks English, informed me they'd gone.'

'Gone where?'

'That's what I'm trying to find out.'

'I'm worried about her, Boog. You didn't see her when she was here, it wasn't our Brigette.'

'I've made a solid connection so hang in there. You'll hear from me as soon as I have something.'

'I'd get on the next plane if I could, but I'm in court every day and my movie starts shooting in four weeks.'

'If I need you, I'll call.'

'Yes, and if it's an emergency I can be there immediately.'

'I'll be in touch.'

At least Boogie knew what he was doing. Lucky felt confident that if anything was going on with Brigette, *he* would find out. She drove home with a lighter heart.

☆ ☆ ☆

'How do you feel it went today?' Howard asked, driving his maroon Bentley along Wilshire.

Sitting next to Howard in his fancy car, Teddy wondered how Price's stuffy lawyer had become his new guardian. Why couldn't he come and go with his dad every day? What was so terrible about that? ''S all right,' he said carefully, although it wasn't all right at all. He'd had a terrible day, listening to the attorneys present their case, painting him as some drunken jerk who'd aided and abetted Mila on her bloodthirsty mission.

'You like Mason, huh? He's a good man?'

He's white. You're white, Teddy thought. *What's not to like?* Both of them were working for his dad. Both of them were highly overpaid. This whole deal must be costing Price a shitload of money.

'Yes,' he lied, although the truth was he considered Mason Dimaggio to be a bossy asshole. What was with the ridiculous suits and hats he wore? And why were they forcing *him*, Teddy Washington, to look like such a geek?

'Your mother's something else,' Howard remarked, a derogatory sneer on his smug, pampered face.

'She used t' be beautiful,' Teddy said defensively.

'Price showed me the wedding pictures the other day,' Howard said, checking out his appearance in the rear-view mirror. 'She was a beauty, all right. Shocking how people let themselves go.'

'Do I havta drive to court with you every day?' Teddy asked, fiddling with the radio control.

'It's the way your father wants it,' Howard replied, swatting Teddy's hand away.

Sure, Teddy thought. *It's what my dad's paying for. That's the only reason you're doin' it.*

As they proceeded down Wilshire, two police cars raced up behind them. Howard drew into the kerb, allowing the two cars to scream their way past. 'This will not be a pleasant experience for the next few weeks, Teddy, but you'll come through it,' he remarked. 'All the wiser I hope.'

' 'S'pose so,' Teddy mumbled, staring out the window at a girl on a bicycle wearing red shorts and a tight tank. She reminded him of Mila.

'Remember to be yourself,' Howard lectured. 'You're a nice boy, not a wild kid. You were led astray. That's our case and we're sticking with it. But you have to back us up. Your demeanour in that courtroom means everything.'

Teddy shifted in his seat. Driving to and from court every day with Howard Greenspan was going to be torture. Fortunately, they were almost home.

As they neared the house, Teddy noticed the two police cars that had roared past them a few minutes ago were now parked outside. 'Why're *they* here?' he asked.

Howard slowed his Bentley, took a look out the window and groaned. 'It's probably something to do with the press,' he said shortly. 'I've *told* Price to control his temper. Let's hope he hasn't hit anybody.'

'Why'd he do that?'

'Because your dad is angry about all the publicity,' Howard said, pulling up behind the second police car. 'He's angry and frustrated. Have you any idea what this is doing to him?'

What about me? Teddy thought. *I'm the one sitting in that courtroom getting accused of all kinds of shit.*

They got out of the gleaming Bentley. Howard locked it and hurried over to a uniformed cop standing outside the house. 'I'm Mr Washington's lawyer,' he said officiously. 'What's happening here?'

The cop shrugged. 'You'd better go inside,' he said.

'Was Mr Washington involved in a fight?'

'There's been a robbery,' the cop said. 'And a rape.'

'Christ!' Howard exclaimed heatedly. 'More bad publicity! This is *all* we need.'

Chapter Seventy-six

THE REALTOR was a petite bottle blonde clad in an expensive Escada suit, diamond-stud earrings, and extremely high heels. In her fifties, she had a permanent smile and an overly friendly manner.

'Mr Golden,' she gushed, as he got out of his car, 'or can I call you Lennie?'

'Sure,' he said, walking up to the front door of the house she was about to show him.

'This is a *most* delightful house,' she said, inserting a key and letting them in. 'It's up for rent, but the owner has said that because it's you he might be prepared to sell, furnishings and all. The house was once rented by Raquel Welch. And last year a very famous young television star lived here for several months.' The woman lowered her voice. 'She insists we protect her privacy, so I'm not allowed to reveal her name.'

Big deal, Lennie thought, checking out the spacious front hallway.

'*Do* look around,' the realtor continued. 'I think you'll find this is an excellent house for you, with the added advantage of a panoramic view of the city. And, of course, all the rooms offer a terrific flow for entertaining.'

He followed her around the one-storey house located high up on Loma Vista. It had three bedrooms, all with bathrooms *en suite*, three entertainment rooms, a large country-style kitchen, a pool, and a tennis court. It was really too big and fancy for what he wanted.

'How much is the owner asking?' he enquired.

'Three million,' she said, as if this was a bargain price. 'However, I'm sure we can get it for less.'

'And the rental is?'

'Twelve thousand per month.'

'I told you over the phone I was looking for something in the six to eight thousand range,' he said, annoyed that she was wasting his time.

'Yes, indeed you did, Mr Golden – Lennie. But when I saw this house, it seemed *so* perfect. You mentioned wanting three bedrooms and a view, and after all, Suzanne Sommers *did* live here.'

He threw her a quizzical look. 'I thought you said Raquel Welch.'

'They *both* lived here,' she said, not batting an eyelash at her obvious lie.

This woman was beginning to irritate him. He'd clearly told her over the phone that eight thousand was his limit, which to his way of thinking was far too much anyway. However, he did not want to spend all his time searching for houses for months on end. His priority was getting Claudia and Leonardo settled and out of his life.

'How about making the owner an offer?' he suggested, checking out the kitchen.

'What kind of offer?' she retaliated, dollar signs lighting her eyes.

'Seven thousand a month.'

She laughed politely. 'Mr Golden – Lennie – they're asking *twelve*.'

'I know,' he said, wandering into the dining room. 'How about compromising at nine?'

'I can put in the offer.'

'I suggest that you do that.'

'And shall we make a provision that if you wish to buy?'

'Yeah, throw that in. Although for three million they don't stand a chance.'

'Property values are rising all the time, Mr Golden,' she lectured. 'I sold three houses this month, all of them fetched over four million.'

'I'm sure,' he said impatiently. 'Anything else you want to show me?'

'No. I'll put in your offer and let you know.'

He felt like he was being taken because he was a celebrity. Shit! Twelve thousand a month! Who was she kidding?

When Lennie arrived back at the hotel, Leonardo was already in bed, and Claudia was in the kitchen fixing pasta. He wasn't hungry, but what the hell? He sat down anyway.

One thing about Claudia, she was a fantastic cook, her Bolognese sauce was beyond delicious and he found himself stuffing down two heaped bowls of pasta without even thinking.

She didn't eat. She hovered, making sure he had everything he needed. Thick crusty garlic bread; a mixed green salad; a cold beer.

Hey, living with Claudia he'd grow fat as a hog. Especially as he wasn't working out because all his equipment – Stairmaster, weights, et cetera – were at the beach-house. Along with Lucky.

His Lucky. The one love of his life.

And what was he doing to get her back? Because if he didn't move fast, he knew that Alex Woods was ready and waiting. The bastard.

☆ ☆ ☆

Duke awoke with a start. He'd fallen asleep behind the wheel of the comfortable green Chevy, parked on the street near the entrance to the garage of the Chateau Marmont. And who could blame him? He'd had a tough day. Stealing two cars. Ransacking the Price Washington mansion. Raping the maid.

He allowed his mind to focus on the maid for a moment. A juicy little piece. She'd squealed like a baby pig at the moment of rear entry. He'd liked that.

A faint smile flitted across his face at the memory. He got off on fear. Other people's. Especially women's.

The truth was he'd done enough for one day and he was genuinely tired. Too tired even to consider offing Lennie Golden. There was always tomorrow. And, besides, he had to think this thing through in a more business-like way.

Maybelline had made a deal with Mila, her cell-mate. The deal was that he got to rob the Washingtons' house in exchange for whacking Lennie Golden. Mila had given Maybelline details about the house – alarm code, safe location, layout – which Maybelline had passed on to him during his last visit.

So what? He could've got in without any of that information. And once he was in, he could've persuaded Consuella to tell him anything he wanted. Especially when he'd had her bent doggie-style over the bathroom stool, and was dousing her big juicy ass with various aftershaves and colognes.

That had been some kick. *Especially* when the mixed scents had hit the tip of his cock, stinging the shit out of him.

Ah . . . but he'd liked the pain. It added to the adventure, and every gig was a new adventure.

So . . . this was not a fair deal. Why should he risk jail-time – not that he'd ever allow himself to get caught again – for such small rewards?

Jesus Christ. Was Maybelline getting soft? He could score big for putting a hit on someone.

Full of these thoughts, he consulted his watch and decided it was way past time to dump the Chevy. Removing a small chamois cloth from his pocket, he dusted every surface he'd touched, then left the car and made his way down the hill on foot, heading for home.

Since Maybelline had screwed their chance of living in the big house with step-grandma Renee, home was now a one-bedroom apartment situated off Hollywood Boulevard. It was not Duke's ideal choice. He knew where his rightful place was – back in the house their grandfather had left them.

Damn Maybelline and her vicious temper.

If only she'd waited for him to come home, it could have all been so easy.

☆ ☆ ☆

Irena sensed trouble long before it happened – she'd always had an antenna for such things. So when she saw the police cars parked outside the house, her first thought was that they'd finally come to arrest her. They'd discovered she'd entered the country with false papers, and were preparing to deport her. She wasn't Irena Kopistani. She was Ludmilla Lamara, a known criminal in Russia.

She'd been waiting twenty years for this to happen.

She walked up to the front door dragging her feet.

A uniformed cop blocked her way. 'Yes?' he said, in a none-too-friendly voice.

'I live here,' she said, studying his broad, beefy face for clues regarding her imminent arrest.

'Your name?'

She hesitated a moment. 'Irena Kopistani,' she said, rubbing her hands together. 'I'm Mr Washington's house-keeper.'

'You'd better go inside.'

'What's happening?' she asked tentatively.

'Detective Solo will fill you in.'

'Where's Mr Washington? Is he all right?'

'He's in the house, ma'am.'

Sometimes she had nightmares that something bad might happen to Price before she could tell him how much he meant to her. She couldn't bear it if he was hurt in any way. He was her only reason for living. The one true love of her life.

Her heart was beating much too fast. She walked through the door into the front hallway, where there was a gathering of unknown faces. She saw Howard Greenspan talking to a tall, haggard-looking man with greasy hair.

'Who's this woman?' the haggard-looking man asked, as she came into view.

'It's all right,' Price said, emerging from the living room. 'Irena's my housekeeper.'

'Good,' the detective said. 'She's the one I want to speak to.'

Irena's heart sank. Irene Kopistani. Ludmilla Lamara. Who did he think she was?

Chapter Seventy-seven

WHEN THE news flashed across the TV screen, Mila was sitting with a couple of Puerto Rican hookers whom she found quite entertaining. Anything to take her mind off her day in court. They were teaching her all kinds of things she hadn't learned in school. Like how to give the mother of all blow-jobs in the back of a moving car, and how to recognize a vice cop when he tried to entrap a girl. Obviously they weren't too good at the second one, because they'd both been arrested during a recent vice bust.

Pandora, one of the hookers, was busy telling stories about her famous clients, when the news broke.

The newscaster, a dour-faced man wearing too much makeup and a bad rug, began relating the story. 'Sometime this afternoon there was an invasion of Price Washington's home in the Hancock Park area of the Wilshire district. Mr Washington was in court at the time, where his son is accused of being involved in a hold-up and the subsequent shooting of TV star Mary Lou Berkeley. An Hispanic maid – alone in the house – was raped and tied up while the house was robbed of jewellery, clothes, and cash. The estimated loss could be in the millions. Police are looking for a white male, early twenties . . .'

'Price Washington,' Pandora purred, stroking her own thigh. 'That dude's about as sexy as they get.'

'I had an NBA player once,' her friend confided. 'All he wanted was a hand job in the alley. He must've liked it, 'cause he came back three nights in a row. Guess I was doin' *somethin'* right.'

Both girls cackled.

Mila got up and returned to her cell where Maybelline was lying on her bunk sucking her hair and staring into space.

'It's all over the news,' Mila announced excitedly.

'What is?' Maybelline said.

'The goddamn robbery. I didn't think Price Washington was *that* important.'

'He's a big star,' Maybelline said.

'You didn't tell me your brother was gonna rape the maid,' Mila said accusingly.

'Oh, that's Duke,' Maybelline said, not at all surprised. 'He has these little . . . habits. Can't break him of them.'

'Rape is a little habit?' Mila said, raising her eyebrows. 'He shouldn't've done that. Now *I* feel responsible.'

'Listen to *you*,' Maybelline snorted, turning nasty. 'You shot some bitch in a car, but you can't stomach my brother raping the stupid maid. What the fuck does it matter to you?'

'I hope he found my gun,' Mila muttered, backing down, because she sensed it was not pretty when Maybelline got pissed.

'If it was where you said it was, he'll have it.'

'How about Lennie Golden? Has he done it yet?'

'Knowing my brother, he's done enough for one day. He'll take care of it tomorrow.'

'Yeah, but if Lennie's called as a witness . . .'

'They won't call him for another few days. There's plenty of time.'

'How do *you* know?'

''Cause the courts drag things out for ever. Don't worry, it'll be taken care of. Duke's a pro.'

Mila was steaming. She wasn't so sure about Duke. The fact that he'd stopped and taken the time to rape the maid infuriated her. What if Irena had been in the house? Would he have raped her too?

Not that she cared about her mother, because Irena sure as hell didn't give a shit about her. Still . . . she hadn't reckoned on her being physically harmed.

Maybe she should get the gun to her lawyer.

Yes, she decided, she'd tell him about it in the morning, then she'd have Maybelline instruct Duke to deliver it.

Right now her trust level was sinking fast. Duke was obviously a maniac, and Maybelline didn't seem to care.

They'd made a deal. And if Maybelline and her crazy brother didn't keep their side of it, they'd both be way sorry.

Chapter Seventy-eight

LUCKY CAUGHT the story on the ten o'clock news. She was shocked. She immediately called Venus, knowing that Venus was friendly with Price Washington.

'What in hell's going on? Has this got anything to do with the case?'

'How do I know?' Venus replied. 'I haven't spoken to Price in weeks.'

'Isn't it kind of weird?' Lucky said. 'His house getting broken into?'

'Not really. Somebody knew he was in court and took advantage of the situation.'

'There's something not quite right about it,' Lucky said. 'Why don't you phone him, see what he has to say?'

'I'm not calling him to find out,' Venus objected. 'That's like *ghoulish*.'

'No, it's not,' Lucky insisted.

'Okay, maybe later.'

Lucky reached for a cigarette. 'How did everything go after I left?' she asked.

'Great. Seven more actors came in to read. One of them was pretty damn hot.'

'Did Alex like him?'

'*Nooo.*'

'He's hard to please.'

'Right. Hard to please and *very* particular.'

'Which is what makes him such a great director.'

'And a huge pain in the ass at times,' Venus said with a dry laugh. 'Although, don't get me wrong, I love working with him. Alex inspires me. He has soul.'

Lucky inhaled deeply, thinking that yes, he did, which was why she was so attracted to him – as a friend, nothing more.

'Now,' she said, 'perhaps you'd like to tell me about ganging up on me today? What was *that* about?'

'It's because Alex and I see what's going on,' Venus explained. 'You're too close to it.' She took a deep breath. 'The deal is this. Alex wants to be with you – no surprise, you've known *that* for the last five years. But he understands that if he's with you, you *cannot* be thinking about Lennie. So until Lennie's history – which we both know he's *not* – Alex realizes he has no chance.'

'Is that why you're both trying to *force* me back with Lennie? It doesn't make sense.'

'What does?' A beat. 'So . . . what d'you think?'

'About what?'

'About Lennie, of course,' Venus said, exasperated. 'You've got to call him, go out, talk things over.'

'I . . . I don't know any more,' Lucky said unsurely. 'I've always felt that the biggest betrayal of all was sleeping with somebody else when you've made the big commitment. I slept around as much as I wanted before I was married, but once you're married that should be it. It's like being on a diet and seeing this incredible chocolate cake, and you're a chocolate freak, so all you want to do is have a bite of that cake. But you know that if you have one small slice, you'll end up eating the whole thing. I know it sounds crazy, but to me that's what fidelity is about.'

'I can dig it,' Venus said. 'You and I both lived our lives like guys. We ran around doing whatever we wanted, and we married guys who'd done the same. Which makes for a real been-there-done-that situation, so nobody's looking around to see what they missed 'cause nobody missed anything!'

'Exactly,' Lucky agreed. 'So when that woman showed up at my door with Lennie's child, how do you think I felt?'

'I know I keep on repeating myself,' Venus said, 'but it's not as if he ran off and had an affair. He was desperate – you've got to take that into consideration.'

'Why?' Lucky said stubbornly.

''Cause it's only fair. And Alex agrees with me. What you need is closure.'

'I guess you could be right.' Lucky sighed. 'Maybe I *will* call him.'

'Best thing you can do,' Venus said. 'Dinner. The two of you. No outside interference. Make sure it's on neutral ground.'

'Good thinking.'

'By the way,' Venus added curiously, 'what *did* Alex mean when he mentioned your one crazy night together?'

'Nothing,' Lucky said quickly.

'You sound guilty,' Venus said gleefully. 'Did something happen between the two of you?'

'If it did – and I'm not *saying* it did – then it would've happened while I thought Lennie was dead.'

'Oh, you *bad* girl,' Venus admonished, loving every moment. 'You *slept* with Alex, didn't you?'

'No, I didn't.'

'Yes, you did!'

'Okay, Venus, enough. I've got to go. Let's talk tomorrow.'

She hung up the phone. Something was bothering her. Price Washington's house getting broken into and the maid getting raped. Could it possibly be connected to the case?

She called Detective Johnson. 'Any connection?' she asked.

'I'm studying the reports now,' he said.

'How about any leads on who did it?'

'Not yet. However, a neighbour did see a man arriving at the house this morning. I'll keep you informed.'

'Thanks,' she said, finally getting off the phone and going into her children's room, where she found little Gino and Maria in the middle of a fierce pillow fight. 'And how're my two little scamps?' she asked, hugging them both.

'Hi, Mommy,' they chorused, out of breath and giggling.

'Hello, you two naughty little rug-rats.'

'Where's Daddy?' Maria demanded.

'I keep on telling you, Daddy's working.'

'Wanna see him,' little Gino chanted. 'Wanna see him! Wanna see him! Wanna see him!'

'You will. You're going to Grand-daddy's this weekend, and Daddy'll be there, too.'

'Supercool!' Maria said, her favourite new word. 'Can we all go swimming together?'

'I'm not coming this weekend, sweetheart,' she explained. 'I've too much work to do here.'

'Oh, Mommy, c'mon,' Maria pleaded. 'I *like* you and Daddy in the pool. You look so pretty together.'

Lucky couldn't help laughing. 'People aren't *pretty* together, darling. They're *nice* together.'

'No, Mommy, you and Daddy are pretty.'

'Well, thank you. I'm glad you think that.'

After reading them a bedtime story, she kissed them both, tucked them into bed, and went back to her bedroom, where she stared at the phone for a while.

Maybe Venus was right. Closure. She needed closure.

☆ ☆ ☆

471

'That was good,' Lennie said, pushing his plate away.

'I'm glad you enjoyed it,' Claudia said, gazing at him with adoring eyes.

He had a horrible feeling she had a crush on him. Of course he knew why. It was because he was there for her, and she'd obviously never had anyone care about her before. He'd been thinking that it was definitely time for her to get out and meet new people.

'I think I've found a house,' he said, standing up from the table.

'A house for us, Lennie?' she asked eagerly.

'No, a house for you and Leonardo.'

'Where will you be?' she asked, disappointed.

'I'll stay here.'

'Why can't you live with *us*?'

'Because, Claudia,' he said patiently, 'I've tried to explain this to you before. I have a wife whom I love very much, and she's not very happy about you turning up here with a child. Now, I understand it's not your fault, but I have to get my life back together. And it's not helping matters that I'm living here with you.'

'I'm sorry, Lennie,' she said, lowering her eyes. 'I have tried to be no trouble. I could not stay in Italy. Leonardo is your son and he needed help.'

'I know, Claudia, I know,' he said, trying to be patient and nice and all the things he didn't feel like being, 'and we're getting him help. I'll speak to the doctors in a day or two, see what their tests have come up with.'

'Thank you, Lennie.'

'This is what I've decided,' he said. 'I'm moving you and Leonardo into the house I've found. Then maybe you should get a job. Your English is pretty good, you shouldn't have any problems. You could be an interpreter, or work at the Italian Embassy.'

'Whatever you say.'

'I say you can have a good life here, Claudia, but you have to realize that it's not going to be with me.'

'I understand,' she murmured, not understanding at all.

'Now I gotta take a shower,' he said, pleased that he'd told her the way it was going to be. 'If the phone rings, pick up, it could be the realtor.'

'Yes, Lennie.'

He went into the bathroom and ran the shower. Tomorrow he would make a concentrated effort to talk to Lucky. This had gone on long enough. As each day passed, they were growing further and further apart, and he couldn't take it any more.

The moment he stepped into the shower, the phone rang.

Claudia picked up. 'Hello?' she said.

On the other end of the line Lucky hesitated for a moment. 'Put Lennie on,' she said at last.

'I'm sorry,' Claudia purred, 'Lennie is in the shower.'

Lucky slammed the phone down.

This was not going to work out.

Chapter Seventy-nine

ONE THING Brigette had tried to learn from Lucky was how to be strong. Obviously she hadn't done such a good job, because if she had, she wouldn't have got into such a devastating predicament.

If only she'd taken Lucky's advice and had the strength of character not to get involved with Carlo. After her previous dismal experiences with men, Lucky had warned her to take great care when entering a new relationship. She should've taken heed of Lucky's philosophy – *fight back or get trampled*. It was a good one.

But Carlo hadn't given her a choice. She'd gone to London to track him down, all set on punishing him. And what had happened? He'd kidnapped her and forced her into becoming a heroin addict. Then, when she was totally addicted and depended on him for everything, he'd *married* her.

She'd really had no choice in the matter because heroin took away the decision-making process. You got up in the morning, took your first shot, and then it was like, okay, here comes another great day – lie back and enjoy it . . . whatever.

So, yes, her life had become a series of dream sequences. And Carlo made sure she always had what she wanted, never depriving her.

And, in some sick way, because of her dependency on

heroin, she'd grown totally dependent on *him*, putting up with his verbal abuse, black rages and sometime physical abuse.

It was only now that she could see the picture clearly. Only now that she realized what he'd done to her, and what an unconscionable monster he was.

Perhaps he'd done her a favour by abandoning her . . . leaving her in the middle of nowhere . . .

He would be punished, for she'd lost his baby, his son. And now that she was no longer pregnant there was nothing to tie them together except a marriage certificate, and her lawyers would soon take care of that. She didn't care how much she had to pay to get rid of him. It would be worth it.

She was doing her best to regain her physical strength, and even though she was still weak with stomach cramps, aching bones and a permanent headache, she was determined to walk out of this place as soon as possible. She knew for sure that she had to get out before Carlo returned.

Who knew what he would do? She would put nothing past him. He might even try to hook her up again. Then once more she'd be trapped. It would be an easy enough task for him to accomplish, because although she hadn't had heroin in a week, it was an addiction she knew she'd probably have to spend the rest of her life fighting.

When she was high, even Carlo being the biggest bastard in the world didn't matter.

Every morning she walked outside and sat by her baby's grave. Her son. Being near him gave her a sense of peace. The poor little soul would have been born addicted, and she could not have taken the pain and suffering the baby would've had to go through.

After a while she began exploring the big old house and the surrounding grounds, eventually discovering a barn in the back, where she found a rusty old bicycle with flat tyres.

After more searching, she came across a pump. It was an exciting discovery, and although she was not mechanically minded, she set about getting the bike into working order.

She had no idea where she was. Carlo had mentioned that they were in the middle of nowhere. But she was sure that if she took a supply of water and cans of food, and followed the road, eventually she'd reach another house or someone who could help her.

She formed a plan in her mind. Two more days of guarding her strength, drinking plenty of nourishing cans of soup from the fast-dwindling supply in the kitchen, and building herself up.

Then she was getting on the bike and leaving.

☆ ☆ ☆

People were drawn towards Boogie. A Vietnam vet with a laidback attitude, tall and lanky, he never presented a threat. Somehow, wherever he was, he always managed to fit in. So when he started hanging out with a group of old men in the village square near the Vitti palace, they accepted him as an American writer, studying other cultures, and allowed him to join in their daily game of boules, and sit around afterwards, drinking bitter black coffee and puffing on strong cigarettes.

Boogie had his eye on one old man in particular, Lorenzo Tiglitali, the houseman from the Vitti family palace. Lorenzo was a gregarious character, short and stocky, with a shock of silver hair, tanned, wrinkled skin, and a wooden leg – a souvenir from the war. He was seventy-two and proud of it, boasting that he'd never had one sick day in forty years of working for the Vitti family.

Lorenzo loved telling tales, and fortunately he spoke very good English. Boogie soon became his best listener.

It was an easy job eliciting information from Lorenzo. He

never stopped talking, carrying on about everything from the price of bread, to how tight his boss was with money.

It didn't take Boogie long to get on to the subject of Carlo.

'That boy!' Lorenzo spat in disgust. 'He's spoiled. No good. Even now he has the American wife he's *still* no good.'

'An American wife, huh?' Boogie asked quietly. 'Do they live at the palace?'

'They did,' Lorenzo said, chugging down a brandy, bought for him by Boogie. 'Now he go to Sardinia with another woman. And the wife . . .' The old man suddenly stopped talking, aware that he might be saying too much.

'What about the wife?' Boogie urged. 'Where is she?'

Lorenzo shrugged, draining his glass of Cognac.

'Another?' Boogie offered.

'I shouldn't . . .'

'Go ahead.'

'Just one more.'

The 'just one more' loosened Lorenzo's tongue. 'His American wife is pregnant, you know. And very rich. Carlo has promised to get the family a few million dollars by the end of the year.'

'No!' Boogie said, feigning surprise.

'Oh, yes,' the old man assured him.

'Tell me about the American girl. Is she happy to be left behind while her husband goes off with other women?'

Lorenzo chuckled. 'She doesn't know about it. He took her to the family hunting lodge in the country.'

'Really? Where's that?'

Lorenzo screwed up his eyes and peered at Boogie. 'Why you so interested?'

'Sometimes I dabble in real estate. I have a friend who might be interested in purchasing a property outside Rome.'

The old man wheezed with laughter. 'Not this place. It's

477

run-down and deserted. The family has no money for upkeep. Maybe when the millions of dollars come they restore it.'

'If it's so run-down and deserted, why would Carlo take his wife there?'

'I heard him telling his mama she would be happy there.'

'Really?' Boogie said, buying the old man yet another Cognac. 'About my friend. Perhaps I should look at this hunting lodge. If you go to your boss with a big enough offer, you could score yourself a healthy commission.'

'I could?' Lorenzo said, his rheumy old eyes popping at the thought.

'Yes,' Boogie said casually. 'Tell me where it is, and I'll go take a look. If I run into the American woman, I'll say I'm a potential buyer. I'm sure she won't object.'

'You'll never find the place,' Lorenzo said.

'If I can find my way through the jungles of Vietnam,' Boogie said, 'I'm sure I can find my way to this house. Here,' he added, pulling out a wad of money, 'let me give you five hundred dollars as good-faith money. If I like the place, you'll get more. If I don't, nothing lost, and you'll be a richer man.'

Lorenzo stared at the money, a greedy expression on his wrinkled old face. His salary had been the same for the last ten years, and he could certainly use something extra. His daughter wanted to go to Milan to be a teacher; his wife was desperate for a new winter coat; his son was married with two children and needed many things.

He grabbed the pile of notes, quickly stuffing them in his pocket. 'Tomorrow I will draw you a map.'

'Good,' Boogie said, sensing it would not do to rush him. 'We have a deal.'

Chapter Eighty

DUKE REVIEWED his stash. He knew he'd done well at the Washington house, but he had not taken the time to ascertain exactly how well. Now he was checking out his spoils.

The safe, which he'd been able to crack – having been taught by a master safe-cracker in jail in Florida – had revealed plenty of treasures. A leather pouch containing twelve expensive Patek Philippe watches, bundles of cash totalling over fifty thousand dollars, some important-looking papers that he would read at a later date, and a leather box full of assorted gold and diamond rings and cufflinks.

He'd also packed a Vuitton suitcase with several custom-made suits, shirts and ties. Even though Price Washington was obviously a much bigger man than he was, Duke liked the idea of hanging these clothes in his closet. Nothing like a three-thousand-dollar suit to give a man a buzz – even if it was just to look at.

He'd also found the shoebox Maybelline had told him to collect. It was exactly where she'd said it would be, hidden in a cupboard above the fridge in the kitchen, unreachable except by step-ladder.

He stared at the shoebox. Maybelline had said not to open it. Fuck that shit. He opened it and discovered a handgun wrapped in a towel. He was smart enough not to get his prints on it.

Very interesting, he thought. *Have to find out more.*

He removed the watches from their pouch and laid them out, admiring them *and* the assorted jewellery. Then he re-counted the money – just to make sure.

He wished he could speak to his sister right now, but she would not be allowed to make a collect call until morning.

Damn! He missed Maybelline. He was miserable without her. They had such a strong connection, and that connection suffered when they were apart.

Maybe he should think about getting her out . . .

☆ ☆ ☆

Mila didn't sleep well. She was disturbed by Maybelline's couldn't-give-a-damn attitude and Duke's rape of the maid. How dare he! How fucking dare he!

Early in the morning she grabbed Maybelline by the arm and said, 'You'd better talk to your brother. I need him to deliver my package today.'

'He's not a delivery boy,' Maybelline snapped, confirming Mila's suspicions that all was not right.

'I didn't say he was,' Mila said, trying to stay calm, 'but my information got him into the house. Now he has to get that package to my lawyer today. I'll give you the address.'

'I'm not sure I like your attitude,' Maybelline said. 'It's a shitty attitude, like we work for you or something.'

'And *I*'m not sure I like yours,' Mila retaliated.

The two girls glared at each other.

'Your brother was supposed to hit Lennie Golden *yester-day*,' Mila said, in a fierce whisper. 'I'd like to know why he didn't.'

'Fuck you,' Maybelline responded. 'Who do you think you're talking to?'

'I thought we were friends,' Mila said, realizing her

precarious position, because now Maybelline's obviously unstable brother had the gun with Teddy's prints on it, and that was a valuable piece of property.

'Don't be so sure of that,' Maybelline said.

'Listen to me,' Mila said, her pinched face darkening with fury. 'If your brother doesn't do what I say, I'll go to the authorities and tell them it was *him* who broke into the house and raped the maid.'

'You can't do that,' Maybelline said, her baby face turning bright red. 'I'll bash your head in before you do that.'

'Let's not fight about it,' Mila said, backing off because all she really wanted was for things to go smoothly. 'We're supposed to be partners in this. The news story said he got a million dollars' worth of stuff. I'm happy for you. All I want is what you promised. He's got to deliver the gun and hit Lennie Golden today. If he does, then everything'll be cool.'

Maybelline didn't say a word.

Mila went off to court still furious. As soon as she saw her lawyer she filled him in about the gun.

'You mean you have a gun with Teddy Washington's prints on it and you're only telling me about it now?' Willard Hocksmith asked incredulously.

She took a step backwards: his foul breath was making her sick. 'Yes,' she said. 'I thought it was smart to save it for later in the trial, when we really needed it.'

'What makes you think there'd even *be* a trial if I had evidence like that?' Willard said, frowning at her stupidity.

'Well, anyway,' she said, 'it's being delivered to your office today.'

'By whom?'

'By this . . . person.'

'What person?'

'Just someone,' she said irritably. 'Don't question me.'

'I *have* to question you, I'm your lawyer. Can't you

understand what's going on here? They've got a witness, Lennie Golden, who swears it was *you* shot the girl. *You*, not Teddy Washington. Now you're telling me you've got a gun with his prints on it? How did you get it?'

'It doesn't matter how I got it,' she said sullenly. 'He shot her. I told you that at the beginning. You should've believed me.'

'And *when* am I supposed to get this gun?'

'Sometime today. You'd better tell them in your office that nobody should open it. It'll be in a shoebox wrapped in a towel.'

'You're a very strange girl,' Willard said.

'Like you're normal,' she muttered.

Chapter Eighty-one

DAY TWO of the trial and the media interest was stronger than ever. Especially with the added attraction of the rape and robbery at Price Washington's house.

Price himself was in shock. He'd known this was going to be an ordeal, but he'd had no idea it would be anything like this. Headline news day after day, the intrusion into his house, the rape, the robbery, the loss of his precious collection of watches and other jewellery. Even worse was the way everybody was talking and writing about him as though they could say whatever they liked, however untrue. He felt used and abused.

And poor Consuella. She'd worked for him for several years and was a nice woman. The fact that the rape had happened to her in his house was devastating.

'You'd better watch out,' Howard said. 'She'll probably sue you.'

'What're you talking about?' Price said. 'I had nothing to do with it.'

'It happened on your premises,' Howard said. 'Some smart shyster will get hold of her and sue you for everything you've got. I hope your personal liability policy is up to date.'

Price was so furious that Teddy had brought all this attention on their family that he could hardly bring himself to speak to him. They'd spent the previous evening in silence

– eating dinner, then going to their respective rooms – barely bidding each other good night.

Because of the interest in his household affairs, the media had now discovered that Irena was Mila's mother. Boy, were they getting off on that one. And Irena was freaked, hiding in her room like a wanted criminal.

Price felt under siege. Every time he attempted to leave the house, he was deluged with press. He'd hired four bodyguards, two for him, and two for Teddy. This fucking case was going to cost him a fortune. He'd already had to postpone several lucrative gigs to deal with it.

The whole thing was bad news. He'd been thinking that after it was over, maybe he'd take Teddy away somewhere – the Virgin Islands or the Bahamas. Somewhere they could chill out and get to know each other better.

He had a bad feeling about the house now. His house that he'd loved for all those years. The house where Teddy was born *and* Mila, and look what had happened to the two of them. Bad karma.

He couldn't get the image of a terrified Consuella, bound and gagged, out of his mind. Her image was haunting him.

He needed a break, and as soon as this was over he was taking one.

'You know, Teddy,' he said to his son before they left for court on the second day, 'I hope this has taught you a real tough lesson. Because I am so fuckin' pissed about this I can't even see straight. You did somethin' really bad. You've brought shame on this family.'

What family? Teddy wanted to say. *We're not a family. There's you, and there's my mom – and she's not family. She's just some fat old publicity-crazy cow.*

Teddy was crushed by his mother's behaviour. He'd hoped she'd be there for him. And she wasn't.

'Sorry, Dad,' he mumbled. But he knew being sorry would never be enough.

☆ ☆ ☆

Steven awoke with Lina cuddled in his arms, still asleep. 'Hey,' he said gently, trying to extract himself. 'I've gotta get up. You can sleep a little longer.'

'I wanna make you breakfast,' she murmured sleepily, clinging to him.

'Oh, no,' he said, laughing. 'I'm not eating fried chicken for breakfast.'

'Don't be mean,' she said, her hand snaking down between his legs. 'I wanna learn to cook for you, Steven. I wanna do all the things I've never done before. You're makin' me into a changed woman.'

'I am?' he said, removing her hand, because much as he was tempted, now was not the time.

'You am,' she said, stretching her long arms above her head. 'Oh, boy,' she sighed. 'Never thought I'd feel like this about anyone, but you're like . . . so solid, you know. I feel safe with you.' As soon as the words escaped her lips, she knew she'd said the wrong thing.

'Mary Lou felt safe with me,' he muttered grimly, 'and look where it got her.' He jumped out of bed and went into his bathroom.

Lina, who found any kind of rejection hard to take, followed him. She was gloriously naked and determined to make him feel good. 'Sorry, sweetie,' she said. 'Didn't mean anything by that . . .'

He attempted to ignore her spectacular body – so sleek and black and perfect.

She rubbed up against him, and suddenly he was lost,

hard as the proverbial rock and way past the point of no return. Lina had that immediate effect on him.

'Got five minutes to spare?' she asked provocatively.

'What makes you think I only need five minutes?' he joked.

Lina was something else.

☆ ☆ ☆

In view of all the publicity about the case, Lucky decided the children should go to Palm Springs earlier than planned. Thank God that Gino loved having them.

She saw them all safely into the station wagon with CeeCee, stood outside and waved them goodbye.

Once they were gone she almost picked up the phone to call Lennie again. But she didn't. If she had to listen to Claudia's lilting voice saying, 'Hello,' one more time, she'd throw up.

You're jealous, a little voice whispered in her head.

Sure I am. Why shouldn't I be? My husband slept with another woman, and that other woman gave birth to his child. I'm not only jealous, I'm furious!

She was still angry, although she'd decided that she *did* want to see him. Alex was right, she could never start another relationship until she had closure with Lennie. Their love affair was too passionate to end on a sour note.

Decisively she grabbed the phone and called him. Once more, Claudia answered.

She refused to give the girl the satisfaction of asking to speak to her own husband, so she hung up again.

Boogie phoned from Europe just as she was leaving the house. 'I've located Brigette,' he said. 'I'm hoping to see her tomorrow.'

'That's good news.'

'It's good and it's bad. Carlo has taken her to a deserted hunting lodge in the country and left her there alone.'

'Where is *he*?'

'I understand he's in Sardinia with a girl.'

'Oh, great.' Lucky sighed. 'Brigette is pregnant, could be doing drugs, and Carlo's running around with another woman. What a winner she found this time. I wish I could get on a plane and come over. I'd like to kick his balls from here to China.'

'Hey, hey, Lucky, tell me how you *really* feel.'

'What's your next move?'

'It's evening here, I'll find the house first thing in the morning.'

'And then?'

'I plan to check on Brigette, make sure she's okay. If she's doing drugs, I'll know.'

'Let's hope Carlo's not around, then maybe she'll tell you. I have a hunch she'll feel more comfortable confiding in you.'

'As soon as I have news I'll call you.'

'Boog, remember this. If she's in any kind of trouble, you've *got* to bring her back.'

'That's the plan.'

'I trust you, Boog.'

'I know you do, Lucky. We've been through a lot together, and I don't come out of retirement easily. But for you – any time.'

'Retirement! Listen to you, you sound like some old man.'

'There are times I feel old.'

'You know, Boog, you're talking far too much. I can remember when you used to be the strong silent type.'

'I'll report in to you later.'

'That's fine. I'll be in court all day, but I'll have my cellphone on.'

'Then I'll keep you informed.'

'Thanks, Boog.'

Chapter Eighty-two

'YOU DIDN'T happen to mention there was a toy in the box,' Duke said, on the phone to his sister.

Maybelline was allowed to make an occasional collect call. Duke was the only person she spoke to. They were both aware that their calls were sometimes taped, and that they had to be careful what they said. Because of this they'd developed a way of speaking in code.

'I didn't tell you 'cause I knew you'd look,' she said. 'I hope you didn't play with it.'

'Why?'

''Cause it's got patterns on it. Teddy Bear patterns.'

'Interesting.'

'Isn't it? Auntie wants you to deliver it to the charity people – the ones she's working with. I think we should keep it. But, in the meantime, take care of that other thing 'cause Auntie's throwing a fit. And you know how close she is to the board.'

'Got it.'

'When?'

'I'll drive by later.'

'Love you, brother.'

'See you Saturday.'

Duke hung up, thinking about Maybelline's hidden messages. She was telling him the gun had Teddy Washington's prints on it, and that he shouldn't deliver it to Mila's lawyer. She was also telling him to go ahead and whack Lennie Golden, otherwise Mila might cause trouble.

Fine with him. He had nothing else to do today. And it wouldn't be the first time he'd sent someone to swim with the fishes. In fact, he had quite a history. Funny that the cops would lock him away for a few lousy rapes, when they could've had him for so much more . . . But, then, nobody had ever said that cops were smart. *He* was smart. Maybelline was smart. The rest of the world were merely stumbling through the day.

He locked all his spoils in a special steel-lined closet he'd had installed in his apartment. It wouldn't do to get *robbed*.

Then he checked his gun and decided exactly how and when he'd take Mr Golden.

Killing someone was such an easy thing to do.

And as long as one didn't get caught, extremely satisfying.

Chapter Eighty-three

HOW TO navigate her way through the crush of press without hitting one of them, that was Lucky's problem. 'Get that fucking microphone out of my face,' she snapped at a vacuous blonde reporter, who jumped back in surprise.

'She used the F-word,' the blonde said to her cameraman, her pretty face shocked.

'She's in the mob,' the man muttered. 'Read it in *Truth and Fact* this week.'

'Far *out*!' the blonde said, her attention shifting towards Price Washington and his entourage of lawyers and body-guards, who'd just arrived.

Safely inside, Lucky got hold of one of the deputies. 'I'd like to see Lennie Golden,' she said. 'Penelope McKay said it's okay.'

The deputy led her to a small room where Lennie sat at a table reading *Newsweek* and sipping coffee from a Starbucks container.

'Hi,' she said, standing in the doorway.

He looked up. 'Uh . . . hi,' he said, surprised and quite delighted by her visit.

'Thought I'd drop by, wish you luck just in case they get to you today,' she said casually.

He put the magazine down and stared at his wife – his gorgeous wife with the jet hair and matching eyes, devastating body and sensual olive skin. His incredible smart, dangerous wife, whom he missed and loved with a passion.

'Come in,' he said.

She did so, shutting the door behind her. 'I hate this place,' she remarked. 'I'll be glad when this is over, won't you?'

'Can't wait.'

'Where did you get the coffee?'

'Round the corner. Want one? I can see if somebody'll go out.'

'It doesn't matter.'

'Have mine,' he said, thrusting it at her.

'Just a sip,' she said, tasting it. 'I didn't have time to make any this morning, what with getting the kids on their way.'

'Where to?'

'Gino's. They're better off in Palm Springs until this is over.' She took a beat. 'You heard about the break-in at Price Washington's?'

'Who didn't?'

Awkward silence.

Lucky opened her purse and removed a pack of cigarettes.

'Thought you were giving it up.'

'I was trying, then this came along,' she said, shaking one out of the pack. 'Did Gino call you?'

'No.'

'He will,' she said, lighting up. 'He's inviting you to spend the weekend. You and your . . . uh . . . other son.' She couldn't bring herself to utter the child's name. 'Just the two of you. Not—'

'I get it,' he interrupted.

'Good,' she said coldly, almost wishing she hadn't come, but glad to see him all the same.

'Yes, Lucky. I do get it. And I'm pleased you're here, because I have several things to tell you.'

'What?' she said, noticing dark circles under his eyes, which meant he hadn't been sleeping well, and neither had she. *I want to kiss him*, a little voice whispered in her head. *I want to hug him and kiss him right now.*

'It's about Claudia . . .'

Oh, Christ, what now? Was he going to tell her he'd fallen in love with the Sicilian girl and wanted to be with her for ever?

Oh, shit! *Here I come, Alex, complete with broken heart.*

'Yes?' she said carefully.

'About me and Claudia,' he said.

'We don't have to go over it again,' she said. 'Especially here.'

'We need to talk. I have to explain everything. I know how upset you are that we're all living at the Chateau Marmont, but I had no choice. What could I do with them? The kid's got a hearing problem, so I've been sending him to doctors. And they had nowhere to go.'

'It's not your responsibility.'

'Yes, it is. I got her pregnant.'

'You don't even know if it's your son or not. She has no proof.'

'Take a look at him, Lucky. He looks exactly like me.'

'Oh,' she said, crushed.

'Anyway, here's the plan,' he said, hoping she'd approve.

'What plan is that?' she said, exhaling smoke.

'I've found a house to put them in, and I want you to come and see it.'

'Why would *I* want to see it?'

'Because you've got to be part of this. It's not me and Claudia and Leonardo against you. It's *us* – you and me – trying to deal with a difficult situation.' He stared at her long and hard. 'I've missed you, sweetheart. I can't tell you how happy I am to see you today.'

'I tried calling you,' she said. 'Only every time I got through, your girlfriend picked up.'

'Will you quit with that girlfriend shit?'

'Just pissing you off. I like to see you rattled.'

She smiled, faintly, but it was enough to give him the encouragement he needed. 'Let's not get into it here,' he said. 'Can you meet me later?'

'Where?'

'At the house I'm renting for Claudia and the kid. The realtor's dropping off the keys at my hotel.'

'Well . . .' she said hesitantly.

'It's important to me that you're part of this, Lucky.'

What did she have to lose? 'Okay,' she said.

'Meet me there at seven. After, we'll go for dinner and talk. I don't know about you, but I can't go on like this – I love you too much to be away from you.' He took a long beat, studying her carefully. 'I know this has been a shock for both of us,' he continued, 'but we've got to face the fact that I *have* a kid, and there's no way I can abandon him.'

'I suppose so,' she said, not sure *how* she felt.

'I'll get you the address,' he said. 'We'll work everything out, trust me on this.'

'I always used to trust you.'

'And you will again. You know you can't shut me out of your life. We belong together. It'll always be that way.'

'Hmm . . .' she said. 'That's what everyone's been telling me.'

'Who's everyone?'

'Your friend, Alex.'

'Not *my* friend.'

'He's on your side. Between him and Venus, they railroaded me into seeing you. They said we either have to be together, or get some closure.'

'I'm here to tell you,' he said forcefully, 'closure ain't

anywhere in our future. Not if *I* have anything to do with it. We'll get through this together, like we've gotten through everything else over the years. We have two incredible kids, and I'm not losing them *or* you.'

'I'd better go,' she said, standing up. 'Penelope McKay let me in as a favour. I'll see you at seven.'

'Do I get a kiss?'

'Don't get carried away,' she said.

He grinned. She couldn't help grinning back.

Both of them had a strong suspicion that everything was going to be all right.

☆   ☆   ☆

Venus and Alex ate breakfast downstairs in the coffee shop. Alex attacked a stack of blueberry pancakes, while Venus settled for strawberry yogurt and herbal tea.

'Mary tracked that actor you were carrying on about,' Alex said. 'He's coming in at noon. If he's as good as you say he is, I want Lucky to see him too.'

'I've got the eye,' Venus said, stealing one of his pancakes with her fingers. 'Just you wait until you see him. If he can act, we're in business.'

Alex squirted more syrup on his pancakes. 'How'd you think Lucky's holding up?' he asked.

'Pretty good, considering what the tabloids are doing to her. Have you seen them?'

'She's pissed, huh?'

'Wouldn't *you* be pissed if you were called a mobster's daughter? Gino was never really a *mobster*, was he?'

'Who the fuck knows?' Alex said, gulping his coffee. 'I like the guy. Who gives a shit if he was connected way back? *I* certainly don't.'

'I think Lucky should sue 'em,' Venus said, sipping her tea.

'Who needs to sue 'em and all that crap?' Alex said. 'You ever had to give a deposition? It's the pits.'

'Yes, Alex, *I* have experienced everything.'

'No doubt about *that*,' he said, quickly getting back on to his favourite subject. 'So what is she doing about Lennie?'

'Taking our advice and meeting with him.'

'Yeah?' he said, not looking too thrilled.

'Hey, listen, we both thought it was a good idea to talk her into it,' Venus said. 'And you're right.'

'We did?' he said quizzically.

'Okay, okay, I *know* you're dying to get into her pants, but as long as she's still lusting after Lennie, it would be a losing proposition for you *and* you know it.'

'So now we'll see,' he said.

'Yes, now we'll see,' Venus repeated.

'What do *you* think's going to happen?' he asked.

'Who knows?' Venus said. 'I mean, Lennie and Lucky, they've always had this kind of love-hate simmering relationship. Very passionate. I'm sure she likes you a lot, Alex. In fact, I know she loves you as a friend. But while Lennie is around, baby, you got no shot.'

'Yeah,' he said ruefully. 'I guess the only way I'll get rid of Lennie is if I put a contract out on him.'

'Very funny,' Venus said. 'You're starting to believe your own scripts.'

Lili joined them at the table, clutching a stack of photographs. 'We have fifteen actors coming in today,' she said, placing the photos in front of Alex. 'The first one's due shortly.'

Alex turned to Venus. 'You sure you want to read with them all?'

'Of course,' she said. 'It's important to test the chemistry. Not that I don't trust your judgement, but me reading with them makes them feel good. It's tough being an actor –

there's nothing worse than rejection, something they're facing all the time. You're a director, you sit there rejecting whoever you want, but can you imagine how *they* feel? *I* know what it's like. *I* had to struggle to get where I am today.'

'Yeah, yeah,' Alex said. 'It's so friggin' tough that when they make it they turn into the asshole pricks of the world, right?'

'It's their revenge for being treated like garbage on the way up,' Venus explained.

'Okay, I get it,' Alex said, calling for the check. 'Let's get this show on the road.'

☆ ☆ ☆

Lucky left the courtroom before the lunchbreak. She was anxious to see what was going on over at the production office. She was also thinking about seeing Lennie that morning, and how nice it had been.

Steven had wanted her to stay with him in the courtroom. 'I need to talk to you about something,' he'd said.

'Not now, Steven,' she'd told him. 'I'll be back later. I promise.'

He'd nodded, not very happy about her leaving.

When she arrived at the production office, Alex was standing outside smoking a cigarette.

'What're you doing out here?' she asked, parking her Ferrari in a convenient spot.

'Waiting for you,' he said.

'Waiting for me? I thought you had a line of actors coming in?'

'I think we've found the right one. It's the guy Venus spotted on TV. He's up there now. I don't want to audition anybody else until you've seen them read the scene together.'

'He's that good?'

'*You* tell me. I might be too close to it. It seems they've got chemistry.'

'I'll be happy to look.'

'And talking of chemistry . . .'

'Yes?'

'I hear you're getting together with Lennie.'

'As a matter of fact, I saw him this morning,' she said. 'We're meeting again tonight.'

'Uh-huh.'

'Thanks for talking me into it, Alex. I know you're right.'

He took her hand. 'Lucky, you're my best friend. I never want that to change.'

'It won't, Alex.'

'The only way it could is if you weren't with Lennie, and I've explained the way I feel about *that*. Now, if you and Lennie *do* get back together, I've made a decision.'

'What decision is that?'

'I'm gonna marry Pia. She's a good girl. Never gives me any crap, is always there, smiling, happy. She's an excellent conversationalist, intelligent, smart, beautiful . . .'

'Hey, I think I should marry her myself,' Lucky said jokingly.

'Seriously, what *do* you think?'

'Seriously?' she said, not sure how she felt at all. 'Uh . . . if that's what you want, then you *should* do it. Although I always thought that getting married had something to do with being in love.'

'How long do you think love lasts?' he asked.

'When you find the right person – for ever.'

☆ ☆ ☆

Upstairs, Venus was chatting away to her new discovery, Billy Melina, twenty years old, a very young combination of Brad Pitt and Johnny Depp.

'Hi, Billy,' Lucky said, entering the room, checking him out, and immediately liking what she saw.

'Nice t' meet you, ma'am,' Billy replied, six feet two, blond and polite with it.

'Billy only got into town six months ago,' Venus explained. 'From Texas.'

'Do you mind running through the scene again with Venus?' Lucky said, taking a seat. 'I'd love to see the two of you together.'

'Sure, ma'am,' Billy said. He had the bluest eyes she'd ever seen, but she wished he'd quit with the ma'am.

Mary leaned in to Lucky. 'We found him on a cancelled series. This kid's going to be big. He has a very special quality. Even Alex thinks so.'

'Really?'

Venus winked at her. 'Okay,' she said, walking over to Billy. 'We're reading the scene that takes place by the pool. Got a feeling you're going to like it a lot.'

'Read away,' Lucky said. 'I can't wait.'

Chapter Eighty-four

GINEE ARRIVED at court on the second day dressed in an orange jumpsuit with too much cleavage, fake diamonds dripping from her ears, wrists and fingers, and leopardskin mules on her feet – the only tiny thing about her. She was accompanied by a camera crew from *Hard Copy*.

Once there, she stood on the steps outside, giving *Hard Copy* an exclusive interview, while a scattering of paparazzi took her picture. She couldn't have been happier.

Price was outraged. So were his lawyers. The three of them huddled in a corner. 'She looks like a Vegas lounge act who's seen better days,' Price complained.

'I'm instructing her not to come here any more,' Howard said. 'This is a bad joke. She's going to turn people against Teddy. She's making a spectacle of herself.'

'I'm not so sure she'll stay away,' Price said. 'She's gettin' off on the attention.'

'We won't pay her,' Howard said. 'It's as easy as that.'

'Not so easy,' Price said. 'Knowin' Ginee, she's gettin' money from the TV show.'

'You're probably right,' Howard agreed. 'Which means we're stuck with her. I'd better talk to her again today.'

'Wish you would,' Price said. 'This is too humiliatin'. People are lookin' at her thinkin', What kind of taste has *he* got?'

'I'll try to slip a couple of your wedding pictures to the tabloids,' Howard said. 'That way they can see she used to be gorgeous.'

'No,' Price said, shaking his head. 'My ego don't need that kinda stroking. I'll survive.'

He'd already decided that he would talk to her himself.

Later in the day he got the opportunity. 'Hey, Ginee,' he said, 'you're supposed t' be lookin' like a mother figure. How about gettin' it together?'

'Why should I look like a goddamn *mother* when I'm on TV?' she demanded. 'They want glamour, pizzazz. *Hard Copy* love me. Tomorrow they're having me sing!'

'You're gonna do *what?*'

'Watch it tomorrow. They're doing one whole segment on little old me!' She smiled triumphantly. 'Now we got *two* stars in the family.'

'Jesus,' he muttered. 'You're really milkin' this. Your own son is in trouble an' all you can think about is yourself.'

'Why shouldn't I?' she said belligerently. 'After you threw me out, I never had a chance.'

'I *didn't* throw you out. We couldn't live together any more, and I paid you plenty over the years. You could've done whatever you wanted t' do.'

'Get it straight, Price. This is my big opportunity, and *nobody's* stoppin' me.'

'Have you talked to your son today? Did you call him at home last night? Tell me this, have you comforted him in any way?'

'Comforted him?' she squealed. 'I hardly even *know* him. Only don't tell that to *Hard Copy*. They think me an' Teddy are real tight. They think I'll get 'em an interview with him. An' you know what? I can get 'em to *pay* for it.'

Price shook his head in disgust. 'Give it a rest, Ginee,' he said. 'Stay home. I don't want you here.'

'Too bad, Price. Teddy is *my* son, and I'll be here every single day.'

☆ ☆ ☆

By lunchtime Mila was getting nervous. 'Has the gun been delivered yet?' she kept on asking Willard.

'You've asked me ten times,' he said. 'I've called the office. Nothing. Who is supposed to be delivering it anyway?'

'A friend of mine,' she said.

'Where did they get it?'

'That's none of your business.'

'It *is* my business, Mila,' he said patiently. 'As your attorney, you're supposed to tell me everything.'

'Why should I?' she asked suspiciously.

'Because I am here to help you.'

'And what if I don't need your help?'

'Of course you need my help,' he said, losing it. 'You're accused of murder, for Chrissakes. Did *you* shoot Mary Lou Berkeley? Or did Teddy?'

'I told you, Teddy did it, and I've got the gun to prove it.'

'Then *get* me the gun.'

'I'm trying to, only it's not so easy when you're locked up in jail.'

Willard shook his head. He didn't know whether to believe her or not. If she'd had this proof all along, why hadn't she produced it before?

God, he wished he could get a job in a decent law firm instead of defending people who had no money.

He stared over at the two high-powered attorneys employed by Price Washington. One day he would like to be just like Mason Dimaggio. Now *that* was a star.

☆ ☆ ☆

Irena hadn't told Price she was coming back to the courtroom on the second day. But, then again, he hadn't questioned her as to why she wasn't in the house when Consuella had been attacked and the house robbed. She didn't care. She just knew that she had to be in court to watch what was going on.

Fortunately, the police being at the house had not been about her, although she'd worried about it all night. What she *didn't* like was the newspapers and tabloids dragging her name up. If they started to investigate . . . if they got a sniff of the real truth . . . she would be deported for sure.

Irena Kopistani had died long ago. If they found that out . . .

She shook her head and stared at the judge, a stern-looking man with white hair and a neat goatee. What if he sentenced Mila to a long jail term? Or even worse, what if he sentenced her to *death*? It was possible.

Irena took a deep breath. She'd made a decision. She was going to tell Price the truth about his daughter. Maybe then Mila would stand a chance.

☆ ☆ ☆

Later in the day, Duke Browning slid into the back of the courtroom, having paid a member of the public for their seat. It had occurred to him that he should get a look at Mila Kopistani. He wanted to see this person who shared Maybelline's cell. He wanted to study this girl who was threatening his precious sister.

She wasn't as pretty as Maybelline, but he had to admit she had something. Kind of a tough, sexy quality that he found quite appealing.

He decided that when and if they called her to the stand, he wanted to be there. He was keeping his eye on this one.

Little did she know that the man sitting at the back of the

court room was preparing to help her. Later that day, he would get rid of Lennie Golden for her, the prosecution's key witness.

And when he did, and she found herself free, he expected her to be suitably grateful.

Chapter Eighty-five

CARLO HAD not expected Isabella to come back into his life. Ah . . . Isabella. Such an exciting beauty for one so young. Twenty-two years old, with delicate features and a ballerina's body, she was his one true love. She was also the reason he'd been banished from Italy, thanks to the death of her eighty-year-old husband. Every finger had pointed towards him because the husband had died under mysterious circumstances. But nobody had any way to prove he was involved.

However, instead of Isabella bonding with Carlo after her husband's death, she'd run off with an overweight opera star.

It had infuriated Carlo beyond control. He had wanted to punish her, but there was nothing he could do. And then he'd been banished to England.

Now, suddenly, Isabella was back in his life. One phone call and he was ready to do anything she wanted, for Isabella was the only woman who had power over him.

'I'm leaving Mario,' she'd told him over the phone. 'I hear that you are married.'

'It means nothing,' he'd said.

'We have much to discuss,' she'd said. 'When can I see you?'

Since Brigette was safely tucked away in the hunting

lodge, he decided he would take a few days to visit Isabella at her vacation house in Sardinia.

'Where are you going?' his mother had demanded.

'I have business to attend to,' he'd said.

'What business?'

'It's personal.'

His mother had looked at him with disgust. She was furious that he had married a foreigner. Even more furious that the American girl was pregnant with his baby.

'You have married a cheap whore,' she'd said, at the time of his marriage.

'No, Mama,' he'd replied. 'I have married one of the richest women in the world. I will get us money for this place. We will live like kings again.'

'You never do anything right,' his mother had complained. 'You might be handsome, but you're useless.'

In all of his thirty-one years he had never heard a word of praise from his mother's lips.

Without giving a second thought to how Brigette was doing all by herself in the middle of the countryside, he got on a plane and flew to Sardinia. The few days he spent with Isabella convinced him that there was no other woman in the world for him.

'Why did you leave me?' he asked.

'I was foolish. Now it is time for us to be together.'

'I have a wife,' he said.

'Divorce her,' she said.

'I have a very rich wife.'

Isabella's interest had immediately perked up. 'A rich wife. This is good, because my inheritance is not as big as I thought.'

'Well,' Carlo said, 'if we play this right, and I stay with this woman perhaps a year or so, I should be able to come away with a fortune.'

'Or she could have an unfortunate . . . accident,' Isabella said. 'Like my husband . . .'

'Your husband was an old man.'

'We need to be together, Carlo,' she said, encouraging him, 'but we both know we cannot be together with no money. We have expensive tastes, and neither of us cares to be without the things that make us happy.'

Isabella had a point. 'Leave it to me,' he said. 'I will work on getting a sum of money that will keep us happy for ever.'

'Do that,' Isabella said. 'Because if you don't, I'll be forced to move on.'

☆ ☆ ☆

Brigette was exhausted. It seemed as though she'd been riding the bike for hours. Perhaps making her own way out of there was a stupid idea. Carlo was right: the hunting lodge was totally isolated and now she was lost. She'd followed the dirt road as far as she could, until eventually it had ended at the edge of a thickly wooded area. Obviously, somewhere along the way, she had taken a wrong turn.

She hadn't realized how weak she was. Two hours out and she was ready to collapse. After losing the baby she'd bled non-stop for twenty-four hours. Not only had it frightened her, it had weakened her even more than the excruciating pain she'd gone through with the drug withdrawal.

She was completely lost. There were no other houses in sight, nothing but bushes and trees and the mud road she was trapped on.

She got off the bike, leaned it against a tree, and sat on the damp ground. This didn't seem possible. It was like being in the wilderness. And on top of everything else the sky was darkening and a drizzle of rain was starting to fall.

She drank some bottled water, trying to decide what to

do next. Without a cellphone, or any other means of communication, she was stranded.

After a while, she got up and climbed back on the bike. There was only one thing to do, and that was to head back in the direction she'd come from.

Boogie decided that maybe he should have brought the old man with him, because Lorenzo was right, the Vittis' hunting lodge was impossible to find. He'd been driving for hours before locating the turn off the main highway that would eventually lead him to the dirt road that would take him to the hunting lodge. But it seemed there were more twists and turns and more side-roads that led nowhere.

Boogie stopped the car and studied the crudely drawn map again. He was determined to find the place before nightfall. It couldn't be *that* difficult.

Chapter Eighty-six

IN SPITE of herself, Lucky was excited. She'd been having all these crazy thoughts about Lennie – divorcing him, starting a new life, maybe even getting together with Alex. But if she was truthful with herself, she knew that Lennie and she were destined to be together for ever.

She smiled to herself. Later she would meet him at the house he planned to rent for Claudia and the boy. And that was a nice thing for him to do, a temporary solution. Lennie had good principles, and at least he was having *her* look at the house, making her part of his decision. Yes, if he put Claudia and the boy in a house of their own, it would certainly make things easier. She wasn't exactly ecstatic about it, but at least she was learning to accept it.

Maybe. She'd see. It would depend on his actions. Lennie was his own man, she'd always respected that about him. He'd never let her take control. Something she found quite easy to do.

She smiled to herself again. God, she'd missed him. She hadn't realized quite how much until she was with him.

Hmm, she thought. If they could get through this, they could get through anything.

☆ ☆ ☆

It was the second day of the trial and he still hadn't been called, so Lennie was able to slip away a few minutes early.

He called Claudia from the car. 'I'm taking you to see the house I've found for you and Leonardo,' he said. 'Be downstairs.'

He had it all planned. He would show Claudia the house, drop her back at the hotel, and return to meet Lucky. That way everybody would be happy.

He felt good about Lucky coming to see him that morning. He knew her doing that meant she was almost ready to forgive him. Not that she had anything to forgive him for. It was something that had happened long ago now. However, he couldn't blame her for being angry and upset that Claudia had turned up with his son. It wasn't exactly an everyday occurrence.

He stopped for a burger on his way to the hotel, suddenly finding himself ravenously hungry. Penelope McKay had told him that they would probably be calling him to the witness stand tomorrow. He was looking forward to telling his story, getting it out there for public consumption. The media were completely ridiculous. It was about time the truth was heard.

When he arrived at the Chateau Marmont, Claudia and Leonardo were waiting dutifully. He ran inside and picked up the house keys from the desk.

Claudia stood beside the car. She looked like she belonged in an old-fashioned Italian movie, with her voluptuous body, flowing chestnut hair and Mediterranean complexion. She shouldn't have any trouble at all finding a man.

Leonardo was wearing his new jeans and a Batman T-shirt. He grinned at Lennie. Lennie grinned back: he was getting fond of the kid. Maybe if he could talk Lucky into it Leonardo could spend some time with them.

Claudia jumped into the car. 'I'm so excited,' she said.

'You should be,' he said. 'This house is costing me a fortune. Wait till you see it.'

He felt good because at least he was doing something for her. He would make sure she was looked after, had enough money, and found a job.

Surely that couldn't piss Lucky off?

☆ ☆ ☆

Outside the hotel, Duke sat in his car watching and waiting. He had this thing about waiting, prolonging the moment. It was like great foreplay. Never rush anything. Always see how long you can string it out.

He'd watched Lennie devour a hamburger, then followed him to the hotel, where a woman and a small boy waited outside.

As soon as Duke set eyes on the woman, he knew he had to have her.

She was the most luscious-looking piece he'd ever seen.

And she would be his. For an hour or two.

He was entitled to *some* fun.

Chapter Eighty-seven

'THERE'S BEEN a big mistake,' Mila said, her pointed face flushed with anger.

'What mistake is that?' Maybelline answered, chewing her hair.

'Your fucking brother didn't deliver the gun today.'

Maybelline shrugged. 'Not my fault,' she said coolly.

'What do you mean, not your fault?' Mila exploded. 'We had an agreement, a bargain. He broke into the Washington house, raped the maid, stole everything he could get his hands on, and now he hasn't delivered my gun. Nor have I heard anything about Lennie Golden yet.'

'Don't worry,' Maybelline said, still calm. 'He's taking care of Lennie Golden tonight.'

'I hope he does. Otherwise everyone will be sorry.'

'Don't threaten me,' Maybelline snapped, her baby face contorted with anger.

'And what about my gun?' Mila said. 'My lawyer's been waiting for it all day. He says that if he'd had the gun before, I wouldn't even have to be locked up like this.'

'I'll speak to Duke,' Maybelline said.

'I thought you already did.'

'Didn't know the gun was so important.'

'Are you serious?' Mila said. '*Of course* you knew.'

'You're making me sorry I ever met you,' Maybelline said.

'What does *that* mean?'

'My brother doesn't have to jump for anybody, especially not *you*.'

'You don't get it, do you?' Mila said. 'The reason your brother got into Price Washington's house was *because* of me.'

'If I have to hear you say that one more time,' Maybelline said, 'I'm gonna scream. He'll hit Lennie Golden tonight. So shut the fuck up.'

'That's all very well,' Mila griped, 'but I need my gun, too. And if he *doesn't* hit Lennie Golden tonight, and I *don't* get my fucking gun, I'm going to the authorities.'

Maybelline stared at her. 'Do you understand who you're fucking with?' she said. 'Do you understand?'

Mila turned her back and walked over to the corner of the cell. She'd had it with this baby-faced cow. Had it with her *and* her stupid brother. If nothing happened by tomorrow, she was telling her lawyer about the break-in.

Fuck *them*! They were screwing with the wrong person. She'd fix them both.

Chapter Eighty-eight

BY CARLO'S reckoning, Brigette would be over the worst. He'd left her alone because it really was her problem, and he wanted no scandal about his wife. This way there were no witnesses, no doctors or nurses saying what a bastard he was to have gotten her hooked in the first place. Who knew what she would have told them?

Now that she was straight, he'd still have control. She was his wife, his pregnant wife at that.

He knew how to tap into Brigette and what she needed. She was the original poor little rich girl with no mother to guide her, an absentee father, and a desperation to be loved.

The truth was that he, Count Carlo Vittorio Vitti, was her saviour. He was the only man who'd been able to give her what she wanted, which was discipline.

She'd probably be mad at him when he arrived back at the hunting lodge, but so what? There was nothing she could do about it.

Now that he had Isabella again, he was a different man. He had a goal to work towards – not just getting Brigette's money, but getting enough so that he and Isabella could be together, for she was the only woman who was his match.

He often thought about their first meeting. She with her

elderly husband, he with one of the more desirable women in Rome. It had been at a party. They'd had sex in the bathroom. Frantic, anonymous sex. She'd laughed, and gone back to her husband's side and kissed him on the mouth, and winked at Carlo behind her husband's back. It was then that he'd known they were two of a kind. So when she'd asked, he'd helped her get rid of the miserable old man. And where had that got him? Exactly nowhere. Two days after the funeral, Isabella had run off with the fat opera singer.

'I only did it to take suspicion away from us,' she'd explained, 'because if people saw us together, they would have surely known it was you who killed my husband.'

'I didn't kill him,' he'd said. 'I assisted *you.*'

Isabella had laughed. 'Whatever.' She had the most seductive laugh in the world.

As soon as he arrived back in Rome, he got in his car and set off to bring Brigette home.

He had a new plan now, and that plan was to travel with her to New York and get her to transfer ten million dollars into a Swiss bank account in his name.

And if she refused . . . she'd be very sorry indeed.

☆ ☆ ☆

Brigette was getting nowhere fast. Exhausted and weak, she navigated a series of dirt roads that led nowhere except into heavily wooded areas. The rain had turned from a drizzle to a steady downpour, and she was soaked through and freezing cold. She started to despair that she was ever going to find her way back to the hunting lodge.

It occurred to her that soon it would be dark, and then what?

She began to panic, pedalling her way to nowhere. Until

suddenly she careened into a tree-trunk and was propelled off the bike, hitting her head on the ground.

She lay to the side of the mud road, unconscious.

And the rain poured down.

Chapter Eighty-nine

CLAUDIA RAN around the house like an excited child discovering Disneyland for the first time. 'It's wonderful, Lennie,' she gasped. 'Much too grand for Leonardo and me. We can't possibly live here.'

'Yes,' he said, pleased she was so thrilled. 'I've rented it for a year. By that time you will have decided what you want to do.'

'But, Lennie, it is so big.'

'I know,' he said. 'I was thinking . . . you talked about your relatives in Sicily . . . maybe somebody could come visit, a sister or something.'

'My family, they do not talk to me,' she said sadly. 'When I had the baby I was a black sheep . . . Is that how you say it in America?'

'Yeah.' He nodded. 'But if you call your mother, some-body – the circumstances are different now, you're in Amer-ica. Surely they'd want to come?'

'I don't know. Lennie, I wish *you* could live here with us.'

'I told you, Claudia,' he said seriously, 'it's impossible. I have my wife, and my own children.'

'But Leonardo *is* your son, Lennie. He was born out of love. You and I, when we were together, it was so . . . special.'

'Claudia,' he said, trying to let her down gently, 'I'm taken. I *have* the woman for me.'

'I understand, Lennie. But sometimes I dream . . .'

'You'll meet somebody else,' he said, veering away from a dangerous subject. 'You're a beautiful woman. There's plenty of guys who'd give anything to be with a woman like you.'

'You think I am beautiful, Lennie?' she asked.

He looked into her glowing face. 'Oh, c'mon, Claudia, you know you are.'

'Thank you.' She put her arms around him and gave him a little hug.

He pushed her gently away and glanced at his watch. Lucky would be here soon. It would not be cool for her to find Claudia hugging him.

Leonardo had gone straight out by the pool, and was sitting on the edge, gazing into the water.

'I hope he can swim,' Lennie said.

Claudia shook her head vigorously. 'He does not swim. Will you teach him?'

'Sure,' he said easily. 'We can all be friends. Once you get to know Lucky you'll love her, and she'll love you. And the kids – well, the kids are something else. Gino and Maria will teach Leonardo to swim in a minute. He needs to spend time with other children.'

'He can't be with other children, Lennie. Because he doesn't hear them, they tease him, call him names.'

'I talked to the doctor. He thinks there's something they can do about his hearing.'

She clasped her hands together. 'Oh, Lennie, that would be so marvellous!'

'It would, wouldn't it?' he said, hoping that everything was going to work out.

☆ ☆ ☆

Duke had parked his car on the street near the house. It was not his car, it was another stolen one. This time he'd taken a Mercedes – striving for a more classy image.

He'd followed Lennie and the woman and the child from the hotel, wondering where they were leading him. And when they'd arrived and parked in the driveway of what seemed to be an empty house with a for-lease sign outside, he couldn't have been more delighted.

This meant he could achieve both of his objectives: do away with Lennie Golden *and* satisfy himself with the woman.

Of course, if the woman saw him shoot Lennie, he'd have to get rid of her too. But Duke didn't mind. There was nothing to connect him with either of them. He would *never* be caught.

He waited five minutes before leaving the Mercedes, locking it carefully behind him. Then he walked up to the house.

The front door was slightly ajar. What was wrong with these people? Didn't anyone consider that there were bad elements in the world who were out to do them harm?

He'd instructed Maybelline *never* to let her guard down. She carried mace, a lethal hunting knife and a stun gun. He'd even taught her some karate.

He pushed open the door and walked inside, straight into a spacious hallway that led through to a huge living room overlooking an azure lap pool.

The boy was sitting outside by the pool. Duke had forgotten about the child. He stared at the boy for a moment, wondering what he should do about him. Then he decided he would face that problem when the time came.

He could hear voices coming from the back of the house.

He took out his gun.
First he would rape the girl.
Then he would kill Lennie Golden.
An audience would make it all the more fun.

Chapter Ninety

'I CAN ONLY stay a minute,' Lucky said, running into the production office.

'Why?' Alex asked. 'Where are you rushing off to?'

'I told you, I'm meeting Lennie.'

He nodded. 'Okay, that's good – I guess. Will you call me later?'

'Will I call you later?' she said mockingly. 'I told you, I'm meeting Lennie. Hopefully I won't be calling anyone later. Where's Venus?'

'She went home. Cooper's getting edgy, says she's spending too much time here.'

'Ah . . . she's giving Coop a taste of what it's like. He was the biggest playboy of all time.'

'Nothing wrong with that,' Alex said.

'Anyway, I just wanted to drop by and go over a few things with you,' Lucky said. 'And to tell you that I definitely approve of Billy Melina. You're right. He's fantastic.'

'Yeah, Billy's got a quality,' Alex said. 'And this is just the beginning. Once I get *my* hands on him . . .'

'Oooh, I've heard what happens when you get your hands on actors. They become nervous wrecks and end up in the psychiatric ward.'

'Yeah, but do I get a performance out of them?'

'You certainly do, Alex.'

'Now listen,' he said, 'how about a drink before you go?'

'Do you think I need one?' she asked, amused.

'Wouldn't do any harm. C'mon, spend a few minutes with me.'

'I don't want to be late. Lennie is showing me the house he's renting for the Sicilian and the kid.'

'Now there's a title for a movie – *The Sicilian and the Kid*.'

'Don't make fun of me, Alex. I'm very vulnerable right now. I'm not used to feeling like this.'

'No, you're not, are you? Lucky Santangelo, mobster's daughter. Fearless in the face of anything.'

'Will you stop? I have a good mind to sue them.'

'Yeah?'

'Why should they be allowed to say whatever they want about people?'

''Cause they know they can get away with it. It'll cost you more money and more time to sue them, so forget about it, it's yesterday's newspaper. Somebody's using it to clean up the rat shit.'

'You're right.'

'How does Gino feel about it?'

'Oh, you know Gino. It's kind of given him a higher profile amongst his friends down in Palm Springs.'

They both laughed.

'Come into my office,' Alex said. 'I'll fix you a Scotch on the rocks, set you up for the night.'

'I guess I could do with a drink.'

'How'd it go this afternoon?'

'Things are plodding along. The media is there in full force. And those two kids are sitting up there like little superstars surrounded by their lawyers. And Steven – Oh, God, I forgot to call him. He wanted to talk to me about something, and we didn't get a chance in court. Can I use your phone?' she asked, following him into his office.

Alex was not the neatest person in the world. There were scripts and CDs, tapes and books stacked everywhere. At the centre of it all was his desk, a huge sprawling dark-wood affair, also piled high with scripts.

He passed her the phone, and opened a desk drawer.

'Somewhere in here I've got a bottle of Scotch,' he muttered. 'Don't keep it out in the open because everybody drinks it.'

'What're *you* – stingy?' she said, laughing.

'Naw, don't like to tempt people.'

She quickly reached Steven's number. A woman answered. 'Jen?' she said.

'No, who's this?'

'*Lina?*' she said. Lina's thick Cockney accent was unmistakable.

'Lucky, is that you?'

'Lina. What are *you* doing at Steven's house?'

'Oh . . . I think we're supposed to be a secret.'

'*What*'s supposed to be a secret?'

'Me and Steven.'

'I'm not quite following you here. Are you telling me that you and Steven are an *item*?'

'I guess so,' Lina said, with an embarrassed giggle. 'Never thought I'd get into this 'ole domestic bit, but I'm 'ere, supportin' him through 'is time of trouble. Making 'im scrambled eggs, massaging 'is feet, an' giving him anything 'e needs.'

'Who'd believe *this*?' Lucky exclaimed. '*You* and Steven.'

'What's so 'ard to believe?'

'Well . . . I mean I didn't think Steven was planning on getting involved with anyone.'

'I'm not just anyone, am I?' Lina said cockily.

'That's true,' Lucky said. 'I guess he was going to tell me, because in court he said he wanted to talk to me about something.'

'Probably me,' Lina said. 'I'm talkable about, aren't I?'

'You certainly are. Wow! This is a shock. But I'm real happy for the two of you. In fact, it's great! Is it *serious*?'

'I moved in,' Lina stated. 'Given up me modelling gigs for a while.'

'Let's have dinner, we should celebrate. Will you tell Steven I called?'

'I'd better not. I'm sure he wants to tell you about us 'imself. 'E should be 'ome soon. Give us a buzz later.'

'I'll do that.' She put down the phone, still in a state of shock. 'Guess what?' she said to Alex, who was busy pouring her an extra large tumbler of Scotch.

'What?' he said.

'My brother has a girlfriend.'

'Your brother Steven?'

'I only have one brother, Alex, and easy on the Scotch. I hardly want to stagger in to see Lennie.'

'Good for Steven,' Alex said.

'I didn't expect it to happen so soon,' Lucky said.

'It's not that soon. And I'm telling you, a man needs a warm body beside him in bed. Especially when you're not so young and horny any more.'

'Is that why you're thinking of marrying Pia? By the way, I meant to ask you, have you mentioned this marriage thing to her?'

'I'll tell her when I'm sure you're not coming back.'

'Very romantic.'

'Who *is* Steven's new girlfriend?'

'Even more peculiar. It's Lina. You know, the super-model?'

'Holy shit!' Alex said. 'Steven and the supermodel. He seems so . . . kind of laid-back and quiet.'

'Before he was married, Steven was a big player. He settled down when he met Mary Lou. It *is* kind of a strange duo, but Lina's really nice, and a lot of fun.'

'Maybe it's exactly what he needs right now,' Alex said, handing her the drink.

She took a couple of gulps and almost gagged.

'Wow! This is strong,' she said. 'Don't you believe in adding water and ice?'

'What do you think this is? A bar?'

She laughed. 'I appreciate the drink, Alex, but I have to go now. Let me know what happens with you and Pia.'

'No, Lucky,' he said. 'You let *me* know what happens with you and Lennie.'

'I'll speak to you tomorrow,' she said. 'What are you doing tonight?'

'Pia is cooking me dinner.'

'There, you see – she *is* the right girl for you. Not only a warm body, but she cooks, too!'

'I'll see *you* in the morning.'

'You got it, Alex.'

Chapter Ninety-one

IT WAS almost dark, and the rain was pounding down. Boogie had been listening to the radio, the newscaster was predicting a big storm. Driving carefully, he noticed car lights up ahead of him on one of the many dirt roads he'd driven down over the last hour. It looked like a Maserati with a lone male driver. He wondered if he should flag the car down and ask directions. Or maybe he should just follow behind. The driver must be heading somewhere in this wilderness, and when he arrived, that would be the time to get directions.

This seemed like the best idea, because if he flashed his lights at the guy, it was highly unlikely he'd stop in this weather.

Boogie was angry with himself. He should have paid Lorenzo to come with him, guide him, but Christ, who'd have thought the place would be this hard to find? Although Lorenzo *had* warned him.

He had a feeling he must be getting near.

Up ahead of him, the Maserati was travelling too fast for the driving rain. Boogie found it easy to keep up – he hadn't taken a course in hazardous conditions for nothing.

It occurred to him that the man driving the car must notice he was being followed. How come he didn't stop and ask what Boogie wanted? Although, since this was Italy, perhaps he thought the car behind him might be driven by a kidnapper.

Boogie hung back, allowing the Maserati to race ahead. He didn't want the guy coming at him with a gun.

Suddenly the Maserati hit something, and for a few seconds the powerful car swerved out of control. The driver didn't stop.

Boogie slowed down to see what he'd hit. Checking it out, he spotted an old bicycle lying across the dirt road.

Something told him to stop. Like Lucky, he always followed his hunches, which is probably why the two of them got along so well.

He knew that if he stopped he'd probably lose the driver up ahead, but somehow he also knew that he had to.

He pulled over, turned off his engine, armed himself with a flashlight, and got out of the car.

The bike was dilapidated and rusty: it could've been lying there for months. Or maybe not.

Boogie began kicking it to the side so he wouldn't have to ride over it. He was surprised it hadn't torn up the Maserati's tyres.

As he was moving the bike, he noticed a flash of golden hair and an arm over to the right.

Christ! There was someone on the ground.

He ran over. A woman was lying there, semi-conscious. He immediately felt her pulse. Thank God she was still alive.

He shone his flashlight on her face and was horrified to discover it was an almost unrecognizable Brigette. She was shivering and shaking, her clothes saturated with rain and mud.

He scooped her up in his arms and carried her to his car.

Her eyelids fluttered open for a moment. She was delirious. 'Where . . . am . . . I? Where's my baby? He'll be all covered in mud, and the grave will float away.'

He laid her down on the back seat of the car, stripping off her wet clothes and wrapping her in his shirt and jacket.

She was shivering uncontrollably, teeth chattering, lips and eyelids blue with cold.

'Don't worry, little Brigette,' he said, remembering her when she was a child. 'Stay with it, we're getting help.'

'I lost the baby,' she sobbed hysterically. 'I lost my baby.'

'It's okay,' he said, running around and jumping into the driver's seat bare-chested. 'We're getting you to a hospital, honey. Hang in there, it won't be long.'

☆ ☆ ☆

Carlo had noticed the car behind him, and it bothered him. What would a car be doing out here at this time of night in the pounding rain?

He had no intention of stopping to find out. He had an uneasy feeling that maybe somehow Brigette had been able to summon help, and someone was coming to get her.

If that happened . . .

He wasn't too far from the house when his Maserati hit something in the middle of the road and veered over to the other side. Fortunately this forced the car behind him to stop, and checking out his rear-view mirror, Carlo roared away. They'd never find the hunting lodge – nobody would unless they knew exactly where they were going.

A few miles on he took a sharp left turn, then two more rights, and finally he was there.

The house was in total darkness since there was no electricity. He'd left Brigette a few candles and some matches, but obviously she wasn't using them. Grabbing a flashlight from the glove box, he jumped out of the car, threw open the front door, and ran into the house.

'Brigette!' he shouted. 'Brigette – where are you?'

No answer. He hurried into the living room, the flashlight making shadows on the wall. Then he saw the dried blood all over the floor. Oh, Christ! What had happened here? Had she killed herself? Was he about to find her dead body somewhere?

He hoped not, for he was under enough suspicion as it was concerning the death of Isabella's husband. If Brigette's body was discovered at the hunting lodge, he'd be the first person at whom they'd point an accusing finger.

Quickly he set about searching the house. Upstairs. Downstairs. All around.

She was not there.

He searched again, shouting out her name.

No Brigette.

How could she escape from this place? She had no phone, no car, no means of communication. It was impossible for her to get away.

And yet . . . she was gone.

He searched one more time, and then he ran out to the Maserati.

He would find his wife. And when he did, she would be very sorry indeed.

Chapter Ninety-two

LUCKY PULLED up at a stop light. She was on her way to see Lennie, which made her feel good. She'd enjoyed her short meeting with Alex, he was still her best friend, but she couldn't believe he'd said that if she got back with Lennie, he was marrying Pia. What was *that* all about? Was he trying to piss her off?

Too bad, Alex. It doesn't piss me off at all. I'm simply worried that you're settling for less than you deserve.

Although who was she to interfere? Maybe Pia was the right one. She'd certainly been with him longer than any of the others, so she obviously made him happy.

Hey – it wasn't Lucky's problem. Right now all she had on her mind was seeing Lennie and working things out. She called Venus on her cellphone.

'Wasn't I right?' Venus crowed, picking up on her private line.

'You were *absolutely* right,' Lucky agreed. 'Billy is great. Between you and Alex, you'll get him doing everything you both want.'

'Let's not forget *you*,' Venus said. '*You*'ll have him running around with his *dick* hanging out. We all know how you like equal nudity on the screen.'

'Quite right too,' Lucky said succinctly, remembering how when she'd taken over Panther, that had been one of her edicts. If the actress takes it off, so must the guy. Boy, there'd been some screaming about *that* one.

'Wait till Cooper gets a look at him,' Venus said. 'He'll throw a jealous fit!'

'Why are you always trying to break Cooper's balls?'

''Cause that's our shtick,' Venus explained, laughing. 'We have fun doing it.'

'So here's the latest,' Lucky said, moving away from the light, which was now green. 'It's juicy stuff.'

'What?' Venus said. 'Tell me immediately.'

'Okay, okay.' A beat. 'Steven has found himself a new girlfriend.'

'I think that's great!' Venus exclaimed. 'Is she nice?'

'Well . . . nice isn't exactly the word I'd use to describe her.'

'Is she *pretty*?'

'Staggeringly gorgeous.'

'Staggeringly gorgeous?' Venus repeated. 'Hmm . . . who is she?'

'Lina.'

'Lina? You mean *the* Lina from the fashion mags and the runway shows, and every gossip column in the world? Isn't she in bed with Charlie Dollar?'

'She sure as hell ain't in bed with him now,' Lucky said. 'She's sharing living quarters with Steven, and from what she says, they've settled into domestic bliss.'

'You've *gotta* be kidding me!' Venus said.

'*I* think it's great,' Lucky said. 'I mean, if you think about it, who's he going to find? Some little bimbo who'll be in Mary Lou's shadow for the rest of her life? Lina has it going for her. She's her own woman.'

'Good for him,' Venus said enthusiastically. 'Does Charlie know?'

'What does he care? He's engaged.'

'Yes, for seven years!'

'Anyway, I gotta go,' Lucky said, pulling up at another red light. 'I'll keep you informed, and I'll see you at lunch tomorrow.'

She caught the guy in the car next to her staring. Oh, God, she hoped he wasn't a journalist. Lately they'd been following her.

As soon as the light changed, she took a few sharp turns at high speed and soon lost him.

Then she set off up Loma Vista to the address Lennie had given her.

☆ ☆ ☆

'Good evening,' Duke said politely.

It was dusk and, since the sun was just beginning to set, he considered it a most appropriate greeting.

Claudia was exploring the bedroom when Lennie saw him. A medium height white man with a baby face. But it wasn't the face Lennie noticed first, it was the gun.

'You really should learn to lock the door behind you,' Duke said mildly, standing in the doorway. 'This *is* Los Angeles. Shit happens.'

Lennie stared at the gun and the baby-faced gunman, and every bad memory of the night with Mary Lou came back. 'Don't hurt anybody,' he said, very slowly. 'We'll do what you want, just don't hurt anybody. I've got a watch, a few hundred dollars, credit cards, and you can take my car. It's parked right outside.'

'That's what I like,' Duke said cheerfully. 'A sensible man. Now, both of you continue being sensible and take your clothes off.'

'What?' Lennie said.

'First throw your money and watch over here, and *then*

remove your clothes,' Duke instructed, savouring every moment.

Claudia was petrified. She gazed at Lennie, seeking protection.

Christ! What was *he* supposed to do? This was a nightmare. The second time in months he'd had a gun in his face. Fuck! No more Mr Nice Guy Liberal. From now on he was carrying a gun at all times, and shooting back just the way Lucky would.

Oh, God, Lucky! She was going to be here soon. If she walked in on this . . . It didn't bear thinking about.

'Listen, man,' Lennie said urgently, throwing over his money, credit cards and watch. 'Take the stuff and go. We're expecting other people.'

'Really?' Duke said, like he couldn't care less. 'Are you going to do as I tell you?' he added, waving the gun in Claudia's direction. 'Or perhaps I should shoot her. What do *you* think, Mr Golden?'

'Take off your dress, Claudia,' Lennie said, in a strained voice, trying to figure out how the gunman knew his name.

She looked at him questioningly. 'What?'

'Take it off,' he repeated. 'He doesn't want us running for help, that's why.'

'Good,' Duke said expansively, as Lennie started removing his shirt. 'You understand me. Sometimes people don't. And then it can get most unfortunate.'

Tentatively Claudia began unbuttoning her dress.

'Step out of it, that's the way,' Duke said encouragingly.

Once again she looked at Lennie. He nodded. She stepped out of her dress.

'Pants off,' Duke said to Lennie.

'You've got what you came for,' Lennie said, wanting to kill him. 'It's not necessary to humiliate us this way.'

'Brave man without a gun,' Duke said. 'I have to admire

that, but you'd better watch the way you speak to me because I'm in charge here. Now get your pants off, and tell her to lose her underwear.'

'Do as he says, Claudia,' Lennie said, his voice even more strained.

'But, Lennie—' she began.

'Do it!' he repeated, remembering saying the same words to Mary Lou, who'd ignored him, and look where it had got her. 'Quickly, Claudia.'

She unhooked her bra and her breasts came tumbling out.

Duke stared at them, licking his lips. 'Nice,' he said. 'Very nice. And all real, huh? You're not one of those silicone whores.' She put her hands up to cover herself. 'Now the panties,' Duke said.

'Lennie . . . I – I don't understand,' she whimpered, almost in tears. 'Why he do this to us?'

'Because I can,' Duke said. 'Now hurry up!'

She stepped out of her panties, vulnerable and exposed.

'You see that bed over there?' he said. 'I want you to take off the sheets and tear them into strips, then I want you to tie your boyfriend up. Got it?'

'Why don't you just take the goddamn money and go?' Lennie said. 'You'll get caught if you stay. People will be here any minute.'

'I'm really scared,' Duke jeered.

Claudia tore up the bed sheets, and Duke instructed her how to tie Lennie up. When she'd completed the task and Lennie was immobilized, Duke ripped the remains of the sheets and strung Lennie with his arms above him to a low ceiling beam so that he was almost suspended, although his feet just about touched the floor.

While he was doing this, Claudia made a vain attempt to attack him. He slapped her away, telling her to sit down and be quiet, or he'd kill her boyfriend.

She did as he asked, fear written all over her face.

When he was sure that Lennie was secure and could not move, he turned his attention back to Claudia. She was definitely a beauty: he planned on taking his time with this one.

He looked around, discovering a sound system built into the wall. He tuned the radio to classical music and turned the volume up loud. Then he sat in a chair and instructed Claudia to dance for him.

She was scared. He could see the fear all over her face and he liked it.

Reluctantly Claudia began to dance.

Duke watched her, soon becoming aroused. She was not skinny, she was rounded and womanly, with large breasts and long legs. He anticipated what he was going to do to her and smiled.

Lennie was watching her too. He had no choice.

'I thought you were a *married* man,' Duke said. 'Is this your piece on the side? Is she a good lay? Does she come easily? Tell me about her, 'cause I plan to fuck her later. And *you*'re going to watch.'

'You're a sick bastard,' Lennie muttered. 'A sick sick bastard.'

'Thank you,' Duke said. 'I'll take that as a compliment.'

Chapter Ninety-three

ARRIVING AT the house on Loma Vista, Lucky pulled up and parked behind Lennie's car. She was glad he was here first. They'd take a quick walk through the house, she'd give it her approval, then the two of them would go out somewhere to talk. She really needed to be with him, living apart was pointless. She knew now that they could work this out.

She got out of her car and walked over to the front door. It was locked. She tried the bell, but it didn't seem to be working, so after a few minutes she made her way around to the back.

It was almost dark, and she was startled to see the young boy out there by himself. Why was Leonardo here? She was not pleased.

As soon as he saw her, he ran up to her, trying to say something.

'Hi,' she said coolly. 'Is your mom around?'

The boy shook his head frantically, pulling at her jacket.

'What *is* it?' she said, irritated.

He began dragging her down the side of the pool towards the back of the house, where lights blazed from the bedroom and loud classical music blared. As they approached, she could see everything through the big glass windows.

She could see Claudia, naked and dancing.

'Oh, my God!' she gasped.

You bastard! Lennie Golden. This is it! I've had it with you.
Without thinking, she turned quickly to leave.

The boy hung on to her jacket, trying to drag her back, making guttural noises in his throat, pointing, desperately attempting to make himself understood.

She turned around, about to tell the stupid kid to leave her alone, when she saw Lennie, almost hanging from a beam, his arms and legs tightly bound.

And she saw the man sitting in a chair, a gun balanced on his knee.

And then she understood.

And she was scared.

And she knew what she had to do.

Grabbing the boy, gesturing for him to be silent, she pulled him along with her as they edged back the way they'd come. At the other end of the pool she pushed him into the bushes. 'Hide!' she whispered vehemently. 'Stay quiet. *Muto! Muto!*'

The boy crouched down, understanding what she was telling him to do.

Adrenalin pumping, Lucky made it to the front of the house and her car. Reaching for her cellphone, she called 911, summoning help, then reached into the glove compartment and took out her gun.

Her mind was racing, a million thoughts. Should she wait for the cops?

No. What if by waiting something happened to Lennie? She had to act now.

Fumbling in her purse she found a credit card and approached the front door. Boogie had taught her, long ago, how to break in to anywhere. Within seconds she'd sprung the lock and was inside the house, entering stealthily, although nobody could possibly have heard her because of the music blasting away.

Her heart was in her throat. This was not the kind of deal

she cared to get involved in – not with three kids at home and responsibilities. But, fuck it, Lennie was in trouble, he needed her. And goddamnit, she was there.

☆ ☆ ☆

Duke was getting bored with the girl's dancing. She was clumsy, not graceful as he had hoped. His sister was graceful. Quick on her feet and light as air. He felt sorry for Maybelline, locked in a jail cell with the girl with the pointed face and mean expression. He couldn't wait for her to get out so they could do things together. And once he'd taken care of step-grandma Renee, they could move back into their house and be a real family again.

'Stop dancing,' he said to the girl. She stopped, frozen with fear. 'Go bend over that stool,' he said, pointing to a chair with no back.

This was the best part, getting them to do whatever he wanted. And today it was even better because he had a reluctant voyeur, trussed up like a Christmas turkey, forced to watch what he didn't want to see.

'For God's sake,' Lennie yelled, 'leave her alone.'

'Why?' Duke said, quite enjoying the fact that Lennie Golden wasn't scared to speak up. 'You saving her for yourself?'

'You son-of-a-bitch motherfucking coward,' Lennie shouted.

'Don't listen to your boyfriend, dear,' Duke said, unfazed. 'Bend over that chair. AND DO IT NOW!'

Claudia jumped to obey him.

'Jesus Christ!' Lennie groaned, anticipating what was to come. 'Don't do this.'

Duke stood up, unzipped his pants, and took out his erect penis. It was small, but capable of doing what he planned.

Slowly he walked towards the chair and a passive Claudia.

☆　☆　☆

Lucky moved like a cat along the corridor leading to the bedroom, holding her gun in front of her. The music was still blaring, blurring her concentration. Fuck it. She was going to nail this perverted bastard, whoever he was.

She reached the bedroom door, which was slightly ajar, and with one fast fluid movement, kicked it open.

Lucky saw Claudia first. Claudia was naked, bent over a stool facing the door. Duke was positioned behind her, about to mount her. Lennie was hanging helplessly by his wrists.

As if in slow motion, Duke jumped off Claudia and reached for his gun, lying on the floor beside him.

'Drop it!' Lucky commanded.

'Who? *Me*?' Duke said, up for the challenge.

'Yes, you.'

'Sorry. No can do.'

She took a long deep breath. Dealing with homicidal maniacs was never her favourite way to spend a day. 'Do it!' she said. 'Or I'll blow your dumb brains all over this god-damn room.'

He turned his gun towards Lennie. 'If you're fast enough,' he said, his finger tightening on the trigger.

And she knew she had to shoot, because if she hesitated, all would be lost.

She let blast, and so did he.

His bullet, meant for Lennie, connected with Claudia, who threw herself in front of Lennie just as Duke fired.

Lucky's bullet penetrated Duke's heart.

He slumped to the ground, a slack smile on his baby face.

It was over.

Chapter Ninety-four

IT WAS past ten when Maybelline was called from her cell to see the warden.

'What's going on?' Mila asked, waking up.

'Dunno,' Maybelline said. She'd decided she hated Mila, they'd been arguing all night.

'Shit!' Mila muttered. 'I hope it's not about me. You'd better be careful what you say.'

Maybelline stalked off without a word. She returned twenty minutes later.

Mila could see something was wrong. 'What's the matter?' she demanded. '*Was* it about me? You didn't tell them anything, did you? 'Cause if you did, I'll fucking kill you!'

'No,' Maybelline said. 'It wasn't about you.'

'Then what was it?' Mila asked. 'They don't pull you out of your cell at night to tell you nothing.'

'It's my brother,' Maybelline said flatly. 'It's Duke.'

'What about him? Did he get Lennie Golden for me today? Is that what happened? Did he hit Lennie and get his sorry ass caught?'

Maybelline looked at her with dead eyes. 'He got killed – that's what happened.'

'Killed?' Mila said blankly. 'How could he get killed?'

540

'He was in a house. Lennie Golden was there. And someone shot Duke.'

'Was it the cops?'

'I feel like my heart has been ripped from my body,' Maybelline said, as if speaking to herself. 'Duke was everything good.' She turned on Mila, her expression fierce. 'If it wasn't for you, he'd never have been there.'

'Don't blame me,' Mila said.

'Ever since you came into this cell I've had nothing but trouble,' Maybelline said. 'And now you've taken away my only reason for living.'

'What did he do with my gun?'

'Your gun?' Maybelline said. 'My *brother* is dead, and you're asking about your *gun*.'

'I'm going to sleep,' Mila said. 'I have to be in court again in the morning. I have to sit there while those dumb lawyers go, "We will prove to you that Mila Kopistani planned this crime, and set out to murder Mary Lou stupid fucking Berkeley."'

'You're the dregs,' Maybelline said. 'If Duke was here now, he'd punish you for your sins.'

'I'm sorry about your brother, but he's left me in the shit. How am I going to get my gun now?'

'If Duke can't punish you, then God surely can,' Maybelline said, her voice rising. 'You are a bitch from hell. My brother is dead because of you!' And with that she reached under her bunk, and produced her one prized possession: a lethal shard of glass.

Maybelline struck out, slitting Mila's throat with one fell swoop.

Mila didn't even see it coming. She fell on to the floor of the cell with a horrifying gurgling sound.

'See how *you* like it,' Maybelline said. 'See how concerned *I* am about *you*.'

She got into her bunk and tried to sleep, while Mila bled to death on the cell floor.

☆ ☆ ☆

Price was reading the *LA Times* in the living room when Irena came in and asked if she might talk to him for a moment.

'Does it have to be now?' he said. 'I'm not feelin' great.'

'I'm sorry,' she said, 'but I must explain something to you. You see, I feel that everything that's happened over these last few months is my fault.'

Christ! He wasn't in the mood. 'Huh?' he said.

'I never treated Mila in the way she expected a mother to treat a daughter,' Irena said. 'I was always cold towards her.'

'What're you talking about?' he said, frowning.

'I resented her from the moment I gave birth,' Irena said, rambling on. 'She – she changed things for me. She came between you and me.'

'Came between us?' His eyebrows rose in surprise. 'Hey, Irena, I know we've had our moments, but I never led you on, never told you anythin' was gonna happen between us.'

'There's something I must tell you.'

'What now?' he said impatiently. The last thing he needed was true confessions from Irena.

'Well, you see, this is the way it happened—'

And just as she was about to tell him the real truth, the phone rang.

Relieved, he grabbed it. 'Yeah? Uh-huh.' He listened carefully for a few minutes. 'Oh, *shit*! Well, what's gonna happen? I – I'll tell her myself. Yeah, I will.' He put the phone down, stood up and held out his arms. 'Come here,' he said.

She walked over to him. 'What?'

He enclosed her in a tight embrace. 'I have kind of . . . shocking news.'

'What *is* it?'

'It's Mila. She was attacked by another inmate. I'm sorry to tell you this, Irena, she's . . . dead.'

EPILOGUE

Six Months Later

'GOOD MORNING,' Lucky said, as Lennie, accompanied by little Gino, Maria and Leonardo, came bounding up the wooden steps from the beach, all four of them wet and sandy, their faces covered in smiles.

She had breakfast laid out on the deck overlooking the ocean. Muffins, fresh fruit, yogurt, French toast and bacon. 'Who's hungry?'

'Me, please!' said Leonardo. Since the successful operation to restore his hearing, he was learning to speak at an alarming rate, picking up all kinds of expressions from little Gino and Maria.

'Then *you* can sit at the head of the table,' she said, giving him a big hug.

Leonardo and she had bonded. Totally inconsolable after the death of his mother, Lucky had been the one he'd clung to. And she had looked after him as if he was her own – which, in a way, he was, because he had Lennie's blood flowing through his veins, and that was enough to make her love him unconditionally.

They'd given Claudia a very moving and special funeral. The service was read in both English and Italian.

After the tragedy, Lucky had expected Lennie to go into another slump. But he hadn't. Instead he'd faced life with a

547

new attitude, brushing up on his shooting skills at the firing range and taking up karate.

She applauded his way of handling it. Action gave him back his power and strength, it made him feel good about himself again.

'*I* wanna sit at the head of the table,' Maria said, pouting.

'Well, *you*'re not going to,' Lucky replied. 'Maybe tomorrow – if you're very, very, *very* good.'

'I can be that!' Maria said, with a cheeky grin.

'I thought so,' Lucky said.

Lennie came up behind her, giving her a warm, sandy hug. 'How's my wife today?' he asked.

'Your wife is fine. How's my husband?'

'All the better for seeing you,' he said, nuzzling her neck.

'Honey?' she said.

'What?'

'We have to leave at noon today, everybody dressed and ready. So don't be clinging to your computer when I say it's time to go.'

'Now would I do that?'

'Yes.'

He grinned and hugged her again. 'Noon. Washed and brushed. No problem.'

'Good. It's not every day we get to go to a wedding.'

☆ ☆ ☆

'You're wearing it!' Brigette insisted.

'I am *not*!' Lina replied.

'Oh, yes, you are.'

Lina took the frilly blue garter and tossed it in the air. It landed in a champagne bucket full of ice.

'*Ooops*, sorry,' she said guiltily. 'Can't wear it now, it's all wet.'

'So are you,' said Brigette, frowning. 'Haven't you ever heard of something borrowed, something blue?'

'Yeah, but not that skank bit of tat thankyouverymuch.'

'You're impossible!'

'That's what Steven says.'

They'd taken over a suite at the Bel Air Hotel and were having fun. The night before they'd hit the town with Kyra, Suzi and Annik, Lina's bridesmaids-to-be. It had been a double celebration. One, Lina's bachelor party. And two, she'd finally made the cover of *Sports World International* and was ecstatic. She was also happy to see Brigette in such good shape. Brigette had cut her blonde hair very short, put on weight and developed a healthy tan.

She seemed at peace with herself, and perfectly content to do nothing for a while, even though her New York agent was begging her to return to work. She'd suffered a terrifying ordeal, and she was taking her time getting over it.

For a while it had been pretty scary. She'd languished in an Italian hospital with pneumonia for almost three weeks before Lucky was allowed to bring her back to America. Boogie had arranged twenty-four-hour guards at the hospital, to make sure that Carlo did not gain access.

Count Vitti had screamed and carried on, until an Italian police official had visited him at the palace and warned him to stay away. 'Miz Santangelo has important friends,' the man said. 'For your own health, do not bother the American girl again.'

Carlo was incensed. The 'American girl' was his wife. He would bother her as much as he wanted. In fact, through his lawyers, he would bother her for ten million dollars. Only then would he go away.

It was not to be. Lucky Santangelo flew in and arranged to see him. They met for drinks in the bar of the Excelsior Hotel. He thought she had come to settle. He was arrogant, prepared to go away for nothing less than the ten million. After all, Brigette was one of the richest women in the world.

Lucky drank champagne, made innocuous small-talk, and finally laid ten crisp one-dollar bills on the table. 'Payment in full,' she said briskly.

'What?' he said, confused.

'And if you value your precious Italian cock, you will *never* attempt to contact Brigette again. The marriage will be annulled.'

He'd stared into her dangerous black eyes and known that she was telling the truth.

'Ask anyone, Carlo. I do not make idle threats.'

He didn't care to fuck with Lucky Santangelo.

He fled to Sardinia to be comforted by his one true love, Isabella.

Too late. She had married a seventy-year-old industrial billionaire and gone to live in Buenos Aires with her new husband.

Carlo was destroyed.

☆ ☆ ☆

Maybelline Browning reported to the authorities everything she knew about Mila Kopistani. She told them how Mila had boasted about shooting Mary Lou Berkeley, and how she'd tricked Teddy Washington into putting his prints on the murder weapon.

She also told them Mila had been threatening her, and that she'd been forced to kill her in self-defence. The result was that by the time she got to court she received only a ten-year sentence.

She didn't care. She had nothing to live for now that Duke was gone.

☆ ☆ ☆

Teddy Washington ended up with eighteen months' probation, which delighted his dad, whose movie had finally come through. To celebrate, Price planned a trip to the Bahamas for him and Teddy – *anything* to get away from Ginee, who was constantly turning up on TV, basking in her own personal fifteen minutes of very dubious fame.

At the last moment Price invited Irena to come along. He felt sorry for her. After all, she'd suffered a devastating loss and he could see how depressed and miserable she was.

Teddy was pissed, but so what? Price knew he could do exactly what he wanted, and right now he wanted the company of a woman who put him before anything and didn't drive him crazy.

☆ ☆ ☆

The children walked down the aisle first. Maria, Carioca and Chyna, the three girls in simple pink dresses with daisies in their hair. Then came the boys, little Gino and Leonardo, resplendent in white shirts and black velvet pants.

The assembled guests oohed and aahed in an appropriate fashion.

'Isn't Chyna the most adorable little girl in the universe?' Venus whispered to Cooper, proud as only a mother could be.

'She needs a sister or a brother,' Cooper said.

'Really?' Venus said, smiling provocatively. 'Well . . . since I'm between movies, we'll have to see what we can do about that!'

Sitting behind them, Pia said to Alex, 'Do you *like* children?'

'From afar,' he answered, glancing over at Lucky, who looked particularly sensational in a red dress. They'd had quite an experience making the movie. Lucky was a hell of a producer, and he hoped, with Lennie's blessing, they would get to work together again soon.

Pia reached for his hand. He still hadn't asked her to marry him, but he was definitely thinking about it.

Gino nudged Paige. 'Get a load of my grandchildren,' he boasted. 'Not bad, huh? A bunch of tough little Santangelos. I love it!'

Next came the bridesmaids, Annik, Kyra and Suzi, three gorgeous supermodels who had every man in the place drooling. They sashayed down the aisle in their deep pink dresses, all long legs, delectable cleavage and, for a change, demure smiles.

The maid of honour, Brigette, was right behind them. So glowingly beautiful that it brought tears to Lucky's eyes. She thought of all her goddaughter had gone through in the last year – the drugs, the miscarriage, her escape from Carlo. It was a miracle that she'd recovered in every way.

Bobby, sitting next to Lucky, his hormones raging, said, 'Wow, Mom! Brig looks *hot*!'

'Calm down, Bobby, she's family,' Lucky admonished. 'You're her uncle!'

'Don't get spaced, Mom, just *looking*. Hey—' he added cheekily, 'd'you think I'm too young for one of the bridesmaids?'

Lucky couldn't help laughing. She was going to have to watch Bobby. He was a womanizer in progress.

Lennie stood next to Steven at the front of the church. He was Steven's best man and proud of it.

Steven couldn't keep still. He was nervous and apprehensive. All the time he kept wondering if somewhere, some-how Mary Lou was watching him. And, if she was, did she approve?

Lina appeared, and a gasp went up. She was a vision in a Valentino wedding gown created especially for her, and on her head was a Harry Winston diamond tiara.

Steven stared down the aisle at his bride-to-be and had no doubt he'd made the right decision.

☆ ☆ ☆

And so Lina and Steven were married, and the assembled guests cheered, and Lennie went to find his wife and when he did, he said, 'I love you, babe. *And* I've had this amazing idea.'

'What idea?' Lucky said, thinking how much she loved him.

'Let's do it again.'

'Let's do *what* again?' she asked, putting her hand up to stroke the back of his neck.

'Have another wedding.'

And she smiled and said, 'Yes,' and knew that as long as there was life, she and Lennie would be together.